THE OTHER

Philippa Gregory is an estab... ... television. She holds a PhD... University of Edinburgh. She ... ...dely praised for her historical novels, including *Earthly Joys, Virgin Earth, A Respectable Trade, The Queen's Fool, The Virgin's Lover, The Constant Princess, The Boleyn Inheritance, The Other Queen,* as well as her works of contemporary suspense. *The Other Boleyn Girl* was adapted for BBC television and is now a major film, starring Scarlett Johansson, Natalie Portman and Eric Bana. Philippa Gregory lives in the North of England with her family and welcomes visitors to her website PhilippaGregory.com

By the same author

PHILIPPA GREGORY

THE OTHER BOLEYN GIRL

HARPER

pp. vi–vii show a fragment of the letter written by Anne Boleyn to Henry VIII
from the Tower of London in 1536, reproduced by permission of the British Library
(OTHO.C.X.228)

pp. 534–535 show a reconstruction of a letter written by Mary Boleyn to the Secretary
of State Thomas Cromwell in 1534. Lettering by Stephen Raw.

HarperCollins*Publishers*
77–85 Fulham Palace Road,
Hammersmith, London W6 8JB

www.harpercollins.com

This paperback edition 2012
1

First published in Great Britain
by HarperCollins*Publishers* 2001

Copyright © Philippa Gregory Ltd 2011

The author asserts the moral right to
be identified as the author of this work

ISBN 978 0 00 792629 9

Set in Postscript Linotype Minion
with Medici Script display by
Rowland Phototypesetting Ltd,
Bury St Edmunds, Suffolk

Printed and bound in Great Britain by
Clays Ltd, St Ives plc

MIX
Paper from
responsible sources

FSC
www.fsc.org

FSC® C007454

For Anthony

been pleasing in y[?]

will

be f[?] leave to hobl[?]

ayde to the trymitie to[?]

to direct you in all

the ——— Tower the 6

...

ing sending ames[?]

Tower willing [?]

ould confesse not

so sayd he must

he did acknow[?]

favours, for ya[?]

Margret [?]

...our eares, let me obteyne
...your grave any furthe
...aue your grave in febr
...ve artions, from my d
...of May.
    your most con
    ever faythfu

    Ann B

...mynde to Queen L...
...e to confesse the
...more, then she f...
...conceale nothing t...
...dge her selfe h...
...my her first hu...
...t tobe his queen

Spring 1521

I could hear a roll of muffled drums. But I could see nothing but the lacing on the bodice of the lady standing in front of me, blocking my view of the scaffold. I had been at this court for more than a year and attended hundreds of festivities; but never before one like this.

By stepping to one side a little and craning my neck, I could see the condemned man, accompanied by his priest, walk slowly from the Tower towards the green where the wooden platform was waiting, the block of wood placed centre stage, the executioner dressed all ready for work in his shirtsleeves with a black hood over his head. It looked more like a masque than a real event, and I watched it as if it were a court entertainment. The king, seated on his throne, looked distracted, as if he was running through his speech of forgiveness in his head. Behind him stood my husband of one year, William Carey, my brother, George, and my father, Sir Thomas Boleyn, all looking grave. I wriggled my toes inside my silk slippers and wished the king would hurry up and grant clemency so that we could all go to breakfast. I was only thirteen years old, I was always hungry.

The Duke of Buckinghamshire, far away on the scaffold, put off his thick coat. He was close enough kin for me to call him uncle. He had come to my wedding and given me a gilt bracelet. My father told me that he had offended the king a dozen ways: he had royal blood in his veins and he kept too large a retinue of armed men for the comfort of a king not yet wholly secure on his throne; worst of all he was supposed to have said that the king had no son and heir now, could get no son and heir, and that he would likely die without a son to succeed him to the throne.

Such a thought must not be said out loud. The king, the court, the whole country knew that a boy must be born to the queen, and born soon. To suggest otherwise was to take the first step on the path that led to the wooden steps of the scaffold which the duke, my uncle, now climbed, firmly and without fear. A good courtier never refers to any unpalatable truths. The life of a court should always be merry.

Uncle Stafford came to the front of the stage to say his final words. I was too far from him to hear, and in any case I was watching the king, waiting for his cue to step forward and offer the royal pardon. This man standing on the scaffold, in the sunlight of the early morning, had been the king's partner at tennis, his rival on the jousting field, his friend at a hundred bouts of drinking and gambling, they had been comrades since the king was a boy. The king was teaching him a lesson, a powerful public lesson, and then he would forgive him and we could all go to breakfast.

The little faraway figure turned to his confessor. He bowed his head for a blessing and kissed the rosary. He knelt before the block and clasped it in both hands. I wondered what it must be like, to put one's cheek to the smooth waxed wood, to smell the warm wind coming off the river, to hear, overhead, the cry of seagulls. Even knowing as he did that this was a masque and not the real thing, it must be odd for Uncle to put his head down and know that the executioner was standing behind.

The executioner raised his axe. I looked towards the king. He was leaving his intervention very late. I glanced back at the stage. My uncle, head down, flung wide his arms, a sign of his consent, the signal that the axe could fall. I looked back to the king, he must rise to his feet now. But he still sat, his handsome face grim. And while I was still looking towards him there was another roll of drums, suddenly silenced, and then the thud of the axe, first once, then again and a third time: a sound as domestic as chopping wood. Disbelievingly, I saw the head of my uncle bounce into the straw and a scarlet gush of blood from the strangely stumpy neck. The black-hooded axeman put the great stained axe to one side and lifted the head by the thick curly hair, so that we could all see the strange mask-like thing: black with the blindfold from forehead to nose, and the teeth bared in a last defiant grin.

The king rose slowly from his seat and I thought, childishly, 'Dear God, how awfully embarrassing this is going to be. He has left it too late. It has all gone wrong. He forgot to speak in time.'

But I was wrong. He did not leave it too late, he did not forget. He wanted my uncle to die before the court so that everybody might know that there was only one king, and that was Henry. There could be only one king, and that was Henry. And there would be a son born to this king – and even to suggest otherwise meant a shameful death.

2

The court returned quietly to Westminster Palace in three barges, rowed up the river. The men on the riverbank pulled off their hats and kneeled as the royal barge went swiftly past with a flurry of pennants and a glimpse of rich cloth. I was in the second barge with the ladies of the court, the queen's barge. My mother was seated near me. In a rare moment of interest she glanced at me and remarked, 'You're very pale, Mary, are you feeling sick?'

'I didn't think he would be executed,' I said. 'I thought the king would forgive him.'

My mother leaned forward so that her mouth was at my ear and no one could have heard us over the creaking of the boat and the beat of the rowers' drum. 'Then you are a fool,' she said shortly. 'And a fool to remark it. Watch and learn, Mary. There is no room for mistakes at court.'

Spring 1522

'I am going to France tomorrow and I shall bring your sister Anne home with me,' my father told me on the stairs of Westminster Palace. 'She's to have a place in the court of Queen Mary Tudor as she returns to England.'

'I thought she'd stay in France,' I said. 'I thought she'd marry a French count or somebody.'

He shook his head. 'We have other plans for her.'

I knew it was pointless to ask what plans they had. I would have to wait and see. My greatest dread was that they would have a better marriage for her than I had made, that I would have to follow the hem of her gown as she swept ahead of me for the rest of my life.

'Wipe that surly look off your face,' my father said sharply.

At once I smiled my courtier's smile. 'Of course, Father,' I said obediently.

He nodded and I curtsied low as he left me. I came up from my curtsey and went slowly up to my husband's bedroom. I had a small looking glass on the wall and I stood before it and gazed at my own reflection. 'It'll be all right,' I whispered to myself. 'I am a Boleyn, that's not a small thing to be, and my mother was born a Howard, that's to be one of the greatest families in the country. I'm a Howard girl, a Boleyn girl.' I bit my lip. 'But so is she.'

I smiled my empty courtier's smile and the reflected pretty face smiled back. 'I am the youngest Boleyn girl, but not the least. I am married to William Carey, a man high in the king's favour. I am the queen's favourite and youngest lady in waiting. Nobody can spoil this for me. Not even she can take this from me.'

Anne and Father were delayed by spring storms and I found myself hoping, childishly, that her boat would sink and she would drown. At the thought of her death I felt a confusing pang of genuine distress mixed with elation. There could hardly be a world for me without Anne, there was hardly world enough for us both.

In any case, she arrived safely enough. I saw my father walking with her from the royal landing stage up the gravelled paths to the palace. Even from the first-floor window, looking down I could see the swing of her gown, the stylish cut of her cloak, and a moment of pure envy swept through me as I saw how it swirled around her. I waited till she was out of sight and then I hurried to my seat in the queen's presence chamber.

I planned that she should first see me very much at home in the queen's richly tapestried rooms, and that I should rise and greet her, very grown-up and gracious. But when the doors opened and she came in I was overcome by a rush of sudden joy, and I heard myself cry out 'Anne!' and ran to her, my skirt swishing. And Anne, who had come in with her head very high, and her arrogant dark look darting everywhere, suddenly stopped being a grand young lady of fifteen years and threw out her arms to me.

'You're taller,' she said breathlessly, her arms tight around me, her cheek pressed to mine.

'I've got *such* high heels.' I inhaled the familiar perfume of her. Soap, and rosewater essence from her warm skin, lavender from her clothes.

'You all right?'

'Yes. You?'

'*Bien sur*! How is it? Marriage?'

'Not too bad. Nice clothes.'

'And he?'

'Very grand. Always with the king, high in his favour.'

'Have you done it?'

'Yes, ages ago.'

'Did it hurt?'

'Very much.'

She pulled back to read my face.

'Not too much,' I said, qualifying. 'He does try to be gentle. He always gives me wine. It's just all rather awful, really.'

Her scowl melted away and she giggled, her eyes dancing. 'How is it awful?'

'He pisses in the pot, right where I can see!'

She collapsed in a wail of laughter. 'No!'

'Now, girls,' my father said, coming up behind Anne. 'Mary, take Anne and present her to the queen.'

At once I turned and led her through the press of ladies in waiting to where the queen was seated, erect in her chair at the fireside. 'She's strict,' I warned Anne. 'It's not like France.'

Katherine of Aragon took the measure of Anne with one of her clear blue-eyed sweeps and I felt a pang of fear that she would prefer my sister to me.

Anne swept the queen an immaculate French curtsey, and came up as if she owned the palace. She spoke in a voice rippling with that seductive accent, her every gesture was that of the French court. I noted with glee the queen's frosty response to Anne's stylish manner. I drew her to a windowseat.

'She hates the French,' I said. 'She'll never have you around her if you keep that up.'

Anne shrugged. 'They're the most fashionable. Whether she likes them or not. What else?'

'Spanish?' I suggested. 'If you have to pretend to be something else.'

Anne let out a snort of laughter. 'And wear those hoods! She looks as if someone stuck a roof on her head.'

'Ssshhh,' I said reprovingly. 'She's a beautiful woman. The finest queen in Europe.'

'She's an old woman,' Anne said cruelly. 'Dressed like an old woman in the ugliest clothes in Europe, from the stupidest nation in Europe. We have no time for the Spanish.'

'Who's we?' I asked coldly. 'Not the English.'

'*Les Français!*' she said irritatingly. '*Bien sur*! I am all but French now.'

'You're English born and bred, like George and me,' I said flatly. 'And I was brought up at the French court just like you. Why do you always have to pretend to be different?'

'Because everyone has to do something.'

'What d'you mean?'

'Every woman has to have something which singles her out, which catches the eye, which makes her the centre of attention. I am going to be French.'

'So you pretend to be something that you're not,' I said disapprovingly.

She gleamed at me and her dark eyes measured me in a way that only Anne could do. 'I pretend no more and no less than you do,' she said quietly. 'My little sister, my little golden sister, my milk and honey sister.'

I met her eyes, my lighter gaze into her black, and I knew that I was smiling her smile, that she was a dark mirror to me. 'Oh that,' I said, still refusing to acknowledge a hit. 'Oh that.'

'Exactly,' she said. 'I shall be dark and French and fashionable and difficult and you shall be sweet and open and English and fair. What a pair we shall be. What man could resist us?'

I laughed, she could always make me laugh. I looked down from the leaded window and saw the king's hunt returning to the stable yard.

'Is that the king on his way?' Anne asked. 'Is he as handsome as they say?'

'He's wonderful. He really is. He dances and rides, and – oh – I can't tell you!'

'Will he come here now?'

'Probably. He always comes to see her.'

Anne glanced dismissively to where the queen sat sewing with her ladies. 'Can't think why.'

'Because he loves her,' I said. 'It's a wonderful love story. Her married to his brother and his brother dying like that, so young, and then her not knowing what she should do or where she could go, and then him taking her and making her his wife and his queen. It's a wonderful story and he loves her still.'

Anne raised a perfectly arched eyebrow and glanced around the room. All the ladies in waiting had heard the sound of the returning hunt and had spread the skirts of their gowns and moved in their seats so that they were placed like a little tableau to be viewed from the doorway when the door was flung open and Henry the king stood on the threshold and laughed with the boisterous joy of an indulged young man. 'I came to surprise you and I catch you all unawares!'

The queen started. 'How amazed we are!' she said warmly. 'And what a delight!'

The king's companions and friends followed their master into the room. My brother George came in first, checked on the threshold at the sight of Anne, held his pleasure hidden behind his handsome courtier's face, and bowed low over the queen's hand. 'Majesty.' He breathed on her fingers. 'I have been in the sun all the morning but I am only dazzled now.'

She smiled her small polite smile as she gazed down at his bent dark curly head. 'You may greet your sister.'

'Mary is here?' George asked indifferently, as if he had not seen us both.

'Your other sister, Anne,' the queen corrected him. A small gesture from her hand, heavy with rings, indicated that the two of us should step forward. George swept us a bow without moving from the prime place near the throne.

'Has she changed much?' the queen asked.

George smiled. 'I hope she will change more with a model such as you before her eyes.'

The queen gave a little laugh. 'Very pretty,' she said appreciatively, and waved him towards us.

'Hello, little Miss Beautiful,' he said to Anne. 'Hello, Mistress Beautiful,' to me.

Anne regarded him from under her dark eyelashes. 'I wish I could hug you,' she said.

'We'll go out, as soon as we can,' George decreed. 'You look well, Annamaria.'

'I am well,' she said. 'And you?'

'Never better.'

'What's little Mary's husband like?' she asked curiously, watching William as he entered and bowed over the queen's hand.

'Great-grandson of the third Earl of Somerset, and very high in the king's favour.' George volunteered the only matters of interest: his family connections and his closeness to the throne. 'She's done well. Did you know you were brought home to be married, Anne?'

'Father hasn't said who.'

'I think you're to go to Ormonde,' George said.

'A countess,' Anne said with a triumphant smile to me.

'Only Irish,' I rejoined at once.

My husband stepped back from the queen's chair, caught sight of us, and then raised an eyebrow at Anne's intense provocative stare. The king took his seat beside the queen and looked around the room.

'My dear Mary Carey's sister has come to join our company,' the queen said. 'This is Anne Boleyn.'

'George's sister?' the king asked.

My brother bowed. 'Yes, Your Majesty.'

The king smiled at Anne. She dropped him a curtsey straight down, like a bucket in a well, head up, and a small challenging smile on her lips. The king was not taken, he liked easy women, he liked smiling women. He did not like women who fixed him with a dark challenging gaze.

'And are you happy to be with your sister again?' he asked me.

I dipped a low curtsey and came up a little flushed. 'Of course, Your Majesty,' I said sweetly. 'What girl would not long for the company of a sister like Anne?'

His eyebrows twitched together a little at that. He preferred the open bawdy humour of men to the barbed wit of women. He looked from me to Anne's slightly quizzical expression and then he got the joke and laughed out loud, and snapped his fingers and held out his hand to me.

'Don't worry, sweetheart,' he said. 'No-one can overshadow the bride in her early years of wedded bliss. And both Carey and I have a preference for fair-haired women.'

Everyone laughed at that, especially Anne who was dark, and the queen whose auburn hair had faded to brown and grey. They would have been fools to do anything but laugh heartily at the king's pleasantry. And I laughed as well, with more joy in my heart than they had in theirs, I should think.

The musicians played an opening chord, and Henry drew me to him. 'You're a very pretty girl,' he said approvingly. 'Carey tells me that he so likes a young bride that he'll never bed any but twelve-year-old virgins ever again.'

It was hard to keep my chin up and my smile on my face. We turned in the dance and the king smiled down on me.

'He's a lucky man,' he said graciously.

'He is lucky to have your favour,' I started, stumbling towards a compliment.

'Luckier to have yours, I should think!' he said with a sudden bellow of laughter. Then he swept me into a dance, and I whirled down the line of dancers and saw my brother's quick glance of approval, and what was sweeter still: Anne's envious eyes as the King of England danced past her with me in his arms.

∾

Anne slipped into the routine of the English court and waited for her wedding. She still had not met her husband-to-be, and the arguments about the dowry and settlements looked as if they would take forever. Not even the influence of Cardinal Wolsey, who had his finger in this as well as every other pie in the bakehouse of England, could speed the business along. In the meantime she flirted as elegantly as a Frenchwoman, served the king's sister with a nonchalant grace, and squandered hours every day in gossiping, riding, and playing with George and me. We were alike in tastes and not far apart in age; I was the baby at fourteen to Anne's fifteen and George's nineteen years. We were the closest of kin and yet almost strangers. I had been at the French court with Anne while George had been learning his trade as a courtier in England. Now, reunited, we became known around the court as the three Boleyns, the three delightful Boleyns, and the king would often look round when he was in his private rooms and cry out for the three Boleyns and someone would be sent running from one end of the castle to fetch us.

Our first task in life was to enhance the king's many entertainments: jousting, tennis, riding, hunting, hawking, dancing. He liked to live in a continual roar of excitement and it was our duty to ensure that he was never bored. But sometimes, very rarely, in the quiet time before dinner, or if it rained and he could not hunt, he would find his own way to the queen's apartments, and she would put down her sewing or her reading and send us away with a word.

If I lingered I might see her smile at him, in a way that she never smiled at anyone else, not even at her daughter the Princess Mary. And once, when I had entered without realising the king was there, I found him seated at her feet like a lover, with his head tipped back to rest in her lap as she stroked his red-gold curls off his forehead and twisted them round her fingers where they glowed as bright as the rings he had given her when she had been a young princess with hair as bright as his, and he had married her against the advice of everyone.

I tiptoed away without them seeing me. It was so rare that they were alone together that I did not want to be the one to break the spell. I went to find Anne. She was walking in the cold garden with George, a bunch of snowdrops in her hand, her cloak wrapped tight about her.

'The king is with the queen,' I said as I joined them. 'On their own.'

Anne raised an eyebrow. 'In bed?' she asked curiously.

I flushed. 'Of course not, it's two in the afternoon.'

Anne smiled at me. 'You must be a happy wife if you think you can't bed before nightfall.'

George extended his other arm to me. 'She is a happy wife,' he said on my behalf. 'William was telling the king that he had never known a sweeter girl. But what were they doing, Mary?'

'Just sitting together,' I said. I had a strong feeling that I did not want to describe the scene to Anne.

'She won't get a son that way,' Anne said crudely.

'Hush,' George and I said at once. The three of us drew a little closer and lowered our voices.

'She must be losing hope of it,' George said. 'What is she now? Thirty-eight? Thirty-nine?'

'Only thirty-seven,' I said indignantly.

'Does she still have her monthly courses?'

'Oh George!'

'Yes she does,' Anne said, matter-of-factly. 'But little good they do her. It's her fault. It can't be laid at the king's door with his bastard from Bessie Blount learning to ride his pony.'

'There's still plenty of time,' I said defensively.

'Time for her to die and him to remarry?' Anne said thoughtfully. 'Yes. And she's not strong, is she?'

'Anne!' For once my recoil from her was genuine. 'That's vile.'

George glanced around once more to ensure that there was no-one near us in the garden. A couple of Seymour girls were walking with their mother but we paid no attention to them. Their family were our chief rivals for power and advancement, we liked to pretend not to see them.

'It's vile but it's true,' he said bluntly. 'Who's to be the next king if he doesn't have a son?'

'Princess Mary could marry,' I suggested.

'A foreign prince brought in to rule England? It'd never hold,' George said. 'And we can't tolerate another war for the throne.'

'Princess Mary could become queen in her own right and not marry,' I said wildly. 'Rule as a queen on her own.'

Anne gave a snort of disbelief, her breath a little cloud on the cold air. 'Oh aye,' she said derisively. 'She could ride astride and learn to joust. A girl can't rule a country like this, the great lords'd eat her alive.'

The three of us paused before the fountain that stood in the centre of the garden. Anne, with her well-trained grace, sat on the rim of the basin and looked into the water, a few goldfish swam hopefully towards her and she pulled off her embroidered glove and dabbled her long fingers in the water. They came up, little mouths gaping, to nibble at the air. George and I watched her, as she watched her own rippling reflection.

'Does the king think of this?' she asked her mirrored image.

'Constantly,' George answered. 'There is nothing in the world more important. I think he would legitimise Bessie Blount's boy and make him heir if there's no issue from the queen.'

'A bastard on the throne?'

'He wasn't christened Henry Fitzroy for no reason,' George replied. 'He's acknowledged as the king's own son. If Henry lives long enough to make the country safe for him, if he can get the Seymours to agree, and us Howards, if Wolsey gets the church behind him and the foreign powers . . . what should stop him?'

'One little boy, and he a bastard,' Anne said thoughtfully. 'One little girl of six, one elderly queen and a king in the prime of his life.' She looked up at the two of us, dragging her gaze away from her own pale face in the water. 'What's going to happen?' she asked. 'Something has to happen. What's it going to be?'

❁

Cardinal Wolsey sent a message to the queen asking us to take part in a masque on Shrove Tuesday which he was to stage at his house, York Place. The queen asked me to read the letter and my voice trembled with excitement over the words: a great masque, a fortress named Chateau Vert, and five ladies to dance with the five knights who would besiege the fort. 'Oh! Your Majesty . . .' I started and then fell silent.

'Oh! Your Majesty, what?'

'I was just wondering if I might be allowed to go,' I said very humbly. 'To watch the revels.'

'I think you were wondering a little more than that?' she asked me with a gleam in her eyes.

'I was wondering if I might be one of the dancers,' I confessed. 'It does sound very wonderful.'

'Yes, you may be,' she said. 'How many ladies does the cardinal command of me?'

'Five,' I said quietly. Out of the corner of my eye I could see Anne sit back in her seat and close her eyes for just a moment. I knew exactly what she was doing, I could hear her voice in my head as loudly as if she was shouting: 'Choose me! Choose me! Choose me!'

It worked. 'Mistress Anne Boleyn,' the queen said thoughtfully. 'The Queen Mary of France, the Countess of Devon, Jane Parker, and you, Mary.'

Anne and I exchanged a rapid glance. We would be an oddly assorted quintet: the king's aunt, his sister Queen Mary, and the heiress Jane Parker who was likely to be our sister-in-law, if her father and ours could agree her dowry, and the two of us.

'Will we wear green?' Anne asked.

The queen smiled at her. 'Oh, I should think so,' she said. 'Mary, why don't you write a note to the cardinal and tell him that we will be delighted to attend, and ask him to send the master of the revels so that we can all choose costumes and plan our dances?'

'I'll do it.' Anne rose from her chair and went to the table where the pen and ink and paper were ready. 'Mary has such a cramped hand he will think we are writing a refusal.'

The queen laughed. 'Ah, the French scholar,' she said gently. 'You shall write to the cardinal then, Mistress Boleyn, in your beautiful French, or shall you write to him in Latin?'

Anne's gaze did not waver. 'Whichever Your Majesty prefers,' she said steadily. 'I am reasonably fluent in both.'

'Tell him that we are all eager to play our part in his Chateau Vert,' the queen said smoothly. 'What a shame you can't write Spanish.'

❧

The arrival of the master of the revels to teach us our steps for the dance was the signal for a savage battle fought with smiles and the sweetest words as to who would play which role in the masque. In the end the queen herself intervened and gave us our parts without allowing any discussion. She gave me the role of Kindness, the king's sister Queen Mary got the plum part of Beauty, Jane Parker was Constancy – 'Well she does cling on so,' Anne whispered to me. Anne herself was Persever-ance. 'Shows what she thinks of you,' I whispered back. Anne had the grace to giggle.

We were to be attacked by Indian women – in reality the choristers of the royal chapel – before being rescued by the king and his chosen friends. We were warned that the king would be disguised and we should take great care not to penetrate the transparent ruse of a golden mask strapped on a golden head, taller than anyone else in the room.

❀

It was a great romp in the end, far more fun than I had expected, much more of a play-fight than a dance. George flung rose petals at me and I drenched him with a shower of rosewater. The choristers were just little boys and they got over-excited and attacked the knights and were swung off their feet and spun around and dumped, dizzy and giggly, on the ground. When we ladies came out from the castle and danced with the mystery knights it was the tallest knight who came to dance with me, the king himself, and I, still breathless from my battle with George, and with rose petals in my headdress and my hair, and sugared fruit tumbling out of the folds of my gown, found that I was laughing and giving my hand to him, and dancing with him as if he were an ordinary man and I little more than a kitchen maid at a country romp.

When the signal for the unmasking should have come the king cried out: 'Play on! Let's dance some more!' and instead of turning and taking another partner he led me out again, a country dance when we went hand to hand and I could see his eyes gleaming at me through the slits in his golden mask. Reckless and laughing, I smiled back up at him and let that sunny approbation sink into my skin.

'I envy your husband when your dress comes off tonight, you will shower him with sweets,' he said in an undertone when the dance brought us side by side as we watched another couple in the centre of the ring.

I could not think of a witty reply, these were not the formal compli-ments of courtly love. The image of a husband being showered with sweets was too domestic, and too erotic.

'Surely you should envy nothing,' I said. 'Surely everything is all yours.'

'Why would that be?' he asked.

'Because you are king,' I started, forgetting that he was supposed to be

13

in impenetrable disguise. 'King of Chateau Vert,' I recovered. 'King for a day. It should be King Henry who envies you, for you have won a great siege in one afternoon.'

'And what d'you think of King Henry?'

I looked up at him, my innocent look. 'He is the greatest king that this country has ever known. It is an honour to be at his court and a privilege to be near him.'

'Could you love him as a man?'

I looked down and blushed. 'I would not dare to think of it. He has never so much as glanced towards me.'

'Oh he has glanced,' the king said firmly. 'You can be sure of that. And if he glanced more than once, Miss Kindness, would you be true to your name and be kind to him?'

'Your . . .' I bit my lip and stopped myself saying: 'Your Majesty'. I looked around for Anne; more than anything, I wanted her by my side and her wits at my service.

'You are named Kindness,' he reminded me.

I smiled at him, peeping up through my golden mask. 'I am,' I said. 'And I suppose I should have to be kind.'

The musicians finished the dance and waited, poised for the king's orders. 'Unmask!' he said and tore his own mask off his face. I saw the king of England, gave a wonderful little gasp and staggered.

'She's fainting!' George cried out, it was beautifully done. I fell into the king's arms as Anne, fast as a snake, unpinned my mask, and – brilliantly – pulled off my headdress so that my golden hair tumbled down like a stream over the king's arm.

I opened my eyes, his face was very close. I could smell the perfume on his hair, his breath was on my cheek, I watched his lips, he was close enough to kiss me.

'You have to be kind to me,' he reminded me.

'You are the king . . .' I said incredulously.

'And you have promised to be kind to me.'

'I didn't know it was you, Your Majesty.'

He lifted me gently and carried me over to the window. He opened it himself and the cold air blew in. I tossed my head and let my hair ripple in the draught.

'Did you faint for fright?' he asked, his voice very low.

I looked down at my hands. 'For delight,' I whispered, as sweet as a virgin in confession.

He bent his head and kissed my hands and then rose to his feet. 'And now we dine!' he called out.

I looked over to Anne. She was untying her mask and watching me with a long calculating look, the Boleyn look, the Howard look that says: what has happened here, and how may I turn it to my advantage? It was as if under her golden mask was another beautiful mask of skin, and only beneath that was the real woman. As I looked back at her she gave me a small secret smile.

The king gave his arm to the queen, she rose from her chair as gay as if she had been enjoying watching her husband flirt with me; but as he turned to lead her away she paused and her blue eyes looked long and hard at me, as if she were saying goodbye to a friend.

'I hope you will soon recover from your faintness, Mistress Carey,' she said gently. 'Perhaps you should go to your room.'

'I think she is light-headed from lack of food,' George interposed quickly. 'May I bring her in to dine?'

Anne stepped forward. 'The king frightened her when he unmasked. No-one guessed for a moment that it was you, Your Majesty!'

The king laughed in delight, and the court laughed with him. Only the queen heard how the three of us had turned her order so that despite her declared wishes, I would be brought in to dine. She measured the strength of the three of us. I was no Bessie Blount, who was next to nobody; I was a Boleyn, and the Boleyns worked together.

'Come and dine with us then, Mary,' she said. The words were inviting but there was no warmth in them at all.

∽

We were to sit where we pleased, the knights of the Chateau Vert and the ladies, all mixed up informally at a round table. Cardinal Wolsey as the host sat opposite the king with the queen at the third point on the table and the rest of us scattered where we chose. George put me next to him and Anne summoned my husband to her side and diverted him, while the king, seated opposite me, stared at me and I, carefully, looked away. On Anne's right was Henry Percy of Northumberland, on George's other side was Jane Parker, watching me intently, as if she were trying to discover the trick of being a desirable girl.

I ate only a little, though there were pies and pasties and fine meats and game. I took a little salad, the queen's favourite dish, and drank wine and water. My father joined the table during the meal and sat beside my mother who whispered quickly in his ear and I saw his glance flick over me, like a horse-trader assessing the value of a filly. Whenever I looked up the king's eyes were on me, whenever I looked away I was conscious of his stare still on my face.

When we had finished, the cardinal suggested that we go to the hall and listen to some music. Anne was at my side and steered me down the stairs so that when the king arrived the two of us were seated on a bench against the wall. It was easy and natural for him to pause to ask me how I did now. Natural that Anne and I should stand as he came past us, and that he should sit on the vacant bench and invite me to sit beside him. Anne drifted away and chattered to Henry Percy, shielding the king and me from the court, most especially from the smiling gaze of Queen Katherine. My father went up to speak to her while the musicians played. It was all done with complete ease and comfort, and it meant that the king and I were all but concealed in a crowded room with music loud enough to drown our whispered conversation, and every member of the Boleyn family well placed to hide what was going on.

'You are better now?' he asked me in an undertone.

'Never better in all my life, sire.'

'I am riding out tomorrow,' he said. 'Would you care to come with me?'

'If Her Majesty can spare me,' I said, determined not to risk the queen's displeasure.

'I will ask the queen to release you for the morning. I shall tell her that you need the fresh air.'

I smiled. 'What a fine physician you would make, Your Majesty. If you can make a diagnosis and provide the cure all in the space of a day.'

'You must be an obedient patient and do whatever I advise,' he warned me.

'I will.' I looked down at my fingers. I could feel his gaze on me. I was soaring, higher than I could have dreamed.

'I may order you to bed for days at a time,' he said, his voice very low.

I snatched a quick look at his intense gaze on my face and felt myself blush and heard myself stammer into silence. The music abruptly stopped. 'Do play again!' my mother said. Queen Katherine looked around for the king and saw him seated with me. 'Shall we dance?' she asked.

It was a royal command. Anne and Henry Percy took their places in a set, the musicians started to play. I rose to my feet and Henry went to sit beside his wife and watch us. George was my partner.

'Head up,' he snapped as he took my hand. 'You look hangdog.'

'She's watching me,' I whispered back.

'Course she is. More to the point *he's* watching you. And most important of all, Father and Uncle Howard are watching you, and they expect you to carry yourself as a young woman on the rise. Up you go, Mistress Carey, and all of us go up with you.'

I raised my head at that and I smiled at my brother as if I were carefree. I danced as gracefully as I could, I dipped and turned and twirled under his careful hand. And when I looked up at the king and the queen they were both watching me.

They held a family conference at my uncle Howard's great house in London. We met in his library where the dark bound books muffled the noise from the streets. Two men in our Howard livery were stationed outside the door to prevent any interruptions, and to ensure that no one stopped and eavesdropped. We were to discuss family business, family secrets. No-one but a Howard could come near.

I was the very cause and subject of the meeting. I was the hub around which these events would turn. I was the Boleyn pawn that must be played to advantage. Everything was concentrated on me. I felt my very wrists throb with a sense of my own importance, and a contradictory flutter of anxiety that I would fail them.

'Is she fertile?' Uncle Howard asked my mother.

'Her courses are regular enough and she's a healthy girl.'

My uncle nodded. 'If the king has her, and she conceives his bastard, then we have much to play for.' I noticed with a sort of terrified concentration that the fur on the hem of his sleeves brushed against the wood of the table, the richness of his coat took on a lustre from the light of the flames of the fire behind him. 'She can't sleep in Carey's bed any more. The marriage has to be put aside while the king favours her.'

I gave a little gasp. I could not think who would say such a thing to my husband. And besides, we had sworn that we would stay together, that marriage was for the making of children, that God had put us together and no man could put us apart.

'I don't . . .' I started.

Anne tweaked at my gown. 'Hush,' she hissed. The seed pearls on her French hood winked at me like bright-eyed conspirators.

'I'll speak to Carey,' my father said.

George took my hand. 'If you conceive a child the king has to know that it is his and none other's.'

'I can't be his mistress,' I whispered back.

'No choice.' He shook his head.

'I can't do it,' I said out loud. I gripped tightly on my brother's comforting clasp and looked down the long dark wood table to my uncle, as sharp as a falcon with black eyes that missed nothing. 'Sir, I am sorry, but I love the queen. She's a great lady and I can't betray her. I promised before God to cleave only to my husband, and surely I shouldn't betray him? I know the king is the king; but you can't want me to? Surely? Sir, I can't do it.'

He did not answer me. Such was his power that he did not even consider replying. 'What am I supposed to do with this delicate conscience?' he asked the air above the table.

'Leave it to me,' Anne said simply. 'I can explain things to Mary.'

'You're a little young for the task of tutor.'

She met his look with her quiet confidence. 'I was reared in the most fashionable court in the world,' she said. 'And I was not idle. I watched everything. I learned all there was to see. I know what is needed here, and I can teach Mary how to behave.'

He hesitated for a moment. 'You had better not have studied flirtation too closely, Miss Anne.'

Her serenity was that of a nun. 'Of course not.'

I felt my shoulder lift, as if I would shrug her away. 'I don't see why I should do what Anne says.'

I had disappeared, though this whole meeting was supposed to be about me. Anne had stolen their attention. 'Well, I shall trust you to coach your sister. George, you too. You know how the king is with women, keep Mary in his sight.'

They nodded. There was a brief silence.

'I'll speak with Carey's father,' my father volunteered. 'William will be expecting it. He's no fool.'

My uncle glanced down the table to Anne and George where they stood either side of me, more like jailers than friends. 'You help your sister,' he ordered them. 'Whatever she needs to ensnare the king, you give her. Whatever arts she needs, whatever goods she should have, whatever skills she lacks, you get them for her. We are looking to the two of you to get her into his bed. Don't forget it. There will be great rewards. But if you fail, there will be nothing for us at all. Remember it.'

❧

My parting with my husband was curiously painful. I walked into our bedroom as my maid was packing my things to take them to the queen's rooms. He stood amid the chaos of shoes and gowns thrown on the bed, and cloaks tossed over chairs, and jewel boxes everywhere; and his young face showed his shock.

'I see you are on the rise, madam.'

He was a handsome young man, one that any woman might have favoured. I thought that if we had not been ordered by our families into

18

this marriage and now out of it that we might have liked each other. 'I am sorry,' I said awkwardly. 'You know that I have to do what my uncle and my father tell me.'

'I know that,' he said bluntly. 'I have to do what they all order as well.'

To my relief, Anne appeared in the doorway, her mischievous smile very bright. 'How now, William Carey? Well met!' It seemed as if it were her greatest joy to see her brother-in-law amid the mess of my things and the wreckage of his own hopes for a marriage and a son.

'Anne Boleyn.' He bowed briefly. 'Have you come to help your sister onwards and upwards?'

'Of course.' She gleamed at him. 'As we all should do. None of us will suffer if Mary is favoured.'

She held his gaze for one fearless moment, and it was he who turned away to look out of the window. 'I have to go,' he said. 'The king bids me to go hunting with him.' He hesitated a moment and then he came across the room to where I stood surrounded by the scatterings of my wardrobe. Gently, he took my hand and kissed it. 'I am sorry for you. And I am sorry for me. When you are sent back to me, perhaps a month from now, perhaps a year, I will try to remember this day, and you looking like a child, a little lost among all these clothes. I will try to remember that you were innocent of any plotting; that today at least, you were more a girl than a Boleyn.'

❁

The queen observed that I was now a single woman, lodged with Anne as my bedfellow in a little room off her chambers, without comment. Her outward manner to me changed not at all. She remained courteous and quiet-spoken. If she wanted me to do something for her: write a note, sing, take her lap dog from the room, or send a message, she asked me as politely as she had ever done. But she never again asked me to read to her from the Bible, she never asked me to sit at her feet while she sewed, she never blessed me when I went to bed. I was no longer her favourite little maid.

It was a relief to go to bed at night with Anne. We drew the curtains around us so that we were safe to whisper in the shadowy darkness without being overheard and it was like France in the days of our childhood. Sometimes George would leave the king's rooms and come to find us, and climb onto the high bed, balance his candle perilously on the bedhead, and bring out his pack of cards or his dice and play with us while the other girls in nearby rooms slept, not knowing that a man was hidden in our chamber.

They did not lecture me about the role I was to play. Cunningly, they waited for me to come to them and tell them that it was beyond me.

I said nothing while my clothes were moved from one end of the palace to the other. I said nothing when the whole court packed and moved to the king's favourite palace, Eltham in Kent, for the spring. I said nothing when my husband rode beside me during the progress and talked to me kindly of the weather and the condition of my horse, which was Jane Parker's, lent under protest, as her contribution to the family ambition. But when I had George and Anne to myself in the garden at Eltham Palace, I said to George:

'I don't think I can do this.'

'Do what?' he asked unhelpfully. We were supposed to be walking the queen's dog, which had been carried on the pommel of the saddle for the day's ride and was thoroughly jolted and sick-looking. 'Come on, Flo!' he said encouragingly. 'Seek! Seek!'

'I can't be with my husband and the king at the same time,' I said. 'I can't laugh with the king when my husband is watching.'

'Why not?' Anne rolled a ball along the ground for Flo to chase after. The little dog watched it go without interest. 'Oh go on, you stupid thing!' Anne exclaimed.

'Because I feel all wrong.'

'D'you know better than your mother?' Anne asked bluntly.

'Of course not!'

'Better than your father? Your uncle?'

I shook my head.

'They are planning a great future for you,' Anne said solemnly. 'Any girl in England would die for your chances. You are on the way to becoming the favourite of the king of England, and you are simpering round the garden wondering if you can laugh at his jokes? You've got about as much sense as Flo here.' She put the tip of her riding boot under Flo's unwilling arse and pushed her gently along the path. Flo sat down, as stubborn and as unhappy as me.

'Gently,' George cautioned her. He took my cold hand and tucked it in the crook of his elbow. 'It's not as bad as you think,' he said. 'William was riding with you today to show that he gives his consent, not to make you feel guilty. He knows that the king must have his way. We all know that. William's happy enough about it. There will be favours for him which you will have been the means of his getting. You're doing your duty by him by advancing his family. He's grateful to you. You're not doing anything wrong.'

I hesitated. I looked from George's brown honest eyes to Anne's averted face. 'There's another thing,' I said, forced to confess.

'What is it?' George asked. Anne's eyes followed Flo but I knew that her attention was turned on me.

'I don't know how to do it,' I said quietly. 'You know, William did it once a week or so, and that in the dark, and quickly done, and I never much liked it. I don't know what it is I am supposed to do.'

George gave a little gulp of laughter and put his arm around my shoulders and gave me a hug. 'Oh, I'm sorry to laugh. But you have it all wrong. He doesn't want a woman who knows what to do. There are dozens of them in every bath house in the City. He wants you. It's you he likes. And he'll like it if you are a little shy and a little uncertain. That's all right.'

'Hulloah!' came a shout from behind us. 'The Three Boleyns!'

We turned and there was the king on the upper terrace, still dressed in his travelling cloak with his hat rakishly set on his head.

'Here we go.' George swept a low bow. Anne and I sank down into our curtseys together.

'Are you not tired from your ride?' the king asked. The question was general but he was looking at me.

'Not at all.'

'That's a pretty little mare you were riding, but too short in the back. I shall give you a new horse,' he said.

'Your Majesty is very kind,' I said. 'She's a borrowed horse. I should be glad to have a horse of my own.'

'You shall pick out your choice in the stables,' he said. 'Come, we can go and look now.'

He held out his arm to me and I put my fingers gently on the rich cloth of his sleeve.

'I can hardly feel you.' He put his hand on my own and pressed it tighter. 'There. I want to know that I have you, Mistress Carey.' His eyes were very blue and bright, he took in the top of my French hood and then my golden-brown hair, smoothed back under the hood, and then my face. 'I *do* want to know that I have you.'

I felt my mouth go dry and I smiled, despite the breathless feeling that was something between fear and desire. 'I am happy to be with you.'

'Are you?' he asked, suddenly intent. 'Are you really? I want no false coin from you. There are many who would urge you to be with me. I want you to come of your own free will.'

'Oh Your Majesty! As if I did not dance with you at Cardinal Wolsey's revels without even knowing that it was you!'

He was pleased with the recollection. 'Oh yes! And you all but fainted when I unmasked and you discovered me. Who did you think it was?'

'I didn't think. I know it was foolish of me. I thought you were perhaps a stranger in court, a new and handsome stranger, and I was so pleased to be dancing with you.'

He laughed. 'Oh Mistress Carey, such a sweet face and such naughty thoughts! You hoped that a handsome stranger had come to court and chose to dance with you?'

'I don't mean to be naughty.' I was afraid for a moment that it was too sugary even for his taste. 'I just forgot how I should behave when you asked me to dance. I am sure I would never do anything wrong. There was just a moment when I –'

'When you?'

'When I forgot,' I said softly.

We reached the stone archway which led into the stables. The king paused in the shelter of the arch and turned me towards him. I could feel myself alive in every part of my body, from my riding boots, slippery on the cobblestones, to my upward glance at his face.

'Would you forget again?'

I hesitated, and then Anne stepped forward and said lightly: 'What horse does Your Majesty have in mind for my sister? I think you'll find she's a good horsewoman.'

He led the way into the stables, releasing me for a moment. George and he looked at one horse and then another. Anne came to my side.

'You have to keep him coming forward,' she said. 'Keep him coming forward but never let him think that you come forward yourself. He wants to feel that he is pursuing you, not that you are entrapping him. When he gives you the choice of coming forward or running away, like then – you must always run away.'

The king turned and smiled at me as George told a stable boy to lead a handsome bay horse from the stall. 'But don't run too fast,' my sister warned. 'Remember he has to catch you.'

☙

I danced with the king that evening before the whole of the court, and the next day I rode my new horse at his side when we went hunting. The queen, seated at the high table, watched us dance together, and when we rode out she waved farewell to him from the great door of the palace. Everyone knew that he was courting me, everyone knew that I would consent when I was ordered to do so. The only person who did not know this was the king. He thought that the pace of the courtship was determined by his desire.

The first rent day came a few weeks later in April when my father was appointed treasurer of the king's household, a post which brought him access to the king's daily wealth which he could peculate as he thought best. My father met me as we went in to dinner, and took me from the queen's train for a quiet word as Her Majesty went to her place at the top table.

'Your uncle and I are pleased with you,' he said briefly. 'Be guided by your brother and sister, they tell me that you are doing well.'

I bobbed a little curtsey.

'This is just the start for us,' he reminded me. 'You've got to have him and hold him, remember.'

I flinched a little from the words of the wedding mass. 'I know,' I said. 'I don't forget.'

'Has he done anything yet?'

I glanced towards the great hall where the king and the queen were taking their place. The trumpeters were in position to announce the arrival of the procession of servers from the kitchen.

'Not yet,' I said. 'Just eyes and words.'

'And you reply?'

'With smiles.' I did not tell my father that I was half-delirious with pleasure at being courted by the most powerful man in the kingdom. It was not hard to follow my sister's advice and smile and smile at him. It was not hard to blush and feel that I wanted to run away and at the same time wanted to draw closer.

My father nodded. 'Good enough. You may go to your place.'

I curtsied again and hurried into the hall just ahead of the servers. The queen looked at me a little sharply, as if she might reprimand me, but then she glanced sideways and caught sight of her husband's face. His expression was fixed, his gaze locked onto me, as I made my way up the hall and took my place among the ladies in waiting. It was an odd expression, intent, as if for a moment he could see nothing and hear nothing, as if the whole of the great hall had melted away for him and all he could see was me in my blue gown with my blue hood and my fair hair smoothed away off my face, and a smile trembling on my lips as I felt his desire. The queen took in the heat of his look, pressed her lips together, smiled her thin smile, and looked away.

❀

He came to her rooms that evening. 'Shall we have some music?' he asked her.

'Yes, Mistress Carey can sing for us,' she said pleasantly, gesturing me forward.

23

'Her sister Anne has the sweeter voice,' the king countermanded. Anne threw me a swift triumphant glance.

'Will you sing us one of your French songs, Miss Anne?' the king asked.

Anne swept one of her graceful curtsies. 'Your Majesty has only to command,' she said, the hint of the French accent strong in her voice.

The queen watched this exchange, I could see that she was wondering if the king's fancy was moving to another Boleyn girl. But he had outwitted her. Anne sat on a stool in the middle of the room, her lute on her lap, her voice sweet – as he said, sweeter than mine. The queen sat in her usual chair, with padded embroidered arms and a cushioned back which she never leaned against. The king did not take the matching chair beside hers, he strolled over to me and took Anne's vacated space, and glanced at the sewing in my hands.

'Very fine work,' he remarked.

'Shirts for the poor,' I said. 'The queen is good to the poor.'

'Indeed,' he said. 'How quickly your needle goes in and out, I should make such a knot of it. How tiny and deft your fingers are.'

His head was bent towards my hands, I found I was looking at the base of his neck and thinking that I should like to touch the thick curling hair.

'Your hands must be half the size of mine,' he said idly. 'Stretch them out and show me.'

I stabbed the needle into the shirts for the poor people and stretched out my hand to show him, palm up, towards him. His gaze never left my face as he put his hand out too, palm to palm towards mine yet not touching. I could feel the warmth of his hand against my hand, but I could not take my eyes from his face. His moustache curled a little around his lips, I wondered if the hair would be soft, like my husband's dark sparse curls, or wiry like spun gold. It looked as if it might be strong and scratchy, his kiss might buff my face to redness, everyone would know we had been kissing. Beneath the little curls of hair his lips were sensual, I could not take my eyes from them, I could not help but think about the touch of them, the taste of them.

Slowly, he brought his hand closer to mine, like dancers closing in a pavane. The heel of his hand touched the heel of mine and I felt the touch like a bite. I jumped a little and I saw his lips curve as he saw that his touch was a shock to me. My cool palm and fingers extended along his, my fingers stopping short of his at the top joints. I felt the sensation of his warm skin, a callus on one finger from archery, the hard palms of a man who rides and plays tennis and hunts and can hold a lance and a sword all the day. I dragged my gaze from his lips and took in his whole face, the bright alertness of his gaze focused on me like a sun through a burning glass, the desire which radiated from him like heat.

'Your skin is so soft.' His voice was as low as a whisper. 'And your hands are tiny, as I thought.'

The excuse of measuring the span of our fingers had long been exhausted, but we remained still, palm to palm, eyes on each other's face. Then slowly, irresistibly, his hand cupped around mine and he held it, gently but firmly within his own.

Anne finished one song and started another, without a change of key, without a break in her voice, keeping the spell of the moment.

It was the queen who interrupted. 'Your Majesty is disturbing Mistress Carey,' she said, with a little laugh as if the sight of her husband handfast with another woman, twenty-three years her junior, was amusing. 'Your friend William will not thank you for making his wife idle. She has promised to hem these shirts for the nuns at Whitchurch nunnery and they are not half done.'

He let me go and turned his head to his wife. 'William will forgive me,' he said carelessly.

'I am going to have a game of cards,' the queen said. 'Will you play with me, husband?'

For a moment I thought she had done it, drawn him away from me by his long-established affection. But as he rose to his feet to do as she wanted, he glanced back and saw me looking up at him. There was almost no calculation in my look – almost none. I was nothing more than a young woman gazing up at a man, with desire in my eyes.

'I shall have Mistress Carey as my partner. Shall you send for George and have another Boleyn for your partner? We could have a matched pair.'

'Jane Parker can play with me,' the queen said coolly.

∽

'You did that very well,' Anne said that night. She was seated by the fire in our bedroom, brushing her long dark hair, her head tipped to the side so that it fell like a scented waterfall over her shoulder. 'The bit with the hands was very good. What were you doing?'

'He was measuring his hand span against mine,' I said. I finished the plait of my fair hair and pulled my nightcap on my head and tied the white ribbon. 'When our hands touched I felt . . .'

'What?'

'It was like my skin was on fire,' I whispered. 'Really. Like his touch could burn me.'

Anne looked at me sceptically. 'What d'you mean?'

The words spilled out of my mouth. 'I want him to touch me. I am absolutely dying for him to touch me. I want his kiss.'

Anne was incredulous. 'You desire him?'

I wrapped my arms around myself and sank onto the stone windowseat. 'Oh God. Yes. I didn't realise this was where I was going. Oh yes. Oh yes.'

She grimaced, her mouth pulled down. 'You'd better not let Father and Mother hear that,' she warned. 'They've ordered you to play a clever game, not moon around like a lovesick girl at twilight.'

'But don't you think he wants me?'

'Oh, for the moment, yes. But next week? Next year?'

There was a tap on our bedroom door and George put his head around it. 'Can I come in?'

'All right,' Anne said ungraciously. 'But you can't stay long. We're going to bed.'

'I am too,' he said. 'I've been drinking with Father. I am going to bed and tomorrow, when I am sober, I shall arise early and hang myself.'

I hardly heard him, I was staring out of the window and thinking of the touch of Henry's hand against my own.

'Why?' Anne asked.

'My wedding is to be next year. Envy me, why don't you?'

'Everyone gets married but me,' Anne said irritably. 'The Ormondes have fallen through and they have nothing else for me. Do they want me to be a nun?'

'Not a bad choice,' George said. 'D'you think they'd take me?'

'In a nunnery?' I caught the sense of the talk and turned around to laugh at him. 'A fine abbess you'd make.'

'Better than most,' George said cheerfully. He went to sit on a stool, missed his seat and thudded down on the stone floor.

'You're drunk,' I accused.

'Aye. And sour with it.'

'There's something about my future wife that strikes me as very odd,' George said. 'Something a little . . .' he searched for the word. 'Rancid.'

'Nonsense,' Anne said. 'She's got an excellent dowry and good connections, she's favourite of the queen and her father is respected and rich. Why worry?'

'Because she's got a mouth like a rabbit snare, and eyes that are hot and cold at the same time.'

Anne laughed. 'Poet.'

'I know what George means,' I said. 'She's passionate and somehow secretive.'

'Just discreet,' Anne said.

George shook his head. 'Hot and cold at once. All the humours muddled up together. I shall live a dog's life with her.'

'Oh marry her and bed her and send her to the country,' Anne said impatiently. 'You're a man, you can do what you like.'

He looked more cheerful at that. 'I could push her down to Hever,' he said.

'Or Rochford Hall. And the king's bound to give you a new estate on your marriage.'

George raised his stone decanter to his lips. 'Anyone want some of this?'

'I will,' I said, taking the bottle and tasting the tart cold red wine.

'I'm going to bed,' Anne said primly. 'You should be ashamed of yourself, Mary, drinking in your nightcap.' She turned back the covers and climbed into bed. She inspected George and me as she folded the sheets around her hips. 'Both of you are a good deal too easy,' she ruled.

George pulled a face. 'Told us,' he said cheerfully to me.

'She's very strict,' I whispered in mock-respect. 'You'd never think she spent half her life flirting in the French court.'

'More Spanish than French, I think,' George said, wantonly provocative.

'And unmarried,' I whispered. 'A Spanish duenna.'

Anne lay down on the pillow, hunched her shoulders and pulled the covers into place. 'I'm not listening, so you can save your breath.'

'Who'd have her?' George demanded. 'Who'd want her?'

'They'll find her someone,' I said. 'Some younger son, or some poor old broken-down squire.' I gave the flask to George.

'You'll see,' came from the bed. 'I'll make a better marriage than either of you. And if they don't forge me one soon, I'll do it for myself.'

George passed the stone flask back to me. 'Drain it,' he said. 'I've had more than enough.'

I finished the last swig of drink and went round to the other side of the bed. 'Goodnight,' I said to George.

'I'll sit here awhile beside the fire,' he said. 'We are doing well, aren't we, us Boleyns? Me betrothed, and you on your way to bedding the king, and little Mademoiselle Parfait here free on the market with everything to play for?'

'Yes,' I said. 'We are doing well.'

I thought of the intent blue gaze of the king on my face, the way his eyes travelled from the top of my headdress down to the top of my gown. I turned my face into the pillow so that neither of them could hear me. 'Henry,' I whispered. 'Your Majesty. My love.'

Next day there was to be a joust in the gardens of a house a little distance from Eltham Palace. Fearson House had been built in the last reign by one of the many hard men who had come to their wealth under the king's father, himself the hardest man of them all. It was a big grand house, free of any castle wall or moat. Sir John Lovick had believed that England was at peace forever and built a house which would not be defended, indeed which could not be defended. His gardens were laid around the house like a chequerboard of green and white: white stones and paths and borders around low knot gardens of green bay. Beyond them lay the park where he ran deer for hunting, and between the park and the gardens was a beautiful lawn kept ready all the year round for the king's use as a jousting green.

The tent for the queen and her ladies was hung in cherry-red and white silk, the queen was wearing a cherry gown to match and she looked young and rosy in the bright colour. I was in green, the gown I had worn at the Shrove Tuesday masque when the king singled me out from all the others. The colour made my hair glow more golden and my eyes shone. I stood beside the queen's chair and knew that any man looking from her to me would think that she was a fine woman, but old enough to be my mother, while I was a woman of only fourteen, a woman ready to fall in love, a woman ready to feel desire, a precocious woman, a flowering girl.

The first three jousts were among the lower men of the court, hoping to attract attention by risking their necks. They were skilled enough, there were a couple of exciting passes, and one good moment when the smaller man unhorsed a bigger rival which made the common people cheer. The little man dismounted and took off his helmet to acknowledge the applause. He was handsome, slight and fair-haired. Anne nudged me. 'Who's that?'

'Only one of the Seymour boys.'

The queen turned her head. 'Mistress Carey, would you go and ask the master of the horse when my husband is riding today and what horse he has chosen?'

I turned to do her bidding, and I saw why she was sending me away. The king was coming slowly across the grass towards our pavilion and she wanted me out of his way. I curtsied and dawdled to the doorway, timing my departure so that he saw me hesitating under the awning. At once he excused himself from a conversation and hurried over. His armour was polished bright as silver, the trimming on it was gold. The leather straps holding his breastplate and armguards were red and smooth as velvet. He looked taller, a commanding hero from long-ago wars. The sun shining on him made the metal burn with light so that I had to step back into the shade and put my hand up to my eyes.

'Mistress Carey, in Lincoln green.'

'You are all bright,' I said.

'You would be dazzling if you were in the darkest of blacks.'

I said nothing. I just looked at him. If Anne or George had been close by they could have prompted me with some compliment. But I was empty of wit, it was all crowded out by desire. I could say and do nothing but just look at him and know that my face was full of longing. And he said nothing too. We stood, gazes locked, intently interrogating each other's faces as if we might understand the other's desire from his eyes.

'I must see you alone,' he said finally.

I did not coquet. 'Your Majesty, I cannot.'

'You don't want to?'

'I dare not.'

He took in a deep breath at that, as if he would sniff out lust itself. 'You could trust me.'

I tore my eyes from his face and looked away, seeing nothing. 'I dare not,' I said again simply.

He reached out and took my hand to his lips and kissed it. I could feel the warmth of his breath on my fingers and, at last, the gentle stroke of the curls of his moustache.

'Oh, soft.'

He looked up from my hand. 'Soft?'

'The touch of your moustache,' I explained. 'I have been wondering how it felt.'

'You have been wondering how my moustache felt?' he asked.

I could feel my cheeks growing warm. 'Yes.'

'If you were kissed by me?'

I dropped my gaze to my feet so that I should not see the brightness of his blue eyes, and gave a little imperceptible nod.

'You have been wishing to be kissed by me?'

I looked up at that. 'Your Majesty, I have to go,' I said desperately. 'The queen sent me on an errand and she will wonder where I am.'

'Where did she bid you go?'

'To your master of horse, to find out what horse you are riding and when you are to ride.'

'I can tell her that myself. Why should you walk around in the burning sun?'

I shook my head. 'It's no trouble to me to go for her.'

He made a little tutting noise. 'And she has servants enough to run around the jousting green, God knows. She has a full Spanish retinue while I am begrudged my little court.'

Out of the corner of my eye I saw Anne coming through the hangings of the queen's room and freeze as she saw the king and me close together.

Gently he released me. 'I shall go to see her now and answer her questions about my horses. What will you do?'

'I'll come in a moment,' I said. 'I need to take a little moment before I go back in, I feel all . . .' I broke off at the impossibility of describing what I was feeling.

He looked at me tenderly. 'You're very young to be playing this game, aren't you? Boleyn or no Boleyn. They'll be telling you what to do and putting you in my way, I suppose.'

I would have confessed to the family's plot to ensnare him but for Anne, waiting in the shadows of the jousting tent. With her watching me, I just shook my head. 'It's no game to me.' I looked away, I let my lip tremble. 'I promise you, it's no game to me, Your Majesty.'

His hand came up, he took my chin and turned my face towards him. For one breathless moment I thought with dread and with delight that he was going to kiss me, in front of everyone.

'Are you afraid of me?'

I shook my head and resisted the temptation to turn my face to his hand. 'I am afraid of what may happen.'

'Between us?' He smiled, the confident smile of a man who knows that the woman he desires is only moments away from his arms. 'Nothing bad will come to you for loving me, Mary. You can have my word on it, if you like. You will be my mistress, you will be my little queen.'

I gasped at that potent word.

'Give me your scarf, I want to wear your favour while I joust,' he said suddenly.

I looked around. 'I can't give it to you here.'

'Send it to me,' he said. 'I'll tell George to come to you, give it to him. I won't wear it so it shows. I'll tuck it into my breastplate. I'll wear it against my heart.'

I nodded.

'So you give me your favour?'

'If you wish,' I whispered.

'I wish it so much,' he said. He bowed and turned towards the entrance of the queen's tent. My sister Anne had disappeared like a helpful ghost.

I gave them all a few minutes and then I went back into the tent myself. The queen gave me a sharp interrogatory look. I sank into a curtsey. 'I saw the king coming to answer your questions himself, Your Majesty,' I said sweetly. 'So I came back.'

'You should have sent a servant in the first place,' the king said abruptly.

'Mistress Carey should not be running round the jousting ground in this sun. It's far too hot.'

The queen hesitated for only a moment. 'I am so sorry,' she said. 'It was thoughtless of me.'

'It's not me you should apologise to,' he said pointedly.

I thought she would balk at that, and from the tension in Anne's body at my side I knew that she too was waiting to see what a Princess of Spain and a Queen of England would do next.

'I am sorry if I inconvenienced you, Mistress Carey,' the queen said levelly.

I felt no triumph at all. I looked across the richly carpeted tent at a woman old enough to be my mother and felt nothing but pity for the pain I would cause her. For a moment I did not even see the king, I saw only the two of us, bound to be each other's grief.

'It is a pleasure to serve you, Queen Katherine,' I said, and I meant it.

For a moment she looked at me as if she understood some of what was in my mind and then she turned to her husband. 'And are your horses fit for today?' she asked. 'Are you confident, Your Majesty?'

'It's me or Suffolk today,' he said.

'You will be careful, sire?' she said softly. 'There's no harm in losing to a rider like the duke; and it would be the end of the kingdom if anything happened to you.'

It was a loving thought, but he took it with no grace at all. 'It would be indeed, since we have no son.'

She flinched and I saw the colour go from her face. 'There is time,' she said, her voice so quiet that I could hardly hear it. 'There is still time . . .'

'Not much,' he said flatly. He turned away from her. 'I must go and get ready.'

He went past me without a glance, though Anne and I and all the other ladies sank down into a curtsey as he passed by. When I rose up the queen was looking towards me, not as if I were a rival, but as if I were still her favourite little maid in waiting who might bring her some comfort. She looked at me as if for a moment she would seek someone who would understand the dreadful predicament of a woman, in this world ruled by men.

George strolled into the room and kneeled before the queen with his easy grace. 'Your Majesty,' he said. 'I have come to visit the fairest lady in Kent, in England and the world.'

'Oh George Boleyn, rise up,' she said, smiling.

'I would rather die at your feet,' he offered.

She gave him a little tap on the hand with her fan. 'No, but you can give me odds for the king's joust if you want.'

'Who would bet against him? He is the finest of horsemen. I will give you a wager of five to two against the second joust. Seymours against Howards. There's no doubt in my mind of the winner.'

'You would offer me a bet on the Seymours?' the queen asked.

'Have them carry your blessing? Never,' George said quickly. 'I would have you bet on my cousin Howard, Your Majesty. Then you can be sure of winning, you can be sure of betting on one of the finest and most loyal families in the country, and you can have tremendous odds as well.'

She laughed at that. 'You are an exquisite courtier indeed. How much do you want to lose to me?'

'Shall we say five crowns?' George asked.

'Done!'

'I'll take a bet,' Jane Parker said suddenly.

George's smile vanished. 'I could not offer you such odds, Mistress Parker,' he said civilly. 'For you have all my fortune at your command.'

It was still the language of courtly love, the constant flirtatiousness which went on in the royal circles night and day and sometimes meant everything, but more often than not meant nothing at all.

'I'd just like to bet a couple of crowns.' Jane was trying to engage George in the witty flattering conversation that he could do so well. Anne and I watched her critically, not disposed to help her with our brother.

'If I lose to Her Majesty – and you will see how graciously she will impoverish me – then I will have nothing for any other,' George said. 'Indeed, whenever I am with Her Majesty I have nothing for any other. No money, no heart, no eyes.'

'For shame,' the queen interrupted. 'You say this to your betrothed?'

George bowed to her. 'We are betrothed stars circling a beautiful moon,' he said. 'The greatest beauty makes everything else dim.'

'Oh run away,' the queen said. 'Go and twinkle elsewhere, my little star Boleyn.'

George bowed and went to the back of the tent. I drifted after him. 'Give it me quick,' he said tersely. 'He's riding next.'

I had a yard of white silk trimming the top of my dress, which I took and pulled through the green loops until it was free and then handed it to George. He whisked it into his pocket.

'Jane sees us,' I said.

He shook his head. 'No matter. She's tied to our interest whatever her opinion. I have to go.'

I nodded and went back into the tent as he left. The queen's eyes rested briefly on the empty loops at the front of my gown, but she said nothing.

'They'll start in a moment,' Jane said. 'The king's joust is next.'

I saw him helped into his saddle, two men supporting him as the weight of his armour nearly bore him down. Charles Brandon, the Duke of Suffolk, the king's brother-in-law, was arming also, and the two men rode out together and came past the entrance to the queen's tent. The king dipped his lance in salute to her, and held it down as he rode past the length of the tent. It became a salute to me, the visor of his helmet was up, I could see him smile at me. There was a tiny flutter of white at the shoulder of his breastplate which I knew was the kerchief from my gown. The Duke of Suffolk rode behind him, dipped his lance to the queen and then stiffly nodded his head to me. Anne, standing behind me, gave a little indrawn breath.

'Suffolk acknowledged you,' she whispered.

'I thought so.'

'He did. He bowed his head. That means the king has spoken to him of you, or spoken to his sister Queen Mary, and she has told Suffolk. He's serious. He must be serious.'

I glanced sideways. The queen was looking down the list where the king had halted his horse. The big charger was tossing his head and sidling while he waited for the trumpet blast. The king sat easily in the saddle, a little golden circlet round his helmet, his visor down, his lance held before him. The queen leaned forward to see. There was a trumpet blast and the two horses leaped forward as the spurs were driven into their sides. The two armoured men thundered towards each other, divots of earth flying out from the horses' hooves. The lances were down like arrows flying to a target, the pennants on the end of each lance fluttering as the gap closed between them, then the king took a glancing blow which he caught on his shield, but his thrust at Suffolk slid under the shield and thudded into the breastplate. The shock of the blow threw Suffolk back off his horse and the weight of his armour did the rest, dragging him over the haunches, and he fell with an awful thud to the ground.

His wife leaped to her feet. 'Charles!' She whirled out of the queen's pavilion, lifting her skirts, running like a common woman towards her husband as he lay unmoving on the grass.

'I'd better go too.' Anne hurried after her mistress.

I looked down the lists to the king. His squire was stripping him of his heavy armour. As the breastplate came off my white kerchief fluttered to the ground, he did not see it fall. They unstrapped the greaves from his legs and the guards from his arms and he pulled on a coat as he walked briskly up the lists to the ominously still body of his friend. Queen Mary was kneeling beside Suffolk, his head cradled in her arms. His squire was stripping off the heavy armour from his master as he lay there. Mary looked up as her brother came closer and she was smiling.

'He's all right,' she said. 'He just swore an awful oath at Peter for pinching him with a buckle.'

Henry laughed. 'God be praised!'

Two men carrying a stretcher ran forward. Suffolk sat up. 'I can walk,' he said. 'Be damned if I'm carried from the field before I'm dead.'

'Here,' Henry said and heaved him to his feet. Another man came running to the other side and the two of them started to walk him away, his feet dragging and then stumbling to keep pace.

'Don't come,' Henry called to Queen Mary over his shoulder. 'Let us make him comfortable and then we'll get a cart or something and he can ride home.'

She stopped where she was bid. The king's page came running up with my kerchief in his hands, taking it to his master. Queen Mary put out her hand. 'Don't bother him now,' she said sharply.

The lad skidded to a halt, still holding my kerchief. 'He dropped this, Your Majesty,' he said. 'Had it in his breastplate.'

She put out an indifferent hand for it and he gave it to her. She was looking after her husband being helped into the house by her brother and Sir John Lovick hurrying ahead of them, opening doors and shouting for servants. Absently she walked back to the queen's pavilion with my kerchief balled up in her hand. I went forward to take it from her and then I hesitated, not knowing what to say.

'Is he all right?' Queen Katherine asked.

Queen Mary found a smile. 'Yes. His head is clear; and no bones broken. His breastplate is hardly dented.'

'Shall I have that?' Queen Katherine asked.

Queen Mary glanced down at my crumpled kerchief. 'This! The king's page gave it me. It was in his breastplate.' She handed it over. She was quite blind and deaf to anything but her husband. 'I'll go to him,' she decided. 'Anne, you and the rest can go home with the queen after dinner.'

The queen nodded her permission and Queen Mary went quickly from the pavilion towards the house. Queen Katherine watched her go, my kerchief in her hands. Slowly, as I knew she would, she turned it over. The fine silk slipped easily through her fingers. At the fringed hem she saw the bright green of the embroidered silk monogram: MB. Slowly, accusingly, she turned towards me.

'I think this must be yours,' she said, her voice low and disdainful. She held it at arm's length, between finger and thumb, as if it were a dead mouse that she had found at the back of a cupboard.

'Go on,' Anne whispered. 'You've got to get it.' She pushed me in the small of my back and I stepped forward.

The queen dropped it as I reached her, I caught it as it fell. It looked a sorry bit of cloth, something you might wash a floor with.

'Thank you,' I said humbly.

∾

At dinner the king hardly looked at me. The accident had thrown him into the melancholy that was such a characteristic of his father, which his courtiers too were learning to fear.

The queen could not have been more pleasant and more entertaining. But no conversation, no charming smiles, no music could lift his spirits. He watched the antics of his Fool without laughing, he listened to the musicians and drank deep. The queen could do nothing to cheer him, because she was partly the cause of his ill-humour. He was looking at her as a woman near her change of life, he saw Death at her shoulder. She might live for a dozen years more, she might live for a score. Death was even now drying up her courses and putting the lines on her face. The queen was heading towards old age and she had made no heirs to follow them. They might joust and sing and dance and play all the day but if the king did not put a boy into Wales as prince then he had failed in his greatest, most fundamental duty to the kingdom. And a bastard on Bessie Blount would not do.

'I am sure that Charles Brandon will soon be well again,' the queen volunteered. There were sugared plums on the table and a rich sweet wine. She took a sip but I thought that she had little relish for it while her husband sat beside her with a face so drawn and dark that he could have been his father who had never liked her. 'You must not feel that you did wrong, Henry. It was a fair joust. And you've taken hits from him before, God knows.'

He turned in his chair and looked at her. She looked back at him and I saw the smile drain from her face at the coldness of his stare. She did not ask him what was the matter. She was too old and wise ever to ask an angry man what was troubling him. Instead, she smiled, a dauntless endearing smile, and she raised her glass to him.

'Your health, Henry,' she said with her warm accent. 'Your health and I must thank God that it was not you that was hurt today. Before now, I have been the one running from the pavilion to the lists with my heart half broken with fear; and though I am sorry for your sister Queen Mary, I have to be glad that it was not you that was hurt today.'

'Now that,' Anne said in my ear, '*that* is masterly.'

It worked. Henry, seduced by the thought of a woman sick with fear over his well-being, lost his dark sulky look. 'I would never cause you a moment of uneasiness.'

'My husband, you have caused me days and nights of them,' Queen Katherine said, smiling. 'But as long as you are well and happy, and as long as you come home at the end of it all; why should I complain?'

'Aha,' Anne said quietly. 'And so she gives him permission and your sting is drawn.'

'What d'you mean?' I asked.

'Wake up,' Anne said brutally. 'Don't you see? She's called him out of his bad temper and she has told him that he can have you, as long as he comes home afterwards.'

I watched him lift his glass in a return toast to her.

'So what happens next?' I asked. 'Since you know everything?'

'Oh he has you for a while,' she said negligently. 'But you won't come between them. You won't hold him. She's old, I grant you. But she can act as if she adores him and he needs that. And when he was little more than a boy she was the most beautiful woman in the kingdom. It'll take a lot to overcome that. I doubt that you're the woman to do it. You're pretty enough and half in love with him, which is helpful, but I doubt that a woman such as you could command him.'

'Who could do it?' I demanded, stung by her dismissal of me. 'You, I suppose?'

She looked at the two of them as if she were a siege engineer measuring a wall. There was nothing in her face but curiosity and professional expertise. 'I might,' she said. 'But it would be a difficult project.'

'It's me that he wants, not you,' I reminded her. 'He asked for my favour. He wore my kerchief under his breastplate.'

'He dropped it and forgot it,' Anne pointed out with her usual cruel accuracy. 'And anyway, what he wants is not the issue. He's greedy and he's spoiled. He could be made to want almost anything. But you'll never be able to do that.'

'Why should I not do that?' I demanded passionately. 'What makes you think that you could hold him and I could not?'

Anne looked at me with her perfectly beautiful face as lovely as if it were carved from ice. 'Because the woman who manages him will be one who never stops for a moment remembering that she is there for strategy. You are all ready for the pleasures of bed and board. But the woman who manages Henry will know that her pleasure must be in managing his thoughts, every minute of the day. It would not be a marriage of sensual lust at all, though Henry would think that was what he was getting. It would be an affair of unending skill.'

The dinner ended at about five o'clock on the cool April evening and they brought the horses around to the front of the house so that we could say goodbye to our host and mount and ride back to Eltham Palace. As we left the banqueting tables I saw the servants tipping the leftover loaves and meats into great panniers which would be sold at a discount at the kitchen door. There was a trail of extravagance and dishonesty and waste that followed the king round the country like slime behind a snail. The poor people who had come to watch the jousting and stayed on to watch the court dine now gathered at the kitchen door to collect some food from the feast. They would be given the broken meats: the slicings from the loaves, the off-cuts from the meats, the puddings which had been half-eaten. Nothing would be wasted, the poor would take anything. They were as economical as keeping a pig.

It was these perks that made a place in the king's household such a joy for his servants. In every place, every servant could perform a little cheat, put a little by. The lowliest server in the kitchen had a little business in crusts of the pastry from the pies, in lard from the basting, in the juices of the gravy. My father was at the top of this heap of off-cuts, now that he was controller of the king's household: he would watch the slice that everyone took of their bit of business, and he would take a slice of his own. Even the trade of lady in waiting who looks as if she is there to provide company and little services for the queen is well-placed to seduce the king under her mistress's nose, and cause her the most grief that one woman can cause to another. She too has her price. She too has her secret work which takes place after the main dinner is over and when the company are looking the other way, and which trades in off-cuts of promises and forgotten sweetmeats of love-play.

We rode home as the light faded from the sky and it grew grey and cool. I was glad of my cloak which I tied round me, but I kept my hood pushed back so that I could see the way before me and the darkening skies above me, and the little pinpricks of stars showing in the pale grey sky. We had been riding for half the journey when the king's horse came alongside mine.

'Did you enjoy your day?' he asked.

'You dropped my kerchief,' I said sulkily. 'Your page gave it to Queen

Mary and she gave it to Queen Katherine. She knew it at once. She gave it back to me.'

'And so?'

I should have thought of the small humiliations which Queen Katherine managed, as part of the duty of queenship. She never complained to her husband. She took her troubles to God; and only then in a very low whispered prayer.

'I felt dreadful,' I said. 'I should never have given it to you in the first place.'

'Well now you have it back,' he said without sympathy. 'If it was so precious.'

'It's not that it was precious,' I pursued. 'It's that she knew without a doubt that it was mine. She gave it back to me in front of all the ladies. She dropped it to the ground, it would have fallen to the floor if I had not caught it.'

'So what has changed?' he demanded, his voice very hard, his face suddenly ugly and unsmiling. 'So what is the difficulty? She has seen us dancing together and talking together. She has seen me seeking your company, you have been handclasped with me before her very eyes. You didn't come to me then with your complaints and your nagging.'

'I'm not nagging!' I said, stung.

'Yes you are,' he said flatly. 'Without cause, and, may I say, without position. You are not my mistress, madam, nor my wife. I don't listen to complaints about my behaviour from anyone else. I am the King of England. If you don't like how I behave then there is always France. You could always go back to the French court.'

'Your Majesty . . . I . . .'

He spurred his horse and it went into a trot and then into a canter. 'I give you goodnight,' he said over his shoulder and he rode away from me with his cloak in a flurry and the plume in his hat streaming, and he left me with nothing to say to him, no way to call him back.

❧

I would not speak to Anne that night though she marched me in silence from the queen's rooms to our own and expected a full account of everything that had been said and done.

'I won't say,' I said stubbornly. 'Leave me alone.'

Anne took off her hood and started to unplait her hair. I jumped onto the bed, threw off my gown, pulled on my night shift and slipped between the sheets without brushing my hair or even washing my face.

'You're surely not going to bed like that,' Anne said, scandalised.

'For God's sake,' I said into the pillow, 'leave me alone.'

'What did he . . . ?' Anne started as she slid into bed beside me.

'I won't say. So don't ask.'

She nodded, turned and blew out her candle.

The smell of the smoke from the snuffed wick blew towards me. It smelled like the scent of grief. In the darkness, shielded from Anne's scrutiny, I turned over, lay on my back staring up at the tester above my head and considered what would happen if the king were so angry that he never looked at me again.

My face felt cold. I put my hand to my cheeks and found that they were wet with tears. I rubbed my face on the sheet.

'What is it now?' Anne asked sleepily.

'Nothing.'

❁

'You lost him,' Uncle Howard said accusingly. He looked down the long wooden dining table in the great hall at Eltham Palace. Our retainers stood on guard at the doors behind us, there was no-one in the hall but a couple of wolfhounds and a boy asleep in the ashes of the fire. Our men in Howard livery stood at the doors at the far end. The palace, the king's own palace, had been made secure for the Howards so that we could plot in private.

'You had him in your hand and you lost him. What did you do wrong?'

I shook my head. It was too secret to spill on the unyielding surface of the high table, to offer up to flint-faced Uncle Howard.

'I want an answer,' he said. 'You lost him. He hasn't looked at you for a week. What have you done wrong?'

'Nothing,' I whispered.

'You must have done something. At the jousting he had your kerchief under his breastplate. You must have done something to upset him after that.'

I shot a reproachful look at my brother George: the only person who could have told Uncle Howard about my scarf. He shrugged and made an apologetic face.

'The king dropped it and his page gave my scarf to Queen Mary,' I said, my throat tight with nervousness and distress.

'So?' my father said sharply.

'She gave it to the queen. The queen returned it to me.' I looked from one stern face to another. 'They all knew what it meant,' I said despairingly. 'When we rode home I told him that I was unhappy at him letting my favour be found.'

Uncle Howard exhaled, my father slapped the table. My mother turned her head away as if she could hardly bear to look at me.

'For God's sake.' Uncle Howard glared at my mother. 'You assured me that she had been properly brought up. Half her life spent in the French court and she whines at him as if she were a shepherd girl behind a haystack?'

'How could you?' my mother asked simply.

I flushed and dropped my head until I could see the reflection of my own unhappy face in the polished surface of the table. 'I didn't mean to say the wrong thing,' I whispered. 'I'm sorry.'

'It's not that bad,' George interceded. 'You're taking too dark a view. He won't stay angry for long.'

'He sulks like a bear,' my uncle snapped. 'Don't you think there are Seymour girls dancing for him at this very moment?'

'None as pretty as Mary,' my brother maintained. 'He'll forget that she ever said a word out of place. He might even like her for it. It shows she's not overly groomed. It shows there's a bit of passion there.'

My father nodded, a little consoled, but my uncle drummed the table with his long fingers. 'What should we do?'

'Take her away.' Anne spoke suddenly. She drew attention at once in the way that a late speaker always does, but the confidence in her voice was riveting.

'Away?' he asked.

'Yes. Send her down to Hever. Tell him that she's ill. Let him imagine her dying of grief.'

'And then?'

'And then he'll want her back. She'll be able to command what she likes. All she has to do –' Anne gleamed her spiteful little smile '–*All* she has to do when she returns is to behave so well that she enchants the most educated, the most witty, the most handsome prince in Christendom. D'you think she can do it?'

There was a cold silence while my mother and my father and my Uncle Howard and even George all inspected me in silence.

'Neither do I,' Anne said smugly. 'But I can coach her well enough to get her into his bed, and whatever happens to her after that is in the hands of God.'

Uncle Howard looked intently at Anne. 'Can you coach her in how to keep him?' he asked.

She raised her head and smiled at him, the very picture of confidence. 'Of course, for a while,' she said. 'He's only a man after all.'

Uncle Howard laughed shortly at the casual dismissal of his sex. 'You have a care,' he urged. 'We men are not where we are today because of some sort of accident. We chose to get into the great places of power, despite the desires of women; and we chose to use those places to make laws which will hold us there forever.'

'True enough,' Anne granted. 'But we're not talking of high policy. We're talking of catching the king's desire. She just has to catch him and hold him for long enough for him to make a son on her, a royal Howard bastard. What more could we ask?'

'And she can do that?'

'She can learn,' Anne said. 'She's halfway there. She is his choice, after all.' The little shrug she gave indicated that she did not think much of the king's choice.

There was a silence. Uncle Howard's attention had moved from me and my future as the brood mare for the family. Instead he was looking at Anne as if he had seen her for the first time. 'Not many maids of your age think as clearly as you.'

She smiled at him. 'I'm a Howard like you.'

'I'm surprised you don't try for him yourself.'

'I thought of it,' she said honestly. 'Any woman in England today would be bound to think of it.'

'But?' he prompted her.

'I'm a Howard,' she repeated. 'What matters is that one of us catches the king. It hardly matters which one. If his taste is for Mary and she has his acknowledged son then my family becomes the first in the kingdom. Without rival. And we can do it. We can manage the king.'

Uncle Howard nodded. He knew that the king's conscience was a domesticated beast, given to easy herding but prone to sudden stubborn stops. 'It seems we have to thank you,' he said. 'You have planned our strategy.'

She acknowledged his thanks, not with a bow, which would have been graceful. Instead, she turned her head like a flower on the stem, a typically arrogant gesture. 'Of course I long to see my sister as the king's favourite. These things are my business quite as much as yours.'

He shook his head as my mother made a shushing noise at her overly confident eldest daughter. 'No, let her speak,' he said. 'She's as sharp as any of us. And I think she's right. Mary must go to Hever and wait for the king to send for her.'

'He'll send,' Anne said knowledgably. 'He'll send.'

❧

I felt like a parcel, like the curtains for a bed, or the plates for the top table, or the pewter for the lower tables in the hall. I was to be packed up and sent to Hever as bait for the king. I was not to see him before I left, I was not to speak to anyone about my going. My mother told the queen that I was overtired and asked for me to be excused from her service for a few days so that I might go home and rest. The queen, poor lady, thought that she had triumphed. She thought that the Boleyns were in retreat.

❁

It was not a long ride, a little more than twenty miles. We stopped to dine at the roadside, eating nothing more than bread and cheese which we had carried with us. My father could have called on the hospitality of any great house along the way, he was well enough known as a courtier high in the favour of the king, and we would have been nobly entertained. But he did not want to break the journey.

The high road was rutted and pitted with potholes, every now and then we saw a broken cart wheel where a traveller had been overturned. But the horses stepped out well enough on the dry ground and every now and then the going was so good that we broke into a canter. The verges on the side of the road were thick with the white of gypsy lace and big-faced white daisies, and lush with the early summer greenness of grass. In the hedges the honeysuckle twisted around the bursting growth of hawthorn and may, at the roots were pools of purple-blue self-heal and the gangly growth of ladies' smock with dainty flowers of white, veined with purple. Behind the hedges in the thick lush pastures were fat cows with their heads down, munching, and in the higher fields there were flocks of sheep with the occasional idle boy watching over them from the shade of a tree.

The common land outside of the villages was mostly farmed in strips and they made a pretty sight where they were gardened in rows with onions and carrots drawn up like a retinue on parade. In the villages themselves the cottage gardens were tumbling confusions of daffodils and herbs, vegetables and primroses, wild beans shooting and hawthorn hedgerows in flower with a corner set aside for a pig, and a rooster crowing on the dunghill outside the back door. My father rode in a quiet satisfied silence when the road took us onto our own land, downhill, through Edenbridge, and through the wet meadowlands towards Hever. The horses went slower as the going grew heavier on the damp road, but my father was patient now we were nearing our estate.

It had been his father's house before it was his; but it went no further back in our family than that. My grandfather had been a man of no more than moderate means who had risen by his own skills in Norfolk, apprenticed to a mercer, but eventually became Lord Mayor of London. For all that we clung to our Howard connection it was only a recent one, and only through my mother who had been Elizabeth Howard, a daughter of the Duke of Norfolk, a great catch for my father. He had taken her to our grand house at Rochford in Essex and then brought her to Hever where she had been appalled at the smallness of the castle, and the cosy poky private rooms.

At once he had set to rebuild it to please her. First he put a ceiling across the great hall, which had been open to the rafters in the old style. In the space he created above the hall he made a set of private rooms for us where we could dine and sit in greater comfort and privacy.

My father and I turned in at the gates of the park, the gatekeeper and his wife tumbling out to make their bow as we went by. We rode past them with a wave, and up the dirt road to the first river, which was spanned by a little wooden bridge. My horse did not like the look of this, she jibbed at it as soon as she heard the echo of her hoofbeats on the hollow wood.

'Fool,' my father said briefly, leaving me to wonder whether he meant me or the horse, and put his own hunter before mine and led the way across. My horse followed behind, very docile when she could see that there was no danger, and so I rode up to the drawbridge of our castle behind my father and waited while the men came out of the guard room to take our horses and lead them away to the stables at the back. My legs felt weak after the long ride when they lifted me down from the saddle but I followed my father across the drawbridge and into the shadow of the gatehouse, under the forbidding thick teeth of the portcullis and into the welcoming little castle yard.

The front door stood open, the yeoman of the ewry and the chief household men came out and bowed to my father, half a dozen servants behind them. My father ran his eyes over them: some were in full livery, some were not, two of the servant girls were hastily untying the hessian aprons they wore over their best aprons underneath, and disclosing some very dirty linen as they did so; the spit boy, peeping out from the corner of the yard, was filthy with deeply engrained dirt and half-naked in his rags. My father took in the general sense of disorder and carelessness and nodded at his people.

'Very well,' he said guardedly. 'This is my daughter Mary. Mistress Mary Carey. You have prepared rooms for us?'

'Oh yes, sir.' The groom of the bedchambers bowed. 'Everything is ready. Mistress Carey's room is ready.'

'And dinner?' my father demanded.

'At once.'

'We'll eat in the private rooms. I'll have dinner tomorrow in the great hall and people can come and see me. Tell them I will dine in public tomorrow. But this evening I won't be disturbed.'

One of the girls came forward and dipped a curtsey to me. 'Shall I show you your room, Mistress Carey?' she asked.

I followed her at my father's nod. We went through the broad front door and turned left along a narrow hall. At the end a tiny spiral stone staircase led us upwards to a pretty room with a small bed hung with curtains of pale blue silk. The windows looked out over the moat and the park beyond. A door out of the room would lead me into a small gallery with a stone fireplace which was my mother's favourite sitting room.

'D'you want to wash?' the girl asked awkwardly. She gestured towards a jug and ewer filled with cold water. 'I could get you some hot water?'

I stripped off my riding gloves and handed them to her. 'Yes,' I said. For a moment I thought of the palace at Eltham and the constant sycophantic service. 'Get me some hot water and see that they bring my clothes up. I want to change out of this riding dress.'

She bowed and left the room by the little stone staircase. As she went I could hear her muttering to herself: 'Hot water. Clothes,' so as not to forget. I went to the windowseat, kneeled up and looked out of the little window through the leaded panes.

I had spent the day trying not to think of Henry and the court I was leaving behind me, but now at this comfortless homecoming I realised that I had not just lost the love of the king, I had lost the luxuries which had become essential to me. I did not want to be Miss Boleyn of Hever again. I did not want to be the daughter of a small castle in Kent. I had been the most favoured young woman in the whole of England. I had gone far beyond Hever and I did not want to come back.

❧

My father stayed no more than three days, long enough to see his land agent and those tenants who urgently wanted to speak to him, time enough to solve a dispute about a boundary post and to order his favourite mare put to the stallion, and then he was ready to leave again. I stood on the drawbridge to bid him farewell and I knew that I must look sorrowful indeed since even he noticed as he swung himself up into the saddle.

'What's the matter?' he demanded, bracingly. 'Not missing court, are you?'

'Yes,' I said shortly. There was no point telling my father that indeed I missed the court, but that I missed most, unbearably, the sight of Henry.

'No-one to blame but yourself,' my father said robustly. 'We have to trust to your brother and sister to set it right for you. If not, then God knows what will become of you. I'll have to get Carey to take you back, and we'll have to hope that he forgives you.'

He laughed aloud at the shocked look on my face.

I drew closer to my father's horse and put my hand on his gauntlet where it rested on the reins. 'If the king asks for me would you tell him that I am very sorry if I offended him?'

He shook his head. 'We play this Anne's way,' he said. 'She seems to think she knows how to manage him. You have to do as you are bid, Mary. You bodged it once, you have to work under orders now.'

'Why should Anne be the one who says how things are done?' I demanded. 'Why d'you always listen to Anne?'

My father took his hand from under my grip. 'Because she's got a head on her shoulders and she knows her own value,' he said bluntly. 'Whereas you have behaved like a girl of fourteen in love for the first time.'

'But I am a girl of fourteen in love for the first time!' I exclaimed.

'Exactly,' he said unforgivingly. 'That's why we listen to Anne.'

He did not trouble to say goodbye to me, but turned his horse away, trotted over the drawbridge and then down the track towards the gates.

I raised my hand to wave in case he looked back; but he did not. He rode straight-backed, looking forward. He rode like a Howard. We never look back. We have no time for regrets or second thoughts. If a plan goes awry we make another, if one weapon breaks in our hands we find a second. If the steps fall down before us we overleap them and go up. It is always onwards and upwards for the Howards; and my father was on his way back to court and to the company of the king without a backwards glance for me.

❦

By the end of the first week I had taken a turn around every walk that there was in the garden and explored the park in every direction from my starting point at the drawbridge. I had started a tapestry for the altar of St Peter's church at Hever and completed a square foot of sky which was very boring indeed, being nothing but blue. I had written three letters to Anne and George and sent them off by messenger to the court at Eltham. Three times he had gone for me and come back with no reply except their good wishes.

By the end of the second week I was ordering my horse out of the stables in the morning and going for long rides on my own, I was too irritable even for the company of a silent servant. I tried to keep my temper hidden. I thanked the maid for any little service she did for me, I sat to eat my dinner and bowed my head when the priest said grace as if I did not want to leap up and scream with frustration that I was trapped in Hever while the court was on the move from Eltham to Windsor and I not with them. I did everything I could to contain the fury that I was so far from court, and so terribly left out of everything.

By the third week I had slid into a resigned despair. I heard nothing from anyone and I concluded that Henry did not want to send for me to return, that my husband was proving intractable and did not want a wife carrying the disgrace of being the king's flirtation – but not his mistress. Such a woman could not add to a man's prestige. Such a woman was best left in the country. I wrote to Anne and to George twice in the second week but still they did not reply. But then, on Tuesday of the third week, I received a scrawled note from George.

> Don't despair – I wager you are thinking yourself quite aban-
> doned by us all. He speaks of you constantly and I remind him
> of your many charms. I should think he will send for you within
> the month. Make sure that you are looking well!
> Geo.
> Anne bids me tell you that she will write in a little while.

George's letter was the only moment of relief during my long wait. As I entered my second month of waiting, the month of May, always the happiest month at court as the season for picnics and journeyings started again, it seemed to me that my days were very long.

I had no-one to talk to, I had no company to speak of at all. My maid chattered to me while she dressed me. At breakfast I dined alone at the top table and spoke only to claimants who came to the house with business for my father to transact. I walked in the garden for a little while. I read some books.

In the long afternoons I had my hunter brought round and I rode in wider and wider sweeps of the countryside. I began to learn the lanes and byways that stretched around my home and even started to recognise some of our tenants on their little farms. I learned their names and started to rein in my horse when I saw a man working in the fields and ask him what he was growing, and how he was doing. This was the best time for the farmers. The hay was cut and drying in windrows, waiting to be pitchforked into great stacks and thatched to keep dry for winter feed. The wheat and barley and rye were standing tall in the fields and growing in height and plumpness. The calves were growing fat on their mothers' milk and the profits from this year's wool sales were being counted in every farmhouse and cottage in the county.

It was a time for leisure, a brief respite in the hard work of the year, and the farmers held little dances on the village green, and races and sports before the main work of harvesting.

I, who had first ridden into the Boleyn estate looking around me and recognising nothing, now knew the country all around the estate wall, the farmers and the crops they were growing. When they came to me at dinner time and complained that such a man was not properly farming his strip which he held by agreement with his village, I knew straightaway what they were speaking of because I had ridden that way the day before and seen the land left to grow weeds and nettles, the only wasted lot among the well-tended common fields. It was easy for me, as I ate my dinner, to warn the tenant that his land would be taken from him if he did not use it for growing a crop. I knew the farmers who were growing hops and the ones who were growing vines. I made an agreement with one farmer that if he should get a good crop of grapes then I would ask my father to send to London for a Frenchman to come on a visit to Hever Castle and teach the art of winemaking.

It was no hardship to ride around every day. I loved being outside, hearing the birds singing as I rode through the woods, smelling the flowering honeysuckle as it cascaded through the hedges on either side of the track. I loved my mare Jesmond, which the king had given me: her eagerness to canter, the alert flicker of her ears, her whinny when she saw me come into the stable yard, a carrot in my hand. I loved the lushness of the meadows by the river, the way they shimmered white and yellow with flowers, and the blaze of red poppies in the wheatfields. I loved the weald and the buzzards circling in the sky in great lazy loops, even higher than larks, before turning on their broad wings and wheeling away.

It was all makeweight, it was all a way of filling the time since I could not be with Henry and could not be at court. But I had a growing sense that if I were never to go to court again, then I could at least be a good and fair landlord. The more enterprising young farmers outside Edenbridge could see that there was a market for lucerne. But they knew no-one who grew it, nor where they could get the seeds. I wrote for them to a farmer on my father's estate in Essex, and got them both seeds and advice. They planted a field while I was there, and promised to plant another when they saw how the crop liked the soil. And I thought, even though I was no more than a young woman, I had done a wonderful thing. Without me they would not have gone further than slapping their hands on the table at the Hollybush and swearing that a man could make some money from the new crops. With my help they were able to try it out, and if they made a fortune then there would be two more men rising up in the world, and if my grandfather's story were anything to go by, then no-one could tell how high they might aspire.

They were glad of it. When I rode out to the field to see how the ploughing was going they came across, kicking the mud off their boots, to explain how they were casting their seed. They wanted a lord who took an interest. In the absence of anyone else: they had me. And they knew well enough that if I took an interest in the crop I might be persuaded to take a share. I might have some money tucked away that I might invest, and then we could all grow prosperous together.

I laughed at that, looking down from my horse into their brown weatherbeaten faces. 'I have no money.'

'You're a great lady at court,' one of them protested. His gaze took in the neat tassels on my leather boots, the inlaid saddle, the richness of my dress and the golden brooch in my hat. 'There's more on your back today than I earn in a year.'

'I know,' I said. 'And that's where it stays. On my back.'

'But your father must give you money, or your husband,' the other man said persuasively. 'Better to gamble it on your own fields than on the turn of a card.'

'I'm a lady. It's none of it mine. Look at you. You're doing well enough – is your wife a rich woman?'

He chuckled sheepishly at that. 'She's my wife. She does as well as I do. But she doesn't own anything of her own.'

'It's the same for me,' I said. 'I do as my father does, as my husband does. I dress as is proper for their wife or their daughter. But I don't own anything on my own account. In that sense I am as poor as your wife.'

'But you are a Howard and I am a nobody,' he observed.

'I'm a Howard woman. That means I might be one of the greatest in the land or a nobody like you. It all depends.'

'On what?' he asked, intrigued.

I thought of the sudden darkening of Henry's face when I displeased him. 'On my luck.'

Summer 1522

In the middle of my third month of exile, the month of June, with the garden of Hever filled with heavy-headed roses and their scent hanging in the air like smoke, I had a letter from Anne.

> *It is done. I have put myself in his way and talked about you.*
> *I have told him that you miss him unbearably and you are pining*
> *for him. I have told him that you have displeased your family*
> *by showing too openly your love for him and you have been sent*
> *away to forget him. Such is the contrary nature of men that he*
> *is much excited at the thought of you in distress. Anyway, you*
> *can come back to court. We are at Windsor. Father says you can*
> *order half a dozen men from the castle to escort you and come*
> *at once. Make sure that you arrive quietly before dinner and*
> *come straight to our room where I will tell you how you are to*
> *behave.*

Windsor Castle, one of Henry's prettiest castles, sat on the green hill like a grey pearl on velvet, the king's standard fluttering from the turret, the drawbridge open, and a continual coming and going of carts and pedlars and brewers' drays and wagons. The court sucked the wealth out of the countryside wherever it rested and Windsor was experienced in servicing the profitable appetites of the castle.

I slipped into a side door and found my way to Anne's rooms, avoiding anyone who knew me. Her room was empty. I settled myself down to wait. As I had expected, at three o'clock she came into the room, pulling her hood off her hair. She jumped when she saw me.

'I thought you were a ghost! What a fright you gave me.'

'You told me to come privately to your room.'

'Yes, I wanted to tell you how things are. I was speaking to the king just a moment ago. We were in the tiltyard watching Lord Percy. *Mon dieu!* It's so hot!'

'What did he say?'

'Lord Percy? Oh he was enchanting.'

'No, the king.'

Anne smiled, deliberately provoking. 'He was asking about you.'

'And what did you say?'

'Let me think.' She tossed her hood on the bed and shook her hair free. It tumbled in a dark wave down her back and she swept it up in one hand to leave her neck cool. 'Oh, I can't remember. It's too hot.'

I was too experienced in Anne's teasing to let her torment me. I sat quietly in the little wooden chair by the empty fireplace and did not turn my head while she washed her face and splashed her arms and neck and tied her hair back again, with many exclamations in French and complaints about the heat. Nothing made me look around.

'I think I can remember now,' she offered.

'It doesn't matter,' I said. 'I'll see him myself at dinner. He can tell me anything he wants to tell me then. I don't need you.'

She bridled at that at once. 'Oh yes you do! How will you behave? You don't know what to say!'

'I knew enough to have him head over heels in love with me and ask for my kerchief,' I observed coolly. 'I should think I know enough to talk to him civilly after dinner.'

Anne stepped back and measured me. 'You're very calm,' was all she said.

'I've had time to think,' I replied levelly.

'And?'

'I know what I want.'

She waited.

'I want him,' I said.

She nodded. 'Every woman in England wants him. I never thought that you would prove exceptional.'

I shrugged off the snub. 'And I know that I can live without him.'

Her gaze narrowed. 'You'll be ruined, if William doesn't take you back.'

'I could bear that too,' I rejoined. 'I liked it at Hever. I liked riding out every day and walking round the gardens. I was on my own there for nearly three months, and I've never been on my own in my whole life before. I realised that I don't need the court and the queen and the king or even you. I liked riding out and looking at the farmland, I liked talking to the farmers and watching their crops and seeing how things grow.'

'You want to become a farmer?' she laughed scornfully.

'I could be happy as a farmer,' I said steadily. 'I'm in love with the king –' I snatched a breath '– oh, very much. But if it all goes wrong, I could live on a little farm and be happy.'

Anne went to the chest at the foot of the bed and drew out a new hood. She watched herself in the mirror as she smoothed back her hair and drew on the headdress. At once her dramatic dark looks took on a new elegance. She knew it, of course.

'If I were in your shoes it would be the king or nothing for me,' she said. 'I'd put my neck on the block for a chance at him.'

'I want the man. Not because he's king.'

She shrugged. 'They're one and the same thing. You can't desire him like an ordinary man and forget the crown on his head. He's the best there is. There is no greater man than him in the kingdom. You'd have to go to France for King Francis or Spain for the emperor to find his equal.'

I shook my head. 'I've seen the emperor and the French king and I wouldn't look twice at either of them.'

Anne turned from the glass and tugged her bodice down a little lower so that the curve of her breasts showed. 'Then you're a fool,' she said simply.

When we were ready she led me to the queen's chambers. 'She'll accept you back, but she won't give you a warm welcome,' Anne threw over her shoulder as the soldiers before the queen's door saluted us, and held the double doors open. The two of us, the Boleyn girls, walked in as if we owned half the castle.

The queen was sitting in the windowseat, the windows flung wide open for the cooler evening air. Her musician was beside her, singing as he played his lute. Her women were around her, some of them sewing, some of them sitting idle, waiting for the summons to dinner. She looked perfectly at peace with the world, surrounded by friends, in her husband's home, looking out from her window over the little town of Windsor and the pewter-coloured curve of the river beyond. When she saw me her face did not change. She was too well-trained to betray her disappointment. She gave me a small smile. 'Ah, Mistress Carey,' she said. 'You are recovered and returned to court?'

I sank into a curtsey. 'If it please Your Majesty.'

'You have been at your parents' home, all this long time?'

'Yes. At Hever Castle, Your Majesty.'

'You must have rested well. There is nothing in that part of the world but sheep and cows, I think?'

I smiled. 'It is farmland,' I agreed. 'But there was much for me to do. I enjoyed riding out and looking at the fields and talking to the men who work them.'

For a moment, I could see that she was intrigued by the thought of the land, which after all her years in England she still only saw as a place for hunting and picnics and the summer progress. But she remembered why I had left court in the first place. 'Did His Majesty order your return?'

I heard a little warning hiss from Anne behind me but I disregarded it. I had a romantic, foolish thought, that I did not want to look this good woman in her honest eyes and lie to her. 'The king sent for me, Your Majesty,' I said respectfully.

She nodded and looked down at her hands where they were quietly clasped in her lap. 'Then you are fortunate,' was all she said.

There was a brief silence. I wanted very much to tell her that I had fallen in love with her husband but I knew that she was far above me. She was a woman whose spirit had been hammered and forged until she could only ring true. Compared with the rest of us she was silver, while we were pewter, a common mixture of lead and tin.

The great double doors swung open. 'His Majesty the king!' the herald announced and Henry strolled into the room. 'I am come to lead you into dinner,' he started, and then he saw me and stopped in his tracks. The queen's considering gaze flicked from his transfixed face to mine and back again.

'Mary,' he exclaimed.

I forgot even to curtsey. I just stared at him.

A little warning tut from Anne failed to recall me. The king crossed the room in three long strides and took my hands in his, and held them to his chest. I felt the scratch of his embroidered doublet under my fingers, the caress of his silk shirt through the slashings.

'My love,' he said in a low whisper. 'You are welcome back to court.'

'I thank you . . .'

'They told me that you were sent away to learn a lesson. Did I do right to say you could come back unlearned?'

'Yes. Yes. Perfectly right,' I stumbled.

'You were not scolded?' he pressed.

I gave a little laugh and looked up at his intent blue gaze. 'No. They were a little cross with me, but that was all.'

'You wanted to come back to court?'

'Oh yes.'

The queen rose to her feet. 'So. Let us go to dinner, ladies,' she said generally. Henry threw a quick glance at her over his shoulder. She held out her hand to him, imperious as a daughter of Spain. He turned to her with the old habit of devotion and obedience and I could not think how to recapture him. I stepped behind her and bent low to arrange the train of her gown while she stood, queenly; despite her stockiness, beautiful; despite the weariness in her face.

'Thank you, Mistress Carey,' she said gently. And then she led us in to dinner with her hand resting lightly on her husband's arm, and he inclined his head to her to hear something she said, and he did not look back at me again.

❧

George greeted me at the end of dinner, strolling to the queen's table where we ladies were seated with wine and sweetmeats before us. He brought me a sugared plum. 'Sweets for the sweet,' he said, planting a kiss on my forehead.

'Oh George,' I said. 'Thank you for your note.'

'You were bombarding me with desperate cries,' he said. 'Three letters I got from you in the first week. Was it so awful?'

'The first week was,' I said. 'But then I became accustomed. By the end of the first month I was rather taking to the country life.'

'Well, we all did our best for you here,' he said.

'Is Uncle at court?' I asked, looking around. 'I don't see him.'

'No, in London with Wolsey. But he knows all that is going on, don't you worry. He said to tell you that he will be hearing reports of you and he trusts you now know how to behave.'

Jane Parker leaned across the table. 'Are you going to be a lady in waiting?' she asked George. 'For you are sitting at our table and on a lady's stool.'

George rose unhurriedly. 'I beg your pardon, ladies. I did not mean to intrude.'

Half a dozen voices assured him that he did not intrude. My brother was a handsome young man and a popular visitor to the queen's rooms. No-one but his sour-tongued betrothed objected to him joining our table.

He bowed over her hand. 'Mistress Parker, thank you for reminding me to leave you,' he said courteously, his irritation clear behind his sweet tones. He bent and kissed me firmly on the lips. 'God speed you, little Marianne,' he whispered in my ear. 'You are carrying the hopes of your family.'

I caught his hand as he was about to go. 'Wait, George, I wanted to ask you something.'

He turned back. 'What?'

I tugged at his hand to make him lean down to me so that I could whisper in his ear. 'Do you think that he loves me?'

'Oh,' he said, straightening up. 'Oh, love.'

'Well, do you?'

He shrugged. 'Whatever does it mean? We write poems about it all day and sing songs about it all night but if there is such a thing in real life I'm damned if I know.'

'Oh George!'

'He wants you, I can tell you that. He's prepared to go through a degree of trouble to have you. If that means love to you then yes, he loves you.'

'That's enough for me,' I said with quiet satisfaction. 'Wants me, and is prepared to go through a degree of trouble. That sounds like love to me.'

My handsome brother bowed. 'If you say so, Mary. If that is good enough for you.' He straightened up and immediately stepped back. 'Your Majesty.'

The king stood before me. 'George, I cannot allow you to spend the evening talking to your sister, you are the envy of the court.'

'I am,' George said with all his courtier charm. 'Two beautiful sisters and not a care in the world.'

'I thought we should have some dancing,' the king said. 'Will you lead out Mistress Boleyn and I will take care of Mistress Carey, here?'

'I should be delighted,' George said. Without looking around for her, he snapped his fingers and, alert as ever, Anne appeared at his side.

'We're to dance,' he said shortly.

The king waved his hand and the musicians struck up a quick country dance so we arranged ourselves in a ring of eight people and started the flowing steps first one way then the other. At the opposite side of the circle I saw George's familiar beloved face and, beside him, Anne's smooth smile. She looked as she did when she was studying a new book. She was reading the king's mood as carefully as she might look at a psalter. She was looking from him to me as if to measure the urgency of his desire. And, while never turning her head, she was checking the mood of the queen, trying to get an idea of what she had seen or what she felt.

I smiled to myself. Anne had met her match in the queen, I thought. No-one could penetrate beneath the veneer of the daughter of Spain. Anne was a courtier beyond all others but she had been born a commoner. Queen Katherine had been born a princess. From the moment she could talk she had been taught to guard her tongue. From the moment she could walk she had been taught to step carefully and speak kindly to both rich and poor, for you never knew when you might need both rich and poor. Queen Katherine had been a player in a highly competitive, highly wealthy court before Anne had even been born.

Anne might look around all she liked to see how the queen was bearing up under the sight of me, close to the king, our gazes locked on each other, desire very hot between us. Anne might look; but the queen never betrayed any emotion more than polite interest. She clapped at the end of the dances and once or twice cried out congratulations. And then suddenly the dance ended, and Henry and I were left stranded without musicians playing, without other dancers encircling us and hiding us. We were left alone, exposed, still handclasped with his eyes on my face and me looking up at him in silence, locked together as if we might stay that way forever.

'Bravo,' said the queen, her voice completely steady and confident. 'Very pretty.'

❀

'He'll send for you,' Anne said that night as we undressed in the room. She shook out her dress and laid it carefully in the chest at the foot of the bed, her hood at the other end, her shoes carefully set side by side under the bed. She pulled on her night shift and sat before the mirror to brush her hair.

She handed the brush to me and she closed her eyes as I set about the long strokes from head to waist.

'Perhaps tonight, perhaps during the day tomorrow. You'll go.'

'Of course I'll go,' I said.

'Well, remember who you are,' Anne warned. 'Don't let him just have you in a doorway or somewhere hidden and hurried. Insist on proper rooms, insist on a proper bed.'

'I'll see,' I said.

'It's important,' she cautioned me. 'If he thinks he can take you like a slut then he'll have you and forget you. If anything, I think you should hold out a little longer. If he thinks you're too easy he'll not have you more than once or twice.'

I took her soft hanks of hair in my hand and plaited them.

'Ow,' she complained. 'You're pulling.'

'Well, you're nagging,' I said. 'Leave me to do it my way, Anne. I've not done so badly so far.'

'Oh that.' She shrugged her white shoulders and smiled at her reflection in the mirror. 'Anyone can attract a man. The trick is to keep him.'

The knock at the door startled us both. Anne's dark eyes flew to the mirror, to my reflected image looking blankly back at her.

'Not the king?'

I was already opening the door.

George was standing there, in the red suede doublet he had worn at dinner, the white fine linen shirt gleaming through the slashings, the red cap embroidered with pearls on his dark head.

'*Vivat! Vivat Marianne!*' He came quickly in and closed the door behind him. 'He asked me to invite you to take a glass of wine with him. I'm to apologise for the lateness of the hour, the Venetian ambassador has only just left. They talked of nothing but war with France and now he is filled with passion for England, Henry and St George. I'm to assure you that you're free to make your choice. You can take a glass of wine and come back to your own bed. You're to be your own mistress.'

'Any offer?' Anne asked.

George raised a supercilious eyebrow. 'Show a little elegance,' he reprimanded her. 'He's not buying her outright. He's inviting her for a glass of wine. We'll fix the price later on.'

I put my hand to my head. 'My hood!' I exclaimed. 'Anne, quick! Plait up my hair.'

She shook her head. 'Go as you are,' she said. 'With your hair down around your shoulders. You look like a virgin on your wedding day. I'm right, aren't I, George? That's what he wants.'

He nodded. 'She's lovely like that. Loosen her bodice a bit.'

'She's supposed to be a lady.'

'Just a bit,' he suggested. 'A man likes a glimpse of what he's buying.'

Anne untied the laces at the back of my bodice until the boned stomacher was a little looser. She tugged it down at the waist so it sat lower and more invitingly. George nodded. 'Perfect.'

She stepped back and looked at me as critically as my father had looked at the mare he had sent to the stallion. 'Anything else?'

George shook his head.

'She'd better wash,' Anne suddenly decided. 'Under her arms and her cunny at least.'

I would have appealed to George. But he was nodding, as intent as a farmer. 'Yes, you should. He has a horror of anything rank.'

'Go on.' Anne gestured to the jug and ewer.

'You two go out,' I said.

George turned for the door. 'We'll wait outside.'

'And your bum,' Anne said as he closed the door. 'Don't skimp on it, Mary. You've got to be clean all over.'

The closing door cut off my response which was not that of a young lady. I washed myself briskly in cold water and rubbed myself dry. I took some of Anne's flower water and patted it on my neck and hair and on the tops of my legs. Then I opened the door.

'Are you clean?' Anne asked sharply.

I nodded.

She looked at me anxiously. 'Go on then. And you can resist for a bit, you know. Show a little doubt. Don't just fall into his arms.'

I turned my face away from her. She seemed to me quite unbearably crass about the whole matter.

'The girl can have a bit of pleasure,' George said gently.

Anne rounded on him. 'Not in his bed,' she said sharply 'She's not there for her pleasure but for his.'

I didn't even hear her. All I could hear was the thud of my heart pounding in my ears and my knowledge that he had sent for me, that I would be with him soon.

'Come on,' I said to George. 'Let's go.'

Anne turned to go back into the room. 'I'll wait up for you,' she said.

I hesitated. 'I might not come back tonight.'

She nodded. 'I hope you don't. But I'll wait up for you anyway. I'll sit by the fire and watch the dawn come in.'

I thought for a moment about her keeping a vigil for me in her spinster bedroom while I was snug and loved in the King of England's bed. 'My God, you must wish it was you,' I said with sudden acute delight.

She did not flinch from it. 'Of course. He is the king.'

'And he wants *me*,' I said, hammering the point home.

George bowed and offered me his arm and led me down the narrow stairs to the lobby before the great hall. We went through it like a pair of interlinked ghosts. No-one saw us pass. There were a couple of the scullions sleeping in the ashes of the fire and half a dozen men dozing head-down on tables around the room.

We went past the top table and through the doors where the king's private rooms began. There was a set of broad stairs richly hung with a beautiful tapestry, the colours drained from the bright silks by the moon-light. There were two men at arms before the presence chamber and they stood aside to let me pass when they saw me with my golden hair let down and the confident smile on my face.

The presence chamber behind the double doors was a surprise to me. I had only ever seen it crowded with people. This was where everyone came to have sight of the king. Petitioners would bribe senior members of the court to allow them to stand here in case the king noticed them and asked them how they did, and what they wanted of him. I had never seen this big vaulted room other than packed with people in their most handsome clothes, desperate for the king's attention. Now it was silent, shadowy. George pressed his hand on my cold fingertips.

Ahead of us were the doors to the king's private chambers. Two men at arms stood with pikes crossed. 'His Majesty commands our presence,' George said briefly.

There was a short chime as the pikes clashed, the two men presented arms, bowed, and swung the double doors open.

∾

The king was seated before the fire, wrapped in a warm robe of velvet trimmed with fur. As he heard the door open he leaped to his feet.

I dropped into a deep curtsey. 'You sent for me, Majesty.'

He could not take his eyes from my face. 'I did. And I thank you for coming. I wanted to see . . . I wanted to talk . . . I wanted to take a little . . .' He broke off finally. 'I wanted you.'

I stepped a little closer. He would smell Anne's perfume from that distance, I thought. I tossed my head and felt the weight of my hair shift. I saw his eyes go from my face to my hair and back again. Behind me, I heard the door closing as George went out without a word. Henry did not even see him go.

'I am honoured, Your Majesty,' I murmured.

He shook his head, not in impatience, but as the gesture of a man who cannot waste time on play. 'I want you,' he said again, flatly, as if that were all that a woman would need to know. 'I want you, Mary Boleyn.'

I took a small step closer to him. I leaned towards him. I felt the warmth of his breath and then the touch of his lips on my hair. I did not move forward or back.

'Mary,' he whispered and his voice was choked with his desire.

'Your Majesty?'

'Please call me Henry. I want to hear my name on your lips.'

'Henry.'

'D'you want me?' he whispered. 'I mean as a man? If I were a farmer on your father's estate, would you want me then?' He put his hand under my chin to lift up my face so that he could look into my eyes. I met his bright blue gaze. Carefully, delicately I put my hand to his face and felt the softness of his curling beard under my palm. At once he closed his eyes at my touch and then turned his face and kissed my hand where it cupped his chin.

'Yes,' I said, caring not at all that it was nonsense. I could not imagine this man as anything but King of England. He could no more deny being king than I could deny being a Howard. 'If you were a nobody and I were a nobody I would love you,' I whispered. 'If you were a farmer with

58

a field of hops I would love you. If I were a girl who came to pick the hops would you love me?'

He drew me closer to him, his hands warm on my stomacher. 'I would,' he promised. 'I would know you anywhere for my true love. Whoever I was and whoever you were, I would know you at once for my true love.'

His head came down and he kissed me gently at first and then harder, the touch of his lips very warm. Then he led me by the hand towards the canopied bed and lay me down on it and buried his face in the swell of my breasts where they showed above the stomacher that Anne had helpfully loosened for him.

⚜

At dawn I raised myself on my elbow and looked out of the leaded panes of the window to where the sky was growing pale and I knew that Anne would be watching for the sun too. Anne would be watching the light slowly filling the sky and knowing that her sister was the king's mistress and the most important woman in England, second only to the queen. I wondered what she made of that as she sat in the windowseat and listened to the first birds tentatively sounding out their notes. I wondered how she felt, knowing that I was the one the king had chosen, the one who was carrying the ambitions of the family. Knowing that it was me and not her in his bed.

In truth, I did not have to wonder. She would be feeling that disturbing mixture of emotions that she always summoned from me: admiration and envy, pride and a furious rivalry, a longing to see a beloved sister succeed, and a passionate desire to see a rival fall.

The king stirred. 'Are you awake?' he asked from half-under the covers.

'Yes,' I said, instantly alert. I wondered if I should offer to leave, but then he emerged head first from the tangle of bedding and his face was smiling.

'Good morrow, sweetheart,' he said to me. 'Are you well this morning?'

I found I was beaming back at him, reflecting his joy. 'I'm very well.'

'Merry in your heart?'

'Happier than I have ever been in my life before.'

'Then come to me,' he said, opening his arms, and I slid down the sheets and into the warm musky-scented embrace, his strong thighs pressing against me, his arms cradling my shoulders, his face burrowing into my neck.

'Oh Henry,' I said foolishly. 'Oh, my love.'

'Oh I know,' he said engagingly. 'Come a little closer.'

☙

I did not leave him till the sun was fully up and then I was in a hurry to be back in my room before the servants were about.

Henry himself helped me into my gown, tied the laces at the back of my stomacher, put his own cloak around my shoulders against the chill of the morning. When he opened the door my brother George was lounging in the windowseat. When he saw the king, he rose to his feet and bowed, cap in hand, and when he saw me behind the king he gave me a sweet smile.

'See Mistress Carey back to her room,' the king said. 'And then send the groom of the bedchamber in, would you, George? I want to be up early this morning.'

George bowed again and offered me his arm.

'And come with me to hear Mass,' the king said at the door. 'You can come with me to my private chapel today, George.'

'I thank you.' George accepted with nonchalant grace the greatest honour that any courtier could receive. The door to the privy chamber closed as I curtsied and then we went quickly through the audience chamber and through the great hall.

We were too late to avoid the lowest of the servants, the lads employed to keep the fires burning were dragging great logs into the hall. Other boys were sweeping the floor, and the men at arms who had slept where they had dined were opening their eyes and yawning and cursing the strength of the wine.

I put the hood of the king's cloak up over my dishevelled hair and we went quickly and quietly through the great hall and up the staircase to the queen's apartments.

Anne opened the door at George's knock and drew us in. She was white-faced with lack of sleep, her eyes red. I took in the delicious sight of my sister on the rack of jealousy.

'Well?' she asked sharply.

I glanced at the smooth counterpane on the bed. 'You didn't sleep.'

'I couldn't,' she said. 'And I hope you slept but little.'

I turned away from her bawdiness.

'Come now,' George said to me. 'We only want to know that all is well with you, Mary. And Father will have to know and Mother and Uncle Howard. You'd better get used to talking about it. It's not a private matter.'

'It's the most private matter in the world.'

'Not for you,' Anne said coldly. 'So stop looking like a milkmaid in springtime. Did he have you?'

'Yes,' I said shortly.

'More than once?'

'Yes.'

'Praise God!' George said. 'She's done it. And I have to go. He asked me to hear Mass with him.' He crossed the room and caught me up into a hard hug. 'Well done. We'll talk later. I have to go now.'

He banged the door indiscreetly as he left and Anne made a little tutting noise and then turned to the chest which held our clothes.

'You'd better wear your cream gown,' she said. 'No need to look the whore. I'll get you some hot water, You'll have to bathe.' She raised her hand to my protests. 'Yes, you will. So don't argue. And wash your hair You have to be spotless, Mary. Don't be such a lazy slut. And get out of that gown and hurry, we have to go to Mass with the queen in less than an hour.'

I obeyed her, as I always did. 'But are you happy for me?' I asked as I struggled out of the stomacher and petticoat.

I saw her face in the mirror, the leap of jealousy veiled by the sweep of her eyelashes. 'I am happy for the family,' she said. 'I hardly ever think about you.'

❀

The king was in his private gallery, overlooking the chapel, hearing matins as we filed past to the queen's adjoining room. Straining my ears I could just hear the mutter of the clerk putting papers before the king for him to glance at and sign as he watched the priest in the chapel below go through the familiar motions of the Mass. The king always did his business at the same time as hearing the morning service, he followed his father in this tradition, and there were many who thought the work was hallowed. There were others, my uncle among them, who thought that it showed that the king was in a hurry to get the work out of the way and that he only ever gave it half his mind.

I kneeled on the cushion in the queen's private room, looking at the ivory gleam of my gown as it shimmered, hinting at the contours of my thighs. I could still feel the warmth of him in the tenderness between my legs, I could still taste him on my lips. Despite the bath which Anne had insisted that I took, I still fancied that I could smell the sweat from his chest on my face and in my hair. When I closed my eyes it was not in prayer, but in a reverie of sensuality.

The queen was kneeling beside me, her face grave, her head erect under the heavy gable hood. Her gown was open a little at the neck so that she might slide her finger inside and touch the hair shirt that she always wore next to her skin. Her sober face was drawn and tired, her head bowed over her rosary, the old slack skin on her chin and cheeks looking weary and pouched under her tightly closed eyes.

The Mass went on interminably. I envied Henry the distraction of the state papers. The queen's attention never wavered, her fingers were never idle on her beads, her eyes were always closed in prayer. Only when the service ended and the priest wiped the chalices in the white cloths and took them away did she give a lingering sigh, as if she had heard something that none of us had ears for. She turned and smiled on all of us, all her ladies, even me.

'And now let us go to break our fast,' she said pleasantly. 'Perhaps the king will eat with us.'

As we filed past his door, I felt myself dawdle, I could not believe that he would let me go by without a word. As if he sensed my desire, my brother George flung open the door at the exact moment that I was lingering and said loudly: 'A good morning to you, my sister.'

In the room behind him Henry looked up quickly from his work and saw me, framed in the doorway, in the cream gown that Anne had chosen for me, with my cream headdress pulling my rich hair off my young face. He gave a little sigh of desire at the sight of me and I felt my colour rise, and my smile warm my face.

'Good day, sire. And good day to you, my brother,' I said softly, while my eyes never left Henry's face.

Henry rose to his feet and stretched out his hand as if to draw me in. He checked himself with a glance at his clerk.

'I'll take my breakfast with you,' he said. 'Tell the queen I will come along in a few moments. Just as soon as I have finished these . . . these . . .' His vague gesture indicated that he had no idea what the papers were.

He came across the room, like a dazed trout swimming towards a poacher's bright lantern. 'And you, this morning, are you well?' he said quietly, for my ears only.

'I am.' I shot a quick, mischievous glance up at his intent face. 'A little weary.'

His eyes danced at the admission. 'Did you not sleep well, sweeting?'

'Hardly at all.'

'Was the bed not to your liking?'

I stumbled, I was never as skilled as Anne at this sort of word-play. In the end I said nothing but what was simply true. 'Sire, I liked it very well.'

'Would you sleep there again?'

In a delicious moment I found the right response. 'Oh sire. I was hoping I would not sleep there again very soon.'

He threw back his head and laughed, he snatched up my hand and, turning it over, pressed a kiss into the palm. 'My lady, you have only to command me,' he promised. 'I am your servant in every way.'

I bowed my head to watch his mouth press my hand, I could not take my eyes from his face. He raised his head and we looked at each other, a long mutual look of desire.

'I should go,' I said. 'The queen will wonder where I am.'

'I shall follow you,' he said. 'Believe it.'

I shot him a quick smile then I turned and ran down the gallery after the queen's ladies. I could hear my heels going tap tap tap on the stones beneath the rushes, I could hear the rustle of my silk gown. I could sense, in every part of my alert body, that I was young and lovely and beloved. Beloved by the King of England himself.

He came to breakfast and smiled as he took his seat. The queen's pale eyes took in the rosy colour of my face, the rich gleam of my cream gown, and looked away. She called for some musicians to play for us while we ate, and for the queen's master of the horse to attend us.

'Will you go hunting today, sire?' she asked him pleasantly.

'Yes, indeed. Would any of your ladies care to follow the hunt?' the king invited.

'I am sure they would,' she said with her usual pleasant tone. 'Mademoiselle Boleyn, Mistress Parker, Mistress Carey? I know you three for keen riders. Would you like to ride with the king today?'

Jane Parker shot a swift malicious gleam at me for being named third. She does not know, I thought, inwardly hugging myself. She can triumph all she likes because she does not know.

'We would be enchanted to ride with the king,' Anne said smoothly. 'All three of us.'

❧

In the great courtyard before the stables the king mounted his big hunter while one of the grooms lifted me up into the saddle of the horse he had given me. I hooked my leg firmly around the pommel and arranged my gown to fall becomingly to the ground. Anne scrutinised me, without missing the tiniest detail, as she always did, and I was pleased when her head, capped with the neatest of French hunting hats with a dainty plume, gave a small approving nod. She called to the groom to lift her up into the saddle and she brought her hunter up beside mine and held him steady while she leaned over.

'If he wants to take you off into the woods and have you, you're to say no,' she whispered. 'Try to remember that you are a Howard girl. You're not a complete slut.'

'If he wants me . . .'

'If he wants you, he'll wait.'

The huntsman blew his horn and every horse in the courtyard stiffened with excitement. Henry grinned across at me like an excited boy and I beamed back. My mare, Jesmond, was like a coiled spring, and when the master of the hunt led the way over the drawbridge we trotted quickly after him, the hounds like a sea of brindle and white around the horses' hooves. It was a bright day but not too hot, a cool wind moved the grass of the meadow as we trotted away from the town, the haymakers leaned on their scythes and watched us pass, doffing their caps as they saw the bright colours of the aristocratic riders, and then dropping to their knees as they saw the king's standard.

I glanced back at the castle. A casement window in the queen's apartments stood open and I saw her dark hood and her pale face looking out after us. She would meet us for dinner and she would smile at Henry and smile at me as if she had not seen us, riding side by side, out for a day's sport together.

The yelping of the hounds suddenly changed in tone and then they fell silent. The huntsman blew his horn, the long loud blast which meant that the hounds had taken a scent.

'Hulloa!' Henry shouted, spurring his horse forward.

'There!' I cried. At the end of the avenue of trees opening before us I saw the outline of a large stag, his antlers held flat on his back as he crashed away from the hunt. At once the hounds streamed out behind him, almost silent except for the occasional bark of excitement. They plunged into the undergrowth and we pulled up the horses and waited. The huntsmen trotted anxiously away from the hunt, criss-crossing the forest by the little rides, hoping to spot the deer break away. Then one of them suddenly stood high in his stirrups and blew a loud note on his horn. My horse reared with excitement at the sound and spun round towards him. I clung gracelessly to the pommel and to a handful of mane, caring nothing how I looked as long as I did not tumble off backwards into the mud.

The stag broke away and was racing for his life across the rough empty ground at the edge of the woods that led to the watermeadows and the river. At once the dogs poured after him and the horses after them in a breakneck race. The hooves pounded all around me, I had my eyes squinted, half-shut, as divots of mud flew up into my face, I crouched low over Jesmond's neck, urging her onwards. I felt my hat tear from my head and tumble away, then there was a hedge before me, white with summer blossom. I felt Jesmond's powerful hindquarters bunch up

64

beneath me and with one great leap she cleared it, hit the ground on the far side, recovered and was pounding into her fastest gallop again. The king was ahead of me, his attention fixed on the stag which was gaining on us. I could feel the ripple of my hair as it shook out from the pins and I laughed recklessly to feel the wind in my face. Jesmond's ears went back to hear me laugh and then forward as we came to another hedge with a nasty little ditch before it. She saw it as I did and checked only for a moment and then made a mighty cat-jump: all four feet off the ground at once in order to clear it. I could smell the perfume of crushed honeysuckle as her hooves clipped the top of the hedge, then we were on and on, even faster. Ahead of me the little brown dot that was the stag plunged into the river and started to swim strongly for the other side. The master of the hunt desperately blew for the hounds not to follow the beast into the water but to come back to him and to run down the bank to keep pace with the quarry to bait it as it came to shore. But they were too excited to listen. The whippers-in surged forward but half the pack were after the deer in the river, some of them swept away by the fast current, all of them powerless in the deep water. Henry pulled up his horse and watched the chaos develop.

I was afraid that it would make him angry but he threw back his head and laughed as if he delighted in the stag's cunning.

'Go then!' he shouted after him. 'I can eat venison here without cooking you! I have a larder of venison!'

Everyone around us laughed as if he had made a wonderful jest and I realised that everyone had been afraid that the failure of the hunt would turn his mood sour. Looking from one bright delighted face to another I thought for one illuminating moment what fools we were to make this one man's temper the very centre of our lives. But then he smiled towards me and I knew that for me at least, there was no choice.

He took in my mud-splashed face and my tumbling tangled hair. 'You look like a maid for country matters,' he said, and anyone could have heard the desire in his voice.

I pulled off my glove and put my hand to my head, ineffectually twisting a knot of hair and tucking it back. I gave him a little sideways smile which acknowledged his bawdiness and yet refused to answer it.

'Oh shush,' I ordered softly. Behind his intent face I saw Jane Parker suddenly gulp as if she had swallowed a horse fly and I saw that she had realised at last that she had better mind her manners around us Boleyns.

Henry dropped from his horse, threw the reins to his groom and came to my horse's head. 'Will you come down to me?' he asked, his voice warm and inviting.

I unhooked my knee and let myself slide down the side of my horse and into his arms. He caught me easily and set me on my feet but he did not release me. Before the whole court kissed me on one cheek and then another 'You are the Queen of the Hunt.'

'We should crown her with flowers,' Anne suggested.

'Yes!' Henry was pleased with the thought and within moments half the court was plaiting honeysuckle garlands and I had a crown of haunting honey perfume to put on my tumbled golden-brown hair.

The wagons came up with the things for dinner and they put up a little tent for fifty diners, the king's favourites, and chairs and benches for the rest, and when the queen arrived, ambling on her steady palfrey, she saw me seated at the king's left hand and crowned with summer flowers.

Next month and England was finally at war with France, a war declared and formal, and Charles, the Emperor of Spain, aimed his army like a lance at the heart of France while the English army in alliance with him marched out of the English fort of Calais, and headed south down the road to Paris.

The court lingered near the City, anxious for news, but then the summertime plague came to London and Henry, always fearful of illness, ruled that the summer progress should start at once. We fled rather than moved to Hampton Court. The king ordered that all the food should be brought from the surrounding country, nothing could come from London. He forbade merchants and traders and artisans to follow the court from the unhealthy stews of the capital. The clean palace on the fresh water must be kept safe from illness.

The news from France was good, and the news from the City was bad. Cardinal Wolsey organised the court to go south and then west, staying at the great houses of the great men, entertained with masques and dinners and hunting and picnics and jousts, and Henry went like a boy, easily diverted by the passing scene. Every courtier living on the route had to play host to the king as if it were his greatest joy instead of his most dreaded expense. The queen travelled with the king, riding by his side through the pretty countryside, sometimes travelling in a litter if she were tired, and though I might be sent for during the night, he was attentive and loving to her during the day. Her nephew was the English army's only ally in Europe, the friendship of her family meant victory to an English army. But Queen Katherine was more to her husband than an ally in wartime. However much I might please Henry, he was still her boy – her lovely indulged spoilt golden boy. He might summon me or any other girl to his room, without disturbing the constant steady affection between them which had sprung from her ability, long ago, to love this man who was more foolish, more selfish, and less of a prince than she was a princess.

Winter 1522

The king kept his court at Greenwich for Christmas and for twelve days and nights there was nothing but the most extravagant and beautiful parties and feastings. There was a Christmas master of the revels – Sir William Armitage – and it was his task to dream up something new for every day. His daily programme followed a delightful pattern of something for us to do out of doors in the morning – a boat race to watch, jousting, or an archery competition, bear baiting, a dog fight, a cocking match, or a travelling show with tumblers and fire-eaters, followed by a great dinner in the hall with fine wine and ale and small beer and every day some enchanting pudding made of sculpted marchpane as fine as a piece of art. In the afternoon there would be a diversion: a play or a talk, some dancing or a masque. We all had parts to play, we all had costumes to wear, we all had to be as merry as we could be, for the king was always laughing this winter and the queen never stopped smiling.

The inconclusive campaign against France had ended with the cold weather, but everyone knew that come the spring there would be another series of battles and England and Spain would jointly venture against their enemy. The King of England and the queen from Spain were united in every sense of the word that Christmas season, and once a week without fail they dined privately together and he slept in her bed that night.

But every other night, also without fail, George would come to the room I shared with Anne and tap on the door and say: 'He wants you,' and I would go to my love, to my king, at the run.

I never stayed for the whole night. There were foreign ambassadors from all over Europe bidden to Greenwich for Christmas and Henry would not show such a snub to the queen before them. The Spanish ambassador in particular was a stickler for etiquette and he was a close friend to the queen. Knowing the part I played at court, he did not like me; and I would not have enjoyed bumping into him coming out of the king's private rooms all flushed and dishevelled. Better by far that I should slip from the king's warm bed and hurry back to my chamber with George yawning at my side, hours before the ambassador arrived to hear Mass.

Anne was always up and waiting for me, with ale ready mulled and the fire banked in to warm our chamber. I would jump into bed and she would throw a woollen wrap around my shoulders and sit beside me and comb out the tangles from my hair while George put another log on the fire and sipped at his own cup.

'It's weary work, this,' he said. 'I fall asleep most afternoons. I cannot keep my eyes open.'

'Anne puts me to bed after my dinner as if I were a child,' I said resentfully.

'What d'you want?' Anne asked. 'To be as haggard as the queen?'

'She's not looking too bonny,' George agreed. 'Is she ill?'

'Just old age, I think,' Anne said uncaringly. 'And the effort of appearing happy all the time. She must be exhausted. Henry takes a lot of pleasing, doesn't he?'

'No,' I said smugly, and the three of us laughed.

'Has he said if he is giving you a special gift for Christmas?' Anne asked. 'Or George? Or any of us?'

I shook my head. 'He hasn't said.'

'Uncle Howard sent a gold chalice wrought with our arms for you to give to him,' Anne said. 'It's safe in the cupboard. It's worth a fortune. I only hope we see some return on it.'

I nodded drowsily. 'He has promised me a surprise.' At once the two of them were alert. 'He wants to take me to the shipyard tomorrow.'

Anne made a grimace of disdain. 'I thought you meant a gift. Are we all to go? The whole court?'

'Just a small party.' I closed my eyes and started to drift off into sleep. I heard Anne get up from the bed and move about the room, unpacking my clothes from the chest and laying them out for the morning.

'You must wear your red,' she said. 'And you can borrow my red cape trimmed with swansdown. It'll be cold on the river.'

'Thank you, Anne.'

'Oh, don't think I'm doing it for you. I am doing this for the advancement of the family. None of this is for you, as yourself.'

I hunched my shoulders against the coldness of her tone but I was too tired to retort. Dimly, I heard George put down his cup and rise from his chair. I heard his soft kiss on Anne's forehead.

'Weary work but everything to play for,' he said quietly. 'Goodnight, Annamaria – I leave you to your duties and go to mine.'

I heard her seductive chuckle. 'The whores of Greenwich are a noble calling, my brother. I shall see you tomorrow.'

∾

Anne's cape looked wonderful over my red riding habit and she lent me her smart little French riding hat as well. Henry, Anne, I, George, my husband William, and half a dozen others rode alongside the river to the shipyard where they were building the king's new ship. It was a bright wintry day, the sun sparkled on the water, the fields either side of the river were noisy with the sound of water birds, the geese from Russia overwintering at our milder watermeadows. Against their continual gabble, the quacking of ducks and the call of snipe and curlew were very loud. We cantered beside the river in a little group, my horse shouldering against the king's big hunter, Anne and George on either side of us. Henry pulled up to a trot and then a walk as we came near to the dock.

The foreman came out as he saw our party approaching and pulled off his hat and bowed low to the king.

'I thought to ride out and see how you do,' the king said, smiling down on him.

'We are honoured, Your Majesty.'

'And how goes the work?' The king swung himself down from the saddle and tossed the reins of his horse to a waiting groom. He turned and lifted me down and tucked my hand into the crook of his elbow and led me to the dry dock.

'So what d'you think of her?' Henry asked me, squinting up at the smooth oak side of the half-built ship as she rested on the great wooden rollers. 'Don't you think she is going to be most lovely?'

'Lovely and dangerous,' I said, looking at the gun doors. 'Surely the French have nothing as good as this.'

'Nothing,' Henry said proudly. 'If I'd had three beauties like this one at sea last year I would have destroyed the French navy as they skulked in port, and I should have been King of England and France in deed as well as word today.'

I hesitated. 'The French army is said to be very strong,' I ventured. 'And Francis very resolute.'

'He's a peacock,' Henry said crossly. 'All show. And Charles of Spain will take him in the south as I come at him from Calais. The two of us will divide France between us.' Henry turned to the shipwright. 'When will she be ready?'

'In spring,' the man answered.

'Is the draughtsman here today?'

The man bowed. 'He is.'

'I have a fancy to have a sketch made of you, Mistress Carey. Will you sit for a moment and let the man take your likeness?'

I flushed with pleasure. 'Of course, if you wish it.'

Henry nodded to the shipwright who shouted from the platform to the quay below us and a man came running. Henry helped me down the ladder and I sat on a pile of newly sawn planks while a young man in rough homespun cloth sketched a quick likeness of my face.

'What will you do with the picture?' I asked curiously, trying to keep still and hold a smile on my lips.

'Wait and see.'

The artist put his paper to one side. 'I have enough.'

Henry put out his hand to me and raised me to my feet. 'Then, sweeting, let's ride home to our dinner. I'll take you home around the water-meadows, there's a good gallop to the castle.'

The grooms were walking the horses around so that they did not catch cold. Henry threw me up into my saddle and then mounted his own horse. He glanced over his shoulder to see that everyone was ready. Lord Percy was tightening Anne's girth. She looked down and gave him her slow provocative smile. Then we all turned and rode back to Greenwich as the sun set primrose and cream in the cold winter sky.

❁

Christmas dinner lasted for nearly all the day and I was sure that Henry would send for me that night. Instead he announced that he would visit the queen and I had to be among the ladies who sat with her, waiting for him to finish drinking with his friends and come to bed in the queen's apartments.

Anne pushed a half-sewn shirt into my hands and sat beside me, firmly planting herself on the skirts of my outspread gown so I could not rise without her letting me up. 'Oh leave me alone,' I said under my breath.

'Take that miserable look off your face,' she hissed. 'Do your sewing and smile as if you were enjoying it. No man is going to desire you when you look as sulky as a baited bear.'

'But to spend Christmas night with her . . .'

Anne nodded. 'D'you want to know why?'

'Yes.'

'Some beggarly soothsayer told him that he would get a son tonight. He's hoping the queen might give him an autumn child. Lord, what fools men are.'

'A soothsayer?'

'Yes. Foretold a son, if he forsook all other women. No need to ask who paid her.'

'What d'you mean?'

'My guess is that we'd find Seymour gold in her pocket if we turned her upside down and shook her very hard. But it's too late for that now. The damage is done. He'll be in the queen's bed tonight and every night till twelfth night. So you had better make sure that when he walks past you to do his duty he remembers what he's missing.'

I bent my head lower over my sewing. Anne, watching me, saw a tear fall on the hem of the shirt and saw me blot it with my finger.

'Little fool,' she said roughly. 'You'll get him back.'

'I hate the thought of him lying with her,' I whispered. 'I wonder if he calls her sweeting, too?'

'Probably,' Anne said bluntly. 'Not many men have the wit to vary the tune. But he'll do his duty by her and then look around again, and if you catch his eye and smile then it will be you again.'

'How can I smile when my heart is breaking?'

Anne gave a little giggle. 'Oh what a tragedy queen! You can smile when your heart is breaking because you are a woman, and a courtier, and a Howard. That's three reasons for being the most deceitful creature on God's earth. Now sshh – here he comes.'

George came in first with a quick smile for me and went to kneel at the queen's feet. She gave him her hand with a pretty blush, she was glowing with pleasure that the king was coming to her. Henry came in next with my husband, William, and with his hand on Lord Percy's shoulder. He walked past me with nothing more than a nod of his head though Anne and I stood as he entered the room and dipped low into a curtsey. He went straight to the queen, kissed her on the lips and then led the way into her privy chamber. Her maids went in with them and shortly came out and closed the door. The rest of us were left outside in silence.

William looked around and smiled at me. 'Well met, good wife,' he said pleasantly. 'Shall you be keeping your present quarters for much longer, d'you think? Or will you want me as a bedfellow again?'

'That must depend on the command of the queen and of our uncle,' George said evenly. His hand slid along his belt to where his sword would hang. 'Marianne cannot choose for herself, as you know.'

William did not rise to the challenge. He gave me a rueful smile. 'Peace,

George,' he said. 'I don't need you to explain it all to me. I should know by now.'

I looked away. Lord Percy had drawn Anne into an alcove and I heard her seductive giggle at something that he said. She saw me watching and said more loudly: 'Lord Percy is writing sonnets to me, Mary. Do tell him that his lines don't scan.'

'It's not even finished,' Percy protested. 'I was just telling you the first line and already you are too critical.'

' "Fair lady – thou dost treat me with disdain – " '

'I think that's a very good start,' I said helpfully. 'How would you go on, Lord Percy?'

'It's clearly not a good start,' George said. 'To start a courtship with disdain is the very worst start you could make. A kind start would be more promising.'

'A kind start would be certainly startling, from a Boleyn girl,' William said with a barb in his tone. 'Depending on the suitor, of course. But now I think of it – a Percy of Northumberland might get a kind start.'

Anne flashed him a look which was something less than sisterly but Henry Percy was so absorbed in his poem that he hardly heard him. 'It goes on with the next line, which I don't have yet, and then it goes something something something something, my pain.'

'Oh! To rhyme with disdain!' George declared provokingly. 'I think I'm beginning to get this.'

'But you must have an image that you pursue throughout the poem,' Anne said to Henry Percy. 'If you are going to write a poem to your mistress you must compare her to something and then twist the comparison round to some witty conclusion.'

'How can I?' Percy asked her. 'I cannot compare you to anything. You are yourself. What should I compare you to?'

'Oh very pretty!' George said approvingly. 'I say, Percy, your conversation is better than your poetry, I should stay on one knee and whisper in her ear, if I was you. You'll triumph if you stick to prose.'

Percy grinned and took Anne's hand. 'Stars in the night,' he said.

'Something something something something, some delight,' Anne rejoined promptly.

'Let's have some wine,' William suggested. 'I don't think I can keep up with this dazzling wit. And who will play me at dice?'

'I'll play,' George said before William could challenge me. 'What will the stakes be?'

'Oh a couple of crowns,' William said. 'I should hate to have you as my enemy for a gambling debt, Boleyn.'

'Or any other cause,' my brother said sweetly. 'Especially since Lord Percy here might write us a martial poem about fighting.'

'I don't think something something something, is very threatening,' Anne remarked. 'And that is all that his lines ever say.'

'I am an apprentice,' Percy said with dignity. 'An apprentice lover and an apprentice poet and you are treating me unkindly. "Fair lady – thou dost treat me with disdain –" is nothing but the truth.'

Anne laughed and held out her hand for him to kiss. William drew a couple of dice from his pocket and rolled them on the table. I poured him a glass of wine and put it by him. I felt oddly comforted to be serving him when the man that I loved was bedding his wife in the room next door. I felt that I had been put aside, and for all I knew I might have to stay to one side.

We played until midnight and still the king did not emerge.

'What d'you think?' William asked George. 'If he means to spend the night with her we might as well go to our beds.'

'We're going,' Anne said firmly. She held out a peremptory hand to me.

'So soon?' Percy pleaded. 'But stars come out at night.'

'Then they fade at dawn,' Anne replied. 'This star needs to veil herself in darkness.'

I rose to go with her. My husband looked at me for a moment. 'Kiss me goodnight, wife,' he ordered.

I hesitated and then I went across the room. He expected me to put a cool kiss on his cheek but instead I bent over and kissed him on his lips. I felt him respond as I touched him. 'Goodnight, husband. And I wish you a merry Christmas.'

'Goodnight, wife. My bed would have been warmer tonight with you in it.'

I nodded. There was nothing I could say. Without intending it, I glanced towards the closed door of the queen's privy chamber where the man I adored slept in the arms of his wife.

'Maybe we'll all end up with our wives in the end,' William said quietly.

'For sure,' George said cheerfully, shovelling his winnings from the table into his cap, and then pouring them into the pocket of his jacket. 'For we will be buried alongside each other, whatever our preferences in life. Think of me, melting to dust with Jane Parker.'

Even William laughed.

'When will it be?' Percy asked. 'Your happy nuptial day?'

'Sometime after midsummer. If I can contain my impatience for that long.'

'She brings a handsome dowry,' William remarked.

'Oh who cares for that?' Percy exclaimed. 'Love is all that matters.'

'Thus speaks one of the richest men in the kingdom,' my brother observed wryly.

Anne held out her hand to Percy. 'Pay no attention, my lord. I agree with you. Love is all that matters. At any rate, that's what I think.'

❧

'No you don't,' I said as soon as the door was shut behind us.

Anne gave me a tiny smile. 'I wish you would take the trouble to see who I am talking to, and not what I am saying.'

'Percy of Northumberland? You are talking of marriage for love to Percy of Northumberland?'

'Exactly. So you can simper at your husband all you like, Mary. When I marry I shall do better than you by far.'

Spring 1523

In the early weeks of the New Year the queen found her youth again, and blossomed like a rose in a warm room, her colour high, her smiles ready. She put aside the hair shirt she usually wore under her gown, and the telltale rough skin at her neck and shoulders disappeared as if smoothed away by joy. She did not tell anyone the cause of these changes; but her maid told another that she had missed one of her courses, and that the soothsayer was right: the queen had taken with child.

Given her past history of not going full term, there was every reason for her to be on her knees, her face turned up to the statue of the Virgin Mary in the little prie dieu in the corner of her privy chamber, and every morning found her there, one hand upon her belly, one hand on her missal, her eyes closed, her expression rapt. Miracles could happen. Perhaps a miracle was happening for the queen.

The maids gossiped that her linen was clean again in February and we began to think that soon she would tell the king. Already he had the look of a man waiting for good news, and he walked past me as if I were invisible. I had to dance before him and attend his wife and endure the smirks of the ladies and know once again that I was nothing more than a Boleyn girl, and not the favourite any more.

'I can't stand it,' I said to Anne. We were sitting by the fireplace in the queen's apartments. The others were walking with the dogs, but Anne and I had refused to go out. The mist was coming off the river and it was a bitterly cold day. I was shivering inside a fur-lined gown. I had not felt well since Christmas night when Henry had gone past me into her room. He had not sent for me since then.

'You are taking it hard,' she observed contentedly. 'That's what comes of loving a king.'

'What else could I do?' I asked miserably. I moved to the windowseat to get more light on my sewing. I was hemming the queen's shirts for the poor, and just because they were for old labouring men did not mean that I was allowed sloppy work. She would look at the seams and if she thought they were clumsily executed she would ask me, very pleasantly, to do them again.

'If she has a child and it's a son then you might as well have stayed with William Carey and started your own family,' Anne observed. 'The king will be at her beck, and your days will be done. You'll just be one of many.'

'He loves me,' I said uncertainly. 'I'm not one of many.'

I turned my head away and looked out of the window. The mist was curling off the river in great coils, like dust under a bed.

Anne gave a hard little laugh. 'You've always been one of many,' she said brutally. 'There are dozens of us Howard girls, all with good breeding, all well taught, all pretty, all young, all fertile. They can throw one after another on the table and see if one is lucky. It's no real loss to them if one after another is taken up and then thrown aside. There's always another Howard girl conceived, there's always another whore in the nursery. You were one of many before you were even born. If he does not cleave to you then you go back to William, they find another Howard girl to tempt him, and the dance starts all over again. Nothing is lost for them.'

'Something is lost for me!' I cried out.

She put her head on one side and looked at me, as if she would sift the reality from the impatience of childish passion. 'Yes. Perhaps. Something is lost for you. Your innocence, your first love, your trust. Perhaps your heart is broken. Perhaps it will never mend. Poor silly Marianne,' she said softly. 'To do one man's bidding to please another man and get nothing for yourself but heartbreak.'

'So who would come after me?' I asked her, turning my pain into taunting. 'Who d'you think the next Howard girl will be that they push into his bed? Let me guess – the other Boleyn girl?'

She flashed me a quick black glance and then her dark eyelashes swept down on her cheeks. 'Not me,' she said. 'I make my own plans. I don't risk being taken up and dropped again.'

'You told me to risk it,' I reminded her.

'That was for you,' she said. 'I would not live my life as you live yours. You would always do as you were bid, marry where you were told, bed where you were ordered. I am not like you. I make my own way.'

'I could make my own way,' I said.

Anne smiled disbelievingly.

'I'd go back to Hever and live there,' I said. 'I wouldn't stay at court. If I am put aside I could go to Hever. At least I will always have that now.'

The door to the queen's apartment opened and I glanced up as the maids came out, lugging the sheets from the queen's bed.

'That's the second time this week she's ordered them to be changed,' one said irritably.

Anne and I exchanged a quick look. 'Are they stained?' Anne demanded urgently.

The maid looked at her insolently. 'The queen's sheets?' she asked. 'You ask me to show you the queen's own bed linen?'

Anne's long fingers went to her purse and a piece of silver changed hands. The maid's smile was triumphant as she pocketed the coin. 'Not stained at all,' she said.

Anne subsided and I went to hold the door open for the two women. 'Thank you,' the second one said, surprised at my politeness to a servant. She nodded to me. 'Rank with sweat, poor lady,' she said quietly.

'What?' I asked. I could hardly believe that she was giving me freely a piece of information that a French spy would pay a king's ransom for, and that every courtier in the land was longing to know. 'Are you saying the queen is having night sweats? That her change of life is on her?'

'If not now then very soon,' the maid said. 'Poor lady.'

❀

I found my father with George in the great hall, head to head while the servants set the great trestle tables for dinner around them. He beckoned me to him.

'Father,' I said, dropping him a curtsey.

He kissed me coolly on the forehead. 'Daughter,' he said. 'Did you want to see me?'

For a chilling moment I wondered if he had forgotten my name. 'The queen is not with child,' I told him. 'She started her course, this day. She missed her other times because of her age.'

'God be praised!' George said exultantly. 'I bet myself a gold crown on this. That is good news.'

'The best,' my father said. 'The best for us, the worst for England. Has she told the king?'

I shook my head. 'She started to bleed this afternoon, she has not seen him yet.'

My father nodded. 'So we have the news before him. Anyone else know it?'

I shrugged. 'The maids who changed her linen, and so anyone who was paying them. Wolsey, I suppose. Perhaps the French might have bought a maid.'

'Then we have to be fast if we want to be the ones to tell him. Should I?'

George shook his head. 'Too intimate,' he said. 'What about Mary?'

'It puts her before him at the very moment of his disappointment,' my father mused. 'Better not.'

'Anne then,' George said. 'It should be one of us to remind him of Mary.'

'Anne can do it,' my father agreed. 'She could turn a polecat off the scent of a mouse.'

'She's in the garden,' I volunteered. 'At the archery butts.'

The three of us walked from the great hall into the bright light of the spring sunshine. There was a cold wind blowing through the yellow daffodils that nodded in the sunshine. We could see the little group of courtiers at the archery butts, Anne among them. As we watched she stepped up, sighted the target, drew her bow and we heard the twang of the string and the satisfying thud as the arrow hit the bullseye. There was a scattering of applause. Henry Percy strode up to the target and plucked Anne's arrow from it and tucked it into his own quiver, as if he would keep it.

Anne was laughing, holding out her hand for her arrow, as she glanced over and saw us. At once, she turned from the company and came towards us.

'Father.'

'Anne.' He kissed her more warmly than he had kissed me.

'The queen has started her courses,' George said bluntly. 'We think that you should tell the king.'

'Rather than Mary?'

'It makes her look low,' my father said. 'Tattling with chambermaids, watching them empty piss pots.'

For a moment I thought that Anne would remark that she did not want to look low either, but she shrugged her shoulders. She knew that serving the Howard family ambition always had a price attached.

'And make sure that Mary is back in his eye,' my father said. 'When he turns against the queen it must be Mary who picks him up.'

Anne nodded. 'Of course.' Only I could have heard the edge in her voice. 'Mary comes first.'

❧

The king came to the queen's rooms that evening as usual to sit beside her at the fireside. We three of us watched him, certain that he must tire of this domestic peace. But the queen was skilful in entertaining him. There was always a game of cards or dice going on, she had always read the most recent books and could venture and defend an interesting opinion. There were always other visitors, learned or well-travelled men who would talk with the king, there was always the best music, and Henry loved good music. Thomas More was a favourite of hers and sometimes the three of them would walk on the flat roofs of the castle and look at the night skies. More and the king would speak of interpretations of the Bible and whether there would ever come a time when it would be right to allow an English Bible that common people could read. And there were always pretty women. The queen was wise enough to fill her rooms with the prettiest women in the kingdom.

This evening was no exception, she entertained him as if he were a visiting ambassador that she had to favour. After he had talked with her for a while someone asked if he would sing and he took the floor and sung us one of his own compositions. He asked for a lady to take the soprano part and Anne reluctantly and modestly came forward and said that she would try. Of course she had it note perfect. They sang an encore, well pleased with themselves, and then Henry kissed Anne's hand and the queen called for wine for our two songsters.

It was nothing more than a touch to his hand and Anne had him a little aside from the rest of the court. Only the queen and us Boleyns knew that the king had been drawn away. The queen called for one of the musicians to play us another air, she had too much sense ever to be caught glaring after her husband as he started another flirtation. She shot one quick look at me to see how I was taking the sight of my sister on the king's arm and I gave her a bland, innocent smile.

'You are becoming a fine courtier, my little wife,' William Carey remarked.

'I am?'

'When you first came to court you were a fresh piece of goods, hardly glazed by the French court, but now the gilt seems to be entering your soul. Do you ever do a thing without thinking twice?'

For a moment I would have defended myself but I saw Anne speak a sentence to the king and saw him glance back at the queen. Anne put her hand gently on his sleeve and said another soft word. I turned away from William, quite deaf to him, and instead watched the man I loved. I saw his broad shoulders bend and drop down, as if half his power had gone from him. He looked at the queen as if she had betrayed him, his face vulnerable as a child. Anne turned so he was shielded from the rest of the court and George went forward to ask the queen if we might dance, to keep the attention away from Anne, pouring sorrow into the king's ear.

I could not bear it, I slipped away from the girls who were clamouring to dance and went to Henry, pushing past Anne to get to him. His face was pale, his eyes tragic. I took his hands and said only: 'Oh my dear.'

He turned to me at once. 'Did you know too? Do all her ladies know?'

'I think so,' Anne said. 'We cannot blame her for not wanting to tell you, poor lady, it was her last hope. It was your last chance, sire.'

I felt his fingers grip my hand a little tighter. 'The soothsayer told me . . .'

'I know,' I said gently. 'She was probably bribed.'

Anne melted away, and the two of us were alone.

'And I lay with her and tried so hard, and hoped . . .'

'I prayed for you,' I whispered. 'For you both. I was so hoping that you would have a son, Henry. Before God, I would rather that she gave you a legitimate son than any other wish in the world.'

'But she cannot now.' His mouth shut like a trap. He looked like a spoilt child, who cannot get what he wants.

'No, not any more,' I confirmed. 'It is over.'

Abruptly he dropped my hands and turned away from me. The dancers parted before his rapid advance as he strode through the sets. He went to the queen, who was seated smiling on her court and said, loud enough for everyone to hear: 'I'm told you are unwell, madam. I could wish you had told me yourself.'

At once she looked to me, her sharp gaze accusing me of betraying her most intimate secret. Minutely I shook my head. She looked for Anne in the dancers and saw her, with George's hand in hers. Blandly, Anne looked back.

'I am sorry, Your Majesty,' the queen said with her immense dignity. 'I should have chosen a more fitting time to discuss this with you.'

'You should have chosen a more immediate time,' he corrected her. 'But since you are unwell I suggest that you dismiss your court and bide by yourself.'

Those of the queen's court who grasped at once what was happening whispered quickly to their neighbours. But most of them stood and stared at the king's sudden storm of bad humour, and at the queen's white-faced endurance.

Henry turned on his heel, snapped his fingers for his friends: George, Henry, William, Charles, Francis, as if he were calling his dogs, and

81

marched out of the queen's rooms without another word. I was pleased to see that of all of them, my brother George swept her the deepest bow. She let them go without a word, and rose and went quietly into her own privy chamber.

The musicians who had been fiddling away sounding more and more ragged, found their tune had died and they looked around for orders.

'Oh go,' I said in sudden impatience. 'Can't you see there'll be no more dancing and no more singing for tonight? Nobody here needs music. God knows, nobody wants to dance.'

Jane Parker looked at me in surprise. 'I'd have thought you'd have been glad. The king on bad terms with the queen, and you ready to be picked up like a bruised peach in the gutter.'

'And I'd have thought you'd have had more sense than to say such a thing,' Anne said roundly. 'To speak thus of your sister-in-law to be! You had better take care or you won't be welcome in this family.'

Jane did not back down to Anne. 'There's no breaking a betrothal. George and I are as good as wed in church. It's just a question of settling the day. You can welcome me or you can hate me, Miss Anne. But you can't forbid me. We are promised before witnesses.'

'Oh what does it matter!' I cried out. 'What does any of it matter?' I turned and ran to my chamber. Anne slipped in after me.

'What's wrong?' she demanded tersely. 'Is the king angry with us?'

'No, though he should be, for we did a nasty piece of work in telling him the queen's secret.'

'Oh aye,' Anne nodded, quite unmoved. 'But he was not angry with us?'

'No, he's hurt.'

Anne went to the door.

'Where are you going?' I asked.

'I'm going to get them to bring the bath here,' she said. 'You're going to wash.'

'Oh Anne,' I said irritably. 'He's heard the worst news in his life. He's in the worst of tempers. He's hardly going to send for me tonight. I can wash tomorrow, if I have to.'

She shook her head. 'I'm taking no chances,' she said. 'You wash tonight.'

❀

She was wrong, but only by a day. The next day the queen sat alone in her room with her ladies and I dined in the privy chamber with my brother, with his friends, and with the king. It was a merry merry evening with music and dancing and gambling. And that night I was in the king's bed once more.

◎

This time Henry and I were all but inseparable. The court knew that we were lovers, the queen knew, even the common people who came out from London to watch us dine knew. I wore his gold bracelet around my wrist, I rode his hunter to hounds. I had a pair of matched diamonds for my ears, I had three new gowns, one of cloth of gold. And one morning in bed he said to me:

'Did you never wonder what came of that sketch that I asked the artist at the shipyard to do?'

'I'd forgotten him,' I said.

'Come here and kiss me and I will tell you why I ordered him to draw you,' Henry said lazily.

He lay back on the pillows of his bed. It was late in the morning but the curtains were still drawn around us, shielding us from the servants coming in to make up the fire, to bring him hot water, to empty the piss pot. I swarmed up the bed towards him, leaning my round breasts against his warm chest, letting my hair tumble forward in a veil of gold and bronze. My mouth came down on his, I inhaled the warm erotic scent of his beard, felt the soft prickle of the hairs around his mouth, pushed deeper against his lips and felt, as much as heard, his little groan of desire as I kissed him hard.

I raised my head and smiled into his eyes. 'There is your kiss,' I whispered throatily, feeling my desire rise with his. 'Why did you order the artist to draw me?'

'I shall show you,' he promised. 'After Mass. We'll ride down to the river and you shall see my new ship and your likeness at the same time.'

'Is the ship ready?' I asked. I was reluctant to move away from him but he pulled back the covers and was ready to rise.

'Yes. We'll see her launched next week sometime,' he said. He drew back the bed curtains a little and shouted for a servant to fetch George. I threw on my gown and my cloak and Henry held my hand to help me down from the bed. He kissed me on the cheek. 'I'll break my fast with the queen,' he decided. 'And then we'll go out and see the ship.'

✤

It was a lovely morning. I was wearing a new riding habit of yellow velvet, made for me with a bolt of cloth the king had given me. Anne was at my side in one of my old gowns. It gave me a fierce joy to see her wearing my hand-me-downs. But then, in the contradictory way of sisters, I admired what she had done with it. She had ordered it to be shortened and re-cut in the French way and she looked stylish. She wore it with a little French hat made from the material she had saved by cutting the skirt straighter. Henry Percy of Northumberland could not keep his eyes off her, but she flirted with equal charm with all of the king's companions. There were nine of us riding out. Henry and I side by side in the lead. Anne behind me with Percy and William Norris. George and Jane, a silent ill-matched couple, next, and Francis Weston and William Brereton came behind, laughing and cracking jokes. We were preceded only by a couple of grooms and followed by four mounted soldiers.

We rode by the river. The tide was coming in and the waves splashed on the shore, white-capped. The seagulls, blown inland, cried and wheeled above our heads, their wings as bright as silver in the spring sunshine. The hedgerows were greening with the fresh colour of spring growth, primroses like pale pats of creamy butter in the sunny spots on the banks. The track alongside the river was hard-packed mud and the horses cantered along at a good easy pace. As we rode, the king sang me a lovesong of his own composing, and when I heard it over the second time I sang it with him and he laughed at my attempt at harmony. I did not have Anne's talent, I knew. But it did not matter. That day nothing mattered, nothing could matter, but that my beloved and I were riding out together in the brightest of sunshine, on a little journey for pleasure, and he was happy, and I was happy in his sight.

We reached the shipyard sooner than I wanted and Henry himself stood beside my horse, lifted me down from the saddle and held me for a swift kiss when my feet were on the ground.

'Sweetheart,' he whispered. 'I have a little surprise for you.'

He turned me around and stepped to one side so that I could see his beautiful new ship. She was almost ready for the sea now, she had the characteristic high poop deck and prow of a fighting ship, built for speed.

'Look,' Henry said, seeing me taking in her lines but not the detail. He pointed to her name carved and enamelled in gold in bold curly letters at the ornate prow. It said: 'Mary Boleyn'.

For a moment I stared, reading the letters of my name but not understanding. He did not laugh at my astounded face, he watched me, seeing my surprise turn to puzzlement and then to dawning understanding.

'You named her for me?' I asked. I could hear my voice quaver. It was an honour too great for me. I felt too young, too small a person altogether to have a ship, and such a ship, named for me. And now everyone in the world would know that I was the king's mistress. There could be no denial.

'I did, sweetheart.' He was smiling. He expected me to be delighted.

He tucked my cold hand under his elbow and urged me to the front of the ship. There was a figurehead, looking out with a proud beautiful profile, looking out over the Thames, out to sea, to France. It was me, with my lips slightly parted, slightly smiling, as if I was a woman to want such an adventure. As if I were not the cat's-paw of the Howard family but a courageous lovely woman in my own right.

'Me?' I asked, my voice a thread above the sound of the water splashing at the side of the dry dock.

Henry's mouth was at my ear, I could feel the warmth of his breath on my cold cheek.

'You,' he said. 'A beauty, like you. Are you happy, Mary?'

I turned to him and his arms came around me and I stood up on tiptoe and buried my face in the warmth of his neck and smelled the sweet scent of his beard and his hair. 'Oh Henry,' I whispered. I wanted my face hidden from him, I knew that he would see no pleasure but a terror at rising so high, so publicly.

'Are you happy?' he insisted. He turned my face up, with a hand under my chin, so that he could scan me as if I were a manuscript. 'It is a great honour.'

'I know.' My smile trembled on my lips. 'I thank you.'

'And you shall launch her,' he promised me. 'Next week.'

I hesitated. 'Not the queen?'

I was fearful of taking her place to launch the newest and greatest ship that he had ever built. But of course it had to be me. How could she launch a ship that bore my name?

He shrugged her away as if they had not been husband and wife for thirteen years. 'No,' he said shortly. 'Not the queen. You.'

I found a smile from somewhere and hoped that it was convincing and that it hid my terrified sense that I was going too far, too fast, and that the end of this road was not the sort of carefree joy that we had felt this morning, but something darker and more fearful. For all that we had ridden, singing out of tune together, we were not a lover and his lass. If my name was on this ship, if I launched it next week, then I was a declared rival to the Queen of England. I was an enemy to the Spanish ambassador, to the whole nation of Spain. I was a powerful force in the court, a threat to the Seymour family. The higher I rose in the king's favour the greater the dangers that opened up around me. But I was a young woman of only fifteen years old. I could not yet revel in ambition.

As if she could read my reluctance, Anne was at my side. 'You do my sister a great honour, sire,' she said smoothly. 'It is a most exquisite ship, as lovely as the woman you named her for. And a strong and powerful ship – like yourself. God bless her and send her against our enemies. Whoever they may be.'

Henry smiled at the compliment. 'She is bound to be a lucky ship,' he said. 'With the face of an angel going before her.'

'D'you think she'll have to fight the French this year?' George asked, taking my hand and giving my fingers a quick hidden pinch to recall me to my work as a courtier.

Henry nodded, looking grim. 'Without doubt,' he said. 'And if the Spanish emperor will move in concert with me, we will follow my plan of our attack in the north of France, as he attacks in the south, then we cannot fail to curb Francis's arrogance. This summer we will do it, without fail.'

'If we can trust the Spanish,' Anne said silkily.

Henry's face darkened. 'It is they who have the greatest need of us,' he said. 'Charles had better remember that. This is not a matter of family or kinship. If the queen is displeased with me for one reason or another she must remember that she is a queen of England first, and a princess of Spain second. Her first loyalty must be to me.'

Anne nodded. 'I should hate to be so divided,' she said. 'Thank God we Boleyns are English through and through.'

'For all your French gowns,' Henry said with a sudden gleam of humour.

Anne smiled back at him. 'A gown is a gown,' she said. 'Like Mary's gown of yellow velvet. But you of all people would know that underneath there is a true subject with an undivided heart.'

He turned to me at that and smiled at me as I looked up at him. 'It is my pleasure to reward such a faithful heart,' he said.

I felt that there were tears in my eyes and I tried to blink them away without him seeing, but one stood on my eyelashes. Henry bent down and kissed it. 'Sweetest girl,' he said gently. 'My little English rose.'

❦

The whole court turned out to launch the ship, the *Mary Boleyn*, and only the queen pleaded an indisposition and stayed away. The Spanish ambassador was there to watch the vessel slip into the water, and whatever reservations he felt about the name of the ship he kept to himself.

My father was in a silent frenzy of irritation at himself, at me, at the king. The great honour which had been done to me and to my family had turned out to have a price attached. King Henry was a subtle monarch in such matters. When my uncle and father had thanked him for the compliment of using their name he thanked them for the contribution that he was sure they would want to make to the fitting out of such a ship which would so redound to their credit as it carried the Boleyn name across the seas.

'And so the stakes go up again,' George said cheerfully as we watched the boat slide over the rollers into the salty river waters of the Thames.

'How can they get any higher?' I asked from the corner of my smiling mouth. 'I have my life on the table.'

The shipyard workers, already half drunk on free ale, waved their caps and cheered. Anne smiled and waved in reply. George grinned at me. The wind stirred the feather in his cap, ruffled his dark curls. 'Now it's costing Father money to keep you in the king's favour. Now it's not just your heart and happiness on the table, my little sister, it's the family fortune. We thought we were playing him for a lovesick fool, but it turns out he's playing us for money lenders. Stakes go up. Father and Uncle will want to see a return for this investment. You see if they don't.'

I turned away from George and found Anne. She was a little distance from the court, Henry Percy beside her as usual. They were both watching the ship as the barges towed her out into the river and then turned her, and, struggling against the current, brought her back alongside the jetty and started to tie her up so that she could be fitted out as she lay in the water. Anne's face was bright with the joy that flirtation always brought her.

She turned and smiled at me. 'Ah, the Queen of the Day,' she said mockingly.

I made a little grimace. 'Don't tease me, Anne. I have had enough from George.'

Henry Percy stepped forward and took my hand and kissed it. As I looked down at the back of his blond head I realised how high my star was rising. This was Henry Percy, son and heir to the Duke of Northumberland. There was no other man in the kingdom who had fairer prospects or a greater fortune. He was the son of the richest man in England, second only to the king, and he was bowing his head to me and kissing my hand.

'She shall not tease you,' he promised me, coming up smiling. 'For I shall take you in to dine. I'm told that the cooks from Greenwich were out here at dawn to get everything ready. The king is going in, shall we follow?'

I hesitated but the queen, who always created a sense of formality, was left behind at Greenwich, lying in a darkened room with a pain in her belly and fear in her heart. There was no-one at the dockside but the feckless idle men and women of the court. No-one cared about precedence, except in the sense that winners must come first. 'Of course,' I said. 'Why not?'

Lord Henry Percy offered his other arm to Anne. 'Shall I have two sisters?'

'I think you would find the Bible forbids it,' Anne said provocatively. 'The Bible orders a man to choose between sisters and to stay with his first choice. Anything else is a cardinal sin.'

Lord Henry Percy laughed. 'I'm sure I could get an indulgence,' he said. 'The Pope would surely grant me a dispensation. With two sisters like this, what man could be made to choose?'

❁

We did not ride home until it was twilight and the stars were starting to come out in the pale grey sky of spring. I rode beside the king, my hand in his, and we let the horses amble along the riverside tow track. We rode under the archway of the palace and up to the opening front door. Then he pulled up his horse and he lifted me down from the saddle and whispered in my ear: 'I wish you were queen for all the days, and not just for one day in a pavilion by the river, my love.'

∾

'He said what?' my uncle asked.

I stood before him, like a prisoner under question before the court. Behind the table in the Howard rooms were seated Uncle Howard, Duke of Surrey, and my father and George. At the back of the room, behind me, Anne was sitting beside my mother. I, alone before the table, stood like a disgraced child before my elders.

'He said that he wished I was queen for all the days,' I said in a small voice, hating Anne for betraying my confidence, hating my father and my uncle for their cold-hearted dissection of lovers' whispers.

'What d'you think he meant?'

'Nothing,' I said sulkily. 'It's just love talk.'

'We need to see some repayment for all these loans,' my uncle said irritably. 'Has he said anything about giving you land? Or something for George? Or us?'

'Can't you hint him into it?' my father suggested. 'Remind him that George is to be married.'

I looked to George in mute appeal.

'The thing is that he's very alert for that sort of thing,' George pointed out. 'Everyone does it to him all the time. When he walks from his privy chamber to Mass every morning, his way is lined with people just waiting to ask him for a favour. I should think what he likes about Mary here is that she's not like that. I don't think she's ever asked for anything.'

'She has diamonds worth a fortune in her ears,' my mother put in sharply from behind me. Anne nodded.

'But she didn't ask for them. He gave them freely. He likes to be generous when it's unexpected. I think we have to let Mary play this her own way. She has a talent for loving him.'

I bit my lip on that, to stop myself saying a word. I did have a talent for loving him. It was perhaps the only talent I had. And this family, this powerful network of men, were using my talent to love the king as they used George's talents at swordplay, or my father's talent for languages, to further the interests of our family.

'Court moves to London next week,' my father remarked. 'The king will see the Spanish ambassador. There's little chance of him making any greater move towards Mary while he needs the Spanish alliance to fight the French.'

'Better work for peace then,' my uncle recommended wolfishly.

'I do. I am a peacemaker,' my father replied. 'Blessed, aren't I?'

❁

The court in progress was always a mighty sight, part-way between a country fair, a market day, and a joust. It was all arranged by Cardinal Wolsey, everything in the court or the country was done by his command. He had been at the king's side at the Battle of the Spurs in France, he had been almoner then to the English army and the men had never lain so dry at night nor eaten so well. He had a grasp of detail that made him attentive to how the court would get from one place to another, a grasp of politics that prompted him as to where we should stop and which lord should be honoured with a visit when the king was on his summer progress, and he was wily enough to trouble Henry with none of these things so the young king went from pleasure to pleasure as if the sky itself rained down supplies and servants and organisation.

It was the cardinal who ruled the precedence of the court on the move. Ahead of us went the pages carrying the standards with the pennants of all the lords in the train fluttering above their heads. Next there was a gap to let the dust settle and then came the king, riding his best hunter with his embossed saddle of red leather and all the trappings of kingship. Above his head flew his own personal standard, and at his side were his friends chosen to ride with him that day: my husband William Carey, Cardinal Wolsey, my father, and then trailing along behind them came the rest of the king's companions, changing their places in the train as they desired, lagging back or spurring forward. Around them, in a loose formation, came the king's personal guards mounted on horses and holding their lances at the salute. They hardly served to protect him – who would dream of hurting such a king? – but they kept back the press of people who gathered to cheer and gawp whenever we rode through a little town or a village.

Then there was another break before the queen's train. She was riding the steady old palfrey which she always used. She sat straight in the saddle, her gown awkwardly disposed in great folds of thick fabric, her hat skewered on her head, her eyes squinting against the bright sunshine. She was feeling ill. I knew because I had been at her side when she had mounted her horse in the morning and I had heard the tiny repressed grunt of pain as she settled into the saddle.

Behind the queen's court came the other members of the household, some of them riding, some of them seated in carts, some of them singing or drinking ale to keep the dust from the road out of their throats. All of us shared a careless sense of a high day and a holiday as the court left Greenwich and headed for London with a new season of parties and entertainments ahead of us, and who knew what might happen in this year?

∿

The queen's rooms at York Place were small and neat and we took only a few days to get unpacked and have everything to rights. The king visited every morning, as usual, and his court came with him, Lord Henry Percy among them. His lordship and Anne took to sitting in the windowseat together, their heads very close, as they worked on one of Lord Henry's poems. He swore that he would become a great poet under Anne's tuition and she swore that he would never learn anything, but that it was all a ruse to waste her time and her learning on such a dolt.

I thought that it was something for a Boleyn girl from a little castle in Kent and a handful of fields in Essex to call the Duke of Northumberland's son a dolt, but Henry Percy laughed and claimed that she was too stern a teacher and talent, great talent, would out, whatever she might say.

'The cardinal is asking for you,' I said to Lord Henry. He rose up, in no particular hurry, kissed Anne's hand in farewell, and went to find Cardinal Wolsey. Anne gathered up the papers they had been working on and locked them in her writing box.

'Does he really have no talent as a poet?' I asked.

She shrugged with a smile. 'He's no Wyatt.'

'Is he a Wyatt in courtship?'

'He's not married,' she said. 'And so more desirable to a sensible woman.'

'Too high, even for you.'

'I don't see why. If I want him, and he wants me.'

'You try asking Father to speak to the duke,' I recommended sarcastically. 'See what the duke says.'

She turned her head to look out of the window. The long beautiful lawns of York Place stretched down below us, almost hiding the sparkle of the river at the foot of the garden. 'I won't ask Father,' she said. 'I thought I might settle matters on my own account.'

I was going to laugh then I realised she was serious. 'Anne, this is not something you can settle for yourself. He's only a young man, you're only seventeen, you can't decide these things for yourselves. His father is certain to have someone in mind for him, and our father and uncle are certain to have plans for you. We're not private people, we're the Boleyn girls. We have to be guided, we have to do as we are told. Look at me!'

'Yes, look at you!' She rounded on me with a sudden flare of her dark energy. 'Married when you were still a child and now the king's mistress. Half as clever as me! Half as educated! But you are the centre of the court and I am nothing. I have to be your lady in waiting. I cannot serve you, Mary. It's an insult to me.'

'I never asked you to . . .' I stammered.

'Who insists that you bathe and wash your hair?' she demanded fiercely.

'You do. But I . . .'

'Who helps you choose your clothes and prompts you with the king? Who has rescued you a thousand times when you've been too stupid and tongue-tied to know how to play him?'

'You. But Anne . . .'

'And what is there in this for me? I have no husband who can be given land to show the king's favour. I have no husband to win high office because my sister is the king's mistress. I get nothing from this. However high you rise I still get nothing. I have to have a place of my own.'

'You should have a place of your own,' I said weakly. 'I don't deny it. All I was saying was that I don't think you can be a duchess.'

'And you should decide?' she spat at me. 'You who are nothing but the king's diversion from the important business of making a son if he can and making war if he can raise an army?'

'I don't say I should decide,' I whispered. 'I just said that I don't think they'll let you do it.'

'When it's done, it's done,' she said with a toss of her head. 'And no-one will know until it's done.'

Suddenly, like a striking snake, she reached out and grabbed my hand in a fierce grip. At once she twisted it behind my back and held me so that I could move neither forward nor backwards but only cry out in pain: 'Anne! Don't! You're really hurting!'

'Well, hear this,' she hissed in my ear. 'Hear this, Mary. I am playing my own game and I don't want you interrupting. Nobody will know anything until I am ready to tell them, and then they will know everything too late.'

'You're going to make him love you?'

Abruptly she released me and I gripped my elbow and my arm where the bones ached.

'I'm going to make him marry me,' she said flatly. 'And if you so much as breathe a word to anyone, then I will kill you.'

❁

After that I watched Anne with more care. I saw how she played him. Having advanced through all the cold months of the New Year at Greenwich, now, with the coming of the sun and our arrival in York Place, she suddenly retreated. And the more she withdrew from him the more he came on. When he came into a room she looked up and threw him a smile which went like an arrow to the centre of the target. She filled her look with invitation, with desire. But then she looked away and she would not look at him again for the whole of the visit.

He was in the train of Cardinal Wolsey and was supposed to wait on His Grace while the cardinal visited the king or the queen. In practice there was nothing for the young lord to do but to lounge around the queen's apartments and flirt with anyone who would talk to him. It was clear that he only had eyes for Anne and she walked past him, danced with anyone who asked her but him, dropped her glove and let him return it to her, sat near him but did not speak to him, returned his poems and told him that she could help him no longer.

She went into the most unswerving of retreats, having been unswervingly in advance, and the young man did not begin to know what he could do to recapture her.

He came to me. 'Mistress Carey, have I offended your sister in some way?'

'No, I don't think so.'

'She used to smile on me so charmingly and now she treats me very coldly.'

I thought for a moment, I was so slow at these things. On the one hand was the true answer: that she was playing him like a complete angler with a fish on the line. But I knew Anne would not want me to say that. On the other hand was the answer Anne would want me to give. I looked into Henry Percy's anxious baby face for a moment of genuine compassion. Then I gave him the Boleyn smile and the Howard answer. 'Indeed, my lord, I think she is afraid to be too kind.'

I saw the hope leap up in his trusting, boyish face. 'Too kind?'

'She was very kind to you, was she not, my lord?'

He nodded. 'Oh yes. I'm her slave.'

'I think she feared that she might come to like you too much.'

He leaned forward as if to snatch the words from my mouth 'Too much?'

'Too much for her own peace of mind,' I said very softly.

He leaped up and took two strides away from me and then came back again. 'She might desire me?'

I smiled and turned my head a little so that he could not see my weariness at this deceit. He was not to be put off. He dropped to his knees before me and peered up into my face.

'Tell me, Mistress Carey,' he begged. 'I have not slept for nights. I have not eaten for days. I am a soul in torment. Tell me if you think that she loves me, if you think that she might love me. Tell me, for pity's sake.'

'I cannot say.' Indeed, I could not. The lies would have stuck in my throat. 'You must ask her yourself.'

He sprang up, like a hare out of bracken with the beagle hounds behind it. 'I will! I will! Where is she?'

'Playing at bowls in the garden.'

He needed nothing more, he tore open the door and ran out of the room. I heard the heels of his boots ring down the stone stairs to the door to the garden. Jane Parker, who had been seated across the room from us, looked up.

'Have you made another conquest?' she asked, getting the wrong idea as usual.

I gave her a smile as poisonous as her own. 'Some women attract desire. Others do not,' I said simply.

❧

He found her at the bowling green, losing daintily and deliberately to Sir Thomas Wyatt.

'I shall write you a sonnet,' Wyatt promised. 'For handing me victory with such grace.'

'No, no, it was a fair battle,' Anne protested.

'If there had been money on it I think I would be getting out my purse,' he said. 'You Boleyns only lose when there is nothing to gain by winning.'

Anne smiled. 'Next time you shall put your fortune on it,' she promised him. 'See – I have lulled you into a sense of safety.'

'I have no fortune to offer but my heart.'

'Will you walk with *me*?' Henry Percy interrupted, his voice coming out far louder than he intended.

Anne gave a little start as if she had not noticed him there. 'Oh! Lord Henry.'

'The lady is playing bowls,' Sir Thomas said.

Anne smiled at them both. 'I have been so roundly defeated that I will take a walk and plan my strategy,' she said and put her hand on Lord Henry Percy's arm.

He led her away from the bowling green, down the winding path that led to a seat beneath a yew tree.

'Miss Anne,' he began.

'Is it too damp to sit?'

At once he swung his rich cloak from his shoulder and spread it out for her on a stone bench.

'Miss Anne . . .'

'No, I am too chilled,' she decided and rose up from the seat.

'Miss Anne!' he exclaimed, a little more crossly.

Anne paused and turned her seductive smile on him.

'Your lordship?'

'I have to know why have you grown so cold to me?'

For a moment she hesitated, then she dropped the coquettish play and turned a face to him which was grave and lovely.

'I did not mean to be cold,' she said slowly. 'I meant to be careful.'

'Of what?' he exclaimed. 'I have been in torment!'

'I did not mean to torment you. I meant to draw back a little. Nothing more than that.'

'Why?' he whispered.

She looked down the garden to the river. 'I thought it better for me, perhaps better for us both,' she said quietly. 'We might become too close in friendship for my comfort.'

He took a swift step from her and then back to her side. 'I would never cause you a moment's uneasiness,' he assured her. 'If you wanted me to promise you that we would be friends and that no breath of scandal would ever come to you, I would have promised that.'

She turned her dark luminous eyes on him. 'Could you promise that no-one would ever say that we were in love?'

Mutely, he shook his head. Of course he could not promise what a scandal-mad court might or might not say.

'Could you promise that we would never fall in love?'

He hesitated. 'Of course I love you, Mistress Anne,' he said. 'In the courtly way. In the polite way.'

She smiled as if she were pleased to hear it. 'I know it is nothing more than a May game. For me, also. But it's a dangerous game when played between a handsome man and a maid, when there are many people very quick to say that we are made for each other, that we are perfectly matched.'

'Do they say that?'

'When they see us dance. When they see how you look at me. When they see how I smile at you.'

'What else do they say?' He was quite entranced by this portrait.

'They say that you love me. They say that I love you. They say that we have both been head over heels in love while we thought we were doing nothing but playing.'

'My God,' he said at the revelation. 'My God, it *is* so!'

'Oh my lord! What are you saying?'

'I am saying that I have been a fool. I have been in love with you for months and all the time I thought I was amusing myself and you were teasing me, and that it all meant nothing.'

Her gaze warmed him. 'It was not nothing to me,' she whispered.

Her dark eyes held him, the boy was transfixed. 'Anne,' he whispered. 'My love.'

Her lips curved into a kissable, irresistible smile. 'Henry,' she breathed. 'My Henry.'

He took a small step towards her, put his hands on her tightly laced waist. He drew her close to him and Anne yielded, took one seductive step closer. His head came down as her face tipped up and his mouth found hers for their first kiss.

'Oh, say it,' Anne whispered. 'Say it now, this moment, say it, Henry.'

'Marry me,' he said.

❀

'And so it was done,' Anne reported blithely in our bedroom that night. She had ordered the bath tub to be brought in and we had gone into the hot water, one after another, and scrubbed each other's backs and washed each other's hair. Anne, as fanatical as a French courtesan about cleanliness, was ten times more rigorous than usual. She inspected my fingernails and toenails as if I were a dirty schoolboy, she handed me an ivory earscoop to clean out my ears as if I were her child, she pulled the lice comb through every lock of my head, reckless of my whimpers of pain.

'And so? What is done?' I asked sulkily, dripping on the floor and wrapping myself in a sheet. Four maids came in and started to bale out the water into buckets so that the great wooden bath could be carried away. The sheets they used to line the bath were heavy and sodden, it all seemed like a great deal of effort for very little gain. 'For all I have heard is more flirtation.'

'He's asked me,' Anne said. She waited till the door was shut behind the servants and then wrapped the sheet more tightly around her breasts and seated herself before the mirror.

There was a knock at the door.

'Who is it now?' I called in exasperation.

'It's me,' George replied.

'We're bathing,' I said.

'Oh let him come in.' Anne started to comb through her black hair. 'He can pull out these tangles.'

George lounged into the room and raised a dark eyebrow at the mess of water on the floor and wet sheets, at the two of us, half naked, and Anne with a thick mane of wet hair thrown over her shoulder.

'Is this a masque? Are you mermaids?'

'Anne insisted that we should bathe. Again.'

Anne offered him her comb and he took it.

'Comb my hair,' she said with her sly sideways smile. 'Mary always pulls.' Obediently, he stood behind her and started to comb through her dark hair, a strand at a time. He combed her carefully, as he would handle his mare's mane. Anne closed her eyes and luxuriated in his grooming.

'Any lice?' she asked, suddenly alert.

'None yet,' he reassured her, as intimate as a Venetian hairdresser.

'So what's done?' I demanded, returning to Anne's announcement.

'I have him,' she said frankly. 'Henry Percy. He has told me he loves me, he has told me that he wants to marry me. I want you and George to witness our betrothal, he can give me a ring, and then it's done and unbreakable, as good as a marriage in a church before a priest. And I shall be a duchess.'

'Good God.' George froze, the comb held in the air. 'Anne! Are you sure?'

'Am I likely to bodge this?' she asked tersely.

'No,' he allowed. 'But still. The Duchess of Northumberland! My God, Anne, you will own most of the north of England.'

She nodded, smiling at herself in the mirror.

'Good God, we will be the greatest family in the country! We'll be one of the greatest in Europe. With Mary in the king's bed and you the wife of his greatest subject, we will put the Howards so high they can never fall.' He broke off for a moment as he thought through to the next step.

'My God, if Mary was to fall pregnant to the king and to have a boy, then with Northumberland behind him he could take the throne as his own. I could be uncle to the King of England.'

'Yes,' Anne said silkily. 'That was what I thought.'

I said nothing, watching my sister's face.

'The Howard family on the throne,' George murmured, half to himself. 'Northumberland and Howards in alliance. It's done, isn't it? When those two come together. They would only come together through a marriage and an heir for both of them to strive for. Mary could bear the heir, and Anne could weld the Percys to his future.'

'You thought I'd never achieve it,' Anne said, pointing a finger at me. I nodded. 'I thought you were aiming too high.'

'You'll know another time,' she warned me. 'Where I aim, I will hit.'

'I'll know another time,' I concurred.

'But what about him?' George warned her. 'What if they disinherit him? Fine place you'll be in then, married to the boy who used to be heir to a dukedom, but now disgraced and owning nothing.'

She shook her head. 'They won't do that. He's too precious to them. But you have to take my part, George; and Father and Uncle Howard. His father has to see that we are good enough. Then they'll let the betrothal stand.'

'I'll do all I can but the Percys are a proud lot, Anne. They meant him for Mary Talbot until Wolsey came out against the match. They won't want you instead of her.'

'Is it just his wealth that you want?' I asked.

'Oh, the title too,' Anne said crudely.

'I mean, really. What d'you feel for him?'

For a moment I thought she was going to turn aside the question with another hard joke which would make his boyish adoration of her seem like nothing. But then she tossed her head and the clean hair flew through George's hands like a dark river.

'Oh, I know I'm a fool! I know he is nothing more than a boy, and a silly boy at that, but when he is with me I feel like a girl myself. I feel as if we are two youngsters, in love and with nothing to fear. He makes me feel reckless! He makes me feel enchanted! He makes me feel in love!'

It was as if the Howard spell of coldness had been broken, smashed like a mirror, and everything was real and bright. I laughed with her and snatched up her hands and looked into her face. 'Isn't it wonderful?' I demanded. 'Falling in love? Isn't it the most wonderful, wonderful thing?'

She pulled her hands away. 'Oh, go away, Mary. You are such a child. But yes! Wonderful? Yes! Now don't simper over me, I can't stand it.'

George took a hank of her dark hair and twisted it onto the top of her head and admired her face in the mirror. 'Anne Boleyn in love,' he said thoughtfully. 'Who'd have believed it?'

'It'd never have happened if he hadn't been the greatest man in the kingdom after the king,' she reminded him. 'I don't forget what's due to me and my family.'

He nodded. 'I know that, Annamaria. We all knew that you would aim very high. But a Percy! It's higher than I imagined.'

She leaned forward as if to interrogate her reflection. She cupped her face in her hands. 'This is my first love. My first and ever love.'

'Please God that you are lucky and that it is your last love as well as your first,' George said, suddenly sober.

Her dark eyes met his in the mirror. 'Please God,' she said. 'I want nothing more in my life but Henry Percy. With that I would be content. Oh – George, I cannot tell you. If I can have and hold Henry Percy I will be so very content.'

∾

Henry Percy came, at Anne's bidding, to the queen's rooms at noon the next day. She had chosen her time with care. The ladies had all gone to Mass, and we had the rooms to ourselves. Henry Percy came in and looked around, surprised at the silence and emptiness. Anne went up to him and took both his hands in hers. I thought for a moment that he looked, not so much courted as hunted.

'My love,' Anne said, and at the sound of her voice the boy's face warmed; his courage came back to him.

'Anne,' he said softly.

His hand fumbled in the pocket of his padded breeches, he drew a ring out of an inner pocket. From my station in the windowseat I could see the wink of a red ruby – the symbol of a virtuous woman.

'For you,' he said softly.

Anne took his hand. 'Do you want to plight our troth now, before witnesses?' she asked.

He gulped a little. 'Yes, I do.'

She glowed at him. 'Do it then.'

He glanced at George and me as if he thought one of us might stop him.

George and I smiled encouragingly, the Boleyn smile: a pair of pleasant snakes.

'I, Henry Percy, take thee, Anne Boleyn, to be my lawful wedded wife,' he said, taking Anne by the hand.

'I, Anne Boleyn, take thee, Henry Percy, to be my lawful wedded husband,' she said, her voice steadier than his.

He found the third finger of her left hand. 'With this ring I promise myself to you,' he said quietly, and slipped it on her finger. It was too loose. She clenched a fist to hold it on.

'With this ring, I take you,' she replied.

He bent his head, he kissed her. When she turned her face to me her eyes were hazy with desire.

'Leave us,' she said in a low voice.

❁

We gave them two hours, and then we heard, down the stone corridors, the queen and her ladies coming back from Mass. We knocked loudly on the door in the rhythm that meant 'Boleyn!' and we knew that Anne, even in a sated sleep, would hear it and jump up. But when we opened the door and went in, she and Henry Percy were composing a madrigal. She was playing the lute and he was singing the words they had written together. Their heads were very close so that they might both see the hand-written music on the stand, but excepting that intimacy, they were as they had been any day these last three months.

Anne smiled at me as George and I came into the room, followed by the queen's ladies.

'We have written such a pretty air, it has taken us all the morning,' Anne said sweetly.

'And what is it called?' George asked.

'"Merrily, merrily",' Anne replied. 'It's called "Merrily Merrily and Onward We Go".'

❧

That night it was Anne who left our bedchamber. She threw a dark cloak over her gown and went to the door as the palace tower bell rang for midnight.

'Where are you going at this time of night?' I demanded, scandalised.

Her pale face looked out at me from under the dark hood. 'To my husband,' she said simply.

'Anne, you cannot,' I said, aghast. 'You will get caught and you will be ruined.'

'We are betrothed in the sight of God and before witnesses. That's as good as a marriage, isn't it?'

'Yes,' I said unwillingly.

'A marriage could be overthrown for non-consummation, couldn't it?'

'Yes.'

'So I'm making it fast,' she said. 'Not even the Percy family will be able to wriggle out of it when Henry and I tell them that we are wedded and bedded.'

I kneeled up in the bed, imploring her to stay. 'But Anne, if someone sees you!'

'They won't,' she said.

'When the Percys know that you and he have been slipping out at midnight!'

She shrugged. 'I don't see the how or where makes much difference. As long as it is done.'

'If it should come to nothing –' I broke off at the blaze of her eyes. In one stride she was across the room and she had her hands at the neck of my nightdress, twisting it against my throat. 'That is why I am doing this,' she hissed. 'Fool that you are. So that it does not come to nothing. So that no-one can ever say that it was nothing. So that it is signed and sealed. Wedded and bedded. Done without possibility of denial. Now you sleep. I shall be back in the early hours. Long before dawn. But I shall go now.'

I nodded and said not a word until her hand was on the ring of the door latch. 'But Anne, do you love him?' I asked curiously.

The curve of her hood hid all but the corner of her smile. 'I am a fool to own it, but I am in a fever for his touch.'

Then she opened the door, and was gone.

Summer 1523

The court saw in the May with a day of revels, planned and executed by Cardinal Wolsey. The ladies of the queen's court went out on barges, all dressed in white, and were surprised by French brigands, dressed in black. A rescue party of freeborn Englishmen, dressed all in green, rowed to the rescue and there was a merry fight with water thrown from buckets, and water cannonade with pigs' bladders filled with water. The royal barge, decorated all over in green bunting and flying a greenwood flag, had an ingenious cannon that fired little water bombs which blasted the French brigands out of the water, and they had to be rescued by the Thames boatmen who were well paid for their trouble and then had to be prevented from joining in the fight.

The queen was thoroughly splashed in the battle and she laughed as merry as a girl to see her husband with a mask on his face and a hat on his head, playing at Robin of Nottingham and throwing a rose to me, as I sat in the barge beside her.

We landed at York Place and the cardinal himself greeted us on shore. There were musicians hidden in the trees of the garden. Robin of Greenwood, half a head taller than anyone else and golden-haired, led me into the dance. I saw the queen's smile never falter as the king took my hand and placed it on his green doublet, over his heart, and I tucked his rose into my hood so that it bloomed at my temple.

The cardinal's cooks had surpassed themselves. As well as stuffed peacock and swan, goose and chicken, there were great haunches of venison and four different sorts of roasted fish, including his favourite, carp. The sweetmeats on the table were a tribute to the May, all made into flowers and bouquets in marchpane, almost too pretty to break and eat. After we had eaten and the day started to grow chilly, the musicians played an eerie little tune and led us up through the darkening gardens into the great hall of York Place.

It was transformed. The cardinal had ordered it swathed in green cloth, fastened at every corner with great boughs of flowering may. In the centre of the room were two great thrones, one for the king and one for the queen, with the king's choristers dancing and singing before them. We all took our places and watched the children's masque and then we all rose and danced too.

We made merry till midnight and then the queen rose and signalled to her ladies to leave the room. I was following in her train when my gown was caught by the king.

'Come to me now,' Henry said urgently.

The queen turned to make her farewell curtsey to the king and saw him, with his hand on the hem of my gown and me hesitating before him. She did not falter, she swept him her dignified Spanish curtsey.

'I give you good night, husband,' she said in her deep sweet tone. 'Good night, Mistress Carey.'

I dropped like a stone into a curtsey to her. 'Good night, Your Majesty,' I whispered, my head down. I wished that the curtsey might take me down further, into the floor, into the ground below the floor, so she could not see my scarlet burning face as I came up.

When I rose up she was gone and he was turned aside. He had forgotten her already, it was as if a mother had left the young people to play at last. 'Let's have some more music,' he said joyously. 'And some wine.'

I looked around. The ladies of the queen's court were gone with her. George smiled reassuringly at me.

'Don't fret,' he said in an undertone.

I hesitated but Henry, who had been taking a glass of wine, turned back to me with a goblet in his hand. 'To the Queen of the May!' he said, and his court, who would have repeated Dutch riddles if he had recited them, obediently replied: 'To the Queen of the May!' and raised their glasses to me.

Henry took me by the hand and led me up to the throne where Queen Katherine had been sitting. I went with him but I could feel my feet drag. I was not ready to sit on her chair.

Gently he urged me up the steps and I turned and looked down at the innocent faces of the children below me, and the more knowing smiles from Henry's court.

'Let's dance for the Queen of the May!' Henry said, and swept a girl into a set and they danced before me, and I, seated on the queen's throne, watching her husband dance, and flirt prettily with his partner, knew that I wore her tolerant mask-like smile on my own face.

A day after the May Day feast Anne came whirling into our room, white-faced.

'See this!' she hissed and threw a piece of paper on the bed.

> *Dear Anne, I cannot come to see you today. My lord cardinal knows everything and I am bidden to explain to him. But I swear I shall not fail you.*

'Oh my God,' I said softly. 'The cardinal knows. The king will know too.'

'So what?' Anne demanded, like a striking adder. 'So what if they all know? It's a proper betrothal, isn't it? Why shouldn't they all know?'

I saw that the paper was shaking in my hand. 'What does he mean, he will not fail you?' I asked. 'If it is an unbreakable betrothal then he cannot fail. There can be no question of failure.'

Anne took three swift steps across the room, came up short against the wall, wheeled around and took three steps back again, prowling like a lion in the Tower. 'I don't know what he means by that,' she spat. 'The boy's a fool.'

'You said you loved him.'

'That doesn't mean he's not a fool.' She reached a sudden decision. 'I must go to him. He'll need me. He'll wilt beneath them.'

'You cannot. You'll have to wait.'

She flung open the clothes press and pulled out her cloak.

There was a thunderous knock on the door and we both froze. In one movement she had the cloak off her shoulders, slammed into the press and she was sitting on it, serene, as if she had been there all the morning. I opened the door. It was a serving man in the livery of Cardinal Wolsey.

'Is Mistress Anne within?'

I opened the door a little wider so he could see her, thoughtfully gazing out over the garden. The cardinal's barge with the distinctive red standards was moored at the bottom of the garden.

'Will you please come to the cardinal in the audience room,' he said.

Anne turned her head and looked at him without replying.

'At once,' he said. 'My lord the cardinal said that you were to come at once.'

She did not flare up at the arrogance of the command. She knew as well as I did that since Cardinal Wolsey ran the kingdom, a word from him carried the same weight as a word from the king. She crossed to the mirror, threw one glance at her reflection. She pinched her cheeks to draw a little colour to them, bit her upper lip and then her lower.

'Shall I come too?' I asked.

'Yes, walk beside me,' she said in a rapid undertone. 'It'll remind him that you have the ear of the king. And if the king is there – soften him if you can.'

'I can't demand anything,' I whispered urgently.

Even at this moment of crisis she shot me a swift patronising smile. 'I know *that*.'

We followed the servant through the great hall and to Henry's audience room. It was unusually deserted. Henry was out hunting, the court with him. The cardinal's men in their scarlet livery were at the doors. They stepped back to let us through and then barred the way once more. His lordship had made sure that we would not be interrupted.

'Mistress Anne,' he said as she entered the room. 'I have heard a most distressing piece of news today.'

Anne stood very still, her hands folded, her face serene. 'I am sorry to hear that, Your Grace,' she said smoothly.

'It seems that my page, young Henry of Northumberland, has presumed on his friendship with you and on the freedom which I allow him to dally in the queen's rooms and prattle of love.'

Anne shook her head, but the cardinal would not let her speak.

'I have told him this day that such freakish sports are not fitting in one who will inherit the counties of the North and whose marriage is a matter for his father, for the king, and for me. He is not a lad on a farm who can tumble the milkmaid into the haystack and no-one think the less. The marriage of a lord as great as he is a matter of policy.' He paused. 'And the king and I make the policy in this kingdom.'

'He asked me for my hand in marriage and I gave it to him,' Anne said steadily. I could see the gold 'B' she wore on the pearl choker around her neck bumping to her rapid heartbeat. 'We are betrothed, my lord cardinal. I am sorry if the match is not to your liking but it is done. It cannot be undone.'

He shot her one dark look from under his plump hat.

'Lord Henry has agreed to submit to the authority of his father and of the king,' he said. 'I am telling you this out of courtesy, Mistress Boleyn, and so that you may avoid giving offence to those set above you by God.'

She went white. 'He never said that. He never said he would submit to his father's authority instead of –'

'Instead of yours? You know, I *did* wonder if that was how it was. Indeed, he did, Mistress Anne. All of this little matter is in the hands of the king and the duke.'

'He is promised to me, we are betrothed,' she said fiercely.

'It was a de futuro betrothal,' the cardinal ruled. 'A promise to marry in the future if possible.'

'It was de facto,' Anne replied unswervingly. 'A betrothal made before witnesses, and consummated.'

'Ah.' One podgy hand was raised in caution. The heavy cardinal's ring winked at Anne as if to remind her that this man was the spiritual leader of England. 'Please do not suggest that such a thing could have happened. It would be too imprudent. If I say that the betrothal was de futuro then that is what it was, Mistress Anne. I cannot be in the wrong. If a lady bedded a man on such slender surety she would be a fool. A lady who had given herself and then found herself abandoned would be totally ruined. She would never marry at all.'

Anne shot a swift sideways glance at me. Wolsey must have been aware of the irony of preaching the virtues of virginity to a woman who was sister to the most notorious adulteress in the kingdom. But his gaze never wavered.

'It would be very injurious to you, Mistress Boleyn, if your affection for Lord Henry persuaded you to tell me such a lie.'

I could see her fighting her rising panic. 'My lord cardinal,' she said, and her voice quavered slightly. 'I would be a good Duchess of Northumberland. I would care for the poor, I would see justice done in the North. I would protect England from the Scots. I would be your friend forever. I would be eternally in your debt.'

He smiled a little, as if the thought of Anne's favour was not the greatest of bribes he had ever been offered. 'You would be a delightful duchess,' he said. 'If not of Northumberland then elsewhere, I am sure. Your father will have to make that decision. It will be his choice where you are wed, and the king and I will have some say in the matter. Rest assured, my daughter in Christ, I will be careful of your wishes. I will bear in mind,' he did not trouble to hide a smile, 'I will bear in mind that you wish to be a duchess.'

He held out his hand and Anne had to step forward, curtsey, and kiss the ring, and then walk backwards from the room.

When the door shut on us she did not say a word. She turned on her heel and headed for the stone staircase down to the garden. She did not speak until we had marched down the pretty winding paths and were deep in a bower of roses which were sprawling around a stone seat and opening their white and scarlet petals to the sunshine.

'What can I do?' she demanded. 'Think! Think!'

I was about to answer that I could think of nothing, but she was not talking to me. She was talking to herself. 'Can I outflank Northumberland?

Get Mary to plead my case with the king?' She shook her head for a moment. 'Mary can't be trusted. She'd bodge it.'

I bit back my indignant denial. Anne strode up and down the grass, her skirts swishing around her high-heeled shoes. I sank down to the seat and watched her.

'Can I send George to stiffen Henry's resolve?' She took another turn. 'My father, my uncle,' she said rapidly. 'It's in their interest to see me rise. They could speak to the king, they could influence the cardinal. They might find me a dowry which would attract Northumberland. They would want me as duchess.' She nodded with sudden determination. 'They must stand by me,' she decided. 'They will stand by me. And when Northumberland comes to London they will tell him that the betrothal is done, and that the marriage has taken place.'

∾

The family meeting was convened in the Howard house in London. My mother and father were seated at the great table, my uncle Howard between them. Myself and George, sharing Anne's disgrace, were standing at the back of the room. And it was Anne who was before the table like a prisoner before the bar. She did not stand with her head bowed as I always did. Anne stood with her head high, one dark eyebrow slightly raised, and she met my uncle's glare as if she were his equal.

'I am sorry that you have learned French practices along with your style of dress,' my uncle said baldly. 'I warned you before that I would have no whisper against your name. Now I hear that you have allowed young Percy improper intimacies.'

'I have lain with my husband,' Anne said flatly.

My uncle glanced at my mother.

'If you say that, or anything like it, ever again, you will be whipped and sent to Hever and never brought back to court,' my mother said quietly. 'I would rather see you dead at my feet than dishonoured. You shame yourself before your father and your uncle if you say such a thing. You make yourself a disgrace. You make yourself hateful to us all.'

Seated behind Anne I could not see her face, but I saw her fingers take in a fold of her gown, as a drowning man might catch at a straw.

'You will go to Hever until everyone has forgotten about this unfortunate mistake,' my uncle ruled.

'I beg your pardon,' Anne said bitingly. 'But the unfortunate mistake is not mine but yours. Lord Henry and I are married. He will stand by me. You and my father must bring pressure to bear on his father, on the cardinal and the king, to let this marriage be made public. If you will do this then I am the Duchess of Northumberland and you have a Howard girl in the greatest duchy of England. I would have thought that gain was worth a little struggle. If I am duchess and Mary has a son then he is the nephew of the Duke of Northumberland and the king's bastard. We could put him on the throne.'

Uncle's gaze flared at her. 'This king executed the Duke of Buckingham two years ago for saying less than that,' he said very quietly. 'My own father signed the death warrant. This is not a king who is careless of his heirs. You will never, ever speak like this again or you will find yourself not at Hever but behind the walls of a nunnery for life. I mean it, Anne. I will not have the safety of this family jeopardised by your folly.'

He had shocked her with his quiet rage. She gulped and tried to recover. 'I will say no more,' she whispered. 'But this could work.'

'Can't be done,' my father said flatly. 'Northumberland won't have you. And Wolsey won't let us leap up that high. And the king will do what Wolsey says.'

'Lord Henry promised me,' Anne said passionately.

My uncle shook his head and was about to rise from the table, the meeting was over.

'Wait,' Anne said desperately. 'We can achieve this. I swear to you. If you will stand by me then Henry Percy will stand by me, and the cardinal and the king and his father will have to come round to it.'

My uncle did not hesitate for a moment. 'They won't. You are a fool. You can't fight Wolsey. There isn't a man in the country who is a match for Wolsey. And we won't risk his enmity. He would put Mary out of the king's bed and pop a Seymour girl in her place. Everything we are striving to do with Mary will be overset if we support you. This is Mary's chance, not yours. We won't have you spoil it. We'll have you out of the way for the summer at least, perhaps for a year.'

She was stunned into silence. 'But I love him,' she said.

There was a silence in the room.

'I do,' she said. 'I love him.'

'That means nothing to me,' my father said. 'Your marriage is the business of the family and you will leave that to us. You'll go to Hever for at least a year's banishment from court and think yourself lucky. And if you write to him, or reply to him, or see him again, then it will be a nunnery for you. A closed order.'

❀

'Well, that didn't go too badly,' George said with forced cheerfulness. He and Anne and I were walking down to the river to get the boat back to

York Place. A servant in Howard livery went before us, pushing beggars and street sellers out of the way, and one came behind to guard us. Anne walked blindly, quite unaware of the eddy of disturbance all down the crowded street.

There were people selling goods from off the backs of carts, bread and fruit and live ducks and hens, fresh up from the country. There were fat London housewives bartering for the goods, quicker-tongued and quicker-witted than the countrymen and -women, who were slow and careful, hoping to get a fair price for their provender. There were pedlars with chapbooks and music sheets in their sacks, cobblers with sets of ready-made shoes trying to persuade people that they would fit all varieties of foot. There were flower sellers and watercress sellers, there were lounging pageboys and chimney sweeps, there were link boys with nothing to do till the dark came, and street sweepers. There were servants idling on their way to and from marketing, and outside every shop there was the wife of the owner, sat plump on her stool, smiling at the passers-by and urging them to step inside and see what was for sale.

George threaded Anne and me through this tapestry of business like a determined bodkin. He was desperate to get Anne home before the storm of her temper broke.

'Went very well indeed, I'd say,' he said staunchly.

We reached a pier leading out into the river and the Howard servant hailed a boat. 'To York Place,' George said tersely.

The tide was with us and we went quickly upriver, Anne looking blindly at the beach on either side strewn with the dirt of the city.

We landed at the York Place jetty and the Howard servants bowed and took the boat back to the City. George swept Anne and me up to our room and finally got the door closed behind us.

At once Anne whirled round on him and leaped like a wildcat. He grabbed her wrists in his hands and wrestled her away from his face.

'Went pretty well!' she shrieked at him. 'Pretty well! When I have lost the man I love, and my reputation as well? When I am all but ruined and shall be buried in the country until everyone has forgotten about me? Pretty well! When my own father will not stand by me and when my own mother swears that she would rather see me dead? Are you mad, you fool? Are you mad? Or just dumb, blind, God-rotting stupid?'

He held her wrists. She made another slash at his face with her nails. I came from behind and pulled her backwards so that she should not stamp on his feet with her high heels. We reeled, the three of us, like drunkards in a brawl, I was crushed against the foot of the bed as she fought me as well as him, but I clung on around her waist, pulling her backwards as George gripped her hands to save his face. It felt as if we were fighting something worse than Anne, some demon that possessed her, that possessed all of us Boleyns: ambition – the devil that had brought us to this little room and brought my sister to this insane distress, and us to this savage battle.

'Peace, for God's sake,' George shouted at her as he fought to avoid her fingernails.

'Peace!' she screamed at him. 'How can I be at peace?'

'Because you've lost,' George said simply. 'Nothing to fight for now, Anne. You've lost.'

For a moment she froze quite still, but we were too wary to let her go. She glared into his face as if she were quite demented and then she threw back her head and laughed a wild savage laugh.

'Peace!' she cried passionately. 'My God! I shall die peacefully. They will leave me at Hever until I am peacefully dead. And I will never ever see him again!'

She gave a great heartbroken wail at that, and the fight went out of her and she slumped down. George released her wrists and caught her to him. She flung her arms around his neck and buried her face against his chest. She was sobbing so hard, so inarticulate with grief that I could not hear what she was saying, then I felt my own tears come as I made out what she was crying, over and over. 'Oh God, I loved him, I loved him, he was my only love, my only love.'

∾

They wasted no time. Anne's clothes were packed and her horse saddled and George ordered to escort her to Hever that same day. Nobody told Lord Henry Percy that she had gone. He sent a letter to her; and my mother, who was everywhere, opened it and read it calmly before thrusting it on the fire.

'What did he say?' I asked quietly.

'Undying love,' my mother said with distaste.

'Should we not tell him that she's gone?'

My mother shrugged. 'He'll know soon enough. His father is seeing him this morning.'

I nodded. Another letter came at midday, Anne's name scrawled on the front in an unsteady hand. There was a smudge, perhaps a tearstain. My mother opened it, granite-faced, and it went the way of the first.

'Lord Henry?' I asked.

She nodded.

I rose from my place at the fireside and sat in the windowseat. 'I might go out,' I said.

She turned her head. 'You'll stay here,' she said sharply.

The old habit of obedience and deference to her had a strong hold on me. 'Of course, my lady mother. But can I not walk in the garden?'

'No,' she said shortly. 'Your father and uncle have ruled that you are to stay indoors, until Northumberland has dealt with Henry Percy.'

'I'm not likely to stand in the way of that, walking in the garden,' I protested.

'You might send a message to him.'

'I would not!' I exclaimed. 'Surely to God you can all see that the one thing, the *one thing* is that I always, always, do as I am told. You made my marriage at the age of twelve, madam. You ended it just two years later when I was only fourteen. I was in the king's bed before my fifteenth birthday. Surely you can see that I have always done as I have been told by this family? If I could not fight for my own freedom I am hardly likely to fight for my sister's!'

She nodded. 'Good thing too,' she said. 'There is no freedom for women in this world, fight or not as you like. See where Anne has brought herself.'

'Yes,' I said. 'To Hever. Where at least she is free to go out on the land.'

My mother looked surprised. 'You sound envious.'

'I love it there,' I said. 'Sometimes I think I prefer it even to court. But you will break Anne's heart.'

'Her heart has to break and her spirit has to break if she is to be any use to her family,' my mother said coldly. 'It should have been done in her childhood. I thought they would teach you both the habits of obedience in the French court but it seems they were remiss. So it has to be done now.'

There was a tap at the door and a man in shabby clothes stood uneasily on the threshold.

'A letter for Mistress Anne Boleyn,' he said. 'For none but her, and the young lord said I was to watch you read it.'

I hesitated, I glanced across at my mother. She gave me a quick nod of her head and I broke the red seal with the Northumberland crest, and unfolded the stiff paper.

> *My wife,*
> *I will not be forsworn if you will stand by the promises we have made to each other. I will not desert you if you do not desert me. My father is most angry with me, the cardinal too,*

and I do fear for us. But if we hold to each other then they must
let us be together. Send me a note, a word only, that you will
stand by me, and I will stand by you.
 Henry.

'He said there should be a reply,' the man said.

'Wait outside,' my mother said to the man, and closed the door in his face. She turned to me. 'Write a reply.'

'He'll know her handwriting,' I said unhelpfully.

She slid a piece of paper before me, put a pen in my hand and dictated the letter.

Lord Henry,
 Mary is writing this for me as I am forbidden to put pen to
paper to you. It is no use. They will not let us marry and I have
to give you up. Do not stand against the cardinal and your father
for my sake for I have told them that I surrender. It was only a
betrothal de futuro and is not binding on either one of us. I
release you from your half-promise and I am released from mine.

'You will break both their hearts,' I observed, scattering sand on the wet ink.

'Perhaps,' my mother said coolly. 'But young hearts mend easily, and hearts that own half of England have something better to do than to beat faster for love.'

Winter 1523

With Anne away I was the only Boleyn girl in the world, and when the queen chose to spend the summer with the Princess Mary it was I who rode with Henry at the head of the court on progress. We spent a wonderful summer riding together, hunting, and dancing every night, and when the court returned to Greenwich in November I whispered to him that I had missed my course and I was carrying his child.

At once, everything changed. I had new rooms and a lady in waiting. Henry bought me a thick fur cloak, I must not for a moment get chilled. Midwives, apothecaries, soothsayers came and went from my rooms, all of them were asked the vital question: 'Is it a boy?'

Most of them answered yes and were rewarded with a gold coin. The eccentric one or two said 'no' and saw the king's pout of displeasure. My mother loosened the laces of my gown and I could no longer go to the king's bed at night, I had to lie alone and pray in the darkness that I was carrying his son.

The queen watched my growing body with eyes that were dark with pain. I knew that she had missed her courses too, but there was no question that she might have conceived. She smiled throughout the Christmas feasts and the masques and the dancing, and she gave Henry the lavish presents that he loved. And after the twelfth night masque, when there was a sense that everything should be made clear and clean, she asked him if she might speak with him privately and from somewhere, God knows where, she found the courage to look him in the face and tell him that she had been clean for the whole of the season, and she was a barren woman.

'Told me herself,' Henry said indignantly to me that night. I was in his bedroom, wrapped in my fur cloak, a tankard of mulled wine in my hand, my bare feet tucked under me before a roaring fire. 'Told me without a moment's shame!'

I said nothing. It was not for me to tell Henry that there was no shame in a woman of nearly forty ceasing her bleeding. Nobody had known better than he that if she could have prayed her way into childbed they would have had half a dozen babies and all of them boys. But he had forgotten that now. What concerned him was that she had refused him what she should have given him, and I saw once again that powerful indignation which swept over him with any disappointment.

'Poor lady,' I said.

He shot me a resentful look. 'Rich lady,' he corrected me. 'The wife of one of the wealthiest men in Europe, the Queen of England no less, and nothing to show for it but the birth of one child, and that a girl.'

I nodded. There was no point arguing with Henry.

He leaned over me to put his hand gently on the round hard curve of my belly. 'And if my boy is in there then he will carry the name of Carey,' he said. 'What good is that for England? What good is that for me?'

'But everyone will know he is yours,' I said. 'Everyone knows that you can make a child with me.'

'But I have to have a legitimate son,' he said earnestly, as if I or the queen or any woman could give him a son by wishing it. 'I have to have a son, Mary. England has to have an heir from me.'

Spring 1524

Anne wrote to me once a week for all the long months of her exile and I was reminded of the desperate letters I had sent her when I had been banished from court. I remembered too that she had not bothered to reply. Now it was me at court and she was in outer darkness and I took a sister's triumph in my generosity in replying to her often, and I did not spare her news of my fertility, and Henry's delight in me.

Our Grandmother Boleyn had been summoned to Hever to be a companion to Anne, and the two of them, the young elegant woman from the French court, and the wise old woman who had seen her husband leap from next to nothing to greatness, quarrelled like cats on a stable roof from morning to night and made each other's lives a complete misery.

If I cannot return to court, I shall go mad,

Anne wrote.

> *Grandmother Boleyn cracks hazelnuts in her hands and drops the shells everywhere. They crunch underfoot like snails. She insists that we walk out in the garden together every day, even when it is raining. She thinks that rainwater is good for the skin, and says this is why Englishwomen have such peerless complexions. I look at her weatherbeaten old leather and know that I would rather stay indoors.*
>
> *She smells quite dreadful and is completely unaware of it. I told them to draw a bath for her the other day and they tell me that she consented to sit on a stool and let them wash her feet. She hums under her breath at the dinner table, she doesn't even know she is doing it. She believes in keeping an open house in the grand old way and everyone, from the beggars of Tonbridge*

to the farmers of Edenbridge, is welcome into the hall to watch us eat as if we were the king himself with nothing to do with our money but give it away.

Please, please, tell Uncle and Father that I am ready to return to court, that I will do their bidding, that they need fear nothing from me. I will do anything to get away from here.

I wrote a reply at once.

You will be able to come to court soon, I am sure, because Lord Henry is betrothed against his will to Lady Mary Talbot. He was said to be weeping when he made his promise. He has gone to defend the Scottish border with his own men from Northumberland under his standard. The Percys have to hold Northumberland safe while the English army goes to France again this summer and, with the Spanish as our allies, finish the work they started last summer.

George's wedding to Jane Parker is to take place this month at last, and I shall ask Mother if you can be present. She will surely not refuse you that.

I am well but very tired. The baby is very heavy and when I try to sleep at night it turns and kicks. Henry is kinder than I have ever known him, and we are both hoping for a boy.

I wish you were here. He is hoping for a boy so much. I am almost afraid as to what will happen if it is a girl. If only there was something one could do to make it be a boy. Don't tell me about asparagus. I know all about asparagus. They make me eat it at every meal.

The queen watches me all the time. I am too big now for concealment and everyone knows it is the king's baby. William has not had to endure anyone congratulating him on our first child. Everyone knows, and there is a sort of wall of silence that makes it comfortable for everyone but me. There are times when I feel like a fool: my belly going before me, breathless on the stairs, and a husband who smiles at me as if we were strangers.

And the queen . . .

I wish to God I did not have to pray in her chapel every morning and night. I wonder what she is praying for, since all hope for her is gone. I wish you were here. I even miss your sharp tongue.

Mary.

115

George and Jane Parker were finally to marry after countless delays in the little chapel at Greenwich. Anne was to be allowed up from Hever for the day, she could sit in one of the high boxes at the back where no-one would see her, but she was not allowed to attend the wedding feast. Most importantly for us, since the wedding was to take place in the morning, Anne had to ride up the day before and the three of us, George, Anne, and I, had the night together from dinner time till dawn.

We prepared ourselves for a night of talking like midwives settling in for a long labour. George brought wine and ale and small beer, I crept down to the kitchen and filched bread, meat, cheese and fruit from the cooks who were happy to pile a platter for me, thinking that it was my seven-month belly which was making me hungry.

Anne was in her cut-down riding habit. She looked older than her seventeen years and finer, her skin was pale. 'Walking in the rain with the old witch,' she said grimly. Her sadness had given her a serenity which had not been there before. It was as if she had learned a hard lesson: that chances in life would not fall into her lap like ripe cherries. And she missed the boy she loved: Henry Percy.

'I dream of him,' she said simply. 'I so wish I didn't. It's such a pointless unhappiness. I am so tired of it. Sounds odd, doesn't it? But I am so tired of being unhappy.'

I glanced across at George. He was watching Anne, his face full of sympathy.

'When is his wedding?' Anne asked bleakly.

'Next month,' he said.

She nodded. 'And then it will be over. Unless she dies, of course.'

'If she dies he could marry you,' I said hopefully.

Anne shrugged. 'You fool,' she said abruptly. 'I can hardly wait for him in the hope that Mary Talbot drops dead one day. I'm quite a card to play once I've lived this down, aren't I? Especially if you give birth to a boy. I'll be aunt to the king's bastard.'

Without meaning to, I put my hands protectively before my belly as if I did not want my baby to hear that it was only wanted if it was a boy. 'It'll carry the name of Carey,' I reminded her.

'But what if it is a boy and born healthy and strong and golden-haired?'

'I shall call him Henry.' I smiled at the thought of a strong golden-haired baby in my arms. 'And I don't doubt but the king will do something very fine for him.'

'And we all rise,' George pointed out. 'As aunts and uncles to the king's son, perhaps a little dukedom for him, perhaps an earldom. Who knows?'

'And you, George?' Anne asked. 'Are you merry, this merry merry night? I had thought you'd be out roistering and drinking yourself into the gutter, not sitting here with one fat lady and one broken-hearted one.'

George poured some wine and looked darkly into his cup. 'One fat lady and one broken-hearted one almost exactly suits my mood,' he said. 'I couldn't dance or sing to save my life. She *is* a most poisonous woman, isn't she? My beloved? My wife-to-be? Tell me the truth. It's not just me, is it? There is something about her that makes you shrink from her, isn't there?'

'Oh nonsense,' I said roundly. 'She's not poisonous.'

'She sets my teeth on edge and she always has,' Anne said bluntly. 'If ever there's tittle-tattle or dangerous scandal, or someone telling tales of someone else, she's always there. She hears everything and she watches everyone, and she's always thinking the worst of everyone.'

'I knew it,' George said glumly. 'God! What a wife to have!'

'She may give you a surprise on your wedding night,' Anne said slyly, drinking her wine.

'What?' George said quickly.

Anne raised an eyebrow over the cup. 'She's very well-informed for a virgin,' she said. 'Very knowledgeable about matters for married women. Married women and whores.'

George's jaw dropped. 'Never tell me she's not a virgin!' he exclaimed. 'I could surely get out of it if she was not a virgin!'

Anne shook her head. 'I've never seen a man do anything that was not from politeness,' she said. 'Who would, for God's sake? But she watches and listens, and she doesn't care what she asks or what she sees. I heard her whispering with one of the Seymour girls about someone who had lain with the king – not you –' she said quickly to me '– there was very worldly talk about kissing with an open mouth, letting one's tongue lick and suchlike, whether one should lie on a king or underneath him, and where one's hands should go, and what could be done to give him such pleasure as he might never forget it.'

'And she knows these French practices?' George asked, astounded.

'She talked as if she did,' Anne said, smiling at his amazement.

'Well, by God!' said George, pouring himself another glass of wine and waving the bottle at me. 'Perhaps I will be a happier husband than I thought. Where your hands should go, eh? And where should they go, Mistress Annamaria? Since you seem to have heard this conversation as well as my lovely wife-to-be?'

'Oh don't ask me,' Anne said. 'I'm a virgin. Ask anyone. Ask Mother or Father or my uncle. Ask Cardinal Wolsey, he made it official. I'm a virgin. I am an attested official sworn-to-it virgin. Wolsey, the Archbishop of York himself, says I am a virgin. You can't be more of a virgin than me.'

'I shall tell you all about them,' George said more cheerfully. 'I shall write to you at Hever, Anne, and you can read my letter aloud to Grandmother Boleyn.'

❁

George was pale as a bride on his wedding morning. Only Anne and I knew it was not from heavy drinking the night before. He did not smile as Jane Parker approached the altar, but she was beaming broad enough for them both.

With my hands clasped over my belly I thought it was a long time since I had stood before the altar and promised to forsake all others and cleave to William Carey. He glanced across at me with a slight smile, as if he too was thinking that we had not foreseen this when we had been handclasped, and hopeful, only four years ago.

King Henry was at the front of the church, watching my brother take his bride, and I thought that my family were doing well out of my heavy belly. The king had come late to my wedding, and more to oblige his friend William than to honour the Boleyns. But he was at the forefront of the well-wishers when this pair turned from the altar and came down the aisle of the church, and the king and I together led the guests into the wedding feast. My mother smiled on me as if I were her only daughter, as Anne left quietly by the side door of the chapel and took her horse and rode home to Hever accompanied only by serving men.

I thought of her riding to Hever alone, seeing the castle from the lodge gate, as pretty as a toy in the moonlight. I thought of the way the track curved through the trees and came to the drawbridge. I thought of the rattle of the drawbridge coming down and the hollow sound that the hoof beats made as the horse stepped delicately on the timbers. I thought of the dank smell of the moat and then the waft of meat cooking on a spit as one entered the courtyard. I thought of the moon shining into the courtyard and the haphazard line of the gable ends against the night sky, and I wished with all my contrary heart that I was squire of Hever and not the pretend queen of a masquing court. I wished with all my heart that I might have been carrying a legitimate son in my belly and that I could have leaned out of the window and looked out over my land, just a little manor farm perhaps, and known that it would be all his by right one day.

But instead I was the lucky Boleyn, the Boleyn blessed by fortune and the king's favour. A Boleyn who could not imagine the boundaries of her son's land, who could not dream how far he might rise.

Summer 1524

I withdrew from the court for the whole of the month of June to prepare for my lying in. I had a darkened room hung with thick tapestries, I should see no light nor breathe fresh air until I emerged six long weeks after the birth of my baby. Altogether I would be walled up for two and a half months. I was attended by my mother and by two midwives, a couple of serving maids and a lady's maid supported them. Outside the chamber, taking turn and turn about night and day, were two apothecaries waiting to be called.

'Can Anne be with me?' I asked my mother as I eyed the darkened room.

She frowned. 'Her father has ordered that she must stay at Hever.'

'Oh, please,' I said. 'It'll be such a long time and I'd like her company.'

'She can visit,' my mother ruled. 'But we can't have her present at the birth of the king's son.'

'Or daughter,' I reminded her.

She made the sign of the cross over my belly. 'Please God it is a boy,' she whispered.

I said nothing more, content to have carried my way by getting Anne to visit me. She came for a day and stayed for two. She had been bored at Hever, infuriated by our Grandmother Boleyn, desperate to get away, even to a darkened room and a sister biding her time by sewing little nightshirts for a royal bastard.

'Have you been over to Home Farm?' I asked.

'No,' she said. 'I've ridden past it.'

'I wondered how they were getting on with their strawberry crop?'

She shrugged.

'And the Peters' farm? Did you go over for the sheep shearing?'

'No,' she said.

'D'you know what hay crop we got this year?'

'No.'

'Anne, what on earth do you do all day?'

'I read,' she said. 'I practise my music. I have been composing some songs. I ride every day. I walk in the garden. What else is there to do in the country?'

'I go round and see the farms,' I remarked.

She raised an eyebrow. 'They're always the same. The grass grows.'

'What d'you read?'

'Theology,' she said shortly. 'Have you heard of Martin Luther?'

'Of course I've heard of him,' I said, stung. 'Enough to know that he's a heretic and his books are forbidden.'

Anne gave her small secretive smile. 'He's not necessarily a heretic,' she said. 'It's a matter of opinion. I have been reading his books and others who think like he does.'

'You'd better keep it quiet,' I said. 'If Father and Mother find you've been reading banned books they'll send you to France again, anywhere to get you out of the way.'

She shrugged. 'No-one pays any attention to me, I'm quite eclipsed by your glory. There is only one way to come to the attention of this family and that is to climb into the king's bed. You have to be a whore to be beloved by this family.'

I folded my hands over my swollen belly and smiled at her, quite unmoved by her malice. 'There's no need to pinch me because my stars have led me here. There was no need for you to set yourself at Henry Percy and onwards to disgrace.'

For a moment the mask of her beautiful face dropped and I saw the longing in her eyes. 'Have you heard from him?'

I shook my head. 'If he wrote to me they'd not let me have the letter,' I said. 'I think he's still fighting against the Scots.'

She pressed her lips together to keep back a little moan. 'Oh God, what if he is hurt or killed?'

I felt my baby stir and I put my warm hands on my loose stomacher. 'Anne, he should be nothing to you.'

Her eyelashes flickered down over the heat in her gaze. 'He is nothing to me,' she replied.

'He's a married man now,' I said firmly. 'You will have to forget him if you ever want to get back to court.'

She pointed at my belly. 'That is the problem for me,' she said baldly. 'All anyone can think of in this family is that you might be carrying the king's son. I have written to Father half a dozen times and he has had his clerk reply to me once. He doesn't think about me. He doesn't care about me. All anyone cares about is you and your fat belly.'

'We'll know soon enough,' I said. I was trying to sound serene but I was afraid. If Henry had got a girl on me and she was strong and lovely then he should be happy enough to show the world that he was potent. But this was no ordinary man. He wanted to show the world that he could make a healthy baby. He wanted to show the world that he could make a boy.

∾

She was a girl. Despite all those months of hoping and whispered prayers and even special Masses said in Hever and Rochford church, she was a girl.

But she was *my* little girl. She was an exquisite little bundle with hands so tiny that they were like the palms of a little frog, with eyes so dark a blue that they were like the sky above Hever at midnight. She had a dusting of black hair on the crown of her head, as unlike Henry's ruddy gold as anything one could imagine. But she had his kissable rosebud mouth. When she yawned she looked like a very king, bored with insufficient praise. When she cried, she squeezed real tears onto her outraged pink cheeks, like a monarch denied his rights. When I fed her, holding her in my arms and marvelling at the insistent powerful sucking on my breast, she swelled like a lamb and slept as if she were a drunkard lolling beside a tankard of mead.

I held her in my arms constantly. There was a wet nurse to attend her, but I argued that my breasts hurt so much that I must let her suckle, and I cunningly kept her to myself. I fell in love with her. I fell completely and utterly in love with her and I could not for a moment imagine that anything would have been any better if she had been a boy.

Even Henry melted at the sight of her when he visited me in the shadowy peace of the birthing room. He picked her up from her cradle and marvelled at the tiny perfection of her face, her hands, her little feet under the heavy embroidered gown. 'We'll call her Elizabeth,' he said, rocking her gently.

'May I choose her name?' I asked, greatly daring.

'You don't like Elizabeth?'

'I had another name in mind.'

He shrugged. It was a girl's name. It did not matter much. 'As you wish. Call her what you like. She's a pretty little thing, isn't she?'

He brought me a purse of gold and a necklace with diamonds. And he brought me some books, a critique of his own work of theology, some heavy works that Cardinal Wolsey had recommended. I thanked him for them and put them to one side, and thought that I would send them to

Anne and ask her to write me a synopsis so that I might bluff my way through a conversation.

We started his visit formally enough, seated on chairs either side of the fireplace, but he took me to the bed and lay beside me and kissed me gently and sweetly. After a little while he wanted to have me and I had to remind him that I was not yet churched. I was not clean. Timidly I touched at his waistcoat and with a sigh he took my hand and pressed it against his hardness. I wished that someone would tell me what he wanted of me. But then he himself guided my touch, and whispered in my ear what he wanted to do, and then after a little while of his movement and my blundering caresses he gave a sigh and lay still.

'Is it enough for you?' I asked timidly.

He turned and gave me his sweet smile. 'My love, it is a great pleasure for me to have you, even like this, after this long time. When you go to be churched don't confess it – the sin is all mine. But you would tempt a saint.'

'And you do love her?' I pressed him.

He gave an indulgent, lazy chuckle. 'Why yes. She's as lovely as her mother.'

He rose up after a few moments and straightened his clothes. He gave me his delicious roguish grin that still delighted me, though half my mind was on the baby in her cradle, and the other half on the ache in my milk-heavy breasts.

'You shall have rooms nearer to mine when you are churched,' he promised me. 'I want you by me all the time.'

I smiled. It was a delicious moment. The King of England wanted me with him, constantly at his side.

'I want a boy off you,' he said bluntly.

❁

My father was angry with me that the baby was a girl – or so my mother said – reporting from an outside world which seemed very remote. My uncle was disappointed but determined not to show it. I nodded as if I cared but I felt only a total delight that she had opened her eyes this morning and looked at me with a sort of bright intensity that made me certain that she had seen me and known me for her mother. Neither my father nor my uncle could be admitted into the birthing room, and the king did not repeat his single visit. There was a sense of this place being a refuge for us, a secret room where men and their plans and their treacheries would not come.

George came, breaking the conventions with his usual comfortable grace. 'Nothing too awful going on in here, is there?' he asked, putting his handsome head around the door.

'Nothing,' I said, welcoming him with a smile and my cheek to kiss. He bent over me and kissed me deeply on the mouth. 'Oh how delicious, my sister, a young mother, a dozen forbidden pleasures all at once. Kiss me again – kiss me like you kiss Henry.'

'Go away,' I said, pushing him off. 'Look at the baby.'

He peered at her as she lay sleeping in my arms. 'Nice hair,' he said. 'What shall you call her?'

I glanced at the shut door. I knew I could trust George. 'I want to call her Catherine.'

'Rather odd.'

'I don't see why. I am her lady in waiting.'

'But it's her husband's baby.'

I giggled, it was impossible for me not to revel in my sense of joy. 'Oh George, I know. But I have admired her from the moment I entered her service. And I want to show her that I respect her – whatever else has happened.'

Still he looked doubtful. 'D'you think she'll understand? Won't she think it's some kind of mockery?'

I was so shocked that I gripped Catherine a little. 'She cannot imagine that I would triumph over her.'

'Here, why are you crying?' George asked. 'There's no reason to cry, Mary. Don't cry, you'll curdle the milk or something.'

'I'm not crying,' I said, ignoring the tears on my cheeks. 'I'm not meaning to cry.'

'Well, stop,' he urged me. 'Stop it, Mary. Mother will come in and everyone will blame me for upsetting you. And they'll say that I shouldn't be here in the first place. Why don't you wait till you come out and then you can see the queen and ask her yourself if she would like the compliment? That's all I'd suggest.'

'Yes,' I said, feeling immediately more cheerful. 'I could do that, and then I might explain.'

'But don't cry,' he reminded me. 'She's a queen, she won't like tears. I bet you've never seen her cry, for all you've been with her day and night for four years.'

I thought for a moment. 'No,' I said slowly. 'D'you know, in these four years, I have never ever seen her cry.'

'You never will,' he said with satisfaction. 'She's not a woman who crumbles into distress. She's a woman of most powerful will.'

∾

My only other visitor was my husband, William Carey. He arrived, gracefully enough, bearing a bowl of early strawberries which he had ordered to be brought up from Hever.

'A taste of home,' he said kindly.

'Thank you.'

He glanced into the cradle. 'They tell me it's a girl and she is well and strong?'

'She is,' I said, a little chilled by the indifference of his tone.

'And what name are you calling her? Other than mine? I assume she is to carry my name, she isn't to be Fitzroy or some other acknowledgement that she is a royal bastard?'

I bit my tongue and bowed my head. 'I am sorry if you are offended, husband,' I said meekly.

He nodded. 'So what name?'

'She is to be Carey. I thought Catherine Carey.'

'As you wish, madam. I have been granted five good stewardships of land, and a knighthood. I am Sir William now, and you are Lady Carey. I have more than doubled my income. Did he tell you?'

'No,' I said.

'I am in the highest of favour. If you had obliged us with a boy I might have looked for an estate in Ireland or France. I might have been Lord Carey. Who knows how high a boy bastard might have taken us?'

I did not reply. William's tone was mild; but the words had a cutting ring to them. I did not think he was truly asking me to celebrate his good fortune in being England's most famous cuckold.

'You know, I had thought to be a great man at the king's court,' he said bitterly. 'When I knew he liked my company, when my star was rising. I hoped to be something like your father, a statesman who might see the whole picture of the scene, who might play his part in arguing at the great courts of Europe, dealing one with the other and always taking his own country's interest as his byword. But no, here I am, rewarded ten times over for doing nothing but looking the other way while the king takes my wife to his bed.'

I kept my silence, and my eyes down. When I looked up he was smiling at me, his ironical half-sad crooked smile. 'Ah, little wife,' he said gently. 'We did not have much time together, did we? We did not bed very well nor very often. We did not learn tenderness or even desire. We only had a little time.'

'I am sorry for that too,' I said softly.

'Sorry that we did not bed?'

125

'My lord?' I said, genuinely confused by the sudden sharpness in his tone.

'It has been suggested, very politely by your kinsmen, that perhaps I had dreamed it all and we did not bed at all. Is that your wish? That I deny ever having had you?'

I was startled. 'No! You know it is not my wishes that are consulted in these matters.'

'And they have not told you to tell the king that I was impotent on our wedding night and every night thereafter?'

I shook my head. 'Why would I say such a thing?'

He smiled. 'To get our marriage set aside,' he suggested. 'So that you are an unmarried woman. And the next baby is Fitzroy and perhaps Henry can be prevailed on to make him legitimate, the son and heir to the throne. Then you are the mother of the next King of England.'

There was a silence. I found I was staring blankly at him. 'They never want me to do that?' I whispered.

'Oh you Boleyns,' he said gently. 'What happens to you, Mary, if they have our marriage set aside and push you forward? It overthrows the state of marriage and it names you, without contradiction, as a whore, a pretty little whore.'

I felt my cheeks blaze but I kept my mouth shut. He looked at me for a moment and I saw the anger drain from his face and be replaced with a sort of weary compassion. 'Say what you have to say,' he recommended me. 'Whatever they order you. If they press you to say that on our bedding night I juggled with silver pomanders all night and never lay between your legs, you can say that, swear it if you have to – and you will have to. You are going to face the enmity of Queen Katherine herself, and the hatred of all of Spain. I shall spare you mine. Poor silly little girl. If it had been a boy in that cradle I think they would have pushed you into perjury the moment you were churched, to get rid of me, and to lure Henry on.'

We looked at each other very steadily for a moment. 'Then, you and I must be the only people in the whole world who are not sorry it is a girl,' I whispered. 'Because I don't want more than I have now.'

He smiled his bitter courtier smile. 'But next time?'

❁

The court went on its midsummer progress, down the dusty lanes to Sussex and on to Winchester and thence to the New Forest so that the king could hunt deer every day from dawn till twilight and then feast on venison every night. My husband went with his king, close at his side, boys together, no thought of jealousy when the court was on the move and the hounds were running ahead of the horses and yelping, and the hawks were coming behind in their special cart with their trainers riding alongside and singing to them to keep them calm. My brother went too, riding alongside Francis Weston, astride a new black hunter, a big strong beast which the king had given him from the royal stables, as a further token of his affection for me and mine. My father was in Europe, as part of the unending negotiations between England, France and Spain, trying to rein in the ambitions of three greedy bright young monarchs all jockeying for the title of the greatest king in Europe. My mother went with the court, with her own little train of servants. My uncle went, with his own men in Howard livery and with a wary eye always for the ambitions and pretensions of the Seymour family. The Percy family were there, Charles Brandon and Queen Mary, the London goldsmiths, the foreign diplomats: all the great men of England abandoned their fields, their farms, their ships, their mining, their trading, and their city houses to go hunting with the king, and not one dared to lag behind in case there was money being granted or land being dispensed, or favours to be had, or the king's dancing eyes might turn on a pretty daughter or a wife and a position might be gained.

I, thank God, was spared it this year, and I was glad to be away, riding slowly down the lanes to Kent. Anne met me in the neat courtyard of Hever Castle, her face as dark as a midsummer storm. 'You must be mad,' she said in greeting. 'What are you doing here?'

'I want to be here with my baby this summer. I need to rest.'

'You don't look like you need a rest.' She scrutinised my face. 'You look beautiful,' she conceded grudgingly.

'But look at her.' I pulled the white lace shawl back from Catherine's little face. She had slept for most of the journey, rocked by the jolting of the litter.

Anne politely glanced. 'Sweet,' she said, without much conviction. 'But why didn't you send her down with the wet nurse?'

I sighed at the impossibility of convincing Anne that there was anywhere better to be than the court. I led the way into the hall and let the wet nurse take Catherine from my arms to change her swaddling clothes.

'And then bring her back to me,' I stipulated.

I sat on one of the carved chairs at the great hall table and smiled at Anne as she stood before me, as impatient as an interrogator.

'I'm not really interested in the court,' I said flatly. 'It's having a baby; you wouldn't understand. It's as if I suddenly know what the purpose of life is. It's not to rise in the king's favour nor to make one's way at court.

Nor even to raise one's family a little higher. There are things that matter more. I want her to be happy. I don't want her to be sent away as soon as she is old enough to walk. I want to be tender with her, I want her to be schooled under my eye. I want her to grow up here and know the river and the fields and the willows in the watermeadows. I don't want her to be a stranger in her own country.'

Anne looked rather blank. 'It's just a baby,' she said flatly. 'And chances are she'll die. You'll have dozens more. Are you going to be like this over all of them?'

I flinched at the thought of it, but she didn't even see. 'I don't know. I didn't know I'd feel like this over her. But I do, Anne. She's the most precious thing in the world. Much more important to me than anything else. I can't think about anything but caring for her and seeing that she is well and happy. When she cries it's like a knife in my heart, I can't bear the thought of her crying at all. And I want to see her grow. I won't be parted from her.'

'What does the king say?' Anne demanded, going to the one central point for a Boleyn.

'I haven't told him this,' I said. 'He was happy enough that I should go away for the summer and rest. He wanted to get off hunting. He was in a fever to go this year. He didn't mind too much.'

'Didn't mind too much?' she repeated incredulously.

'He didn't mind at all,' I corrected myself.

Anne nodded, nibbling her fingers. I could almost see the calculations of her brain as she picked over what I was saying. 'Very well then,' she said. 'If they don't insist that you go to court I don't see why I should worry. It's more amusing for me to have you here, God knows. You can chatter to that merciless old woman at least and spare me her unending talk.'

I smiled. 'You really are very disrespectful, Anne.'

'Oh yes, yes, yes,' she said impatiently, drawing up a stool. 'But now tell me all the news. Tell me about the queen, and I want to know what Thomas More has said about the new tract from Germany. And what are the plans for the French? Is it to be war again?'

'I am sorry.' I shook my head. 'Someone was talking about it the other night but I wasn't listening.'

She made a little noise and leaped to her feet. 'Oh very well then,' she said irritably. 'Talk to me about the baby. That's all you're interested in, isn't it? You sit with your head half-cocked listening for her all the time, don't you? You look ridiculous. For heaven's sake sit up straight. The nurse won't bring her back any quicker for you looking like a hound on point.'

I laughed at the accuracy of her description. 'It's like being in love. I want to see her all the time.'

'You're always in love,' Anne said crossly. 'You're like a big butter ball, always oozing love for someone or other. Once it was the king and we did very well out of that. Now it's his baby, which will do us no good at all. But you don't care. It's always seep seep seep with you: passion and feeling and desire. It makes me furious.'

I smiled at her. 'Because you are all ambition,' I said.

Her eyes gleamed. 'Of course. What else is there?'

Henry Percy hovered between us, tangible as a ghost. 'Don't you want to know if I have seen him?' I asked. It was a cruel question and I asked it hoping to see pain in her eyes, but I got nothing for my malice. Her face was cold and hard, she looked as if she had finished weeping for him and as if she would never weep for a man again.

'No,' she said. 'So you can tell them when they ask that I never mentioned his name. He gave up, didn't he? He married another woman.'

'He thought you'd abandoned him,' I protested.

She turned her head away. 'If he'd been a proper man he'd have gone on loving me,' she said, her voice harsh. 'If it had been the other way round I'd never have married while my lover was free. He gave in, he let me go. I'll never forgive him. He's dead for me. I can be dead for him. All I want to do is to get out of this grave and get back to court. All that there is left for me is ambition.'

❧

Anne, Grandmother Boleyn, Baby Catherine and I settled down to spend the summer together in enforced companionship. As I grew stronger and the pain in my privates eased, I got back on my horse and started to ride out in the afternoons. I rode all around our valley and up to the hills of the Weald. I watched the hay meadows turn green again after their first cut, and the sheep grow white and fluffy with new wool. I wished the reapers joy at the harvest when they went into the wheatfields to sickle the first of the crop and saw them load the grain into great carts and take it to the granary and the mill. We ate hare one night after the reapers had sent in the dogs after the animals trapped in the last stand of wheat. I saw the cows separated from their calves for weaning and felt my own breasts ache with sympathy when I saw them crowding around the gate and trying to break through the thick-set hedges, barging and tossing their heads and bellowing for their babies.

'They'll forget, Lady Carey,' the cowman said to me consolingly. 'They won't cry for more than a few days.'

I smiled at him. 'I wish we could leave them a little longer.'

'It's a hard world for man and beast,' he said firmly. 'They have to go, or how will you get your butter and your cheese?'

The apples swelled round and rosy in the orchard. I went into the kitchen and asked the cook to make us great fat apple dumplings for our dinner. The plums grew rich and dark and split their skins, and the lazy late-summer wasps buzzed around the trees and grew drunk on the syrup. The air was sweet with honeysuckle and the heady perfume of fruit fattening on the bough. I wanted the summer never to end. I wanted my baby always to stay this small, this perfect, this adorable. Her eyes were changing colour from the dark blue of birth to a darker indigo, almost black. She would be a dark-eyed beauty like her sharp-tempered aunt.

She smiled now when she saw me, I tested her over and over again, and I grew quite cross with my Grandmother Boleyn who claimed that a baby was blind until two or three years of age and that I was wasting my time hanging over her cradle, and singing to her, and spreading a carpet under the trees and lying on it with her and spreading her little fingers to tickle her palms, and taking up her tiny fat foot to nibble her toes.

The king wrote to me once, describing the hunting and the kills he had made. It sounded as if there would not be a deer left in the New Forest by the time he was satisfied. At the end of the letter he said that the court would be back at Windsor in October, and Greenwich for Christmas, and that he expected me there, without my sister of course, and without our baby to whom he sent a kiss. Despite the tenderness of the kiss to our child, I knew that the joy of my summer with my baby was at an end, whatever my wishes might be; and that like a peasant woman who has to leave her child and go back to the field, it was time for me to go back to my work.

Winter 1524

I found the king at Windsor in merry mood. The hunting had gone well, the company had been excellent. There was a rumour about a flirtation with one of the queen's new ladies, one Margaret Shelton, a Howard cousin of mine, newly come to court, and another story, more comical than true, about a lady who took every fence neck and neck with the king until, in sheer despair of outriding her, he had her behind a bush, and rode away before she had rearranged her dress. She was stuck on the ground until someone came by who would lift her back up into the saddle, and her hope of taking my place was over.

There were bawdy tales of drinking bouts and my brother George had a bruise over one eye after a brawl in a tavern, and some running joke about a young page who had been besotted with George and had been sent home in disgrace after penning him a dozen lovesick sonnets all signed Ganymede. All in all the gentlemen of the court had been merry and the king himself was in high spirits.

He snatched me up and held me tight and kissed me hard when he saw me, before all the court, though, thank God, the queen was not there. 'Sweetheart, I have missed you,' he said exuberantly. 'Tell me that you have missed me too.'

I could not help but smile into his bright eager face. 'Of course,' I said. 'And I hear on all sides that Your Majesty has amused yourself.'

There was a little guffaw from the king's most intimate friends and he grinned a little sheepishly himself. 'My heart ached for you night and day,' he said with the exquisite mock courtesy of courtly love. 'I pined in outer darkness. And you are well? And our baby?'

'Catherine is very beautiful and grows well and strong,' I said with a tiny stress on her name to prompt him. 'She is most beautifully fashioned, a true Tudor rose.'

My brother George stepped forward and the king released me so that George could kiss my cheek.

'Welcome back to court, my sister,' he said cheerily. 'And how is the little princess?'

There was a moment of stunned silence. The smile was wiped from Henry's face. I gaped at George in blank horror at the terrible error he had made. He spun on his heel in a flash and turned to the king: 'I call little Catherine a princess because she is fawned over as if she were a queen in the making. You should see the clothes that Mary has sewn for her, embroidered with her own hands. And the bed linen that the little empress reclines on! Even her swaddling clouts have her initials. You would laugh, Your Majesty. You would laugh to see her. She is a little tyrant at Hever, it must all be done to her direction. She is a veritable cardinal. She is a pope of the nursery.'

It was a wonderful recovery. Henry relaxed and laughed at the thought of the little baby's dictatorship, all the courtiers instantly echoed his laughter with their own smiles and titters at George's description of the baby.

'Is it really so? Do you indulge her so much?' the king asked me.

'She is my first,' I excused myself. 'And all her clothes will be used again for the next one.'

It was a perfect note to hit. At once Henry thought of the next one and we had moved onwards. 'Oh yes,' he said. 'But what will the princess do with a rival in the nursery?'

'I hope she will be too small to know much about it,' George suggested smoothly. 'She might have a little brother before she is more than a year old. There are only months between Mary and Anne, remember. We are fertile stock.'

'Oh George, for shame,' my mother said, smiling. 'But a little boy at Hever would bring us all such joy.'

'Me too,' said the king, looking at me with warm eyes. 'A little boy would be a great joy to me.'

❀

As soon as my father came home from France there was another family conference. This time I had a chair placed for me before the table. I was no longer a girl under instruction, I was a woman with the king's favour. I was no longer their pawn. I was at the very least a castle, a player in the game.

'Say she conceives again and this time it is a boy,' my uncle said softly. 'Say the queen is prompted by her own conscience to retire and set him free to remarry. He would be very tempted by a pregnant mistress.'

For a moment I thought I had dreamed this plan, and then I knew I had been waiting for this moment. My husband William had warned me of this, and it had stayed in the back of my mind as a thought too awful to contemplate.

'I am married already,' I observed.

My mother shrugged. 'No more than a few months. It was hardly consummated at all.'

'It was consummated,' I said steadily.

My uncle raised his eyebrow to prompt my mother.

'She was young,' my mother said. 'How would she know what was happening? She could swear it was never fully done.'

'I can't do it.' I spoke to my mother and then I turned to my uncle. 'I dare not do it. I can't take her throne, I can't take her place. She's a princess three times over, and I'm just a Boleyn girl. I swear to you: I can't do it.'

It was nothing to him. 'You need do nothing out of the ordinary,' he said. 'You will marry as you are bid, as you did once before. And I will order all the rest.'

'But the queen will never retire,' I said desperately. 'She has said so herself, she told me herself. She said she would die first.'

My uncle exclaimed, pushed his chair back and took a step to look out of the window. 'She's in a strong position at the moment,' he conceded. 'While her nephew is in alliance with England, nobody can upset that agreement, least of all Henry, for a baby not yet conceived. But the moment the war against France is won, and the spoils divided, then she is nothing but a woman too old for him who can never give him an heir. She knows, as we all do, that she has to go.'

'When the war is won, perhaps,' my father worried. 'But we dare not risk a breach with Spain just now. I have spent all this summer trying to broker such an alliance and make it stick.'

'Which comes first?' my uncle asked drily. 'Country or family? Because we cannot use Mary as we should, without risking the well-being of the country.'

My father hesitated.

'Of course, you're not blood kin,' my uncle said, quietly venomous. 'Only a Howard by marriage.'

'Family comes first,' my father said slowly. 'It must do.'

'Then we may have to sacrifice the alliance with Spain against France,' my uncle said coldly. 'It is more important to us to get rid of Queen Katherine than it is to make peace in Europe. It is more important to get our girl into the king's bed than to save the lives of Englishmen. There are always more men who can be pressed for soldiers. But this chance for us Howards comes once in a century.'

Spring 1525

We heard the news from Pavia in March. A messenger burst in upon the king in the early morning while he was still half-dressed, and he came running like a boy to the queen, a herald flying before him to hammer on the door of the queen's apartments and shout: 'His Majesty is coming: the king!' so that we tumbled out of our rooms in different states of undress and only the queen was composed and elegant in a gown thrown over her nightshirt. Henry banged the door coming into the room and ran through us, while we twittered like an aviary of blind thrushes, straight to his queen. He did not even look at me, though I was deliciously rumpled with my hair in a cloud of gold around my face. But it was not to me that Henry raced with the best news he had ever heard. He brought the news to his queen, to the woman who had made for him an unbreakable alliance with her country of Spain. He had been unfaithful to her many times, he had been unfaithful to their policy many times. But when it triumphed, in this moment of intense joy, it was to her that he took the news, it was Katherine who was queen in his heart once more.

He threw himself at her feet and snatched up her hands and covered them with kisses and Katherine laughed like a girl again and cried out with impatience: 'What is it? Tell me! Tell me! What is it?' while Henry could do nothing more than say:

'Pavia! God be praised! Pavia!'

He leaped to his feet and danced her around the room, jumping like a boy. The gentlemen of his train came running in, he had outstripped them in the race to get to the queen. George came tumbling into the room with his friend Francis Weston, saw me and came to my side.

'What on earth is going on?' I asked, smoothing my hair back and tying my skirt around my waist.

'A great victory,' he said. 'A decisive victory. The French army is said to be all but destroyed. France lies open before us. Charles of Spain can have his pick of the south, we shall overrun the north. France is no more. It is destroyed. It will be the Spanish empire up to the borders of the English kingdom in France. We have hammered the French army into the ground and we are the unquestioned masters of France, and joint rulers of most of Europe.'

'Francis defeated?' I asked disbelievingly, thinking of the ambitious dark prince who had been the rival of our golden king.

'Smashed to pieces,' Francis Weston confirmed. 'What a day for England! What a triumph!'

I looked across at the king and queen. He was no longer attempting to dance, he had lost the rhythm of the steps, instead he had wound her in his arms and was kissing her forehead, her eyes and her lips. 'My dearest,' he said. 'Your nephew is a great general, this is a great gift he has given us. We will have France at our feet. I shall be King of England and France in reality as well as title. And Richard de la Pole is dead – his threat to my throne is dead with him. King Francis himself is taken prisoner, France is destroyed. Your nephew and I are the greatest kings in Europe and our alliance will own everything. Everything that my father planned from you and your family has been given to us this day.'

The queen's face was radiant with joy, the years were stripped off her with his kisses. She was rosy, her blue eyes sparkling, her waist supple in his grasp.

'God bless the Spanish and the Spanish princess!' Henry bellowed suddenly and all the men of his court shouted it back to him in a full-throated reply.

George glanced sideways at me. 'God bless the Spanish princess,' he said quietly.

'Amen,' I said, and I found it in my heart to smile at her glow as she rested her head against her husband's shoulder and smiled on her cheering court. 'Amen, and God keep her as happy as she is at this moment.'

∾

We were drunk with victory, that dawn and the four dawns that followed. It was like the twelfth night revels in the middle of March. From the leads of the castle we could see the beacon bonfires burning all the way to London and the city itself was red against the night sky with fires at every street corner and men spit-roasting carcasses of beef and lamb. We could hear church bells pealing, a constant chime as everyone in the country celebrated the total defeat of the oldest enemy of England. We ate special dishes which were given new names to mark the occasion: Pavia Peacock and Pavia Pudding, Spanish Delight, and Charles Blancmange. Cardinal Wolsey ordered a special High Mass of celebration in St Paul's and every church in the land gave thanks for the victory at Pavia and the emperor who had won it for England – Charles of Spain, the beloved nephew of Queen Katherine.

There was no question now of who sat at the right hand of the king. It was the queen, who walked through the great hall wearing deepest crimson and gold with her head high and a little smile on her lips. She did not flaunt her return to favour. She took it as she had taken her eclipse: as the nature of royal marriage. Now that her star was risen again she walked as proudly as she had ever done when in shadow.

The king fell in love with her all over again as a thanksgiving for Pavia. He saw her as the source of his power in France, as the source of his joy at the victory. Henry was first and foremost a spoiled child; when he was given a wonderful present, he loved the giver.

He would love the giver of a gift right up to the moment that the present bored him, or it broke, or it failed to be what he wanted. And towards the end of March the first signs came to us that Charles of Spain might prove a disappointment.

Henry's plan had been that they should divide France between them, tossing only a share of the spoils to the Duke of Bourbon, and that Henry should become King of France in reality and take the old title which the Pope had conferred on him so many years ago. But Charles of Spain was in no hurry. Instead of making plans for Henry to go to Paris to be crowned King of France, Charles went to Rome for his own coronation as Holy Roman Emperor. And worse even than this was that Charles showed no interest in the English plan to capture the whole of France. He had King Francis as a prisoner; but now he was planning to ransom him back to France, to return him to the throne which had been so recently destroyed.

'In God's name, why? Why would he?' Henry bellowed at Cardinal Wolsey in a great explosion of rage. Even the most favoured gentlemen of the king's inner circle flinched. The ladies of the court visibly cowered. Only the queen, on her chair by the side of the king at the top table of the great hall, was impassive, as if the most powerful man in the country was not shaking with uncontrollable fury only one foot from her.

'Why would the mad Spanish dog betray us so? Why would he release Francis? Is he mad?' He turned on the queen. 'Is he insane, your nephew? Is he playing some costly double game? Is he double-crossing me, as your father would have double-crossed mine? Is there some vile traitorous blood in these Spanish kings? What's your answer, madam? He writes to you, doesn't he? What did he write last? That he wants to release our worst enemy? That he is a madman or just a fool?'

She glanced at the cardinal to see if he would intercede; but Wolsey was no friend of the queen after this turn of events. He stayed dumb and met her sharp look of appeal with diplomatic serenity.

Isolated, the queen had to face her husband without support. 'My nephew does not write to me of all his plans. I did not know he was thinking of releasing King Francis.'

'I should hope not!' Henry yelled, bringing his face very close to hers. 'For you would be guilty of treason at the very least if you knew that the worst enemy this country has ever seen was to be set free by your nephew.'

'But I did not know,' she said steadily.

'And Wolsey tells me that he is thinking of jilting Princess Mary? Your own daughter! What d'you say to that?'

'I did not know,' she said.

'Excuse me,' Wolsey remarked softly. 'But I think Her Majesty has forgotten the meeting she had with the Spanish ambassador yesterday. Surely he warned you that the Princess Mary would be rejected.'

'Rejected!' Henry bounded from his chair, too inflamed to sit still. 'And you knew, madam?'

The queen rose, as she must, when her husband was on his feet. 'Yes,' she said. 'The cardinal is correct. The ambassador did mention that there were doubts over the betrothal of the Princess Mary. I did not speak of it because I would not believe it until I had heard it from my nephew himself. And I have not.'

'I am afraid there is no doubt at all,' Cardinal Wolsey interpolated.

The queen turned a steady gaze on him, noting that the cardinal had exposed her to her husband's rage, and had done it twice, and wilfully. 'I am sorry that you should think so,' she said.

Henry flung himself into his chair, too enraged to speak. The queen remained standing and he did not invite her to sit. The lace at the top of her gown stirred with her steady breath, she merely touched the rosary that hung from her waist with her forefinger. She could not be faulted for dignity or presence.

Henry turned to her, icily angry. 'Do you know what we will have to do, if we want to seize this opportunity which God has given to us and which your nephew is about to throw away?'

She shook her head in silence.

'We will have to raise a huge tax. We will have to muster *another* army. We will have to mount another expedition to France, and we will have to fight another war. And we will have to do this alone, alone and without support because your nephew, *your nephew*, madam, fights and wins one of the most lucky victories that could ever come to a king, and then plays ducks and drakes with it, skims it away off the waves as if victory was a pebble on the beach.'

Even at that, she did not move. But her patience only inflamed him more. He leaped down from his chair again and there was a little gasp as he flung himself towards her. For a moment I even thought he might strike her but it was a pointing finger, not a fist, which she got in the face. 'And you do not order him to be faithful to me?'

'I do,' she said through half-closed lips. 'I commend him to remember our alliance.'

Behind her, Cardinal Wolsey shook his head in denial.

'You lie!' Henry yelled at the queen. 'You are a Spanish princess more than an English queen!'

'God knows that I am a faithful wife and Englishwoman,' she replied.

Henry flung himself away and there was a sudden flurry as the court threw themselves out of his path and dropped into curtseys and bows. His gentlemen bowed briskly to the queen and followed his impetuous progress; but he checked at the door. 'I shall not forget this,' he shouted back at the queen. 'I shall neither forgive nor forget your nephew's insult to me, nor shall I forgive or forget your behaviour, your damned treasonous behaviour.'

She sank slowly and beautifully into her deep regal curtsey and held it like a dancer until Henry swore and banged out of the door. Only then did she rise up and look thoughtfully around her, at all of us who had witnessed her humiliation and who now looked away from her that she might not claim our service.

❀

At dinner the next night I saw the king's eyes on me as I walked demurely into the great hall behind the queen. After dinner, when they cleared a space for dancing, he came over to me, walking past the queen, all but turning his back on her as he stood before me and claimed me for a dance.

There was a little rustle of attention as he took me out on the dance floor. 'The volte,' Henry said over his shoulder and the other dancers, who had been readying to form into a set and dance with us, fell back and formed a circle to watch instead.

It was a dance like no other, a dance of seduction. Henry did not take his blue eyes off my face, he danced towards me, stamped his foot and clapped his hands as if he would strip me naked then and there before the whole court. I banished the thought of the watching queen from my mind. I kept my head up and my eyes fixed on the king, and I danced towards him, the sly tripping steps, with a sway of my hips and a turn of my head. We faced one another and he snatched me up in the air and held me, there was a ripple of applause, he lowered me gently to my feet and I felt my cheeks burning with a potent combination of self-consciousness, triumph, and desire. We parted to the beat of the tabor and then came back as the dance turned our steps towards each other again. Once again he threw me up in the air and this time slid me down, so that my body was pressed against his. I felt him down every inch of my body: his chest, his hose, his legs. We paused, our faces so close that if he had leaned forward he could have kissed me. I felt his breath on my face and then he said very quietly: 'My chamber. Come at once.'

He took me to bed that night, and most of the nights that followed, with a steady desire. I should have been happy. Certainly my mother and my father and my uncle and even George were delighted that I was the king's first choice once more, and that everyone in the court was once again gravitating towards me. The ladies of the queen's chamber were as deferential to me as they were to her. Foreign ambassadors bowed to me as deeply as if I were a princess, the gentlemen of the king's bedchamber wrote sonnets to the gold of my hair and the curl of my lips, Francis Weston wrote a song for me and everywhere I went there were people ready to do me a service, to assist me, to pay court to me, and always, always to whisper to me that if I could mention a little thing to the king they would be greatly obliged to me.

I followed George's advice and I always refused to ask the king for anything, even for myself, and so he was comfortable with me in a way that he could never be with anyone else. We made an odd little domestic haven behind the closed door of the privy chamber. We dined alone, after the dinner had been served in the great hall. We had the company only of the musicians and perhaps one or two chosen friends. Thomas More would take Henry up on to the leads and look at the stars and I would go too, looking up at the dark night sky and thinking that the same stars were shining down on Hever, gleaming through the arrow-slit windows to light my baby's sleeping face.

I missed my course in May, and in June I missed again. I told George who put his arm around me and pressed me close to him. 'I'll tell Father,' he said. 'And Uncle Howard. Pray God that it's a boy this time.'

I wanted to tell Henry myself but they decided that news so momentous and so rich with the possibility of profit should come from my father to the king, that the Boleyns could garner the full credit for my fertility. My father asked for a private audience; and the king, thinking it was something to do with Wolsey's long negotiations with France, drew him into a window embrasure, out of the court's hearing, and invited him to speak. My father spoke a short, smiling sentence, and I saw Henry look from my father to me, where I sat with the ladies, and then heard his loud whoop of delight. He rushed across the room and was about to snatch me up when he suddenly checked himself for fear of hurting me, and caught my hands instead, and kissed them.

'Sweetheart!' he exclaimed. 'The best news! The best I could hear!'

I glanced around at the agog faces, and then back to the king's joy.

'Your Majesty,' I said carefully. 'I am so glad to make you happy.'

'You could do nothing to make me more joyful,' he assured me. He urged me to my feet and drew me to one side. To one woman the ladies craned forward and simultaneously looked away, desperate to know what was going on and equally desperate not to appear to be eavesdropping. My father and George stepped before the king and started talking loudly about the weather and how soon the court would leave on its summer progress, blocking out the whispered conversation between the king and me.

Henry pressed me into the windowseat and laid his hand gently on my stomacher. 'Not laced too tight?'

'No,' I said, smiling up at him. 'It is very early days yet, Your Majesty. I hardly show.'

'Pray God it is a boy this time,' he said.

I smiled up at him, with all the Boleyn recklessness. 'I am sure it is,' I said. 'Remember that I never said so with Catherine. But this time I am sure of it. I am sure that he will be a boy. Perhaps we will call him Henry.'

❀

The reward for my pregnancy came quickly to my family that summer. My father became Viscount Rochford and George became Sir George Boleyn. My mother became a viscountess and entitled to wear purple. My husband had another grant of land to add to his growing estate.

'I am to thank you for this I think, madam,' he said. He had chosen to sit beside me at dinner and serve me with the very best cuts of meat. Looking up the hall to the high table I saw that Henry's eyes were on me and I smiled up at him.

'I am glad to be of service to you,' I said politely.

He leaned back in his chair and smiled at me but his eyes were dull, drunkard's eyes, filled with regret. 'And so we spend another year with you at court and me in the king's train and we never meet, and we rarely talk. You are a mistress and I a monk.'

'I did not know that you had chosen a celibate life,' I observed mildly.

He had the grace to smile. 'I am married and not married,' he pointed out. 'Where am I to get heirs for my new lands if not on my wife?'

I nodded. There was a brief silence. 'Yes, you're right. I am sorry,' I said shortly.

'If you have a girl and his interest wanes they will send you home to me. You will be my wife again,' William remarked conversationally. 'How do you think we shall fare? Us and the two little bastards?'

My eyes flew to his face. 'I don't like to hear you speak like that.'

'Careful,' he cautioned me. 'We're being watched.'

At once my face glazed with an empty social smile. 'Watched by the king?' I asked, carefully not looking around.

'And your father.'

I took a piece of bread and nibbled it, turned my head as if we were talking of nothing important. 'I don't like to hear you talk of my Catherine like that,' I said. 'She bears your name.'

'And that should make me love her?'

'I think you would love her if you saw her,' I said defensively. 'She is a most beautiful child. I don't see how you could fail to love her. I hope to be with her this summer at Hever. She will be learning to walk.'

The hard look left his face. 'And is that your greatest wish, Mary? You, the mistress of the King of England? And your greatest wish is that you could live in a little manor castle and teach your daughter to walk?'

I gave a little laugh. 'Absurd, aren't I? But yes. I would like nothing more than to be with her.'

He shook his head. 'Mary, you correct me,' he said gently. 'When I think that I have been abused by you and I am angry with you and this wolfpack of your family I suddenly see that we are all of us doing very well off you. All of us are thriving very handsomely and in the middle of it all, like a piece of soft manchet bread nibbled by ducks, is you, being eaten alive by every one of us. Perhaps you should have married a man who would have loved and kept you and given you a baby that you could have suckled yourself, without interruption.'

I smiled at the picture.

'Don't you wish you had married a man like that? Sometimes I wish you had. I wish that you had married a man who would have loved you and kept you, whatever the advantages to handing you over. And when I am drunk and sad I sometimes wish that I had had the courage to have been that man.'

I let the silence extend until the attention of our neighbours had been distracted by something else.

'What's done is done,' I said gently. 'It was all decided for me before I was old enough to think for myself. I am sure, my lord, that you were right to do as the king desired.'

'I will exert my power to do one thing,' William said. 'I will get him to consent to you going to Hever this summer. I can do that for you at least.'

I looked up. 'I would be so glad,' I whispered. I felt my eyes filling with tears at the thought of seeing Catherine again. 'Oh, my lord. I would be so glad of that.'

❧

William was as good as his word. He spoke to my father, he spoke to my uncle, and then finally he spoke to the king. And I was allowed to Hever for the whole of the summer so that I could be with Catherine and walk with her in the apple orchards of Kent.

George came to visit without warning twice through the summer months, riding into the castle courtyard hatless and in his shirtsleeves, sending the housemaids into a frenzy of desire and anxiety. Anne would ply him with questions as to what was doing at court, and who was seeing whom, but he was quiet and weary and often during the heat of midday he would go up the stone stairs to the little chapel alongside his room where the watery reflections from the moat beneath danced on the white-washed ceiling, and he could kneel in silence and pray or daydream as he wished.

He was most ill-suited in his wife. Jane Parker never came with him to Hever, he would not allow her. These days with us were to be unsullied by her bright curious gaze, her avaricious desire for scandal.

'She really is a monster,' he remarked idly to me. 'She is quite as bad as I had feared.'

We were seated in the heart of the ornamental garden before the main entrance of the castle. Around us the hedges and plants were sculpted like a painting, each bush in its place, each plant blowing just so. We three were sprawled on the stone seat before the fountain which pattered soothingly, like rain on a roof, as George rested his dark head in my lap and I leaned back and closed my eyes.

Anne at the end of the stone bench looked at us. 'How bad?'

He opened his eyes, too lazy to sit up. He raised his hand and counted off her sins on his fingers. 'One, she's vilely jealous. I can't step out of the door without her watching me go, and she shows her jealousy by mock battles.'

'Mock?' Anne queried.

'You know,' he said impatiently. He adopted a falsetto whine. '"If I see that lady look at you again, Sir George, I shall know what to think of you! If you dance with that girl one more time, Sir George, I shall have words with her and with you!"'

'Oh,' Anne said. 'How vile.'

'Two,' he said, continuing the list. 'She's light-fingered. If there's a shilling in my pocket that she thinks I won't miss, it disappears. If there's a bauble lying around she snaps it up like a magpie.'

Anne was enchanted. 'No, really? I missed some gold ribbon once. I always thought she took it.'

'Three,' he continued. 'And worst of all. She chases me round the bed like a bitch on heat.'

I snorted with surprised laughter. 'George!'

'She does,' he confirmed. 'Scares the life out of me.'

'You?' Anne asked scornfully. 'I'd have thought you'd be glad.'

He sat up and shook his head. 'It's not like that,' he said earnestly. 'If she was hot I wouldn't mind, provided she kept her heat indoors and didn't shame me. But it's not like that. She likes . . .' He broke off.

'Oh do tell!' I begged.

Anne silenced me with a quick frown. 'Ssh. This is important. What does she like, George?'

'It's not like lust,' he said uneasily. 'I can deal with lust. And it's not variety – I like a little taste of the wild myself. But it's as if she wanted some kind of power over me. The other night she asked me if I would like a maid brought in. She offered to bring me in a girl and worse: she wanted to watch.'

'She likes to watch?' Anne demanded.

He shook his head. 'No, I think she likes to arrange. I think she likes to listen at doors, to spy through keyholes. I think she likes to be the one that makes things happen and watches others at the business. And when I said "no" . . .' He stopped abruptly.

'What did she offer you then?'

George flushed. 'She offered to get me a boy.'

I gave a little shriek of scandalised laughter, but Anne was not laughing at all.

'Why would she offer you that, George?' she asked quietly.

He looked away. 'There's a singer at court,' he said shortly. 'A lad so sweet, pretty as a maid but with the wit of a man. I've said nothing and done nothing. But she saw me laugh with him once and clap him on the shoulder – and she thinks everything is lust.'

'This is the second lad whose name has been linked with yours,' Anne observed. 'Was there not some pageboy? Sent back to his home last summer?'

'That was nothing,' George said.

'And now this?'

'Nothing again.'

'A dangerous nothing,' Anne said. 'A dangerous brace of nothings. Wenching is one thing but you can be hanged for this.'

We were silent for a moment, a dark little group under a midsummer blue sky. George shook his head. 'It's nothing,' he reiterated. 'And it's my own business. I'm sickened by women, by the constant desire and talk of women. You know all the sonnets and all the flirting and all the empty promises. And a boy is so clean and so clear . . .' He turned away. 'It's a whim. I won't regard it.'

Anne looked at him, her eyes narrowed with calculation. 'It's a cardinal sin. You'd better let this whim go by.'

He met her gaze. 'I know it, Mistress Clever,' he said.

'What about Francis Weston?' I asked.

'What about him?' George rejoined.

'You're always together.'

George shook his head impatiently. 'We're always in service to the king,' he corrected me. 'We're forever waiting for the king. And all there is to do is to flirt with the girls at court and talk scandal with them. It's no wonder I am sick of it. The life I live makes me weary to the soul of the vanity of women.'

Autumn 1525

When I returned to court in the autumn a family conference was convened. I noted wrily that this time I had one of the big carved chairs with arms, and a velvet cushion in the seat. This year I was a young woman who might be carrying the king's son in her belly.

They decided that Anne might come back to court in the spring.

'She's learned her lesson,' my father said judicially. 'And with Mary's star rising so high we should have Anne at court. She should be married.'

My uncle nodded, and they moved on to the more important topic of what might be in the king's mind since the same settlement which had ennobled my father had also made Bessie Blount's boy a duke. Henry Fitzroy, a little lad of only six, was the Duke of Richmond and Surrey, the Earl of Nottingham and Lord High Admiral of England.

'It's absurd,' my uncle said flatly. 'But it shows how his mind is working. He's going to make Fitzroy the next heir.'

He paused. He looked round the table at the four of us: my mother and father, George and me. 'It tells us that he's getting truly desperate. He must be thinking of a new marriage. It's still the safest, fastest way to an heir.'

'But if Wolsey brokers a new marriage he'll never favour us,' my father observed. 'Why should he? He's no friend of ours. He'll look for a French princess, or Portuguese.'

'But what if she has a son?' my uncle asked, nodding towards me. 'When the queen is out of the way? Here's a girl of good birth, as good as Henry's mother's. Pregnant for the second time by him. Every chance in the world that she might be carrying his son. If he marries her he has an heir. At once. A complete solution.'

There was a silence. I looked around the table and saw that they were all nodding. 'But the queen will never leave,' I said simply. It was always me that reminded them of that one fact.

'If the king has no need of her nephew, then the king has no need of her,' my uncle said brutally. 'The Treaty of the More which has taken Wolsey so much trouble has opened the door for us. Peace with France is the end of the alliance with Spain, is the end of the queen. Whether she wills it or no, she is no more than any unwanted wife.'

He let the silence hang in the room. It was outright treason that we were talking now and my uncle feared nothing. He looked me in the face and I felt the weight of his will like a thumb pressed on my forehead. 'The end of the alliance with Spain is the end of the queen,' he said. 'The queen is going whether she likes it or not. And you are going into her place, whether you like it or not.'

I searched my soul for courage and I rose to my feet and went behind my chair so that I could hold onto the thick carved wooden back. 'No,' I said, and my voice came out steadily and strong. 'No, Uncle, I am sorry but I can't do it.' I looked down the long dark wood table and met his gaze, as sharp as a falcon with black eyes that missed nothing. 'I love the queen. She's a great lady and I can't betray her. I cannot take her place. I cannot push her out and take the place of the Queen of England. It's to overthrow the order of things. I daren't do it. I can't do it.'

He smiled at me, his wolfish smile. 'We are making a new order,' he said. 'A new world. There is talk of the end of the authority of the Pope, the map of France and Spain is being redrawn. Everything is changing, and here we are, at the very front of the change.'

'If I refuse?' I asked, my voice very thin.

He gave me his most cynical smile that left his eyes as cold as wet coals. 'You don't,' he said simply. 'The world's not changed that much yet. Men still rule.'

Spring 1526

Anne was finally allowed back to court and took over my duties as lady in waiting to the queen as I grew weary. It was a hard pregnancy this time, the midwives swore that it was because I was carrying a big strong boy and he was sapping my strength. I certainly felt the weight of him when I walked around Greenwich, always longing for my bed.

When I lay in bed the weight of the baby pressed on my back so that my feet and toes would seize with the cramps and I would suddenly cry out in the night, and Anne would groggily wake and burrow down to the end of the bed to massage my clenched toes.

'For God's sake go to sleep,' she said angrily. 'Why do you toss and turn the whole time?'

'Because I cannot get comfortable,' I snapped back. 'And if you cared more for me and less for yourself you would get me an extra pillow for my back and a drink, instead of lying there like a fat bolster.'

She giggled at that and sat up in the darkness and turned to see me. The embers of the fire lit the bedroom.

'Are you really ill, or just making a fuss over nothing?'

'Really ill,' I said. 'Truly, Anne, I ache in every bone in my body.'

She sighed and got out of bed and took the candle to the glowing fire and lit it. She held it close to my face so that she could see me.

'You're as white as a boggart,' she said cheerfully. 'You look old enough to be my mother.'

'I am in pain,' I said steadily.

'D'you want some hot ale?'

'Yes please.'

'And another pillow?'

'Yes please.'

'And a piss as usual?'

'Yes please. Anne, if you had ever carried a child you would know what this feels like. I swear to you it's no small matter.'

'I can see that it is not,' she said. 'I only have to look at you to know that you feel like a woman of ninety years old. God knows how we will keep the king if this goes on.'

'I don't have to do anything,' I said irritably. 'All he ever looks at these days is my belly.'

Anne thrust the poker in the fire and set the ale at the hearthside with a couple of mugs. 'Does he play with you?' she asked interestedly. 'When you go to his room after dinner?'

'Not once in the past month,' I said. 'The midwife said that I should not.'

'Sound advice to the mistress of a king,' Anne muttered irritably, bending over the fire. 'I wonder who paid her to tell you that? You're such a fool to listen.' She drew the hot poker from the embers and thrust it into the jar of ale where it hissed and seethed. 'What did you tell the king?'

'The baby matters more than anything.'

Anne shook her head and poured the ale. 'We matter more than anything else,' she reminded me. 'And no woman has ever kept a man by giving him children. You have to do both, Mary. You can't stop pleasing him just because he's got a child on you.'

'I can't do everything,' I said plaintively. She passed my cup and I took a sip. 'Anne, all I really want to do is to rest and let this baby grow strong inside me. I have been at one court or another since I was four years old. I am tired of dancing, I am tired of feasting, I am tired of watching jousting and dancing in the masque and being amazed to see that the man who looks exactly like the king in disguise is indeed the king in disguise. If I could, I would go back to Hever tomorrow.'

Anne piled back into bed beside me, mug in hand. 'Well you can't,' she said flatly. 'You've got everything to play for now. If the queen is set aside, then there's no knowing how far you might rise. You've come this far. You have to go on.'

I paused for a moment, looking at her over the top of my mug. 'Hear me,' I said softly. 'My heart's not in it.'

She met my gaze. 'That's as may be,' she said frankly. 'But you're not free to choose.'

❁

It was a cold winter, and that made it worse for me. Cooped up indoors with nothing to think of but each new strange pain every day, I started to fear the birth. I had carried my first baby in such happy ignorance;

but now I knew that before me was the month of darkness and enclosure, and after that the interminable pain with the midwives threatening to pull the baby out of me, while I clung to the sheets tied to the bedposts and screamed with terror and pain.

'Smile,' Anne would snap at me when the king came to my rooms, and the ladies around me would flutter and take up a lute or a tabor. And I would try to smile but the ache in my back and the constant need to use the piss pot made my smile fade and I drooped on my stool.

'Smile,' Anne would say under her breath. 'And sit up straight, you lazy slut.'

Henry looked across at the two of us. 'Lady Carey, you look weary,' he said.

Anne gleamed at him. 'She is carrying a heavy burden,' she said with a smile. 'And who should know it better than Your Majesty?'

He looked a little surprised. 'Maybe,' he said. 'You are forward, madam.'

Anne did not blink. 'I should think any woman would move forward to Your Majesty,' she said with a little sparkle. 'Unless she had good cause to make haste away.'

He was intrigued. 'And would you haste away, Mistress Anne?'

'Never too fast,' she said quickly.

He laughed out loud at that and the ladies, Jane Parker among them, looked over to see what I had said to amuse him. He patted my knee. 'I am glad we brought your sister back to court,' he said. 'She will keep us merry.'

'Very merry,' I said as sweetly as I could.

ᘯ

I said nothing to Anne until we were on our own and she was undressing me at bedtime. She unlaced the tight ties on my bodice and I sighed with relief as my swollen belly was released. I scratched at the skin and saw the red weals left by my nails, and I straightened my back trying to ease the ache that I had with me always.

'And what d'you think you're doing with the king?' I asked acidly. 'Hasting away, are you?'

'Open your eyes,' she said tersely. She helped me out of my skirt and into my nightgown. My new maid poured water into an ewer and under Anne's critical scrutiny I washed myself as thoroughly as I could be bothered in the cool water.

'And your feet,' Anne ordered.

'I can't even see my feet, much less wash them.'

Anne gestured for the bowl to be lifted down to the floor so that I could sit on the stool while the maid washed my feet.

'I'm doing as I'm told,' Anne said coldly. 'I thought you would see it at once.'

I closed my eyes, enjoying the sensation of having my dirty feet soaped. Then I heard the warning note in her voice. 'Told by whom?'

'By our uncle. By our father.'

'To do what?'

'To keep the king's mind on you, to keep him engaged with you. To keep you before him.'

I nodded. 'Well, of course.'

'And failing that, to flirt with him myself.'

I sat up straighter and paid a little more attention. 'Uncle told you to flirt with the king?'

Anne nodded.

'When did he tell you this? Where?'

'He came down to Hever.'

'He went all the way to Hever in midwinter to tell you to flirt with the king?'

She nodded, unsmiling.

'Good God, did he not know that you would do it anyway? That you flirt as naturally as you breathe?'

Anne gave an unwilling laugh. 'Clearly not. He came to tell me that our first task, yours and mine, is to make sure that wherever the king goes for diversion during your confinement and after the birth, it is not into the petticoats of a Seymour girl.'

'And how am I to prevent this?' I demanded. 'I will be in the birthing chamber for half the time.'

'Exactly. I am to prevent it for you.'

I thought for a moment and went straight to the anxiety of my childhood. 'But what if he comes to like you best?'

Anne's smile was as sweet as poison. 'What matter? So long as it is a Boleyn girl?'

'Uncle Howard thinks this? Does he think nothing of me, in childbed, while my sister is set on to flirt with the father of my child?'

Anne nodded. 'Yes. Exactly. He thinks nothing of you at all.'

'I didn't want you to come back to court to be my rival,' I said sulkily.

'I was born to be your rival,' she said simply. 'And you mine. We're sisters, aren't we?'

She did it beautifully, with such light charm that no-one even knew it was being done. She played cards with the king and she played so well that she only ever lost by a couple of points. She sang his songs and preferred them to any written by any other man. She encouraged Sir Thomas Wyatt and half a dozen others to hang around her so that the king learned to think of her as the most alluring young woman in the court. Wherever Anne went there was a continual ripple of laughter and chatter and music – and she moved in a court which was hungry for entertainment. In the long winter days all the courtiers had an absolute duty to keep the king entertained; but Anne was the courtier without match. Only Anne could get through the day being fascinating and charming and challenging and always look as if she was being nothing but herself.

Henry sat with me, or with Anne. He called himself a thorn between two roses, a poppy between two ripe ears of wheat. He rested his hand on the small of my back as he watched her dance. He followed the score where I held it in my broadening lap as she sang a new song for him. He staked me when I played cards against her. He watched her take the choicest cuts of meat from her plate and put them on mine. She was sisterly, she was tender, she could not have been sweeter or more attentive to me.

'You are the lowest of things,' I said to her one night as she combed her hair before the mirror and then plaited it into one thick dark rope.

'I know,' she said complacently, looking at her reflection.

There was a tap outside and George put his head around the door. 'Can I come in?'

'Come,' Anne said. 'And shut the door, there's a gale blowing down that corridor.'

Obediently, George closed the door for her, and waved a pitcher of wine at the two of us. 'Anyone share a glass of wine with me? Not Milady Fruitfulness? Not Milady Spring?'

'I thought you'd have gone down to the stews with Sir Thomas,' Anne remarked. 'He said he was roistering tonight.'

'The king kept me back,' George said. 'Wanted to ask me about you.'

'Me?' Anne said, suddenly alert.

'Wanted to know how you might respond to an invitation.'

Without realising it I had spread my fingers like claws on the red silk sheet of the bed. 'What sort of invitation?'

'To his bed.'

'And you said?' Anne prompted him.

'As I've been bid. That you're a maid and the flower of the family. There'll be no bedding before you're wed. Whoever asks.'

'And he said?'

'Oh.'

'That was all?' I pressed George. 'He just said "Oh"?'

'Yes,' George said simply. 'And followed Sir Thomas's boat down the river to visit whores. I think you have him on the run, Anne.'

She lifted her nightdress high and got into bed. George watched her naked feet with a connoisseur's gaze. 'Very nice.'

'I think so,' she said complacently.

~

I went into the birthing chamber in the middle of January. What went on while I was enclosed in darkness and silence I did not need to know. I heard there was a joust and Henry carried a favour under his surcoat that was not given to him by me. On his shield he wore the motto 'Declare, I dare not!' which puzzled half the court, thinking it was meant as a compliment to me, but an odd misfiring compliment since I saw neither joust nor motto, locked in the shadowy silence of the birthing chamber with no court and no musicians but just a gaggle of old ladies drinking ale and biding their time: my time actually.

And there were those who thought my star was very high on the rise: 'Declare, I dare not!' was a signal to the court a son and heir might be declared. Only a very few people thought to look from the king, jousting with the ambiguous promise on his shield, to my sister as she sat at the queen's shoulder, her dark eyes on the horsemen, the smallest of smiles on her lips, the tiniest consciousness in the turn of her head.

She visited me that evening, and complained of the stuffiness of the chamber and the darkness of the room.

'I know,' I said shortly. 'They say it has to be like this.'

'I don't see why you bear it,' she said.

'Think a moment,' I counselled her. 'If I insist on having the curtains drawn and the windows open and then I lost the baby or it is born dead, what d'you think our lady mother would say to me? The king's anger would be sweet in comparison.'

Anne nodded. 'You can't afford to do one thing wrong.'

'No,' I said. 'It's not all pleasure being the king's sweetheart.'

'He wants me. He is on the brink of telling me so.'

'You'll have to step back if I have a boy,' I warned her.

She nodded. 'I know. But if it is a girl they may tell me to step onwards.'

I leaned back on the pillows, too weary to argue. 'Step onwards or back, for all I care.'

She looked at my hugely rounded belly with unsympathetic curiosity. 'You are gross. He should have named a barge after you, not a warship.'

I looked at her bright animated face and the exquisite hood which drew her hair back from her smooth complexion. 'When they launch snakes you shall have your namesake,' I promised her. 'Go away, Anne. I'm too tired to quarrel with you.'

She rose at once and went to the door. 'If he desires me instead of you, then you will have to help me as I have helped you,' she warned me.

I closed my eyes. 'If he desires you then I shall take my new baby, God willing, and go to Hever and you can have the king, and the court, and day after day of envy and spite and gossip with my blessing. But I don't think he is a man who will bring his woman much joy.'

'Oh I shan't be his woman,' she said disdainfully. 'You don't think I'd be a whore like you, do you?'

'He'll never marry you,' I predicted. 'And even if he would, you should think twice. You look at the queen before you aim for her chair. You look at the suffering in that woman's face and ask yourself if marriage to her husband is likely to bring you joy.'

Anne paused before opening the door. 'You don't marry a king for joy.'

❧

I had one more visitor in February. My husband William Carey came to see me early one morning, while I was breaking my fast on bread and ham and ale.

'I did not mean to interrupt you as you ate,' he said politely, hovering in the doorway.

I waved my hand at my maid. 'Take it away.' I felt at a disadvantage, so fat and heavy against his sleek handsomeness.

'I came to bring you the king's good wishes. He asked me to tell you that he has kindly given me some stewardships. I am in your debt, once again, madam.'

'I'm glad.'

'I understand from this generosity that I am to give your child my name?'

I shifted a little awkwardly in the bed. 'He has not told me what he wants. But I would have thought . . .'

'Another Carey. What a family we are making!'

'Yes.'

He took my hand and kissed it as if he suddenly repented of teasing me. 'You are pale and you look weary. Is it not so easy, this time?'

I felt tears prickling under my eyelids at his unexpected kindness. 'No. It is not so easy this time.'

'Not afraid?'

I put my hand on my swelling belly. 'A little.'

'You'll have the best midwives in the kingdom,' he reminded me.

I nodded. There was no point in saying that I had been attended by the best midwives before and they had spent three nights standing around the bed telling the most evil tales any woman ever had to hear about the deaths of babies.

William turned to the door. 'I will tell His Majesty that you are looking bonny and blithe.'

I smiled a shallow smile. 'Please do, and give him my obedient duty.'

'He's much engaged with your sister,' William remarked.

'She's a very engaging woman.'

'You're not afraid she might take your place?'

I gestured at the dark chamber and the heavy hangings on the bed, the hot fire and my own lumpish body. 'My God, husband, any woman in the world could take my place with my blessing if she would do it this morning.'

He laughed out loud at that, swung his hat to me in his bow, and went out through the door. I lay for a while in silence, watching the hangings of the bed move slowly in the still air. It was February, my baby was not due until the middle of the month. It felt like a lifetime.

Thank God he came early. And thank God he was a boy. My little baby boy was born on the fourth day of February. A boy: the king's acknowledged healthy boy; and the Boleyns had everything to play for.

Summer 1526

But they could not play me.

'What in God's name is wrong with you?' my mother demanded. 'It has been three months since the birth, and you are as white as if you were sickening for the plague. Are you ill?'

'I cannot stop bleeding.' I looked into her face for some sympathy. She was blank and impatient. 'I am afraid I will bleed to death.'

'What do the midwives say?'

'They say that it will stop in time.'

She tutted at that. 'You're so fat,' she complained. 'And you're so . . . you're so dull, Mary.'

I looked up at her and felt my eyes fill with tears. 'I know,' I said humbly. 'I feel dull.'

'You have given the king a son.' My mother was trying to be encouraging but I could hear her impatience. 'Any woman in the world would give her right hand to do what you have done. Any woman in the world would be up and out of her bed and at his side, laughing at his jests and singing his songs, and riding out with him.'

'Where is my son?' I asked flatly.

She hesitated for a moment, confused. 'You know where. At Windsor.'

'D'you know when I last saw him?'

'No.'

'Two months ago. I came back from churching and he was gone.'

She was completely blank. 'But of course he was taken away,' she said. 'Of course we made arrangements that he should be cared for.'

'By other women.'

'Why should that matter?' My mother was genuinely uncomprehending. 'He is well cared for, and named Henry for the king.' She could not keep the exultation from her voice. 'With everything before him!'

'But I miss him.'

For a moment it was as if I were speaking another language altogether, something incomprehensible: Russian or Arabic.

'Why?'

'I miss him and I miss Catherine.'

'And this is why you are so dull?'

'I am not dull,' I said flatly. 'I am sad. I am so sad that I want to do nothing but lie on my bed and put my face into my pillows and weep and weep.'

'Because you miss your child?' My mother had to have confirmation, the thought was so strange to her.

'Did you never miss me?' I cried out. 'Or if not me, then Anne? We were taken away from you when we were little more than babies and sent to France. Did you not miss us then? Someone else taught us to read and write, someone else picked us up when we fell, someone else taught us to ride on our ponies. Did you never think that you would have liked to have seen your children?'

'No,' she said simply. 'I could not have found you a better place than the royal court of France. I would have been a poor mother if I had kept you at home.'

I turned away. I could feel my tears very wet on my cheeks.

'If you could see your baby would you be happy again?' my mother asked.

'Yes,' I breathed. 'Oh yes, Mother, yes. I would be happy if I could see him again. And Catherine.'

'Well, I will tell your uncle,' she said grudgingly. 'But you must be really happy: smiling, laughing, dancing blithe, pleasing to the eye. You must win the king back to your side.'

'Oh, has he strayed so very far?' I asked acidly.

She did not look ashamed, not for a moment. 'Thank God Anne has him in her toils,' she said. 'She plays with him like you might tease the queen's dog. She has him on a thread.'

'Why not use her then?' I demanded spitefully. 'Why bother with me at all?'

The swiftness of her answer warned me that this had already been decided at a family council.

'Because you have the king's son,' she said simply. 'Bessie Blount's bastard is made Duke of Richmond, our Baby Henry has as good a claim. It is nothing to annul your marriage to Carey, and next to nothing to annul the marriage to the queen. We are looking to have him marry you. Anne was our decoy while you were in childbed. But we are placing our fortunes with you.'

157

She was silent for a moment as if she expected me to respond with joy. When I said nothing she spoke again, a little more sharply. 'So get up now, and get the maid to brush your hair and lace you tightly.'

'I can come to dinner because I am not ill,' I said grimly. 'They say the bleeding does not matter and perhaps it does not. I can sit near the king and I can laugh at his jokes and ask him to sing for us. But I cannot be merry in my heart, Mother. Do you understand me at all? I cannot make myself merry any more. I have lost my joy. I have lost my joy. And no-one but me even knows what this feels like, and how dreadful it is.'

She looked at me with a hard determined stare. 'Smile,' she ordered me.

I drew back my lips and felt my eyes fill with tears.

'That's good enough,' she said. 'Stay like that, and I will make arrangements for you to see your children.'

❧

My uncle came to my new rooms after dinner. He looked around with some pleasure, he had not seen how richly I was housed since I came out of the birthing chamber. Now I had a privy chamber as large as the queen's and four ladies of my household to sit with me. I had a pair of personal maids for my service and a pageboy. The king had promised me a musician of my own. Behind the privy chamber was my bedchamber which I shared with Anne, and a little retiring room where I could go to read and be alone. Most days I went in there, closed the door tightly behind me and wept without anyone seeing.

'He's keeping you very fine.'

'Yes, Uncle Howard,' I said politely.

'Your mother says you are pining for your babies.'

I bit my lip to try to stop the tears coming to my eyes.

'What in God's name are you looking like that for?'

'Nothing,' I whispered.

'Smile then.'

I showed him the same gargoyle face that had satisfied my mother and he stared at me rudely and then nodded. 'Well enough. Don't think you can be idle and spoiled just because you have his boy. The baby is no use to us unless you take the next step.'

'I can't make him marry me,' I said quietly. 'He's still married to the queen.'

He snapped his finger. 'Good God, woman, d'you know nothing? That never mattered less. He's one step away from war with her nephew now.

He's all but in alliance with France and the Pope and Venice against the Spanish emperor. Are you so ignorant that you don't know that?'

I shook my head.

'You should make it your business to know these things,' he said sharply. 'Anne always does. The new alliance will fight against Charles of Spain and if they start to win then Henry will join them. The queen is the aunt of the enemy of all of Europe. She has no influence with him any more. She is the aunt of a pariah.'

I shook my head in disbelief. 'It's not long since Pavia when she was the country's saviour.'

He snapped his fingers. 'Forgotten. Now, as to you. Your mother says that you are not well?'

I hesitated. The impossibility of confiding in my uncle was very apparent to me. 'No.'

'Well, you have to be back in the king's bed by the end of this week, Mary. You do that or you'll never see your children again. D'you understand?'

I gave a little gasp at the cruelty of the bargain and he turned his hawk-face towards me and looked at me with his dark eyes. 'I'll settle for nothing less.'

'You cannot forbid me the sight of my children,' I whispered.

'You'll find that I can.'

'I have the king's favour.'

His hand slammed the table with a sound like a pistol shot. 'You do not! That is my very point! You do not have the king's favour, and without it, you do not have mine. Get back into his bed and you can do whatever you like. You can ask him to set up a nursery for you, you can dandle your babies on the throne of England. You can banish me! But outside his bed you are nothing but a silly used whore that no-one cares for.'

There was a dead silence in the room.

'I understand,' I said stiffly.

'Good.' He moved away from the fireplace and pulled down his jerkin. 'You'll thank me for this on your coronation day.'

'Yes,' I said. I could feel my knees giving way. 'May I sit?'

'No,' he said. 'Learn to stand.'

❂

That night there was dancing in the queen's rooms. The king had brought his musicians to play for her. It was apparent to everyone that though he sat beside her, he was there to enjoy watching her ladies as they danced. Anne was among them. She was wearing a gown of dark blue, a new gown, and she had a matching hood. She was wearing her usual necklace of pearls with the 'B' in gold as if she wanted to flaunt her status as a single woman.

'Dance,' George said to me very quietly, his mouth next to my ear. 'They're all waiting for you to dance.'

'George, I dare not. I'm bleeding. I might faint.'

'You have to get up and dance,' he said. He looked at me with a bright smile on his face. 'I swear it, Mary. You have to do it or you're lost.' He held out his hand.

'Hold me tight,' I said. 'If I start to fall then catch me.'

'Into the breach. Come on. It has to be done.'

He led me to join the circle of dancers. I saw Anne's quick gaze take in the strength of George's grip under my elbow, and the whiteness of my face. For a moment she turned her back and I knew she would have been happy to see me drop to the floor. But then she saw the gaze of our uncle upon us, and our mother's bright demanding stare, and she gave up her place to me in the set of dancers, summoning her partner Francis Weston away, and George led me down the line towards the king and I looked up and smiled at His Majesty.

I danced that set, and then the next, and then the king himself came towards us and said to George: 'I'll take your place and dance with your sister, if she's not too tired.'

'She'd be honoured.'

I smiled radiantly. 'I could dance all night if Your Majesty was my partner.'

George bowed and stepped back. I saw him take a fold of Anne's dress in his fingers and draw her away to the wall of the room.

The king and I touched hands, turned towards each other, and started the dance. The steps drew us close and then led us apart, his eyes never left me.

Beneath the tight lacing of my stomacher my belly ached as if I were filled with poison. I could feel the sweat trickling down between my tightly strapped breasts. I kept smiling my bright mirthless smile. I thought if I could get Henry alone I might persuade him to let me see my children at Hever when he went hunting this summer. The thought of my baby son made my breasts prickle with pain as the milk tried to flow under the tight strapping. I smiled as if I were filled with joy. I looked across the circle of dancers at the father of my children and I smiled at him as if I could not wait to lie with him for his own sake, and not for what he could do for me and mine.

∾

Anne supervised my washing that evening with a spiteful efficiency which caused her to slap me with a cold washing sheet, and complain of the bloodstained water.

'Good God, you disgust me,' she said. 'However will he bear it?'

I wrapped myself in a sheet and combed my own hair before she could fly at me with the lice comb and rip the hairs from my head under the pretext of making me clean.

'Perhaps he won't send for me,' I said. I was so tired from the dancing and from patiently standing for half an hour while Henry took his formal leave of the queen that I wanted to do nothing more than to tumble into bed.

There was a tap at the door, George's knock. He put his head around the door. 'Good,' he said, seeing me washed and half-naked. 'He wants you. You can just put on a robe and come.'

'He's a brave man then,' Anne said spitefully. 'Her breasts still leak milk, she's still bleeding, and at the smallest thing she bursts into tears.'

George giggled like a boy. 'Bless you, Annamaria, you are the sweetest sister. I should think she wakes every day and thanks God she has a bedfellow like you to comfort and cheer her.'

Anne had the grace to look discomfited.

'And I have something for the bleeding,' he said. He pulled a small piece of wadding from his pocket. I looked at it with suspicion.

'What is it?'

'One of the whores told me about it. You push it up your cunny and it stops the bleeding for a while.'

I made a face. 'Doesn't it get in the way?'

'She says not. Do it, Marianne. You have to get into his bed tonight.'

'Look away then,' I said. George turned to the window and I went to the bed and struggled with unskilful fingers to do as he told me.

'Let me,' Anne said crossly. 'God knows I do everything else for you.'

She thrust the stuff up inside me and then pushed again. I let out a hoarse gasp of pain and George half-turned. 'No need to murder the girl,' he said mildly.

'It's got to go up, hasn't it?' Anne demanded, flushed and cross. 'She's got to be plugged, hasn't she?'

George offered me a hand. I tumbled off the bed, wincing with pain. 'Good God, Anne, if you ever leave court you could set up as a witch,' he said pleasantly. 'You have all the gentleness already.'

She scowled at him.

'Why are you so sour?' he asked as I tied the gown around me and stepped into my shoes with the high scarlet heels.

'Nothing,' Anne said.

'Oho!' he said with sudden understanding. 'I see it all, little Mistress Anne. They've told you to step back and leave him to Mary. You are to be nothing more than lady in waiting to the old queen while your sister mounts up to the throne.'

She scowled at him, her beauty completely erased by jealousy. 'I am nineteen years of age,' she said bitterly. 'Half the court thinks I'm the most beautiful woman in the world. All of them know that I am the wittiest and the most stylish. The king cannot take his eyes off me. Sir Thomas Wyatt has gone to France to escape me. But my sister, a year younger than me, is married and has two children by the king himself. When is it going to be my turn? When am I to be wed? Who is going to be the match for me?'

There was a little silence. George put his hand to her flushed cheek. 'Oh Annamaria,' he said tenderly. 'There couldn't be a match for you. Not the King of France himself or the Emperor of Spain. You are a perfect piece, finished in every way. Be patient. When you are sister to the Queen of England we could look anywhere. Better to secure Mary where she might be well-placed to serve you, than throw yourself away on some paltry duke.'

She gave an unwilling chuckle at that and George bent his dark head and brushed her cheek with his lips. 'You are,' he assured her. 'You are indeed utterly perfect. We all of us adore you. Keep it up, for God's sake. If anyone ever knows what you are truly like in private we'll all be lost.'

She drew back and would have slapped him but he jerked his head out of the way and laughed at her and snapped his fingers to me. 'Come on, little queen in the making!' he said. 'All ready? All prepared?' He turned to Anne. 'He can get his cock up, yes? You've not packed her too tight, like a ship's keel?'

'Of course,' she said crossly. 'But I should think it'll hurt like the devil.'

'Well, we won't worry about that, will we?' George smiled at her. 'After all, this is our meal ticket and our fortune that we are sending to his bed, hardly a girl at all. Come, child! You have work to do for us Boleyns, and we are counting on you!'

He kept up a flow of chatter as we went through the great hall and up the shadowy stairs to the king's chambers. When we entered Cardinal Wolsey was sitting with Henry and George drew me to a windowseat and brought me a glass of wine while we waited for the king and his most trusted counsellor to finish their low-voiced talk.

'Probably counting the scraps from the kitchen,' George whispered to me mischievously.

I smiled. The cardinal's attempts to make the king's court run with less waste was a source of continual amusement to those courtiers, my family among them, whose comfort and profit came from exploiting its folly and extravagance.

Behind us, the cardinal bowed and nodded to his page to gather up his papers. He nodded to George and to me as George led me forward to sit in his chair by the fireside.

'I shall bid you goodnight, Your Majesty, madam, sir,' he said and left the room.

'Will you take a glass of wine with us, George?' the king asked.

I shot a swift glance of appeal to my brother.

'I thank Your Majesty,' George said and poured wine for the king, for me, and for himself. 'You are working late, sire?'

Henry waved a dismissive hand. 'You know how the cardinal is,' he said. 'Unceasing in his labours.'

'Deadly dull,' George suggested impertinently.

The king chuckled disloyally. 'Deadly dull,' he agreed.

❁

He sent George away by eleven o'clock and we were in bed by midnight. He caressed me gently and praised the plumpness of my breasts and the roundness of my belly, and I stored his words up so that when my mother next reproached me for being fat and dull I could claim that the king liked me this way. But it was no joy to me. Somehow, when they had taken my baby away they had stolen away a part of me too. I could not love this man, knowing that he would not listen to me, knowing that I was not allowed even to show him my sadness. He was the father of my children and yet he would have no interest in them until they were old enough for him to use as counters in the game of inheritance. He had been my lover for years and yet it had been my task to make sure that he never knew me. As he lay on me, and moved inside me, I felt as lonely as if I were the ship which bore my name, out all alone at sea.

Henry fell asleep almost as soon as he had done, breathing heavily, half-sprawled across me with his beard hot against my neck, his sour breath in my face. I could have screamed at the weight and the smell of him but I lay very still. I was a Boleyn. I was not some slut of a kitchen maid who could not bear a little discomfort. I lay still and thought of the moon shining on the moat of Hever Castle and wished myself in my own little room in the comfort of my bed. I took care not to think of my children: little Catherine in her bed at Hever, or Henry in his crib at Windsor. I could not risk tears when I was in the king's bed. I must be ready to turn to him with a smile whenever he might wake.

To my surprise he stirred at about two in the morning. 'Light a candle,' he said. 'I can't sleep.'

I rose from the bed and felt myself ache in every bone of my body from the discomfort of lying unmoving under his weight. I stirred up the logs of the fire and then lit a candle from the flame. Henry sat up and pulled the covers around his naked shoulders. I put on my robe and sat by the fire and waited to know what his pleasure might be.

I noted with dread that he did not look happy. 'What is the matter, my lord?'

'Why d'you think the queen could not give me a son?'

I was so surprised at this turn of thought that I could not answer quickly and smoothly, like a courtier. 'I don't know. I'm sorry, sire. It's too late for her now.'

'I know that,' he said impatiently. 'But why didn't it happen before? When I married her I was a young man of eighteen and she was twenty-three. She was beautiful, beautiful, I can't tell you. And I was the handsomest prince in Europe.'

'You still are,' I said swiftly.

He gave me a little complacent smile. 'Not Francis?'

I waved away the French king. 'Nothing compared with you.'

'I was virile,' he said. 'And potent. Everyone knows that. And she took with child straightaway. D'you know how soon after the wedding she felt her baby quicken?'

I shook my head.

'Four months!' he said. 'Think of it. I had her in foal in the first month of marriage. How is that for potency?'

I waited.

'Stillborn,' he said. 'Only a girl. Stillborn in January.'

I looked away from his discontented face to the flames of the fire.

'She took again,' he said. 'This time a boy. Prince Henry. We had him christened, we had a tournament in his honour. I've never been happier in my life. Prince Henry, named for me and for my father. My son. My heir. Born the first of January. He was dead by March.'

I waited, chilled at the thought of my Henry, taken away from me, who too might be dead in three months. The king was far away from me, back in the past when he had been a youth not much older than I was now.

'Another baby on the way before I went to war against the French,' he said. 'Miscarried in October. An autumn loss. It took the shine off the victory against the French. It took the shine off her. Two years after that, in the spring: another baby born dead, another boy. Another baby who would have been Prince Henry if he had lived. But he didn't live. None of them lived.'

'You had the Princess Mary,' I reminded him in a half-whisper.

'She came next,' he said. 'And I was sure that we had broken the pattern. I thought – God knows what I hoped for – but I had a thought that there had been some ill luck, or some illness, or some such thing that had worked itself out. That once she could bear one baby who lived then others would follow. But it took two years for her even to conceive after Mary. And then it was a baby girl – and born dead.'

I took a breath, I had been holding my breath listening to this familiar story. The terrible listing of the babies' deaths by their father was as painful as watching his wife on her prie dieu naming the lost ones over her rosary.

'But I knew,' Henry said, heaving himself off his pillows and turning to me, his face no longer filled with sorrow but flushing with anger, 'I knew that I was potent and fertile. Bessie Blount had my boy while the queen was labouring over the last dead baby. Bessie had a boy from me while all I had from the queen were little corpses. Why should that be? Why should that be?'

I shook my head. 'How should I know, sire? It's the will of God.'

'Yes,' he said with satisfaction. 'Exactly so. You are right, Mary. That is what it is. It has to be.'

'God could not wish such a thing on you,' I said, choosing my words with care, studying his profile in the darkness, longing for Anne's advice. 'Of all the princes in Christendom you must be his favourite.'

He turned to look at me, his blue eyes robbed of their colour in the darkness. 'So what could be wrong?' he prompted me.

I found I was gaping at him, my mouth half-open like an idiot dawdling on a village stile, trying to think of what he might want me to say.

'The queen?'

He nodded. 'My marriage to her was cursed,' he said simply. 'It must have been so. Cursed from the beginning.'

I bit back my instant denial.

'She was my brother's wife,' he said. 'I should never have married her. I was advised against it, but I was young and headstrong and I believed her when she swore that he had never had her.'

I was on the brink of telling him that the queen was incapable of a lie. But I thought of us Boleyns and our ambitions, and I held my peace.

'I should never have married her,' he said. He repeated it once, twice, and then his face crumpled like a tearful boy and he put his arms out to me and I hurried to the bedside to hold him. 'Oh God, Mary, see how I am punished? Our two children, and one of them a boy, and Bessie's

165

Henry born out of wedlock; but no son to follow behind me on the throne unless he has the courage and the skill to fight his way through. Or else the Princess Mary takes it and holds it and England has to bear whatever husband I can get for her. Oh God! See how I am punished for the Spanish woman's sin! See how betrayed I am! And by her!'

I felt his tears wet upon my neck and I held him close to me and rocked him as if he had been my baby. 'You still have time, Henry,' I whispered. 'You're a young man. And potent and virile. If the queen should release you then you can still have an heir.'

He was inconsolable. He sobbed like a child and I rocked him, no longer trying to assure him of anything but just to caress him and pet him and whisper, 'There. There. There,' until his storm of tears blew out and he fell asleep, still in my arms, with his eyelashes dark with the wetness of his tears and his rosebud mouth downturned.

Again I did not sleep. His head rested heavily in my lap, my arms supported him around his shoulders, I spent the night willing myself not to move. This time my mind was busy. For the first time I had heard of a threat to the queen, from lips other than those of my family. This was the word of the king; and that was far more serious for the queen than anything that had gone before.

❧

Henry stirred before dawn and pulled me down into the bed with him. He had me quickly, without even opening his eyes and dozed off to sleep again and then woke as the groom of the bedchamber came in with the ewers of hot water for him to wash, and the pageboy came to stir the fire. I drew the curtains of the bed around the two of us and put on my robe and stepped into my high-heeled shoes.

'Will you hunt with me today?' Henry asked.

I straightened my back which was stiff from holding his weight all night long, and smiled as if I were not weary through and through. 'Oh yes!' I said delightedly.

He nodded. 'After Mass,' he said, dismissing me.

I went out. George was waiting for me in the ante-room, faithful as ever, swinging a gilt pomander stuffed with herbs and sniffing at it. He took a second look at my face as I came from the king's room.

'Trouble?' he asked.

'Not for us.'

'Oh good. Who for?' he asked cheerfully, drawing my arm through his and strolling by my side through the room and then down the stairs to the great hall.

'Will you keep it secret?'

He made an uncertain face. 'Just tell me and let me be the judge.'

'D'you think I am an utter fool?' I asked irritably.

He gave me his most engaging smile. 'Sometimes,' he said. 'Now tell me, what is the secret?'

'It's Henry,' I said. 'He wept last night for being accursed by God in not having sons.'

George stopped his stride. 'Accursed? Did he say accursed?'

I nodded. 'He thinks that God will not give him sons because he married his brother's wife.'

A look of pure delight illuminated my brother's face. 'Come,' he said. 'Come at once.'

He drew me down the second stairs to the old part of the palace.

'I'm not dressed.'

'Doesn't matter. We're going to Uncle Howard.'

'Why?'

'Because the king has finally got to where we want him to be. At last. At last.'

'We want him to think that he's accursed?'

'Good God, yes.'

I stopped and would have pulled my hand from the crook of his elbow but he held me tight and pulled me onwards. 'Why?'

'You are a fool as I thought,' he said simply, and hammered on my uncle's door.

It swung open. 'This had better be important,' my uncle said with threatening courtesy before the door revealed us. 'Come in.'

George thrust me in and closed the door behind us.

My uncle was seated before the little fire in his privy chamber, a pot of ale beside him, a sheaf of papers before him, wearing his fur-lined robe. No-one else was stirring in his household. George took a quick glance around the room. 'Is it safe to speak?'

My uncle nodded and waited.

'I've just brought her from the king's bed,' he said. 'The king told her that he is childless because of the will of God. He's calling himself accursed.'

My uncle's sharp gaze switched to my face. 'He said that? He said accursed?'

I hesitated. Henry had wept in my arms, had held me as if I were the only woman in the world who could pity his pain. Something of the sense of betrayal must have shown in my face because my uncle laughed shortly, kicked a log into a spurt of flame on the fire, and gestured to George to seat me on a stool at the fireside. 'Tell me,' he said, with quiet menace. 'If you want to see your babies at Hever this summer. Tell me, if you want to see your son before he is breeched.'

I nodded, drew a breath, and told my uncle word for word what the king had said to me in the silence and privacy of his bed, what I had answered, and how he had wept and slept. My uncle's face was like a death mask in marble. I could read nothing from it. Then he smiled.

'You can write to the wet nurse and tell her to take your baby to Hever. You will visit him within the month,' he said. 'You've done very well, Mary.'

I hesitated, but he waved me away. 'You can go. Oh, one thing. Are you hunting with His Majesty today?'

'Yes,' I said.

'If he speaks more of it today, or at any time, do as you are doing. Just play on.'

I hesitated. 'How is that?'

'Delightfully stupid,' he said. 'Don't prompt him at all. We have scholars who can advise him on theology, and lawyers who can advise him on divorce. You just keep on being sweetly stupid, Mary. You do it beautifully.'

He could see that I was insulted and he smiled past me to George. 'She is much the sweeter of the two,' he said. 'You were right, George. She is the perfect step on our upward stair.'

George nodded, and swept me from the room.

I found I was shaking with a mixture of distress at my own disloyalty and anger at my uncle. 'A step?' I spat out.

George offered me his arm and I took it and he pressed his hand down on my trembling fingers. 'Of course,' he said gently. 'It is our uncle's task to think of the family moving upwards and upwards. Each one of us is nothing more than a step on the way.'

I would have pulled away from him but he held me tightly. 'I don't want to be a step!' I exclaimed. 'If I could be one thing I would be a small farm-owner in Kent with my two children sleeping in my bed at night and my husband a good man who loves me.'

In the shadowy courtyard George smiled down at me, turned my face towards him with one finger under my chin and kissed me lightly on the lips. 'We all would,' he assured me with joyful insincerity. 'We are all simple people at heart. But some of us are called to great things and you are the greatest Boleyn at court. Be happy, Mary. Think how sick this news will make Anne.'

I rode out that day with the king on a long hunt that took us along the river for miles, chasing a deer which the hounds finally pulled down in the water. I was nearly crying with exhaustion by the time we got back to the palace and there was no time to rest. That evening there was a picnic by the river with musicians on barges and a tableau of the queen's ladies. The king, the queen, her ladies in waiting, and I watched from the shore as three barges came slowly upriver, a haunting song drifting across the fast-flowing water. Anne was on one barge, scattering rose petals into the flow, posed at the front like a figurehead, and I saw that Henry's eyes did not leave her. There were other ladies on the boat who stood beside her and flirted with their skirts as they were helped to disembark. But only Anne had that deliciously self-conscious way of walking. She moved as if every man in the world was watching her. She walked as if she were irresistible. And such was the power of her conviction that every man at court did look at her, did find her irresistible. When the last note of the music had finished and the gentlemen who had been on the rival barge sprang ashore there was a little rush towards her. Anne stood back on the gangplank and laughed as if she were surprised at the foolishness of the young men of the court, and I saw a smile on Henry's lips at the arpeggio of her laughter. Anne tossed her head and walked away from them all, as if no-one could be good enough to please her, and went straight towards the king and queen and swept them a curtsey.

'Did the tableau please Your Highnesses?' she asked, as if it had been her treat laid before them, and not a dance of the queen's ordering to entertain the king.

'Very pretty,' the queen said dampeningly.

Anne shot one blaze of a look at the king from under lowered eyelashes. Then she swept another low curtsey and strolled over towards me and sat on the bench at my side.

Henry returned to his conversation with his wife. 'I shall visit the Princess Mary when I am on progress this summer,' he said.

The queen hid her surprise. 'Where will we meet her?'

'I said I will meet her,' Henry said coldly. 'And she will come to wherever I command.'

She did not flinch. 'I should like to see my daughter,' she persisted. 'It is many months since I was last with her.'

'Perhaps,' Henry said, 'she can come to you. Wherever you are.'

The queen nodded, noting, as every member of the court strained to hear, that she was not to travel with the king this summer.

'Thank you,' the queen said with simple dignity. 'You are very good.

She writes to me that she is making much progress in her Greek and Latin. I hope you will find that she is an accomplished princess.'

'Greek and Latin will be of little help to her in the making of sons and heirs,' the king said shortly. 'She had better not be growing into a stooped scholar. It is a princess's first duty to be the mother of a king. As you know, madam.'

The daughter of Isabella of Spain, one of the most intelligent and educated women in Europe, folded her hands in her lap and looked down at the rich rings on her thin fingers. 'I know it indeed.'

Henry sprang to his feet and clapped his hands. The musicians broke off at once and waited to know his command. 'Play a country dance!' he said. 'Let's dance before dinner!'

At once they started a bright infectious jig and the courtiers turned to take their places. Henry came towards me, I rose up to dance with him but he only smiled at me, and held out his hand to Anne. Eyes downcast, she went past me without a glance. Dismissively, her gown brushed my knees as if I should have drawn further back, out of her way, as if everyone should always step back to let Anne through. Then she was gone and as I looked up I met the queen's eyes. She looked blankly at me as I might look at a rivalry of birds fluttering in the dovecote. It was not as if it mattered. They would all be eaten in time.

❧

I was in a fever for the court to set off on its summer progress so that I might go to Hever to my children, but we were delayed as Cardinal Wolsey and the king could not agree where the court should go first. The cardinal, deep in negotiations with England's new allies of France, Venice and the Pope, against the Spanish, wanted the court to stay close to London, so that he might reach the king easily if matters came to war.

But there was plague in the city and plague in all the port towns, and Henry was terrified of illness. He wanted to go far out into the countryside where the water was sweet and where the crowds of supplicants and beggars would not follow him from the city stews. The cardinal argued as best he could, but Henry, running from sickness and death, was unstoppable. He would go as far as Wales itself to see the Princess Mary, but he would not stay near London.

I was allowed to go nowhere without the king's express permission and George's escort. I found them both playing at tennis in the hot sunshine of the enclosed court. As I watched, a good hit from George bounced on the overhanging roof with a crack and rolled into the court but Henry was already there and struck it powerfully into the corner.

George acknowledged the shot with a hand thrown up like a swordsman and served again. Anne was sitting at the side of the court, in the shade with a few other ladies in waiting, as posed and as cool as little statues in a fountain, all exquisitely dressed, all awaiting favour. I gritted my teeth against my instant desire to sit beside her, to outshine her, and instead I stood at the back, waiting for the king to finish the game.

He won, of course. George took him to the final point and then lost convincingly. All the ladies clapped and the king turned, flushed and smiling, and saw me.

'I hope you did not stake your brother.'

'I would never gamble against Your Majesty at any game of skill,' I said. 'I am too careful of my little fortune.'

He smiled at that, and took a napkin from his page to mop his rosy face.

'I am here to ask a favour,' I said quickly before anyone could interrupt us. 'I want to see our son, and our daughter, before the court leaves on its travels.'

'God knows where we are to go,' Henry said, a frown puckering his face. 'Wolsey keeps saying . . .'

'If I might go today I could be back within the week,' I said quietly. 'And then travel with you, wherever you decide to go.'

He did not want me to leave him. His mouth lost its smile. I shot a quick look at George, prompting him to help me.

'And you can come back and tell us how the baby is faring!' George said. 'And if he is as handsome and strong as his father. Does the nurse say that he is fair?'

'As golden as a Tudor,' I said quickly. 'But no-one can tell me that he is more handsome than his father.'

We had caught Henry on the cusp of his mood before he fell into ill humour. The smile returned. 'Ah, you are a flatterer, Mary.'

'I should so like to see him well cared for before I go away with you, Your Majesty,' I said.

'Oh very well,' he said negligently. His eyes went past me to Anne. 'I shall find something to do.'

All the other ladies around her smiled when they saw him look in their direction. The more daring tossed their heads and turned their shoulders and coquetted like trained ponies in a ring. Only Anne glanced at him, and then looked away, as if his attention were a matter of indifference. She looked away and smiled at Francis, and the turn of her head was as inviting as any other woman's whispered promise. Francis was at her side in a moment and her hand was taken, and carried to his mouth for a kiss.

I saw the king's face darken, and I marvelled at Anne's recklessness. The king put the napkin around his neck and opened the door of the tennis court. At once the ladies, all surprised, rose to their feet and sank into their curtseys. Anne glanced around, leisurely reclaimed her hand from Sir Francis's caress, and swept a little curtsey of her own.

'Did you see any of the game at all?' the king asked her abruptly.

Anne rose up from the curtsey and smiled into his face as if his disfavour meant nothing. 'I watched about half,' she said negligently.

His face darkened. 'Half, madam?'

'Why would I watch your opponent, Your Majesty? When you are on the court?'

There was a second of silence and then he laughed aloud and the court sycophantically laughed with him, as if they had not been holding their breath at her impertinence just a second before. Anne smiled her dazzling mountebank smile.

'The game would make no sense to you then,' Henry said. 'Since you see only half the play.'

'I see all the sun and none of the shadow,' she riposted. 'All the day and none of the night.'

'You call me the sun?' he asked.

She smiled at him. 'Dazzling,' she whispered and the word was the most intimate of blandishments. 'Dazzling.'

'You call me dazzling?' he asked.

She opened her eyes wide as if his misunderstanding surprised her. 'The sun, Your Majesty. The sun is dazzling today.'

Hever was a small grey turretted island among the green lushness of the fields of Kent. We entered the park through a gate carelessly left open at the east end and rode towards the castle as the sun set behind it. The jumbled red-tiled roofs glowed in the golden light, the grey stone of the walls was reflected in the still waters of the moat so it looked like two castles, one floating on another, like a dream world of my home. There were a pair of wild swans on the moat, nebs nibbling against each other, making a heart shape with their arched necks. Their mirrored reflection made four swans, the reflected castle flickering in the water around them.

'Pretty,' George said shortly. 'Makes you wish we could be here all the time.'

We skirted the moat and crossed the flat planked bridge where the track went over the river. A brace of snipe darted up from the reeds and made my tired horse flinch at their clatter. They had cut the hay in the meadows on either side of the river and the sweet green smell hung on the evening air. Then we heard a shout and a couple of my father's men in their livery tumbled out of the guard room and arrayed themselves on the drawbridge, shading their eyes against the light.

'It's the young lord, and my lady Carey,' one of the soldiers exclaimed. A lad at the back turned and ran with the news into the courtyard, and we slowed the horses down to a walk as the bell rang and the guards came rushing out of the guard room and the servants scrambled into the inner courtyard.

George shot me a rueful smile at the inefficiency of our soldiers, and reined back his horse so that I could go across the drawbridge first and under the portcullis in the arched gateway. Everyone was running into the courtyard, from the lads who turned the spit in the kitchen in their dirt and rags, to the housekeeper who was opening the doors to the great hall and calling sharply to a servant inside.

'My lord, Lady Carey,' she said, coming forward. The yeoman of the servery stepped forward with her and they both bowed. A groom caught my reins and the captain of the guard helped me as I dropped from the saddle.

'How is my baby?' I asked the housekeeper.

She nodded to the stairway in the corner of the courtyard. 'There he is.'

I turned quickly, the wet nurse was bringing my baby out into the sunlight. First of all I had to absorb his growth. I had last seen him when he was just a month old, and he had been a small baby at birth. Now, I could see his cheeks had become rounded and rosy pink. The wet nurse had her hand cupped over his fair head, and I felt a pang of jealousy so powerful that it made me almost sick at the sight of her big red workaday hand on the head of the king's son, my son. He was tight-swaddled, rolled in bandages, strapped on his swaddling board. I held out my arms to him and his nurse passed him over to me, like a meal on a platter.

'He is well,' the nurse said defensively.

I held him up so I could see his face. His little hands and arms were strapped to his sides, his swaddling even held his head still. Only his eyes could move and they took in my face, scanning from my mouth to my eyes and then taking in the sky behind me and the ravens whirling around the tower above my head.

'He is lovely,' I whispered.

George, dismounting in a more leisurely fashion from his horse, tossed the reins to a stable lad and looked over my shoulder. At once the dark blue eyes switched to scrutinise the new face.

'Looking at his uncle,' George said with satisfaction. 'Good. Mark me well, lad. We shall make each other's fortune. Isn't he a Tudor, Mary? He's the very spit of the king. Well done.'

I smiled looking at the rosy cheeks and the golden hair which gleamed in threads from under the lace cap, at the dark blue eyes which looked from George's face to mine with such calm confidence. 'He is, isn't he?'

'It's odd.' George lowered his voice to a whisper for my ears only. 'Just think, we might swear fealty to this little scrap. He might be King of England one day. He might be the greatest man in Europe and you and I might have all our dependence on him.'

I tightened my grip on the board and felt the warm little body strapped tight to the wooden frame. 'Please God keep him safe, whatever his future,' I whispered.

'Keep us all safe,' George returned. 'For it will not be an easy road to get him onto the throne.'

He took the baby from me and handed him casually to his nurse, as if he were impatient of speculating, and led me towards the front door of the house. I checked, just on the doorstep was a tiny girl of two years old, dressed in the short clothes of babyhood, looking up at me. A woman had firm grip of her hand. Catherine, my daughter, looked up into my face as if I were a stranger.

I dropped to my knees on the stone cobbles of the courtyard. 'Catherine, d'you know who I am?'

Her little pale face trembled but did not crumple. 'My mother.'

'Yes,' I said. 'I wanted to come and see you before but they would not let me. I have missed you, my daughter. I have wanted to have you with me.'

She glanced upwards at the maidservant holding her little hand. A squeeze of her palm told her to reply. 'Yes, Mother,' she said in a small voice.

'Did you remember me at all?' I asked. The pain in my voice was evident to everyone within earshot. Catherine looked up to the maid who held her hand, she looked back to my face. Her lip trembled, her face crumpled, she burst into tears.

'Oh God,' George said wearily. His firm hand under my elbow forced me up and over the threshold into my home, then he pushed me firmly towards the great hall. The fire was lit, even though it was midsummer, and the big chair before the fire was occupied by Grandmother Boleyn.

'How do,' George said succinctly. He turned on the household which had followed us into the hall. 'Out. And go about your business,' he said shortly.

174

'What's the matter with Mary?' my grandmother asked him.

'Heat, and sun,' George improvised at random. 'And horse riding. After giving birth.'

'Is that all?' she asked acidly.

George thrust me into a chair and dropped into a seat himself. 'Thirst,' he said pointedly. 'I should think that she is half-dead for a glass of wine. I know that I am, madam.'

The old lady beamed at his rudeness and gestured at the heavy sideboard behind her. George got to his feet and poured a glass of wine for me and one for himself. He downed his in one gulp and poured another.

I rubbed my face with the back of my hand and looked around. 'I want Catherine brought to me,' I said.

'Leave it,' George counselled me.

'She hardly knows me. She looks as if she has forgotten me altogether.'

'That's why I said leave it.'

I would have argued but George persisted. 'She would have been dragged out of her nursery when they heard the bell, and stuffed into her best gown and taken downstairs and told to greet you politely. Poor child was probably sick with fright. Lord, Mary, don't you remember the fuss when we knew that Father and Mother were coming? It was worse than going to court for the first time. You used to vomit in terror and Anne used to go around in her best dress for days at a time. It's always terrifying when your mother comes to see you. Give her a little while to become comfortable again and then go quietly to her room and sit with her.'

I nodded at the good sense, and settled back into my chair.

'All well at court?' the old lady asked. 'How is my son? And your mother?'

'Well,' George said briefly. 'Father has been in Venice for the last month, working for the alliance. Wolsey's business. Mother is well, in attendance on the queen.'

'The queen well?'

George nodded. 'She's not on progress with the king this year. Much diminished at court.'

The old lady nodded at the familiar story of a woman travelling too slowly towards her death. 'And the king? Is Mary still his favourite?'

'Mary or Anne,' George said, smiling. 'He seems to have a taste for Boleyn girls. Mary is still favourite.'

My grandmother turned her acute bright gaze on me. 'You're a good girl,' she said approvingly. 'How long are you here for?'

'A week,' I said. 'That's all I was allowed.'

'And you?' she asked, turning to George.

'I think I'll stay a few days,' he said idly. 'I had forgotten how pretty Hever is in summer. I might stay and take Mary home when we have to go back to court.'

'I shall be with the children all day,' I warned him.

'That's all right,' he smiled. 'I shan't need company. I shall write. I think I shall become a poet.'

❧

I took George's advice and did not approach Catherine until I had gone to my little room, up the tiny winding stair, washed my face in the bowl of water, and looked out of the leaded windows over the darkening parkland around the castle. I saw a flicker of white of a barn owl and heard his interrogative hoot, and then the answer from his mate in the woods. I heard a fish jump in the moat, and saw the stars start to prick silver dots in the blue-grey sky. Then, and only then, I went to the nursery to find my daughter.

She was seated in front of the fire on her stool, a bowl of milk with bread on her lap, her spoon suspended halfway to her mouth as she listened to the talk over her head as her nursemaid gossiped with another maid. When they saw me, they leaped to their feet and Catherine would have dropped her bowl if the nursemaid had not been quick to snatch it from her. The other maid disappeared with a flick of her gown, and the nursemaid seated herself beside Catherine and made a fine show of watching my daughter eat, and making sure that she was not too close to the fire.

I took a seat and said nothing, until the fuss subsided a little and I could watch Catherine as she spooned the last of her supper. Her nursemaid took the bowl out of her hands and I nodded to her to leave the room and she went without saying another word.

I felt in the pocket of my gown. 'I have brought you a little present,' I said. It was an acorn on a string, cleverly carved into a face. The little cup of the acorn made a hat on the head. At once she smiled and put out her hand for it. Her palm was plump like a baby's still, her fingers tiny. I put the acorn into her hand and felt the softness of the skin.

'Shall you give him a name?' I asked.

A little frown puckered the smoothness of her forehead. Her golden-bronze hair was pulled away from her face and half-hidden by her night-cap. I gently touched the ribbon of the nightcap and then the golden ringlets which bobbed below the brim. She did not flinch from my touch, she was all-absorbed in the acorn.

'What shall I call him?' Her blue eyes flashed up at me.

'He's from an oak tree. He is an acorn,' I said. 'That's the tree that the king wants us all to plant. It grows into strong wood for his ships.'

'I shall call him Oakey,' she said with decision. She clearly had no interest in the king or his ships. She twitched the string and the little acorn bobbed. 'Dancing,' she said with satisfaction.

'Would you like to sit on my lap with Oakey and I could tell you a story about him going to a great revel and dancing with all the other acorns?' I asked.

For a moment she hesitated.

'The hazelnuts came too,' I said temptingly. 'And the chestnuts. It was a great woodland ball. I think the berries were there.'

It was enough. She rose from her stool and came towards me and I lifted her onto my lap. She was heavier than I remembered: a child of solid flesh and bone, not the dream child that I thought of night after night. I put her on my knee and felt the warmth and strength of her. I rested my cheek against the warm cap and felt her curls tickle my neck. I inhaled the sweet scent of her skin, that wonderful baby-child scent.

'Tell,' she commanded and sat back to listen, as I started the story of the Woodland Revel.

❁

We had a wonderful week together: George, the babies and me. We walked in the sunshine and took picnics out into the hay meadows where the soft grass was starting to grow through the stubble again. When we were out of sight of the castle I would strip the swaddling off Baby Henry and let him kick his legs in the warm air and move freely. I would play ball with Catherine, and hide and seek: not a very challenging game in an open meadow, but she was still at the age where she believed that if she shut her eyes and buried her head under a shawl then she could not be seen. And George and Catherine ran races in which he was more and more outrageously handicapped so at first he had to hop, and then he had to crawl, and at the end of the week he could only be trundled along on his hands with me holding his feet in order to make it fair, so that she could win on her unsteady little feet.

The night we were due to go back to court I could not eat my dinner, I was so sick with grief, I could not bring myself to tell her that I was leaving. I stole away in the dawn like a thief and told her nursemaid to tell her when she woke that her mother would come back again as soon as she could, and to be a good girl and look after Oakey. I rode until midday in a haze of misery and did not notice that it had been raining since we set out until George remarked at noon: 'For pity's sake let's get out of this rain and find something to eat.'

He had halted before a monastery where the bell was starting to toll for Nones and he dropped to the ground and lifted me down from the saddle. 'Have you cried all the way?'

'I suppose so,' I said. 'I can't bear to think of . . .'

'Don't think of it then,' he said briskly. He stood back while one of our men rang the big bell and announced us to the gatekeeper. When the big gate swung open George marched me into the courtyard and up the steps to the refectory. We were early, there were only a couple of monks laying out pewter plates on the table and pewter mugs for ale or wine.

George snapped his fingers at one of them and sent him scurrying for wine for the two of us, and then pressed the cold metal goblet into my hand. 'Drink up,' he said firmly. 'And stop crying. You have to be at court tonight and you can't arrive with a white face and red eyes. They'll never let you go again if it makes you ugly. You're not a woman who can please herself.'

'You show me a woman in the world who can please herself,' I said, passionately resentful, and made him laugh.

'No,' he said. 'I don't know one. How glad I am that Baby Henry and me are men.'

❧

We did not get to Windsor until evening and then we found the court on the brink of departure. Not even Anne could spare time from her packing to inspect me. She was in a flurry of preparation and I saw two new gowns disappearing into her box.

'What are those?'

'Gift from the king,' she said shortly.

I nodded, saying nothing. She shot me a sideways smile and then put in the matching hoods. I saw, as she undoubtedly meant that I should, that at least one was thickly sewn with seed pearls. I went to the windowseat and watched her put her cape over the top of them all and then call for her maid to come and strap up the box. When the girl had come and the porter followed her to lug the box away, Anne turned to me challengingly: 'So?'

'What's going on?' I asked. 'Gowns?'

She turned, her clasped hands behind her back, demure as a schoolgirl. 'He's courting me,' she said. 'Openly.'

'Anne, he is my lover.'

Lazily, she shrugged. 'You weren't here, were you? You'd strolled off to Hever, you wanted your children more than him. You weren't exactly . . .' She paused. 'Hot.'

'And you are?'

She smiled, as if at some inner jest. 'There is a certain heat in the air, this summer.'

I set my teeth on my temper. 'You were supposed to keep him interested in me, not fling him off course.'

She shrugged again. 'He's a man. Easier to interest than turn away.'

'I am curious about one thing,' I said. If the words had been knives I would have thrown them blade-first into her self-satisfied, smiling face. 'Clearly, you have his attention if he is giving you such gifts. You have moved upwards at court. You are the favourite.'

She nodded, her satisfaction hung around her like the warm scent of a stroked cat.

'Clearly you do this despite the fact that he is my acknowledged lover.'

'I was told to,' she said insolently.

'You were not told to supplant me,' I said sharply.

She shrugged, all innocent. 'I can't help it if he desires me,' she said, her tone like milk. 'The court is filled with men who desire me. Do I encourage them? No.'

'It's me you're talking to, remember,' I said grimly. 'Not one of your fools. I know that you encourage everybody.'

She gave me that same bland smile.

'What d'you hope for, Anne? To be his mistress? To push me out of my place?'

At once the smug joy in her face was replaced by an absorbed thoughtfulness. 'Yes, I suppose so. But it's a risk.'

'Risk?'

'If I let him have me, the chances are he'll lose interest. He's hard to hold.'

'I don't find him so.' I scored a small point.

'You get nothing. And he married off Bessie Blount to a nobody when he had finished with her. She gained nothing from it either.'

I bit my tongue so hard that I could taste the blood in my mouth. 'If you say so, Anne.'

'I think I'll hold out. Hold out till he sees that I am not a Bessie Blount, and not a Mary Boleyn. A greater thing by far. Hold out till he sees that he has to make me an offer, a very great offer.'

I paused for a moment. 'You'll never get Henry Percy back if that's what you're hoping,' I warned her. 'He won't give you Percy for your favour.'

She was across the room in two great strides and she snatched both of my wrists, her fingernails digging in. 'You never mention his name again,' she hissed. 'Never!'

I wrenched my hands away, and grabbed her by the shoulders. 'I'll say what I want to you,' I swore. 'Just as you say what you want to me. You're accursed, Anne, you lost your one love and now you want anything that's not yours. You want anything that's mine. You've always wanted anything that was mine.'

She pulled out of my grip and flung open the door. 'Leave me,' she ordered.

'You can go,' I corrected her. 'This is *my* room, remember.'

For a moment we glared at each other, stubborn as cats on the stable wall, full of mutual resentment and something darker, the old sense between sisters that there is only really room in the world for one girl. The sense that every fight could be to the death.

I moved away first. 'We're supposed to be on the same side.'

She slammed the door shut. 'It's our room,' she stipulated.

The lines between Anne and me were now clearly drawn. All our childhood it had been a question as to which of us was the best Boleyn girl, now our girlhood rivalry was to be played out on the greatest stage in the kingdom. By the end of the summer one of us would be the acknowledged mistress of the king; the other would be her maid, her assistant, perhaps her Fool.

There was no way I could defeat her. I would have plotted against her but I had no allies and I had no power. None of my family saw any disadvantage in the king having me in his bed at night and Anne on his arm every day. To them it was an ideal situation, the clever Boleyn girl as his companion and advisor, the fecund Boleyn girl as his lover.

Only I saw what it cost her. At night, after dancing and laughing and continually drawing the attention of the court to her, she would sit before the mirror and pull off her hood and I would see her young face drained and exhausted.

Often George would come to our room and bring a glass of port wine for her and the two of us. George and I would put her into bed, draw the sheets up under her chin and watch her as she drained the glass and the colour came slowly back into her cheeks.

'God knows where this is taking us,' George muttered to me one evening as we watched her sleep. 'The king is besotted with her; the court is mad about her. What in God's name is she hoping for?'

Anne stirred in her sleep.

'Hush,' I said, drawing the curtains around the bed. 'Don't wake her. I can't stand another moment of her, I really cannot.'

George cocked a bright look at me. 'That bad?'

'She sits in my place,' I said flatly.

'Oh, my dear.'

I turned my head away. 'Everything I have gained she has taken from me,' I said, my voice low with passionate resentment.

'But you don't want him so much now, do you?' George asked.

I shook my head. 'That doesn't mean I want to be pushed aside by Anne.'

He strolled with me to the door with his hand round my waist, idly resting on my hip. He kissed me full on the lips like a lover. 'You know you're the sweetest.'

I smiled at him. 'I know I am a better woman than her. She's ice and ambition, and she would see you on the gallows before surrendering her ambition. And I know that in me he has a lover who loves him for himself. But Anne has dazzled him, and dazzled the court, and dazzled even you.'

'Not me,' George said gently.

'Uncle likes her best,' I said resentfully.

'He likes nobody. But he wonders how far she might go.'

'We all wonder that. And what price she's prepared to pay. Especially if it's me that pays it.'

'It's not an easy dance she's leading,' George admitted.

'I hate her,' I said simply. 'I could happily watch her die of her ambition.'

❧

The court was to visit the Princess Mary at Ludlow Castle and we travelled due west all summer. She was only ten but she was old for her years, educated and schooled in the formal strict style which her mother had known at the Spanish court. She had a priest and a set of tutors, a lady companion and her own household in Wales where she was princess. We expected a dignified little woman, a girl on the brink of womanhood.

What we saw was someone very different.

She came into the great hall where her father was at dinner and had the ordeal of walking from doorway to high table with the eyes of everyone upon her. She was tiny, as small as a six-year-old, a perfect little doll with pale brown hair under her hood and a grave pale-skinned face. She was as dainty as her mother had been when she had first come to England, but she was tiny, a little child.

The king greeted her tenderly enough but I could see the shock on his face. He had not seen her for more than six months, he had expected her to have grown and bloomed into womanhood. But this was no princess who could be married within a year and sent to her new home, confident that within another two or three years she would be ready to bear children. This was a child herself, and a pale thin shy little child at that.

He kissed her and she was seated at his right hand at the high table where she looked down the hall and saw every eye on her. She ate hardly anything. She drank not at all. When he spoke to her she answered in whispered monosyllables. Undoubtedly she was learned, we had all her tutors troop in one after another to assure the king that she could speak Greek and Latin, and compile addition tables and knew the geography of her principality and of the kingdom. When they played some music and she danced she was graceful and light on her feet. But she did not look like a girl who was robust and buxom and fertile. She looked like a girl who could quite easily fade away, catch a little cold and die of it. This was the only legitimate heir to the throne of Henry's father, and she did not look strong enough to lift the sceptre.

George came for me early that night in Ludlow Castle. 'He's foul with temper,' he warned.

Anne stirred in our bed. 'Not happy with his little dwarf?'

'It's amazing,' George remarked. 'Even half-asleep, you're still as sweet as poison, Anne. Come on, Mary, he can't be kept waiting.'

Henry was standing by the fire when I entered, one foot resting against a log, pushing it deeper into the red embers. He barely glanced up as I came into the room then he stretched out one peremptory hand for me and I went swiftly into his arms.

'This is a blow,' he said softly into my hair. 'I had thought that she would be grown, nearly a woman. I had thought to marry her to Francis or even to his son, and bind us with an alliance to France. A girl is no good for me, no good at all. But a girl who cannot even be married!' He broke off, abruptly turned away and took two swift angry steps across the room. A game of cards was laid out on the table, the hands face down, half-finished. With one angry swipe he knocked them off the table, knocked the table over. At the crash there was a shout from the guard outside the door.

'Your Majesty?'

'Leave me!' Henry bellowed back.

He rounded on me. 'Why would God do this to me? Why such a thing to me? No sons and a daughter who looks like the next winter might blow her away? I have no heir. I have no-one to come after me. Why would God do such a thing to me?'

I kept silent and shook my head, waiting to see what he wanted.

'It's the queen, isn't it?' he said. 'That's what you're thinking. That's what they're all thinking.'

I did not know whether to agree or disagree. I kept a wary watch on him and held my peace.

'It's that damned marriage,' he said. 'I should never have done it. My father didn't want it. He said she could stay in England as a widowed princess, ours for the ordering. But I thought . . . I wanted . . .' He broke off. He did not want to remember how deeply and faithfully he had loved her. 'The Pope gave us a dispensation but it was a mistake. You can't dispense against the word of God.'

I nodded gravely.

'I should not have married my brother's wife. Simple as that. And because I married her I have been accursed with her barrenness. God has not given this false marriage his blessing. Every year he has turned his face from me and I should have seen it earlier. The queen is not my wife, she is Arthur's wife.'

'But if the marriage was never consummated . . .' I started.

'Makes no difference,' he said sharply. 'And anyway, it was.'

I bowed my head.

'Come to bed,' Henry said, suddenly weary. 'I cannot stomach this. I have to be free of sin. I have to tell the queen to leave. I have to cleanse myself of this dreadful sin.'

Obediently, I went to the bed and slipped my cloak from my shoulders. I turned back the sheets and got into bed. Henry fell to his knees at the foot of the bed and prayed fervently. I listened to the muttered words and found that I was praying too: one powerless woman praying for another. I was praying for the queen now that the most powerful man in England was blaming her for leading him into mortal sin.

Autumn 1526

We returned to London, to Greenwich, one of the king's most beloved palaces, and still his dark mood did not lift. He spent much time with clerics and with advisors, some people thought that he was preparing another book, another study of theology. But I, who had to sit with him most nights while he read and wrote, knew that he was struggling with the words of the Bible, struggling to know whether it was the will of God that a man should marry his brother's widow – and thus care for her; or whether it was the will of God that a man should put his brother's widow away – because to look on her with desire was to shame his brother. God on this occasion was ambiguous. Different passages in the Bible said different things. It would take a college full of theologians to decide which rule should take precedence.

It seemed obvious to me that a man should marry his brother's widow so that his brother's children could be brought up in a godly home and a good woman well cared for. Thank God that I did not venture this opinion at Henry's evening councils. There were men disputing in Greek and Latin, going back to original texts, consulting the fathers of the church. The last thing they wanted was a bit of common sense from an immensely ordinary young woman.

I was no help to him. I could be no help to him. It was Anne who had the brain he needed, and Anne alone who had the ability to turn some theological tangle into a joke that could make him laugh, even as he puzzled over it.

They walked together, every afternoon, her hand tucked in the crook of his elbow, their heads as close together as a pair of conspirators. They looked like lovers but when I lingered beside them I would hear Anne say: 'Yes, but St Paul is very clear in his discussion of this . . .' and Henry would reply: 'You think that is what he means? I always thought that he was referring to another passage.'

George and I would walk behind them, malleable chaperones, and I watched as Anne pinched Henry's arm to drive home a point or shook her head in disagreement.

'Why does he not just tell the queen that she must leave?' George asked simply. 'There's not a court in Europe that would condemn him. Everyone knows he has to have a son.'

'He likes to think well of himself,' I explained, watching the turn of Anne's head and hearing her ripple of low laughter. 'He could not bring himself to turn off a woman just because she's become old. He has to find a way to see that it is God's will that he leaves her. He has to find a greater authority than his own desires.'

'My God, if I was a king like him I'd follow my desires and I wouldn't worry myself whether it was God's will or no,' George exclaimed.

'That's because you're a grasping greedy Boleyn. But this is a king who wants to do the right thing. He can't move forward until he knows that God is on his side.'

'And Anne is helping him,' George observed mischievously.

'What a keeper of a conscience!' I said spitefully. 'Your immortal soul would be safe in her hands.'

They called a family conference. I had been waiting for it. Ever since we had come home from Ludlow my uncle had been watching the two of us, Anne and I, with a silent intensity. He had been with the court this summer, he had seen how the king spent his days with Anne, how he was irresistibly drawn to wherever she might be. But how habitually he summoned me to him at nightfall. My uncle was baffled by the king's desire for us both. He did not know how Henry should be steered, to do the best for the Howards.

George and Anne and I were ranged before the big table in my uncle's room. He sat on the other side of it, my mother beside him on a smaller chair.

'The king obviously desires Anne,' my uncle began. 'But if she merely supplants Mary as the favourite then we are no further on. Worse off, in fact. For she's not even married, and while this is going on no-one can have her, and once it's finished she's worthless.'

I looked to see if my mother flinched at this discussion of her oldest daughter. Her face was stern. This was family business, not sentiment.

'So Anne must withdraw,' my uncle ruled. 'You're spoiling the game for Mary. She's had a girl and a boy off him and we have nothing to show for it but some extra lands . . .'

'A couple of titles,' George murmured. 'A few offices . . .'

'Aye. I don't deny it. But Anne is taking the edge off his appetite for Mary.'

'He has no appetite for Mary,' Anne said spitefully. 'He has a habit for Mary. A different thing. You're a married man, Uncle, you should know that.'

I heard George's gasp. My uncle smiled at Anne and his smile was wolfish.

'Thank you, Mistress Anne,' he said. 'Your quickness of wit would much become you, if you were still in France. But since you are in England I have to remind you that all English women are required to do as they are bid, and look happy while doing it.'

Anne bowed her head and I saw her colour up with temper.

'You're to go to Hever,' he said abruptly.

She started up. 'Not again! For doing what?'

'You're a wild card and I don't know how to play you,' he said with brutal frankness.

'If you leave me at court I can make the king love me,' she promised desperately. 'Don't send me back to Hever! What is there for me?'

He raised his hand. 'It's not forever,' he said. 'Just for Christmas. It's obvious that Henry's very taken with you but I don't know what we can do with this. You can't bed him, not while you're a maid. You have to be married before you can go to his bed, and no man of any sense will marry you while you are the king's favourite. It's a mess.'

She bit back her reply and dropped a tiny curtsey. 'I am grateful,' she said through her teeth. 'But I cannot see that sending me to Hever for Christmas all on my own, far from the court, far from the king, is going to help my chances to serve this family.'

'It gets you out of the way so you don't spoil the king's aim. As soon as he is divorced from Katherine he can marry Mary. Mary, with her two bonny babies. He can get a wife and an heir in one ceremony. You just muddle the picture, Anne.'

'So you would paint me out?' she demanded. 'Who are you now? Holbein?'

'Hold your tongue,' my mother said sharply.

'I'll get you a husband,' my uncle promised. 'From France if not from England. Once Mary is Queen of England she can get a husband for you. You can take your pick.'

Anne's fingernails dug into her clenched hands. 'I shan't have a husband as her gift!' she swore. 'She won't ever be queen. She's risen as far as she can go. She's opened her legs and given him two children and *still* he does not care for her. He liked her well enough when he was courting her, can't you see? He's a huntsman, he likes the chase. Once Mary was caught the sport was over, and God knows, never was a woman easier caught. He's used to her now, she's more a wife than a mistress – but a wife without honour, a wife without respect.'

She had said exactly the wrong thing. My uncle smiled. 'Like a wife? Oh I hope so. So I think we'll have a little rest from you for now and see what Mary can do with him when you're not there. You've been rivalling Mary and she is our favourite.'

I curtsied with a sweet smile to Anne. 'I am the favourite,' I repeated. 'And she is to disappear.'

Winter 1526

I sent Christmas fairings for my babies in Anne's trunk when she went down to Hever. To Catherine I sent a little marchpane house with roof tiles of roasted almonds and windows of spun sugar. I begged Anne to give it to Catherine on twelfth night and tell her that her mother loved her and missed her and would come again soon.

Anne dropped down into her hunter's saddle as gracelessly as a farmer's wife riding to market. There was no-one to watch her, there was no benefit to being light and laughing.

'God knows why you don't defy them and go down, if you love your babies so much,' she said, tempting me to trouble.

'Thank you for your good advice,' I said. 'I am sure you meant it for the best.'

'Well, God knows what they think you can do without me here to advise you.'

'God knows indeed,' I replied cheerfully.

'There are women that men marry and there are women that men don't,' she pronounced. 'And you are the sort of mistress that a man doesn't bother to marry. Sons or no sons.'

I smiled up at her. I was so much slower in wits than Anne that it was a great joy to me when once in a while a weapon came to my sluggish hand. 'Yes,' I said. 'I expect you're right. But there is clearly a third sort and that is the woman that men neither marry nor take as their mistress. Women that go home alone for Christmas. And that seems to be you, my sister. Good day.'

I turned on my heel and left her and she had nothing to do but to nod to the soldiers who were to ride with her and trot out through the gateway and down the road to Kent. A few flakes of snow swirled in the air as she went.

It was clear what would become of the queen as soon as we were settled in Greenwich for the feast of Christmas. She was to be neglected and ignored and everyone in the court knew that she was out of favour. It was a vile thing to see, like an owl being mobbed in daytime by the lesser birds.

Her nephew, the Emperor of Spain, knew something of what was going on. He sent a new ambassador to England, Ambassador Mendoza, a wily lawyer who might be relied on to represent the queen to her husband, and to bring Spain and England into accord once more. I saw my uncle in a whispered conference with Cardinal Wolsey and guessed that he was not smoothing Ambassador Mendoza's way.

I was right. For all of the Christmas feast the new ambassador was not allowed to come to court, his papers were not recognised, he was not allowed to make his bow to the king, he was not allowed even to see the queen. Her messages and letters were watched, she could not even receive presents without them being inspected by the grooms of the bedchamber.

Christmas went into twelfth night and still the new Spanish ambassador was not allowed to see the queen. Not until mid-January did Wolsey stop his cat-and-mouse game and acknowledge that Ambassador Mendoza was indeed a genuine representative of the Emperor of Spain and might bring his papers to court and his messages to the queen.

I was in the queen's rooms when a page came from the cardinal to say that the ambassador had asked to attend on her. The colour rose to her cheeks, she leaped to her feet. 'I should change my gown, but there's no time.'

I stood behind her chair, the only lady attending her, everyone else was walking in the garden with the king.

'Ambassador Mendoza will bring me news of my nephew.' The queen seated herself in her chair. 'And I trust he will create an alliance between my nephew and my husband. Families should not quarrel. There has been an alliance between Spain and England for as long as I can remember. It's all wrong when we are divided.'

I nodded and then the door opened.

It was not the ambassador with his retinue, bringing gifts and letters and private documents from her nephew. It was the cardinal, the queen's greatest enemy, and he led the ambassador into her room as a mountebank might lead a dancing bear. The ambassador was captured. He could not speak to the queen alone, any secrets he might have carried in his luggage had been ransacked long ago. This was not a man who would bring the king back into alliance with Spain. This was not a man who could bring the queen back to her true status at court. This was a man all but kidnapped by the cardinal.

Her hand, when she gave it to him to kiss, was steady as a rock. Her voice was sweet and perfectly modulated. She greeted the cardinal with pleasant courtesy. No-one would ever have known from her behaviour that it was her doom that came in that day, along with the sulky ambassador and the smiling cardinal. She knew at that moment that her friends and her family were powerless to help her. She was horribly, vulnerably, completely alone.

❧

There was a joust at the end of January, and the king refused to ride. George was chosen to carry the royal standard instead. He won for the king, and got a new pair of leather gloves by way of thanks.

That night I found the king in a sombre mood, wrapped in a thick gown before the fire of his chamber, with a bottle of wine half-empty beside him and another empty bottle lolling in the white ash of the fireplace and draining its lees into a red puddle.

'Are you well, Your Majesty?' I asked cautiously.

He looked up and I saw that his blue eyes were bloodshot, his face slack.

'No,' he said quietly.

'What's the matter?' I spoke to him as tenderly and easily as I might speak to George. He did not seem like a king of terror tonight. He was a boy, a sad boy.

'I didn't ride in the joust today.'

'I know.'

'And I won't ride again.'

'Ever?'

'Perhaps never.'

'Oh, Henry, why not?'

He paused. 'I was afraid. Isn't that shameful? When they started to strap me into my armour I realised that I was afraid.'

I didn't know what to say.

'It's a dangerous business, jousting,' he said resentfully. 'You women in the stands with your favours and your wagers, listening to the heralds sound the trumpets, you don't realise. It's life or death if you're down in the joust. It's not play down there.'

I waited.

'What if I die?' he asked blankly. 'What if I die? What happens then?'

For one dreadful moment I thought that he was asking me about his immortal soul. 'No-one knows for certain,' I said hesitantly.

'Not that.' He waved it away. 'What becomes of the throne? What becomes of my father's crown? He put this country together after years of fighting, no-one thought that he could do it. No-one but him could have done it. But he did it. And he had two sons. Two sons, Mary! So when Arthur died there was still me to inherit. He made the kingdom safe by his work on the battlefield and his work in bed. I inherited a kingdom as safe as it could be: secure borders, obedient lords, a treasury filled with gold, and I have no-one to hand it on to.'

His tone was so bitter that there was nothing I could say. I bowed my head.

'This business of a son is wearing me down. I walk every day in unholy terror that I will die before I can get a son to put on the throne. I cannot joust, I cannot even hunt with a light heart. I see a fence before me and instead of throwing my heart over and trusting to my horse to jump clean I have this flash before my eyes and I see myself dead of a broken neck in a ditch and the crown of England hanging on a thorn bush for anyone to pick up. And who could do it? Who would do it?'

The agony in his face and in his voice was too much for me. I reached for the bottle and refilled his glass. 'There's time,' I said, thinking how my uncle would like me to say such a thing. 'We know that you are fertile with me. Our son Henry is the very picture of you.'

He huddled his cape around him a little closer. 'You can go,' he said. 'Will George be waiting to take you back to your room?'

'He always waits,' I said, startled. 'Don't you want me to stay?'

'I am too dark in my heart tonight,' he said frankly. 'I have had to face the prospect of my own death and it does not make me feel like playing between the sheets with you.'

I curtsied. At the doorway I paused and looked back at the room. He had not seen me go. He was still hunched in his chair, wrapped in his cloak, staring at the embers as if he would see his future in the red ashes.

'You could marry me,' I said quietly. 'And we have two children already, and one of them a boy.'

'What?' He looked up at me, his blue eyes hazy with his own despair.

I knew that my uncle would have wanted me to press forward. But I was never a woman who could press forward like that.

'Goodnight,' I said gently. 'Goodnight, sweet prince,' and I left him with his own darkness.

Spring 1527

The queen's fall from power became more and more visible. In February the court entertained envoys from France. They were not delayed while their papers were scrutinised, they were welcomed with feastings and banquets and all sorts of parties, and it soon became clear that they were in England to arrange for the marriage of Princess Mary to either King Francis of France or to his son. Princess Mary was summoned from the quiet retreat of Ludlow Castle and presented to the envoys, encouraged to dance and to play and to sing and to eat. My God! How they made that child eat! As if she might swell in size before their very eyes in time to be of a marriageable girth within the months of the negotiations. My father, home from France in their train, was everywhere – advising the king, translating for the envoys, in secret conference with the cardinal as to how they should re-draw the alliances of Europe, and finally, plotting with my uncle how the family could be advanced through these turbulent times.

They decided between the two of them that Anne should be returned to court. People were starting to wonder why she had gone away. My father wanted the French envoys to see her. My uncle stopped me on the stair on my way to the queen's rooms to tell me that Anne would be returning.

'Why?' I asked, as close to rudeness as I dared. 'Henry was speaking to me of his desire for a son only the other night. If she comes back she'll spoil everything.'

'Did he speak of your son?' he asked me bluntly, and at my silence he shook his head. 'No. You make no progress with the king, Mary. Anne was right. We move forward not at all.'

I turned my head and looked out of the window. I knew I looked sullen. 'And where d'you think Anne will take you?' I burst out. 'She won't work for the good of the family, she won't do as she is bid. She'll go for her own profits and her own lands and her own titles.'

He nodded, stroking the side of his nose. 'Aye, she's a self-seeking woman. But he keeps asking for her, he's hot for her in a way he never was for you.'

'He has two children by me!'

My uncle's dark eyebrows shot up at my raised voice. At once I dropped my head again. 'I am sorry. But what more can I do? What can Anne do that I have not done? I have loved him and bedded him and borne him two strong children. No woman could do more. Not even Anne, though she's so precious to everyone.'

'Perhaps she can do more,' he said, ignoring my irrelevant spite. 'If she were to conceive a child by him right now, he might marry her. He's so desperate for her he might do that. He's desperate for her, he's desperate for a child, the two desires might come together.'

'And what about me?' I cried.

He shrugged. 'You can go back to William,' he said as if it did not matter at all.

A few days later, Anne returned to court as discreetly as she had left and within the day was the centre of everyone's attention. I had my bedfellow and my companion again, and I found myself tying the laces of her dresses when we woke in the morning and combing her hair at night. She commanded my service just as once she had been forced to give me hers.

'Didn't you fear I would have won him back?' I asked curiously as I was brushing her hair before we went to bed.

'You don't matter,' she said confidently. 'Not for a moment. This is my spring, this will be my summer. I will have him dancing at the end of my string. Nothing will set him free of my spell. It doesn't matter what you do, it doesn't matter what any woman does. He is besotted. He is mine for the taking.'

'Just for the spring and the summer?' I asked.

Anne looked thoughtful. 'Oh, who can hold a man for long? He's on the very crest of the wave of his desire, I can hold him there; but at the end of it, the wave has to break. No-one stays in love forever.'

'If you want to marry him you'll have to hold him for a lot longer than a couple of seasons. D'you think you can hold him for a year? For two?'

I could have laughed aloud to see the confidence drain from her face.

'By the time he gets free to wed, *if* he ever gets free to wed, he won't be hot for you any more anyway. You'll be on the wane, Anne. You'll be half-forgotten. A woman who has had her best years, has reached her mid-twenties, and still unmarried.'

She thumped down in the bed and slapped the pillow. 'Don't you ill-wish me,' she said crossly. 'My God, sometimes you sound like an Edenbridge crone. Anything could happen for me, I can make anything happen for me. It is you who'll be on the wane, because it is you who is too lazy to make your own destiny. But I wake every day with an utter determination to have my own way. Anything could happen for me.'

By May the business with the French envoys was all but finished. Princess Mary was to marry either the French king or his second son as soon as she was a woman. They held a great tennis tournament to celebrate and Anne was made mistress of the order of the players and made great work of a chart listing all the men of the court with their names on little flags. The king found her poring over it with one little flag absent-mindedly pressed to her heart.

'What have you there, Mistress Boleyn?'

'The order of the tennis tournament,' she said. 'I have to match each gentleman fairly so that all can play and we are certain of a true winner.'

'I meant what have you there, in your hand?'

Anne started. 'I forgot I was holding it,' she said quickly. 'Just one of the names. I am placing the names in the order of play.'

'And who is the gentleman that you hold so close?'

She managed to blush. 'I don't know, I had not looked at the name.'

'May I?' He held out his hand.

She did not give him the little flag. 'It means nothing. It was just the flag that was in my hand as I was puzzling. Let me put it where it should be on the board and we'll consider the order of play together, Your Majesty.'

He was alert. 'You seem ashamed, Mistress Boleyn.'

She flared up a little. 'I am ashamed of nothing. I just don't want to seem foolish.'

'Foolish?'

Anne turned her head. 'Please let me put this name down and you can advise me on the order of play.'

He put out his hand. 'I want to know the name on the flag.'

For an awful moment I thought that she was not play-acting with him. For an awful moment I thought he was about to discover that she was cheating so that our brother George had the best place in the draw. She was so completely confused and distressed by his pressing to know the name that even I thought that she had been caught out. The king was like one of his best pointer dogs on the scent. He knew that something was being hidden and he was racked by his curiosity and his desire.

'I command it,' he said quietly.

With tremendous reluctance Anne put the little flag into his outstretched hand, swept a curtsey and walked away from him. She did not look back; but once she was out of sight we all heard her heels patter and her dress swish as she ran away from the tennis court back up the stone-flagged path to the castle.

Henry opened his hand and looked at the name on the flag that she had been holding to her breast. It was his own name.

Anne's tennis tournament took two days to complete and she was everywhere, laughing, ordering, umpiring and scoring. At the end there were four matches left to play: the king against our brother George, my husband William Carey against Francis Weston, Thomas Wyatt, newly returned from France, against William Brereton, and a match between a couple of nobodies which would take place while the rest of us were dining.

'You had best make sure that the king doesn't play Thomas Wyatt,' I said to Anne in an undertone as our brother George and the king went onto the court together.

'Oh why?' she asked innocently.

'Because there's too much riding on this. The king wants to win in front of the French envoys and Thomas Wyatt wants to win in front of you. The king won't take kindly to being beaten in public by Thomas Wyatt.'

She shrugged. 'He's a courtier. He won't forget the greater game.'

'The greater game?'

'Whether it is tennis or jousting or archery or flirtation the game is to keep the king happy,' she said. 'That's all we are here for, that's all that matters. And we all know that.'

She leaned forward. Our brother George was in place, ready to serve, the king alert and ready. She raised her white handkerchief and dropped it. George served, it was a good one, it rattled on the roof of the court and dropped down just out of Henry's reach. He lunged for it and got it back over the net. George, quick on his feet and twelve years younger than the king, smashed the ball past the older man and Henry raised his hand and conceded the point.

The next serve was an easy one for the king to reach and he did a smooth passing shot that George did not even attempt to chase. The play ebbed and flowed, both men running and hitting the ball as hard as they could, apparently giving no quarter and allowing no favours. George was steadily and consistently losing but he did it so carefully that anyone watching would have thought the king the better player. Indeed, he probably was the better player in terms of skill and tactics. It was only that George could have outrun him twice over. It was only that George was lean and fit, a young man of twenty-four, while the king was a man with a thickening girth, a man heading towards the middle years of his life.

They were near the end of the first set when George sent up a high ball. Henry leaped to smash it past George and take the point but then he fell and crashed down on the court and let out a terrible cry.

All the ladies of the court screamed, Anne was on her feet at once, George jumped the net and was first at the king's side.

'Oh God, what is it?' Anne called.

George's face was white. 'Get a physician,' he shouted. A page went flying up to the castle, Anne and I hurried to the gate of the court, tore it open and went in.

Henry was red-faced and cursing with the pain. He reached for my hand and clung to it. 'Damnation. Mary, get rid of all these people.'

I turned to George. 'Keep everyone out.'

I saw the quick embarrassed look Henry shot towards Anne and realised that the pain he was suffering was less than the injury to his pride at the thought of her seeing him on the ground with tears squeezing from under his eyelids.

'Go, Anne,' I said quietly.

She did not argue. She withdrew to the gate of the tennis court and waited, as the whole court waited, to hear what had struck the king down in the very moment of his triumphant shot.

'Where is the pain?' I asked him urgently. My terror was that he would point to his breast or to his belly and it would be something torn inside him, or his heart missing its beat. Something deep and irreparable.

'My foot,' he said, choking on the words. 'Such a fool. I came down on the side of it. I think it's broken.'

'Your foot?' The relief made me almost laugh out loud. 'My God, Henry, I thought you were dead!'

He looked up at that and grinned through his scowl. 'Dead of tennis? I have given up jousting to keep myself safe and you think that I might be dead of tennis?'

I was breathless with relief. 'Dead of tennis! No! But I thought perhaps ... it was so sudden, and you went down so fast ...'

'And at the hand of your brother!' he finished, and then suddenly the three of us were howling with laughter, the king's head cradled in my lap, George gripping his hands, and the king torn between the intense pain of his broken foot and the ludicrous thought that the Boleyns had attempted to assassinate him with tennis.

The French envoys were due to leave, their treaties signed, and we were to have a great masque and party to bid them farewell. It was to take place in the queen's apartments, without her invitation, without even her desire. The master of the revels merely arrived and abruptly announced that the king had ordered that the masque should take place in her rooms. The queen smiled as if it was the very thing that she wanted and let him measure up for awnings and tapestries and scenery. The queen's ladies were to wear gowns of gold or silver and to dance with the king and his companions who would enter disguised.

I thought how many times the queen had pretended not to recognise her husband when he came into her rooms disguised, how many times she had watched him dance with her ladies, how often he had led me out before her and that now she and I would watch him dance with Anne. Not a flicker of resentment crossed her face for even a moment. She thought that she would choose the dancers, as she had always done before, a little piece of patronage, one of the many ways to control the court. But the dancing master already had a list of the ladies who were to play the parts. They had been named by the king, and the queen was left with nothing to do, she was a cipher in her own rooms.

It took them all day to prepare for the masque, and the queen had nowhere to sit while they hammered the draperies into the wooden panelling. She retired to her privy chamber while the rest of us tried on our gowns and practised our dance, too excited to care that we could hardly hear the beat of the music over the noise of the workmen. The queen went to bed early to get away from the noise and the disruption while the rest of us feasted late in the hall.

The next day the French envoys came to dine at noon in the great hall. The queen sat at Henry's right hand but his eyes were on Anne. The trumpets sounded and the servers marched in like soldiers, all in step in their bright liveries, bringing dish after dish to the top table and then to the other tables in the hall. It was a feast of quite ludicrous proportions, every sort of beast had been killed and gutted and cooked to demonstrate the wealth of the king and the richness of his kingdom. The pinnacle of the feast was the dish of fowls with a peacock cooked and presented all in its feathers, a great towering piece of fancy. It was stuffed with a swan which had been stuffed with chicken which had been stuffed with a lark. The carver's task was to get a perfect slice from every bird without disturbing the beauty of the dish. Henry took a taste of everything but I saw Anne refuse all that she was offered.

Henry beckoned the server with one crook of his finger and whispered in his ear. He sent Anne the heart of the dish, the lark. She looked up as if she were surprised – as if she had not been following every move that he had made – and she smiled at him and bowed her head in thanks. Then she tasted the meat. As she put a small slice in her smiling mouth, I saw him shudder with desire.

After dinner the queen and her ladies, Anne and I among them, retired from the great hall and hurried to our rooms to change. Anne and I helped each other lace into the tight stomachers of our cloth of gold gowns, and Anne complained as I pulled her laces tight.

'Too much lark,' I said unsympathetically.

'Did you see how he watches me?'

'Everyone saw.'

She pushed her French hood far back on her head so that her dark hair showed, and straightened the gold 'B' that she always wore round her neck.

'What d'you see when my hood is set back like this?'

'Your smug face.'

'A face without a line on it. Hair that is glossy and dark without one thread of grey.' She stepped back from the mirror and admired the golden gown. 'Dressed like a queen,' she said.

There was a knock on the door and Jane Parker put her head into the room. 'Talking secrets?' she asked hungrily.

'No,' I said unhelpfully. 'Just getting ready.'

She opened the door and slipped inside. She was wearing a silver gown, cut low to show her breasts, and then tugged down a bit lower still; and a silver hood. When she saw how Anne was wearing her hood she at once went to the mirror and pushed her own back a little. Anne winked at me behind her back.

'He does favour you above all others,' she said confidentially to Anne. 'Anyone can see that he desires you.'

'Indeed.'

Jane turned to me. 'Doesn't it make you feel jealous? Isn't it odd bedding a man who desires your sister?'

'No,' I said shortly.

Nothing would halt the woman. Her speculation was like the slime trail after a snail. 'I would find it very odd. And then, when you come from his bed, you get into bed with Anne and the two of you are side by side and all but naked. He must wish he could come to your room and have both of you at once!'

I was stunned. 'That's filthy talk. His Majesty would be much offended.'

She gave a smile which would have been better in a bawdy house than in a lady's room. 'Of course, there's only one man who comes in here to the two beautiful sisters, after their bed time, and that's my husband. I know he visits most nights. For sure he's never in my bed.'

'Good God, who can blame him!' Anne exclaimed roundly. 'For I'd rather sleep with a worm than have you whispering in my ear all the night. Go, Jane Parker, and take your foul mouth and your worse mind to the necessary room where it belongs. Mary and I are going to dance.'

❧

Almost as soon as the French envoys were gone, as if he had been waiting for quietness and secrecy, Cardinal Wolsey created a hidden court of law and summoned witnesses, prosecutors, and defendants. He was judge, of course. That way it seemed to be Wolsey, only Wolsey, acting on principle and not on instruction. That way a divorce could be ordered by the Pope, and not requested by the king. Amazingly, Wolsey's court remained a secret. No-one except those ferried quietly downriver to Westminster knew of it. Not Mother, always alert for the family's benefit, not Uncle Howard, the spymaster. Not I, warm from the king's bed, not Anne, enfolded in his confidence. Most importantly, not even the queen knew of her court. For three days they had an innocent woman's marriage on trial and she did not even know it.

For Wolsey's secret court at Westminster was to try Henry himself for cohabiting unlawfully with the wife of his dead brother Arthur: a charge so grave and a court so preposterous that they must have been pinching themselves as they swore themselves in and watched their king walk, head penitently bowed, into the dock, accused of sin by his own Lord Chancellor. Henry confessed that he had married his brother's wife on the basis of a mistaken papal dispensation. He said that at the time, and after, he had 'grave doubts'. Wolsey unblinkingly ordered that the matter should be put before a papal legate – his unbiased self – and the king agreed, named a lawyer and withdrew from the proceedings. The court sat for three days and then summoned theologians to give evidence that it was unlawful to marry the wife of a dead brother. My uncle's spy network finally picked up news of the secret court when he heard of an inquiry made to the Bishop of Lincoln. At once Anne, George and I were summoned before him to his rooms at Windsor.

'Divorced for what purpose?' he demanded, his voice tight with excitement.

Anne was almost panting at the news. 'He must be doing it for me. He must be planning to set aside the queen for me.'

'Has he proposed?' my uncle demanded, straight to the point.

She met his gaze. 'No. How can he? But I will wager any prize you like that he will ask me the moment he is free of the queen.'

My uncle nodded. 'How long can you hold him?'

'How long can it take?' Anne countered. 'The court is in session now. It will hand down a judgement, the queen will be set aside, the king will be free at last; and *voilà*! Here am I!'

Despite himself he smiled at her assurance. '*Voilà*. So you are,' he concurred.

'So you agree, it is to be me.' Anne drove a bargain with him. 'Mary shall leave court or stay as I require. The family will support me with the king, as I need. We play this only for my benefit. There is no choice, Mary is not reinstated, you do not urge her on. I am the only Boleyn girl we put forward.'

My uncle looked at my father. My father looked from one daughter to the other and shrugged. 'I doubt either of them,' he said flatly. 'Surely he'll aim higher than a commoner. Clearly it won't be Mary. She's had her heyday and he's cooled towards her.'

I felt myself chilled all through at this loveless analysis. But my father did not even look at me. This was business. 'So it won't be Mary. But I doubt very much if his passion for Anne will take him forward in preference to a French princess.'

My uncle thought for a moment. 'Which do we support?'

'Anne,' my mother recommended. 'He's mad for Anne. If he can rid himself of his wife this month I think he might have Anne.'

My uncle looked from my sister to me as one might choose an apple to eat. 'Anne then,' he said.

Anne did not even smile. She just gave a little sigh of relief.

My uncle pushed back his chair and rose to his feet.

'What about me?' I asked awkwardly.

They all looked towards me as if for a moment they had forgotten I was there.

'What about me? Am I to go to his bed if he sends for me? Or am I to refuse?'

My uncle did not decide. That was the moment when I felt Anne's supremacy. My uncle, the head of my family, the fount of authority in my world, looked to my sister for her decision.

'She can't refuse,' she said. 'We don't want some slut getting into his bed and diverting him. He must keep Mary as his mistress for the nights and he'll go on falling in love with me during the day. But you must be dull, Mary, like a dull wife.'

'I don't know I can do that,' I said irritably.

Anne gave her sexy gurgle of laughter. 'Oh you can,' she said with a sly sideways smile at my uncle. 'You can be wonderfully dull, Mary. Don't underrate yourself.'

I saw my uncle hide a smile and I felt my cheeks burn with rage. George leaned towards me and I felt his comforting weight against my shoulder, as if to remind me that it would do me no good to protest.

Anne raised an eyebrow at my uncle and he nodded that we could leave. She led the way from the room, I followed the hem of her gown as I had always dreaded that I would have to do. I kept my eyes down as she led us out into the sunshine and walked up by the archery butts and looked out over the garden and the steeply stepped terraces down to the moat, and then the little town and the river beyond. George touched my hand with his fingers but I hardly felt him. I was consumed with rage that I had been put aside for my sister. My own family had decided that I was to be the whore and she was to be the wife.

'So I shall be queen,' Anne said dreamily.

'I shall be brother-in-law to the King of England,' George said, as if he could hardly believe it.

'And what shall I be?' I spat. I would not be the king's favourite, I would not be the centre of the court. I would lose the place I had worked for ever since I was twelve years old. I would be last year's whore.

'You'll be my lady in waiting,' Anne said sweetly. 'You'll be the other Boleyn girl.'

❈

No-one knew how much the queen knew of the disaster which was being prepared for her. She was a queen of ice and stone in these spring days, while the cardinal trawled the universities of Europe for evidence against a wife who was completely innocent of any sin. As if to challenge the fates the queen started work on yet another new altar cloth, a match of the one she had started before; the two of them would be a massive project which would take years, and a full court of ladies in waiting, to complete. It was as if everything, even her sewing, must demonstrate to the world that she would live and die as queen of

England. How else could it be? No queen had ever been set aside before.

She had asked me to help her by blocking in the blue sky above the angels. It had been drawn for her by a Florentine artist and was very much in the new style, with luscious rounded bodies half-hidden by the angels' feathery wings, and bright expressive faces on the shepherds around the crib. It was as good as a play to look at the drawing the artist had made, the people were as vivid as if they were alive. I was glad that it would not be me who had to follow the tiny detailed lines with my needle. Long before the sky was done Wolsey would have passed sentence, the Pope confirmed it and she would be divorced and in a nunnery, and the nuns could sew the difficult draperies and the feathery wings while we Boleyns closed the trap on the bachelor king. I finished one long hank of blue silk for a tiny square of sky and took my needle to the light of the narrow window when I suddenly saw the brown head of my brother race up the steps which ran around the moat and then he was out of sight, though I craned forward to see why he was running.

'What is it, Lady Carey?' the queen asked from behind me, her voice absolutely expressionless.

'My brother running in,' I said. 'May I go down and see him, Your Majesty?'

'Of course,' she said calmly. 'If there is important news you might bring it straight to me, Mary.'

I kept the needle in my hand as I left the room and hurried down the stone steps to the great hall. George had just burst in through the door.

'What's happened?' I asked.

'I must find Father,' he said. 'The Pope's been captured.'

'What?'

'Where is Father? Where is he?'

'Perhaps with the clerks.'

At once George turned to go to their offices. I hurried after him and grabbed his sleeve but he pulled himself free. 'Wait, George! Captured by who?'

'By the army of Spain,' he said. 'Mercenaries, in the employ of Charles of Spain, and the word is that they ran out of control, they sacked the Holy City and captured His Holiness.'

I stood stock still for a moment, shocked into silence. 'They'll let him go,' I said. 'They couldn't be so . . .' The very words failed me. George was almost hopping from one foot to another in his urgency to run onwards.

'Think!' he counselled me. 'What does it mean if the Pope is captured by the armies of Spain? What does it mean?'

I shook my head. 'That the Holy Father is in danger,' I said feebly. 'You cannot capture the Pope . . .'

George laughed out loud. 'Fool!' He took me by the hand and pulled me after him, up the stairs to the offices of the clerks. He hammered on the door and put his head around it. 'Is my father here?'

'With the king,' someone replied. 'In his privy chamber.'

George spun on his heel and ran back down the stairs. I picked up the long skirt of my gown and pattered after him. 'I don't understand.'

'Who can grant the king a divorce?' George demanded, pausing on the turn of the stair. He looked up at me, his brown eyes ablaze with excitement. I hesitated above him, like a defender of the circular stair.

'Only the Pope,' I stumbled.

'Who holds the Pope?'

'Charles of Spain, you say.'

'Who is Charles of Spain's aunt?'

'The queen.'

'So d'you think the Pope is going to grant the king a divorce now?'

I paused. George jumped up two steps and kissed my open mouth. 'Silly girl,' he said warmly. 'This is disastrous news for the king. He's never going to get free of her. It's all gone awry and we Boleyns gone awry with it.'

I snatched at his hand as he would have run away from me. 'So why are you so happy? George! If we are ruined? Why are you so merry?'

He laughed up at me. 'I'm not happy, I'm maddened,' he half-shouted. 'For a moment I had started to believe our own madness. I had started to believe that Anne would be his wife and the next Queen of England. And now I am sane again. Thank God. That is why I laugh. Now let me go, I have to tell Father. I had the news from a boatman come upriver with a message for the cardinal. Father will like to know first, if I can find him.'

I let him go, in his wildness there was no holding him.

I heard his boots rattle down the stone stairs and then the bang of the opening door of the great hall, a few hasty steps across the stone floor of the hall, the yelp of a dog as he kicked it aside, and then the door creaked shut. I sank down on the stairs, where he had left me, the queen's embroidery needle still in my hand, wondering where we Boleyns were now, since all the power had shifted back to the queen again.

George had not told me whether or no I might tell the queen and I judged it safer to say nothing when I went back to her rooms. I smoothed out my face, pulled down the stomacher of my dress, and composed myself before I opened the door.

She knew already. I could tell by the way the altar cloth was flung aside and she was standing at the window, looking out, as if she could see all the way to Italy and her victorious young nephew who had promised to love and reverence her, riding in triumph into Rome. When I came in the room she shot one quick cautious glance at me and then gave a little giggle, when she saw my stunned expression.

'You have heard the news?' she guessed.

'Yes. My brother was running to my father with it.'

'It will make a difference to everything,' she asserted. 'Everything.'

'I know it.'

'And your sister will be in such a difficult position when she hears,' she said slyly.

An irresistible giggle escaped me. 'She called herself a storm-tossed maiden!' I said with a wail of laughter.

The queen clapped her hand to her mouth. 'Anne Boleyn? Storm-tossed?'

I nodded. 'Gave him a jewel engraved with a maiden in a storm-tossed boat!'

The queen crammed the knuckles of her hand into her mouth. 'Hush! Hush!'

We heard the noise of people outside the door and in one quick movement she was back in her place, the big frame of embroidery pulled towards her, her heavy gable hood bent over her work, her face grave. She glanced at me and nodded me towards my work. I took the needle and thread that I had carried all this while, so that when the guards opened the door the queen and I were industriously stitching in silence.

It was the king himself, without companions. He came in, saw me, checked for a moment and then came on, as if he was glad to have me as a witness for what he might say to his wife of so many years.

'It appears that your nephew has committed the most awful of crimes,' he said without preamble, his voice hard and angry.

She raised her head. 'Your Majesty,' she said, and sank into a curtsey.

'I say, the most awful of crimes.'

'Why, what has he done?'

'His army has captured the Holy Father and imprisoned him. A blasphemous act, a sin against St Peter himself.'

A small frown creased her weary face. 'I am sure he will release the Holy Father and restore him at once,' she said. 'Why would he not?'

'He would not, because he knows that if he holds the Pope in his power then he holds all of us in his hand! He knows that we are cat's-paws! He seeks to rule us all by ruling the Pope!'

The queen's head was turned to her work again but I could not take my gaze from Henry. This was a new man, one I had not seen before. He was not angry in his usual red rage. He was coldly angry; today he had all the power of a grown man who has been a tyrant since eighteen.

'He is a very ambitious young man,' she concurred sweetly. 'As you were at his age, I remember.'

'I did not seek to command all of Europe and destroy the plans of greater men!' he said, bitingly.

She looked up at him and smiled with her constant, pleasant confidence. 'No,' she agreed. 'It is almost as if he is divinely guided, is it not?'

ℂℴ

My uncle ruled that we should all behave as if we were not defeated. So, as if nothing had gone wrong for us, as if the Boleyns were not overthrown, the laughter, the music and the flirtations continued in Anne's rooms. No-one called them my rooms any more, though they had once been given to me and furnished for me. Just as the queen had become a ghost, I had become a shadow. Anne had lived and bedded with me; but now she was the substance and I was the shadow. It was Anne who called for cards, and Anne who called for wine, and Anne who looked up and smiled that sleek confident smile when the king came into the room.

There was nothing I could do but take second place and smile. The king might bed me at night, but all the day he was Anne's. For the first time in all the long while that I had been his lover I felt like a whore indeed, and it was my own sister who shamed me.

The queen, left alone for much of the time, continued work on the altar cloth, spent hours before her prie dieu, and met constantly with her confessor, John Fisher, the Bishop of Rochester. For many hours he was with the queen and when he came out of her chamber he was grave and quiet. We used to watch him walk down the cobbled hill to his boat on the river and laugh at his slow pace. He walked with his head bent, as if weighed down by thought.

'She must have sinned like the devil,' Anne remarked. Everyone listened, waiting for the jest.

'Oh why?' George prompted her.

'Because she confesses for hours every day,' Anne exclaimed. 'God knows what that woman must have done, but she confesses for longer than I dine!'

There was a roar of easy, sycophantic laughter, and Anne clapped her hands and called for music. Couples lined up to dance. I stayed at the window, watching the bishop walk away from the castle and from the queen and wondered indeed what the two of them did discuss in such length. Could it be that she knew exactly what the king was planning? Could it be that she was hoping to turn the church, the very church in England, against him?

I squeezed past the dancers and went to the queen's rooms. As usual these days, there was silence; no music pouring from the open windows, the doors were shut where they used to be flung wide open to visitors. I opened them and went in.

Her receiving room was empty. The altar cloth was where she had left it, spread over stools. The sky was only half-finished, it would never be done while she had no-one to work with her. I wondered that she could bear to sew alone at one corner and see the yards and yards of empty material ahead of her. The fire was out in the hearth, the place was cold. I had a moment of real apprehension. For a moment I thought – what if she has been taken? It was a mad thought, for who could arrest a queen? Where could a queen be taken? But just for a moment I thought that the silence and emptiness of the room could only mean one thing, that Henry had suddenly snapped, and, refusing to wait for a moment longer, had sent his soldiers to take her away.

Then I heard a tiny sound. It was so pitiful that I thought it was the wail of a child. It came from her privy chamber.

I didn't stop to think, there was something in that heartbroken cry that would call to anyone; I opened the door, and went in.

It was the queen. Her head was buried in the rich covers on her bed, her hood pushed askew. She was kneeling as if to pray but she had the covers stuffed into her mouth and all the sound that she could make was this dreadful, heartbroken keening. The king was standing behind her, hands on hips like an executioner on Tower Green. He glanced over his shoulder at the sound of the opening door and saw me; but he showed no sign of recognition. His face was blank and stern, like a man driven beyond himself.

'And so I must tell you that the marriage was indeed unlawful and must and will be annulled.'

The queen raised her tearstained face from the bed. 'We had a dispensation.'

'A Pope cannot dispense with the law of God,' Henry said firmly.

'It is not the law of God . . .' she whispered.

'Don't argue with me, madam,' Henry interrupted. He feared her intelligence. 'You must learn that you will no longer be my wife and my queen. You must step aside.'

She turned her tearstained face to him. 'I cannot step aside,' she said.

'Even if I wished to. I am your wife and your queen. Nothing can prevent that. Nothing can put it aside.'

He headed for the door, desperate to be away from her agony. 'I have told you, so you have heard it from my own lips,' he said at the doorway. 'You cannot complain that I have not been honest with you. I have told you that this is how it must be.'

'I have loved you for years,' she cried after him. 'I gave my womanhood to you. Tell me, in what way have I offended you? What have I ever done which was displeasing?'

He was nearly gone, I pressed back against the panelled wall so that he could get past me; but at that final plea he checked and turned for a moment.

'You had to give me a son,' he said simply. 'You did not do that.'

'I tried! God knows, Henry! I tried! I bore you a son, that he did not live was no fault of mine. God wanted our little prince in heaven; that was no fault of mine.'

The pain in her voice shook him, but he moved away. 'You had to give me a son,' he repeated. 'I have to have a son for England, Katherine. You know that.'

Her face was bleak. 'You have to reconcile yourself to God's will.'

'It is God himself who has prompted me to this,' Henry shouted. 'God himself has warned me that I must leave this false marriage of sin and start again. And if I do, I shall have a son. I know it, Katherine. And you –'

'Yes?' she said, as quick as her own greyhound on the scent, all her courage suddenly flaring up. 'What for me? A nunnery? Old age? Death? I am a Princess of Spain and the Queen of England. What can you offer me instead of these?'

'It is God's will,' he repeated.

She laughed at that, a dreadful sound, as wild as her crying had been. 'God's will that you should turn aside from your true wedded wife and marry a nobody? A whore? The sister of your whore?'

I froze, but Henry was gone, pushing past me out of the door. 'It is God's will and my will!' he shouted from the outer chamber, and then we heard the door slam.

I crept backwards, desperate that she should not know that I had seen her cry, desperate that she should not see me, whom she had named as his whore. But she raised her head from her hands and said simply:

'Help me, Mary.'

In silence I went forward. It was the first time in the seven years that I had known her that she had asked for help. She put out her arm to be dragged to her feet and I saw that she could hardly stand. Her eyes were bloodshot with crying.

'You should rest, Your Majesty,' I said.

'I cannot rest,' she replied. 'Help me to my prie dieu and give me my rosary.'

'Your Majesty . . .'

'Mary,' she croaked, her voice hoarse from that dreadful gape-mouthed whimpering. 'He will destroy me, he will disinherit our daughter, he will ruin this country, and he will send his immortal soul to hell. I have to pray for him, for me, and for our country. And then I have to write to my nephew.'

'Your Majesty, they will never let a letter reach him.'

'I have ways to send it to him.'

'Don't write anything that could be held against you.'

She checked at that, hearing the fear in my voice. And then she smiled an empty bitter smile that did not reach her eyes. 'Why?' she asked. 'Do you think it can be worse than this? I cannot be charged with treason, I am the Queen of England, I *am* England. I cannot be divorced, I am the wife of the king. He has run mad this spring and he will recover by autumn. All I have to do is get through the summer.'

'The Boleyn summer,' I said, thinking of Anne.

'The Boleyn summer,' she repeated. 'It cannot last more than a season.'

She grasped the velvet upholstered prayer cushion of the prie dieu with her age-spotted hands and I knew that she could hear and see nothing in this world any more. She was close to her God. I went out quietly, closing the door behind me.

❁

George was in the shadows of the queen's public rooms, lurking like an assassin. 'Uncle wants you,' he said shortly.

'George, I cannot go. Make an excuse for me.'

'Come on.'

I stepped into the shaft of light streaming in through the open window and I blinked at the brightness. Outside I could hear someone singing and Anne's carefree ripple of laughter.

'Please George, tell him you couldn't find me.'

'He knows you were with the queen. I was ordered to wait until you came out. Whenever that was.'

I shook my head. 'I can't betray her.'

George crossed the room with three swift steps, got hold of me under my elbow and marched me towards the door. He went so fast I had to run to keep up with him and as he strode down the stairs I would have lost my footing but for his vice-like grip on my arm.

'What's your family?' he demanded through clenched teeth.

'Boleyn.'

'What's your kin?'

'Howards.'

'What's your home?'

'Hever and Rochford.'

'What's your kingdom?'

'England.'

'Who's your king?'

'Henry.'

'Then serve them. In that order. Did I say the Spanish queen once in that list?'

'No.'

'Remember it.'

I struggled against his determination. 'George!'

'Every day I give up my desires for this family,' he said in a savage undertone. 'Every day I dance attendance on one sister or the other and play pander to the king. Every day I deny my own desire, my own passion, I deny my own soul! I make my life a secret to myself. Now you come.'

He pushed me through the door of Uncle Howard's private room without knocking. My uncle was seated at his desk, the sunlight falling brightly on his papers, a posy of early roses before him on the table. He glanced up when I came in and his keen gaze took in my rapid breathing and the distress in my face.

'I need to know what passed between the king and the queen,' he said without preamble. 'A maid said you were in there with them.'

I nodded. 'I heard her cry and I went in.'

'She cried?' he demanded incredulously.

I nodded.

'Tell me.'

For a moment I was silent.

He looked at me once more and there was a world of power in his dark piercing gaze. 'You tell me,' he repeated.

'The king told her that he is seeking an annulment because the marriage is invalid.'

'And she?'

'She accused him of Anne, and he did not deny it.'

A flame of fierce joy leaped into my uncle's eyes. 'How did you leave her?'

'Praying,' I said.

My uncle rose from the desk and walked around to me. Thoughtfully, he took my hand and spoke quietly. 'You like to see your children in the summer, don't you, Mary?'

My longing for Hever, for little Catherine and for my baby boy, made me dizzy. I closed my eyes for a moment and I could see them, I could feel them in my arms. I could smell that sweet baby smell of clean hair and sun-warmed skin.

'If you serve us well in this I shall let you go to Hever for the whole summer while the court is on progress. You can spend all summer with your children and no-one will trouble you. Your work will be done, I will release you from court. But you must assist me in this, Mary. You must tell me exactly what you think the queen plans to do.'

I gave a little sigh. 'She said that she would write to her nephew. She said she knew a way to get a letter to him.'

He smiled. 'I expect you to find out how she sends letters to Spain and to come and tell me. Do that and you shall be with your children a week later.'

I swallowed my sense of treachery.

He went back to his desk and turned to his papers. 'You can go,' he said carelessly.

∾

The queen was at the table when I came into the room. 'Ah, Lady Carey, can you light another candle for me? I can hardly see to write.'

I lit another candlestick and put it close to her paper. I could see she was writing in Spanish.

'Would you send for Señor Felipez?' she asked me. 'I have an errand for him.'

I hesitated but she raised her head from the paper and gave me a little nod so I curtsied and went to the door where a manservant was on guard. 'Fetch Señor Felipez,' I said shortly.

In a moment he came. He was a yeoman of the ewery, a middle-aged man who had come over from Spain when Katherine was married. He had stayed in her household and despite marrying an Englishwoman and siring English children, he had never lost his Spanish accent nor his love of Spain.

I showed him into the room and the queen glanced at me. 'Leave us,' she said. I saw her fold the letter and seal it with her own sealing ring, the pomegranate of Spain.

I stepped outside the door and sat in a windowseat and waited like the spy I was until I saw him come out, tucking the letter into his jerkin, and then wearily I went to find Uncle Howard and tell him everything.

Señor Felipez left court next day and my uncle found me walking up the twisting path to the summit of Windsor Castle.

'You can go to Hever,' he said briefly. 'You've done your work.'

'Uncle?'

'We'll pick up Señor Felipez as he sets sail from Dover for France,' he said. 'Far enough from the court for no word of it to get back to the queen. We'll have her letter to her nephew and that will be her ruin. It'll be proof of treason. Wolsey's at Rome, the queen will have to agree to a divorce to save her own skin. The king will be free to remarry. This summer.'

I thought of the queen's belief that if she could only hold on till autumn, she would be safe.

'Betrothal this summer, public wedding and coronation when we all return to London in the autumn.'

I swallowed. The icy knowledge that my sister would be Queen of England and I would be the king's discarded whore froze me inside. 'And I?'

'You can go to Hever. When Anne is queen you can come back to court and serve as her lady in waiting, she'll need her family around her then. But for now your work is done.'

'Can I go today?' was all I asked.

'If you can find someone to take you.'

'Can I ask George?'

'Yes.'

I curtsied to him and turned to walk up the hill, my pace quicker.

'You did well with Felipez,' my uncle said as I hurried away. 'It's bought us the time that we needed. The queen thinks that help is on its way but she is all alone.'

'I am glad to serve the Howards,' I said shortly. It was better that no-one ever knew that I would have buried the Howards, every one of them, except George, in the great family vault and never thought that there was a loss.

George had been riding with the king and was not willing to get back into the saddle again. 'I have a thick head. I was drinking and gambling last night. And Francis is impossible . . .' He broke off. 'I won't set out for Hever today, Mary, I can't stand it.'

I took his hands in mine and made him look me in the face. I knew there were tears in my eyes and I did nothing to stop them flowing down my cheeks. 'George, please,' I said. 'What if Uncle changes his mind? Please help me. Please take me to my children. Please take me to Hever.'

'Oh, don't,' he said. 'Don't cry. You know I hate it. I'll take you. Of course I'll take you. Send someone down to the stables and tell them to saddle our horses and we'll start at once.'

Anne was in our room when I burst in to pack a few things in a bag and to see the chest corded up to send on after me in a wagon.

'Where are you going?'

'Hever. Uncle Howard says I can.'

'But what about me?' she demanded.

At the desperate tone in her voice I looked at her more closely. 'What about you? You have everything. What in God's name do you want more?'

She dropped to the stool before the little looking glass, rested her head on her hands and stared at herself. 'He's in love with me,' she said. 'He's mad for me. I spend all my time bringing him close and holding him off. When he dances with me I can feel his hardness like a codpiece. He's desperate to have me.'

'So?'

'I have to keep him like that, like a sauce pot on a charcoal burner. I have to keep him at the simmer. If he boils over what would become of me? I'd be scalded to death. If he cools off and goes and dips his wick somewhere else then I have a rival. That's why I need you here.'

'To dip his wick?' I repeated her crude image.

'Yes.'

'You'll have to manage without,' I said. 'You have only a few weeks. Uncle says that you'll be betrothed this summer and married this autumn. I've played my part, and I can go.'

She did not even ask me what part I had played. Anne always had a vision like a lantern with the shutters down. She only ever shone in one direction. It was always Anne and then the Boleyns and then the Howards. She would never have needed the catechism that George shouted at me to remind me of my loyalties. She always knew where her interests lay.

'I can do it for a few weeks more,' she said. 'And then I shall have it all.'

Summer 1527

After George left me at Hever I heard nothing from either him or Anne as the court made its progress through the English countryside in the sunny days of that perfect summer. I did not care. I had my children and my home to myself and no-one watched me to see if I looked pale or jealous. No-one whispered to another behind a shielding hand that I was in better or worse looks than my sister. I was free of the constant observation of the court, I was free of the constant struggle between the king and the queen. Best of all, I was free from my own constant jealous tally between Anne and myself.

My children were of an age where the whole day could fly by in a set of tiny activities. We fished in the moat with pieces of bacon on strings. We saddled up my hunter and each child took a turn in sitting on her for a walk. We went on expeditions across the castle drawbridge and into the garden to pick flowers or into the orchard for fruit. We ordered a cart lined with hay and I took the reins myself and drove us out of the park all the way to Edenbridge and drank small ale in the house there. I watched them kneel for Mass, their eyes round at the raising of the Host. I watched them as they fell asleep at the end of the day, their skin flushed with sunshine, their long eyelashes sweeping their plump cheeks. I forgot that there was such a thing as court and king and favourite.

Then, in August, I had a letter from Anne. It was brought to me by her most trusted groom, Tom Stevens, who had been born and bred in Tonbridge. 'From my mistress, to be given to your own hands,' he said reverently on his knee before me in the dining hall.

'Thank you, Tom.'

'And none but you has seen it,' he said.

'Very good.'

'And none but you will see it for I shall stand guard over you while you read it and then put it in the fire for you and we shall watch it burn, my lady.'

I smiled but I began to feel uneasy. 'Is my sister well?'

'As a young lamb in the meadow.'

I broke the seal and spread the papers.

> *Be glad for me for it is done and my fate is sealed. I have it. I am to be Queen of England. He asked me to marry him this very night and promised that he will be free within the month, when Wolsey is acting Pope. I had Uncle and Father join us at once, saying that I wanted to share my joy with my family, and so there are witnesses and he cannot withdraw. I have a ring from him which I am to keep hid for the meantime but it is a betrothal ring and he is sworn to be mine. I have done the impossible. I have caught the king and sealed the fate of the queen. I have overturned the order. Nothing will ever be the same for any woman in this country again.*

> *We are to be married as soon as Wolsey sends word that he has annulled their marriage. The queen will know of it on our wedding day, and not before. She is to go to a nunnery in Spain. I don't want her in my country.*

> *You can be happy for me and for our kin. I shall not forget that you helped me to this and you will find that you have a true friend and sister in Anne, Queen of England.*

I rested the letter on my lap and looked at the embers of the fire. Tom stepped forward.

'Shall I burn it now?'

'Let me read it once more,' I said.

He stepped back but I did not look at the excited scrawl of black ink again. I did not need to remind myself what she had written. Her triumph was in every line. The end of my life as the favourite of the English court was complete. Anne had won and I had lost and a new life would start for her, she would be, as she already signed herself: Anne, Queen of England. And I would be next to nothing.

'So, at last,' I whispered to myself.

I handed Tom the letter and watched him push it to the very centre of the red embers. It twisted in the heat and browned and then blackened. I could still read the words: *I have overturned the order. Nothing will ever be the same for any woman in this country again.*

I did not need to keep the letter to remember the tone. Anna triumphant. And she was right. Nothing would be the same for any woman in this country again. From this time onwards no wife, however obedient, however loving, would be safe. For everyone would know that if a wife such as Queen Katherine of England could be put aside for no reason, then any wife could be put aside.

The letter burst suddenly into bright yellow flame, I watched it burn to soft white ash. Tom put a poker into the fire and mashed it into dust.

'Thank you,' I said. 'If you go to the kitchen they will give you food.' I drew a silver coin from my pocket and gave it to him. He bowed and left me looking at the little specks of white ash floating on the smoke up the chimney and out to the night sky, which I could see through the great arch of brick and soot.

'Queen Anne,' I said, listening to the words. 'Queen Anne of England.'

I was watching over the children having their morning nap when I saw a horseman with grooms, from the high window. I hurried down, expecting George. But the horse that came clattering into the courtyard belonged to my husband, William. He smiled at my surprise.

'Don't blame me for being the harbinger of gloom.'

'Anne?' I asked.

He nodded. 'Outflanked.'

I led him into the great hall and seated him in my grandmother's chair nearest the fire.

'Now,' I said, when I checked that the door was shut and the room empty. 'Tell me.'

'You remember Francisco Felipez, the queen's servant?'

I nodded, admitting nothing.

'He requested safe conduct from Dover to Spain but it was a feint. He had a letter from the queen to her nephew and he tricked the king. He went by specially hired ship out of London that very morning and by sea to Spain. By the time they realised they'd lost him he'd gone. He's got the queen's letter to Charles of Spain; and all hell has broken loose.'

I found my heart was pounding. I put my hand to my throat as if I would still it. 'What sort of hell?'

'Wolsey's still in Europe but the Pope is forewarned and won't have him as deputy. None of the cardinals will support him and even the peace deal has fallen through. We're back at war with Spain. Henry's sent his secretary flying off to Orvieto, straight to the Pope's prison, to ask him to annul the marriage himself, and allow Henry to marry any woman he pleases, *even* one whose sister he has had, *even* one he has had. Either a whore herself or a whore's sister.'

I gasped. 'He's getting permission to marry a woman he's had? Dear God, not me?'

William's sharp laugh barked out. 'Anne. He's making provision for bedding her before marriage. The Boleyn girls don't come out of this very well, do they?'

I sat back in my chair and took a little breath. I did not want my husband to taunt me about unchastity. 'And so?'

'And so it all rests with the Holy Father who is reposing in the care of the queen's nephew at Orvieto Castle and very very unlikely, I would think – wouldn't you? – to issue a papal bull which legitimises the most unchaste behaviour one can think of: sleeping with a woman, sleeping with her sister, and marrying one of them. Least of all to a king whose legitimate wife is a woman of unsullied reputation, whose nephew holds the power in Europe.'

I gasped. 'So the queen has won?'

He nodded. 'Again.'

'How is Anne?'

'Enchanting,' he said. 'First up in the morning. Laughing and singing all day, delighting the eye, diverting the mind, up with the king to hear Mass, riding out with him all day, walking in the gardens with him, watching him play tennis, sitting beside him while the clerks read the letters to him, playing word games, reading philosophy with him and discussing it like a theologian, dancing all night, choreographing masques, planning entertainments, last to bed.'

'She is?' I asked.

'A perfect perfect mistress,' he said. 'She never stops. I should think she's dead on her feet.'

There was a silence. He drained his cup.

'So we are as we were,' I said disbelievingly. 'No further forward at all.'

He smiled his warm smile at me. 'No, I think you are worse than you were,' he said. 'For now you are out in the open and every huntsman knows the quarry. The Howards have broken cover. Everyone knows now that you are playing for the throne. Before, you all looked as if you were only after wealth and places, much like the rest of us, only a touch more predatory. Now we all know that you are aiming for the highest apple on the tree. Everyone will hate you.'

'Not me,' I said fervently. 'I'm staying here.'

He shook his head. 'You're coming to Norfolk with me.'

I froze. 'What d'you mean?'

'The king has no use for you, but I have. I married a girl and she is still my wife. You shall come with me to my home and we shall live together.'

'The children . . .'

'Will come with us. We shall live as I wish.' He paused. 'As *I* wish,' he repeated.

I got to my feet, I was suddenly afraid of him, this man whom I had married and bedded and never known. 'I still have powerful kin,' I warned him.

'You should be glad of it,' he said. 'For if you had not, I would have put you aside five years ago when you first crammed cuckold's horns on my head. This is not a good time for wives, madam, I think you and your family will find in the mess you have made you may all slip and tumble down.'

'I have done nothing but obey my family and my king.' My voice was steady, I did not want him to know that I was afraid.

'And now you will obey your husband,' he said, his voice all silk. 'How glad I am that you have such years of training.'

❧

> Anne –
> William says that us Boleyns are lost and he is taking me and
> the children to Norfolk. For pity's sake speak to the king for me,
> or to Uncle Howard or to Father, before I am taken away and
> cannot get back.
> M

I slipped down the little stone stairs that led into my father's study and from there out into the courtyard. I beckoned one of the Boleyn men and told him to ride with my note to the court which would be somewhere on the road between Beaulieu and Greenwich.

He tipped his hat to me and took the letter. 'Make sure it gets to Mistress Anne,' I said. 'It is important.'

We had dinner in the great hall. William was urbane as ever, the perfect courtier, keeping up a stream of news and gossip about the court. Grandmother Boleyn could not be comforted. She was resentful, but she did not dare openly to complain. Who could tell a man that he might not take his wife and children to his home?

As soon as they brought the candles in she heaved herself to her feet.

'I'm for my bed,' she said sulkily. William rose to his feet and bowed to her as she left the room.

Before he sat he reached inside his doublet and took out a letter. I recognised my writing at once. It was my letter to Anne. He tossed it down on the table before me.

'Not very loyal,' he remarked.

I picked it up. 'Not very polite to stop my servants and read my letters.'

He smiled at me. 'My servants and my letters,' he said. 'You are my wife. Everything that is yours is mine. Everything that is mine I keep. Including the children and the woman who carries my name.'

I sat opposite him and I put my hands flat on the table. I drew a breath to steady myself. I reminded myself that although I was a woman of only nineteen years, for four and a half of those years I had been the mistress of the King of England, and I had been born and bred a Howard.

'Now hear this, husband,' I said steadily. 'What is past, is past. You were happy enough to get your title and your lands and your wealth and the favour of the king, and we all know why those came to you. I have no shame in it, you have no shame in it. Anyone in our position would have been glad of it, and both you and I know that it is no sinecure earning and keeping the king's favour.'

William looked taken aback at my sudden frankness.

'The Howards will not fall over this mischance of Wolsey's. It is Wolsey's miscalculation, not ours. The game is far from over yet, and if you knew my Uncle Howard as well as I do you would be in no hurry to assume that he is defeated.'

William nodded.

'I am very sure that our enemies are at our heels, that the Seymours are ready to take our place at a moment's notice, that already some Seymour girl somewhere in England is being primed to take the king's eye. That's always true. There's always a rival. But right now, whether or not he is free to marry her, Anne's star is in the ascendancy, and all of us Howards – and you too, husband – serve our own interests best if we support her rise.'

'She looks like she is skating on melting ice,' he said abruptly. 'She is trying too hard. She is sweating to keep her place at his side, she never lets up for a moment. Anyone watching carefully could see it.'

'What does it matter who sees it, as long as he does not?'

William laughed. 'Because she can't keep it up. She is dancing him at her fingertip ends, she can't do that forever. She might have held him till the autumn but no woman can do it forever. No man can be held the way she will have to hold him. She could hold him for weeks; but now Wolsey has failed it might be months. It could be years.'

I was checked for a moment at the thought of Anne getting old while making merry. 'But what else can she do?'

'Nothing,' he said with a wolfish grin. 'But you and I can go to my house and start to live as a married couple. I want a son who looks like me, not a little blond Tudor. I want a daughter with my dark eyes. And you are going to give them to me.'

I bowed my head. 'I won't be reproached.'

He shrugged. 'You will bear whatever treatment I give you. You are my wife, are you not?'

'Yes.'

'Unless you too would like an annulment, since marriage seems to be out of fashion? You could be enclosed in a nunnery if you wish?'

'No.'

'Then go to my bed,' he said simply. 'I shall be up in a minute.'

I froze at that. I had not thought of it. He looked at me over the top of his cup of wine. 'What?'

'Can we wait till we get to Norfolk?'

'No,' he said.

I undressed slowly, wondering at my own reluctance. I had bedded with the king a dozen times when I felt no desire at all but merely followed his wishes and satisfied him. Every time in this last year when I knew that he desired Anne, I had forced myself to hold him and whisper 'sweetheart' and known myself to be a whore – and the man a fool not to know the false coin from the real.

So I was no thirteen-year-old virgin as I had been when I had first been put to bed with this man to consummate the marriage. But I was not yet a woman of such cynicism that I could prepare without dread for bed with a man who seemed half-enemy. William had a score to settle with me, and I was afraid of him.

He took his time. I climbed slowly into bed and feigned sleep when the door opened and he came in. I heard him moving around the room, stripping naked and getting into bed beside me. I felt the weight of the covers lift as he pulled them up around his bare shoulders.

'Not asleep then?'

'No,' I admitted.

In the darkness his hands came out for me and found my face, stroked my neck to my shoulders, and thence to my waist. I was wearing my linen shift but I could feel the coldness of his hands through the fine cloth. I heard his breathing come a little faster. He pulled me towards him and I yielded, and spread myself ready for him as I always did for Henry. For a moment I checked, thinking that I did not know what to do for any man but Henry.

'You're not willing?' he asked.

'Of course I am willing. I am your wife,' I said levelly.

I feared he might trap me into a refusal which would allow him to put me aside; but his little sigh of disappointment showed me that he was genuinely hoping for a warmer response. 'We'll sleep then.'

I was so relieved that I dared not say a word in case he changed his mind. I lay perfectly still until he turned his back on me, pulled the covers up over his shoulders, thumped his head down on the pillows and was quiet. Then, and only then, did I let my belly unknot and wiped the insincere Howard smile from my face. I let myself drift into sleep. I had survived another night, I was still at Hever, the Howards had everything to play for. Anything might happen tomorrow.

We were woken by a knocking on the door. I was up and out of bed before William could wake and catch my hand. I opened the door and said sharply: 'Hush. My lord is sleeping,' as if that were my only concern and not that I was determined to get out of his bed as quickly as possible.

'Urgent message from Mistress Anne,' the servant said and offered me a letter.

I dearly wanted to throw on a cloak and read it far away from William but he was awake and sitting up. 'Our dear sister,' he said with a mocking smile. 'And what does she say?'

I had no choice but to open the letter before him and hope to God that Anne was thinking of someone else for once in her selfish life.

> Sister,
> The king and I bid you and your husband come to meet us
> at Richmond where we will all be merry.
> Anne

William held out his hand for the letter. I handed it over.

'She guessed I was coming for you when I left court,' he observed. I said nothing. 'And so hip-hop, with one bound you are free of me,' he said bitterly. 'And we are back where we were.'

He had spoken my very thought but behind the hardness of his tone I saw his hurt. Cuckold's horns are not a comfortable headdress and he had been wearing them now for five years. Slowly I went to the bed. I put out my hand to him. 'I am your wedded wife,' I said gently. 'And I never forgot it, though our lives took us far apart. If we ever have to be married in very truth, William, you will find me a good wife to you.'

He looked up at me. 'Is this a Howard speaking who fears the turning of the tide and thinks that life as Lady Carey would be a safer bet than being the other Boleyn girl when the first Boleyn girl is ruined?'

His guess was so precise that I had to turn my head rather than risk him seeing the truth in my eyes. 'Oh, William,' I said reproachfully.

He drew me down to him and turned my face towards him with his finger under my chin. 'Dearest wife,' he said sarcastically.

I closed my eyes rather than meet his scrutiny and then, to my surprise, felt the warmth of his face and tender, gentle little kisses on my lips. I felt desire well up in me like a long-forgotten spring. I put my hands around his neck and pulled him a little closer.

'I made a bad beginning last night,' he said gently. 'So not now, and not here. But perhaps somewhere soon, don't you think, little wife?'

I smiled up at him, hiding my relief at not being taken to Norfolk. 'Somewhere soon,' I agreed. 'Whenever you wish, William.'

Autumn 1527

Anne at Richmond was queen in all but name. She had new apartments, which were adjacent to the king's, she had ladies in waiting, she had a dozen new gowns, she had jewels, she had a couple of hunters to ride out with the king, she sat with him when his counsellors discussed the matters of the country with him, she had her own chair at his side. Only in the great hall when the true queen came in to dinner was Anne demoted to a table on the floor of the hall while Katherine sat down to dinner in her majesty.

I was to sleep in Anne's apartments, partly to give her countenance so that no-one might think that the king's constant companionship meant that they were lovers, but in truth, to help her keep him at arm's length. He was desperate to have her, arguing that since they were betrothed they might bed. Anne played every trick she could summon. She protested her virginity and said that she would never forgive herself if she gave away her maidenhead before marriage, though God knew how much she desired him. She said that she would never forgive herself if she did not come before him on their wedding night a maid untouched – though God knew how much she desired him. She said that if he loved her as much as he said he did he would love the holy purity of her soul – though God knew la la la – and she said that she was afraid, that she both yearned for and shrank from him, that she needed time.

'How long can it take?' she snarled at George and me. 'For God's sake! For some damn clerk to ride to Rome, get a paper signed and ride back? How long can it take?'

We were tucked away in our bedroom at the back of her privy chamber, the only private place in the whole of the palace. Everywhere else we were on unending public show. Everyone watched Anne for the slightest clue that the king was losing interest, or that he had finally had her. She was scanned by a hundred eyes for any sign of either desertion or pregnancy. George and I felt like her bodyguard some days, on other days like today we felt like jailers. She was prowling up and down in the small space, swishing between bed and window, unable to stop moving, unable to stop muttering.

George caught her hands and brought her to a standstill. One glance over her head warned me to grab her from behind if she went into one of her rages.

'Anne, be calm. We have to go out and watch the boatmen race at any moment. You have to be calm.'

She quivered in his grip and then the anger went out of her and her shoulders slumped. 'I'm so tired,' she whispered.

'I know,' he said steadily. 'But this could go on for a long while yet, Anne. You're playing for the greatest prize in the world. You have to prepare yourself for a long game of skill.'

'If she would only die!' she suddenly flared up.

George's glance went at once to the solid wooden door. 'Hush. She might,' he said. 'Or Wolsey might have pulled it off. He could be sailing up the river right now, and you could be wed tomorrow and in the king's bed tomorrow night and pregnant the next morning. Be at peace, Anne. Everything rests on you keeping your looks.'

'And your temper,' I supplemented quietly.

'You dare advise me?'

'He won't stand for tantrums,' I warned her. 'He's spent all his married life with Katherine and she never raised so much as an eyebrow at him, let alone her voice. He'll let you go far because he's mad for you. But he won't stand for one of your scenes.'

She looked as if she might flare up again, but then she nodded as she acknowledged the sense of it. 'Yes, I know. That's why I need you two.'

We both stepped a little closer to her, George still grasping her hands, and I put my hands on her hips and held her tightly.

'I know,' George said. 'We're in this together. This is for all of us: Boleyns and Howards. We all rise or fall on this. We're all waiting and playing the long game. You have to lead the charge, Anne. But we're all behind you.'

She nodded and turned to the new large mirror mounted on the wall, reflecting the light from the gardens and the river outside. She pushed back her hood, she straightened the pearl necklace. She turned her head and looked sideways at her reflection and tried that mischievous, promising smile. 'I'm ready,' she said.

We made way for her as if she were queen already. As she went out of the door with her head held high George and I exchanged a swift look of players who have pushed the principal on stage, and we followed behind her.

My husband was on the royal barge to watch the boatmen race and he smiled at me and made a place beside him on the bench. George joined the young men of the court, Francis Weston among them. I glanced to see that Anne was seated beside the king. By the flighty turn of her head and her sideways glance at him I could see that she was in full control of herself and of him, once more.

'Walk with me in the gardens before dinner,' my husband said quietly in my ear.

At once I was alert. 'Why?'

He laughed at me. 'Oh, you Howards! Because I like your company, because I ask it of you. Because we are man and wife and we may live as man and wife any day now.'

I smiled ruefully. 'I don't forget it.'

'Perhaps you will learn to anticipate it with pleasure?'

'Perhaps,' I said sweetly.

He looked out over the river where the afternoon sun was sparkling on the water. The boats of the noblemen all manned by their liveried rowers were drawn up under the starter's orders. They made a colourful sight with the oars held high like trumpets, waiting for the command to start. They all looked towards the king, who took a scarlet silk kerchief and gave it to Anne. She stepped up to the edge of the royal barge and held it high over her head. For a moment she held the pose, well aware that all eyes were on her. From where I was sitting with William we could see her in profile, her head flung back, her hood well back from her face, her pale skin flushing with pleasure, her dark green gown tight around her breasts and slim waist. She was the very essence of desire. She dropped the red kerchief and the boats leaped forward under the thrust of the oars. She did not go back to her seat at the king's side, she had a moment where she forgot to play the queen. She leaned over the rail so that she could see as the Howard boat pulled ahead of the Seymours.

'Come on, Howards!' she suddenly shouted. 'Come on!'

As if they heard her call above all the other shouting from the riverbank the rowers quickened their stroke and the boat surged forward, paused, and surged forward again to a quicker tempo than the Seymours'. I was on my feet now, everybody was cheering, the royal barge dipped precariously as the whole court forgot its dignity and crowded onto one side and yelled for their favourite house. The king himself, laughing like a boy again with his arm around Anne's waist, was watching, careful not to shout for one lord or another, but clearly willing the Howards to win since that would delight the girl in his arms.

They went faster, the oars a blur of splashing water and light, and at the line they were unquestionably half a length before the Seymours. There was a great drum roll and a blast of trumpets to tell the Seymours that it was all over for them, that we had won the boat race, that we had won the race to be the first family in the kingdom, and that it was our girl in the arms of the king with her eye on the throne of England.

☙

Cardinal Wolsey came home, not in triumph with an annulment in his pocket, but in disgrace, and found that he could not even talk to Henry alone. The man who had managed every single thing from the amount of wine served at banquets to the terms of the peace with France and Spain found that he had to make his report before Anne and Henry, side by side, as if they were joint monarchs. The girl he had scolded for unchastity and for aiming too high sat at the right hand of the King of England and looked at him with narrowed eyes as if she were not very impressed with what he had to say.

The cardinal was too old and wily a courtier to let any surprise show on his face. He bowed very pleasantly to Anne and made his report. Anne smiled very equably and listened, leaned forward, whispered a little poison in Henry's ear, and listened some more.

❀

'Idiot!' she stormed in our little room. I was sitting on the bed, my feet drawn out of the way. She was on her track running from window to bedpost like one of the lions in the Tower, I thought idly that she would leave a mark on the polished floorboards and we could show it to those who like relics and signs. We could call it 'Anne's Martyrdom to Time'.

'He's a fool, and we have got nowhere!'

'What does he say?'

'That it is a serious matter to put aside the aunt of the man who holds the Pope and half of Europe in his grasp, and that, God willing, Charles of Spain will be defeated by Italy and France together when they go to war, and that England should promise support but not risk a man nor loose an arrow.'

'We wait?'

She threw her hands above her head and screamed. 'We wait? No! You can wait! The cardinal can wait! Henry can wait! But I have to dance on the spot, I have to be seen to make progress while actually making none.

I have to retain the illusion of things happening, I have to make Henry feel more and more intensely loved, I have to give him the belief that things are getting better and better because he is a king and all his life everyone has told him that he shall have the very best. He has been promised cream and gold and honey, I cannot give him "wait". How am I to keep going? How am I to do it?'

I wished that George was here. 'You'll manage,' I said. 'You'll go on as you have been going. You've done wonderfully well, Anne.'

She gritted her teeth. 'I will be old and exhausted before this is done.'

Gently I took her and turned her towards her grand Venetian glass mirror. 'Look,' I said.

Anne could always be comforted by the sight of her own beauty. She paused and took a breath.

'And you're brilliant as well,' I reminded her. 'He is always saying that you have the sharpest mind in the kingdom and if you were a man he would have you for cardinal.'

She smiled a little sharp feral smile. 'That must please Wolsey.'

I smiled back, my face next to hers in the mirror, the two of us, as ever, a contrast in looks, in colouring, in expression. 'I'm sure,' I said. 'But there's nothing Wolsey can do.'

'He doesn't even see the king without an appointment now,' she gloated. 'I've seen to that. They don't wander off together for their friendly little talks as they used to. Nothing is decided without me being there. He cannot come to the palace for a meeting with the king without notifying the king and notifying me. He is pushed out of power and I am inside it.'

'You've done wonderfully well,' I said, the words sickening me as they soothed her. 'And you have years and years ahead of you, Anne.'

Winter 1527

William and I slipped into a comfortable routine which was almost domestic, though it revolved around the wishes of the king and of Anne. I still slept in her bed at night and to all intents and purposes lived with her in the rooms that we shared. To the outer world we were both still the queen's ladies in waiting, no more and no less than the others.

But from morning to night Anne was with the king, as close to his side as a newly wed bride, as a chief counsellor, as a best friend. She would return to our chamber only to change her gown or lie on the bed and snatch a rest while he was at Mass, or when he wanted to ride out with his gentlemen. Then she would lie in silence, like one who has dropped dead of exhaustion. Her gaze would be blank on the canopy of the bed, her eyes wide open, seeing nothing. She would breathe slowly and steadily as if she were sick. She would not speak at all.

When she was in this state I learned to leave her alone. She had to find some way to rest from the unending public performance. She had to be unstoppably charming, not just to the king but to everyone who might glance in her direction. One moment of looking less than radiant and a rumour storm would swirl around the court and engulf her, and engulf us all with her.

When she rose up from her bed and went to the king, William and I would spend time together. We met almost as strangers and he courted me. It was the oddest, simplest and sweetest thing that an estranged husband has ever done for an errant wife. He sent me little posies of flowers, sometimes sprigs of holly leaves and the rose-pink berries of yew. He sent me a little gilt bracelet. He wrote me the prettiest poems praising my grey eyes and my fair hair and asking for my favour as if I were his lady love. When I sent for my horse to ride out with Anne I would find a note tucked into my stirrup leather. When I pulled back my sheets to get into bed with Anne at night I would find a sweetmeat wrapped in gilt paper. He showered me with little gifts and little notes and whenever we were together at a court banquet or at the archery butts, or watching the players on the tennis court, he would lean towards me and whisper out of the side of his mouth:

'Come to my room, wife.'

I would giggle as if I were his new mistress instead of a wife of many years' standing and I would step back from the crowd, and a few moments later he would slip away, to meet in the confined space of his bedchamber on the west wall of Greenwich Palace. Then he would take me in his arms and say delightfully, promisingly: 'We have only a moment, my love, only an hour at the most: so this shall be all for you.'

He would lie me on the bed, unlace my tight stomacher, caress my breasts, stroke my belly, and pleasure me in every way he could think of until I cried out in joy: 'Oh William! Oh my love! You are the best, you are the best, you are the very very best.'

And at that moment, with the smile of the well-praised man through all the ages, he would let himself pour into me and rest on my shoulder with a shuddering sigh.

For me it was desire, and only a small part calculation. If Anne should fall, and we Boleyns fall with her, then I would be very glad to have a husband who loved me and who had a handsome manor in Norfolk, a title and wealth. And besides, the children carried his name, and he could order them to his house at a moment's notice if he so pleased. I would have told the devil himself that he was the best, the very very best, if it kept me with my children.

❧

Anne was merry at the Christmas feast. She danced as if nothing would stop her from dancing all day and all night. She gambled as if she had a queen's fortune to lose. She had an understanding with me and with George; we immediately returned the money later, in private. But when she lost to the king her hard-earned money disappeared into the royal purse and was never seen again. And she had to lose to him whenever they played: he hated it when anyone else won.

He showered her with gifts and with honour, he led her out at every dance. She was the crowned queen in every masque. But still Katherine sat at the head table and smiled on Anne as if the honour was in her gift, as if Anne was her deputy, by her consent. And the Princess Mary, the little thin white-faced princess, sat beside her mother and smiled at Anne as if she were enormously amused at this light-footed pretender to the throne.

'God, I hate her,' Anne said, as she was getting undressed at night. 'She is the very image of them both, the moon-faced thing.'

I hesitated. There was no point in arguing with Anne. Princess Mary had grown to be a girl of rare prettiness, with a face so filled with character and determination that you could not doubt for a moment that she was her mother's daughter through and through. When she looked down the hall at Anne and at me it was as if she looked straight through us, as if we were nothing but clear panes of Venetian glass and all she wanted to know was what might be beyond. She did not seem to envy us, nor see us as rivals to her father's attention or even as a danger to her mother's place. She saw us as a pair of light women, so insubstantial that the wind might blow us away in a merciful puff.

She was a witty girl, only eleven years old but capable of making a pun or turning a jest in English, French, Spanish or Latin. Anne was quick and a scholar, but she had not had the teaching of this little princess and she envied her that too. And the girl had all of her mother's presence. Whether or not Anne ever became queen she had been born and bred to be a snapper-up of privilege and place. Princess Mary had been born to rights that we could only dream of. She had an assurance that neither of us could ever learn. She had a grace that came from absolute confidence in her position in the world. Of course Anne hated her.

'She's nothing,' I said comfortingly. 'Let me brush your hair.'

There was a quiet tap at the door and George slid into the room before we could call out 'Enter'.

'I'm in a terror of being seen by my wife,' he said by way of excuse. He waved a bottle of wine at us and three pewter cups. 'She's been dancing and she's hot tonight. She all but ordered me to our bed. If she saw me come in here she'd be wild.'

'She's bound to have seen you.' Anne took a glass of George's wine. 'She misses nothing, that woman.'

'She should have been a spy. She would have loved to have been a spy specialising in fornication.'

I giggled and let him pour me a measure of wine. 'Wouldn't take much skill to track you down,' I pointed out. 'You're always in here.'

'It's the only place I can be myself.'

'Not the whorehouse?' I asked.

He shook his head. 'I don't go any more, I've lost my taste for it.'

'Are you in love?' Anne asked cynically.

To my surprise he glanced away and flushed. 'Not I.'

'What is it, George?' I asked.

He shook his head. 'Something and nothing. Something I cannot tell you and nothing I dare to do.'

'Someone at court?' Anne demanded, intrigued.

He pulled up a stool before the fire and looked deep into the embers. 'If I tell you, then you must swear to tell no-one.'

We nodded, absolutely sisters in our determination to know everything.

'More than that, you won't even say anything to each other when I am gone. I don't want your comments behind my back.'

This time we hesitated. 'Swear to not even talk among ourselves?'

'Yes, or I say nothing.'

We hesitated, and then curiosity overcame us. 'All right,' said Anne, speaking for us both. 'We swear.'

His young handsome face crumpled and he buried his face into the rich sleeve of his jacket. 'I'm in love with a man,' he said simply.

'Francis Weston,' I said at once.

His silence told me that I had guessed right.

Anne's face was one of stunned horror. 'Does he know?'

He shook his head, still buried among the rich red velvet of his embroidered sleeve.

'Does anyone else know?'

Again his brown head shook.

'Then you must never give any hint of it, never tell anyone,' she ordered him. 'This must be the first and last time you speak of it to anyone, even to us. You must cut him out of your heart and mind and never even look at him again.'

He looked up at her. 'I know it's hopeless.'

But her advice was not for his benefit. 'You endanger me,' she said. 'The king'll never marry me if you bring shame to us.'

'Is that it?' he demanded, in sudden rage. 'Is that all that matters? Not that I am in love and tumbled like a fool into sin. Not that I can never be happy, married to a snake and in love with a heartbreaker, but only, *only*, that Mistress Anne Boleyn's reputation must be without blemish.'

At once she flew at him, her hands spread like claws, and he caught her wrists before she could rake his face. 'Look at me!' she hissed. 'Didn't I give up my only love, didn't I break my heart? Didn't you tell me then that it was worth the price?'

He held her away but she was unstoppable. 'Look at Mary! Didn't we take her from her husband and me from mine? And now you have to give up someone too. You have to lose the great love of your life, as I have lost mine, as Mary lost hers. Don't whimper to me about heartbreak, you murdered my love and we buried it together and now it is gone.'

George was struggling with her and I gripped her from behind, pulling her off him. Suddenly, the fight went out of her and the three of us stood still, like masquers forming a tableau, me, hugging her waist, him holding her wrists, her stretched hands still inches from his face.

'Good God, what a family we are,' he said wonderingly. 'Good God, what have we come to?'

'It's where we're going that matters,' she said harshly.

George met her gaze and nodded slowly, like a man taking an oath 'Yes,' he sighed. 'I won't forget.'

'You'll give up your love,' she stipulated. 'And never mention his name again.'

Again the defeated nod.

'And you'll remember that nothing matters more than this, my road to the throne.'

'I'll remember.'

I felt myself shudder, and I let go her waist. There was something in that whispered pledge that felt not like a pact with Anne but like a promise to the devil.

'Don't say it like that.'

They both looked at me, the matching brown dark eyes of the Boleyns, the long straight noses, that impertinent quirky little mouth.

'It's not worth life itself,' I said, trying to make light of it.

Neither of them smiled.

'It is,' Anne said simply.

Summer 1528

Anne danced, rode, sang, gambled, sailed on the river, went picnicking, walked in the gardens and played in the tableau as if she had no care in the world. She grew whiter and whiter. The shadows under her eyes went darker and darker and she started to use powder to hide the hollows under her eyes. I laced her more and more loosely as she lost weight, and then we had to pad her gown to make her breasts show plump as they used to.

She met my eyes in the mirror as I was lacing her and she looked every inch the older sister. She looked years older than me.

'I'm so tired,' she whispered. Even her lips were pale.

'I warned you,' I said without sympathy.

'You'd have done the same if you had the wit and the beauty to hold him.'

I leaned forward so that my face was close to hers and she could see the bloom on my cheeks and my eyes bright, and my colour high beside her own drawn fatigue. 'I don't have wit or beauty?' I repeated.

She turned to the bed. 'I'm going to rest,' she said ungraciously. 'You can go.'

I saw her into bed, and then I went out, running down the stone stairs to the gardens outside. It was a wonderful day, the sun was bright and warm and the light was sparkling on the river. The little boats plying across the river wove in and out of the bigger ships waiting for the tide to set sail for the sea. There was a light wind coming upriver and it brought the smell of salt and adventure into the well-kept garden. I saw my husband walking with a couple of men on the lower terrace and I waved at him.

At once, he excused himself and came towards me, resting one foot on the flight of steps and looking up at me.

'How now, Lady Carey? I see you are as beautiful as ever this day.'

'How are you, Sir William?'

'I am well. Where is Anne, and the king?'

'She's in her room. And the king is going out to ride.'

'So are you at liberty?'

'As a bird in the sky.'

He smiled at me, his secret knowing smile. 'May I have the pleasure of your company? Shall we take a little walk?'

I went down the steps towards him, enjoying the sensation of his eyes on me. 'Certainly.'

He drew my hand into the crook of his arm and we walked along the lower terrace, he matched his pace to mine and leaned towards me to whisper in my ear. 'You are the most delicious thing, my wife. Tell me we don't have to walk for too long.'

I kept my face forward but I could not help but giggle. 'Anyone who saw me come from the palace will know I have been in the garden for no more than half a moment.'

'Oh but if you are obeying your husband,' he pointed out persuasively. 'An admirable thing in a wife.'

'If you order me,' I suggested.

'I do,' he said firmly. 'I absolutely command you.'

I caressed the fur trim of his doublet with the back of my hand. 'Then what can I do but obey?'

'Excellent.' He turned and guided us in by one of the little garden doors and the moment it was shut behind us he took me in his arms and kissed me, and then led me up to his bedroom where we made love for all of the afternoon while Anne, the lucky Boleyn girl, the favoured Boleyn girl, lay sick with fear on her spinster bed.

❁

That evening there was an entertainment and a dance. Anne as usual had the leading part and I was one of the dancers. Anne was paler than ever, white-faced in a silver gown. She was such a ghost of her former beauty that even my mother noticed. She summoned me with a crook of her finger from where I was waiting to say my piece in the play and dance my dance.

'Is Anne ill?'

'No more than usual,' I said shortly.

'Tell her to rest. If she loses her looks she will lose everything.'

I nodded. 'She does rest, Mother,' I said carefully. 'She lies on her bed, but there is no resting from fear. I have to go and dance now.'

She nodded and let me go. I circled the hall and then made my entrance in the masque. I was a star descending from the western sky and blessing the earth with peace. It was some kind of reference to the war in Italy and I knew the Latin words but had not troubled myself with the meaning. I saw Anne grimace and knew that I had pronounced something wrong. I should have felt ashamed but my husband, William, winked at me and stifled a laugh. He knew that I should have been learning my lines when I had been in bed with him that afternoon.

The dance was completed and a handful of strange gentlemen entered the room wearing masks and dominoes and picked out their partners to dance. The queen was amazed. Who could they be? We were all amazed, and none more so than Anne who smiled when a thick-set man, taller than most of the rest, asked her to dance with him. They danced together till midnight and Anne laughed at her own surprise when at unveiling she discovered that it was the king. She was still as white as her gown at the end of the evening, not even the dancing had flushed her skin.

We went to our room together. She stumbled on the stair and when I put out a hand to steady her I felt her skin was cold and wet with sweat.

'Anne, are you sick?'

'Just tired,' she said faintly.

In our room when she washed the powder off her face I could see that her colour had drained to that of vellum. She was shivering, she did not want to wash or comb her hair. She tumbled into bed and her teeth chattered. I opened the door and sent a servant running for George. He came, pulling his cape over his nightshirt.

'Get a doctor,' I said. 'This is more than tiredness.'

He looked past me into the room where Anne was hunched up in bed, the covers piled around her shoulders, her skin as yellow as a little old lady, her teeth chattering with cold.

'My God, the sweat,' he said, naming the most terrifying illness after the plague itself.

'I think so,' I said grimly.

He looked at me with fear in his eyes. 'What will happen to us if she dies?'

❧

The sweat had come to court with a vengeance. Half a dozen people who had been dancing were in their chambers. One girl had already died, Anne's own maid was sick as a dog in the rooms which she shared with half a dozen others, and while I was waiting for the physician to send some medicines for Anne, I had a message from William telling me not to come near him, but to take a bath with spirit of aloes in the water, for he had the sweat and prayed to God that he had not given it to me.

I went along to his chamber and spoke to him from the doorway. He had the same yellowish tinge to his face as Anne, and he too was piled with blankets and still shivering with cold.

'Don't come in,' he ordered me. 'Don't come any closer.'

'Are you being cared for?' I asked.

'Yes, and I'll take a wagon to Norfolk,' he said. 'I want to be home.'

'Wait a few days and go when you are better.'

He looked at me from the bed, his face contorted with the pain of the illness. 'Ah, my silly child-wife,' he said. 'I can't afford to wait. Care for the children at Hever.'

'Of course I will,' I said, still not understanding him.

'D'you think we made another baby?' he asked.

'I don't know yet.'

William closed his eyes for a moment as if he were making a wish. 'Well, whatever happens is in the hands of God,' he said. 'But I should have liked to have made a true Carey on you.'

'There'll be plenty of time for that,' I said. 'When you are better.'

He gave me a little smile. 'I'll think of that, little wife,' he said tenderly, though his teeth still chattered. 'And if I am not at court for a while, do you take care of yourself and of our children.'

'Of course,' I said. 'But you will come back, as soon as you are better?'

'The moment I am well again I will come back,' he promised. 'You go to Hever and be with the children.'

'I don't know when they'll let me go.'

'Go today,' he advised. 'There'll be uproar when they know how many people have taken the sweat. It's very bad, my love. It's very bad in the City. Henry will be off like a hare, mark my words. No-one will look for you for a week, and you can be safe with the children in the country. Find George and get him to take you. Go now.'

I hesitated for a moment, tempted to do as he told me.

'Mary, if this was the last thing I told you to do I could not be more serious. Go to Hever and care for the children while the court is sick. It would be very bad if your babies were to lose both mother and father to the sweat.'

'But what d'you mean? You won't die?'

He managed a smile. 'Of course not. But I'll be happier in my mind on my journey to my home if I know you are safe. Find George and tell him that I commanded you to go, and him to escort you safely.'

I took half a step inside the room.

'Don't come any closer!' he snapped. 'Just go!'

His tone was rude, and I turned on my heel and went out of the room in something of a pet and closed the door behind me with a little slam, so that he should know that I was offended.

It was the last time that I ever saw him alive.

❀

George and I had been at Hever for little more than a week when Anne arrived travelling almost alone, in an open wagon. She was faint with exhaustion when she arrived and neither George nor I had the courage to nurse her ourselves. A wise woman from Edenbridge came in and took her to the tower room and sent for enormous portions of food and wine, some of which, we hoped, were actually eaten by Anne. The whole country was either sick or in a terror of sickness. Two maids left the castle to nurse their parents in nearby villages and both of them died. It was a most fearsome disease and George and I woke every morning in a sweat of terror and spent the rest of the day wondering if we too were destined to die.

The king, at the first signs of sickness, had left at once and gone to Hunsdon. That in itself was bad enough for the Boleyns. The court was in chaos, the country gripped by death. Worse for us: Queen Katherine was well, the Princess Mary was well, and the two of them, with the king, travelled together for the whole of the summer, as if they were the only ones blessed by heaven, untouched in a sea of sickness.

Anne fought for life, as she had fought for the king, a long dogged battle in which she brought all her determination to bear against almost impossible odds. Love letters came from the king, marked Hunsdon, Tittenhanger, Ampthill, recommending one cure or another, promising that he had not forgotten her and that he still loved her. But clearly, the divorce could not progress while there was no business being done at all, when even the cardinal himself was sick. It was half-forgotten and the queen was at the king's side and their engaging little princess was their best companion and greatest entertainment. Everything had somehow stopped for the summer and Anne's sense of the flying of time, and Anne's desperation, were nothing to a man whose greatest fear was illness, and who was miraculously blessed with good health amid a sea of misery.

By our good fortune, the Boleyn luck, the sweat did not come to Hever and the children and I were safe in the familiar green fields and meadows. I had a letter from William's mother which told me that he had reached his home, as he had wanted, before he had died. It was a short cold letter which at the end congratulated me on being a free woman again; as if she rather thought that my marriage vows had never constrained me very much in the past.

I read the letter in the garden, on my favourite seat, looking towards the moat and the stone walls of the castle. I thought of the man I had cuckolded and who, in the last few months, had become such a delightful lover and husband. I knew that I had never given him his due. He had been married to a child and left by a girl, and when I came back to him as a woman it was always with an element of calculation in my kiss.

Now I realised that his death had set me free. If I could escape another husband, I might buy a little manor farm on my family's lands in Kent or Essex. I might have land that I could call my own and crops that I could watch grow. I might at last become a woman in my own right instead of the mistress of one man, the wife of another, and the sister of a Boleyn. I might bring up my children under my own roof. Of course, I had to get some money from somewhere, I had to persuade some man, Howard, Boleyn, or king, to give me a pension so that I could raise my children and feed myself, but it might be possible for me to gain enough to be a modest widow living in the country on my own little farm.

'You cannot really want to be a nobody,' George exclaimed as I outlined this plan as we were walking together in the woods. The children were hiding behind trees and stalking us as we walked slowly ahead of them. We were to play the parts of a pair of deer. George was wearing a bunch of twigs in his hat to signify antlers. Now and then we could hear little Henry's irresistible chuckle of excitement as he crashingly approached, believing himself completely unseen and unheard. I could not help thinking of his father's enthusiasm for disguises and how he too always thought that people were baffled by the simplest stratagem. Now, I indulged my son and pretended that I did not hear his noisy dash from tree to tree nor see him run from shadow to bush.

'You have been the favourite of the court,' George protested. 'Why would you not want to make a grand marriage? Father or Uncle could get the pick of England for you. When Anne becomes queen then you could have a French prince.'

'It's still woman's work whether it's done in a great hall or in the kitchen,' I said bitterly. 'I know it well enough. It's earning no money for yourself and everything for your husband and master. It's obeying him as quickly and as well as if you were a groom of the servery. It's having to tolerate anything he chooses to do, and smile as he does it. I've served Queen Katherine in these last few years. I've seen how life has been for her. I wouldn't be a princess, not even for a princess's dowry. I wouldn't even be a queen. I have seen her shamed and humiliated and insulted, and all she could do was kneel on her prie dieu, pray for a little help, and get to her feet and smile at the woman who was triumphing over her. I don't think much of that, George.'

Catherine behind us made an excited little rush and caught at my gown. 'Caught you! I caught you!'

George turned and lifted her up, tossed her in the air and handed her to me. She was heavy now, a firm-bodied little four-year-old smelling of sunshine and leaves.

'Clever girl,' I said. 'You are a great hunter.'

'And what about her?' George asked. 'Would you deny her a great place in the world? She will be the Queen of England's niece. Think of that.'

I hesitated. 'If women could only have more,' I said longingly. 'If we could have more in our own right. Being a woman at court is like forever watching a pastrycook at work in the kitchen. All those good things, and you can have nothing.'

'What about Henry then?' he said, temptingly. 'Your Henry is the nephew of the King of England, known well enough as his son. If (God forbid) Anne does not have a son, then Henry could claim the throne of England, Mary. Your son is the son of a king, and he could be his heir.'

I did not glow at the thought. I looked fearfully into the wood where my staunch little boy was struggling to keep up with us and muttering to himself hunting songs of his own composing.

'Please God he is safe,' was all I said. 'Please God he is safe.'

Autumn 1528

Anne survived her illness and grew stronger in the clean air of Hever. When she came from her chamber I still would not sit with her, I was so afraid of taking the sickness to my children. She tried to be witty about my fears but there was an edge to her voice. She had felt betrayed by the king when he had fled the court, and she was mortally offended that he had spent the summer with Queen Katherine and with the Princess Mary.

She was determined to find him as soon as the cooler weather came, and the sweating sickness passed away. I was hoping that I might be overlooked in the rush to get Anne on the throne.

'You have to come back with me,' Anne said flatly.

We were at our favourite seat by the moat of the castle. Anne was seated on the stone bench, George sprawled on the grass before her. I was seated on the grass, leaning back against the bench, watching my children solemnly paddling their little feet in the water. It was shallow water at the bank, but I could not take my gaze off them.

'Mary!' Anne's voice was sharp.

'I heard you,' I said, not turning my head.

'Look at me!'

I glanced up at her.

'You have to come back with me, I can't manage without you.'

'I don't see why –'

'I do,' George said. 'She has to have a bedfellow that she can trust. When she closes her bedroom door behind her she has to know that no-one is going to prattle to the queen that she's crying, or tell Henry that she's furious. She's acting a part every day of her life, she needs a band of travelling players to be with. She has to have some people around her that she can know, that can know her. It can't be all masquerade.'

'Yes,' Anne said, surprised. 'That's just how it is. How did you know?'

'Because Francis Weston is a friend to me,' George said frankly. 'I need someone to whom I am not brother or son or husband.'

'Nor lover,' I prompted.

He shook his head. 'Just friend. But I know how Anne needs you, because I need him.'

'Well I need my children,' I said stubbornly. 'And Anne manages well enough without me.'

'I am asking you as my sister.' Something in her tone made me look at her a little more closely. This illness had knocked some of the arrogance out of her, she sounded for a moment like a woman who needed a sister's tenderness. Slowly, very slowly, in an unfamiliar gesture, Anne stretched out her hand to me.

'Mary . . . I can't do this on my own,' she whispered. 'It nearly killed me last time. I knew something would break inside me if I had to keep going. And now I have to go back to court and it will start all over again.'

'Can't you keep the king without such effort?'

She leaned back and closed her eyes. For a moment she did not look like the most determined, the most brilliant young woman in a brilliant court. She looked like an exhausted girl who has seen the depths of her own fear. 'No. The only way I know is always to be the best there is.'

I reached out and touched her hand and felt her fingers grip mine. 'I'll come and help.'

'Good,' she said quietly. 'I do need you, you know. Stay beside me, Mary.'

∾

Back at court, at Bridewell Palace, the game had changed again. The Pope, weary at last of the endless demands from England, was sending an Italian theologian, Cardinal Campeggio, to London to resolve finally and absolutely the matter of the king's marriage. Far from being threatened by this new development the queen seemed to welcome it. She was looking well. There was a glow on her skin from the summer sun and she had been happy in the company of her daughter. The king, shaken by his terror of infection, had been easy to entertain. Together they had discussed the cause of the illness which had swept the country, planned measures for prevention, and composed special prayers which they had ordered to be said in every church. Together they had worried about the health of the country which they had ruled for so long. Anne, though never far from the king's thoughts, lost some of her glamour when she was merely one of the many sick. Once again, the queen was his only constant and reliable friend in a dangerous world.

I could see the difference in her the moment we came into her apartment in the palace. She wore a new gown of dark red velvet which suited the warm colour of her skin. She did not look like a young woman – she would never be a young woman again; but she had a confident poise which Anne could never learn.

She welcomed Anne and me with a faint ironic smile. She inquired after my children, she asked after Anne's health. If she thought for a moment that the country would have been a better place if the sweat had carried off my sister, as it had taken so many others, there was no sign of that in her face.

In theory, we were still her ladies in waiting, though the presence chamber and the privy chamber which had been allocated to us were almost as large as the queen's own rooms. Her ladies flitted from her rooms to ours, to the king's presence chambers. The steady discipline of the court was breaking down, there was a sense now that almost anything could happen. The king and queen were on terms of quiet courtesy. The papal legate was on his way from Rome but taking an inordinate time over the journey. Anne was back at court indeed, but the king had spent a happy summer without her, it might be that his passion had cooled.

No-one dared to predict which way events might move and so there was a steady stream of people arriving to pay their respects to the queen and moving from her rooms to visit Anne. They crossed with another flow whose money was on the other horse. There was even talk that Henry would, in the end, come back to me and our growing nursery. I paid no attention until I heard my uncle had laughed with the king about his handsome boy at Hever.

I knew well enough, as did Anne, as did George, that my uncle never did anything by accident. Anne took George and me into her privy chamber and stood before us to accuse us.

'What's going on?' she demanded.

I shook my head but George looked shifty.

'George?'

'It's always true that your stars rise and fall in opposition,' he said awkwardly.

'What d'you mean?' she asked frostily.

'They had a meeting of the family.'

'Without me?'

George flung up his hands like a defeated fencer. 'I was summoned. I didn't speak. I didn't say a thing.'

Anne and I were on him at once. 'They met without us there? What are they saying? What do they want now?'

George put us both at arm's length. 'All right! All right! They don't

241

know which way to jump. They don't know which way to go. They didn't want Anne to know for fear of offending her. But now that you are so luckily widowed, Mary, and he lost interest in Anne this summer, they are wondering if he might not be brought round to you again.'

'He did not lose interest!' Anne swore. 'I won't be supplanted.' She rounded on me. 'You she-dog! This would be your plan!'

I shook my head. 'I've done nothing.'

'You came back to court!'

'You insisted on it. I've hardly looked at the king, I've hardly said two words to him.'

She turned from me and pitched face down on the bed as if she could not bear to look at either of us. 'But you've got his son,' she wailed.

'That's it really,' George said gently. 'Mary's got his son and now she's free to marry. The family think that the king might settle for her. And his dispensation applies to either of you. He can marry her if he wants.'

Anne rose up from the pillows, tearstained.

'I don't want him,' I said, exasperated.

'It doesn't matter, does it?' she said bitterly. 'If they tell you to go forward then you will go forward and take my chair.'

'As you took mine,' I reminded her.

She sat up. 'One Boleyn girl or the other.' Her smile was as bitter as if she had been biting on a lemon. 'We might either of us be Queen of England and yet we'll always be nothing to our family.'

Anne spent the next weeks entrancing the king all over again. She drew him away from the queen, away even from his daughter. Slowly the court came to realise that she had won him back. There was nobody but Anne.

I watched the seduction with the detachment of a widow. Henry gave Anne a London house of her own. Durham House on The Strand, her own apartments over the tiltyard at Greenwich Palace for the Christmas season. The king's council publicly ruled that the queen should not dress too finely nor go out to be seen by the people. It was apparent to everyone that it was only a matter of time before Cardinal Campeggio ruled for divorce, Henry could marry Anne, and I could go home to my children and make a new life.

I was still Anne's chief confidante and companion and one day in November she insisted that she and George and I walk by the flooded river at Greenwich Palace.

'You must be wondering what will become of you, now that you have no husband,' Anne started. She seated herself on a bench and looked up at me.

'I thought I would live with you while you need me, and then go back to Hever,' I said cautiously.

'I can ask the king to allow that,' she said. 'It is in my gift.'

'Thank you.'

'And I can ask him to provide for you,' she said. 'William left you almost nothing, you know.'

'I know,' I said.

'The king used to pay William a pension of one hundred pounds a year. I can have that pension transferred to you.'

'Thank you,' I repeated.

'The thing is,' Anne said lightly, turning her collar up against the cold wind, 'I thought I would adopt Henry.'

'You thought what?'

'I thought I would adopt little Henry as my own son.'

I was so astounded, I could only look at her. 'You don't even like him very much,' I said, the first foolish thought of a loving mother. 'You never even play with him. George has spent more time with him than you.'

Anne glanced away, as if seeking patience from the river and the jumbled roof tops of the City beyond. 'No. Of course. That's not why I would adopt him. I don't want him because I like him.'

Slowly, I started to think. 'So that you have a son, Henry's son. You have a son who is a Tudor by birth. If he marries you then in the same ceremony he gets a son.'

She nodded.

I turned and took a couple of steps, my riding boots crunching on the frozen gravel. I was thinking furiously. 'And of course, this way, you take my son away from me. So I am less desirable to Henry. In one move you make yourself the mother of the king's son and you take away my great claim to his attention.'

George cleared his throat, and leaned against the river wall, arms folded across his chest, his face a picture of detachment. I rounded on him. 'You knew?'

He shrugged. 'She told me after she'd done it. She did it as soon as we told her that the family thought that you might take the eye of the king again. She only told Father and Uncle after the king had agreed and the deed was done. Uncle thought it a keen bit of play.'

I found my throat dry and I swallowed. 'A keen bit of play?'

'And it means that you are provided for,' George said fairly. 'It puts your son close to the throne, it concentrates all the benefits on Anne, it's a good plan.'

'This is *my* son!' I could hardly say the words, I was choking on my grief. 'He is not for sale like some Christmas goose driven into market.'

George rose from the wall and put his arm around my shoulders, turned me to face him. 'No-one's selling him, we're making him all but a prince,' he said. 'We're claiming his rights for him. He could be the next King of England. You should be proud.'

I closed my eyes and felt the onshore wind on the cold skin of my face. I thought for a moment that I might faint or vomit, and more than anything else I longed for that, to be struck down so sick that they had to take me home to Hever and leave me there forever with my children.

'And Catherine? What about my daughter?'

'You can keep Catherine,' Anne said precisely. 'She's only a girl.'

'If I refuse?' I looked up into George's dark honest eyes. I trusted George, even though he had kept this from me.

He shook his head. 'You can't refuse. She's done it legally. Signed and sealed already. It's done.'

'George,' I whispered. 'This is my boy, my little boy. You know what my boy is to me.'

'You'll still see him,' George said consolingly. 'You'd be his aunt.'

It was like a physical blow. I staggered, and would have lost my footing but for George's arm. I turned to Anne who was sweetly silent, the smuggest of small smiles curving her lips. 'It's everything for you, isn't it?' I said, shaken by the depth of my hatred. 'You have to have everything, don't you? You have the King of England at your beck and call and you have to have my son too. You're like a cuckoo that eats all the other babes in the nest. How far do we all have to go for your ambition? You'll be the death of us all, Anne.'

She turned her head away from the hatred on my face. 'I have to be queen,' was all she said. 'And you all have to help me. Your son Henry can play his part in the advancement of this family and we will help him upwards, in return. You know that's how it is, Mary. Only a fool rails against the way the dice fall.'

'They're weighted dice when I play with you,' I said. 'I shan't forget this, Anne. On your deathbed I'll remind you that you took my son because you were afraid that you could not make one of your own.'

'I can make a son!' she said, stung. 'You did it! Why shouldn't I?'

I gave a little triumphant laugh. 'Because you're older every day,' I said spitefully. 'And so is the king. Who knows that you can make a child at all? I was so fertile with him that I had two children from him one after another, and one the most beautiful boy that God ever put on this earth. You'll never have a boy like my Henry, Anne. You know in your very bones that you'll never have a boy to match him. All you can do is steal my son because you know you'll never have your own.'

She was so white that she looked as if the sweat had come back to her. 'Stop it,' George said. 'Stop it, you two.'

'Never say that again,' she hissed at me. 'It's to curse me. And if I fall, then you go down too, Mary. And George, and all of us. Never dare to say that again or I'll have you sent to a nunnery and you'll never see either of your children again.'

She leaped up from her seat and swirled away in a ripple of fur-trimmed brocade. I watched her run up the path to the palace and thought what a dangerous enemy she was. She could run to Uncle Howard, she could run to the king. Anne had the ear of everyone who might command me. And if she wanted my son, if she wanted my life, she had only to tell either of them and it would be done.

George put his hand on mine. 'I'm sorry,' he said awkwardly. 'But at least this way your children stay at Hever and you can see them.'

'She takes everything,' I said. 'She has always taken everything. But I will never forgive her this.'

Spring 1529

Anne and I were in the hall of Blackfriars monastery, hidden by a curtain at the back. We could not stay away. Nobody who had the smallest pretext to be in court could bear to stay away. Nothing like it had ever happened in England before. It was the place they had chosen to hear the evidence for and against the marriage of the King and Queen of England, a most extraordinary hearing, a most extraordinary event.

The court was at Bridewell Palace – just next door to the monastery. The king and queen would sit down to dinner in the great hall of Bridewell every night, and every day they would go to the court at Blackfriars and hear if their marriage had ever been valid, in all its long loving twenty years' duration.

It was a dreadful day. The queen was dressed in one of her finest gowns, she had clearly decided to defy the council's command that she dress very plain. She was in her new red velvet gown with a petticoat of golden brocade. Her sleeves and the hem of the gown were trimmed with the rich black fur of sable. Her dark red hood framed her face and she did not look weary and sad, as she had done for the past two years; she looked fiery and animated, ready for battle.

When the king was asked to speak to the court he said that he had had doubts about the validity of the marriage from the very beginning and the queen interrupted him – as no-one else in the world would dare to do – and said, very reasonably, that he had left his doubts silent for a long time. The king raised his voice and continued to the end of his prepared speech, but he was rattled.

He said that he had over-ruled his own doubts because of the great love he felt for the queen, but he could not ignore his anxieties any more. I felt Anne beside me tremble like a horse held in from the hunt. 'Such nonsense!' she whispered passionately.

They called the queen to reply to the king's statement. The court crier called her name: once, twice, three times; but she ignored him completely though he stood beside her throne and shouted. She walked through the court, her head very high, and she went straight to Henry, seated on his throne. She kneeled before him. Anne craned around the curtain: 'What's she doing?' she demanded. 'She can't do that.'

I could hear the queen though we were right at the back of the court. Every word was perfectly clear though her accent was as strong as ever.

'Alas, sir,' she said gently, almost intimately. 'Where have I offended you? I take God and all the world to witness that I have been to you a true, humble and obedient wife. These twenty years and more I have been your true wife, and by me you have had many children though it pleased God to call them out of this world. And when you had me at the first I was a true maid, without touch of man –'

Henry shifted in his seat and looked to the head of the court, imploring them to interrupt her, but she never took her eyes from his face.

'If that is true or not I put to your conscience.'

'She can't do this!' Anne hissed disbelievingly. 'She has to call her lawyers to give evidence. She can't speak to the king in public.'

'She is, though,' I said.

There was complete silence in the hall, everyone was listening to the queen. Henry, pressed against the back of his throne, was pale with embarrassment. He looked like a fat spoiled child confronted by an angel. I found that I was smiling at the sight of her, I found I was grinning, though it was my family whose cause was sinking with every word she spoke. I was near to delighted laughter because Katherine of Aragon was speaking out for the women of the country, for the good wives who should not be put aside just because their husbands had taken a fancy to another, for the women who walked the hard road between kitchen, bedroom, church and childbirth. For the women who deserved more than their husband's whim.

Katherine referred her cause to God and the law, and there was uproar when she finished speaking. The cardinals hammered for order, the clerks shouted, and the excitement spread to the people outside the hall and in the streets outside the barred gates of the monastery who repeated her words one to another and then shouted in a great clamour of support for Katherine, the true Queen of England.

And Anne, at my side, burst into tears, laughing and crying at the same time. 'She will be my death or I will be hers!' she swore. 'I will see her dead, please God, before she is the end of me.'

Summer 1529

It should have been Anne's summer of triumph. Cardinal Campeggio's court to hear the matter of the marriage was finally in session, its decision a certainty however persuasive the queen might be. Cardinal Wolsey was Anne's declared friend and chief supporter, the King of England was as much in love as ever, and the queen, after her one triumphant moment, had stepped back, even failing to appear in the court again.

But there was no joy for Anne. When she heard that I was packing to go to Hever to spend the summer with my children she came into the room as if all the fiends in hell were biting at her heels.

'You can't leave me while the cardinals' court is still sitting, I have to have you beside me.'

'Anne, I do nothing. I don't understand half of it and the rest of it I don't want to hear. All this stuff about what Prince Arthur said the morning after their wedding night, and all this servants' gossip from a lifetime ago. I don't want to hear it, it makes no sense to me.'

'You think I want to hear it?' she demanded.

I should have been warned by the wildness in her voice. 'You must do, for you're always in court,' I said reasonably. 'But they'll be finished soon, won't they? They'll say that the queen was married to Prince Arthur, the marriage consummated, and the marriage between her and Henry invalid. Then it's done. What d'you need me here for?'

'Because I'm afraid!' she suddenly burst out. 'I'm afraid! I'm afraid all the time. You can't leave me here alone, Mary. I need you here.'

'Now, Anne,' I said persuasively. 'What is there to fear? The court is not hearing the truth nor looking for it. It is under the command of Wolsey who is the king's man through and through. It is under the command of Campeggio, who has orders from the Pope to see this business to the finish. Your path is straight before you. If you don't want to be here at Bridewell Palace, then go to your new house in London. If you don't want to sleep alone then you have six ladies in waiting. If you are fearful of the king and some new girl at court, then order him to send her away. He does everything that you want. Everyone does everything that you want.'

'You don't!' Her voice was sharp and resentful.

'I don't have to, I'm only the other Boleyn girl. No money, no husband, no future unless you say so. No children unless I am allowed to see them. No son . . .' My voice quavered for a moment. 'But I am allowed to go to see them, and I am going to go, Anne. You can't stop me. No power in the world can stop me.'

'The king can stop you,' she warned me.

I turned to face her and my voice was like iron. 'Hear this, Anne. If you tell him to ban me from my children, I will hang myself with your gold girdle in your new palace of Durham House and you will be accursed forever. There are some things which are too great for even you to play with. You cannot stop me seeing my children this summer.'

'*My* son,' she stressed.

I had to swallow back my rage, I had to hold back my desire to push her out of the damned window and let her break her selfish neck on the stone flags of the terrace below. I took a breath and then I had myself under control. 'I know it,' I said steadily. 'And now I am going to him.'

❧

I went to say goodbye to the queen. She was alone in her silent rooms, stitching at the huge altar cloth. I hesitated in the doorway. 'Your Majesty, I am come to bid you farewell, I am going to my children for the summer.'

She looked up. We were both aware that I no longer needed to ask for her permission to be absent from court.

'You are fortunate to see so much of them,' she said.

'Yes.' I knew she was thinking of the Princess Mary, who had been kept from her since last Christmas.

'But your sister has taken your son,' she remarked.

I nodded. I did not trust myself to speak.

'Mistress Anne plays a strong hand. She wants my husband and your son as well. She wants a full suit.'

I did not dare even look up, I feared that she would see the deep resentment in my eyes.

'I shall be glad to go away this summer,' I said quietly. 'It is good of Your Majesty to spare me.'

Queen Katherine showed me a small flash of a smile. 'I am so well served,' she said ironically. 'I shall hardly miss you in the crowds that gather around me.'

I stood awkwardly, not knowing what to say in the silent rooms which I had once known so happy and so busy. 'I hope to serve Your Majesty again when I come back to court in September,' I said carefully.

She put her needle to one side and looked at me. 'Of course you will serve me. I shall be here. There is no doubt of that.'

'No,' I agreed, traitorous to my fingertips.

'You have never been anything other than courteous and a good servant to me,' she said. 'Even when you were young and very foolish you were a good girl, Mary.'

I felt myself swallow my guilt. 'I wish I had been able to do more,' I said, very low. 'And there were times when I was sorry that I had to serve others, and not Your Majesty.'

'Oh, you mean Felipez,' she said easily. 'Dear Mary, I knew you would tell your uncle or your father, or the king. I made sure that you saw the note and knew who was to be the messenger. I wanted them to watch the wrong port. I wanted them to think they had caught him. He got the message to my nephew. I chose you as my Judas. I knew you would betray me.'

I flushed a deep mortified scarlet. 'I cannot ask you to forgive me,' I whispered.

The queen shrugged. 'Half of the ladies in waiting report to the cardinal or to the king or to your sister every day,' she said. 'I have learned to trust no-one. For the rest of my life I will know that I can trust no-one. I shall die a woman who has been disappointed in my friends. But I am not disappointed in my husband. He is ill advised at the moment, he is dazzled at the moment. But he will come to his senses. He knows that I am his wife. He knows that he can have no other wife but me. He will come back to me.'

I rose up. 'Your Majesty, I am afraid that he never will. He has given his word to my sister.'

'It is not his to give away,' she said simply. 'He is a married man. He cannot promise anything to another woman. His word is my word. He is married to me.'

There was nothing more I could say. 'God bless Your Majesty.'

She smiled a little sadly, as if she knew as well as I did that this was goodbye. She would not be at court when I returned. She raised her hand in blessing over my head as I curtsied to her. 'God grant you a long life and much joy of your children,' she said.

Hever was warm in the sunshine and Catherine had learned to write all of our names, to spell out her little book, and to sing a song in French. Henry, determinedly ignorant, would not even rid himself of the little lisp which made him say 'w' for 'r'. I should have corrected him more severely but I found him too enchanting. He called himself 'Henwy' and he called me his 'deawest' and it would have been a mother with a heart of stone who could have told him he was speaking wrongly. Nor did I tell him that I was his mother only by grace; in law he was Anne's son. I could not bring myself to tell him that he had been stolen from me and I had been forced to let him go.

George stayed with us in the country for two weeks, as relieved as I was to be away from the court which was waiting, like the hounds in a ring around a wounded doe, for the moment that the queen could be dragged down. Neither of us wanted to be there the moment that the cardinals' court ruled against the innocent queen and sent her in disgrace from the country that she had called her home. And then George received a letter from our father.

> *George,*
> *It has gone awry. Campeggio announced today that he can take no decision without the Pope. The court is adjourned, Henry is black with rage and your sister beside herself.*
> *We are all to leave on progress at once and the queen is to be left behind in disgrace.*
> *You and Mary must come and be with Anne, no-one but you can manage her temper.*
> *Boleyn.*

'I shan't go,' I said simply.

We were sitting together in the great hall after dinner. Grandmother Boleyn had gone to bed, the children were fast asleep in their own little beds after a day of running and hiding and playing catch.

'I'll have to,' George said.

'They said I could spend the summer with my children. They promised me that.'

'If Anne needs you –'

'Anne always needs me, she always needs you. She always needs all of us. She is trying to do something impossible – push a good woman out of marriage, push a queen off her throne. Of course she needs an army. You always need an army for a treasonous insurrection.'

George glanced to see that the doors to the hall were shut. 'Careful.'

I shrugged. 'This is Hever. This is why I come to Hever. So that I can speak. Tell them that I was sick. Tell them I might have the sweat. Tell them I said I would come as soon as I am well again.'

'This is our future.'

I shrugged my shoulders. 'We've lost. Everyone knows it but us. Katherine will keep the king, as in very justice she should. Anne will become his mistress. We'll never make it to the throne of England. Not in this generation. You'll have to hope that Jane Parker gives you a pretty girl. And you can throw her into that den of wolves and see who snaps her up.'

He laughed shortly at that. 'I'll leave tomorrow. We cannot all surrender.'

'We've lost,' I said flatly. 'No shame in surrender when you are completely and utterly defeated.'

> *Dear Mary,*
>
> *George tells me that you do not come to court because you think my cause is lost. Be very careful to whom you say this. Cardinal Wolsey will lose his house, his lands and his fortune, he will be displaced from the Lord Chancellorship, he will be a ruined man because he failed in my business. So do not you forget that you too are to work at my business, and I will not tolerate a servant with half a heart.*
>
> *I have the king under my thumb and dancing to my bidding. I am not going to be defeated by two old men and their lack of courage. You speak too soon when you speak of my defeat. I have staked my life on becoming Queen of England. I have said that I shall do it, and I will do it.*
>
> *Anne*
>
> *Come to Greenwich in the autumn without fail.*

Autumn 1529

Everything that Anne had threatened against Wolsey came true, and it was our Uncle Howard with the Duke of Suffolk, the king's dear friend and brother-in-law, who had the pleasure of taking the Great Seal of England off the disgraced cardinal. They would have the pickings of his enormous fortune too.

'I said I would bring him down,' Anne remarked smugly to me. We were reading in the windowseat of her presence chamber of her new London house: Durham House. By standing at the window and craning her head Anne could just see York Place where the cardinal had once reigned supreme and where she had courted Henry Percy.

There was a tap at the door. Anne looked at me to answer for her. 'Come in!' I called.

It was one of the king's pages, a handsome young man of about twenty. I smiled at him, his eyes danced at the attention. 'Sir Harold?' I asked politely.

'The king begs his sweet mistress to accept this gift,' the youth said and dropped to one knee before Anne, holding out a small box.

She took it from him and opened it. She gave a little satisfied purr at the contents.

'What?' I asked, unable to restrain my curiosity.

'Pearls,' she said shortly. She turned to the page. 'Tell the king that I am honoured by his gift,' she said. 'And that I will wear them at dinner tonight to thank him myself. Tell him,' she smiled as if at some private joke, 'that he will find he has a kind mistress and not a cruel one.'

The young man nodded solemnly, got to his feet, made a deep bow to Anne and a flirtatious bob to me, and took himself out of the room. Anne closed the box and tossed it across to me. I looked at the pearls, they were magnificent, set on a chain of gold.

'What did your message mean?' I asked. 'That you will be kind and not cruel?'

'I can't give myself to him,' she said, as prompt as any huckster who knows the value to a penny. 'But we had words this morning because he wanted to take me into his privy chamber after Mass and I would not go.'

'What did you say?'

'I lost my temper,' she confessed. 'I swore that he wanted to treat me as a whore and dishonour me and dishonour himself and destroy any chance we had of a proper decision from Rome. If anyone thinks that I am his whore then I will never supplant Katherine. I'd be no better than you.'

'You lost your temper?' I asked, going at once to the worst part of this. 'What did he do?'

'Fell back,' Anne said ruefully. 'Shot out of the room like a cat scalded by a falling pan. But see what comes of it? He cannot bear me to be displeased with him. I have him dancing like a boy for me.'

'At the moment,' I said warningly.

'Oh, tonight I shall be kind as I promised. I shall dress and sing and dance only for him.'

'And after dinner?'

'I let him touch me,' she said unwillingly. 'I let him stroke my breasts and I let him put his hand up my skirt. But I never take off my gown for him. I really don't dare.'

'D'you pleasure him?'

'Yes,' she said. 'He insists on it and I can't see how to avoid it. But sometimes – ' She rose from the windowseat and paced to the centre of the room. 'When he has stripped off his hose he pushes it into my hand and I hate him for it. It feels like an insult to me, to use me like this and then . . .' She broke off, speechless with temper. 'Then he reaches his pleasure and he spouts like a stupid whale, such a mess and wetness and I think . . .' She slammed her fist into her palm. 'I think God, oh God – I need a baby and there is all this going to waste! Going to waste in my hand when it should be in my belly! For God's sake! Apart from it being a sin, it's such madness!'

'There's always more,' I said practically.

The look she turned on me was haunted. 'There's not always more of me,' she said. 'He's mad to touch me now but he's been waiting three years. What if we have to wait another three years? How am I to keep my looks? How am I to stay fertile? He might well be lusty till he is sixty, but what about me?'

'Does he not think badly of you?' I asked. 'These are whore's tricks you are playing with him.'

Anne shook her head. 'I have to do something to keep him hot for my touch. I have to keep him coming forward and hold him off, all at the same time.'

'There are other things you can do,' I volunteered.

'Tell me.'

'You can let him watch you.'

'Let him watch me do what?'

'Let him watch you while you touch yourself. He loves that. It makes him almost weep with lust.'

She looked intensely uncomfortable. 'For shame.'

I laughed shortly. 'You let him watch you undress, one thing then another, very slowly. Last of all you lift your shift and put your fingers to your cunny and open it up to show him.'

She shook her head. 'I couldn't do it . . .'

'And you can take him in your mouth.' I hid my amusement at her shrinking.

'What?' She looked at me with unveiled disgust.

'You can kneel before him and take it in your mouth. He loves that too.'

'You've done that with him?' she demanded, her nose wrinkled.

I looked her straight in the eye. 'I was his whore,' I said. 'And our brother has his stewardships and our father is a wealthy man because of it. When he lay on his back I would lie on him and kiss him down from his mouth to his parts and then lick his parts like a cat lapping at milk. Then I would take him in my mouth and suck on it.'

Anne's face was a picture of curiosity and revulsion. 'And did he like that?'

'Yes,' I said, brutally frank. 'He adored it; it gave him as great a pleasure as anything else. And you can look as if you cannot bear the thought of it, you can set yourself up as high as you like; but if you have to hold him with whore's tricks then you had better learn some new whore's tricks and do them well.'

For a moment I thought that she would flare up, but she went quiet and nodded her head.

'I'm sure that the queen never did such a thing,' she said with deep resentment.

'No,' I said, exercising my constant resentment for a brief moment. 'But she was his beloved wife that he married for love; and you and I are just whores.'

The tricks Anne learned to play with the king soothed his temper, but made her more irritable than ever. I opened the door to her chamber one day and I heard her voice raised in a breaking storm.

Henry was facing the door as I came in, and the look that he shot me was almost pleading. I stared aghast as Anne railed at him. She had her back to me, she did not even hear the door click, she was in such a rage as to be blind and deaf except to her own loud words.

'And then to find that she, *she*! is still sewing your shirts, and she mocks me with this, she took them out in front of me and asked me to thread her needle. Asked me before all the ladies to thread the needle as if I were some serving woman.'

'I never asked her . . .'

'Oh? What happens? Does she go to your rooms and steal your shirts away in the night? Does the groom of the bedchamber filch them and pass them on to her? Do you sleepwalk and carry them to her by accident?'

'Anne, she is my wife. She has sewed my shirts for twenty years. I had no idea that you would object. But I will tell her that I don't want her to do them any more.'

'You had no idea that I would object? Why don't you go back to her bed and see if I object to that! I sew as well as she does, a good deal better actually, since I am not so old and short-sighted that someone else has to thread my needle for me. But you do not bring your shirts to me. You snub me . . .' Her voice quavered. 'Before the whole court you snub me by taking your shirts to her.' She grew stronger with indignation. 'You might as well say to the world: this is my wife and the woman I trust, and this is my mistress who is for the night and for play.'

'Before God . . .' the king started.

'Before God . . . you have hurt me with this, Henry!'

At the quaver in her voice he was quite unmanned. He opened his arms to her but she shook her head. 'No, no, I won't run to you and have you kiss my tears away and make me tell you that it doesn't matter. It does matter, it matters more than anything.'

She put her hand to her eyes and walked past him, she opened the door to her privy chamber and went in without even glancing at him. In the silence that followed we heard her close the door and turn the key in the lock.

The king and I looked at each other.

He looked stunned. 'Before God, I never meant to hurt her.'

'About some shirts?'

'The queen still sews my shirts for me. Anne didn't know. She has taken it badly.'

'Oh,' I said.

Henry shook his head. 'I shall tell the queen she shall no longer sew them for me.'

'I think that would be wise,' I said gently.

'And when she comes out, will you tell her that I was much grieved to have caused her so much pain? And tell her that the offence will never be repeated?'

'Yes,' I said. 'I'll tell her.'

'I shall send for a goldsmith and have him make her something pretty,' he said, warming to the thought. 'And when she is happy again she will forget that this quarrel ever took place.'

'She will be happy by the time she has rested,' I said hopefully. 'Of course it's hard for her, waiting to be married to you. She loves you so very much.'

For a moment he looked like the boy who had been in love with Katherine. 'Yes, that's why she calls up such a storm. Because she loves me so much.'

'Of course,' I reassured him. The last thing I wanted was for Henry to see how disproportionate Anne's anger was to the facts.

He looked tender again. 'I know. I have to be patient with her. And she's very young, and she knows almost nothing of the world.'

I kept my mouth shut, thinking of the young girl I had been when my family had handed me over to him, and how I had never been allowed a whispered protest, let alone a temper tantrum.

'I'll get her some rubies,' he said. 'A virtuous woman, rubies, you know.'

'She'll like that,' I said with certainty.

❁

Henry gave her rubies, and she rewarded him with more than a smile. She came back to her room very late one night with her gown all dishevelled and her hood in her hand. I had been asleep in bed, I never waited up for her as she used to do for me. She pulled the covers off me to make me wake up and unlace her.

'I did what you said and he adored it,' she said. 'And I let him play in my hair and with my breasts.'

'So you are friends again,' I said. I unlaced her stomacher and pulled the petticoat over her head.

'And Father is to become an earl,' Anne said with quiet satisfaction. 'Earl of Wiltshire and Ormonde. I am to be Lady Anne Rochford and George will be Lord Rochford. Father is to go back to Europe to make the peace, and Lord George our brother is to go with him. Lord George our brother is to become one of the king's most favoured ambassadors.'

I gasped at this tumble of favours. 'An earldom for Father?'

'Yes.'

'And George will be Lord Rochford! How grand for him, he'll love it! And an ambassador!'

'As he has always wanted.'

'And me?' I asked. 'What is there for me?'

Anne fell into bed and let me pull her shoes off her feet and peel down her stockings. 'You stay as the widow Lady Carey,' she said. 'Just the other Boleyn girl. I can't do everything, you know.'

Christmas 1529

The court was to meet at Greenwich, and the queen was to be present. She was to receive every honour and Anne was not to be seen.

'What now?' I asked George. I sat on his bed while he lounged in the windowseat. His man was packing his trunks for his trip to Rome, and every now and then George would look up and shout at his impassive servant: 'Not the blue cape, it has the moth.' Or: 'I hate that hat, give it to Mary for young Henry.'

'What now?' He repeated my question.

'I've been summoned to the queen's apartments and I am to live in my old room in her wing of the palace. Anne is to be in her rooms at the tiltyard all on her own. I think Mother is to stay with her, but I, and all the ladies in waiting, are to wait on the queen, not on Anne.'

'It can't be a bad sign,' George said. 'He's expecting a lot of people out of the City to watch them dine over the days of Christmas. The last thing he can afford are the merchants and the city traders saying that he is incontinent. He wants everyone to think that he has chosen Anne for the benefit of England, not for lust.'

I glanced a little nervously at the servant.

'Joss is all right,' George said. 'Rather deaf, thank God. Aren't you, Joss?' The man did not turn his head.

'Oh well, leave us,' George said. Still the man went on, stolidly packing.

'All the same you should take care,' I said.

George raised his voice. 'Leave us, Joss. You can finish later.'

The man started, looked round, bowed to George and to me, and went out.

George left the windowseat and sprawled on the bed at my side. I pulled his head down so that it rested in my lap and made myself comfortable against the headboard.

'D'you think it will ever happen?' I asked idly. 'It feels as if we have been planning this wedding for a hundred years.'

He had closed his dark eyes but now he opened them and looked up at me. 'God knows,' he said. 'God knows what it will have cost when it does come: the happiness of a queen, the safety of the throne, the respect of the people, the sanctity of the church. Sometimes it seems to me as if you and I have spent our lives working for Anne, and I don't even know what we have gained from it.'

'And you an heir to an earldom? To two earldoms?'

'I wanted to go on crusade and murder unbelievers,' he said. 'I wanted to come home to a beautiful woman in a castle who would worship me for my courage.'

'And I wanted a hop field and an apple orchard and a sheep run,' I said.

'Fools,' George said, and closed his eyes.

He was asleep in a few minutes. I held him gently, watching his chest rise and fall, and then I leaned my head back against the brocade covering the headboard and closed my eyes and drifted into sleep myself.

Still in my dream I heard the door opening and I lazily opened my eyes. It was not George's servant returning, it was not Anne coming to look for us. It was a stealthy turning of the handle and a sly opening of the door and then Jane, George's wife, now Lady Jane Rochford, put her head into the room and looked around for us.

She did not jump when she saw us on the bed together, and I – still half-asleep and frozen into stillness with a sort of fear at her furtiveness – did not move either. I kept my eyelids half-closed and I watched her through my eyelashes.

She kept very still, she did not enter nor leave, but she took in every inch of us: George's head turned into my lap, the spread of my legs under my gown. My head tipped back, my hood tossed on the windowseat, my hair tumbled about my sleeping face. She took us in as if she were studying us to paint a miniature, as if she were collating evidence. Then, as silently as she had come, she slid out again.

At once I shook George and put my hand over his mouth as he woke.

'Sssh. Jane was here. She may still be outside the door.'

'Jane?'

'For God's sake, Jane! Your wife, Jane!'

'What did she want?'

'She said nothing. She just came in and looked at us, asleep together on the bed, she looked all around and then she crept away.'

'She didn't want to wake me.'

'Perhaps,' I said uncertainly.

'What's the matter?'

'She looked – odd.'

'She always looks odd,' he said carelessly. 'On the scent.'

'Yes, exactly,' I said. 'But when she looked at us I felt quite . . .' I broke off, I could not find the words. 'I felt quite dirty,' I said eventually. 'As if we were doing something wrong. As if we were . . .'

'What?'

'Too close.'

'We're brother and sister,' George exclaimed. 'Of course we're close.'

'We were on the bed asleep together.'

'Of course we were asleep!' he exclaimed. 'What else should we be doing together on the bed? Making love?'

I giggled. 'She makes me feel like I shouldn't even be in your room.'

'Well, you should,' he said stoutly. 'Where else can we talk without half the court as well as her prowling round and listening? She's just jealous. She'd give a king's ransom to be on the bed with me in the afternoon, and I'd as soon put my head into a mantrap as into her lap.'

I smiled. 'You don't think she matters at all?'

'Not at all,' he said lazily. 'She's my wife. I can manage her. And the way the fashion is for marriage, I might just throw her off and marry a pretty one instead.'

❧

Anne absolutely refused to spend the Christmas feast at Greenwich if she were not to be the centre of the attention. Although Henry tried again and again to explain to her that it was for the good of their cause she railed at him for preferring the queen at his side.

'I shall go!' she threw at him. 'I shan't stay here and be insulted by neglect. I shall go to Hever. I shall spend the Christmas feast there. Or perhaps I shall go back to the French court. My father is there, I could spend a happy time there, I think. I was always very much admired in France.'

He went white as if she had knifed him. 'Anne, my own love, don't say such things.'

She rounded on him. 'Your own love? You don't even want me at your side on Christmas Day!'

'I want you there, on that day and every day. But if Campeggio is even now reporting to the Pope I want everyone to know that I am putting the queen aside for the purest of reasons, for the very best of reasons.'

'And I am impure?' she demanded, snatching at the word.

The quickness of wits that she had brought to flirtation was now being exercised on Henry as a weapon. And he was as helpless now as he had been then.

'My own true love, you are an angel to me,' he said. 'And I want the rest of the world to know it. I have told the queen that you shall be my wife because you are the finest that England can offer. I told her that.'

'You discuss me with her?' She gave a little breathy scream. 'Oh no! This is to add insult to insult. And she tells you that I am not, perhaps. She tells you that when I was her lady in waiting I was no angel. She tells you that I am not fit to make your shirts, perhaps!'

Henry dropped his head in his hands. 'Anne!'

She spun away from him and turned to the window. I kept my head down over the book I was supposed to be reading and passed my finger along the line of the words but I saw nothing. Covertly, the two of us, king and former mistress, both watched her. The strain in her shoulders made her shudder for a couple of sobs, and then her shoulders eased, and she turned back to him. Her eyes were shining with tears, her anger had flushed colour into her cheeks. She looked aroused. She went towards him and she took his hands.

'Forgive me,' she cooed. 'Forgive me, love.'

He looked up at her as if he could not believe his luck. He opened his arms and she slithered onto his lap and wound her arms around his neck.

'Forgive me,' she whispered.

As quietly as I could I rose from my seat and went to the door. Anne nodded for me to leave, and I went out. As I closed the door behind me I heard her say: 'But I shall go to Durham House and you shall pay for me to keep Christmas there.'

❀

The queen welcomed me back into her rooms with a small triumphant smile. She thought, poor lady, that Anne's absence meant a weakening of Anne's influence. She had not heard, as I had, the list of penances that Anne had set her lover to pay for her absence from court. She did not know, as the rest of the court knew only too well, that Henry's politeness to her over the Christmas feast was to be a matter of form.

She found it out soon enough. He never dined with her alone in her rooms. He never spoke to her unless someone was watching. He never danced with her at all. Indeed, he excused himself from much of the dancing and merely watched the dancers. There were some new girls at court who were twirled by their partners under his eyes, a new Percy heiress, a new Seymour girl. From every county in England that could gain a place at court came a new girl to enchant the king and perhaps get a chance at the throne. But the king was not to be diverted. He sat beside his wife looking drawn, and he thought of his mistress.

That night the queen knelt for a long while before her prie dieu and the other ladies fell asleep in their seats waiting for her to dismiss us and send us to our beds. When she rose up and turned around there was only me still awake.

'Half a dozen Peters,' she said, looking at their neglect of her in her time of sadness.

'I am sorry for it,' I said.

'Whether she is here or whether she is gone seems to make no difference,' she said with a forlorn wisdom. She bowed her head under the weight of the hood and I stepped forward and slipped off the pins and lifted it from her head. Her hair was very grey now, I thought she had aged more in this last year than she had done in the previous five.

'It is just a passion that he will overcome,' she said, more to herself than to me. 'He would tire of her, as he tired of them all. Bessie Blount, you, Anne is only one of a line.'

I did not reply.

'As long as he does not fall into a sin against the Holy Church, while she has her spell on him,' she continued. 'It's the one thing that I pray for, that he does not sin. I know he will come back to me.'

'Your Majesty,' I said quietly. 'What if he does not come? What if they annul your marriage and he marries her? Do you have somewhere to go? Have you secured your own safety if it all goes wrong?'

Queen Katherine turned her tired blue eyes on me as if she saw me for the first time. She held out her arms so that I could unlace the top part of her gown and then turned round so that I could slip it off her shoulders. Her skin was scraped raw by the irritation of her hair shirt. I made no remark, she did not like us ladies even to see it.

'I do not prepare for defeat,' she said simply. 'It would be to betray myself. I know that God will turn Henry's mind back to me and we will be happy together again. I know that my daughter will be Queen of England and she will be one of the finest queens that ever reigned. Her grandmother was Isabella of Castile – no-one can doubt that a woman can rule a kingdom. She will be a princess that everyone will remember, and the king will be Sir Loyal Heart at my death as he was once in my girlhood.'

She went to her privy chamber and the maid, who was dozing before the fire, jumped up and took her gown and hood from my arms.

'God bless you,' the queen said. 'You can tell the others to go to bed now. I shall expect them all to come with me to Mass in the morning. And you too, Mary. I like my ladies to come to Mass.'

Summer 1530

I rode down the road to Hever surrounded by a jogging army of serving men, the Howard standard before and behind me, and any other travellers on the road crowded into the ditch as we went by. The hedges and grass at the roadside were dusty already, it had been a dry spring, all the signs that it would be a bad year for the plague. But at a distance from the road the hay was sweet, already cut and stacked in some fields, and the wheat and barley were knee-high and starting to fatten. The hop fields were green and the grass in the apple orchards was drifted with petals like snow.

I sang as we rode along, there was such joy for me in riding through the English countryside, with my back to the court, on the way to my children. The men were commanded by a gentleman in my uncle's train, William Stafford, and he rode beside me for some of the way.

'This dust is dreadful,' he remarked. 'As soon as we are clear of the town I'll order the men to ride behind you.'

I stole a little sideways glance at him. He was a handsome man, broad-set with an honest open face. I imagined that he was a Stafford ruined on the execution of the disgraced Duke of Buckingham. He certainly looked like a man who had been born and bred to something more.

'I thank you for escorting me. It is important to me to see my children.'

'I should think there was nothing more important. I have neither wife nor child, but if I did have I would not leave them.'

'Why have you never married?'

He gave me a smile. 'I never met a woman I liked enough.'

There was nothing in it; there was something in it. I found I wanted to ask him what a woman would have to do to please him. He was foolish to be so choosy in women. Most men would marry a woman who could bring them either wealth or good connections. And yet William Stafford did not look like a fool.

When we stopped for our dinner he was by my horse to lift me down and he held me for a moment, to keep me steady, when I was on my feet.

'All right?' he asked gently. 'You've been a long time in the saddle.'

'I'm all right. Tell the men we won't stay too long to dine, I want to get on to Hever before nightfall.'

He led me into the inn. 'I hope they can find something good for your dinner. They promised a chicken but I'm afraid it might be a scrawny old goose.'

I laughed. 'Anything! I could eat anything, I am so hungry. Will you dine with me?'

For a moment I thought he would say yes, but then he made a little bow and said: 'I'll eat with the men.'

I felt a little piqued that he refused my invitation. 'As you wish,' I said coolly and went into the low-ceilinged room of the inn. I warmed my hands at the fire, and glanced out of the little leaded pane window. In the stable yard he was watching the men take the tack off the horses and rub them down before they got their dinners. He was a good-looking man, I thought. A pity that he had such bad manners.

∾

This summer I had decided that Henry's golden curls should be cut and Catherine should come out of short clothes and go into proper gowns. Henry too should wear a doublet and hose. If it had been left to me I might have given them another year in their baby clothes but Grandmother Boleyn was insistent that the two of them should leave their infancy behind, and she was quite capable of writing to Anne and saying that I was not bringing up her ward properly.

Henry's hair was softer than hat feathers. He had long golden curls which fell to his shoulders in ringlets and framed his bright little face. No mother in the world could have seen them cut without tears, he was my baby, and the last thing I wanted was for him to leave behind his curls and his baby plumpness, the last thing I wanted was to see any change in the way he held out his arms to be picked up, the unsteady rushing of his fat little legs.

He, of course, was all for it, and he wanted a sword, and his own pony. He wanted to go to the court of France like George, and learn to fight. He wanted to go on crusade and learn to joust, he wanted to grow up as fast as he could, while I wanted to hold him in my arms, my baby forever.

William Stafford came upon us at our favourite place, on the stone bench facing towards the moat and the castle. Henry had run around all morning and was now frankly sleepy, cuddled into my arms, his thumb creeping into his mouth. Catherine was paddling her bare feet in the moat.

He saw at once that there were tears in my eyes but he merely hesitated and said quietly, in order not to wake my boy: 'I am sorry to disturb you, I was coming to tell you that we're returning to London now, and to ask if you had any messages that you wanted to send.'

'I have some fruit and some vegetables for my mother in the kitchen.'

He nodded and then hesitated, irresolute. 'Forgive me,' he said awkwardly. 'I can see that something has made you cry. Is there anything I can do? Your uncle put you in my care. It is my duty to know if someone has offended you.'

That made me chuckle. 'No. It is just that Henry has to be breeched and I have so loved having him as a little baby. I don't want either him or my little Catherine to grow up. If I had a husband he would have taken Henry and cut his curls without my permission. As it is, I have to see it done myself.'

'D'you miss your husband?' he asked curiously.

'A little.' I wondered how much Stafford knew of my marriage that had hardly been a marriage at all. 'We were not much together.' That was about as honest and as tactful as I could manage, and his small judicial nod did not tell me whether he had understood me or not.

'I meant now,' he said, showing me that he was cleverer than I had allowed. 'Now that you no longer have the favour of the king. Now would be the time that you would expect to have another child with your husband, isn't it? And start again?'

I hesitated. 'I suppose so.' I was reluctant to discuss my future with someone who was only a gentleman in my uncle's train, ten a penny if truth were told, little more than a common adventurer if one was to be unkind.

'But it's not a very comfortable situation for a woman like you, a young woman of twenty-two with two young children. You've your whole life ahead of you and yet your future is tied to your sister's. You are in her shadow. You, who were once the favourite of everyone.'

It was such a bleak and accurate summary of my life that I rather choked at the vista he opened up for me. 'That's how it is for women,' I said, stung into honesty. 'It's not what one would choose – I grant you that. But women are the very toys of fortune. If my husband had lived then he would have been granted great honours. My brother is Lord George, my father an earl, and I would have shared in his prosperity. But

267

as it is I am still a Boleyn girl and a Howard, I'm not penniless. I have prospects.'

'You're an adventurer,' he said. 'Like me. Or, at any rate, you could be. While your family is so fixed on Anne, and her future is so unreliable, you could make your own future. You could make your own choice. They have forgotten to manage you for a moment. In this moment you might be free.'

I turned my attention to him. 'Is that why you are unmarried? So that you can be free?'

He smiled at me, a gleam of white teeth in his brown face. 'Oh yes,' he said. 'I owe no man a living, I owe no woman a duty. I am your uncle's man, I wear his livery, but I don't see myself as his serf. I'm a freeborn Englishman, I go my own way.'

'You're a man,' I said. 'It's different for a woman.'

'Yes,' he acknowledged. 'Unless she was to marry me. Then we could make our own way together.'

I laughed quietly, and gathered little Henry closer to me. 'You would make your own way on precious little money if you married to disoblige your lord, and without the blessing of her parents.'

Stafford was not at all put out. 'There are worse beginnings than that. I think I'd rather have a woman who loved me stake her life on my ability to care for her, than have her father bind me up with a dowry and a contract.'

'And what would she get?'

He looked me straight in the face. 'My love.'

'And this is worth a breach with her family? With your lord? With her family's kin?'

He glanced away to where the swallows were building their little mud-cups of nests under the turrets of the castle. 'I should like a woman who was free as a bird. I should like a woman who came to me for love, and who wanted me for love, and cared for nothing more than me.'

'You would have a fool as a wife,' I said sharply.

He turned back to me and smiled. 'Just as well that I have never yet met a woman I wanted,' he said. 'So there are no fools rather than two.'

I nodded. It seemed to me that I had triumphed in the exchange but that it was somehow unresolved. 'I hope to remain unmarried for a while,' I said. Even to my own ears I sounded uncertain.

'I hope you do too,' he said oddly. 'I bid you farewell, Lady Carey.' He bowed and was about to go. 'And I think that you will find that your boy is still your little boy whether he is in breeches or short clothes,' he

268

said gently. 'I loved my mother till the day she died, God bless her, and I was always her little boy – however big and disagreeable I became.'

I should not have worried about the loss of Henry's curls. When they were shorn, I could see once more the exquisite rounded shape of his head, the tender vulnerable neck. He no longer looked like a baby, he looked like the smallest most engaging little boy. I liked to cup his head in the palm of my hand and feel the warmth of him. In his adult clothes he looked every inch a prince and, despite myself, I started to think that he might one day sit on the throne of England. He was the king's son, he was adopted by the woman who might well one day take the title of Queen of England – but more than any of this, he was the most golden princely boy I had ever seen. He stood like his father, hands on hips, as if he owned the world. He was the sweetest-tempered boy that any mother has ever called to her and seen come running through a meadow, following her voice as trustingly as a hawk to the whistle. He was a golden child this summer and when I saw the boy he was, and the young man that he might become, I did not grieve any more for the baby he had been.

But I did learn that I wanted another child. The beauty of him as a boy meant that I had lost my baby and I thought of how it would be to have a baby that was not another pawn in the great game of the throne, but wanted for itself alone. How it would be to have a baby with a man who loved me and who looked forward to the child we might have together. That thought took me back to court in a very quiet and sombre mood.

William Stafford came to escort me to Richmond Palace and insisted that we leave early in the morning so that the horses could rest at midday. I kissed my children goodbye and came out into the stable yard where Stafford lifted me up into the saddle. I was crying at leaving them and, to my embarrassment, one of my tears fell on his upturned face. He brushed it with a fingertip but instead of wiping his hand on his breeches he put his finger to his lips and licked it.

'What are you doing?'

At once he looked guilty. 'You shouldn't have dropped a tear on me.'

'You shouldn't have licked it,' I burst out in reply.

He didn't answer, nor did he move away immediately. Then he said: 'To horse,' and turned from me and swung into his own saddle. The little cavalcade moved out of the courtyard of the castle and I waved at my boy and my girl, kneeling up at their bedroom window to see me go.

We rode over the drawbridge with our horses' hooves sounding like thunder on the hollow wooden boards, and down the long sweeping road to the end of the park. William Stafford edged his horse forward beside mine.

'Don't cry,' he said abruptly.

I glanced sideways at him and wished he would go and ride with his men. 'I'm not.'

'You are,' he contradicted me. 'And I cannot escort a weeping woman all the way to London.'

'I'm not a weeping woman,' I said with some irritation. 'But I hate to leave my children and know that I will not see them again for another year. A whole year! I should think I might be allowed to feel a little sad at leaving them.'

'No,' he said staunchly. 'And I'll tell you why. You told me very clearly that a woman has to do as her family bids her. Your family has bidden you to live apart from your children, even to give your son into your sister's keeping. To fight them and to take your children back makes better sense than to weep. If you choose to be a Boleyn and a Howard then you might as well be happy in your obedience.'

'I'd like to ride alone,' I said coldly.

At once he spurred his horse forward and ordered the men at the front of the escort to fall back. They all went back six paces behind me and I rode in silence and in loneliness all the way up the long road to London, just as I had ordered.

Autumn 1530

The court was at Richmond and Anne was all smiles after a happy summer in the country with Henry. They had hunted every day and he had given her gift after gift, a new saddle for her hunter and a new set of bow and arrows. He had ordered his saddler to make a beautiful pillion saddle so that she could sit behind him, her arms around his waist, her head against his shoulder so that they could whisper together as they rode. Everywhere they went they were told that the country was admiring them, favouring their plans. Everywhere they were greeted with loyal addresses, poems, masques and tableaux. Every house welcomed them with a shower of petals and freshly strewn herbs beneath their feet. Anne and Henry were assured over and over again that they were a golden couple with a certain future. Nothing could possibly go wrong for them.

My father, home from France, decided to say nothing to disturb this picture. 'If they're happy together then thank God for it,' he remarked to my uncle. We were watching Anne at the archery butts on the terrace above the river. She was a skilful archer, she looked as if she might take the prize. Only one other lady, Lady Elizabeth Ferrers, looked as if she might outshoot my sister.

'It's a pleasant change,' my uncle said sourly. 'She has the temper of a stable cat, your daughter.'

My father chuckled comfortably. 'She takes after her mother,' he said. 'All the Howard girls jump one way or another as soon as you look at them. You must have had some fights with your sister when you were children.'

Uncle Howard looked cool and did not encourage the intimate note. 'A woman should know her place,' he said icily.

Father exchanged a quick look with me. The regular episodes of uproar in the Howard household were well-known. It was hardly surprising.

Uncle Howard had openly kept a mistress from the moment that his wife had given him his sons. My aunt swore that she had been nothing more than the laundry woman to the nursery and that to this day the two of them could only couple if they were lying on dirty sheets. The hatred between her and her husband was a constant feature of court, and it was as good as a play to see him lead her in on state occasions when they had to keep up the semblance of unity and appear in public together. He held the very tips of her fingertips, and she turned her head away from him as if he smelled of unwashed hose and dirty ruffs.

'We're not all blessed with your happy touch with women,' my father said.

My uncle shot one surprised look at him. He had been head of the family for so long that he was used to deference. But my father was an earl in his own right now, and his daughter, who at that very moment loosed an arrow and saw it fly straight to the heart of the target, could be queen.

Anne turned, smiling from her shot, and Henry, unable to keep from her, leaped to his feet out of the chair and hurried down to the butts and kissed her on the mouth, before all the court. Everyone smiled and applauded, Lady Elizabeth concealed as well as she could any sense of pique that she had lost to the favourite, and received a small jewel from the king while Anne took a little headdress shaped like a golden crown.

'A crown,' my father said, watching the king hold it out to her.

In an intimate, confident gesture Anne pulled off her hood and stood before us all with her dark hair tumbling back from her forehead in thick glossy ringlets. Henry stepped forward and put the crown on her head. There was a pause of absolute silence.

The tension was broken by the king's Fool. He danced behind the king and peeped around him at Anne. 'Oh Mistress Anne!' he called. 'You aimed for the eye of the bull, but you hit very true at another part. The bull's b . . .'

Henry rounded on him with a roar of laughter and aimed a cuff which the Fool dodged. The court exploded in laughter and Anne, beautifully blushing, the little archery crown glinting on her black hair, shook her head at the Fool, wagged her finger at him, and then turned her face in confusion to Henry's shoulder.

I was sharing a bedroom with Anne in the second best rooms that Richmond Palace could offer. They were not the queen's apartments, but they were the next best. There seemed to be an unwritten rule that Anne might commandeer a set of rooms and furnish them as richly as the queen, almost as richly as the king, but she was not yet allowed to live in the queen's own rooms, even though the queen was never there. New protocols had to be invented all the time in this court which was not like any other before.

Anne was sprawled on the ornate bed, careless of creasing her gown.

'Good summer?' she asked me idly. 'Children well?'

'Yes,' I said shortly. I would never again speak willingly of my son to her. She had forfeited her right to be his aunt when she had laid claim to be his mother.

'You were watching the archery with Uncle,' she said. 'What was he talking about?'

I thought back. 'Nothing. Saying you and the king were happy.'

'I have told him that I want Wolsey destroyed. He's turned against me. He's supporting the queen.'

'Anne, he lost the Lord Chancellorship, surely that's enough.'

'He's been corresponding with the queen. I want him dead.'

'But he was your friend.'

She shook her head. 'We both played a part to please the king. Wolsey sent me fish from his trout pond, I sent him little gifts. But I never forgot how he spoke to me about Henry Percy, and he never forgot that I was a Boleyn, an upstart like him. He was jealous of me, and I was jealous of him. We have been enemies from the moment I came home from France. He didn't even see me. He didn't even understand what power I have. He still does not understand me. But at his death, he will. I have his house, I will have his life.'

'He's an old man. He's lost all his wealth and his titles that were his great pride and joy. He's retiring to his see at York. If you want your revenge, you can leave him to rot. That's revenge enough.'

Anne shook her head. 'Not yet. Not while the king still loves him.'

'Is the king to love nobody but you? Not even the man who has guarded him and guided him like a father for years?'

'Yes. He is to love nobody but me.'

I was surprised. 'Have you come to desire him?'

She laughed in my face. 'No. But I would have him see no-one and speak to no-one but me, and those I could trust. And who can I trust?'

I shook my head.

'You – perhaps. George – always. Father – usually. Mother – sometimes, Uncle Howard – if it suits him. Not my aunt, who has gone over to Katherine. Perhaps the Duke of Suffolk but not his wife Mary Tudor who can't bear to see me rise so high. Anyone else? No. That's it. Perhaps some men are tender-hearted to me. My cousin Sir Francis Bryan, perhaps Francis Weston from his friendship with George. Sir Thomas Wyatt cares for me still.' She raised one other finger in silence and we both knew that we were thinking of Henry Percy, so far away in Northumberland, determinedly never coming to court, ill with unhappiness, living in the middle of nowhere with the wife he had married under protest. 'Ten,' she said quietly. 'Ten people who wish me well against a whole world that would be glad to see me fall.'

'But the cardinal can do nothing against you now. He has lost all his power.'

'Then this is the very time when he is ripe to be destroyed. Now that he has lost all his power and he is a defeated old man.'

❦

It was some plot hatched between the Duke of Suffolk and Uncle Howard but it bore Anne's hallmark. My uncle had evidence of a letter from Wolsey to the Pope and Henry, who had been disposed to recall his old friend to high office, turned once more against him and ordered his arrest.

The lord that they sent to arrest him was Anne's choice. It was Anne's final gesture to the man who had called her a foolish girl and an upstart. Henry Percy of Northumberland went to Wolsey at York and said that he was charged with treason and must travel the long road back to London and stay not in his wonderful palace of Hampton Court which now belonged to the king, not in his beautiful London home of York Place which was now renamed Whitehall and belonged to Anne; instead he was to go, like a traitor, to the Tower and await his trial, as others had gone before him and taken the short walk to the scaffold.

Henry Percy must have felt a harsh joy to send to Anne the man who had separated them, now sick with exhaustion and despair. It was no fault of Henry Percy's that Wolsey escaped them all by dying on the road and the only satisfaction that Anne could take was that it was the boy she had loved who told the man that had parted them that her vengeance had come at last.

Christmas 1530

The queen met the court at Greenwich for Christmas and Anne held her rival Christmas feast in the dead cardinal's old palace. It was an open secret that after the king had dined in state with the queen he would quietly slip out, summon the royal barge and be rowed to the stairs at Whitehall where he would eat another supper with Anne. Sometimes he took some chosen courtiers with him, me among them, and then we had a merry night on the river, wrapped up warm against the biting cold wind, with the stars bright above us as we rowed home and sometimes a huge white moon lighting our way.

I was one of the queen's ladies again and I was shocked to see the change in her. When she raised her head and smiled for Henry she could no longer summon any joy into her eyes. He had knocked it out of her, perhaps forever. She still had the same quiet dignity, she still had the same confidence in herself as a Princess of Spain and Queen of England, but she would never again have the glow of a woman who knows that her husband adores her.

One day we were sitting together at the fireside of her apartment, the altar cloth spread from one side of the hearth to the other. I was working on the blue sky which was still unfinished, and she, unusually for her, had left the blue and moved on to another colour. I thought that she must be weary indeed if she left a task unfinished. Usually she was a woman who would persist, whatever it cost her.

'Did you see your children this summer?' she asked.

'Yes, Your Majesty,' I said. 'Catherine is in long dresses now and is learning French and Latin, and Henry's curls are cut.'

'Will you send them to the French court?'

I could not conceal the pang of anxiety. 'Not yet at any rate. They're still so very young.'

She smiled at me. 'Lady Carey, you know that it is not how young they are, nor how dear. They have to learn their duty. As you did, as I did.'

I bowed my head. 'I know that you're right,' I said quietly.

'A woman needs to know her duty so that she may perform it and live in the estate to which God has been pleased to call her,' the queen pronounced. I knew that she was thinking of my sister, who was not in the estate to which God had been pleased to call her, but was instead in some glorious new condition, earned by her beauty and her wit, and maintained now by an inveterate campaign.

There was a knock at the door and one of my uncle's men stood in the doorway.

'A gift of oranges from the Duchess of Norfolk,' he said. 'And a note.'

I rose to receive the pretty basket with the oranges arranged in their dark green leaves. There was a letter marked with my uncle's seal laid on the top.

'Read the note,' the queen said. I put the fruit down on the table and opened the letter. I read aloud: '"Your Majesty, having received a fresh barrel of oranges from the country of your birth I take the liberty of sending the pick of them to you with my compliments."'

'How very kind,' the queen said calmly. 'Would you put them in my bedchamber, Mary? And write a reply to your aunt in my name to thank her for her gift.'

I rose and carried the basket into her room. There was a rug in the doorway and I caught my heel in it. As I staggered to regain my footing the oranges tumbled everywhere, rolling over the floor like a schoolboy's marbles. I swore as quietly as I could, and hurriedly started to pile them back into the basket before the queen came in and saw what a mess I had made of a simple task.

Then I saw something that made me freeze. In the bottom of the basket was a tiny twist of paper. I smoothed it out. It was covered in small numbers, there were no words at all. It was in code.

I stayed there, on my knees with the oranges all around me, for a long time. Then I slowly packed them back in their arrangement and put the basket on a low chest. I even stepped back to admire them and alter their position. Then I put the note in my pocket and went back into the room to sit with the woman that I loved more than any other in the world. I sat beside her, and stitched her tapestry, and wondered what smouldering disaster I had in the pocket of my gown and what I should do with it.

I had no choice. From start to finish I had no choice. I was a Boleyn. I was a Howard. If I did not cleave to my family then I was a nobody with no means to support my children, no future, and no protection. I took the note to my uncle's rooms and I laid it before him on the table.

❧

He had the code broken in half a day. It was not a very complicated conspiracy. It was only a message of hope from the Spanish ambassador, whispered to my aunt, and passed on by her to the queen. Not a very effectual conspiracy. It was a plot in a desert. It meant nothing but some comfort to the queen, and now I had been the instrument in taking that comfort from her.

When the news of it all came out with a great quarrel in my uncle's apartments as he shouted at his wife that she was a traitor against the king and against him, and then there was a royal remonstrance from the king himself to my aunt, I went to the queen. She was in her room, looking out of the window at the frozen garden below her. Some people wrapped warm in furs were walking down to the river where the barges were waiting for them, going to visit my sister in her rival court. The queen, standing in silence, alone in her room, watched them go, the Fool capering round them, one of the musicians strumming a lute and singing them on their way.

I dropped to my knees before her.

'I gave the duchess's note to my uncle,' I confessed baldly. 'I found it in the oranges. If it had not come to my hand I would never have searched for it. I always seem to betray you, but it is never my intention.'

She glanced at my bowed head as if it did not much matter. 'I don't know anyone who would have done any different,' she observed. 'You should be on your knees to your God, not to me, Lady Carey.'

I did not rise. 'I want to beg your pardon,' I said. 'It is my destiny to belong to a family whose interests run counter to yours. If I had been your lady in waiting at another time you would never have had to doubt me.'

'If you had not been tempted you would not have fallen. If it was not in your interests to betray me then you would have been loyal. Go away, Lady Carey, you are no better than your sister who pursues her own ends like a weasel and never glances to one side or the other. Nothing will stop the Boleyns gaining what they want, I know that. Sometimes I think she will stop at nothing, even my death, to do it. And I know that you will help her, however much you love me, however much I loved you when you were my little maid – you will be behind her every step of her way.'

'She's my sister,' I said passionately.

'And I am your queen,' she said, like ice.

My knees ached on the floorboards but I did not want to move.

'She has my son in her keeping,' I said. 'And my king at her beck and call.'

'Go away,' the queen repeated. 'Soon the Christmas feast will be over and we will not meet again till Easter. Soon the Pope will come to his decision and when he tells the king that he has to honour his marriage to me then your sister will make her next move. What have I to expect, d'you think? A charge of treason? Or poison in my dinner?'

'She wouldn't,' I whispered.

'She would,' the queen said flatly. 'And you would help her. Go away, Lady Carey, I don't want to see you again till Easter.'

I rose to my feet and backed away, at the doorway I swept her a deep curtsey, as low as one would offer to an emperor. I did not show her my face, which was wet with tears. I bowed in shame. I went from her room and shut her door and left her alone, looking out over the frozen garden at the laughing court setting off down river to honour her enemy.

The gardens were quiet with most of the court absent. I thrust my cold hands deep into the fur of my sleeves and walked down to the river, my head lowered, my cheeks icy with my tears. Suddenly, a pair of down-at-heel boots stopped before me.

I looked up slowly. A good pair of legs if a woman cared to observe, warm doublet, brown fustian cape, smiling face: William Stafford.

'Not gone with the court to visit your sister?' he asked without a word of greeting.

'No,' I said shortly.

He took a closer look at my downturned face.

'Are your children all right?'

'Yes,' I said.

'What is it then?'

'I've done a bad thing,' I said, narrowing my eyes against the glare of the winter sunshine on the water, looking upriver to where the merry court was rowing away.

He waited.

'I discovered something about the queen and I told my uncle.'

'Did he think it was a bad thing?'

278

I laughed shortly. 'Oh no. So far as he is concerned I am a credit to him.'

'The duchess's secret note,' he guessed at once. 'It's all over the palace. She's been banished from court. But nobody knows how she was detected.'

'I . . .' I started awkwardly.

'No-one will learn it from me.' Familiarly he took my cold hand and tucked it in the crook of his elbow and led me to walk beside the river. The sun was bright on our faces, my hand, trapped between his arm and his body, grew warmer.

'What would you have done?' I asked. 'Since you keep your own counsel and pride yourself so much on being your own man.'

Stafford gave me the most delighted sideways gleam. 'I did not dare to hope that you remembered our talks.'

'It's nothing,' I said, slightly flustered. 'It means nothing.'

'Of course not.'

He thought for a moment. 'I think I would have done as you did. If it had been her nephew planning an invasion then it would have been essential to read it.'

We paused at the boundary of the palace gardens. 'Won't we open the gate and go on?' he asked temptingly. 'We could go to the village and have a mug of ale and a pocketful of roasted chestnuts.'

'No. I have to go to dinner tonight, even though the queen has dismissed me till Easter.'

He turned and walked beside me, saying nothing, but with my hand pressed warmly to his side. At the garden door he stopped. 'I'll leave you here,' he said. 'I was on my way to the stable yard when I saw you. My horse has gone lame and I want to see that they are fomenting her hoof properly.'

'Indeed, I don't know why you delayed for me at all,' I said, a hint of provocation in my voice.

He looked at me directly and I felt my breath come a little short. 'Oh I think you do,' he said slowly. 'I think you know very well why I stopped to see you.'

'Mr Stafford . . .' I said.

'I so hate the smell of the liniment they put on the hoof,' he said quickly. He bowed to me and was gone before I could laugh or protest or even acknowledge that he had trapped me into flirting with him when it had been my hope to entrap him.

Spring 1531

With the death of the cardinal the church quickly learned that it had lost not only one of its greatest profiteers, but also its great protector. Henry fined the church with an enormous tax that emptied the treasuries and made the clergy realise that the Pope might still be their spiritual leader, but their leader on earth was a good deal closer to home and a good deal more powerful.

Not even the king could have done it on his own. Supporting Henry's attack on the church were the brightest thinkers of the age, the men in whose books Anne believed, who demanded that the church return to early purity. The very people of England, ignorant of theology, were not prepared to support their priests or their monasteries against Henry when he spoke of the right of English people to a church of England. The church at Rome seemed very much the church of Rome: a foreign institution, dominated at the moment by a foreign emperor. Better by far that the church should answer firstly to God, and be ruled, as everything else in the country was ruled, by the King of England. How else could he be king?

No-one outside the church would argue with this logic. Inside the church only Bishop Fisher, the queen's old stubborn faithful confessor made any protest when Henry named himself the supreme head of the church of England.

'You should refuse to allow him to court,' Anne said to Henry. They were seated in a window embrasure in the audience chamber of the palace of Greenwich. She lowered her voice only a little out of deference to the petitioners waiting to see him and the court all around them. 'He's always creeping into the queen's rooms to whisper for hours. Who's to say she's confessing and he's praying? Who knows what advice he is giving her? Who knows what secrets they are plotting?'

'I cannot deny her the rites of the church,' the king said reasonably. 'She would hardly plot in the confessional.'

'He's her spy,' Anne said flatly.

The king patted her hand. 'Peace, sweetheart,' he said. 'I am head of the church of England, I can rule on my own marriage. It is all but done.'

'Fisher will speak against us,' she fretted. 'And everyone will listen to him.'

'Fisher is not supreme head of the church,' Henry repeated, savouring the words. 'I am.' He looked over to one of the petitioners. 'What d'you want? You can approach me.'

The man came forward holding out a piece of paper, some quarrel about a will that the court of wards had been unable to resolve. Father, who had brought the man to court, stood back and let him make his petition. Anne slipped from Henry's side to Father, touched his sleeve and whispered. They broke apart and she came back to the king, smiling.

I was laying out the cards for us to play a game. I looked around for a gentleman to take the fourth hand. Sir Francis Weston stepped forward and bowed to me. 'Can I stake my heart?' he asked.

George was watching the two of us, smiling at Sir Francis's flirtatiousness, his eyes very warm.

'You have nothing to stake,' I reminded him. 'You swore to me you lost it when you saw me in my blue gown.'

'I got it back when you danced with the king,' he said. 'Broken but returned.'

'It's not a heart but a battered old arrow,' Henry remarked. 'You're always loosing it off and then going to get it back again.'

'It never finds its target,' Sir Francis said. 'I am a poor marksman beside Your Majesty.'

'You're a poor card player as well,' Henry said hopefully. 'Let's play for a shilling a point.'

❧

A few nights later, Bishop Fisher was sick, and nearly died of his sickness. Three men at his dinner table died of poison, others in his household were sick too. Someone had bribed his cook to put poison in his soup. It was only his good luck that Bishop Fisher had not wanted the soup that evening.

I did not ask Anne what she had said to Father in the doorway, nor what he had replied. I did not ask her if she had any hand in the bishop's

281

sickness and the deaths of three innocent men at his table. It was not a little thing, to think that one's sister and one's father were murderers. But I remembered the darkness of her face as she swore that she hated Fisher as much as she had hated the cardinal. And now the cardinal was dead of shame, and Fisher's dinner had been salted with poison. I felt as if this whole matter, which had started as a summer flirtation, had grown too dark and too great for me to want to know any secrets. Anne's dark-tempered motto, 'Thus it will be: grudge who grudge', seemed like a curse that Anne was laying on the Boleyns, on the Howards, and on the country itself.

❧

The queen was in the centre of the court for the Easter feast, as she had predicted. The king dined with her every night, all smiles so that the people who had come out from the City to see the king and queen dine would go to their homes and say it was a shame that a man in the very prime of his life should be entrapped by a woman so much older and so grave-looking. Sometimes she would withdraw early from dinner and her ladies had to choose whether to go with her or to stay in the hall. I always left with her when she withdrew. I was weary of the endless gossip and scandal of the court, of the spite of the women and of the brittle charm of my sister. And I feared what I might see if I stayed. It was a more unreliable place than the court I had joined with such high hopes when I had been the only Boleyn girl in England, and a newly wed wife with great hopes of my husband and my life with him.

The queen accepted my service without comment; she never mentioned my earlier betrayal. Only once she asked me if I would not rather be in the hall, watching the entertainment or dancing.

'No,' I said. I had picked up a book and was about to offer to read to her as she sat and sewed the altar cloth. Almost all the blue sky was completed, it was remarkable how fast and accurately she had worked. The cloth was spread like a gown over her lap, tumbling down in a swirl of rich blue to the floor, she had only the last corner of sky to stitch.

'You have no interest in dancing?' she asked me. 'You, a young widow? Have you no suitors?'

I shook my head. 'No, Your Majesty.'

'Your father will be looking for another match for you,' she said, stating the obvious. 'Has he spoken to you?'

'No. And matters are . . .' There was no way that I could complete the sentence as a proper courtier. 'Matters are very unsettled for us.'

Queen Katherine gave a little snort of genuine laughter. 'I had not thought of that,' she admitted. 'What a great gamble for a young man! Who knows how far he might rise with you? Who knows how far he might fall?'

I smiled rather wanly and showed her the spine of the book. 'Did you want me to read, Your Majesty?'

'D'you think I am safe?' she asked me abruptly. 'You would warn me if my life was in danger, would you not?'

'Safe from what?'

'From poison.'

I shivered as if the spring evening had suddenly turned damp and chilly. 'These are dark times,' I said. 'Very dark times.'

'I know it,' she said. 'And they started so very well.'

She spoke of her fear of poison to no-one but me, but her ladies observed that she fed a little of her breakfast to her greyhound Flo, before eating it herself. One of them, a Seymour girl – Jane – remarked that it would get fat and that it was bad training for a dog to be fed at the table. Someone else laughed that the love of little Flo was all that the queen had left. I said nothing. I would willingly have had the queen test her food on any of them. We could have lost Jane Seymour and she would not have been much missed.

So when they brought news that Princess Mary was sick, my first thought, like the queen's, was that her pretty, clever daughter had been poisoned. Probably by my sister.

'He says she is very ill,' the queen said, reading the physician's letter. 'My God, he says that she has been sick for eight days, she can keep nothing down.'

I forgot royal protocol and took her hand which was shaking so hard that the paper crackled in her hand. 'It can't be poison,' I whispered urgently. 'It would benefit no-one to poison her.'

'She's my heir,' the queen said, her face as white as the letter. 'Would Anne have her poisoned to frighten me into a nunnery?'

I shook my head. I could not say for sure what Anne might do now.

'Either way I must go to her.' She strode to the door and flung it open. 'Where will the king be?'

'I'll find out,' I said. 'Let me go. You can't go running round the palace.'

'No,' she said with a moan of pain. 'I cannot even go to him and ask him to let me see our daughter. What shall I do if that woman says no?'

For a moment I had no reply. The thought of the Queen of England desperately asking if my upstart sister would let her see her own child, and that child a Princess Royal, was too much, even for this topsy-turvy world. 'It is not her word, Majesty. The king loves the Princess Mary, he would not want her to be sick without her mother to care for her.'

🏵

Anne already knew that the princess was ill. Anne knew everything now. My uncle's spy system, always a superb network, had recruited a servant in every household in England, and its findings were dedicated to the service of my sister. Anne knew that the Princess Mary was sick with distress. The little girl lived alone with no company but servants and her confessor, she spent hours on her knees praying God to turn her father's love back to her mother, his wife. She was sick with grief.

That night, when the king came to the queen's apartments he was primed with his answer. 'You can go and see the princess if you like, and stop there,' he said. 'With my blessing. With my thanks. And so farewell.'

The queen's high colour drained from her cheeks, leaving her looking sick and haggard. 'I would never leave you, my husband,' she whispered. 'I was thinking of our child. I was thinking that you would want to know that she was well cared for.'

'She's only a girl,' he said, a world of spite in his voice. 'You were not so quick to care for our son. You were not so effective a nurse for our son, as I remember?'

She gave a little gasp of pain but he went on. 'So. Are you coming to dinner, madam? Or are you going to your daughter?'

She recovered herself with an effort. She drew herself up to her little height, took the arm that he offered and he led her into dinner as a queen. But she could not play-act as he did. She looked down the body of the hall and saw my sister at her table, her little court about her. Anne felt the queen's dark gaze upon her and looked up. She gave her a radiant confident smile, and the queen, seeing Anne's unconcealed pleasure, knew who she should thank for the king's cruelty. She dropped her head and crumbled a slice of bread without eating any.

That night there were many people who said that a young handsome king should not be matched with a woman who looked old enough to be his mother and was miserable as sin into the bargain.

🙵

Queen Katherine did not leave the tiltyard that was now the court until she was thoroughly beaten. It would have made any woman but my sister feel ashamed to watch the queen find the courage to confront her husband. Only days after she first heard the news that the Princess Mary was sick, she was dining with the king in private, with the ladies of her chamber and the gentlemen of his, a couple of ambassadors and Thomas Cromwell, who was everywhere at the moment. Thomas More was there too, looking very much as if he wished he was not.

They had taken away the meats, and set the voiding course of fruit and dessert wine. The queen turned to the king and asked him – as if it were a simple request – to send Anne away from court. She called her 'a shameless creature.'

I saw the face of Thomas More and knew I had the same stunned expression. I could not believe that the queen should challenge His Majesty in public. That she, whose case even now was before the Pope in Rome, should have the courage to face her husband in his own chamber and politely ask that he set aside his mistress. I could not think why she was doing it, and then I knew. It was for Princess Mary. It was to shame him into letting her go to the princess. She was risking everything to see her daughter.

Henry's face flushed scarlet with anger. I dropped my gaze to the table and I prayed to God that the rage did not turn on me. With my head low I stole a sideways glance and I saw Ambassador Chapuys in the same pose. Only the queen, her hands clasped on the arms of her chair so that they should not tremble, kept her head up, kept her eyes on his suffused face, kept her face schooled to a look of polite inquiry.

'Before God!' Henry raged at her. 'I will never send Lady Anne away from court. She has done nothing to offend any right-thinking man.'

'She is your mistress,' the queen observed quietly. 'And that is a scandal to a God-fearing household.'

'Never!' Henry's shout became a roar. I flinched, he was as terrifying as a baited bear. 'Never! She is a woman of absolute virtue!'

'No,' the queen said calmly. 'In thought and in word, if not in deed, she is shameless and brazen, and no company for a good woman or a Christian prince.'

He leaped to his feet, and still she did not shrink back.

'What the devil do you want of me?' he yelled into her face. His spittle showered her cheeks. She did not blink or turn away. She sat in her chair as if she were made of rock while he was a terrifying spring tide, raging into shore.

'I want to see the Princess Mary,' she said quietly. 'That is all.'

'Go!' he bellowed. 'Go! For God's sake! Go! And leave us all in peace. Go and stay there!'

Slowly, Queen Katherine shook her head. 'I would not leave you, not even for my daughter, though you will break my heart,' she said quietly.

There was a long painful silence. I looked up. There were tears on her face but her expression was completely calm. She knew that she had just surrendered the chance to see her child, even if her child was dying.

Henry glared at her with absolute hatred for a moment and the queen turned her head and nodded to a server behind her. 'More wine for His Majesty,' she said coolly.

Angrily, the king leaped to his feet and pushed back his chair. It scraped like a scream on the wooden floor. The ambassador and the lord chancellor and the rest of us rose uncertainly with him. Henry dropped back into his chair as if he were exhausted. We dipped up and down, lost. Queen Katherine looked at him, she seemed as drained as he did by their quarrel, but she was not beaten.

'Please,' she said very quietly.

'No,' he replied.

❁

A week later and she asked him again. I was not with her when that scene was played out but Jane Seymour told me, very wide-eyed with horror, that the queen had stood her ground when the king had raged. 'How could she dare?' she asked.

'For her child,' I said bitterly. I looked at Jane's young face and thought that before I had my son I had been as great a fool as this ninny. 'She wants to be with her daughter,' I said. 'You wouldn't understand.'

Not until the princess was said by her doctors to be near to death, and asking every day when her mother was coming, did Henry release the queen. He ordered that Princess Mary should be taken by litter to Richmond Palace and the queen could meet her there. I went down to the stable yard to see her off.

'God bless Your Majesty and the princess.'

'At least I can be with her,' was all she said.

I nodded and stepped back and the cavalcade went past me, the queen's standard in front, half a dozen horsemen following the flag, and next came the queen and a couple of her ladies, then the outriders, and then she was gone.

William Stafford was on the other side of the stable yard, watching me waving farewell.

'So, at last, she can see her daughter.' He strolled across to where I stood, holding my dress away from the mud. 'They say that your sister swears that the queen will never return to court. She says that the queen so foolishly loves her daughter that she has gone to her and lost the crown of kingdom in one ride.'

'I don't know that, or anything else,' I said stubbornly.

286

He laughed, his brown eyes gleaming at me. 'You seem very ignorant today. Do you not rejoice in your sister's rise to greatness?'

'Not at this price,' I said shortly, and I turned and walked away from him.

I had barely gone half a dozen steps before he was beside me. 'And what of you, Lady Carey? I have not seen you for days. D'you ever look for me?'

I hesitated. 'Of course I don't look for you.'

He fell into step beside me. 'I don't expect it,' he said with sudden earnestness. 'I might joke with you, madam. But I know very well that you're far above me.'

'I am,' I said ungraciously.

'Oh I know it,' he assured me again. 'But I thought that we quite liked each other.'

'I cannot play these games with you,' I said gently. 'Of course I don't look for you. You are in service to my uncle and I am the daughter of the Earl of Wiltshire –'

'A rather recent honour,' he supplemented quietly.

I frowned, a little distracted by the interruption. 'Whether it is today's honour or goes back a hundred years makes no difference,' I said. 'I am the daughter of an earl and you are a nobody.'

'But what of you, Mary? Leaving aside the titles? Do you, Mary, pretty Mary Boleyn, never look for me? Never think of me?'

'Never,' I said flatly, and left him standing in the archway to the stable yard.

Summer 1531

The court moved to Windsor and the queen brought the Princess Mary, still very pale and thin, back with her to the castle. The King could not help but be tender to his only legitimate child. His attitude to his wife mellowed, and then hardened again, depending on whether he was with my sister or at the bedside of their daughter. The queen, sleepless with praying and nursing the princess, was never too weary to greet him with a smile and a curtsey, was always a steady star in the firmament of the court. She and the princess was to rest at Windsor for the summer.

She smiled at me when I came in with a posy of early roses. 'I thought the Princess Mary might like these by her bedside,' I said. 'They smell very sweet.'

Queen Katherine took them from me and sniffed at them. 'You are a countrywoman,' she said. 'None of my other ladies would think of picking flowers and bringing them indoors.'

'My children love to bring flowers into their rooms,' I said. 'They make crowns and necklaces from daisies. When I kiss Catherine goodnight I often find buttercups on her pillow where they have fallen from her hair.'

'The king has said that you can go to Hever while the court is travelling?'

'Yes.' I smiled at her accurate reading of my contentment. 'Yes, and stay there all the summer.'

'So we shall be with our children then, you and I. You will come back to court in the autumn?'

'I will,' I promised. 'And I will come back to your service if you want me, Your Majesty.'

'And then we start again,' she said. 'Christmas when I am unchallenged queen and summer when I am deserted.'

I nodded.

'She holds him, doesn't she?' She looked out of the windows which faced towards the garden and the river. In the distance we could see the king with Anne, walking on the riverside path before they rode out on their summer progress.

'Yes,' I said shortly.

'What's her secret, d'you think?'

'I think they're very alike.' My distaste for the two of them crept into my tone. 'They both know exactly what they want and they both stop at nothing to get it. They both have the ability to be absolutely single-minded. It's why the king was such a great sportsman. When he chased a stag he saw nothing in his whole heart but the stag. And Anne is the same. She schooled herself to follow only her interest. And now their desires are the same. It makes them . . .' I paused, thinking of the right word. 'Formidable,' I said.

'I can be formidable,' the queen said.

I gave her a sideways glance. If she had not been queen I would have put my arm around her shoulders and hugged her.

'Who knows it better than I? I have seen you stand up to the king in one of his rages, I have seen you take on two cardinals and the Privy Council. But you serve God, and you love the king, and you love your child. You don't think absolutely singly, "what is it that *I* want?"'

She shook her head. 'That would be the sin of selfishness.'

I looked towards the two figures by the river's edge, the most selfish two people that I knew. 'Yes.'

∾

I went down to the stable yard to make sure that they had the trunks loaded and my horse ready for us to start next morning and found William Stafford checking the wheels of the wagon.

'Thank you,' I said, a little surprised to find him there.

He straightened up and turned his bright smile on me. 'I am to escort you. Did your uncle not say?'

'I am sure he said someone else.'

His smile broadened to a grin. 'It was. But he is not fit to ride tomorrow.'

'Why not?'

'He's ill with drink.'

'Drunk now, and not fit to ride tomorrow?'

'I should have said he will be ill with drink.'

I waited.

'He will be ill with drink tomorrow, because he is going to be dead drunk tonight.'

'And you can foresee the future?'

'I can foresee that I will be pouring the wine,' he chuckled. 'May I not escort you, Lady Carey? You know that I will make sure that you arrive safely.'

'Of course you may,' I said, a little flustered. 'It's just that . . .'

Stafford was very quiet, I had the impression that he was listening to me not just with his ears but with all his senses.

'Just what?' he prompted.

'I would not want you hurt,' I said. 'You cannot be anything more to me than a man in my uncle's service.'

'But what should prevent us liking each other?'

'The gravest of trouble with my family.'

'Would that matter so very much? Would it not be better to have a friend, a true friend, however lowly, than be a grand lonely woman at her sister's beck and call?'

I turned away from him. The thought of being in Anne's service grated on me, as it always did.

'So, shall I escort you to Hever tomorrow?' he asked, deliberately breaking the spell.

'If you like,' I said ungraciously. 'One man is much the same as another.'

He choked on a laugh at that, but he did not argue with me. He let me go and I went from the stable yard rather wanting him to run after me and tell me that he was not the same as any other man, and that I might be very sure of that.

❁

I went up to my room and found Anne adjusting her riding hat before the mirror, glittery with excitement.

'We're going,' she said. 'Come out and bid us farewell.'

I followed her down the stairs, taking care not to step on the long hem of her rich red velvet gown.

We came out of the two huge double doors and there was Henry, already mounted on his horse with Anne's dark hunter waiting restlessly beside him. I noted with horror that my sister had kept the king waiting while she adjusted her hat.

He smiled. She might do anything. Two young men sprang forward to help her up into the saddle and she coquetted for a moment, choosing which one might have the privilege of putting his cupped hands under her boot.

The king gave the signal to start and they all moved off. Anne looked over her shoulder and waved at me. 'Tell the queen we've gone,' she called.

'What?' I asked. 'You surely bid her goodbye?'

She laughed. 'No. We've just gone. Tell her we're gone and she's left all alone.'

I could have run after her and pulled her off her horse and slapped her for that piece of spite. But I stayed where I was on the doorstep, smiling at the king and waving at my sister, and then, as the horsemen and wagons and outriders and soldiers and the whole household clattered past me, I turned and went slowly into the castle.

I let the door bang shut behind me. It was very very quiet. The hangings had gone from the walls, some of the tables had been taken from the great hall and the place was filled with the echoes of silence. The fire had died down in the grate, there were no men at arms to throw on extra logs and call for more ale. The sunlight filtered in through the windows and threw slabs of yellow light on the floor and the dust motes danced in the light. I had never been in a royal palace and heard nothing before. Always the place was alive with noise and work and business and play. Always there were servants scolding, and orders being shouted down the stairs, and people begging for admission or for some favour, musicians playing, dogs barking, and courtiers flirting.

I went up the stairs to the queen's apartments, my heels tapping on the flagstones. I knocked on the door and even my fingertips on the wood seemed unnaturally loud. I pushed it open and thought for a moment that the room was vacant. Then I saw her. She was at the window, watching the road winding away from the palace. She could see the court which had been her court, led by the husband who had been her husband, and all her friends and servants, goods, furniture and even the household linen, winding away down the road from the castle, following Anne Boleyn on her big black hunter, leaving her alone.

'He's gone,' she said wonderingly. 'Without even saying goodbye to me.'

I nodded.

'He's never done such a thing before. However bad it has been he always comes to me for my blessing before he goes away. I thought sometimes that he was like a boy, like my boy, that however much he might go away he would always want to know that he could come back to me. He would always want my blessing on any journey he made.'

A troop of horsemen clattered alongside the baggage train, urging the drivers to close up and keep better order. We could hear the noise of the wheels from the queen's window. She was spared nothing.

There was a clatter of boots on the stair and a sharp tap on the half-open door. I went to answer it. It was one of the king's men with a letter with the royal seal.

She turned at once, her face lit up with joy, and ran across the room to take it from his hand. 'There! He didn't leave without a word. He has written to me,' she said, and took it over to the light and broke the seal.

I watched her grow old as she read it. The colour drained from her cheeks and the light went from her eyes and the smile left her lips. She sank down into the windowseat and I pushed the man from the room and shut the door on his staring face. I ran over to her and knelt at her side.

The queen looked down at me but she did not see me, her eyes were filled with tears. 'I am to leave the castle,' she whispered. 'He is sending me away. Cardinal or no cardinal, Pope or no Pope, he is sending me into banishment. I am to be gone within a month and our own daughter is to go too.'

The messenger tapped on the doorway and cautiously put his head inside the door. I leaped to my feet and would have slammed the door in his face for impertinence, but the queen put her hand on my sleeve.

'Any reply?' he asked. He did not even call her 'Your Majesty'.

'Go where I may, I remain his wife, and I will pray for him,' she said steadily. She rose to her feet. 'Tell the king that I wish him well on his journey, that I am sorry not to have said goodbye to him, if he had told me he was leaving so soon I should have made sure that he did not leave without his wife's blessing. And ask him to send a message to tell me that he is in good health.'

The messenger nodded, shot a quick apologetic look at me, and got himself out of the room. We waited.

The queen and I went to the window. We could see the man on his horse ride the length of the baggage train which was still winding down the river road. He vanished from sight. Anne and Henry, perhaps handclasped, perhaps singing together, would be far ahead on the road to Woodstock.

'I never thought it would end like this,' she said in a small voice. 'I never thought he would be able to leave me without saying goodbye.'

❧

It was a fine summer for the children and for me. Henry was five and his sister seven years old and I decided that they should each have a pony of their own; but nowhere in the county could I find a pair of good ponies small enough and docile enough for us. I had mentioned this plan to William Stafford as we rode to Hever and so I was not wholly surprised when I saw him returning, uninvited, a week later, riding up the lane with a small fat pony on either side of his rangy hunter.

The children and I had been walking in the meadows before the moat. I waved to him and he turned off the lane and rode along the side of the moat towards us. As soon as Henry and Catherine saw the ponies they were leaping with excitement.

'Wait,' I cautioned them. 'Wait and see. We don't know that they'll be any good. We don't know that we want to buy them.'

'You're right to be cautious. I'm such a huckster,' William Stafford said, sliding from his saddle and dropping to the ground. He took my hand in his and brought it to his lips.

'Wherever did you find them?'

Catherine had the rope of the little grey pony and was petting its nose. Henry was behind my skirt, eyeing the chestnut with a mixture of intense excitement and fear.

'Oh you know, on the doorstep,' he said idly. 'I can send them back if you don't like them.'

At once there was a wail of protest from Henry, still behind my skirts. 'Don't send them back!'

William Stafford dropped to one knee to be on a level with Henry's bright face. 'Come out, lad,' he said kindly. 'You'll never make a horseman hiding behind your mother.'

'Does he bite?'

'You have to feed him with your hand flat,' William explained. 'Then he can't bite.' He flattened Henry's hand and showed him how a horse crops.

'Does he gallop?' Catherine asked. 'Gallop like mother's horse?'

'He can't go as fast, but he does gallop,' William answered. 'And he can jump.'

'Can I jump with him?' Henry's eyes were like trenchers.

William straightened up and smiled at me. 'You have to learn to sit on him first, walk, trot and canter. Then you can go on to jousting and jumping.'

'Will you teach me?' Catherine demanded. 'You will, won't you? Stay here with us all the summer and teach us how to ride?'

William's smile was shamelessly triumphant. 'Well I should like to, of course. If your mother says that I may.'

At once the two children turned to me. 'Say yes!' Catherine begged.

'Please!' Henry urged me.

'But I can teach you to ride,' I protested.

'Not to joust!' Henry exclaimed. 'And you ride sideways. I need to ride straight. Don't I, sir? I need to ride straight because I'm a boy and I'm going to be a man.'

William looked at me over the top of my son's bobbing head. 'What d'you say, Lady Carey? Can I stay for the summer and teach your son to ride straight?'

I did not let him see my amusement. 'Oh very well. You can tell them in the house to prepare a room if you like.'

Every morning William Stafford and I would walk for hours with the children seated on their little ponies walking beside us. After dinner we would put the ponies on long lunge reins and let them walk, trot and then canter in a circle while the two children clung on like a pair of little burrs.

William was unendingly patient with them. He made sure that every day they learned a little more, and I suspected that he also made sure that they did not learn too fast. He wanted them to ride on their own by the end of the summer, but not before.

'D'you have no home of your own to go to?' I asked unkindly as we walked back to the castle one evening, each of us leading a pony. The sun was sinking behind the turrets and it looked like a little fairytale palace with the windows winking with rosy light and the sky all pale and cloud-striped behind it.

'My father lives in Northampton.'

'Are you his only son?' I asked.

He smiled at that key question. 'No, I am a second son: good for nothing, milady. But I am going to buy a little farm if I can, in Essex. I have a mind to be a landowner of a small farm.'

'Where will you find the money?' I asked curiously. 'You can't do very well from my uncle's service.'

'I served on a ship and took a little prize money a few years ago. I have enough to start. And then I shall find a woman who would like to live in a pretty house amid her own fields and know that nothing – not the power of princes nor the malice of queens – can touch her.'

'Queens and princes can always touch you,' I said. 'Else they would not be queens and princes.'

'Yes, but you can be so small as to be of no interest to them,' he said. 'Our danger would be your son. While they see him as the heir to the throne then we would never be out of their sights.'

'If Anne has a boy of her own she'll give mine up,' I said. Without realising it I had followed the train of his thoughts just as I had fallen into step beside him.

Cunningly he said nothing to alert me. 'Better than that, she'll want him away from the court. He could be with us and we could bring him up as a little country squire. It's not a bad life for a man. Perhaps the best life there is. I don't like the court. And these last few years you never know where you are.'

We reached the drawbridge and in accord helped the children from their saddles. Catherine and Henry ran ahead into the house as William and I led their ponies round to the stable yard. A couple of lads came out to take them from us.

'Coming to dinner?' I asked casually.

'Of course,' he said and threw me a little bow and was gone.

❧

It was only in my room, as I kneeled and prayed that night and found my mind wandering, as it always does, that I realised that I had let him talk to me as if I would be the woman who would want a pretty house amid my own fields, and William Stafford in my married bed.

> *Dear Mary,*
>
> *We are to come to Richmond for autumn and then Greenwich for winter. The queen will not be under the same roof as the king, ever again. She is to go to Wolsey's old house, The More in Hertfordshire, and the king is to give her a court of her own there, so she need not complain of being ill-treated.*
>
> *You are no longer to be in her service, you will serve me alone.*
>
> *The king and I are confident that the Pope is in terror of what the king might do to the church in England. We are certain that he will rule in our favour as soon as the courts reconvene in the autumn. I am preparing myself for an autumn wedding and a coronation soon after. It is all but complete – grudge who will grudge it!*
>
> *Uncle has been very cold towards me and the Duke of Suffolk has quite turned against me. Henry sent him away from us this summer and I was glad to have him taught a lesson. There are too many people envying me and watching me. I want you at Richmond when I arrive, Mary. You may not go to the que – to Katherine of Aragon at The More. And you may not stay at Hever. I am doing this for your son as much as for myself and you will help me.*
>
> *Anne.*

Autumn 1531

That autumn when I returned to court I realised that the queen was finally thrown down. Anne had convinced Henry that there was no longer any point in keeping up the appearance of being a good husband. They might as well show their brazen faces to the world and defy anyone to come against them.

Henry was generous. Katherine of Aragon lived in great state at The More and she entertained visiting ambassadors as if she were still a beloved and honoured queen. She had a household of more than two hundred people, fifty of them maids in waiting. They were not the best of the young women: those all flocked to the king's court and found themselves attached to Anne's household. Anne and I had a merry day in allocating young women that we disliked to the queen's court, we got rid of half a dozen Seymours that way, and laughed at the thought of Sir John Seymour's face when he found out.

'I wish we could send George's wife to wait on the queen,' I said. 'He would be happier if he came home and found her gone.'

'I'd rather have her here where I can see her than send her to somewhere that she might cause more trouble. I want no-one around the queen but nonentities.'

'You can't still fear her. You have all but destroyed her.'

Anne shook her head. 'I'll not be safe until she is dead,' she said. 'Just as she will not be safe until I am dead. It is not just a matter now of a man or a throne, it is as if I am her shadow and she is mine. We are locked together till death. One of us has to win outright and neither of us can be sure that we have won or lost until the other is dead and in the ground.'

'How could she win?' I demanded. 'He won't even see her.'

'You don't know how much people hate me,' Anne whispered, I had to lean close to hear. 'When we are on our progress we go from house to house now, and never stop in the villages. People have heard the rumours from London and they no longer see me as a pretty girl who rides beside the king, they see me as the woman who destroyed the happiness of the queen. If we linger in a village then people shout against me.'

'No!'

She nodded. 'And when the queen came into the City and gave a banquet there was a mob outside Ely Palace and they were all calling out blessings on her and promising her that they would never bow the knee to me.'

'A handful of sulky servants.'

'What if it's more than that?' Anne asked bleakly. 'What if the whole country hates me? What d'you think the king feels when he hears them booing and cursing me? D'you think a man like Henry can bear to be cursed when he rides out? A man like Henry, who has been used to praise ever since he was a child?'

'They'll get accustomed,' I said. 'The priests will preach in the churches that you are his wife, when you give them a son they'll turn round in a moment, you'll be the saviour of the country.'

'Yes,' she said. 'It all hangs on that, doesn't it? A son.'

❁

Anne was right to fear the mob. Just before Christmas we went up the river from Greenwich to dinner with the Trevelyans. It was not an outing of the court. Nobody knew that we were going. The king was dining in private with a couple of ambassadors from France and Anne took a fancy to go into the City. I went with her, with a couple of the king's gentlemen and a couple of the other ladies. It was cold on the river and we were wrapped up warmly in furs. No-one on the banks could even have seen our faces as the boat stopped at the Trevelyans' stairs and we disembarked.

But somebody saw us, and somebody recognised Anne, and before we had even started eating there was a servant running into the hall and whispering to Lord Trevelyan that there was a mob coming towards the house. His quick glance at Anne told us all who they were coming for. She rose at once from the table, her face as white as her pearls.

'You'd better go,' his lordship said ungallantly. 'I cannot promise your safety here.'

'Why not?' she asked. 'You can close your gates.'

'For Christ's sake, there are thousands of them!' His voice was sharp with fear. Now we were all on our feet. 'This isn't a gang of apprentice lads, it's a mob coming, they are swearing to hang you from the rafters. You had better get to your boat and go back to Greenwich, Lady Anne.'

She hesitated for a moment, hearing his determination to get her away from his home.

'Is the boat ready?'

Someone ran from the hall shouting for the boatmen.

'Surely we can beat them off!' Francis Weston said. 'How many men have you got here, Trevelyan? We can take them on, teach them a lesson, and then have our dinner.'

'I have three hundred men,' his lordship started.

'Well then – let's arm them and . . .'

'The mob is eight thousand, and growing as they pass through every street.'

There was a stunned silence. 'Eight thousand?' Anne whispered. 'Eight thousand people marching against me in the streets of London?'

'Quickly,' Lady Trevelyan said. 'For God's sake, get to your boat.'

Anne snatched her cape from the woman and I grabbed another, it wasn't even mine. The ladies who had come with us were crying with fear. One of them ran away upstairs, she was afraid to be on the river in case they came after us on the dark waters. Anne raced out of the house and through the black garden. She flung herself into the boat and I was right behind her. Francis and William were with us, the rest threw the mooring ropes into the boat and pushed it off. They wouldn't even come with us.

'Get your heads down and keep covered,' one of them shouted.

'And take the royal standard down.'

It was a shameful moment. One of the boatmen snatched out his knife and cut the ropes holding the royal standard for fear that the people of England should see their own king's flag. He fumbled with it and then it slipped from his hand and fell overboard. I watched it turn in the water and sink down.

'Never mind that! Row!' Anne shouted, her face veiled in her furs.

I ducked down beside her and we clung together. I could feel her trembling.

We saw the mob as we pulled out into the swirling current. They had lit torches and we could see the bobbing flares reflected in the dark river. The string of lights seemed to go on for ever. Over the water we could hear them shouting curses on my sister. At each violent shout there was a roar of approval, a roar of naked hatred. Anne shrank lower in the boat, held onto me yet more tightly and shook with fear.

The boatmen rowed like men possessed, they knew that none of us would survive an attack on the boat in this weather. If the mob even knew that we were out on the dark water they would heave up cobblestones and throw them, they would chase down the banks to get to us, they would find boats to commandeer and they would be after us.

'Row faster!' Anne hissed.

We made ragged progress, too afraid to beat a drum or shout the rhythm. We wanted to slip past the mob, shielded by the darkness. I peered over the edge of the boat and saw the lights pause, hesitate, as if they were looking out into the darkness, as if they could sense with the preternatural awareness of a savage beast that the woman they wanted was muffling her sobs of terror into her furs only yards away from them.

Then the procession went on, to the Trevelyans' house. It wound along the curve of the river, the torches stretching for what seemed like miles. Anne sat up and pushed back her hood. Her face was aghast.

'D'you think he'll protect me against that?' she demanded fiercely. 'Against the Pope – yes – especially when it means that he gets the tithes of the church into his own keeping. Against the queen – yes – especially when it means that he gets a son and heir. But against his own people, if they come for me with torches and ropes in the night? D'you think he'll stand by me then?'

❧

It was a quiet Christmas at Greenwich that year. The queen sent the king a beautiful cup of gold and he sent it back to her with a cold-hearted message. We felt her absence all the time. It was like a home when a beloved mother is missing. It was not that she had been sparkling or brilliant or provocative as Anne always, wearisomely, was – it was just that she had always been there. Her reign had gone on for so long that there were very few people who could remember the English court without her.

Anne was determinedly bright and enchanting and active. She danced and she sang, she gave the king a set of darts in Biscayan fashion and he gave her a room full of the most expensive fabrics for her gowns. He gave her the key to the room and watched her as she went in and exclaimed in delight at the rich swathes of colour swagged from one golden pole to another. He showered gifts on her, on all of us Howards. He gave me a beautiful shirt with a collar of blackwork. But still, it was more like a wake than Christmas. Everyone missed the steadying presence of the queen and wondered what she was doing at the lovely house which had belonged to the cardinal, who had been her enemy till the very last when he had finally found the courage to acknowledge that she was in the right.

Nothing could lift people's spirits, though Anne wore herself to a shadow trying to be merry. At night she would lie beside me in the bed and even in her sleep I would hear her muttering, like a woman quite insane.

I lit the candle one night and held it up to see her. Her eyes were closed, dark eyelashes sweeping her white cheeks. Her hair was tied back under a nightcap as bleached as her skin. The shadows under her eyes were violet as pansies, she looked frail. And all the time her bloodless lips, parted in a smile, were muttering introductions, jests, quick quips. Every now and again she would turn her head restlessly on the pillow, that enchanting turn of her head that she did so well, and she would laugh, a horrid breathy sound from a woman so driven that even in her deepest dreams she was trying to make a celebration come alive.

She started to drink wine in the morning. It brought colour to her face and a brightness to her eyes, it lifted her from her intense fatigue and nervousness. Once she thrust a bottle at me when I came into her rooms with Uncle following me. 'Hide it,' she hissed desperately and turned to him with the back of her hand against her mouth so that he would not smell the drink on her breath.

'Anne, you have to stop,' I said when he had gone. 'Everyone watches you all the time. People are bound to see, and they will tell the king.'

'I can't stop,' she said darkly. 'I can't stop anything, not for a moment. I have to go on and on and on, as if I am the happiest woman in the world. I am going to marry the man I love. I am going to be Queen of England. Of course I am happy. Of course I am wonderfully happy. There couldn't be a happier woman in England than me.'

❧

George was due to come home in the New Year and Anne and I decided on a private dinner in her grand rooms to welcome him. We spent the day consulting with the cooks and ordering the very best that they had, and then the afternoon lingering in the windowseats waiting to see George's boat coming up the river with the Howard standard flying. I spotted it first, dark against the dusk, and I did not say a word to Anne but slipped from the room and ran down the stairs so that when George disembarked and came up the landing stage I was alone, into his arms, and it was me that he kissed and whispered: 'Good God, sister, I am glad to be home.'

When Anne saw that she had lost the chance of taking first place she did not run after me but waited to greet him in her rooms, before the great arching mantelpiece when he bowed and next kissed her hand and only then folded her into his arms. Then the women were dismissed and we were the three Boleyns together again, as we had always been.

George had told us all his news over dinner and he wanted to know everything that had happened since he had been away from court. I noticed that Anne was careful what she told him. She did not tell him that she could not go into the City without an armed guard. She did not tell him that in the country she had to ride swiftly through peaceful little villages. She did not tell him that the night after Cardinal Wolsey had died she had designed and danced in a masque entitled 'Sending the Cardinal to Hell' which had shocked everyone who saw it by its tasteless triumphing over the king's dead friend and its outright bawdiness. She did not tell him that Bishop Fisher was still against her and that Bishop Fisher had nearly died of poison. When she did not tell him these things I knew, as I had in truth known before, that she was ashamed of the woman that she was becoming. She did not want George to know how deep this canker of ambition had spread inside her. She did not want him to know that she was not his beloved little sister any more but a woman who had learned to throw everything, even her mortal soul, into the battle to become queen.

'And what about you?' George asked me. 'What's his name?'

Anne was blank. 'What are you talking about?'

'Anyone can see – surely I've not got it wrong? – Marianne is glowing like a milkmaid in springtime. I would have put a fortune on her being in love.'

I blushed a deep scarlet.

'I thought so,' my brother said with deep satisfaction. 'Who is it?'

'Mary has no lover,' Anne said.

'I suppose she might have her eye on somebody without your permission,' George suggested. 'I suppose somebody might have picked her out without applying to you, Mistress Queen.'

'He'd better not,' she said, without a trace of a smile. 'I have plans for Mary.'

George let out a soundless whistle. 'Good God, Annamaria, anyone would think you were anointed already.'

She rounded on him. 'When I am, I will know who my friends are. Mary is my lady in waiting and I keep good order in my household.'

'Surely she can make her own choice now.'

Anne shook her head. 'Not if she wants my favour.'

'For God's sake, Anne! We're family. You're where you are because Mary stepped back for you. You can't turn around now and act like a

Princess of the Blood. We put you where you are. You can't treat us like subjects.'

'You are subjects,' she said simply. 'You, Mary, even Uncle Howard. I had my own aunt sent from court, I had the king's brother-in-law sent from court. I had the queen herself sent from court. Is there anyone who has any doubt that I can send them into exile if I wish? No. You may have helped me to be where I am –'

'Helped you! We bloody well pushed you!'

'But now I am here I will be queen. And you will be my subjects and in my service. I will be the queen and mother to the next King of England. So you had better remember that, George, for I won't tell you again.'

Anne rose up from the floor and swept towards the door. She stood before it, waiting for someone to open it for her, and when neither of us sprang up she flung it open herself. She turned on the threshold. 'And don't call me Annamaria any more,' she said. 'And don't call her Mari-anne. She is Mary, the other Boleyn girl. And I am Anne, Queen Anne to be. There is a world of difference between us two. We don't share a name. She is next to nobody and I will be queen.'

She stalked out, not troubling to close the door behind her. We could hear her footsteps going to her bedroom. We sat in silence while we heard her chamber door slam.

'Good God,' George said, heartfelt. 'What a witch.' He got up and closed the door against the cold draught. 'How long has she been like this?'

'Her power has grown steadily. She thinks she is untouchable.'

'And is she?'

'He's deeply in love. I should think she is safe, yes.'

'And he still hasn't had her?'

'No.'

'Good God, what do they do?'

'Everything, but the deed. She daren't allow it.'

'Must be driving him crazy,' George said with grim satisfaction.

'Her too,' I said. 'Almost every night he is kissing her and touching her and she is all over him with her hair and her mouth.'

'Does she speak to everyone like this? Like she spoke to me?'

'Far worse. And it is costing her friends. Charles Brandon is against her now, Uncle Howard is sick of her; they have quarrelled outright, at least a couple of times since Christmas. She thinks she is so safe in the king's love that she needs no other protection.'

'I won't tolerate it,' George said. 'I'll tell her.'

I maintained my look of sisterly concern, but my heart leaped at the

302

thought of a gulf opening up between Anne and George. If I could get George on my side, I would have a real advantage in any fight to regain the ownership of my son.

'And truly, is there no-one that has caught your eye?' he asked.

'A nobody,' I said. 'I would tell no-one but you, George – so keep it as a secret.'

'I swear,' he said, taking both my hands and drawing me closer. 'A secret, on my honour. Are you in love?'

'Oh no,' I said, drawing back at the very thought of it. 'Of course not. But he pays me a little attention and it's nice to have a man make a fuss of you.'

'I'd have thought the court was full of men making a fuss of you.'

'Oh they write poetry and they swear they will die of love. But he . . . he is a little more . . . real.'

'Who is he?'

'A nobody,' I said again. 'So I don't think about him.'

'Pity you can't just have him,' George said with brotherly candour.

I did not reply. I was thinking of William Stafford's engaging intimate smile. 'Yes,' I said very quietly. 'A pity, but I can't.'

Spring 1532

George, ignorant of the change of the temper of the people, invited Anne and me to ride out with him, down the river, to dine at the little ale house and come home again. I waited for Anne to refuse, to tell him that it was no longer safe for her to ride out alone; but she said nothing. She dressed in an unusually dark gown, she wore her riding hat pulled down over her face, and she laid aside her distinctive necklace with the golden 'B'.

Pleased to be back in England riding out with his sisters, George did not notice Anne's discreet behaviour and dress. But when we stopped at the ale house the slatternly old woman who should have been serving us took a sideways glance at Anne and then went away. Moments later the master of the house came out, wiping his hands on an apron of hessian, and announced that the bread and cheese he had been going to set before us had spoiled, there was nothing in his house we could eat.

George would have flared up, but Anne put a hand on his sleeve and said that it was no matter, we should go to the monastery nearby and eat there. He let himself be guided by her, and we ate well enough. The king was an object of terror now in every abbey and monastery in the land. Only the servants, less politically astute than the monks, glanced askance at Anne and at me, and speculated in whispers as to which was the old whore and which was the new.

Riding home, the cold sun on our backs, George spurred his horse forward and rode beside me. 'Everyone knows then,' he said flatly.

'From London to far out into the country,' I said. 'I don't know how far the news has gone.'

'And I don't see anyone throwing his hat in the air and shouting huzzah?'

'No, you won't see that.'

'I'd have thought a pretty English girl would have pleased people? She's pretty enough, isn't she? Waves her hand as she goes by, gives out alms, all the rest of it?'

'She does all that,' I said. 'But the women have a stubborn liking for the old queen. They say that if the King of England puts a loyal honest wife aside because he fancies a change, then no woman is safe.'

George was silent for a moment. 'Do they do more than mutter?'

'We were caught in a riot in London. And the king says it's not safe for her to go into the City at all. She is hated, George, and they say all sorts of things about her.'

'Things?'

'That she is a witch and has enchanted the king by sorcery. That she is a murderess and would poison the queen if she could. That she has made him impotent with all other women so he has to marry her. That she blasted the children in the queen's womb and put barrenness on the throne of England.'

George went a little pale and his hand on the rein clenched into the old sign against witchcraft – thumb between the two first fingers to make the sign of the cross. 'They say this publicly? Might the king hear of it?'

'The worst of it is kept from him, but someone is bound to tell him sooner or later.'

'He wouldn't believe a word of it, would he?'

'He says some of it himself. He says he is a man possessed. He says that she has enchanted him and that he can't think about another woman. It's love talk when he says it, but when it gets out – it's dangerous.'

George nodded. 'She should do more good works and not be so damned . . .' He broke off, searching for the word. 'Sensual.'

I looked ahead. Even on horseback, even when she was riding with no-one but her family, Anne swayed in the saddle in a way that made you want to take her by the waist.

'She's a Boleyn and a Howard,' I said frankly. 'Underneath the great name, we're all bitches on heat.'

❧

William Stafford, waiting at the gateway to Greenwich Palace when we rode in, tipped his hat to me and caught my secret smile. When we had dismounted and Anne had led the way in, he was at the doorway and he drew me to one side.

'I was waiting for you,' he said, without further greeting.

'I saw.'

'I don't like you riding without me, the country's not safe for the Boleyn girls.'

'My brother took care of us. It was good to be out without a great retinue.'

'Oh, I can offer you that. Simplicity I can offer in abundance.'

I laughed. 'I thank you.'

He kept his hand on my sleeve to keep me by him. 'When the king and your sister marry then you will be married to a man of their choosing.'

I looked into his square, tanned face. 'And so?'

'And so, if you wanted to marry a man with a pretty little manor and a few fields around it you should make haste to do so before your sister's wedding. The later that you leave it the harder it will be.'

I hesitated. I moved away from the touch of his hand and I turned away. I smiled at him, sideways under my eyelashes. 'But no-one has asked me,' I sweetly explained. 'I shall have to reconcile myself to being a widow all my days. No-one has asked me to marry him at all.'

For once he was lost for words. 'But I thought . . .' he began. A delighted laugh escaped me. I swept him a deep curtsey, and turned for the palace. As I climbed the stairs I glanced back to see him fling his hat to the ground and kick it, and I knew the joy that every woman knows, when she has got a handsome man on the run.

❁

I did not see him again for a week though I dawdled in the stable yard, and in the garden, and at the river where he might have found me. When my uncle's train went by one day I watched them but I could not pick him out from the two hundred men in matching Howard livery. I knew I was behaving like a fool; but I thought that there was no harm in looking for a handsome man and teasing him.

I did not see him for a week, and then not for another week. My uncle and I were watching the king and Anne playing at bowls one warm April morning and I said casually: 'Do you still have that man – William Stafford – in your service?'

'Oh yes,' my uncle said. 'But I have given him leave for a month.'

'Gone from court?'

'He has a fancy to marry, he tells me. He has gone to speak to his father and to buy a place for his new wife.'

I felt the ground shift. 'I thought he was married already,' I said, choosing the safest thing to say.

'Oh no, a terrible philanderer,' my uncle said, his mind half on the king and Anne. 'One of the ladies of the court was quite besotted with him, thought she would marry him and give up the life of court to live with him and a flock of hens. Can you imagine it!'

'Foolish.' My mouth was dry. I swallowed a little.

'And all the time he's betrothed to some country girl, I don't doubt,' my uncle said. 'Waiting for her to come of age, I expect. He's off to marry this month and then he'll come back to me. He's a good man, very reliable. He took you to Hever, didn't he?'

'Twice,' I said. 'And he found me the children's ponies.'

'He's good at things like that,' my uncle said. 'He should go far. I might raise him up to run my stables, be my master of horse.' He paused, and suddenly turned his dark gaze on me like a bright lantern. 'Didn't flirt with you, did he?'

The look I returned to him was one of absolute indifference. 'A man in your service? Of course not.'

'Good,' my uncle said, unimpressed. 'He's a rogue given half a chance.'

'He won't have a chance with me,' I said.

❧

Anne and I were ready for bed, dressed in our night shifts, the maids dismissed, when there was the familiar tap at the door. 'Could only be George,' Anne said. 'Come in.'

Our handsome brother lounged at the door with a pitcher of wine in one hand and three glasses in the other. 'I come to worship at the shrine of beauty.' He was quite drunk.

'You can come in,' I said. 'We are wonderfully beautiful.'

He kicked the door shut behind him. 'Much better by candlelight,' he said, surveying the two of us. 'Good God, Henry must go mad to think that he had the one of you and wants the other and can have neither.'

Anne was never pleased to be reminded that the king had been my lover. 'He is always attentive to me.'

George rolled his eyes at me. 'Drink?'

We all took a glass and George threw another log on the fire. There was a whisper of sound from the other side of the door. George, suddenly lithe and quick, was up at the door and tore it open. Jane Parker stood there, just straightening up from where she had been bending to put her eye to the keyhole.

'My dear wife!' George said with a voice like honey. 'If you want me in your bed you don't have to crawl around my sister's rooms, you can just ask.'

She flushed to the roots of her hair and peered past him to Anne, in bed, her gown slipping from her naked shoulder, and me in my nightdress at the fireside. There was something about the way she looked at the three of us that made me flinch. She always made me feel ashamed, as if I had

307

been doing something wrong. But it was as if she would collude with us. She looked as if she wanted to know dirty secrets, and share them.

'I was passing the door and I heard voices,' she said awkwardly. 'I was afraid that someone was disturbing Lady Anne. I was just about to knock to make sure that her ladyship was all right.'

'You were going to knock with your ear?' George asked, puzzled. 'With your nose?'

'Oh leave it, George,' I said suddenly. 'There is nothing wrong, Jane. George came to have a drink with us and say goodnight. He'll come to your room in a moment.'

She looked very far from grateful for my intervention. 'He can come or not as he likes,' she said. 'He can stay here all night if that is his pleasure.'

'Leave me,' Anne said simply. She spoke as if she would not descend to brawl with Jane.

George bowed in obedience and smartly shut the door in Jane's face. He turned and put his back to it and, without caring that she would certainly hear, laughed aloud. 'What a little snake!' he cried. 'Oh Mary, you shouldn't rise to her. Follow Anne's lead: "Leave me." Good God! It was tremendous: "Leave me."'

He came back to the fireside and poured us all wine. He handed the first glass to me and the second to Anne and then he held up his own to toast us both.

Anne did not raise her glass and she did not smile at him. 'Next time,' she observed, 'you will serve me first.'

'What?' he asked, confused.

'When you pour a glass of wine, it comes first to me. When you open my bedroom door you ask me if I want to admit the visitor. I am going to be queen, George, and you must learn to serve me as a queen.'

He did not flare up at her as he had done when he was freshly home from Europe. Even in that short time he had seen that Anne had great power. She did not care if she quarrelled with her uncle, or with any of the men at court that could have been her allies. She did not care who hated her, as long as the king was at her beck and call. And she could ruin any man she chose.

George put his glass down on the hearth and crawled up on the bed so that he was on his hands and knees, with his face just inches from hers. 'My little queen in waiting,' he purred.

Anne's face softened at his intimacy.

'My little princess,' he whispered. Gently he kissed her on the nose and then the lips. 'Don't be a shrew with me,' he begged her. 'We all know that you are the first lady of the kingdom, but be sweet to me, Anne. We'll all be so much happier if you are sweet to me.'

Unwillingly, she smiled. 'You must show me every respect,' she warned him.

'I will lie beneath your horse's hooves,' he promised her.

'And never take liberties.'

'I would rather die.'

'Then you can come here and I will be sweet to you,' she said.

He leaned forward and kissed her again. Her eyes closed and her lips smiled and then parted. I watched as he pressed closer, and his finger went to her bare shoulder and stroked her neck. I watched, quite fascinated and quite horrified, as his fingers went into her smooth dark hair and pulled her head back for his kiss. Then she opened her eyes with a little sigh. 'Enough.' And she pushed him gently off the bed. George returned to his place at the fireside and we all pretended that it was nothing more than a brotherly kiss.

❁

The next day Jane Parker was as confident as ever. She smiled at me, she curtsied at Anne and handed her cape as Anne was about to go out walking by the river with the king.

'I would have thought you would have been displeased this day, my lady.'

Anne took the cape. 'Why?'

'The news,' Jane said.

'What news?' I asked, so that Anne did not appear curious.

Jane answered me, but she watched Anne. 'The Countess of Northumberland is divorcing Henry Percy.'

Anne staggered for a moment and went white.

'Oh!' I cried, to draw the attention to me and from Anne. 'What a scandal! Why should she divorce him? What an idea! How very wrong of her.'

Anne had recovered, but Jane had watched her. 'Why,' Jane said, in a voice like silk. 'She says that their marriage was never valid at all. She says that there was a pre-contract. She says that all along he has been married to you, Lady Anne.'

Anne's head went up and she smiled at Jane. 'Lady Rochford, you do bring me the most extraordinary tidings. And you do choose the strangest of times to bring them to me. Last night you were creeping and listening at my door, and now you are as filled with bad news as a dead dog with maggots. If the Countess of Northumberland is unhappy in her marriage then I am sure that we all grieve for her.' There was a little murmur from the ladies, more like avid curiosity than sympathy. 'But if she wants to claim that Henry Percy was betrothed to me then it is simply not true. In either case, the king is waiting for me and you are delaying me.'

Anne tied her own cape and swept from the room. Two or three of her ladies followed her, as they should all have done. The rest held back, circling Jane Parker for more scandal.

'Jane, I am sure the king will want to see you attending Lady Anne,' I said spitefully.

At once she had to go, she followed Anne from the room and the others trailed behind her.

I picked up my skirts and ran like a schoolgirl to my uncle's apartments.

He was at his desk, though it was early in the afternoon. A clerk stood at his elbow, writing memoranda as my uncle dictated. My uncle frowned when I put my head around the door and then motioned me in and gestured that I should wait.

'What is it?' he asked. 'I am busy. I've just heard that Thomas More is unhappy with the king's matter against the queen. I didn't expect him to like it but I was hoping his conscience could swallow it. I'd give a thousand crowns not to have Thomas More openly against us.'

'It's something else,' I said tersely. 'But important.'

My uncle waved the clerk from the room.

'Anne?' he asked.

I nodded. We were a family business now and Anne was our goods for sale. My uncle knew, without me telling him, that if I ran to his rooms first thing in the afternoon, then it was a crisis in our trading.

'Jane just said that the Countess of Northumberland is to petition for divorce against Henry Percy,' I said in a rush. 'Jane said that she is arguing he was pre-contracted to Anne.'

'Damnation,' my uncle swore.

'Did you know?'

'Of course I knew she had it in mind. I thought she was going to plead desertion or cruelty or buggery or something. I thought we had moved her away from the pre-contract business.'

'We?'

He scowled at me. 'We. Doesn't matter who, does it?'

'No.'

'And how does Jane know?' he demanded irritably.

310

'Oh Jane knows everything. She was listening at Anne's door last night.'

'What could she have heard?' he asked, the spymaster in him always alert.

'Nothing,' I said staunchly. 'George was there and we were doing nothing but talking and drinking a glass of wine.'

'No-one but George?' he asked sharply.

'Who else could it be?'

'That's what I'm asking you.'

'You cannot doubt Anne's chastity.'

'She spends her life spinning her toils around men.'

Even I could not let this injustice go. 'She spins her toils around the king, as you ordered.'

'So where is she now?'

'In the garden with the king.'

'Go to her straightaway and tell her to deny everything with Henry Percy. No betrothal of any sort, no pre-contract. Just a boy and a girl in springtime and a green affection. A pageboy making eyes at a lady in waiting. Nothing more than that, and never returned by her. Just him. Have you got that?'

'There are those who know different,' I warned him.

'They're all bought,' he said. 'Except Wolsey, and he's dead.'

'He might have told the king, back then, before anyone knew that the king would fall in love with Anne.'

'He's dead,' my uncle said with relish 'He can't repeat it. And everyone else will fall over themselves to assure the king that Anne is as chaste as the Virgin Mary. Henry Percy quicker than anyone. It's only that damned wife of his who is so desperate to get out of that marriage that she'd risk everything.'

'Why does she hate him so?' I wondered.

He gave a sharp bark of laughter. 'Good God, Mary, you are the most delightful fool. Because he *was* married to Anne, and she knows it. Because he was in love with Anne, and she knows it. And because losing Anne turned his head to melancholy and he has been a man destroyed ever since. No wonder she doesn't want to be his wife. Now go and find your sister and lie your head off. Open those beautiful eyes of yours and tell lies for us.'

I found the king and Anne at the riverside walk. She was talking earnestly to him and his head was inclined towards her as if he could not risk missing a single word. She glanced up when she saw me coming. 'Mary

311

will tell you,' she said. 'She was my bedfellow then when I was nothing more than a girl new to court.'

Henry looked up at me and I could see the hurt in his face.

'It's the Countess of Northumberland,' Anne explained 'Spreading slander about me to save herself from a marriage that she has grown tired of.'

'What can she be saying?'

'The old scandal. That Henry Percy was in love with me.'

I smiled at the king with all the warmth and confidence I could muster. 'Of course he was, Your Majesty. Don't you remember what it was like when Anne first came to court? Everyone was in love with her. Henry Percy among them.'

'There was talk of a betrothal,' Henry said.

'With the Earl of Ormonde?' I asked quickly.

'They couldn't agree the dowry and the title,' Anne said.

'I meant between you and Henry Percy,' he persisted.

'There was nothing,' she said. 'A boy and a girl at court, a poem, a few words, nothing at all.'

'He wrote three poems to me,' I said. 'He was the most idle page that the cardinal ever had. He was always writing poems to everyone. What a shame that he has married a woman with no sense of humour. But thank God she had no love of poetry or she would have run away even sooner!'

Anne laughed but we could not turn Henry off his course.

'She says there was a pre-contract,' he persisted. 'That you and he were betrothed.'

'I have told you we were not.' Anne contradicted him with a little edge to her voice.

'But why should she say it if it is not so?' Henry demanded.

'To rid herself of her husband!' Anne snapped.

'But why choose that lie, rather than another? Why not say he was married to Mary here? If she had his poems too?'

'I expect she will,' I said wildly, hoping to delay the explosion from Anne. But her temper was rising up in her and she could not stop it. She pulled her hand from the crook of his arm.

'What are you suggesting?' she demanded. 'What are you saying of me? Are you calling me unchaste? When I stand here and swear to you that I have never, ever looked at another man? And now you – of all people in the world – accuse me of being pre-contracted! You! Who sought me out and courted me with another wife still living? Which of us is the more likely to be a bigamist, think you? A man with a wife tucked away in a beautiful house in Hertfordshire, fawned on by her own court, visited by everyone, a queen in exile, or the girl who once had a poem written to her?'

'My marriage is invalid!' Henry shouted back at her. 'As every cardinal in Rome knows!'

'But it took place! As every man, woman and child in London knows. You spent enough money on it, God knows. You were merry enough about it then! But nothing took place for me, no promises were made, no rings were given, nothing nothing nothing! And you torment me with this nothing.'

'Before God!' he swore. 'Will you listen to me?'

'No!' she screamed, quite beyond control. 'For you are a fool and I am in love with a fool and the more fool me. I will not listen to you but you will listen to every spiteful worm that would spit poison in your ear!'

'Anne!'

'No!' she cried and flung herself away from him.

In two swift strides he was after her and had caught her to him. She lashed out at him and hit him on the padded shoulders of his jacket. Half the court flinched to see the monarch of England assaulted, no one knew what to do. Henry grabbed her hands and slammed them behind her back, holding her so that her face was as close to him as if they were making love, her body pressed to his, his mouth close enough to bite or to kiss. I saw the look of avid lust that spread over him the moment he had her close.

'Anne,' he said again in a quite different voice.

'No,' she repeated, but she was smiling.

'Anne.'

She closed her eyes and tipped back her head and let him kiss her eyes and her lips. 'Yes,' she whispered.

'Good God,' George said in my ear. 'Is this how she plays him?'

I nodded as she turned in his arms and they walked together, hip to hip, his arm around her shoulders, her arm around his waist. They looked as if they wished they were walking to the bedroom instead of walking by the river. Their faces were alight with desire and satisfaction, as if the quarrel had been a storm like the storm of lovemaking.

'Always the rage and then the making up?'

'Yes,' I said. 'It is instead of the rage of making love, don't you think? They both get to shout and cry and then end up quietly in each other's arms.'

'He must adore her,' George said. 'She flies at him and then she nestles. My God, I've never seen it so clearly. She is a passionate whore, isn't she? I'm her brother and I'd have her now. She could drive a man crazed.'

313

I nodded. 'She always gives in; but always at least two minutes too late. She always pushes it to the very limit and beyond.'

'It's a damned dangerous game to play with a king who has absolute power.'

'What else can she do?' I asked him. 'She has to hold him somehow. She has to be a castle that he besieges over and over again. She has to keep the excitement up somehow.'

George slipped my hand into his arm and we followed the royal couple along the path. 'And what of the Countess of Northumberland?' he asked. 'She'll never get her annulment on the grounds that Henry Percy was pre-contracted to Anne?'

'She might as well wait to be widowed,' I said crudely. 'We can't let any slur be attached to Anne. The Countess will be married forever to a man who has always been in love with someone else. She'd have done better to never be a countess at all but to marry a man who loved her.'

'Are you all for love these days?' George asked. 'Is this the advice of the nobody?'

I laughed as if I did not care. 'The nobody has gone,' I said. 'And good riddance. The nobody meant nothing, as I should have foreseen.'

Summer 1532

The nobody, William Stafford, came back to my uncle's service in June. He came to find me to tell me that he was back at court and that he would escort me to Hever when I was ready to leave.

'I have already asked Sir Richard Brent to ride with me,' I said coldly.

I had the pleasure of seeing him look taken aback. 'I thought you might allow me to stay and take the children out riding.'

'How kind of you,' I said icily. 'Perhaps next summer.' I turned and walked away from him before he could think of anything to say to keep me. I felt his gaze on my back and felt that I had repaid him in some measure for flirting with me and treating me like a fool while all along he was planning to marry someone else.

∾

Sir Richard stayed only a few days, which was a relief to both of us. He did not like me in the country where I was distracted by my children and interested in my tenants. He preferred me at court where I had nothing to do but flirt. To his half-hidden relief he was summoned back by the king to help to plan for a royal trip to France.

'I am desolated to have to leave you,' he said, waiting for them to lead his horse round from the stables while we stood in the sunshine by the moat. The children dropped twigs into the water on one side of the drawbridge and were waiting for them to float through. I laughed while I watched them.

'That will take forever,' I said. 'It's not a fast-flowing stream.'

'William made us boats with a sail,' Catherine said to me, not taking her eye off her twig. 'They went whichever way the wind was blowing.'

I turned my attention back to my desolate lover. 'We will miss you, Sir Richard. Please give my regards to my sister.'

'I shall tell her that the country suits you as green velvet wrapped around a diamond,' he said.

'Thank you,' I replied. 'Do you know if the whole court is to go to France?'

'The noblemen and the king and the Lady Anne and her ladies in waiting,' he said. 'And I have to arrange all the staging posts in England to be ready for such a progress.'

'I'm sure they could trust the work to no more competent gentleman,' I said. 'For you brought me here with great comfort.'

'I could take you back again,' he offered.

I put my hand down to feel Henry's warm cropped head. 'I'll stay here for a little longer,' I said. 'I like to be in the country for the summer.'

I had not thought how I should get back to court, I was so happy with the children, so warmed by the sun of Hever, so much at peace in my little castle, under the skies of my home. But at the end of August I received a terse note from my father to tell me that George would come for me the next day.

We had a miserable supper. My children were pale and huge-eyed at the prospect of parting. I kissed them goodnight and then I sat by Catherine's bed waiting for her to sleep. It took a long time. Catherine forced her eyes open, knowing that once she slept the night would come, and next day I would be gone; but after an hour, not even she could stay awake any longer.

I ordered my maids to pack my gowns and my things and see that they were loaded onto the big wagon. I ordered the steward to pack cider and beer that my father would welcome, and apples and other fruit that would be an elegant gift for the king. Anne had wanted some books and I went to pick them out of the library. One was in Latin and I took a long time puzzling out the title to make sure that I had the right one. The other was a theology book in French. I put them carefully with my little jewel box. Then I went to bed and cried into my pillow because my summer with my children was cut short.

I was mounted and waiting for George with the wagon loaded and ready when I saw the column of men riding down the lane towards the drawbridge. Even at that distance I knew it was not George but him.

'William Stafford,' I said, unsmiling. 'I was expecting my brother.'

'I won you,' he said. He swept his hat from his head and beamed at me. 'I played him at cards and won the right to come and fetch you back to Windsor Castle.'

'Then my brother is forsworn,' I said disapprovingly. 'And I am not a chattel to be put on a gambling table of a common inn.'

'It was a most uncommon inn,' he said, needlessly provocative. 'And after he lost you he lost a very handsome diamond and a dance with a pretty girl.'

'I want to leave now,' I said rudely.

He bowed, crammed his hat on his head and signalled to the men to turn. 'We slept at Edenbridge last night so we are fresh for the journey,' he said.

My horse fell into pace beside his. 'Why didn't you come here?'

'Too cold,' he said shortly.

'Why, you have had one of the best rooms every time you have stayed here!'

'Not the castle. There's nothing wrong with the castle.'

I hesitated. 'You mean me.'

'Icy,' he confirmed. 'And I have no idea what I have done to offend you. One moment we were talking of the joys of country living and the next you are a flake of snow.'

'I don't have the least idea what you mean,' I said.

'Brrr,' he said and sent the column forward into a trot.

He kept up a punishing pace until it was midday and then he called a halt. He lifted me down from my horse and opened the gate into a field by a river. 'I brought food for us to eat,' he said. 'Come and walk with me while they are getting it ready.'

'I'm too tired to walk,' I said unhelpfully.

'Come and sit then.' He spread his cape on the ground in the shade of a tree.

I could not argue any more. I sat on his cape and I leaned back against the friendly roughness of the bark and looked at the sparkling river. A few ducks dabbled in the water near us, in the reeds at the far side was the furtive dodging of a pair of moorhen. He left me for a few moments and when he came back he was carrying two pewter mugs of small ale. He gave one to me and drew a gulp from his own.

'Now,' he said, with every appearance of a man settling down to talk. 'Now, Lady Carey. Please tell me what I have done to offend you.'

It was on the tip of my tongue to tell him that he had not offended me at all, that since there was nothing between us from start to finish, nothing could be lost.

'Don't,' he said hastily, as if he could see all of this in my face. 'I know

I tease you, lady, but I never meant to distress you. I thought we were halfway to understanding each other.'

'You were openly flirting with me,' I said crossly.

'Not flirting, I've been courting you,' he corrected me. 'And if you object to that then I can do my best to stop, but I have to know why.'

'Why did you leave court?' I asked abruptly.

'I went to see my father, I wanted to have the money he had promised me on marriage, and I wanted to buy a farm, in Essex. I told you all about it.'

'And you are planning marriage?'

For a moment he scowled then all at once his face cleared. 'Not with anyone else!' he cried out. 'What did you think? With you! You cloth-head girl! With you! I've been in love with you from the moment I first saw you and I have racked my brains as to how I could find a place fit for you and make a home good enough for you. Then when I saw how you love it at Hever I thought that if I were to offer you a manor house, a pretty farm, you might consider it. You might consider me.'

'My uncle said you were buying a house to marry a girl,' I gasped.

'You!' he cried out again. 'You're the girl. Always you. Never anyone but you.'

He turned to me and for a moment I thought that he would snatch me up to him. I put my hand out to fend him off and at that tiny gesture he at once checked. 'No?' he asked.

'No,' I said shakily.

'No kiss?' he said.

'Not one,' I said, trying to smile.

'And no to the little farmhouse? It faces south and it nestles in the side of a hill. It's got good land all around it, it's a pretty building, half-timbered and a thatched roof, and stables in a courtyard round the back. A herb garden and an orchard and a stream at the bottom of the orchard. A paddock for your hunter and a field for your cows.'

'No,' I said, sounding more and more uncertain.

'Why not?' he asked.

'Because I am a Howard and a Boleyn and you are a nobody.'

William Stafford did not flinch from my bluntness. 'You would be a nobody too, if you married me,' he said. 'There's a great comfort in it. Your sister is set to be queen. D'you think she will be happier than you?'

I shook my head. 'I cannot escape who I am.'

'And when are you happiest now?' he asked me, knowing the answer already. 'In winter when you are at court? Or in summer when you are with the children at Hever?'

'We would not have the children at your farm,' I said. 'Anne would take them. She wouldn't let the king's son be brought up by two nobodies in the middle of nowhere.'

'Until she has a son of her own, and at that moment she'll never want to see him again,' he said shrewdly. 'She'll have other ladies in waiting, your family will find other Howard girls. Drop out from their world and you'll be forgotten within three months. You can choose, my love. You don't have to be the other Boleyn girl for all your life. You could be the absolutely one and only Mistress Stafford.'

'I don't know how to do things,' I said feebly.

'Like what?'

'Make cheese. Skin chickens.'

Slowly, as if he did not want to startle me, he knelt beside me. He took my unresisting hand and lifted it to his lips. He turned it over and opened up the fingers so that he could kiss the palm, the wrist, each fingertip. 'I will teach you how to skin chickens,' he said gently. 'And we will be happy.'

'I don't say yes,' I whispered, closing my eyes at the sensation of his kisses on my skin and the warmth of his breath.

'And you don't say no,' he agreed.

At Windsor Castle Anne was in her presence chamber surrounded by tailors and haberdashers and seamstresses. Great bolts of rich fabrics were thrown over chairs and spread out in the windowseat. The place looked more like the Clothmakers' Hall on a feast day than the queen's rooms, and for a moment I thought of the careful housekeeping of Queen Katherine, who would have been shocked to her soul by the wanton richness of the silk and velvets and cloth of gold. 'We leave for Calais in October,' Anne said, two seamstresses pinning folds of material around her. 'You'd better order some new gowns.'

I hesitated.

'What?' she snapped.

I did not want to speak out in front of the tradesmen and the ladies in waiting. But it seemed that I had no choice. 'I cannot afford new gowns,' I said quietly. 'You know how my husband left me, Anne. I have only a small pension, and what Father gives me.'

'He'll pay,' she said confidently. 'Go to my cupboard and pull out my old red velvet and that one with the silver petticoat. You can have them made over for you.'

Slowly I went to her privy chamber and lifted the heavy lid to one of her many chests of clothes.

She waved me towards one of the seamstresses. 'Mrs Clovelly can rip it back and make it new for you,' she said. 'But make sure that it's fashionable. I want the French court to see us all looking very stylish. I don't want anything dowdy and Spanish about my ladies.'

I stood before the woman as she measured me.

Anne glanced around. 'You can all go,' she said abruptly. 'All except Mrs Clovelly, and Mrs Simpter.'

She waited until they had cleared the room. 'It's getting worse,' she said, her voice very low. 'That's why we're home early. We couldn't travel around at all. Everywhere we went there was trouble.'

'Trouble?'

'People shouting names. In one village, half a dozen lads throwing stones at me. And the king at my side!'

'They were stoning the king?'

She nodded. 'Another little town we couldn't even go in. They had a bonfire in the town square and they were burning me in effigy.'

'What did the king say?'

'At first he was furious, he was going to send in the soldiers, teach them a lesson; but it was the same at every village. There were too many. And what if the people started fighting against the king's soldiers? What would happen then?'

The seamstress turned me round with a gentle touch on my hips. I moved as she bid me but I hardly knew what I was doing. I had been brought up in the steady peace of Henry's reign; I could hardly take in the thought of English men rising up against this king.

'What does Uncle say?'

'He says to thank God that we have only the Duke of Suffolk to fear as an enemy, because when the king is stoned and insulted in his own kingdom then a civil war will follow swift behind.'

'Suffolk is our enemy?'

'Absolutely declared,' she said shortly. 'He says that I have cost the king the church, will he lose the country as well?'

I turned once more and the seamstress kneeled back and nodded. 'Shall I take these gowns and re-model them?' she asked in a whisper.

'Take them,' I said.

She picked up her materials and her sewing bag and went from the room. The seamstress hemming Anne's gown put in the final stitch and snipped off the thread.

'My God, Anne,' I said. 'Was it really everywhere?'

'Everywhere,' she said grimly. 'They turned their backs on me in one village, they hissed at me in another. When we rode down the country lanes the boys scaring crows cried out against me. The goose girls spat on the road before me. When we went through any market town the women at the stalls threw stinking fish and rotten vegetables in our way. When we went to stay at a house or a castle we had a mob of people following behind us, abusing us, and we had to shut the gates against them.' She shook her head. 'It was worse than a nightmare. When our hosts came out to greet us their faces would fall to see half their tenants in the road shouting out against the lawful king. We came to every door with a train of unhappiness. We can't go into the City of London, and now we can't go into the country either. We are hiding in our own palaces, where the people can't get to us. And they are calling her Katherine the Well-Beloved.'

'What does the king say?'

'He says we won't wait for the ruling from Rome. As soon as Archbishop Warham dies, then he will appoint a new archbishop who will marry us and we'll just do it, whether Rome rules in our favour or not.'

'What if Warham lingers?' I asked nervously.

Anne laughed harshly. 'Oh don't look like that! I won't send him soup! He's an old man, he's been in his bed most of this summer. He'll die soon and then Henry will appoint Cranmer and he will marry us.'

I shook my head disbelievingly. 'As easily as that? After all this time?'

'Yes,' she said. 'And if the king was more of a man and less of a schoolboy he could have married me five years ago and we could have had five sons by now. But he had to make the queen see that he was right, he had to make the country see that he was right. He has to be seen to be doing the right thing, whatever the truth of the matter. He's a fool.'

'You'd better not say that to anyone but me,' I cautioned her.

'Everyone knows,' she said stubbornly.

'Anne,' I said. 'You had better watch your tongue and your temper. You could still fall, even now.'

She shook her head. 'He's going to give me a title in my own right, and a fortune that no-one can take from me.'

'What title?'

'Marquess of Pembroke.'

'Marchioness?' I thought I had not heard her properly.

'No.' Her face glowed with pride. 'Not a title that you give to a woman who is married to a marquess. The title that a person can hold in their own right. Marquess. I am to be Marquess, and no-one can take that away from me. Not even the king himself.'

I closed my eyes on a surge of pure jealousy. 'And the fortune?'

'I am to have the manors of Coldkeynton and Hanworth in Middlesex, and lands in Wales. They'll bring me about a thousand pounds a year.'

'A thousand pounds?' I repeated, thinking of my annual pension of one hundred pounds.

Anne gleamed. 'I shall be the richest woman in England and the most noble,' she said. 'Rich in my own right, noble in my own right. And then I will be queen.'

She laughed as she realised how bitter her triumph was for me. 'You must be happy for me.'

'Oh, I am.'

∾

Next morning the stable yard was in a great fuss and bother, the king was hunting and everyone had to go with him. The hunters were being brought out of their stables and the hounds were waiting in a corner of the great yard, whipped in by the huntsmen but forever dashing off to one corner or another, sniffing and yowling with excitement. Grooms were running round with straps and buckles and helping their masters into the saddles. Stable lads were out with cloths to give shining haunches and glossy necks one last polish. Henry's black hunter, arching its neck and pawing the ground, was by the mounting block, waiting for the king.

I looked everywhere for William Stafford, then I felt the lightest of touches at my waist and a warm voice in my ear said: 'I was sent on an errand, I ran back all the way.'

I turned around to see him. I was almost in his arms. We were so close that if he moved forward half an inch we would have touched all down the length of our bodies. I closed my eyes for a moment in desire at the scent of him, and when I opened them I saw his eyes dark with lust for me.

'For God's sake, step back,' I said shakily.

Unwillingly he released one hand and stepped half a pace back from me. 'Before God, I have to marry you,' he said. 'Mary, I am beyond myself. I have never been like this in my life before. I cannot go another moment without holding you.'

'Ssshh,' I whispered. 'Put me up in the saddle.'

I had thought that if I was up there and out of his way then the weakness in my knees and the dizziness in my head would matter less. Somehow I got into the saddle, crooked my leg around the pommel and arranged my riding habit so that it fell as it should. He pulled the hem straight, and cupped my foot in his hand. He looked up at me, his face filled with determination.

'You have to marry me,' he said simply.

I glanced around, at the wealth of the court, the bobbing feathers in the hats, the velvets and silks – all dressed like princes, even for a day in the saddle. 'This is my life,' I said, trying to explain. 'This has been my home since I was a little girl. First the French court and now here. I have never lived in an ordinary house, I have never stayed in the same room for a whole year. I am a courtier from a family of courtiers. I can't become a country wife at the snap of your fingers.'

There was a blast of horns and the king, very broad but smiling, came out of the castle door with Anne at his side. Her quick glance raked the courtyard and I snatched my foot back from William's grasp and met her gaze with a blandly innocent smile. The king was helped onto his horse, he sat heavily in the saddle for a moment, and then gathered the reins and was ready, and everyone who was still on foot scrambled into the saddle and jockeyed for the best position in the cavalcade, the gentlemen trying to be close to Anne, the ladies riding, as if by accident, alongside the king.

'Are you not coming?' I asked urgently.

'Do you want me to?'

Slowly the horsemen were leaving the courtyard, jostling and waiting at the arched gateway.

'You'd better not. My uncle is out today, and he sees everything.'

William stepped back and I saw the light die from his eyes. 'As you wish.'

For all the world I would have jumped off my horse and kissed the smile back into his face. But he bowed, and stepped back to lean against the wall and watched the hunt and me ride out and away from him. He did not even call to me when he would see me again. He let me go.

Autumn 1532

Anne was enthroned as Marquess of Pembroke with all the ceremony of a coronation, in the king's presence chamber at Windsor Castle. He sat in his throne flanked by my uncle and Charles Brandon, the Duke of Suffolk, newly forgiven and returned to court in time to witness Anne's triumph. Suffolk looked as if he was chewing on lemons, his smile was so bitter, my uncle was torn between joy at the wealth and the prestige for his niece and his increasing hatred of her arrogance.

Anne wore a gown of red velvet trimmed with the white fluffy fur of ermine. Her hair, dark and glossy as a racehorse's mane, was spread over her shoulders like a girl on her wedding day. Lady Mary, the duke's daughter, held the robe of state, and the rest of Anne's ladies, Jane Parker, me, the other dozen or so, all dressed in our best, followed in her train and stood behind in sycophantic silence while the king tied the robe of state about her shoulders, and put a gold coronet on her head.

At the banquet George and I sat side by side and looked up to our sister, seated beside the king.

He did not ask if I was envious. It was an answer too obvious to be worth inquiry. 'I don't know another woman who could have done it,' he said. 'She has a unique determination to be on the throne.'

'I never had that,' I said. 'The only thing I've ever wanted from childhood was not to be overlooked.'

'Well you can forget that,' George said with brotherly frankness. 'You'll be overlooked now for the rest of your life. We'll both be as nothing. Anything I achieve will be seen as her gift. And you'll never match her. She's the only Boleyn anyone will ever know of or remember. You'll be a nobody forever.'

It was the word 'nobody'. At the very word the bitterness drained out of me, and I smiled. 'You know, there might be some joy in being a nobody.'

We danced till late and then Anne sent all the ladies to their beds but me.

'I'm going to him,' she said.

She did not need to explain what she meant. 'Are you sure?' I asked. 'You're still not married.'

'Cranmer will be installed any day,' she said, 'I'm going to France as his consort and Henry has insisted that they treat me as queen. He's given me the title of Marquess and the lands, and I cannot keep saying no.'

'Good God, you want to!' I suddenly understood her impatience. 'Do you love him at last?'

'Oh no!' she exclaimed impatiently, as if it were irrelevant. 'But I have kept him at arm's length so long that he has been driven nearly mad, and me too. Sometimes I have been so aroused by his desire and his pulling and teasing of me that I could have done it with a stable lad. And I have his promise, I can see my way to the throne. I want to do it now. I want to do it tonight.'

I poured water for her into the ewer and warmed a drying sheet for her while she washed. 'What will you wear?'

'The gown I was wearing to dance,' she said. 'And the coronet. I'll go to him like a queen.'

'George had better take you.'

'He's coming, I already told him.'

She finished washing and took the sheet from me to pat herself dry. Her body in firelight and candlelight was as beautiful as a wild animal. There was a tap on the door. 'Let him in,' she said.

I hesitated. She was tying her skirt around her waist but apart from that she was naked. 'Go on,' she said wilfully.

I shrugged and opened the door. George recoiled at the sight of his sister, her dark hair tumbled over her naked breasts.

'You can come in,' she said carelessly. 'I'm nearly ready.'

He threw one shocked interrogative look at me and came into the room and dropped into the chair at the fireside.

Anne, holding the stomacher across her naked breasts and belly, turned her bare back to George to lace her up. He rose to his feet and threaded the laces through the holes in the criss-cross pattern. At every insertion of the thread his hand brushed her skin and I saw her close her eyes in pleasure at the continual caress. George's face was dark, he was scowling as he did her bidding. 'Anything else?' he asked. 'Tie your shoes for you? Polish your boots?'

'Don't you want to touch me?' she taunted him. 'I'm good enough for the king.'

'You're good enough for the bagnio,' he said brutally. 'Get your cape, if you're coming.'

'But I *am* desirable,' she said, confronting him.

George hesitated. 'Why on earth ask me? Half the court was weak at the knees this evening. What more do you want?'

'I want everyone,' she said, unsmiling. 'I want you to say that I am the best, George. I want *you* to say it here, in front of Mary.'

He gave his low chuckle. 'Oh the old rivalry,' he said slowly. 'Anne, Marquess of Pembroke, you are the most desired and the richest girl in the family. You have eclipsed us both in success. You will shortly eclipse your revered father and uncle in terms of pride and position. What more do you want?'

She had been glowing with his praise but at that question she looked suddenly afraid, as if she remembered the curses of the fishwives and the shouts of 'Whore!' from the market traders. 'I want everyone to know it,' she said.

'Shall I take you to the king?' George asked pragmatically.

Anne put her hand on his arm and I saw him tense at the turn of her head and her sidelong smile. 'Wouldn't you rather take me to your chamber?'

'If I wanted to be beheaded for incest – yes.'

She gave her sexy little laugh. 'Very well then. To the king. But remember, George, you are my courtier, like all the others.'

He bowed and led her from the room. I listened to them cross the presence chamber and then go down the stairs, and I waited till I heard the door at the bottom of the stairs bang shut. I thought that Anne's desire to be first with everyone must be powerful indeed if she would pause to torment her own brother on the very night of her bedding the king.

❧

She came back at daybreak, huddled into her clothes, just as I used to do. George brought her back and together we stripped her and pushed her into bed. She was too weary to speak.

'So it's done,' I said as her eyes closed.

'Several times, I should think,' he said. 'I waited outside the chamber and slept in the chair and a couple of times in the night they woke me with their crying out and panting. Please God we get an heir from it.'

'And no doubt that he'll marry her? He won't tire of her now he has her?'

'Not inside six months. And now she's getting some pleasure for herself and not having to fight him off all the time she might be sweeter to him, and – please God – sweeter to us.'

'If she's much sweeter to you she'll be in your bed as well as the king's.'

George stretched and yawned and smiled lazily down at me from his extended height. 'She was hot,' he said. 'And she could take it out on no-one else. She was hot and once that wears off then please God she has a baby in her belly and a ring on her finger and a crown on her head. *Vivat Anna*! And grudge who grudges it – it's done.'

I left Anne sleeping and thought that I might see William Stafford if I went to my uncle's rooms at this hour in the morning. The castle was stirring, the lanes approaching the kitchen were crowded with the wagons bringing cords of firewood and charcoal from the woods, fruit and vegetables from the market, and meat, milk and cheese from the farms. In my uncle's rooms there was the bustle of a great household setting about the day. The maids had finished sweeping and cleaning in the presence chamber and the scullions were loading the fireplaces with logs and blowing on the embers to make them flame up.

My uncle's gentlemen were housed in half a dozen small rooms off the great hall, his men at arms slept in the guard room. William could be anywhere. I walked through the presence chamber and nodded at a couple of the gentlemen I knew and tried to look as if I were waiting to see my uncle or my mother.

The door to my uncle's privy chamber opened and George came out in a rush.

'Oh good,' he said on seeing me. 'Is Anne still asleep?'

'She was when I left her.'

'Go to her and wake her up. Tell her that the clergy has submitted to the king, or at least enough of them to mean that we have won, but Thomas More has announced that he has resigned his post. The king will learn it during Mass today when he receives More's letter, but she should be forewarned. The king is bound to take it hard.'

'Thomas More?' I repeated. 'But I thought he was on our side?'

My brother tutted at my ignorance. 'He promised the king never to comment publicly on the dissolution of the marriage. But it's obvious what he thinks, isn't it? He's a lawyer, a logical man, he's hardly likely to be convinced by the twisting of the truth that's been going on in a thousand universities in Europe.'

'But I thought he wanted the church reformed?' I asked. Not for the first time I was adrift in the sea of politics which was my family's natural element.

'Reformed; not taken to pieces and headed by the king,' my brother said quickly. 'Who knows better than Thomas More that the king is not fit to play Pope? He's known him from childhood. He'd never accept Henry as the heir to St Peter.' My brother laughed shortly. 'It's a ridiculous notion.'

'Ridiculous? I thought we supported it.'

'Of course we do,' he said. 'It means that Henry can rule on his own marriage, he can marry Anne. But no-one but a fool would think that there was the least justification for it in law, in morality, or in common sense. Look, Mary, don't worry. Anne understands all this. Just go and wake her and tell her that More is resigning and the king will learn of it this morning and she is to be calm. That's what my uncle said. Anne must be calm.'

I turned to do as he bid me, and just at that very moment, William Stafford came into the hall, shrugging on his doublet. He paused when he saw me and made me a low bow. 'Lady Carey,' he said. He bowed to my brother. 'Lord Rochford.'

'Go,' my brother said to me and gave me a little push. He ignored William. 'Go and tell her.'

There was nothing I could do but hurry from the room without even being able to touch William's hand and say 'good morning' to him.

❧

Anne and the king were closeted alone for most of the morning, considering what the resignation of Thomas More might mean to them. My father and uncle were with them, and Cranmer and Secretary Cromwell, all the men attached to Anne's cause, all determined that the king should take the power and the profit of the church in England. Anne and the king came out to dinner in very good harmony and she sat at his right hand as if she were already queen.

After dinner the two of them went to his privy chamber and everyone was sent away. George raised an eyebrow at me with a little smile and whispered: 'As long as a little prince comes out of it, eh, Mary?' and then went strolling off to play at cards with Francis Weston and a couple of the others. I went out into the garden to sit in the sunshine and look at the river, and all the time I knew that I was longing for William Stafford.

As if I had summoned him, he was suddenly there before me.

'Were you looking for me this morning?' he asked.

'No,' I said, lying as quick as a courtier. 'I was looking for my brother.'

'Whatever the case, I have come looking for you,' he offered. 'And glad I am to find you. Very glad, my lady.'

I moved a little on the seat and gestured that he might sit beside me. The moment he was within touching distance I felt my heart hammer. There was a scent about him, a warm sweet male scent that lingered about his hair and his soft brown beard. I found that I was leaning towards him and I made myself sit back.

'I am to come with your uncle to Calais,' he said. 'Perhaps I can be of service to you on the journey.'

'Thank you,' I said.

There was a brief silence.

'I am sorry about the stable yard,' I said. 'I was afraid of Anne seeing us together. While she has the guardianship of my son I dare not offend her.'

'I understand,' William said quickly. 'It was just the moment – I had hold of your little riding boot. I didn't want to let go.'

'I can't be your lover,' I said in a very low voice. 'Clearly not.'

He nodded. 'But were you looking for me this morning?'

'Yes,' I whispered, honest at last. 'I couldn't go for another minute without seeing you.'

'I have been hovering in this garden and outside the marquess's chambers all of the day, hoping to see you,' he said. 'I've been out here so long that I thought of getting a spade and doing something useful in the time while I was waiting.'

'Gardening?' I said with a gurgle of laughter, thinking of Anne's face if I were to announce that I was in love with the man who dug the garden. 'That hardly helps.'

'No,' he said, sharing my amusement. 'But I was hanging round the ladies' chambers like a pimp so it's the better of the two. Mary, what shall we do? What is your desire?'

'I don't know,' I said, speaking nothing but the truth. 'I feel as if this is a sort of madness which I am going through and if I had a true friend they would tie me down until it had passed.'

'You think it will pass?' he asked, as if it were an interesting viewpoint that he had not considered.

'Oh yes,' I said. 'It is a fancy, isn't it? It is just that it happened to both of us at once. I have taken a fancy to you and if you had not liked me,

I would have mooned around a little and made sheep's eyes at you for a while, and then got over it.'

He smiled at that. 'I should have liked that. Couldn't you do that anyway?'

'We will laugh at this later.'

I expected him to argue. In truth I was counting on him to argue that this was a real love, an undying love, and persuade me that I had to follow my heart whatever the cost.

But he nodded. 'A fancy, then? And nothing more?'

'Oh,' I said, surprised.

William rose to his feet. 'How soon do you expect to recover?' he asked conversationally.

I stood close to him. I was drawn to him as if every bone in my body needed his touch whatever my mouth might say.

'Just think a little,' he said to me gently. His mouth was so close to my ear that his breath stirred the tendril of hair which had escaped from my hood. 'You could be my love, you could be my wife. We would have Catherine, would we not? They would not take her away from you? And as soon as Anne has her own son she will give you Henry back, our boy.'

'He's not our boy,' I said, clinging to common sense with difficulty under this low-voiced torrent of persuasion.

'Who bought him his first pony? Who made him his first sailing boat? Who taught him to tell the time by the sun?'

'You,' I admitted. 'But no-one but you and me would consider that.'

'He might.'

'He's only a little boy, he has no say in anything. And Catherine will never have a say in anything. She'll be just another Boleyn girl who will be sent where they want her.'

'Then break the pattern for yourself, and we'll rescue the children too. Don't you be just another Boleyn girl for a day longer. Come and be Mrs Stafford, the one and only most beloved Mrs Stafford, who owns her fields outright and her little farmhouse, and is learning to make cheese and skin a chicken.'

I laughed and at once he caught at my hand and pressed his thumb against my palm. Despite myself my fingers closed on his hand and we stood for a moment, handclasped in the warm sunshine, and I thought, like a lovesick girl: 'This is heaven.'

There was a footstep behind us and I dropped his hand as if it had burnt me and whipped around. Thank God it was George and not that spying wife of his. He looked from my blushing face to William's impassive expression and raised an eyebrow.

'Sister?'

'William here is just telling me that my hunter has strained her fetlock,' I said at random.

'I've poulticed it,' William said quickly. 'And Lady Carey can borrow one of the king's horses while Jesmond is recovering. Shouldn't be more than a day or two.'

'Very good,' George said. William bowed and left us.

I let him go. I did not have the courage, even before George whom I would have trusted with any other secret, to call him back. William walked away, his shoulders a little stiff with resentment.

George followed my gaze after him. 'A little lust stirring in the lovely Lady Carey?' he asked idly.

'A little,' I conceded.

'Is this the nobody that meant nothing?'

I smiled ruefully. 'Yes.'

'Don't,' he said simply. 'Anne has to be immaculate between now and her wedding day, especially now that she is bedding the king. We are all of us on show. If you have a little lust for the man, then sit on it, my sister, for until Anne is married we have to be as chaste as angels, and she has to be head seraphim.'

'I'm hardly likely to roll in the hay with him,' I protested. 'My reputation is as good as anyone's. Certainly better than yours.'

'Then tell him to stop looking at you as if he wanted to eat you alive,' George said. 'The man looks completely besotted.'

'Does he?' I said eagerly. 'Oh George, does he?'

'God help us,' George said. 'Coal on the fire. Yes, I'm afraid he does. Tell him to keep it to himself until Anne is married and Queen of England and then you can choose for yourself.'

❀

There was an explosive row going on in Anne's privy chamber. George and I, coming in from a ride, froze in the presence chamber and looked around at Henry's gentlemen and Anne's ladies, who were all maintaining a wonderful pretence of not listening while straining to hear every word through the thick door. I heard Anne's scream of rage over Henry's rumble of discontent.

'What use has she of them? What use? Or is she to come back to court at Christmas again? Is she to sit in my place and am I to be thrown down now that you have had me?'

'Anne, for God's sake!'

'No! If you loved me at all I would not have had to ask! How can I go to France in anything but the queen's jewels? What does it say if you take me to France as a marquess with nothing but a handful of diamonds?'

'They're hardly a handful . . .'

'They're not the crown jewels!'

'Anne, some of those were bought for her by my father for her first marriage, they are nothing to do with me . . .'

'They are everything to do with you! They are England's jewels, given to the queen. If I am to be queen then I must have them. If she is queen then she can keep them. Choose!'

We all heard Henry's goaded roar. 'For God's sake, woman, what do I have to do to please you? You have had every honour that a woman could dream of! What d'you want now? The gown off her back? The hood off her head?'

'All that and more!' Anne yelled back at him.

Henry flung open the door, we all began talking with tremendous animation, started upon seeing him, and dropped into our bows.

'I shall see you at dinner,' he said icily over his shoulder to Anne.

'You will not,' she said very loudly. 'For I shall be long gone. I shall take my dinner on the road and my breakfast at Hever. You do not treat me with disdain.'

At once he turned back to her and the door swung behind him. We all strained forward to hear what we could not see. 'You would not leave me.'

'I will not be half a queen,' she said passionately. 'Either you have me or not at all. Either you love me or not at all. Either I am all yours or I am nobody's. I will have no half-measures with you, Henry.'

We heard the rustle of her gown as he crushed her to him and her little sigh of delight.

'You shall have every diamond in the Tower, you shall have her diamonds and her barge as well,' he promised huskily. 'You shall have your heart's desire, since you have given me mine.'

George stepped forward and closed the door. 'Anyone for a game of cards?' he asked cheerfully. 'I think we may have to wait for some time.'

There was a ripple of half-suppressed laughter and someone produced a pack of cards and someone else a pair of dice. I sent the page running for the musicians to make some noise to drown whatever indiscreet sighs came from Anne's privy chamber. I was as busy and as bustling as I could be to make sure that the court was at play while my sister and the king made love. I did everything I could do, so that I did not have to think of the queen, moved to her new and less comfortable house, being told by a messenger from the king that she had to hand over her royal jewels, her very own rings, bracelets and necklaces, and every little token of love that he had ever given her, because my sister wanted to wear them to France.

❧

It was an enormous expedition, the greatest ever undertaken by Henry's court since the journey to the Field of the Cloth of Gold; and it was in every way as extravagant and ostentatious as that fabled event had been. It had to be – Anne was determined that anything that Katherine had seen and done must be bettered by her; so we rode through England from Hanbury to Dover like emperors. A troop of horse went ahead of us to clear any malcontents out of the road, but the sheer weight of the expedition and the number of horses, carriages, wagons, soldiers, men at arms, serving men, camp followers and the beauty of the ladies on horseback and their gentlemen companions stunned most of the country into amazed silence.

✿

We had a clear sailing across the Channel. The ladies went below, Anne retired to her cabin and slept for much of the voyage. The gentlemen were up on deck, wrapped in their riding coats, watching the horizon for other ships and sharing jugs of hot wine. I came up on deck and leaned over the ship's rail, and watched the movement of the waves rolling beneath the prow of the boat and listened to the creaking of the timbers.

A warm hand covered my cold one. 'Are you feeling well?' William Stafford whispered in my ear. 'Not sick?'

I turned towards him and smiled. 'Not at all, praise God. But all the sailors say that this is a very calm crossing.'

'Please God it stays that way,' he said fervently.

'Oh! My knight errant! Don't tell me that you are ill?'

'Not very,' he said defensively.

I wanted to take him in my arms. I thought for a moment what a test of love it is, when the beloved is less than perfect. I would never have thought that I could be drawn to a man suffering from seasickness and yet here I was, longing to fetch spiced wine for him and wrap him up warm.

'Come and sit down.' I glanced around. We were as unobserved as one might ever be in this court which was a very mine of gossip and scandal. I led him to a rolled pile of sails and settled him against the mast so that he might lean back. I tucked his cloak around him as carefully as if he had been my boy Henry.

'Don't leave me,' he said in a tone so plaintive that for a moment I thought that he was teasing me, but I met a look of such limpid innocence that I touched his cheek with my cold fingers.

'I'm just going to get us some hot spiced wine.' I went to the galley where the cooks were heating wine and ale and serving chunks of bread, and when I came back William moved up on the roll of sail so that I could sit beside him. I held the cup while he ate the bread and then we shared the wine, sip for sip.

'Are you better?'

'Of course, is there anything I can do for you?'

'No, no,' I said hastily. 'I was just pleased that you look better. Can I get you some more mulled wine?'

'No,' he said. 'Thank you. I think I should like to sleep.'

'Could you sleep if you leaned back against the mast?'

'No, I don't think I could.'

'Or if you lay down on the sail?'

'I think I'd roll off.'

I glanced around. Most people had gone over to the leeward side of the boat and were dozing or gambling. We were all but alone. 'Shall I hold you?'

'I should like that,' he said softly, as if he were almost too ill to speak.

We exchanged seats, I went with my back to the mast and then he put his dear curly-haired head into my lap and put his arms around my waist and closed his eyes.

I sat stroking his hair and admiring the softness of his brown beard and the flutter of his eyelashes on his cheek. His head was warm and heavy on my lap, his arms tight around my waist. I felt the total contentment that I always knew when we were close together. It was as if my body had yearned for him all of my life, whatever my mind might have been thinking; and that at last, I had him.

I tipped my head back and felt the cold sea air on my cheeks. The rocking of the boat was soporific, the muted creak and hush of the wind in the sheets and the sails. The noise grew fainter and fainter as I fell asleep.

I woke to the warmth of his touch, his head nuzzling my crotch, rubbing against my thighs, his hands exploring inside my cape, stroking my arms, my waist, my neck, my breasts. As I sleepily opened my eyes to this flood of sensation, he lifted his head and kissed my bare neck, my cheek, my eyelids, and then finally, passionately, my mouth. His mouth was warm and sweet and lingering, his tongue slid between my lips and stirred me. I wanted to eat him, I wanted to drink him, I wanted him to kiss me and then bear me down onto the holystoned boards of the deck and to have me, then and there, and never let me go.

When he loosened his grip on me and would have released me it was me who put my hands behind his head and pulled his mouth towards me again, it was my desire which drove us onwards, not his.

'Is there a cabin? A bunk? Anywhere we can go?' he asked me breathlessly.

'The ladies have all the accommodation, and I gave my bunk away.'

He gave a little groan of frustrated desire and then ran his hands through his hair and laughed at himself. 'Good God, I am like a cunt-struck page!' he said. 'I am shaking with desire.'

'Me too,' I said. 'Oh God, me too.'

William got to his feet. 'Wait here,' he ordered me, and disappeared down into the body of the ship. He came back with a cup of small ale which he offered to me first, and then took a long draught himself.

'Mary, we must marry,' he said. 'Or you must take full responsibility for me going insane.'

I laughed weakly. 'Oh my love.'

'Yes I am,' he said fervently.

'You are what?'

'I am your love. Say it again.'

For a moment I thought I might refuse and then I knew I was weary of denying the truth. 'My love.'

He smiled at that, as if for the moment it was enough for him. 'Come here,' he said, opening his cape like a wing and summoning me to the rail of the ship. Obediently, I went and stood beside him and he put his arm and his warm riding cape around my shoulders and held me close to him. Under the shelter of the cape I slid my hand around his waist, and unseen by any but seagulls, I rested my head on his shoulder and we stood there, swaying hip to hip with the motion of the ship for a long peaceful time.

'And there's France,' he said finally.

I looked ahead and could see the dark shape of the land and then gradually the quayside and the masts of the boats and the walls and the castle of the English fortress of Calais.

Reluctantly, he released me. 'I shall come and find you as soon as we are settled.'

'I shall look for you.'

We stood apart, there were people coming up on deck, marvelling at the smoothness of the crossing and looking over the narrowing strait of water to Calais.

'Do you feel all right now?' I asked, out of arm's reach, feeling the habitual coldness of my life take the place of that passionate intimacy.

For one moment William had the grace to look confused. 'Oh, my seasickness, I had forgotten it.'

I suddenly realised I had been tricked. 'Were you ever ill at all? No! You never were! It was all a scheme to get me to sit beside you and to wrap you up and to hold you while you slept.'

He was delightfully shamefaced, he dropped his head like a scolded boy and then I saw the gleam of his smile. 'But you tell me, my Lady Carey,' he challenged me. 'Did you have the happiest six hours of your life, just now? Or did you not?'

I bit my tongue. I paused and thought. There must have been in my life a dozen happy moments. I had been the beloved of a king, I had been reclaimed by a loving husband, and I had been the more successful sister for many years. But the happiest six hours?

'Yes,' I said simply, conceding him everything. 'Those were the happiest six hours of my life.'

❧

We docked the ship in a bustle of noise and activity and the harbourmaster and the sailors and dockers all came down to the quayside to watch the king and Anne disembark and cheer them as they touched English soil in France. Then we all went up to hear Mass in the chapel of St Nicholas with the governor of Calais, who made a great fuss, treating Anne with the same courtesy as if she were a crowned queen. But whatever the governor might say and do to appease her in her anxious hunt for reassurance, the King of France was not so amenable and Henry had to leave Anne behind in Calais while he rode out to meet Francis.

'He's such a fool,' Anne muttered to herself, looking out of the window of Calais Castle as Henry rode out at the head of his men at arms, his hat off his head to bow in acknowledgement to the crowd, and then turning in the saddle to wave up to the castle in the hope that she would be watching him.

'Why?'

'He must have known that the Queen of France wouldn't meet with me, she's a Spanish princess like Katherine. And then he let the Queen of Navarre refuse to meet me as well. She should never have been asked but it gave her the chance to say that she would not.'

'Did she say why not? She was always so kind to us when we were little.'

'She said my behaviour was a scandal,' Anne said shortly. 'Good God,

336

how these women do put on airs when they are married and safe. You would think none of them ever struggled to catch a husband.'

'So will we not see King Francis at all?'

'We cannot meet him officially,' Anne said. 'There's no lady to meet me.' She drummed her fingers on the windowsill. 'Katherine was greeted by the Queen of France herself and everyone says now how friendly they were.'

'Well, you're not queen yet, you know,' I said injudiciously.

The look she turned on me was like ice. 'Yes,' she said. 'I know that. I have observed that over the last six years. I have had a little while to become aware of that, thank you. But I will be. And when I next come to France as queen I shall make her sorry for this insult to me, and when Margaret of Navarre seeks to marry her children to my sons I will not forget that she called me a scandal.' She looked hard at me. 'And I shall not forget that you are always very quick to point out that I am not yet queen.'

'Anne, I was only saying . . .'

'Then you should be silent and try thinking before you speak for once,' she snapped.

❁

Henry invited King Francis of France back to the English fort of Calais and for two days we ladies in waiting, with Anne at our head, had to content ourselves with peeping from the castle window at the French king, and seeing nothing more of his fabled good looks than the top of his head. I expected Anne to be in a state of absolute fury at being excluded but she was smiling and secretive, and when Henry came to her room every night after dinner he was welcomed with such pleasant humour that I was certain that she had something planned.

She set us to rehearsing a special dance which was to be led in by her and then to include the seated diners, who would be summoned to dance with us. It was obvious that she was planning to enter the king's banquet with the King of France and dance with him.

Some of the younger ladies wondered how she dared run against the conventions, but I knew that she would have had her plan approved by Henry. His surprise when she entered would be as counterfeit as all the amazement that Queen Katherine had learned to show when her husband had entered her rooms so many times in his disguises. It made me feel old and world-weary to think that we had pretended for years not to recognise the king, and now Anne would play the same games, and the court would still have to admire them.

Despite the demands of riding with Anne in the morning and dancing with her and the ladies in the afternoon I found time every noon to stroll in the streets of Calais where, at a little alehouse, I would always find William Stafford waiting for me. He would draw me inside, away from the prying eyes of the street, and set a mug of small ale before me.

'All well, my love?' he would ask me.

I would smile at him. 'Yes. And with you?'

He nodded. 'I am to ride out with your uncle tomorrow, I have news of some horses he might like. But the prices are absurd. Every French farmer is determined to fleece an English lord this season, for fear we never come again.'

'He said that he might make you master of his horse. That would be a good thing for us, wouldn't it?' I said wistfully. 'We could see each other more easily if you had charge of my horse, and we could ride together.'

'And marry of course,' he said, teasing me. 'Your uncle would be delighted if the master of his horse married his niece. No, my love, I don't think it would be a good thing for us at all. I don't think there's any way for us at court.' He touched my cheek. 'I don't want to see you every day by luck. I want to see you every night and day because we are married and living in the same house.'

I was silent.

'I will wait for you,' William said softly. 'I know that you are not ready now.'

I looked up at him. 'It's not that I don't love you. It's the children, and my family, and Anne. More than anything else – it's Anne. I don't know how I can leave her.'

'Because she needs you?' he asked, surprised.

I gave a little gurgle of laughter. 'Good God! No! Because she won't let me go. She needs me in her sight, so that she knows that she is safe.' I broke off, unable to explain to him the long determined rivalry between the two of us. 'Any triumph she has is halved if I am not there to see it. And anything that goes wrong for me, any slight or humiliation, she is quick to perceive and she would even be quick to revenge – oh! – but inside her heart is singing to know that I have taken a blow.'

'She sounds like a devil,' he said, loyal to me.

I giggled again. 'I wish I could say yes,' I confessed. 'But to tell you the truth, it is the same for me. I am as envious of her as she is of me. But I have seen her rise and rise. I will never do better than her now. I have come to accept it. I know that she caught and held the king when I could not. But I also know that I didn't really want to. After I had my son, I wanted nothing but to be with my children and far from the court, and the king is so –'

'So?' he prompted.

'He's so desirous. Not just of love; but of everything. He's like a child himself and when I had a child of my own, a real child, I found I had no patience with a man who wanted to be diverted like a child. When once I saw King Henry was as selfish as his own little son, I couldn't really love him any more. I couldn't look at him but with impatience.'

'But you didn't leave him.'

'You don't leave the king,' I said simply. 'He leaves you.'

William nodded, acknowledging the truth of it.

'But when he left me for Anne I saw him go without regret. And when I dance with him now, or dine with him, or walk and talk with him, I do my job as a courtier. I let him think that he is the most delightful man in the world and I look up at him and I smile and I give him every reason to think that I am still in love with him.'

William's arm came around my waist and held me rather tightly. 'But you're not,' he specified.

'Let me go,' I whispered. 'You're squeezing me too tight.'

His grip tightened a little more.

'Oh very well,' I said. 'No, of course not. I am doing my job as a Boleyn girl, as a Howard courtier. Of course I don't love him.'

'And do you love anyone at all?' he asked conversationally. His grip around my waist was as fierce as ever.

'Nobody,' I said provocatively.

One finger under my chin forced my face up and his bright brown gaze scanned me as if he would look into my soul.

'A nobody,' I specified.

His kiss, when it came, was as light on my mouth as the brush of a warm feather.

❧

That night, Henry and Francis dined privately at Staple Hall. The ladies in waiting, with Anne leading the way, slipped out from the castle with cloaks around our fine gowns and hoods up over our headdresses. We gathered in the hall outside the chamber and put off our cloaks and helped each other put on our golden dominoes, our golden masks, and our golden hoods. There were no mirrors in the hall so I could not see what I looked like but the others around me were a blaze of gold and I knew I was glittering among them. Anne in particular, her dark eyes glinting through the slits of the golden mask shaped like the face of a hawk, looked rich and wild, her dark hair falling to her shoulders under the golden veil of the hood.

We waited for our cue and then ran in to do our dance. Henry and King Francis could not take their eyes from her. I danced with Sir Francis Weston who whispered appalling suggestions in my ear in French, under the transparent pretext that he thought I was a French lady who would welcome such invitations, and I saw George leading out another lady in his haste to avoid dancing with his wife.

The dance ended and Henry turned to one dancer and unveiled her, then, ceremonially, went around the room taking the visors off all the masked ladies and coming lastly to Anne.

'Ah, the Marquess of Pembroke,' King Francis said with every appearance of surprise. 'When I knew you before you were Mistress Anne Boleyn and the prettiest girl at my court then, just as you are the most beautiful woman at my friend Henry's court now.'

Anne smiled and turned her head towards Henry to smile at him.

'There was only one girl who could ever match you and that was the other Boleyn girl,' King Francis said, looking around for me. Anne's moment of triumph abruptly dissolved and she gestured me to come forward as if she wished she were showing me to a scaffold. 'My sister, Your Majesty,' she said shortly. 'Lady Carey.'

Francis kissed my hand. '*Enchanté*,' he whispered seductively.

'Let's dance again!' Anne said suddenly, irritated as I knew she would be by any attention paid to me. At once the musicians struck a chord, and for the rest of the night the court made merry and everyone took a great deal of trouble to ensure that Anne was happy.

❁

That evening concluded the formal visit to France and the following day we spent in packing up the goods for the journey home. The wind was against us and we had to linger in Calais, sending every morning to the master of the ship to ask if he could get out of harbour on this day, or the next. Anne and Henry hunted and entertained themselves as well as if they had been in England. Better, actually, since in France there was no-one to cat-call when Anne rode down the street or to shout 'whore' at her horse's hooves. And in the delay William and I were free to meet.

We rode out every afternoon on a firm sand beach to the west of the town, which stretched almost as far as the eye could see. Sometimes the horses would strain to gallop on the hard sand at the water's edge and we let them have their heads and fly away. Then we would ride up into the dunes, and William would lift me down from the saddle, spread his cape on the ground and the two of us would lie together, arms around each other, kissing and whispering until I was near to weeping with desire.

There were many afternoons when I was tempted to untie the laces of his breeches and let him have me, without ceremony, like a country girl under the seductive sun with only the cry of seagulls to distract us. He kissed me till my mouth was sore with kissing, my lips swollen and chapped, and all the long evening when I had to dine with the ladies without him, I could still feel the bruises from his passionate biting when I put my lips to a cool glass to drink. He touched me all over my body, without shame. His hands unlaced my stomacher at the back so that he could slide it down to my hips, and caress my naked breasts. He bent his brown curly head and suckled at me till I cried out with pleasure and thought that I would rise up in more and more pleasure until I could hardly bear another moment of it, and then he would plunge his head into my belly and bite me hard on the navel so I flinched with pain and pushed him away and found that I was screaming and fighting him off instead of sighing.

He would wrap me warmly and lie beside me unmoving for long moments until my hunger for him subsided a little. Then he would turn me over and lie his long lean body against my back, take off my cap and lift a handful of hair, so that he could nibble at the nape of my neck and press himself against me so that I felt his hardness even through my gown and underskirt, and I knew myself to be pressing back like a whore, as if to beg him to do the deed, and do it without permission, for I could not say 'Yes'. And God knew that I would not say 'No'.

He would thrust against me, pause, and thrust again, and I would press back, knowing and longing for what would happen next, he would go faster and I would find myself rising towards pleasure, and getting to a point where I could not stop whether I would or no – and then, before I had reached my pleasure, before he had so much as touched me skin to skin, he would pause and give a little sigh and lie down beside me again and gather me to him and kiss my eyelids, and hold me till I stopped trembling.

Every day while the wind blew onshore and kept the ships in the harbour we rode out into the sand dunes and made love which was not making love but which was the most passionate of courtships. And every day I hoped, against myself, that today would be the day when I would whisper 'Yes' or that he would force me to it. But every day he stopped just a second, just a moment, before my consent, and enfolded me in his arms and soothed me as if I were racked with pain instead of desire –

and there were many days when I could not have told the one from the other.

We were walking the horses out of the dunes and back to the beach on the twelfth day when William suddenly paused and looked up. 'The wind's changed.'

'What?' I asked stupidly. I was still dazed with pleasure. I did not know that there was a wind. I was hardly aware of the sand beneath my riding boots, the breakers on the beach, the warmth of the evening sun on my left cheek.

'It's offshore,' he said. 'They'll be able to sail.'

I rested my arm on my horse's neck. 'Sail?' I repeated.

He turned and saw my dazed expression and laughed at me. 'Oh sweetheart, you are far away, aren't you? Remember we cannot sail for England because we are waiting for a favourable wind? This is it. The wind's changed. We'll sail tomorrow.'

The words finally sunk into my understanding. 'So what do we do?'

He looped his horse's reins over his arm and came around to my horse to lift me up into the saddle.

'Set sail, I suppose.' He cupped his hands underneath my boot and tossed me up into the saddle. I recognised the ache in my body as unfulfilled desire, more desire, another day of desire, the twelfth day of unfulfilled desire.

'And then what?' I persisted. 'We can't meet like this at Greenwich.'

'No,' he agreed pleasantly.

'So how shall we meet?'

'You can find me in the stable yard, or I can find you in the garden. We've always managed, have we not?' He mounted his own horse, lightly; he was not trembling like me.

I could not find the words. 'I don't want to meet you like that.'

William adjusted his stirrup leather, frowning slightly, then he straightened up and gave me a polite, rather distant smile.

'I could escort you to Hever in the summer,' he offered.

'That's seven months away!' I exclaimed.

'Yes.'

I rode a little closer to him, I could not believe he was indifferent. 'Don't you want to meet me every afternoon like this?'

'You know I do.'

'Then how is it to be done?'

He gave me a little half-teasing smile. 'I don't think it can be done,' he said gently. 'There are too many enemies of the Howards who would be quick to report you for light behaviour. There are too many spies in your uncle's train for me to be undetected for long. We've been lucky, we've had our twelve days, and they've been very sweet. But I don't think we can have them again in England.'

'Oh.'

I turned my horse's head and felt the sun warm on my back. The waves washed in gently and my horse, fretting a little, shied as they splashed her fetlocks and knees. I could not hold her steady, I could not command her. I could not command myself.

'I think I shan't stay in your uncle's service.' William drew his horse up alongside mine.

'What?'

'I think I'll go to my farm and try my hand as a farmer. It's all there waiting for me. I'm tired of court. I'm not suited to the life. I'm too independent a man to serve a master, even a great family like yours.'

I straightened up a little. The Howard pride helped. I put back my shoulders and I lifted my chin. 'As you wish,' I said, as cold as he.

He nodded and let his horse drop a little back. We rode towards the walls of the town like a lady and her escort. The entranced lovers of the sand dune were far behind us, we were the Boleyn girl and the Howards' man returning to court.

The sallyport was still open, it was not yet dusk, and we rode side by side through the cobbled streets up to the castle. The gates were open, the drawbridge down, we rode straight into the stable yard. There were men watering the horses and rubbing them down with wisps of straw. The king and Anne had returned half an hour before and their horses were being walked till they were cool before being fed and watered. There was no chance at all of a private conversation.

William lifted me down from the saddle and at the touch of his hands on my waist, his body against mine, I was filled with a sudden fierce yearning for him, so acute that I gave a little cry of pain.

'Are you all right?' he asked, setting me on my feet.

'No!' I said fiercely. 'I am not all right. You know that I am not.'

For a moment he too was shaken out of calmness. He caught my hand and roughly pulled me back to him. 'How you are feeling now is how I have been feeling for months,' he swore in a passionate undertone. 'How you are feeling now is how I have been feeling night and day since I first saw you, and I expect to go on feeling like this for the rest of my life. Think about it, Mary. And you send for me. Send for me when you know that you cannot live without me.'

I twisted my hand out of his grip and I pulled myself away. I half-expected him to come after me but he did not. I walked so slowly that if he had as much as whispered my name I would have heard him, and turned. I walked away from him though my feet dragged at every step. I went through the archway to the castle door though every inch of my body was crying out to stay with him.

$$\sim$$

I wanted to go to my room and weep but as I went through the great hall George rose up out of a chair and said: 'I've been waiting for you, where've you been?'

'Riding,' I said shortly.

'With William Stafford,' he accused me.

I let him see my red eyes and the quiver of my mouth. 'Yes. So?'

'Oh God,' George said, brother-like. 'Dear God no, you silly whore. Go and wash and get that look off your face, anyone can guess what you've been doing.'

'I've done nothing!' I exclaimed in sudden passion. 'Nothing! And much good it has done me!'

He hesitated. 'Just as well. Hurry up.'

I went to my room and splashed water on my eyes and rubbed my face on a drying sheet. When I came into Anne's presence chamber there were half a dozen ladies playing cards, and George waiting, very sombre, in the window embrasure.

He gave a quick cautious look around the room and then tucked my hand under his arm and led me away to the picture gallery which ran the length of the great hall but was empty at this time of the day.

'You've been seen,' he said. 'You can't have thought you'd get away with it.'

'With what?'

He stopped short, and looked at me with a seriousness I had never seen before. 'Don't be pert,' he urged me. 'You were seen coming out of the sand dunes with your head on his shoulder and his arm around your waist and your hair all blowing loose in the wind. Don't you know that Uncle Howard has spies everywhere? Didn't you think that you would be bound to be caught?'

'What's going to happen?' I asked fearfully.

'Nothing, if it stops here. That's why it's me telling you, and not Uncle or Father. They don't want to know. As far as you're concerned, they don't know. It's just between you and me and it need go no further.'

'I love him, George,' I said very quietly.

He put his head down and ploughed on down the gallery, dragging me with him by my hand in his arm. 'Doesn't make any difference to people like us. You know that.'

'I can't sleep, I can't eat, I can't do anything but think about him. At night I dream of him, all day I wait to see him, and when I do see him my heart turns over and I think I will faint with desire.'

'And he?' George asked, drawn into this despite himself.

I turned my head away so he should not see the sudden pain in my face. 'I thought he felt the same. But today, when the wind changed, he said we would sail for England and we would not be able to see each other as we had done in France.'

'Well, he's right,' George said brutally. 'And if Anne had been doing her business then neither you nor half a dozen other of the ladies would have been dawdling around France flirting with men in your train.'

'It's not like that,' I flared up. 'He's not a man in my train. He's the man I love.'

'D'you remember Henry Percy?' George suddenly demanded.

'Of course.'

'He was in love. More than that, he was betrothed, more than that: he was married. Did it save him? No. He's stuck in Northumberland, married to a woman who loathes him, still in love, still heartbroken, still hopeless. You can choose. You can be in love and heartbroken, or you can make the best you can of it.'

'Like you?' I said.

'Like me,' he said grimly. Despite himself he looked down the gallery to where Sir Francis Weston was leaning over Anne's shoulder, following a music score. Sir Francis felt our gaze on him and looked up. For once he forgot to smile at me, he looked past me at my brother and there was a deep intimacy in the gaze.

'I never follow my desire, I never consult it,' George said grimly. 'I have put my family first and it costs me a heartbeat, every day of my life. I do nothing which might cause Anne embarrassment. Love does not come into it for us Howards. We are courtiers first and foremost. Our life is at court. And true love has no place at court.'

Sir Francis gave a distant little smile when George did not acknowledge him, and turned his attention back to the music.

George pinched my cold fingers as they rested on his arm. 'You have to stop seeing him,' he said. 'You have to promise on your honour.'

'I can't promise on my honour, for I have no honour,' I said bleakly. 'I was married to one man and I cuckolded him with the king. I went back to him and he died, before I had a chance to tell him that I might love him. And now when I find a man that I could love heart and soul, you ask me to promise on my honour not to see him – and I do so promise. On my honour. There is no honour left in us three Boleyns at all.'

'Bravo,' George said. He took me in his arms and kissed me on the mouth. 'And heartbreak becomes you. You look delicious.'

❁

We sailed the next day. I looked for William on the deck and when I saw him, carefully not looking at me, I went below with the other ladies and curled up in a nest of cushions and went to sleep. More than anything else I wanted to sleep the next half year away until I could go to Hever and see my children again.

Winter 1532

The court held Christmas at Westminster and Anne was the hub of every activity. The master of the revels staged masque after masque when she was hailed as Queen of Peace, Queen of Winter, Queen of Christmas. She was called everything but Queen of England, and everyone knew that title would follow very soon. Henry took her to the Tower of London and she had her pick of the treasury of England, as if she were a princess born.

She and Henry now had adjoining apartments. Brazenly, they retired to his room or hers together at night and they emerged together in the morning. He bought her a fur-lined black satin robe to greet the visitors who came into his bedchamber. I was released from my post as chaperone and bedfellow and found myself alone at night for the first time since girlhood. It was a pleasure of sorts to be able to sit by my little fire and know that Anne would not be storming into the room in a temper. But I found I was lonely. I spent long nights daydreaming in front of the fire, and many cold afternoons, looking out of the window at the grey winter rain. The sunshine and the sand dunes of Calais seemed like a million years away. I felt that I was turning to ice, just like the sleet on the tiled roofs.

I looked for William Stafford among my uncle's men and someone told me that he had gone to his farm to see to the lifting of the turnips and the killing of the old beasts. I thought of him, going about his little farmstead, setting things to rights, dealing with real things while I lingered at court, enmeshed in gossip and scandal and thinking of nothing but the pleasure of two idle selfish people and how to entertain them.

In the middle of the twelve-day Christmas feast Anne came to me and asked what signs would tell a woman that she had conceived. We counted the days of her courses and she was due within the week; she was already determined to be sick in the mornings and unable to eat the fat off the meat, but I told her it was too early to know.

She counted the days. Sometimes I could see her holding herself very still and I knew that she was willing herself to be with child.

The day came when she might have bled, and that night she put her head around the door of my room and said triumphantly: 'I am clean. Does that mean I have a baby?'

'One day proves nothing,' I said ungraciously. 'You have to wait a month at least.'

The next day passed, and the next. She did not tell Henry of her hopes but I imagined that he could count like any other man. They both started to have the look of a couple balancing on air like rope dancers at a fair. He did not dare to ask her, but he came to me and asked me if Anne had missed her course.

'Only by a week or two, Your Majesty,' I said respectfully.

'Shall I send for a midwife?' he asked.

'Not yet,' I advised. 'Better to wait for the second month.'

He looked anxious. 'I should not lie with her.'

'Perhaps just be very gentle,' I advised.

He frowned in his anxiety, and I thought that their desire for this baby would rob all the joy from their mating before they were even wed.

In January it was clear that Anne had missed a month for certain, and she told the king that she thought that she might be with his child.

It was touching to see him. He had been so long married to a barren woman, the thought of a fertile wife was damp ploughland in a dry August to him. They were very quiet together, very strange to each other. They had been passionate quarrellers, passionate lovers, and now they wanted to be friends. Anne wanted to rest quietly, she had a terror of doing anything that might disturb the process which was going on in secret in her body. Henry wanted to sit beside her, as if his presence might continue what he had started. He wanted to hold her and walk beside her, and save her from any exertion at all.

He had seen too many pregnancies end in a mess of crying women and disappointment. He had celebrated some live births and had the joy stolen from him by inexplicable deaths. Now he thought that Anne's ready fertility vindicated him completely. God had cursed him for marrying his brother's wife and now God was lifting the curse by making his wife-to-be (his first wife, in Henry's adaptable conscience) so fertile that she conceived within months of lying with him. He treated her with immense tenderness and respect, and he rushed through a new law, so that they might be legally married, under the new English law, in the new English church.

It took place in almost complete secrecy in Whitehall, Anne's London house, the home of her dead adversary, the cardinal. The king's two witnesses were his friends, Henry Norris and Thomas Heneage, and William Brereton attended him. George and I were commanded to make it seem as though Anne and the king were dining in his privy chamber. We thought the most agreeable way to do this was to order the very best dinner for four and have it served to us sitting in the king's own chamber. The court, watching great dishes going in and out, came to the conclusion that it was a private dinner for the Boleyns and the king. It was a petty revenge for me, to sit in Anne's chair and eat off her plate while she was marrying the King of England, but it amused me. To tell the truth, I tried on her black satin bedgown too, while she was safely out of the way, and George swore that it suited me very well.

Spring 1533

A few months later and the business was done. Anne, forever holding her swelling belly, was publicly announced as the official wife of the king by no less an authority than Archbishop Cranmer, who held the briefest of inquiries into the marriage of Queen Katherine and Henry and discovered that it had always been null and void. The queen did not even attend the court which traduced her name and dishonoured her. She was clinging to her appeal to Rome, and ignoring the English decision. For a moment, foolishly enough, I had looked for her when the announcement was made, thinking that she might be there, defiant in her red gown as she had been defiant before. But she was far away writing to the Pope, to her nephew, to her allies, begging them to insist that her case be tried fairly, before honourable judges in Rome.

But Henry had passed a law, another new law, which said that English disputes could only be judged in English courts. Suddenly, there could be no legal appeal to Rome. I remembered telling Henry that Englishmen would like to see justice done in an English court, never dreaming that English justice would come to mean Henry's whim, just as the church had come to mean Henry's treasury, just as the Privy Council had come to mean Henry and Anne's favourites.

Nobody at the Easter feast mentioned Queen Katherine. It was as if she had never been. Nobody remarked upon it when the stonemasons set to work chipping away the pomegranates of Spain, which had been in place for so long that the stone had weathered like a mountain that has always been there. Nobody asked what Katherine's new title would be, now that there was a new queen in England. Nobody spoke of her at all, it was as if she had died a death so shameful that we were all trying to forget her.

Anne nearly staggered under the weight of the robes of state and the diamonds and jewels in her hair, on her train, on the hem of her gown and laden around her throat and arms. The court was absolutely at her service, and clearly unenthusiastic. George told me that the king planned to have her crowned at Whitsun which this year would fall in June.

'In the City?' I asked.

'It'll be a performance to put Katherine's coronation in the shade,' he said. 'It has to be.'

William Stafford did not return to court. I minded the tone of my voice very carefully and asked my uncle, while we were watching the king play at bowls, whether he had made William Stafford his master of horse because I would dearly love to have a new hunter for the season.

'Oh no,' he said, hearing the lie the moment that it was out of my mouth. 'He has gone. I had a little word with him after Calais. You won't see him again.'

I kept my face very still and I did not gasp or flinch. I was a courtier as well as he, and I could take a hit and still ride on. 'Has he gone to his farm?' I asked, as if I did not much care one way or another.

'That, or ridden off to the crusades,' my uncle said. 'Good riddance.'

I turned my attention to the game and when Henry made a good throw I clapped very loudly and said: 'Hurrah!' Someone offered me a bet but I refused to bet against the king and caught a quick smile from him for that little piece of flattery. I waited till the game was over and when it was clear that Henry was not going to summon me to walk with him, I slipped away from the crowd around him and went to my room.

The fire was out in the little fireplace. The room faced west and was gloomy in the morning. I sat up on my bed and huddled the clothes over my feet and put a blanket around my shoulders like a poor woman in a field. I was miserably cold. I tightened the blanket around me but it did not warm me. I remembered the days on the beach at Calais, the smell of the sea and the gritty sand under my back and in my linen while William touched me and kissed me. In those nights in France I dreamed of him, and woke every morning quite weak with longing, with sand on my pillow from my hair. Even now, my mouth still yearned for his kisses.

I had meant my promise to George. I had said that I was, before anything else, a Boleyn and a Howard through and through; but now, sitting in the shadowy room, looking out over the grey slates of the city, and up at the dark clouds leaning on the roof of Westminster Palace, I suddenly realised that George was wrong, and my family was wrong, and that I had been wrong – for all my life. I was not a Howard before anything else. Before anything else I was a woman who was capable of passion and who had a great need and a great desire for love. I didn't want the rewards for which Anne had surrendered her youth. I didn't want the arid glamour of George's life. I wanted the heat and the sweat and the passion of a man that I could love and trust. And I wanted to give myself to him: not for advantage, but for desire.

Hardly knowing what I was doing, I rose up from the bed and kicked the clothes aside. 'William,' I said to the empty room. 'William.'

∾

I went down to the stable yard and I ordered my horse to be brought from her stall and said that I was going to Hever to see my children. It was a certainty that my uncle would have a pair of eyes and ears listening and watching in the stable yard but I hoped to be gone before a message could be got to him. The court had gone from the bowling green to dinner, and I thought that if I was lucky, I might be away before any spy found my uncle at liberty to deliver the report which told him that his niece had left for her home without an escort.

It was dark within a couple of hours, that cold spring dark that comes on first very grey and then quickly as black as winter. I was hardly clear of the city, coming into a little village that called itself Canning where I could see the high walls and porter's door of a monastery. I hammered on the door and when they saw the quality of my horse, they took me in and showed me to a small white-washed cell and gave me a slice of meat, a slice of bread, a piece of cheese and a cup of small ale for my dinner.

In the morning they offered me exactly the same fare to break my fast and I took Mass on a rumbling belly, thinking that Henry's fulminations against the corruption and wealth of the church should make allowances for little communities like this.

I had to ask for directions to Rochford. The house and the estate had been in the Howard family for years but we seldom visited it. I had been there only once, and that by river. I had no idea of the road. But there was a lad in the stable who said that he knew his way to Tilbury, and the monk who served as master of the horse for the couple of riding mules and the draft horses for ploughing said that the boy could ride with me on an old cob to show me the way.

He was a nice lad, called Jimmy, and he rode bareback, kicking his bare heels against the dusty sides of his old horse, singing at the top of his voice. We made an odd couple: the urchin and the lady, as we rode along the track beside the river. It was hard riding, the track was dust and pebbles in some places, mud in others. Where it crossed the streams

352

which flowed to the Thames there were fords and sometimes deceptive quagmires where my horse shied and fretted at the shifting sand and sucking mud beneath her feet and only the steadiness of Jimmy's old hack kept her going on. We ate our dinner at a farm in a village called Rainham. The goodwife offered me a boiled egg and some black bread as being all that the house could afford. Jimmy ate bread with nothing else, and seemed well pleased. There were a couple of dried apples for our dessert and I nearly laughed as I thought of the dinner I was missing at the palace at Westminster, with the half-dozen side dishes and the dozens of meat dishes served on gold platters.

I was not nervous. For the first time ever I felt as if I had taken my life into my own hands and I could command my own destiny. For once I was obedient neither to uncle nor father nor king, but following my own desires. And I knew that my desire led me, inexorably, to the man I loved.

I did not doubt him. I did not think for one moment that he might have forgotten me, or taken up with some drab from the village, or married an heiress picked out for him. No, I sat on the tailboard of a wheel-less wagon and watched Jimmy spitting apple pips up into the air, and for once I had the sense to trust.

We rode for a couple more hours after dinner and came into the little market town of Grays as it started to get dark. Tilbury was further down the road, Jimmy assured me, but if I wanted Rochford, beyond Southend, he had a notion that I could cut away from the river and ride due east.

Grays boasted a little ale house, no farmhouse of any size, but a good manor house, drawn back from the road. I toyed with the idea of riding up to the manor house and claiming my right, as a benighted traveller, to their hospitality. But I was afraid of my uncle's influence, which stretched all over the kingdom. And I was starting to become uneasy about the dust in my hair and the dirt on my face and clothes. Jimmy was as filthy as a street urchin, no house of any quality would have put him anywhere but in the stable.

'We'll go to the ale house,' I decided.

It was a better place than it at first appeared. It profited from the traffic to and from Tilbury where travellers from the capital frequently chose to embark, rather than wait for the tide or the barges to take their ships up to the pool of London. They could offer me a bed with curtains in a shared room, and Jimmy a straw mattress in the kitchen. They killed and cooked a chicken for my dinner and served it with wheaten bread and a glass of wine. I even managed to wash in a basin of cold water so my face was clean, even if my hair was filthy. I slept in my clothes, and kept my riding boots under my pillow for fear of thieves. In the morning I had the uneasy sense that I smelled, and a string of fleabites across my belly under my stomacher which itched more and more infuriatingly as the day went on.

I had to let Jimmy go in the morning. He had promised only to show me the way to Tilbury, and it was a long ride back for a little lad on his own. He was not in the least daunted by it. He hopped from the mounting block onto the bowed back of his hack and accepted a coin from me, and a hunk of bread and cheese for his dinner on the road. We rode out together till our paths diverged and he pointed me on the track towards Southend, and then went westwards himself, back towards London.

It was empty countryside that I rode through alone. Empty and flat and desolate. I thought that farming this land would be very different from being enfolded in the fertile weald of Kent. I rode briskly, and kept a good look about me, apprehensive that the desolate road through the marshes could be haunted by thieves. In fact, the sheer emptiness of the countryside was my friend. There were no highwaymen since there were no travellers to steal from. In the hours from dawn till noon I saw only a little lad scaring crows from a newly sown vegetable patch, and in the distance a ploughman churning the mud on the edge of the marsh, a plume of seagulls rising up like smoke behind him.

The going was slow as the track went through the marshes and became waterlogged and muddy. The wind blew in from the river bringing the smell of brine. I passed a couple of villages which were little more than mud, shaped into houses, with mud walls and mud roofs. A couple of children stared and then ran after me, crying with excitement as I went past, and they were the colour of mud, too. It was getting to be dusk as I rode into Southend and I looked around for somewhere that I could spend the night.

There were a few houses, and a small church, and the priest's house beside it. I tapped on the door and the housekeeper answered me with a discouraging scowl. I told her that I was travelling and asked her for hospitality and she showed me, with the most unwilling air, into a small room which adjoined the kitchen. I thought that if I had been a Boleyn and a Howard I would have cursed her for her rudeness, but instead I was a poor woman, with nothing in the world but a handful of coins and an absolute determination.

'Thank you,' I said, as if it were an adequate lodging. 'And can I have some water to wash in? And something to eat?'

The chink of the coins in my purse changed her refusal to an assent and she went to fetch me water and then a bowl of meat pottage, which looked and tasted very much as if it had been in the pot for a couple of days. I was too hungry to care, and too tired to argue. I ate it up and wiped the wooden trencher clean with a piece of bread, and then I fell into the little pallet bed and slept till dawn.

She was up in the morning in the kitchen, sweeping the floor and riddling the fire to cook her master's breakfast. I borrowed a drying sheet from her and went out into the yard to wash my face and hands. I washed my feet too, under the pump, scolded all the time by a flock of chickens. I very much wanted to strip off my clothes and wash all over, and then wear clean clothes, but I might as well have wished for a litter and bearers to take me the last few miles. If he loved me, he would not mind a little dirt. If he did not love me, then the dirt would be nothing to me – compared with that catastrophe.

The housekeeper was curious at breakfast as to what I was doing travelling alone. She had seen the horse and my gown and knew what both would be worth. I said nothing, slipped a slice of bread into the pocket of my gown, and went out to saddle my horse. When I was mounted and ready to go I called her out to the yard. 'Can you tell me the way to Rochford?'

'Out of the gate and turn left down the track,' she said. 'Just keep heading eastwards. You should be there in about an hour. Who was it you wanted to see? The Boleyn family are always at court.'

I mumbled a reply. I did not want her to know that I, a Boleyn, had ridden out such a long way for a man who had not even invited me. As I grew nearer to his home I was more and more fearful and I did not need any witnesses to my boldness. I clicked to my horse, and rode out of the yard, turned left, as she had told me, and then straight into the rising sun.

Rochford was a little hamlet of half a dozen houses gathered around an ale house at a crossroads. My family's great house was set back behind high brick walls with a good-sized park around it. I could not even see it from the road. I had no fear that any of the house servants would see me, and no-one would recognise me if they did.

An idle youth of about twenty lounged against a cottage wall and watched the empty lane. It was very flat and windy. It was very cold. If this had been a test of knight errantry it could not have been more discouraging. I put up my chin and called to the man: 'William Stafford's farm?'

He took the straw from his mouth and strolled over towards my horse.

I turned the horse a little, so that he could not put his hand on the reins. He stepped back when the powerful hindquarters moved around, and pulled his forelock.

'William Stafford?' he repeated in complete bewilderment.

I brought out a penny from my pocket and held it between my gloved finger and thumb. 'Yes,' I said.

'The new gentleman?' he asked. 'From London? Appletree Farm,' he said, pointing up the road. 'Turn right, towards the river. Thatched house with a stable yard. Apple tree by the road.'

I flipped the coin towards him and he caught it with one hand. 'You from London too?' he asked curiously.

'No,' I said. 'From Kent.'

Then I turned and rode up the road looking out for the river, an apple tree, and a thatched house with a stable yard.

The ground fell away from the road towards the river. At the river's edge there were reed beds and a flight of ducks suddenly quacked in alarm and up sprang a heron, all long legs and bow-shaped breast, flapping his huge wings and then settling a little further downstream. The fields were hedged with low quickset and hawthorn, at the water's edge the ragged meadows showed yellow, probably spoiled with salt, I thought. Nearer the road they were dull and green with the fatigue of winter, but in spring I thought William might get a good grass crop off them.

On the far side of the road the land was higher and ploughed. Water was glinting in every furrow, this would always be wet land. Further north I could see some fields planted with apple trees. There was a big old solitary apple tree leaning over the road and the branches brushed low. The bark was silvery grey, the twigs chunky with age. A bush of green mistletoe was thick in one fork in a branch and, on an impulse, I rode my horse up to it and picked a sprig, so I was holding that most pagan plant in my hand as I turned off the road and went down the little track to his farmhouse.

It was a little farmhouse, like a child might draw. A long low house, four windows long along the upper storey, two and a central doorway on the lower. The doorway was like a stable door, top and bottom. I imagined that in the not very distant past the farmer's family and the animals would all have slept inside together. At the side of the house was a good stable yard, cobbled and clean, and a field with half a dozen cows beside it. A horse nodded over the gate and I recognised William Stafford's hunter that had galloped beside me on the sandy beaches at Calais. The horse whinnied when he saw us, and mine cried back as if she too remembered those sunny days at the end of autumn.

At the noise the front door opened and a figure came out of the dark interior and stood, hands on hips, watching me ride down the road. He did not move or speak as I rode up to the garden gate. I slipped down from the saddle unaided, and opened his gate without a word of welcome from him. I hitched the reins to the side of the gate and, with the mistletoe still in my hand, I walked up to him.

After all this long journey, I found I had nothing to say. My whole sense of purpose and determination scattered the moment I saw him.

'William,' was all that I managed, and I held out the little twig of mistletoe with the white buds as if it was a tribute.

'What?' he asked unhelpfully. He still made no move towards me.

I pulled off my hood and shook out my hair. I was suddenly, over-whelmingly conscious that he had never seen me anything but washed and perfumed. And here I was, in the same gown I had worn for three days, flea-bitten, lousy, dusty and smelling of horse and sweat, and hopelessly, helplessly inarticulate.

'What?' he repeated.

'I've come to marry you, if you still want me.' There seemed to be no way to mitigate the baldness of the words.

His expression gave nothing away. He looked at the road behind me. 'Who brought you?'

I shook my head. 'I came alone.'

'What's gone wrong at court?'

'Nothing,' I said. 'It's never been better. They're married and she's with child. The Howards never had fairer prospects. I will be aunt to the King of England.'

William gave a short barking laugh at that, and I looked down at my filthy boots and the dust on my riding habit and laughed too. When I looked back up his eyes were very warm.

'I have nothing,' he warned me. 'I am a nobody, as you rightly said.'

'I have nothing but a hundred pounds a year,' I said. 'I'll lose that when they know where I have gone. And I am nobody without you.'

He made a quick gesture with his hand as if he would draw me to him, but still he held back. 'I won't be the cause of your ruin,' he said. 'I won't have you become the poorer for loving me.'

I felt myself tremble at his nearness, at my desire for him to hold me. 'It doesn't matter,' I said urgently. 'I swear to you that it doesn't matter to me any more.'

He opened his arms to me at that, and I stepped and half-fell forward. He snatched me up and crushed me against him, his mouth on mine, his demanding kisses all over my dirty face, on my eyelids and cheeks and lips and then finally plunging into my open longing mouth. Then he lifted me up into his arms and carried me across the threshold of his house, and up the stairs into the bedroom, into the clean linen sheets of his duckdown bed, and into joy.

Much later he laughed at the fleabites, and he brought me a great wooden bath which he filled with water and set before the big fire in the kitchen, and combed my hair for lice while I lolled my head back and soaked in the hot sweet-smelling water. He put my stomacher and skirt and linen to one side for washing and insisted that I dress in his shirt and a pair of his trousers which I kilted in around my waist and rolled up the legs like a sailor on deck. He turned out my horse into the meadow where she rolled with pleasure at being rid of the saddle, and cantered around with William's hunter, bucking and kicking like a filly. Then he cooked me a big bowl of porridge with yellow honey, and cut me a slice of wheaten bread with creamy butter, and a slab of thick soft Essex cheese. He laughed at my travels with Jimmy and scolded me for setting off without an escort, and then he took me back to bed and we made love all the afternoon till the sky darkened and we were hungry again.

We ate dinner by candlelight in the kitchen. In my honour, William killed an old chicken and spit-roasted it. I was armed with a pair of his gauntlets and delegated to turn the spit while he sliced bread and drew the small ale, and went to the cool pantry for butter and cheese.

When we had eaten we drew up our stools to the fire and drank to each other, and then sat in a rather surprised silence.

'I can't believe this,' I said after a little while. 'I thought no further than getting to you. I didn't think about your home. I didn't think what we would do next.'

'And what d'you think now?'

'I still don't know what to think,' I confessed. 'I suppose I will become accustomed. I shall be a farmer's wife.'

He leaned forward and tossed a slab of peat on the fire. It settled with the others and started to glow red. 'And your family?' he asked.

I shrugged.

'Did you leave a note?'

I shook my head. 'Nothing.'

He cracked a laugh. 'Oh my love, what were you thinking of?'

'I was thinking of you,' I said simply. 'I just suddenly realised how much I loved you. All I could think of was that I should come to you.'

William reached across and stroked my hair. 'You're a good girl,' he said approvingly.

I gave a little gurgle of laughter. 'A good girl?'

'Yes,' he said, unabashed. 'Very.'

I leaned back against his caress and his hand strayed from my head to the nape of my neck. He took it in a firm grasp and shook me gently, like a mother cat might hold a kitten. I closed my eyes and melted into his touch.

'You can't stay here,' he said softly.

I opened my eyes in surprise. 'No?'

'No.' He lifted his hand to forestall me. 'Not because I don't love you, because I do. And we must be married. But we have to get the most we can from this.'

'D'you mean money?' I asked, a little dismayed.

He shook his head. 'I mean your children. If you come to me without a word of warning, without the support of anyone, you'll never get your children. You'll never even see them again.'

I pressed my lips together against the pain. 'Anne can take them from me at any moment, anyway.'

'Or return them,' he reminded me. 'You said she was breeding?'

'Yes. But –'

'If she has a son she'll have no need of yours. We need to be ready to pick him up when she drops him.'

'D'you think I might get him back?'

'I don't know. But you have to be at court to play for him.' His hand was warm on my shoulders through the linen of the shirt. 'I'll come back with you,' he said. 'I can leave a man to run the farm for a season or two. The king will give me a place. And we can be together until we see which way the wind is blowing. We'll get the children if we can, and then we'll get clear and come back here.' He hesitated for a moment and I saw a shadow cross his face. He looked uncomfortable. 'Is it good enough for them here?' he asked shyly. 'They're used to Hever, and there's your family's own great house just up the lane. They're gentry born and bred. This is only a little place.'

'They'll be with us,' I said simply. 'And we'll love them. They'll have a new family, a sort of family that no nobleman has ever had before. A father and a mother who married for love, who chose each other despite wealth and position. It should be better for them, not worse.'

'And you?' he asked. 'It's not Kent.'

'It's not Westminster Palace either,' I said. 'I took my decision when I realised that nothing would compensate me for not being with you. I realised then that I need you. Whatever else it costs, I want to be with you.'

The grip on my shoulders tightened and he drew me off my stool and onto his lap. 'Say it again,' he whispered. 'I think that I am dreaming this.'

'I need you,' I whispered, my eyes searching his intent face. 'Whatever else it costs, I want to be with you.'

'Will you marry me?' he asked.

I closed my eyes and leaned my forehead against the warm column of his neck. 'Oh yes,' I said. 'Oh yes.'

We were married as soon as my gown and my linen were washed and dried since I refused absolutely to go to the church in his breeches. The priest knew William, and opened the church for us the very next day and performed the service with absent-minded speed. I didn't mind. I had been married first at the royal chapel in Greenwich Palace with the king in attendance and the marriage had been a cover for a love affair within a few years, and had ended in death. This wedding, so simple and easy, would take me to a quite different future: a house of my own with a man that I loved.

We walked back to the farmhouse hand in hand and we had a wedding feast of freshly baked bread and a ham which William had smoked in his chimney.

'I shall have to learn how to do all of this,' I said uneasily, looking up to the rafters where the three remaining legs of William's last pig were hanging.

He laughed. 'It's easy enough,' he said. 'And we'll get a girl in to help you. We'll need a couple of women working here when the babies come.'

'The babies?' I asked, thinking of Catherine and Henry.

He smiled. 'Our babies,' he said. 'I want a house filled with little Staffords. Don't you?'

We set off back to Westminster the next day. I had already sent a note upriver to George, imploring him to tell Anne and my uncle that I had been taken ill. I said that I had been so afraid that it was the sweat that I left court without seeing them, and had gone to Hever until I recovered.

It was a lie too late, and too unlikely to convince anyone who thought about it, but I was gambling on the fact that with Anne married to the king and pregnant with his child, no-one would be thinking or caring very much what I did at all.

We went back to London by barge, with the two horses loaded with us. I was reluctant to go. I had meant to leave court and live with William in the country, not to disrupt his plans and take him away from his farm. But William was determined. 'You'll never settle without your children,' he predicted. 'And I don't want your unhappiness on my conscience.'

'So it's not an act of generosity at all,' I said with spirit.

'Last thing I want is a miserable wife,' he said cheerfully. 'I've tried to ride with you from Hever to London, remember. I know what a sad little drab you can be.'

∾

We caught an incoming tide and an onshore wind and we made good time upriver. We landed at Westminster stairs and I walked up while William went round to the jetty to unload the horses. I promised to meet him on the stairs to the great hall within the hour; by that time I should have discovered how the land lay.

I went straight to George's rooms. Oddly, his door was locked and so I tapped on it, the Boleyn knock, and waited for his response. I heard a scuffling and then the door swung open. 'Oh it's you,' George said.

Sir Francis Weston was with him, straightening his doublet as I came into the room.

'Oh,' I said, stepping back.

'Francis took a fall from his horse,' George said. 'Can you walk all right now, Francis?'

'Yes, but I'll go and rest,' he said. He bowed low over my hand and did not comment on the state of my gown and cape which bore all the signs of hard wear and home washing.

As soon as the door was shut behind him I turned to George. 'George, I'm so sorry, but I had to go. Did you manage to lie for me?'

'William Stafford?' he asked.

I nodded.

'I thought as much,' he said. 'God, what fools we both are.'

'Both of us?' I asked, warily.

'In our different ways,' he said. 'Went to him and had him, did you?'

'Yes,' I said shortly. I did not dare trust even George with the explosive news that we were married. 'And he's come back to court with me. Will you get him a place with the king? He can't serve Uncle again.'

'I can get him something,' George said doubtfully. 'Howard stock is very high at the moment. But what d'you want with him at court? You're bound to be found out.'

'George, please,' I said. 'I've asked for nothing. Everyone has had places or land or money from Anne's rise, but I have asked for nothing except my children, and she has taken my son. This is the first thing I've ever asked for.'

'You'll get caught,' George warned. 'And then disgraced.'

'We all have secrets,' I said. 'Even Anne herself. I've protected Anne's secrets, I'd protect you, I want you to do the same for me.'

'Oh very well,' he said unwillingly. 'But you must be discreet. No more riding out together alone. For God's sake don't get yourself in pup. And if Uncle finds a husband for you, you'll have to marry. Love or no.'

'I'll deal with that when it happens,' I said. 'And you'll get him a place?'

'He can be a gentleman usher to the king. But make very sure that he knows it is my favour that has bought it for him, and that he keeps his ears and eyes open in my interest. He's my man now.'

'No he's not,' I said with a sly smile. 'He's very much mine.'

'Good God, what a whore,' my brother laughed, and pulled me into his arms.

'And am I safe? Did they all believe I went to Hever?'

'Yes,' he said. 'Nobody noticed you gone at all for a day. They asked me if I had taken you to Hever without permission and it seemed the safest thing to say yes, until I knew what the devil you were doing. I said you feared that the children were ill. When I got your note the lie was already told, and so I've stuck to it. Everyone thinks that you dashed off to Hever and I took you. It's not a bad lie and it should hold.'

'Thank you,' I said. 'I'd better go and change my gown before anyone sees me like this.'

'You'd better throw it away. You're a mad romp, you know, Marianne. I never thought you had it in you. It was always Anne who insisted on going her own way. I thought you would do as you are told.'

'Not this time,' I said, blew him a kiss, and left him.

❁

I met William as I had promised; but it was odd and uncomfortable to have to stand at arm's distance and speak like strangers when I wanted his arms around me and his kisses in my hair.

'George lied for me already, so I am safe. And he says he can get you the post of gentleman usher to the king.'

'How I rise in the world!' William said sardonically. 'I knew that marriage to you would benefit me. Farmer to gentleman usher in one day.'

'The block the next day if you don't mind your tongue,' I warned him.

He laughed and took my hand and kissed it. 'I'll go and find some lodgings just outside the walls and we can spend every night together even if we have to spend our days apart like this.'

'Yes,' I said. 'I want that.'

He smiled at me. 'You're my wife,' he said gently. 'I'm not going to let you go now.'

❧

I found Anne in the queen's chambers, starting work with her ladies on an enormous altar cloth. The sight was so reminiscent of Queen Katherine that for a moment I blinked, and then I saw the crucial differences. Anne's ladies were all Howard family members or our chosen favourites. Prettiest of the girls was undoubtedly our cousin Madge Shelton, the new Howard girl at court, wealthiest and most influential was Jane Parker, George's wife. The very air of the room was different: Queen Katherine often had one of us reading to her, from the Bible or from some book of sermons. Anne had music, there were four musicians playing as I came in, and one of the ladies lifted her head and sang as she worked.

And there were gentlemen in the room. Queen Katherine, brought up in the strict seclusion of the Spanish royal court, was always formal – even after years in England. The gentlemen visited with the king, they were always made welcome and always royally entertained – but in general the courtiers did not linger in the queen's rooms. What flirtations there were took place in the unsupervised freedom of the gardens or out hunting.

The state kept by Anne was far more merry. There were half a dozen men in the room; Sir William Brereton was there, helping Madge to sort the embroidery silks into colours, Sir Thomas Wyatt was in the window-seat listening to the music, Sir Francis Weston was looking over Anne's shoulder and praising her sewing, and in a corner of the room Jane Parker was in whispered talk with James Wyville.

Anne barely glanced up when I came in, in a clean green gown. 'Oh you're back,' she said indifferently. 'Are the children well again?'

'Yes,' I said. 'It was only a rheum.'

'It must be lovely at Hever,' Sir Thomas Wyatt remarked from the windowseat. 'Are the daffodils out by the river?'

'Yes,' I lied quickly. 'In bud,' I corrected myself.

'But the fairest flower of Hever is here,' Sir Thomas said, looking over at Anne.

She glanced up from her sewing. 'And also in bud,' she said provocatively, and the ladies laughed with her.

I looked from Sir Thomas to Anne. I had not thought that she would have even hinted at her pregnancy, especially before gentlemen.

'Would that I were the little bee that played in the petals,' Sir Thomas said, continuing the bawdy jest.

'You would find the flower closed quite tight against you,' Anne said.

Jane Parker's bright eyes turned from one player to the other as if she were watching tennis. The whole game suddenly seemed to me a waste of the time that I could have been spending with William, yet another masque in the unending make-believe of the court. I was hungry for real love now.

'When do we move?' I asked, breaking into the flirtation. 'When do we go on progress?'

'Next week,' Anne said indifferently, snipping a thread. 'We go to Greenwich, I believe. Why?'

'I'm tired of the City.'

'How restless you are,' Anne complained. 'Only just back from Hever and you want to be off again. You need a man to tie you down, sister. You've been a widow for too long.'

At once I subsided into the windowseat beside Sir Thomas. 'No indeed,' I said. 'See, I am as quiet as any sleeping cat.'

Anne laughed shortly. 'Anyone would think that you had an aversion to men.'

The ladies laughed at the note of malice.

'Just a disinclination.'

'You never had a reputation for being disinclined,' Anne said cattily.

I smiled back at her. 'You never had a reputation for being willing. But now, see, we are both happy.'

She bit her lip at that retort, and I saw her think of snubs which she could make in reply, and reject half of them for being too bawdy, or too near to the truth of her own status as a royal mistress no better than I had been.

'Praise God for it,' she said piously and bent her head to her work.

'Amen,' I returned, as sweet as she.

❁

They were long days for me at Westminster in Anne's court. I could see William only by chance during the day. As a gentleman usher he was required to be in close attendance to the king. Henry took a liking to him, consulted him about horses and often rode with him at his side. I thought it ironic that my William, a man completely unsuited to the life of court, should find himself so favoured. But Henry liked straightforward speech as long as it agreed with him.

Only at night could William and I be alone together. He had hired some rooms just across the road from the great palace of Westminster, an attic in the very rafters of an old building. When we lay awake after making love I could hear the sleepy birds settling in their nests in the thatch. We had a little pallet bed, a table and two stools, a fireplace where we warmed up our dinner from the palace, and nothing more. We wanted nothing more.

I woke at dawn every morning to his touch, the delight of his warmth and the heady smell of his skin. I had never before lain with a man who had loved me completely, for myself, and it was a dizzy experience. I had never lain with a man whose touch I adored without any need to hide my adoration, or exaggerate it, or adjust it at all. I simply loved him as if he were my one and only lover, and he loved me too with the same simplicity of appetite and desire which made me wonder what I thought I had been doing all those years when I had been dealing in the false coin of vanity and lust. I had not known then that all along there had been this other currency of pure gold.

∾

Anne's coronation was overshadowed by a violent quarrel with our uncle. I was in her room when he raged at her, swearing that she had become so great in her own mind that she forgot who put her there. Anne, infuriatingly smug, put her hand on her swelling belly and told him that she was great in her body, and that she was very well aware who had put it there.

'By God, Anne, you will remember your family,' he swore.

'How should I forget them? They are around me like wasps around a honeypot. Every time I step, I trip over one of you, asking for another favour.'

'I don't ask,' he snapped. 'I have rights.'

She turned her head at that. 'Not over me! You are speaking to your queen.'

'I am speaking to my niece who would have been banished from the court in disgrace for bedding Henry Percy if it were not for me,' he spat at her.

She leaped to her feet as if she would fly at him.

'Anne!' I cried out. 'Sit! Be still!' I looked at my uncle. 'She *must* not be upset! The baby!'

He looked murderously at her, then he got his temper under control. 'Of course,' he said with stilted politeness. 'Sit, Anne. Be calm.'

She sank down into her seat again. 'Never speak of that,' she hissed at him. 'I swear it, uncle or no uncle, if you raise that old slander against me I will have you out of court.'

'I am Earl Marshal,' he said through his teeth. 'I was one of the greatest men in England when you were still in the nursery.'

'And before Bosworth your father was a traitor in the Tower,' she said triumphantly. 'Remember, as I do, that we are Howards together. If you are not on my side, I am not on yours. You could see the inside of the Tower again at one word from me.'

'Say it,' he spat at her and stalked from the room without a bow. She stared after him. 'I hate him,' she said very quietly. 'I will see him broken to a nobody.'

'Don't think that,' I said hastily. 'You need him.'

'I need no-one,' she said flatly. 'The king is wholly mine. I have his heart, I have his desire, and I am carrying his son. I need no-one.'

❁

The quarrel with Uncle Howard was still not mended when he arrived to escort Anne to her coronation in the City. It was to be, as George had predicted, the finest coronation that anyone had ever seen. Anne had ordered them to burn away the pomegranate crest on Queen Katherine's barge as if Katherine had been a usurper, instead of rightful queen. In their place was Anne's own coat of arms and her initials entwined with Henry's. People mocked even that – saying that they read HA HA! and the last laugh was on poor England. Anne's new motto was everywhere: 'the most happy'. Even George had snorted when he first heard it. 'Anne, happy?' he said. 'When she is Queen of Heaven and has pulled down the Virgin Mary herself.'

We went by barges to the Tower of London, flying flags of gold and white and silver, and the king was waiting for us at the great watergate. They held our barge steady as Anne disembarked, and I watched her, almost as if she was a stranger to me. She rose off her throne and glided down the gangplank as if she had been a queen born and bred. She was wonderfully gowned in silver and gold with a fur cape around her shoulders. She did not look like my sister, she did not look like any mortal woman at all. She carried herself as if she were the greatest queen that had ever been born.

We spent two nights in the Tower and on the first there was a great dinner and entertainment at which Henry gave out honours to celebrate the day. He made eighteen Knights of the Bath and gave out a dozen knighthoods, three of them to his favourite gentlemen ushers, including my husband. William came to find me, after the king had tapped him on the shoulder with his sword and given him the kiss of fealty. He led me out for a dance where we could mingle with the court and hope that no-one would notice the queen's sister dancing with a gentleman usher.

'Well then, my Lady Stafford,' he said softly. 'How is this for ambition?'

'Vaulting,' I said. 'You will be as high as a Howard, I know it.'

'Actually I am glad of it,' he said, reverting to a low confidential whisper as we watched the pair of dancers in the middle of the circle. 'I did not want you to be lowered by marrying me.'

'I would have married you if you had been a peasant,' I said firmly.

He chuckled at that. 'My love, I saw how upset you were about the fleabites. I don't think you would have married me if I had been a peasant at all.'

I turned to laugh at him and then I caught a furious glance from George who was paired to dance with Madge Shelton. At once I steadied myself. 'George is watching us.'

William nodded. 'He'd do better to take care of himself.'

'Oh why?'

It was our turn to dance. William took me to the centre of the circle and we danced together, three steps one way, three steps the other. It was a courtship dance, it was hard to perform without drawing close and locking our gaze. I kept reminding myself not to let my face show my delight in him. William was less discreet than me. Every time I stole a glance at him his eyes were on me as if he would eat me up. I was relieved when we danced around the line of the circle and out under an arch of arms, and the dance became general again.

'What about George?'

'Bad company,' William said shortly.

I laughed out loud. 'He's a Howard, and a friend of the king,' I said. 'He's supposed to be in bad company.'

I saw him change tack. 'Oh, it's nothing, I suppose.'

The musicians reached the end and played a final chord. I drew William to the side of the hall.

'Now tell me truly what you mean.'

'Sir Francis Weston is forever with him,' William said, driven to speak. 'And he has a bad reputation.'

At once I was on my guard. 'You'll have heard of nothing but a young man's wildness.'

'More,' William said shortly.

'What more?'

William looked about him as if he wanted to escape this inquisition. 'I've heard they're lovers.'

I took a little breath.

'You knew?'

I nodded, saying nothing.

'My God, Mary.' William took a step away from me, and then came back to my side. 'You did not tell me? Your own brother deep in sin and you didn't tell me?'

'Of course not,' I exclaimed. 'I don't hold him up to shame. He is my brother. And he might change.'

'You give him loyalty before me?'

'As well as you,' I said swiftly. 'William, this is my brother. We are the three Boleyns, we all three need each other. We all three know a dozen things, a score of things which are the greatest of secrets. I am not yet wholly Lady Stafford.'

'Your brother is a sodomite!' he hissed at me.

'And still my brother!' I grabbed his arm, careless of who might see us, and dragged him to an alcove. 'He is a sodomite, and my sister is a whore, and perhaps a poisoner, and I am a whore. My uncle has been the falsest of friends, my father a time-server, my mother – God knows – some even say she had the king before the two of us! All of this you knew or you could have deduced. Now tell me, am I good enough for you? For I knew that you were a nobody and I came to find you all the same. If you want to rise to be a somebody in this court you will get blood or shit on your hands. I have had to learn this through a hard apprenticeship since I was a little girl. You can learn it now if you have the stomach.'

William gasped at my vehemence and stepped back to take me in. 'I didn't mean to distress you.'

'He is my brother. She is my sister. Come what will, they are my kin.'

'They could be our enemies both,' he warned.

'They could be my enemies till death and they would still be my brother and sister,' I said.

We paused.

'Kin and enemies all at once?'

'Perhaps,' I said. 'It depends on how this great gamble goes.'

William nodded.

'So what do they say about him?' I asked more steadily. 'What did you hear?'

'It's not widely known, thank God, but they say there is a secret court within a court, they circle your sister, they are her closest friends, but at the same time they are lovers among themselves. Sir Francis is one, Sir William Brereton another. Hard gamblers, great horse-riders, men who will do anything for a dare, anything that brings them pleasure or excitement – and George is among them. They're always around the queen, it's her rooms where they meet and flirt and play. So Anne is compromised too.'

I looked across the hall at my brother. He was leaning over the back of Anne's throne and whispering in her ear. I saw her tilt her head to his intimate whisper and giggle.

'This life would corrupt a saint, never mind a young man.'

'He wanted to be a soldier,' I said sadly. 'A great crusader, a knight with a white shield riding out against the infidel.'

William shook his head. 'We'll save the boy Henry from this if we can,' he said.

'My son?'

He nodded. 'Our son. We'll try to give him a life of some purpose, not idleness and pleasure-seeking. And you had better warn your brother and your sister that their circle of friends are the subject of whispers, and he the worst.'

❧

Anne entered the City the following day, I helped her to dress in her white gown with a white surcoat and a mantle of white ermine. She wore her dark hair loose about her shoulders with a golden veil and circlet of gold. She rode into London on a litter pulled by two white ponies with the Barons of the Cinque Ports holding a canopy of cloth of gold over her head, and the whole court, dressed in their finest, following on foot behind her. There were triumphal arches, there were fountains pouring wine, there were loyal poems at every stopping point, but the whole procession wound through a city of terrible silence.

Madge Shelton was beside me as we walked behind Anne's litter in the silence which grew increasingly ominous as we went down the narrow streets to the cathedral. 'Good God, this is dreadful,' she muttered.

London was sulking, the people were out in their thousands but they did not wave flags or call blessings or shout Anne's name. They stared at her with a dreadful hungry curiosity as if they would see the woman who had wrought such a change in England, such a change in the king, and who had finally cut the very mantle of queenship into her own gown.

If her entrance to the City was bleak, her coronation on the second day of silent celebrations was no better. This time she wore crimson velvet trimmed with the softest whitest fur of ermine with a mantle of purple, and a face like thunder.

'Aren't you happy now, Anne?' I asked as I twitched her train straight.

She showed a smile which was more a grimace. 'The most happy,' she said bitterly, quoting her own motto. 'The most happy. I should be, shouldn't I? I have everything I ever wanted, and it was only me, first and last, who believed that I could get it. I am queen, I am the wife of the King of England. I have thrown down Katherine and taken her place. I should be the happiest woman in the world.'

'And he loves you,' I said, thinking of how my life was transformed by being loved by a good man.

Anne shrugged her shoulders. 'Oh yes,' she said indifferently. She touched her belly. 'If only I could know it was a boy. If only I could have been crowned with a prince already in the nursery.'

Gently I patted her shoulder, awkward at the intimacy. Since we had stopped sharing a bed we seldom touched. Since she had a household of maids I no longer brushed her hair or laced her gown. She was intimate still with George but she had grown apart from me; and the theft of my son had left an unspoken resentment between us. I felt odd that she should confide a weakness to me. The polished veneer of queenship had spread over Anne like a glaze over a figurine.

'Not long to wait,' I said gently.

'Three months.'

There was a knock at the door and Jane Parker came in, her face bright with excitement. 'They're waiting for you!' she said breathlessly. 'It's time. Are you ready?'

'I beg your pardon?' Anne said glacially. At once my sister disappeared behind the mask of queenship. Jane dropped into a curtsey. 'Your Majesty! I beg your pardon! I should have said that they are waiting for Your Majesty.'

'I'm ready,' Anne said and rose to her feet. The rest of her court came into the room and the ladies in waiting arranged the long train of her cape, I straightened her headdress, and spread her long dark hair over her shoulders.

Then my sister, the Boleyn girl, went out to be crowned Queen of England.

I spent the night of Anne's coronation with William in my bedroom in the Tower. I should have had Madge Shelton to share my bed but she whispered to me that she would be gone all night so while the feasting of the court went on, William and I crept away to my room, locked the door, threw another log on the fire, and slowly, sensually, undressed and made love.

We woke through the night made love and dozed again in a sleepy cycle of arousal and satisfaction, and by five o'clock in the morning, when it was starting to get light, we were both deliciously exhausted and ravenous with hunger.

'Come on,' he said to me. 'Let's go out and find something to eat.'

We pulled on our clothes and I put on a cape with a hood to hide my face and we crept from the sleeping Tower into the streets of the City. Half the men of London seemed to be drunk in the gutters from the free wine that had poured from the fountains to celebrate the triumph of Anne. We stepped over limp bodies all the way up the hill to the Minories.

We walked hand in hand, careless of being seen in this city which was sick with drink. William led the way to a baker's shop and stepped back to see if smoke was coming from the crooked chimney.

'I can smell bread,' I said, snuffing at the air and laughing at my own hunger.

'I'll knock him up,' William said and hammered on the side door.

A muffled shout from inside answered him and the door was thrown open by a man with a red face smeared with white flour.

'Can I buy a loaf of bread?' William asked. 'And some breakfast?'

The man blinked at the brightness of the light in the street. 'If you have the money,' he said sulkily. 'For God knows I have squandered all of mine.'

William drew me into the bakehouse. It was warm inside and smelled sweet. Everywhere was covered with a fine dust of white flour, even the table and the stools. William swept a seat with his cape and set me down on it.

'Some bread,' he said. 'A couple of mugs of small ale. Some fruit if you have it, for the lady. A couple of eggs, boiled, a little ham perhaps? A cheese? Anything nice.'

'This is my first batch of the day,' the man grumbled. 'I have hardly broken my own fast. Never mind running around slicing ham for the gentry.'

A little chink and the gleam of a silver coin changed everything.

'I have some excellent ham in my larder and a cheese just up from the country that my own cousin made,' the baker said persuasively. 'And my wife shall rise and pour you the small ale herself. She's a good brewer, there's not a better taste in all of London.'

'Thank you,' William said gracefully as he sat down beside me and winked, and rested his arm comfortably around my waist.

'Newly wed?' the man asked, shovelling loaves out of the oven and seeing William's gaze on my face.

'Yes,' I said.

'Long may it last,' he said doubtfully, and turned the loaves onto the wooden counter.

'Amen to that,' William said quietly, and drew me to him and kissed me on the lips and whispered privately in my ear: 'I am going to love you like this forever.'

❧

William saw me into the little wicket gate to the Tower before going down to the river, hiring a river boatman and entering through the watergate. Madge Shelton was in our room when I got in, but too absorbed in brushing her hair and changing her gown to wonder where I had been so early in the morning. Half the court seemed to be waking up in the wrong beds. The triumph of Anne, the mistress who had become a wife, was an inspiration to every loose girl in the country.

I washed my face and hands and dressed ready to go with Anne and the other ladies to matins. Anne, in her first day of queenship, was dressed very richly in a dark gown with a jewelled hood and a long string of pearls twisted twice around her neck. She still wore her golden 'B' for Boleyn, and carried a prayerbook encased in gold leaf. She nodded when she saw me and I dropped into a deep curtsey and followed the hem of her gown as if I was honoured to do so.

After Mass and after breakfast with the king, Anne started to reorganise her household. Many of Queen Katherine's servants had transferred their loyalty without much inconvenience, like the rest of us they would rather be attached to a rising star than to the lost queen. My eye was caught by the name Seymour.

'Are you having a Seymour girl as your lady in waiting?' I asked curiously.

'Which one?' George asked idly, pulling the list towards him. 'That Agnes is said to be a terrible whore.'

'Jane,' Anne said. 'But I shall have Aunt Elizabeth, and Cousin Mary. I should think we have enough Howards to outweigh the influence of one Seymour.'

'Who asked for her place?' George inquired.

'They're all asking for places,' Anne said wearily. 'All of them, all of the time. I thought one or two women from other families would be a sop. The Howards can't have everything.'

George laughed. 'Oh, why not?'

Anne pushed her chair back from the table and rested her hand on her belly and sighed. George was alert.

'Tired?' he asked.

'A little gripe.' She looked at me. 'It doesn't matter, does it? Little nips of pain? They don't mean anything?'

'I had quite bad pains with Catherine, and she went full term, and then an easy birth.'

'They don't mean that it'll be a girl though, do they?' George said anxiously.

I looked at the two of them, the matching long Boleyn noses and long faces and those eager eyes. They were the same features that had looked back at me from my own mirror for all of my life, except that now I had lost that hungry expression.

'Be at peace,' I said gently to George. 'There's no reason in the world why she should not have the most beautiful son. And worrying is the worst thing she can do.'

'As well tell me not to breathe,' Anne snapped. 'It's like carrying the whole future of England in my belly. And the queen miscarried over and over again.'

'Because she was not his proper wife,' George said soothingly. 'Because their marriage was never valid. Of course God will give you a son.'

Silently, she stretched her hand across the table. George gripped it tight. I looked at both of them, at the absolute desperation of their ambition, still riding them as hard as when they were the children of a small lord on the rise. I looked at them and knew the relief of my escape.

I waited for a moment and then I said, 'George, I have heard some gossip about you which is not to your credit.'

He looked up with his merry, wicked smile. 'Surely not!'

'It is serious,' I said.

'Who have you been listening to?' he returned.

'Court whispers,' I said. 'They say that Sir Francis Weston is part of a wild circle, you among them.'

He glanced quickly at Anne, as if to see what she knew.

She looked inquiringly at me. She was clearly ignorant of what was being said. 'Sir Francis is a loyal friend.'

'The queen has spoken.' George tried to make a joke.

'Because she doesn't know the half of it, and you do,' I snapped back.

Anne was alerted by that. 'I have to be all but perfect,' she said. 'I can't let them have anything that they could whisper to the king against me.'

George patted her hand. 'It's nothing,' he soothed her again. 'Don't fret. A couple of wild nights and a little too much to drink. A couple of bad women and some high gambling. I'd never be a discredit to you, Anne, I promise.'

'It's more than that,' I said flatly. 'They say that Sir Francis is George's lover.'

Anne's eyes widened, she reached for George at once. 'George, no?'

'Absolutely not.' He took her hand in a comforting clasp.

She turned a cold face to me. 'Don't come to me with your nasty stories, Mary,' she said. 'You're as bad as Jane Parker.'

'You had better take care,' I warned George. 'Any mud thrown at you sticks to us all.'

'There's no mud,' he replied, but his eyes were on Anne's face. 'Nothing at all.'

'You had better be sure,' she said.

'Nothing at all,' he repeated.

We left her to rest and went out to find the rest of the court who were playing quoits with the king.

'Who spoke of me?' George demanded.

'William,' I said honestly. 'He was not spreading scandal. He knew I would be afraid for you.'

He laughed carelessly, but I heard the strain in his voice. 'I love Francis,' he confessed. 'I can't see a finer man in the world, a braver sweeter better man never lived – and I cannot help but desire him.'

'You love him like a woman?' I asked awkwardly.

'Like a man,' he corrected me swiftly. 'A more passionate thing by far.'

'George, this is a dreadful sin, and he will break your heart. This is a disastrous course. If our uncle knew . . .'

'If anyone knew, I'd be ruined outright.'

'Can you not stop seeing him?'

He turned to me with a crooked smile. 'Can you stop seeing William Stafford?'

'It's not the same!' I protested. 'What you're describing is not the same! Nothing like it. William loves me honourably and truly. And I love him. But this –'

'You're not without sin, you're just lucky,' George said brutally. 'It is luck to love someone who is free to love you in return. But I don't. I just desire him, desire him and desire him; and I wait for it to burn out.'

'Will it burn out?' I asked.

'Bound to,' he said bitterly. 'Everything I have ever gained has always turned to ashes after a little while. Why should this be any different?'

'George,' I said, and put my hand out to him. 'Oh my brother . . .'

He looked at me with those hard hungry Boleyn eyes. 'What?'

'This will be your undoing,' I whispered.

'Oh probably,' he said carelessly. 'But Anne will save me. Anne and my nephew the king.'

Summer 1533

Anne would not release me to go to Hever in the summer when she was expecting her baby in August. The court would not progress around the manor houses of England, nothing would happen as it should. I was in such a bitter rage of disappointment that I could hardly bear to be in the same room as her; but I had to be in the same room as her every day, and listen to her endless, endless speculation of what sort of a king her baby might be. Everyone had to wait on Anne. Everyone had to bow to her. Nothing mattered more than Anne and her belly. She was the focus of everything and she would plan nothing. In such confusion, the court could decide nothing, could go nowhere. Henry could hardly bear to be parted from her, even to go hunting.

At the start of July George and my uncle were sent to France as emissaries to the French king to tell him that the heir to the English throne was about to be born, and to take him some pledges and promises in case the Spanish emperor moved against England at this fresh insult to his aunt. They would go on to a meeting with the Pope in which the deadlock that held England frozen might be broken. I went to Anne to ask her again if she might spare me too, as soon as she went into her confinement.

'I want to go to Hever,' I said quietly. 'I need to see my children.'

She shook her head. She was lying in the bay of the window of her room on a day bed they had pushed into the embrasure for her. All the windows stood open to catch the breeze as it came up the river, but she was still sweating. Her gown was laced firmly, her breasts, pressed by the stomacher, were swollen and uncomfortable. Her back ached, even supported by cushions embroidered with seed pearls.

'No,' she said shortly.

She saw that I was about to argue with her. 'Oh stop it,' she said irritably. 'I can order you as a queen to do what I shouldn't have to even ask as a sister. You ought to want to be with me. I visited you when you were confined.'

'You stole my lover while I was giving birth to his son!' I said flatly.

'I was told to. And you would have done the same if our roles had been turned. I need you, Mary. Don't go wandering off when you're needed.'

'What d'you need me for?' I demanded.

She lost her flushed colour and went waxy white. 'What if it kills me?' she whispered. 'What if it gets stuck and I die of it?'

'Oh Anne . . .'

'Don't pet me,' she said irritably. 'I don't want your sympathy. I just want you here to protect me.'

I hesitated. 'What d'you mean?'

'If they can get the baby out by killing me, I wouldn't give you a groat for my life,' she said brutally. 'They'd rather have a live Prince of Wales than a live queen. They can get another queen. But princes are rare in this market.'

'I won't be able to stop them,' I said feebly.

She gleamed at me under her eyelids. 'I know you're a broken reed. But at least you could tell George and he would work on the king to make them save me.'

Her bleak view of the world made me pause. But then I thought of my own children. 'After your baby is born, and you are well – then I go to Hever,' I stipulated.

'After the baby is born you can go to hell if you like,' she said levelly.

❀

Then there was nothing to do but wait. But in the hot days when it seemed as if nothing was happening, the most appalling news arrived from Rome. The Pope had finally ruled against Henry. Astoundingly: the king was to be excommunicated.

'What?' Anne demanded.

Lady Rochford, George's newly ennobled wife Jane Parker, had brought the news. Like a buzzard to carrion, she was always first. 'Excommunicated.' Even she looked stunned. 'Every Englishman loyal to the Pope should disobey the king,' she said. 'Spain can invade. It would be a holy war.'

Anne was whiter than the pearls at her neck.

'Go out,' I said suddenly. 'How dare you come in here and upset the queen?'

'Some will say that she is not the queen.' Jane went for the door. 'Won't the king put her aside now?'

'Go!' I said fiercely, and ran to Anne. She had her hand on her belly as if she would shield the baby from the disastrous news. I pinched her cheeks, and watched her eyelids flutter.

'He'll stand by me,' she whispered. 'Cranmer himself married us. Crowned me. They can't say it is all to be put aside.'

'No,' I said as staunchly as I could, thinking that yes, perhaps they could put it all aside, for who could deny the Pope when he held the keys of heaven in his hand? The king must surrender. And the first thing he would have to surrender would be Anne.

'Oh God, I wish George was here,' Anne said with a little wail of despair. 'I wish he was home.'

Two days later, George came home from France with a brief panic-stricken letter from our uncle, demanding to know what should be done next in the negotiations to resolve a crisis which had suddenly become a disaster. The king sent George straight back to France again with orders for my uncle to break off the talks and come home. We would all wait and see what would happen.

The days grew hotter, they drew up plans for the defence of England against a Spanish invasion, the priests preached calm from the pulpits but wondered which side they should be on. Many churches simply bolted their doors in the crisis and no-one could confess or pray, bury their dead or christen their babies. Uncle Howard begged the king to let him go back to France and implore Francis to persuade the Pope to lift the excommunication. I never before saw him look so terrified. But George, the steadiest of us all, turned all his attention to Anne.

It was as if he thought that the king's immortal soul and the future of England were too great for him. The one place where he could be effective was to keep the baby growing in Anne's belly. 'This is our guarantee,' he said quietly to me. 'Nothing secures our safety more than a boy baby.'

He spent every morning with Anne, sitting with her on the day bed in the window embrasure. When Henry came into the room George would wander away, but when Henry was gone again, Anne would lean back on the pillows and look for our brother. She never showed Henry the strain she suffered. She remained for him the fascinating woman she had always been. She would show him her temper if he crossed her, quick enough. But she never showed him her fear. She never showed her fear to anyone but to George and me. Henry had her sweetness and her charm and her flirtatiousness. Even eight months with child Anne could flick her eyes sideways in a way which would make a man catch his breath. I used to watch her talking with Henry, and see that every gesture, every inch of her was devoted to delighting him.

No wonder that when he left the room to go hunting she leaned back on the pillows and summoned me to take off her hood and stroke her forehead. 'I'm so hot.'

Henry did not go hunting alone, of course. Anne might be fascinating but not even she could hold him when she was eight months pregnant and forbidden to go to his bed. Henry was flirting openly with Lady Margaret Steyne and it was not long before Anne knew of it.

When he visited her one afternoon he got a sharp welcome.

'I wonder you dare show your face to me,' she greeted him in a hiss as he sat down beside her. Henry glanced around the room and the gentlemen of the court at once moved a little further away and pretended to be deaf while the ladies turned their heads to give the royal couple the illusion of privacy.

'Madam?'

'I hear you've bedded some slut,' Anne said.

Henry looked around and saw Lady Margaret. A glance at William Brereton prompted that most experienced of courtiers to offer Lady Margaret his arm. He swept her out of the room for a walk by the river. Anne watched them go with a glare which would have frightened a lesser man.

'Madam?' Henry inquired.

'I won't have it,' she warned him. 'I won't tolerate it. She must leave court.'

Henry shook his head and rose to his feet. 'You forget to whom you speak,' he pronounced. 'And ill temper is not suitable to your condition. I shall bid you good day, madam.'

'You forget to whom you speak!' Anne retorted. 'I am your wife and the queen and I will not be overlooked and insulted in my own court. That woman is to leave.'

'No-one orders me!'

'No-one insults me!'

'How have you been insulted? The lady has never paid you anything but the greatest of attention and politeness, and I remain your most obedient husband. What is the matter with you?'

'I won't have her at court! I shall not be so treated.'

'Madam,' Henry said, at his most chilling. 'A better lady than you was treated far worse and never complained to me. As you well know.'

For a moment, absorbed in her own temper, she did not catch the reference. And when she did she flung herself out of her chair to her feet. 'You cite her to me!' she screamed at him. 'You dare compare me to that woman who was never your wife?'

'She was a Princess of the Blood,' he shouted back. 'And she would never, never have reproached me. She knew that a wife's whole duty is to mind her husband's comfort.'

Anne slapped her hand on the curve of her belly. 'Did she give you a son?' she demanded.

There was a silence. 'No,' Henry said heavily.

'Then princess or not, she was no use. And she was not your wife.'

He nodded. Henry, and indeed all of us, sometimes had trouble remembering that most debatable fact.

'You are not to distress yourself,' he said.

'Then do not you distress me,' she answered smartly.

Reluctantly, I drew closer. 'Anne, you should sit down,' I said as quietly as I could. Henry turned to me with relief. 'Yes, Lady Carey, keep her quiet. I am just going.' He gave a little bow to Anne and left the room abruptly. Half the gentlemen swirled out with him, half of them were caught unawares and stayed. Anne looked at me.

'What did you interrupt for?'

'You can't risk the baby.'

'Oh! The baby! All anyone thinks about is the baby!'

George drew close to me and took Anne's hand. 'Of course. All our futures depend on it. Yours as well, Anne. Be still now, Mary's right.'

'We should have fought it out to the end,' she said resentfully. 'I should not have let him go until he promised to send her from court. You should not have interrupted us.'

'You can't fight it through to the end,' George pointed out to her. 'You can't end up in bed till you've been birthed and churched. You have to wait, Anne. And you know that he'll have someone else while he's waiting.'

'But what if she keeps him?' Anne wailed, her glance sliding past me, knowing full well that she had taken him from me when I was in childbirth.

'She can't,' George said simply. 'You're his wife. He can't divorce you, can he? He's only just got rid of t'other one. And if you have his son he'd have no reason to. Your winning card is in your belly, Anne. Hold it close and play it right.'

She leaned back against the chair. 'Send for some musicians,' she said. 'They can dance.'

George snapped his fingers and a pageboy jumped forward.

Anne turned to me. 'And you tell Lady Margaret Steyne that I don't want her in my sight,' she said.

❧

The court took to the river that summer. We had never been near to the Thames in the summer months before, and the master of the revels devised water battles and water masques and water entertainments for Henry and his new queen. One night they had a battle of fire at twilight on the water and Anne watched it from a little tented palace on the bank. The queen's men won and then there was dancing on a little stage built out over the river. I danced with half a dozen men and then I looked around for my husband.

He was watching me, he was always watching me for the moment when we could slip away together. One discreet tilt of his head, one secret smile and we were gone into the shadows for a kiss and a hidden touch and sometimes, when it was dark and when we could not resist each other, we would take our pleasure, hidden in the darkness by the river with the sound of faraway music to disguise my moan of pleasure.

I was a clandestine lover and it was that which made me alert for George. He too would take part in the first half-dozen dances and establish his presence at the centre of things. Then he too would step back, back, back from the circle of light into the obscurity of the garden. Then I would see that Sir Francis was missing too and know that he had taken my brother off somewhere, perhaps to his room, perhaps to the stews of the City for some wild doings, perhaps gambling, or riding in the moonlight, or for some rough embracing. George might reappear in five minutes, or he might be gone all night. Anne, who thought he was roistering as he always had done, accused him of flirting with the maids around the court and George laughed and disclaimed as he always had done. Only I knew that a more powerful and more dangerous desire had my brother in its grasp.

In August Anne announced that she would retire for her confinement and when Henry came to visit her in the morning, after hearing Mass, he found that the rooms were in chaos with furniture being moved in and out, and all the ladies in a great toil of activity.

Anne sat on a chair among all the confusion and ordered what she wanted. When she saw Henry come in she inclined her head but did not rise to curtsey to him. He did not care, he was besotted with his pregnant queen, he dropped like a boy to kneel beside her, to put his hands on her great round belly and look up into her face.

'We need a christening gown for our son,' she said without preamble. 'Does she have it?'

'She' meant only one thing in the royal vocabulary. 'She' was always the queen that had disappeared, the queen that no-one ever mentioned, the queen that everyone tried not to remember, sitting in that chair, preparing for her own confinement in that room, and forever turning to Henry with her sweet deferential smile.

'It's her own,' he said. 'Brought from Spain.'

'Was Mary christened in it?' Anne demanded, already knowing the answer.

Henry frowned at the effort of recovering a memory. 'Oh yes, a great long white gown, richly embroidered. But it was Katherine's own.'

'Does she have it still?'

'We can order a new gown,' Henry said pacifically. 'You could draw it yourself, and the nuns could sew it for you.'

A toss of Anne's head indicated that this would not do. 'My baby is to have the royal gown,' she said. 'I want him christened in the gown that all the princes have worn.'

'We don't have a royal gown . . .' he said hesitantly.

'I'll warrant!' she snapped. 'Because she has it.'

Henry knew when he was beaten. He bent his head and kissed her hand, clenched on the arm of the chair. 'Don't distress yourself,' he urged her. 'Not so near your time. I'll send to her for it. I swear I will. Our little Edward Henry shall have everything you might want.'

She nodded, she found her sweet smile, she touched the nape of his neck with her fingertips as he bowed to her.

The midwife came to them and swept a curtsey. 'Your room is ready now,' she said.

Anne turned to Henry. 'You'll visit me every day,' she said. It sounded more like an order than a request.

'Twice a day,' he promised. 'The time will pass, sweetheart, and you must rest for the coming of our son.'

He kissed her hand again and left her, and I drew close as the two of us went to the threshold of her bedchamber. Her great bed had been moved in, and the walls hung with thick tapestries to exclude any noise or sunshine or fresh air. They had put rushes down on the floor with rosemary for scent, and lavender for relief. They had moved all the other furniture out of the room except for one chair and table for the midwife. Anne was expected to stay in bed for one whole month. They had lit a fire although it was midsummer and the room was stifling. They had lit candles so that she could read or sew, and they had put the cradle ready at the foot of the bed.

Anne recoiled on the threshold of the darkened stuffy room. 'I can't go in there, it's like a prison.'

'It's only for a month,' I said. 'Perhaps less.'

'I'll suffocate.'

'You'll be fine. I had to do it.'

'But I'm the queen.'

'All the more reason.'

The midwife came up behind me and said: 'Is it all to your liking, Your Majesty?'

Anne's face was white. 'It's like a prison.'

The midwife laughed and ushered her into the room. 'They all say that. But you'll be glad of the rest.'

'Tell George I'll want to see him later,' Anne said over her shoulder to me. 'And tell him to bring someone entertaining. I'm not going to be all alone in here. I might as well be imprisoned in the Tower.'

'We'll dine with you,' I promised 'If you rest now.'

With Anne withdrawn from court the king returned to his normal pattern of hunting every morning from six till ten and then coming in for his dinner. In the afternoon he would visit Anne and then there would be entertainments laid on for him in the evening.

'Who does he dance with?' Anne demanded, as sharp as ever though she lay hot and tired and heavy in the darkened room.

'No-one in particular,' I said. Madge Shelton had taken his eye and the Seymour girl, Jane. Lady Margaret Steyne was peacocking about in half a dozen new gowns. But none of this would matter if Anne had a boy.

'And who hunts with him?'

'Just his gentlemen,' I lied. Sir John Seymour had bought his daughter a most handsome grey hunter. She had a dark blue gown to ride in and she looked well in the saddle.

Anne looked suspiciously at me. 'You're not chasing after him yourself, are you?' she asked nastily.

I shook my head. 'I've no desire to alter my station in life,' I said honestly enough. Carefully, I kept my thoughts from William. If I let myself think of the set of his shoulders or the way he stretched when he was naked in the morning light, then I knew that my desire would show in my face. Anyone could read it, I was too much his woman.

'And you watch the king for me?' Anne insisted. 'You do watch him, Mary?'

'He's waiting for the birth of his son, like the rest of the court,' I said. 'If you have a boy then nothing can touch you. You know that.'

She nodded and closed her eyes and leaned back on the pillows. 'God, I wish it was over,' she said pettishly.

'Amen,' I said.

Without my sister's keen eyes on me I was free to spend time with William. Madge Shelton was frequently missing from my bedroom and she and I had developed an informal arrangement of always knocking at the door, and turning away from it immediately if it was locked from the inside. Madge was only a young girl but she had grown up quickly at court. She knew that her chances of a good marriage depended on the careful balance of catching a man's desire without letting a shadow fall on her own reputation. And it was a wilder harder-living court than the one I had come to as a girl.

George's deceits worked as well. He and Sir Francis with William Brereton and Henry Norris were at a loose end without the queen in her court. They went hunting with Henry in the morning and sometimes they would be summoned to his council in the afternoon but mostly they were idle. They flirted with the queen's ladies, they slipped up the river to the City, and they disappeared for unexplained nights. I caught him once in the early morning. I had been watching the sunshine on the river when a rowboat tied up to the palace landing stage and George paid off the boatman and came quietly up the garden path.

'George,' I said, stepping out from my seat in the roses.

He gave a start. 'Mary!' At once his thoughts went to Anne. 'Is she all right?'

'She's well. Where have you been?'

He shrugged his shoulders. 'We went for a little entertainment,' he said. 'Some friends of Henry Norris. We went dancing and dining, a little gambling.'

'Was Sir Francis there?'

He nodded.

'George –'

'Don't reproach me!' he said quickly. 'No-one else knows. We keep it quiet enough.'

'If the king found out you would be banished,' I said flatly.

'He won't find out,' he said. 'I know you heard of it but that was a groom who was gossiping. He's silenced. Dismissed. That's the end of it.'

I took his hand and looked in his dark Boleyn eyes. 'George, I fear for you.'

He laughed, his courtier's brittle laugh. 'Don't,' he said. 'I have nothing to fear. Nothing to fear, nothing to look for, and nowhere to go.'

❀

Anne did not get her royal christening gown. They wrote to the queen with proposals for her separation from the king. They addressed her as

Dowager Princess and she tore the parchment of the declaration with an angry pen-stroke when she crossed through the title. They threatened her that she would never see the Princess Mary her daughter again. They moved her to the most desolate of palaces: Buckden in Lincolnshire. Still she would not recant. Still she would not admit the possibility that she had not been the king's lawful wife. In such an impasse, the christening gown seemed to matter very little and after she refused to part with it, saying that it was her own property brought from Spain, Henry did not insist.

I thought of her, in a cold house on the edge of the Fens. I thought of her, separated from her daughter as I was parted from my son by the ambition of the same woman. I thought of her unswerving determination to do right in the sight of God. And I missed her. She had been like a mother to me when I had first come to court and I had betrayed her as a daughter will betray her mother, and yet never stop loving her.

Autumn 1533

Anne's pains started at dawn and the midwife called me straightaway into the birthing chamber. I had to half-fight my way through courtiers and lawyers and clerks and officers of the court in the presence chamber outside the room. Nearest the door were the ladies in waiting assembled to assist the queen in her confinement, in fact doing nothing but frightening each other with nightmare stories of difficult births. Princess Mary was among them, her pale face screwed up into her habitual scowl of determination. I thought Anne cruel to make Katherine's daughter a witness of the birth of the child that would disinherit her. I gave her a little smile as I went past her and she gave me that curious, half-hearted curtsey which was now her trademark. She could trust nobody, she would trust nobody ever again.

Inside the room it was like a scene from hell. They had rigged up ropes on the bedposts and Anne was clinging onto them like a drowning woman. The sheets were already stained with her blood, and the midwives were brewing a caudle on the fire which was stoked high with logs. Anne was naked from the waist down. She was sweating and crying out with fear. Two other ladies in waiting were reciting their prayers in an irritating anxious drone and every now and again Anne would let out a shriek of renewed pain.

'She must rest,' one of the midwives said to me. 'She's fighting it.'

I stepped up to the bed and waited. 'Anne, rest,' I said. 'This is going to go on for hours.'

'It's you, is it?' she said, throwing back her hair. 'Thought you'd get up, did you?'

'I came as soon as I was called. Do you want me to do anything for you?'

'I want you to do this for me,' she said, her wit as sharp as ever.

I laughed. 'Not I!'

She stretched a hand to me and when I held it, she clung on. 'God help me, I am in terror,' she whispered.

'God will help you,' I said. 'You're having a Christian prince, aren't you? You're giving birth to a boy that is going to be the head of the church in England, aren't you?'

'Don't leave me,' she said. 'I am ready to vomit with fear.'

'Oh you'll vomit,' I said cheerfully. 'It gets an awful lot worse than this before it is better.'

∽

Anne was in labour for all of the day and then her pains grew faster and it was clear to us all that the baby was coming. She stopped fighting and went vague and dreamy, her body doing the work for her. I held her up and the midwife spread the cloth for the baby and then gave a shout of joy as the head broke out of Anne's straining body, and then with a slither and a rush the whole baby was born. 'God be praised,' the woman said.

She bent her head and sucked at the baby's mouth and we heard a choking little cry. Both Anne and I strained to see.

'Is it the prince?' Anne gasped, her voice croaky with screaming. 'He is to be Prince Edward Henry.'

'A girl,' the midwife said, determinedly cheerful.

I felt Anne's full weight as she slumped with disappointment and I heard myself whisper: 'Oh God, no.'

'A girl,' the midwife said again. 'A strong healthy girl,' she repeated as if to reconcile us to our disappointment.

For a moment I thought Anne had fainted. She was as white as death itself. I lowered her back against the pillows and stroked the hair back from her sweating face. 'A girl.'

'A live baby is the main thing,' I said, trying to fight my own sense of despair.

The midwife wrapped the baby in the cloth and patted her. Both Anne and I turned our heads at the wailing penetrating cry.

'A girl,' Anne said in horror. 'A girl. What good is a girl to us?'

❀

George said the same when I told him. Uncle Howard swore out loud and called me a useless jade and my sister a stupid whore when I took the news to him. The whole fortunes of the family had depended on this small accident of birth. If Anne had given birth to a boy we would have been the most powerful family in England with a stake in the throne forever. But she had a girl.

Henry, always the king, always unpredictable, did not complain. He took the baby on his lap and praised her blue eyes and her strong sturdy little body. He admired the little details of her hands, the dimples of her knuckles, the tiny perfection of her fingernails. He told Anne that next time they should have a boy, that he was happy to have another princess, and such a perfect little princess, in his household. He ordered that the letters which were to have gone out announcing the birth of a prince should have a double 's' added to them, to tell the King of France and the Emperor of Spain that the King of England had a new daughter. He gritted his teeth and tried not to think what they would say in the courts of Europe. They would laugh at all of England, for going through such an upheaval in order for the king to get a girl on a commoner. But I admired him, that evening, when he took my sister in his arms and kissed her hair and called her sweetheart. I understood him: he was too proud to let anyone know that he had been disappointed. I thought that he was a man of intense vanity, of dangerous whims, and despite all of that – or perhaps *because* all of that – a great king.

I got to my bedroom after thirty-six hours without sleep, and with the anger and despair of my father, my uncle, and my brother ringing in my ears, and found William there with a little meat pie on the fireside table and a pitcher of small ale.

'I thought you'd be tired and hungry,' he said by way of greeting.

I fell into his arms and buried my face into the comforting smell of his linen. 'Oh William!'

'Trouble?'

'They are all so angry, and Anne is in despair, and no-one has looked at the baby but the king and he held her for a few moments only. And it all seems so dreadful. Oh God, if she had only been a boy!'

He patted my back. 'Hush, my love. They'll all come round. And they'll make another child. A son next time, perhaps.'

'Another year,' I said. 'Another year before Anne is free of fear and before I can be free of her.'

He drew me to the table, sat me before it and pressed the spoon into my hand. 'Eat,' he said. 'Everything will seem much better when you have eaten and slept.'

'Where's Madge?' I asked fearfully, looking at the door.

'Roistering in the hall like a drunkard,' he said. 'The court prepared a feast to welcome the prince and was going to eat it whatever happened. Madge won't be back for hours, if she comes at all.'

I nodded and ate my dinner as he bid me. When I had finished he drew me onto the bed and kissed my ear and my neck and my eyelids very gently and very tenderly until I forgot all about Anne and the unwanted baby girl and turned in his arms and let him hold me. I fell asleep like that, fully dressed, lying on the covers of the bed, torn between sleep and desire. I fell asleep and I dreamed of him making love to me, even as he held me and stroked my face, all the night long.

∾

As soon as Anne recovered from the birth she was engrossed in arranging for the care of the little Princess Elizabeth at Hatfield Palace, where a royal nursery was to be established under the charge of our aunt, Lady Anne Shelton, Madge's discreet mother. The Princess Mary, who had been seen to smile behind her hand at Anne's discomfiture in having a girl was to go too, far away from her father and her proper place at court.

'She can wait on Elizabeth,' Anne said carelessly. 'She can be her maid in waiting.'

'Anne,' I said. 'She's a princess in her own right. She can't serve your daughter, it's not right.'

Anne gleamed at me. 'Fool,' she said simply. 'It is all part of the same thing. She must be seen to go where I bid her, she must serve my daughter, that way I know that I am queen indeed and Katherine is forgotten.'

'Can't you rest?' I asked. 'Surely you don't have to be always plotting?'

She gave me a bitter thin smile. 'You don't think that Cromwell rests, do you? You don't think that the Seymours rest, do you? You don't think that the Spanish ambassador and his network of spies and that accursed woman are all resting, saying to themselves: "Well, she has married him and given birth to a useless girl so although we have everything to play for we'll rest." Do you?'

'No,' I said unwillingly.

She looked at me for a moment. 'One might better ask how you manage to look so plump and pleased with yourself when according to reason you should be struggling on a small pension and wasting away.'

I could not hold back a choke of laughter at her gloomy vision of me. 'I manage,' I said shortly. 'But I should like to see my children at Hever now, if you would let me go for a visit.'

'Oh go,' she said, weary of the request. 'But be back at Greenwich in time for Christmas.'

I went to the door quickly, before she could change her mind. 'And tell Henry that he is to go to a tutor, he must be educated properly,' she said. 'He can go later this year.'

I stopped, my hand on the door frame. 'My boy?' I whispered.

'*My* boy,' she corrected me. 'He can't play for all his childhood, you know.'

'I thought . . .'

'I have arranged for him to study with Sir Francis Weston's son and William Brereton's. They're learning well, I'm told. It's time he was with boys of his own age.'

'I don't want him with them,' I said instantly. 'Not the sons of those two.'

She raised one dark eyebrow. 'They are gentlemen of my court,' she reminded me. 'Their sons will be courtiers too, they might be his courtiers one day. He should be with them. It is my decision.'

I wanted to scream at her but I pinched my fingertips and I kept my voice soft and sweet. 'Anne. He's only a little boy still. He is happy with his sister at Hever. If you want him educated I will stay there, I will educate him . . .'

'You!' she laughed. 'As well ask the ducks on the moat to teach him to quack. No, Mary. I have decided. And the king agrees with me.'

'Anne . . .'

She leaned back and looked at me through slitted eyes. 'I take it that you do want to see him at all this year? You don't want me to send him to his tutor at once?'

'No!'

'Then go, sister. For I have taken my decision and you weary me.'

❁

William watched me as I stormed up and down the confines of our narrow lodging-house room. 'I'll kill her,' I swore.

He had his back to the door, he checked that the casement window was shut against eavesdroppers.

'I'll kill her! To put my boy, my precious boy, with the sons of those sodomites! To prepare him for a life at court! To order the Princess Mary to wait on Elizabeth and send my boy into exile in the same breath! She is mad to do this! She is insane with ambition. And my boy . . . my boy . . .'

My throat was too tight for words. My knees gave way beneath me, I laid my face on the covers of our bed and sobbed into them.

William did not move from his post at the door, he let me weep. He waited until I raised my head and wiped my wet cheeks with my fingers. Only then did he step forward and kneel on the floor near me so that I crawled, hands and knees, beaten down by my distress, into his arms. Then he held me gently and rocked me as if I were a baby myself.

'We'll get him back,' he whispered into my hair. 'We'll have a wonderful time with him, we'll send him off to his tutors, and then we'll get him back. I promise it. We'll fetch him back, sweetheart.'

Winter 1533

For her New Year's present to the king Anne commissioned a most extravagant gift. The goldsmiths brought it to the great hall and spent the morning setting it up. When they came to the queen's apartments to tell her that she might come and see it Anne beckoned to George and to me and said we might come too.

We ran down the stairs to the great hall, Anne ahead of us, so that she could fling open the doors and see our faces. It was a most astounding sight: a fountain made of gold inlaid with diamonds and rubies. At the foot of the fountain were three naked women, also wrought of gold, and from their teats spouted springs of more water.

'My God,' said George, truly awed. 'How much did it cost you?'

'Don't ask,' Anne said. 'It is very grand, isn't it?'

'Grand.' I didn't add: 'But vilely ugly,' though I could tell from George's stunned expression that he thought the same.

'I thought the ripple of the water would be soothing. Henry can have it in his presence chamber,' Anne said. She went closer to the edifice and touched it. 'They have wrought it very fine.'

'Fertile women gushing water,' I said, looking at the three gleaming statues.

Anne smiled at me. 'An omen,' she said. 'A reminder. A wish.'

'Pray God a prediction,' George said grimly. 'Any signs yet?'

'Not yet,' she said. 'But it's bound to happen soon.'

'Amen,' George and I said together, devout as Lutherans. 'Amen.'

❧

Our prayers were answered. Anne missed her time in January and then in February again. When the asparagus shoots showed in spring the queen ate them at every meal for they were known to make a boy. People started to wonder. No-one knew for sure. Anne went around with a half-smile on her face and revelled in being the very centre of attention once again.

Spring 1534

The court's plans for a summer progress were delayed again while Anne, at the very centre of the whirlpool of gossip, was well-pleased to sit serenely with her hand on her belly and let them all wonder. The place was alive with gossip. George, my mother, and I were pestered for news from the courtiers who wanted to know if she were indeed with child, and when she might be brought to bed. No-one liked to be close to the plague-ridden streets of London in the hot weather; but the thought of the queen's confinement and the opportunities for advancement that a solitary king might provide were a powerful draw.

We were to be at Hampton Court for the summer, as far as anyone knew, and a proposed trip to France to cement the treaty with Francis was postponed.

Our uncle called a family meeting in May but he did not summon Anne, she was far beyond his ordering now. However, driven by curiosity, she timed her arrival at his rooms to the very second, so that we were all seated and waiting when she entered the room. She hesitated in the doorway, perfectly poised, Uncle rose from his seat at the head of the table to fetch a chair for her, but the moment his place was vacant she walked grandly and slowly to the head of the table and seated herself without a word of thanks. I giggled, a tiny suppressed sound, and Anne flashed me a smile. There was nothing she loved more than the exercise of her power that had been bought at so high a price.

'I asked the family to meet together to discover what are your plans, Your Majesty,' my uncle said smoothly. 'It would help me to know if you are indeed with child, and when you expect to be confined.'

Anne raised a dark eyebrow as if his question was an impertinence. 'You ask that of *me*?'

'I was going to ask your sister or your mother, but since you are here

I might as well ask you directly,' he said. He was not in the least overawed by Anne. He had served more frightening monarchs: Henry's father and Henry himself. He had faced cavalry charges. Not even Anne at her most regal would frighten him.

'In September,' she said shortly.

'If it is another girl he will show his disappointment this time,' my uncle observed. 'He has had trouble enough making Elizabeth his heir over Mary. The Tower is filled with men who refuse to deny Mary. And Thomas More and Fisher are certain to join them. If you had a boy then nobody would deny his rights.'

'It will be a boy,' Anne said positively.

Uncle smiled at her. 'So we all hope. The king will take a woman when you are in your final months.' Although Anne raised her head to speak he would not be interrupted. 'He always does, Anne. You must be calmer about these things, not rail at him.'

'I shall not tolerate it,' she said flatly.

'You will have to,' he said, as uncompromising as she was.

'He never looked away from me in all the years of our courtship,' she said. 'Not once.'

George raised an eyebrow to me. I said nothing. Apparently, I did not count.

My uncle gave a short laugh and I saw my father smile.

'Courtship is different. Anyway, I've chosen the girl to divert him,' my uncle said. 'A Howard girl.'

I felt the sweat break out on me. I knew that I had gone white when George suddenly hissed: 'Sit up!' out of the corner of his mouth.

'Who?' Anne said sharply.

'Madge Shelton,' Uncle said.

'Oh, Madge,' I said, my heart pounding with relief and my cheeks blazing as the colour came rushing back. 'That Howard girl.'

'She'll keep him busy and she knows her place,' my father said judicially, not at all as if he were handing another niece over to adultery and sin.

'And your influence is undiminished,' Anne spat.

My uncle smiled. 'That is true of course, but who would you rather? A Seymour girl? Given that it is a certainty, isn't it best for us that it should be a girl who'll do our bidding?'

'It depends on what you bid her,' Anne said shortly.

'To divert him while you are confined,' my uncle said smoothly. 'Nothing else.'

'I won't have her setting herself up as his mistress, I won't have her in the best rooms, wearing jewels, in new gowns, flaunting herself around me,' Anne warned.

'Yes, you of all women would know how painful that can be for a good wife,' my uncle concurred.

Anne's dark eyes flashed at him. He smiled. 'She shall divert the king during your confinement, and when you are back at court she will disappear,' he promised. 'I shall see that she makes a good marriage and Henry will forget her as easily as he takes her up.'

Anne drummed her fingers on the table. We could all see that she was fighting with herself. 'I wish I could trust you, Uncle.'

'I wish you would.' He smiled at her unwillingness. He turned to me and I felt the familiar tremor of fear at his attention. 'Madge Shelton beds with you, doesn't she?'

'Yes, Uncle,' I said.

'Tell her how to go along, tell her how to manage herself.' He turned to George. 'And you keep the king's attention on Anne and on Madge.'

'Yes, sir,' George said easily, as if he had never wished for any career other than that of a pander in the royal harem.

'Good,' Uncle said, rising to his feet to signal that the meeting was at an end. 'Oh, and one other thing . . .' We all obediently waited on his word, except Anne, who was looking out of the window at the gardens in the sunshine and the court playing bowls, with the king at the centre of all the attention, as always.

'Mary,' Uncle remarked.

I flinched at the mention of my name.

'I think we should have her married, don't you?'

'I'd be pleased to see her betrothed before her sister is brought to bed,' my father remarked. 'That way there's no uncertainty if Anne fails.'

They did not look at Anne, who might be pregnant with a girl and thus diminish our bartering strength in the marriage market. They did not look at me, who was to be traded like a farmer's cow. They looked at each other, merchants with a deal to make.

'Very well,' our uncle said. 'I'll speak to Secretary Cromwell, it's time she was wed.'

❁

I got away from Anne and George, and found my way to the king's rooms. William was not in the presence chamber and I dared not go looking for him in the privy chamber. A young man strolled by with a lute, Sir Francis Weston's musician, Mark Smeaton. 'Have you seen Sir William Stafford?' I asked him.

He made a pretty bow to me. 'Yes, Lady Carey,' he said. 'He's still playing at bowls.'

I nodded and went towards the great hall. As soon as I was out of his sight I took one of the little doors that led out to the broad terrace before the palace and then down the stone steps to the garden. William was picking up the balls, the game had ended. He turned and smiled at me. The other players hailed me and challenged me to a game.

'Oh, very well,' I said. 'What are the stakes?'

'A shilling a game,' William said. 'You have fallen among desperate gamblers, Lady Carey.'

I felt in my purse and put down my shilling and then took a ball and rolled it carefully along the grass. It was nowhere near. I stepped back to make a place for another player and found William at my elbow.

'All well?' he asked quietly.

'Well enough,' I said. 'But I have to be alone with you as soon as we can.'

'Oh, I feel it myself,' he said with a laugh at the back of his voice. 'But I didn't know you were so shameless.'

'Not for that!' I said indignantly and then had to stop and look away before anyone could see me laugh and blush. I longed to touch him, I could hardly stand beside him and not reach out for him. I took a careful step away from him as if to see the game more clearly.

I was knocked out early on, and William took care to lose soon after. We left our shillings on the green for the eventual winner and strolled, as if to take the air, down the long gravel path towards the river. The windows of the palace overlooked the garden, I did not dare touch him or let him take my arm. We walked side by side, like courteous strangers. Only when I stepped up to the landing stage could he touch my elbow, as if to hold me steady, and then he kept hold of me. That simple contact of his hand on my arm warmed me all through.

'What is it?' he asked.

'It's my uncle. He's planning my marriage.'

At once his face was dark. 'Soon? Does he have a husband in mind?'

'No. They're considering.'

'Then we must be ready for when they find someone. And when they do we must just confess, and hope to brazen it out.'

'Yes.' I paused for a moment, glanced at his profile and back to the river. 'He frightens me,' I said. 'When he said he wanted to see me married, in that moment I thought that I would have to obey him. I always have obeyed him, you see. Everybody always obeys him. Even Anne.'

'Don't look like that my love, or I will take you in my arms in full view of the whole palace. I swear to you that you are mine and I will let no-one take you from me. You are mine. I am yours. No-one can deny that.'

'They took Henry Percy from Anne,' I said. 'And she was as much married as us.'

'He was a young lad,' William said. 'No man comes between me and mine.' He paused for a moment. 'But we may have to pay for it. Would Anne stand your friend? If we have her support then we are safe.'

'She won't be pleased,' I said, knowing full well the intense concentrated selfishness of my sister. 'But it doesn't hurt her.'

'Then we wait until we are cornered, and then we confess,' he said. 'And in the meantime we will be as charming as we can be.'

I laughed, 'To the king?' thinking he meant to deploy courtier's skills.

'To each other,' he said. 'Who matters the most to me in the whole world?'

'Me,' I said with quiet joy. 'And you for me.'

❧

We spent the night in each other's arms in the room of a little inn. When I woke and turned to him he was already moving towards me. We fell asleep wrapped in each other as if we could not bear to part, even in sleep we could not bear to let each other go. When I woke in the morning he was still on top of me, still inside me, and when I moved underneath him I felt him stir with desire for me again. I closed my eyes and let myself drift away while he loved me until the early morning sun came brightly through the shutters and the noise from the courtyard downstairs warned us that we should get back to the palace.

He came up the river with me in a little wherry, and left me at the landing stage so that he could disembark further downriver and stroll home half an hour behind me. I thought I would get in by the garden door and creep up to my room in time to appear for morning Mass but when I got to my door George appeared from nowhere and said: 'Thank God you're back, another hour or two and everyone would have known.'

'What is it?' I asked quickly.

His face was grim. 'Anne's taken to her bed.'

'I'll go to her,' I said and ran quickly down the corridor. I knocked at the door to Anne's bedroom and put my head inside. She was quite alone in the imposing chamber, white and wan on the bed.

'Oh you,' she said unpleasantly. 'You might as well come in.'

I stepped into the room and George shut the door firmly behind us. 'What's the matter?' I asked.

'I'm bleeding,' she said shortly. 'And I've got gripping pains, like the pains of childbirth. I think I'm losing it.'

The blank horror of her words was too much for me to take in. I was powerfully aware of my dishevelled hair and the scent of William on every inch of my skin. The contrast between last night's loving and this dawning disaster was too much for me. I turned to George.

'We should get a midwife,' I said.

'No!' Anne hissed like a snake. 'Don't you see? If we call in that crowd, we tell the world. At the moment no-one knows for sure whether I am with child or not; It's all rumour. I can't risk them knowing I lost it.'

'This is wrong,' I said flatly to George. 'This is a baby we are talking about here. We can't let a baby die for fear of scandal. Let's move her to a back room, a little room, nothing fine. And cover her face, and draw the curtains. I'll get a midwife and tell her it's a maid at court. Nobody important.'

George hesitated. 'If it's a girl it's not worth the risk,' he said. 'If it's another girl, it'd be better dead.'

'For God's sake, George! This is a baby. This is a soul. This is our kith and kin. Of course we should save her if we can.'

His face was hard, for a moment he did not look like my beloved brother at all, he looked like one of the iron-featured men at court who would sign the death warrant for anyone, provided that they were themselves secure.

'George!' I cried. 'If this is another Boleyn girl she has a right to live as much as Anne or me.'

'All right,' he said reluctantly. 'I'll move Anne. You get a midwife and make sure you're discreet. Who will you send?'

'William,' I said.

'Oh God: William!' he said irritably. 'Does he have to know everything about us? Does he know a midwife? How will he find one?'

'He'll go to the bath house,' I said bluntly. 'They must need midwives there in a hurry. And he'll keep his mouth shut for love of me.'

George nodded and went to the bed. I heard him start to whisper an explanation to Anne in a tender low voice, and her murmured reply, and I ran from the room to the back door of the palace where I expected William to stroll in at any moment.

❁

I caught him on the threshold and sent him out to find a midwife. He was back within the hour with a surprisingly clean young woman, with a small sack of bottles and herbs.

I took her to the little room where George's pageboys slept and she looked around the darkened room and recoiled. In some grotesque moment of fancy George and Anne had raided the palace costume box to find a mask to hide her well-known face. Instead of a simple disguise they had found a golden bird face mask, which she had worn in France to dance with the king. Anne, panting with pain, half-lit by guttering candles, lay back on a narrow bed, her huge belly straining under the sheet and above it a glittering gold mask with a face like a hawk, a great gilt beak and flaring eyebrows. It was like a scene from some dreadful morality painting with Anne's face like a depiction of greed and vanity, with her dark eyes glittering through the holes in the proud gold face at the head of the bed, while below her vulnerable white thighs were parted over a mess of blood on the sheets.

The midwife peered at her, taking care to touch her very little. She straightened up and asked a string of questions about the pains, how fast they were coming, how strong they were, how long they were lasting. Then she said she could make a posset which would put Anne to sleep and that might save the child. Her body would rest and perhaps the child would rest too. She did not sound hopeful. The expressionless beak of the golden mask turned from the woman to George's drawn face; but Anne herself said nothing.

The midwife brewed up the posset over the fire and Anne drank from a mug of pewter. George held her until she leaned back against his shoulders, the dreadful gleaming mask looking wildly triumphant, even as the midwife gently covered her up. The woman went to the door and George laid Anne gently down and followed us out. 'We can't lose her, we can't bear to lose her,' George said, and for a moment I heard the passion in his voice.

'Pray for her then,' the woman said shortly. 'She's in the hands of God.'

George said something indistinguishable and turned back to the bedroom. I let the woman out of the door and William escorted her down the long dark corridor to the palace gates. I returned to the room and George and I sat either side of the bed while Anne slept and moaned in her sleep.

∾

We had to get her back into her own room, and then we had to give it out that she was unwell. George played cards in her presence chamber as if he had not a care in the world and the ladies flirted and gamed and diced as if everything was the same as usual. I sat with Anne in her bedchamber, and sent a message to the king in her name that she was tired and would see him before dinner. My mother, alerted by George's loud insouciance and my disappearance, came to find Anne. One sight of her in a drugged sleep with blood on the sheets and she went white around the mouth.

'We did the best that we could,' I said desperately.

'Does anyone else know?' she demanded.

'No-one. Not even the king.'

She nodded. 'Keep it that way.'

The day wore on. Anne started to sweat and I began to doubt the wise woman's poooot. I put my hand on her forehead and felt the heat burn against my palm. I looked at my mother. 'She's too hot,' I said. My mother shrugged.

I turned back to Anne. She was rolling her head on the pillow, and then without warning, she lifted up, curved herself inwards and gave a great groan. My mother ripped back the covers and we saw the sudden flood of blood and a mass of something. Anne dropped back on the pillows and cried out, a heartbroken pitiful cry, and then her eyelids fluttered and she was still.

I touched her forehead again, and put my ear to her breast. Her heart was beating steadily and strongly, but her eyes were shut. My mother, her face like stone, was bundling up the stained sheets, wrapping them around the mess. She turned to where the fire was burning, a little summertime fire.

'Stoke it up,' she said shortly.

I hesitated, glancing to Anne. 'She's so hot.'

'This is more important,' she said. 'This has to be gone before anyone has even the slightest idea of it.'

I put the poker into the fire and turned over the hot embers. My mother knelt at the fireside and ripped the sheet into a strip and laid it on the flames, it curled and burned with a hiss. Patiently, she ripped another and another, until she came to the very centre of the bundle, the awful dark mess which had been Anne's baby. 'Put on kindling,' she said shortly.

I looked at her in horror. 'Shouldn't we bury . . . ?'

'Put on kindling,' she spat at me. 'How long d'you think any of us will last if everyone knows that she cannot carry a baby?'

I looked into her face and measured the power of her will. Then I piled the fire with the little scented fir cones, and when they burned up brightly we packed the guilty bundle onto the flames and sat back on our heels like a pair of old witches and watched all that was left of Anne's baby go up the chimney like some dreadful curse.

When the sheet was burned, and the sizzling mess gone too, my mother threw on some more fir cones and some herbs from the floor to purify the smell of the room, and only then did she turn back to her daughter.

Anne was awake, leaning up on one elbow to watch us, her eyes glassy.

'Anne?' my mother said.

With an effort my sister turned her gaze up to her.

'Your baby is dead,' my mother said flatly. 'Dead and gone. You have to sleep and get well. I expect you to be up within the day. Do you hear me? If anybody asks you about the baby you will say that you made a mistake, that there was no baby. There never has been a baby and you never announced one. But for a certainty, one will come soon.'

Anne turned a blank look to her mother. For a moment I was seized with a dreadful fear that the posset and the pain and the heat had driven her mad, and that she would forever look without seeing, hear without understanding.

'The king too,' my mother said, her voice cold. 'Just tell him you made a mistake, that you were not with child. A mistake is innocent enough but a miscarriage is proof of sin.'

Anne's face never changed. She did not even protest her innocence. I thought she was deaf. 'Anne?' I said gently.

She turned to me, and when she saw my shocked eyes, and the smuts on my face, I saw her expression alter. She understood that something very terrible had taken place.

'Why are you in such a mess?' she asked coldly. 'It's not as if anything has happened to you, has it?'

'I'll tell your uncle,' my mother said. She paused at the threshold and looked at me. 'What has she done that this should happen?' she asked as coldly as if she were inquiring after a broken piece of china. 'She must have done something to lose her child like this. D'you know what it was?'

I thought of the days and nights of seducing the king and breaking the heart of his wife, of the poisoning of three men and the destruction of Cardinal Wolsey. 'Nothing out of the ordinary.'

My mother nodded and went from the room without touching her daughter, without another word to either of us. Anne's empty gaze came back to me, her face as blank as the gold hawk mask. I kneeled at the head of her bed and held out my arms. Her expression never altered but she leaned slowly towards me and rested her heavy head on my shoulder.

It took us all that night and the next day to get Anne back on her feet again. The king kept away, once we gave out that she had a cold. Not so my uncle, he came to the doorway of her bedchamber as if she were still nothing more than a Boleyn girl. I saw her eyes darken with rage at his disrespect.

'Your mother has told me,' he said shortly 'How could such a thing happen?'

Anne turned her head. 'How should I know?'

'You consulted no wise women to conceive? You tried no potions or herbs or anything? You invoked no spirits and did no spells?'

Anne shook her head. 'I would not touch such things,' she said. 'You can ask anyone. Ask my confessor, ask Thomas Cranmer. I have a care to my soul as much as you.'

'I have more of a care for my neck,' he said grimly. 'Do you swear it? For I may have to swear for you one day.'

'I swear it,' Anne said sulkily.

'Get up as soon as you can and conceive another, and it had better be a boy.'

The look she turned on him was so filled with hatred that even he recoiled. 'Thank you for that advice,' she snarled. 'It is something that had occurred to me before. I have to conceive as swiftly as possible and it has to go full term and it has to be a boy. Thank you, Uncle. Yes. I know that.'

She turned her face away from him to the rich hangings on her bed. He waited for a moment and then he smiled his grim hard-faced smile at me, and went away. I closed the door and Anne and I were alone.

Her eyes, when she looked at me, were filled with fear. 'But what if the king cannot get a legitimate son?' she whispered. 'He never did it with her. I will get all the blame and what will happen to me then?'

Summer 1534

In the first days of July I was sick in the mornings and my breasts were tender to the touch. William, kissing my belly in a dark-shaded room one afternoon, patted me with his hand and said quietly: 'What d'you think, my love?'

'About what?'

'About this round little belly.'

I turned my head away so he could not see me smile. 'I hadn't noticed.'

'Well I have,' he said bluntly. 'Now tell me. How long have you known?'

'Two months,' I confessed. 'And I have been torn between joy and fear, for this will be our undoing.'

He gathered me into the fold of his arm. 'Never,' he said. 'This is our firstborn Stafford and a cause for the greatest of joy. I couldn't be more pleased. A son to bring the cows in or a daughter to do the milking, what a clever girl you are.'

'D'you want a boy?' I asked curiously, thinking of the constant theme of the Boleyns.

'If you have one,' he said easily. 'Whatever you have in there, my love.'

I was released from court to meet my children at Hever in July and August while Anne and the king went off. William and I had the best summer we had ever spent together with the children, but when the time came to go back to court I was carrying the baby so high and so proudly that I knew I would have to tell Anne the news and hope that she would shield me from my uncle's rage in my pregnancy, as I had shielded her miscarriage from the king.

I was lucky when I arrived at Greenwich. The king was out hunting and most of the court with him. Anne was sitting in the garden, on a turf bench, an awning over her head and a group of musicians playing to her. Someone was reading love poetry. I paused for a moment and took a second look at them. They were all older than I had remembered. This was no longer the court of a young man. They were all seasoned in a way that they had not been when Queen Katherine had been on the throne. There was a hint of extravagance and glamour about them all, there were a great deal of pretty words being spoken and a certain heat in the group which was not all late-summer sunshine and wine. It had become a sophisticated court, an older court; I could almost have said corrupt. It felt as if anything could happen.

'Why, here is my sister,' Anne remarked, shading her eyes with her hand. 'Welcome back, Mary. Have you had enough of the country?'

I kept my riding cloak loosely about me. 'Yes,' I said. 'I have come seeking the sunshine of your court.'

Anne giggled. 'Very nicely put,' she said. 'I shall have you trained as a true courtier yet. How is my son Henry?'

I gritted my teeth on that, as she knew I would. 'He sends his love and duty to you. I have a copy of a letter he has written to you in Latin. He is a bright boy, his schoolmaster is pleased with him, and he has learned to ride very well this summer.'

'Good,' Anne said. Clearly, I was not worth tormenting for she turned from me to William Brereton. 'If you cannot do better with "love" than "dove" I shall have to award the prize to Sir Thomas.'

'Shove?' he suggested.

Anne laughed. 'What? My sweetest queen, my only love, I long to give you a hearty shove?'

'Love is impossible,' Sir Thomas remarked. 'In poetry as in life, nothing goes with it.'

'Marriage,' Anne suggested.

'Clearly love does not go with marriage, marriage is quite another thing. For a start it is three beats as opposed to one. And for another it has no music to it.'

'My marriage has music,' Anne said.

Sir Thomas bowed his head. 'Everything that you do has music,' he pointed out. 'But still the word does not rhyme with anything helpful.'

'The prize goes to you, Sir Thomas,' Anne said. 'You need not flatter me as well as make poetry.'

'It is no flattery to tell the truth,' he said, kneeling before her. Anne gave him a little gold chain from her belt and he kissed it and tucked it away in the pocket of his doublet.

'Now,' Anne said. 'I shall go and change my gown before the king comes home from his hunting wanting his dinner.' She rose to her feet and looked around at her ladies. 'Where is Madge Shelton?'

The silence which greeted her told her everything. 'Where is she?'

'Hunting with the king, Your Majesty,' one of the ladies volunteered.

Anne raised an eyebrow and glanced at me, the only member of her court who knew that Madge had been appointed as the king's mistress by our uncle but only for the duration of Anne's confinement. Now it seemed that Madge was making progress on her own account.

'Where's George?' I asked her.

She nodded, it was a key question. 'With the king,' she said. We knew that George could be trusted to protect Anne's interests.

Anne nodded and turned to the palace. The lightness of the afternoon had faded at the first mention of the king with another woman. Anne's shoulders were set, her face grim. I walked at her side as we went up to her rooms. As I had hoped, she gestured that the ladies in waiting should wait in the presence chamber and she and I went into her privy chamber alone. As soon as the door was closed I said: 'Anne, I have something to tell you. I need your help.'

'What now?' she said. She seated herself before a golden mirror and pulled her hood from her head. Her dark hair, as lovely and lustrous as ever, tumbled down over her shoulders. 'Brush my hair,' she said.

I took a brush and swept it through the dark locks, hoping to soothe her. 'I have married a man,' I said simply. 'And I am carrying his child.'

She was so still that for a moment I thought she had not heard me, and in that moment I hoped to God that she had not. Then she turned around on the stool and her face was like thunder. 'You have done what?' She spat out the question.

'Married,' I said.

'Without my permission?'

'Yes, Anne. I'm very sorry.'

Her head came up, her eyes met mine in the mirror. 'Who?'

'Sir William Stafford.'

'William Stafford? The king's usher?'

'Yes,' I said. 'He has a small farm near Rochford.'

'He is nothing,' she said. I could hear her temper rising in her voice. 'The king knighted him,' I said. 'He is Sir William.'

'Sir William Nothing!' she said again. 'And you are with child?'

I knew it was that she would hate the most. 'Yes,' I said humbly.

She leaped to her feet and dragged the cloak away so that she could see the broad spread of my stomacher. 'You whore!' she swore at me. Her hand came back, I froze, ready to take the blow, but when it came

I felt my neck snap back with the force of it. It threw me backwards against the bed, and she stood over me like a fighter. 'How long has this been going on? When will this next bastard of yours be born?'

'In March,' I said. 'And he is no bastard.'

'D'you think to mock me, coming into my court with a belly on you like a fat brood mare? What d'you mean to do? You mean to tell the world that *you* are the fertile Boleyn girl and I am all but barren?'

'Anne . . .'

Nothing would stop her.

'Showing the world that you are in pup again! You insult me by even being here. You insult our family.'

'I married him,' I said, I could hear my voice shake a little at her anger. 'I married him for love, Anne. Please, please don't be like this. I love him. I can go from court, but please let me see . . .'

She did not even let me finish. 'Aye, you'll go from court!' she cried. 'To hell for all I care. You'll go from court and never come back to it.'

'My children,' I finished breathlessly.

'You can say goodbye to them. I'll not have my nephew brought up by a woman who has no pride in her family and no knowledge of the world. A fool who is dragged through life by her lust. Why marry William Stafford? Why not a lad from the stable? Why not the miller at Hever mill? If all you want is a good thumping why stop at one of the king's men? A soldier in the ranks would do as well.'

'Anne, I warn you.' The anger was creeping into my own voice even as my cheek still throbbed with the heat from her blow. 'I will not take this. I married a good man for love, I did no more than the Princess Mary Tudor did when she married the Duke of Suffolk. I married once to oblige my family, I did as they bid me when the king looked my way, and now I want to please myself. Anne – only you can defend me against our uncle and father.'

'Does George know?' she demanded.

'No. I told you he does not. I only came to you. Only you can help me.'

'Never,' she swore. 'You have married a poor man for love, you can eat love, you can drink it. You can live off it. Go to his little farm in Rochford and rot there, and when Father or George or I come down to Rochford Hall make very sure that you are nowhere in our sight. You are banished from court, Mary. You have ruined yourself and I will set a seal on it. You are gone. I have no sister.'

'Anne!' I cried, utterly aghast.

She turned a furious face to me. 'Shall I call the guards and have you thrown out of the gates?' she demanded. 'For I swear I will do so.'

I fell to my knees. 'My son,' was all I could say.

'*My* son,' she said vindictively. 'I will tell him that his mother is dead and that he is to call me mother. You have lost everything for love, Mary. I hope it brings you joy.'

There was nothing I could say. I rose awkwardly to my feet, my heavy belly making it hard for me to rise. She watched me struggle as if she would sooner push me down than help me. I turned to the door and hesitated with my hand on the handle in case she should change her mind. 'My son . . .'

'Go,' she said. 'You are dead to me. And don't approach the king or I shall tell him what a whore you have been.'

I slipped out of the door and went to my bedroom.

Madge Shelton was changing her dress before the looking glass. She turned when she heard me come in, a bright smile on her young face. She took one look at my grim expression and I saw her eyes widen. That one look said everything that was different between our ages, between our positions, between our places in the Howard family. She was a young girl with everything to sell and I was a woman twice married who would have three children at twenty-seven, cast out by my family and nothing to turn to but one man on a little farm. I was a woman who had her chance and botched it.

'Are you sick?' she asked.

'Ruined,' I said shortly.

'Oh,' she said with all the doltishness of vain youth. 'Sorry.'

I found a grim little laugh. 'That's all right,' I said dourly. 'It's a bed of my own making.'

I threw my riding cloak on the bed and she saw the broad lacing of my stomacher. She gave a little gasp of horror.

'Aye,' I said. 'I'm carrying a baby, and I am married, if you want to know.'

'The queen?' she asked in a half-whisper, knowing, as we all knew, that the one thing this queen hated was fertile women.

'Not best pleased,' I said.

'Your husband?'

'William Stafford.'

A gleam in her dark eyes told me that she had noticed more than she had said. 'I'm so pleased for you,' she said. 'He's a handsome man and a good man. I thought you liked him. So all these nights . . . ?'

'Yes,' I said shortly.

'What happens now?'

'We'll have to make our own way in the world,' I said. 'We'll go to Rochford. He has a little farm there. We might do nicely.'

'On a little farm?' Madge asked incredulously.

'Yes,' I said with sudden energy. 'Why not? There are other places to live than in palaces and castles. There are other tunes to dance to other than the court's music. We don't always have to wait on a king and queen. I have spent all my life at court, wasted my girlhood and womanhood here. I am sorry that I shall be poor but I am damned if I will miss the life here.'

'And your children?' she asked.

The question knocked the wind out of me like a blow to the belly. My knees buckled and I sank to the floor, holding myself tight, as if my heart would break out of me. 'Oh, my children,' I said in a whisper.

'Does the queen keep them?' she asked.

'Yes,' I said. 'Yes. She keeps my son.' I could have said more, and that very bitter. I could have said that she kept my son because she could have none of her own. That she had taken from me everything that she ever could take, she would always take everything from me. That she and I were sisters and deadly rivals and nothing would ever stop us from end-lessly eyeing the other's plate and fearing that the other had the biggest portion. Anne wanted to punish me for refusing to dance in her shadow. And she knew that she had chosen the one forfeit in the world that I could not bear to pay.

'At least I will escape her,' I said. 'And escape this family's ambition.'

Madge looked at me wide-eyed, as worldly as a fawn. 'But escaped to what?'

∾

Anne was quick to announce my departure. My father and mother would not even see me before I left court. Only George came down to the stable yard to watch my trunks being loaded onto a cart, and William help me up into the saddle and then mount his own hunter.

'Write to me,' George said. He was scowling with worry. 'Are you well enough to travel all that way?'

'Yes,' I said.

'I'll take care of her,' William assured him.

'You've not done a wonderful job so far,' George said unpleasantly. 'She's ruined, she's stripped of her pension, and she's banned from court.'

I saw William's hand tighten on the reins and his horse sidled. 'Not my doing,' William said levelly. 'That's the spite and ambition of the queen and the Boleyn family. In any other family in the land Mary would be allowed to marry a gentleman of her choice.'

'Stop it,' I said quickly, before George could reply.

George took a breath and bowed his head. 'She's not been best treated,' he conceded. He looked up at William, seated high on the horse above him, and smiled his rueful, charming Boleyn smile. 'We had our minds on targets other than her happiness.'

'I know,' said William. 'But I do not.'

George looked wistful. 'I wish you would tell me the secret of true love,' he said. 'Here's the two of you riding off the very edge of the world and yet you look as if someone has just given you an earldom.'

I put my hand out to William and he gripped it hard. 'I just found the man I love,' I said simply. 'I could never have had a man who loved me more, nor a more honest man.'

'Go then!' George said. He pulled off his cap as the wagon lurched forward. 'Go and be happy together. I'll do the best I can to get you your place and your pension.'

'Just my children,' I said. 'That's all I want.'

'I'll speak to the king when I can, and you can write. Write to Cromwell perhaps, and I'll talk to Anne. It's not forever. You'll come back, won't you? You'll come back?'

There was an odd tone to his voice; not at all as if he were promising me my safe return to the centre of the kingdom, more as if he feared being without me. He did not sound like one of the greatest men at a great court, he sounded more like a boy abandoned in a dangerous place.

'Keep yourself safe!' I said, suddenly shivering. 'Keep out of bad company, and watch over Anne!'

I had not been mistaken. The expression on his face was one of fear. 'I'll try.' His voice rang with hollow confidence. 'I will try!'

The wagon went out under the archway and William and I rode side by side after it. I looked back at George and he seemed very young and far away. He waved at me and called something, but over the grinding of the wheels on the cobbles and the ringing of the horses' hooves I could not hear.

We came out onto the road and William let his horse lengthen his stride so that we overtook the slow-moving wagon and were clear of the dust from its wheels. My hunter would have trotted to keep up, but I steadied her into a walk. I rubbed my face with the back of my glove and William looked sideways at me. 'No regrets?' he asked gently.

'I just fear for him,' I said.

He nodded. He knew too much about George's life at court to offer me a glib reassurance. George's love affair with Sir Francis, their indiscreet circle of friends, their drinking, their gambling, their whoring, was slowly coming to be an open secret. More and more men at court were taking their pleasures more and more wildly, George among them.

'And for her,' I said, thinking of my sister who had banished me like a beggar and so left herself with only one friend in the world.

William leaned over and put his hand over mine. 'Come on,' he said, and we turned our horses' heads to the river and rode down to meet the waiting boat.

❁

We disembarked at Leigh early in the morning. The horses were cold and fretting after the long river journey and we walked them up the lane, north to Rochford. William took us down the little track which led cross-country to his farm. The early morning mist swirled damp and cold over the fields, it was the very worst time of year to come to the country. It would be a long waterlogged icy winter in the little farmhouse, a long way from anywhere. The dampness on my skirts now would hardly dry out for six months.

William glanced back at me. He smiled. 'Sit up, sweetheart, and look about you. The sun's coming out, and we'll be all right.'

I managed a smile and I straightened my back and pressed my horse onwards. Ahead of me I could see the thatched roof of his farmhouse, and then, as we came over the rise of a hill, the whole pretty little fifty acres, laid out below us with the river lapping up to the bottom fields and the stable yard and barn as neat and as trim as I remembered it.

We rode down the lane and William dismounted to open the gate. A small boy emerged from nowhere and looked doubtfully at the two of us. 'You can't come in,' he said firmly. 'This belongs to Sir William Stafford. A great man at court.'

'Thank you,' William said. 'I am Sir William Stafford and you can tell your mother that you are a fine gatekeeper. Tell her that I am come home, and brought my wife, and that we need bread and milk and some bacon and cheese.'

'You are Sir William Stafford, for sure?' the boy confirmed.

'Yes.'

'Then she'll probably kill a chicken as well,' he said, and legged it across the fields to the little cottage set half a mile away on the lane.

I rode Jesmond through the gate and pulled up in the stable yard. William helped me from the saddle and threw the reins over a hitching post while he took me into the house. The door to the kitchen was open, and we stepped over the threshold together.

'Sit down,' William said, pressing me into a chair by the fireside. 'I'll soon get this lit.'

'Not at all,' I said. 'I'm going to be a farmer's wife, remember. I'll light the fire and you can see to the horses.'

He hesitated. 'D'you know how to light a fire, my little love?'

'Go away!' I said in mock indignation. 'Out of my kitchen. I need to set things to rights here.'

∾

It was like playing at house, like my children might do in a den made of bracken, and at the same time it was a real house, and a real challenge. There was kindling laid in the grate and a tinder box so it did not take me more than about fifteen minutes of patient, painstaking work to get the fire lit and the little flames licking around the wood. The chimney was cold but the wind was in the right quarter so it soon started to draw. William came in from the horses just as the lad returned from the cottage bringing a parcel of food wrapped up in a muslin cloth. We spread the whole thing out on the wooden table and made a little feast of it. William opened a bottle of wine from his cellar under the stairs, and we drank to each other's healths and to the future.

❁

The family who had been farming the fields for William while he had been at court had served him well. The hedges were in good trim, the ditches clear, the meadow fields had been cut for hay and the hay was safely in the barn. The older animals of the herd of cows and sheep would be slaughtered through the autumn, and their meat would be salted or smoked. We had chickens in the yard, we had doves in the cote, and a limitless supply of fish from the stream. For a few pence we could go down to the river and buy sea fish from the fishermen. It was a prosperous farm and an easy place to live.

The urchin's mother, Megan, came over to the farmhouse every day to help me with the work and to teach me the skills I needed to know. She taught me how to churn butter and how to make cheese. She taught me how to bake bread and to pluck a chicken, a dove, or a game bird. It should have been easy and delightful to learn such important skills. I was absolutely exhausted by it.

I felt the skin on my hands grow dry and hard and saw, in the small sliver of looking glass, my face slowly colour with the sun and the wind. I fell into my bed at the end of every day and I slept without dreaming: the sleep of a woman on the edge of exhaustion. But though I was tired

412

at the end of each day I felt I had achieved something, however small. I liked the work since it put food on our table or pence in our savings jar. I liked the feeling that we were building a place together, claiming the land as our own. I liked learning the skills that a poor woman was taught from childhood and when Megan asked me did I not miss my fine clothes and fancy gowns at court, I remembered the endless drudgery of dancing with men I did not like, and flirting with men I did not desire, playing cards and losing a small fortune, and forever trying to please everyone around me. Here there was just William and I, and we lived as easily and as joyfully as two birds in a hedge – just as he had promised.

My only sorrow was the loss of my children. I wrote to them every week and once a month I wrote to George or to Anne, wishing them well. I wrote to Secretary Thomas Cromwell asking him to intervene with my sister and ask her if we might come back to court. But I would not in any way apologise for the choice I had made. I would not sweeten my request with an apology. The words froze on my pen, I could not say that I regretted loving William, for every day I loved him more. In a world where women were bought and sold as horses I had found a man I loved; and married for love. I would never suggest that this was a mistake.

Winter 1535

At Christmas I had a letter from my brother, George.

> *Dear Sister,*
>
> *I send you greetings of the season and hope that it finds you as well in your farmhouse as I am at court. Perhaps better.*
>
> *Matters here are gone a little sour for our sister. The king has been riding and dancing with a Seymour girl – you remember Jane? The one who always looks down: so sweetly; and upwards: so surprised? The king has been seeking her right under the nose of our sister and she is not best pleased. She has rung a few storms over his head but she does not move him to tears as she once did. He can tolerate her displeasure, he just goes away from her. You can imagine what this does to her temper.*
>
> *Our uncle, taking warning from the king's straying, has been putting Madge Shelton in his way, and His Majesty is torn between the two of them. Since they are both ladies in waiting the queen's rooms are in continual uproar and the king finds it safer to go hunting a good deal and leave the ladies to cry and scream and scratch each other's faces undisturbed.*
>
> *Anne is sick with fear and I cannot tell what will be the outcome. She never thought when she overthrew a queen that thereafter all queens would be unsteady. She has no friend at court but me. Father, Mother and Uncle are all in favour of putting Madge forward, to keep the king's eye from the Seymour girl. This leaves a very sour taste with Anne, who accuses the family of seeking to supplant her*

with a new Howard girl. She misses you, but she will not say it.

I speak of you but there is nothing I can tell her which would reconcile her to your marriage. If you had married a prince and been unhappy she would have stood your dearest friend. What breaks her heart is thinking of you finding love, while she is in the greatest court of Europe, frightened and unhappy.

I get richer every day and my wife is a curse to me and my friend is my delight and my torment. This court would corrupt a saint and neither Anne nor I were saints to begin with. She is desperately lonely and frightened and I long for what I cannot have and am forced to keep my desires hidden. I am weary and angry and this Christmas season seems to offer little to us Boleyns unless Anne can get herself with child again. Write to me to tell me of your news. I hope you are as happy as I imagine you to be.

> *Your brother*
> *George.*

William and I celebrated the Christmas feast with a great haunch of venison. I took care not to ask where the beast had been killed. My family's parkland at Rochford Hall was well-stocked and ill-guarded, and there was little doubt in my mind that I had just bought my own deer. But since neither Father nor Mother sent me greetings I thought that I might award myself a gift from their wealth, and I bought the deer at a knock-down price, and a brace of pheasants too. The work of the farm did not stop for the twelve days but we found time to go to Christmas Mass, to see the mummers at Rochford, to drink a wassail cup with our neighbours, and to walk alone beside the river while the seagulls cried over our heads and a cold wind blew up the estuary.

In the iron days of February I prepared for my lying in. This time I would not be a grand lady at court, I would not have to take to my room for a month. I might do as I pleased. William was more apprehensive than I, he insisted that we send for a midwife to stay at the house with us from the last days of the month, to make sure that there was no danger of the baby coming while we were cut off by snow. I laughed at his anxiety but I did as he wished and an old woman, more like a witch than a midwife, came and stayed with us from the first days of March, and watched over me.

I was glad that William had been so careful when I woke one morning and found the room filled with a brilliant white light. It had snowed in the night and it was still snowing, thick white flakes which blew soundlessly out of a grey sky, and swirled around the yard. The world was transformed into a place of utter silence and magic. The hens hid inside their coop, only their three-toed tracks in the yard showed that they had ventured out looking for food. The sheep huddled at the gate, brown and dirty against the whiter field. The cows crowded into the barn and their field was bleached lawn. I sat at the window, feeling my belly churn as the baby moved inside me, and watched the drifts swell and curve along the hedge. It looked as if not a flake was landing, as if they were just swirling and blowing around the house, but every hour the peaks and troughs of the snowdrifts grew higher and more exotically sculpted. When I looked down from the window, the flakes were white as duck feathers, but when I craned my neck and looked up, they were like scraps of grey lace, dirty against a dull sky.

'Setting in,' William said. He had wrapped sacking around his legs and boots and he stood in the little porch outside the door untying it and kicking off the snow. I came slowly down the stairs and smiled at him. He was arrested by the sight of me. 'Are you well?'

'Dreamy,' I said. 'I have been watching the snow all the morning.'

He exchanged one swift meaningful glance with the midwife who was making porridge at the fire, and then he hopped across the kitchen floor in his bare feet and drew me into a chair at the fireside. 'Are your pains coming?' he asked.

I smiled. 'Not yet. But I think it will be today.'

The midwife slopped porridge into a big bowl and passed it to me with a spoon. 'Sup up then,' she said encouragingly. 'We'll all need our strength.'

❧

In the end it was an easy birth. My baby girl came in only four hours of labour and the midwife wrapped her in a warm white sheet and put her to my breast. William, who was at my side for every moment of the four hours, put his hand on her little bloodstained head and blessed her, his mouth trembling with emotion. Then he lay down on the bed beside me. The old woman threw a cover over the three of us and left us warm, wrapped in each other's arms, fast asleep.

We did not wake until the baby stirred and cried two hours later and then I put her to my breast and felt the familiar, wonderful sensation of a beloved child feeding. William tucked a shawl around my shoulders and went downstairs to fetch me a cup of mulled ale. It was still snowing,

I could see the white flakes against the darker sky from the bed. I snuggled down into the warmth and leaned back against the goosefeather pillows and knew that I was a woman blessed indeed.

Spring 1535

Dear Sister,

The queen our sister commands me to tell you that she is with child once more and that you are to come to court to help her but that your husband must stay at Rochford and the baby with him. She will not see either. Your pension will be restored to you and you may be allowed to see your children at Hever this summer.

That is the message I have been ordered to give you, and I tell you as well that we need you at Hampton Court. Anne expects her confinement in the autumn of this year. We will go on progress this summer but not very far. She is anxious to have you with her, because she is desperate to keep this child, as you can imagine, and she wants a friend at court as well as me. In truth, at the moment, she is the loneliest woman in the world. The king is quite taken up with Madge who goes everywhere in a new gown for every day of the week. There was a family conference held the other day by our uncle to which neither I nor Father nor Mother was bid. The Sheltons went. I leave you to imagine what Anne and I made of that. Anne is still queen, but she is no longer favourite either with the king or with her own family.

I warn you of one other thing before you arrive. The city is in an uneasy mood. The oath of succession has driven five good men to the Tower of London and to their deaths and it may drive more. Henry has discovered that his power is without limits and now there is neither Wolsey nor Queen Katherine nor Thomas More to keep him steady. The court itself is a wilder

place than when you knew it before. I have been in the forefront
of it, and it sickens me. It is like a runaway cart and I cannot
see how to leap clear. It is not a happy place that I am bidding
you visit. No – that I am begging you to visit.

As inducement, I can promise you a summer with your chil-
dren, if Anne is well enough to let you leave her.
George.

I took the letter with the heavy Boleyn seal to my husband where he was in the yard, milking a cow with his head pressed against her warm flank and the milk hissing into the bucket.

'Good news?' he asked, reading my bright face.

'I am allowed back to court. Anne is with child again and she wants me there.'

'And your children?'

'I can see them this summer if she will release me.'

'Thank God,' he said simply, and he turned his head to the cow's belly and closed his eyes for a moment and I realised, as I had not fully known before, that he had been suffering for me in the loss of my children.

'Any forgiveness for me?' he asked after a little while.

I shook my head. 'You're forbidden. But I suppose you could just come with me.'

'I'd be sorry to leave the farm again for long.'

I chuckled. 'Have you become a rustic, my love?'

'Arr,' he said. He rose from the milking stool and patted the cow on the rump. I held open the gate for her and she went out into the field where the spring grass was coming through rich and green. 'I'll come to court with you, whether they say so or not; and when the summer comes, we'll come back here.'

'After Hever,' I stipulated.

He smiled at me and his warm hand closed on mine as it rested on the top of the gate. 'After Hever, of course,' he said. 'When is the queen's baby due?'

'In the autumn. But no-one knows.'

'Pray God this time she can carry it.' He hesitated for a moment and then dipped a ladle into the warm milk. 'Taste,' he commanded.

I did as I was bid and drank a draught of the warm foamy milk.

'Good?'

'Yes.'

'D'you want it in the dairy for churning?'

'Yes,' I said. 'I thought I'd do it myself.'

'I don't want you getting too tired.'

I smiled at his concern. 'I can do it.'

'I'll carry it in for you,' he said tenderly. And he led the way into the dairy where our baby, named Anne to please her aunt, wrapped tight in her swaddling, was asleep on the bench.

The royal barge was sent to bring me back to Hampton Court. William, the wet nurse, and myself embarked at Leigh very grand in our court clothes. Our horses were to follow later. The imposing nature of our send-off was rather spoiled by my husband who kept shouting last-minute instructions to Megan's husband who would care for the farm while we were away.

'I am sure he would have remembered the shear the sheep,' I remarked mildly when William finally settled down into his seat and stopped hanging over the rail and bawling like a seaman. 'When their coats grew very long, he would probably have noticed.'

He grinned. 'I am sorry. Did I disgrace you?'

'Well, since you are a member of the royal family, I do think you might find a way to behave which is not quite like a drunk farmer on market day.'

He was quite unrepentant. 'Beg your pardon, Lady Stafford,' he said. 'I swear, when we get to Hampton Court I shall be discretion itself. Where shall I sleep, for instance? Would a hayloft in your stable be sufficiently humble?'

'I thought we might take a little house in the town. And I'll come every day for most of the day.'

'And you had better come home to sleep at night,' he said emphatically. 'Or I shall come up to the palace and fetch you. You're my wife now, my acknowledged wife. I expect you to act like one.'

I smiled and turned my head away so that he should not see the amusement in my face. Pointless to remind my straightforward deter-mined husband, that my previous marriage had been a court marriage and I had all but never slept in my husband's bed, and no-one had been in the least surprised.

'Makes no difference,' he said, with his intuitive knowledge of my thoughts. 'No difference at all how your first marriage was. This is my marriage, and I want my wife in my bed.'

I laughed aloud and snuggled back into his arms. 'It's where I want to be,' I confessed. 'Why would I ever want to be anywhere else?'

The royal barge went smoothly upriver, the rowers keeping to the rhythmic beat of the drum, the tide, rushing inwards, carrying us as fast as a cantering horse. The familiar landmarks came into sight, the great square white tower and the yawning mouth of the watergate at the Tower of London. The bridge was a dark shadow across the river like a doorway opening up to the beauty of the waterside palaces and their gardens and all the bustle and excitement of the central waterway of a great city. The little wherries and ferries and fishing boats criss-crossed the river before us, at Lambeth the great ponderous horse ferry hesitated while we went swiftly by. William pointed to a great grey heron nesting awkwardly in some trees at the water's edge and a cormorant as it upended and dived, a dark acquisitive shadow under water.

Many faces turned in the direction of the royal barge but there were few smiles. I remembered riding in the barge with Queen Katherine and how everyone had pulled off their hats as we went by and the women curtsied, and the children kissed their hands and waved. There had been a trust that the king was wise and strong and that the queen was beautiful and good and that nothing could go wrong. But Anne and the Boleyn ambition had opened a great crack in that unity and now everyone could see into the void. They could see now that the king was no better than some paltry little mayor of a fat little town, who wanted nothing more than to feather his own nest, and that he was married to a woman who knew desire, ambition and greed and longed for satisfaction.

If Anne and Henry had expected the people to forgive them then they must be disappointed. The people would never forgive. Queen Katherine might be all but a prisoner in the cold marshes of Huntingdonshire, but she was not forgotten. Indeed, every day that there was no new christening of a new heir for England, her banishment seemed more and more pointless.

I lay back against William's comforting shoulder and dozed. I heard our baby cry after a little while and I woke to see the wet nurse clasping her close and feeding her. My own breasts, firmly bound, ached in longing, and William tightened his grip around my waist and kissed the top of my head. 'She's well cared for,' he said gently. 'And no-one will ever take her away from you.'

I nodded. I could order her to be brought to me at any time of the day or night. She was my child in a way that my other two had never been. There was no point in telling him that when I saw her blue intent eyes that I grieved even more for the two I had lost. She could not take their place, she only reminded me that I was a mother of three and that though I might have a warm little bundle in my arms, there were two children of mine somewhere else in the world, and I did not even know where my son lay his head at night.

It was twilight before we saw the great pier of Hampton Court and the great iron gates behind them. The drummer gave an extra roll of drums and we saw the watermen tumbling along the pier making ready for us to land. There was a brief cursory fanfare to honour the king's standard, and then the barge was docked and we were landed and William and I were back at court.

Discreetly, William, our baby and the wet nurse took the tow path down to the village and left me to enter the palace on my own. He squeezed my hand briefly before he turned away. 'Be brave,' he said with a smile. 'Remember, she needs you now. Don't sell your services too cheap.'

I nodded, gathered my cloak around me and turned to face the great palace.

I was shown in as if I were a stranger, up the great stairs to the queen's apartments. When the guards opened the door and I walked in there was a moment of dead silence and then a storm of female enthusiasm burst about my head. Every woman in the room touched my shoulders, my neck, the sleeves of my gown, the hood over my hair, and remarked how well I was looking, how motherhood became me, how the country air suited me and how delightful it was to see me back at court. Every single woman was my dearest friend, my sweetest cousin, I should have my pick of bedchambers, everyone wanted to share with me. It was so delightful for them to see me back at court that I could only be amazed that they had managed so long without me, not one of them ever writing, not one of them ever asking my sister for clemency.

And was I indeed married to William Stafford? And did he indeed have a manor farm? Just the one? Just one? But a large place? No? How odd! And did we have a baby? A boy or a girl? And who were the godparents and the sponsors? And what was her name? And where were William and the baby now? At court? No? Well, how curious.

I fended off the questions with all the skill that I could manage and looked around for George. He was not there. The king had ridden out late with just a handful of hard-drinking hard-riding favourites and they were not yet back. The ladies had changed for dinner and were awaiting the return of the men. Anne was in her privy chamber, alone.

I took my courage in my hands and went to her door. I tapped on it and turned the handle, and went in.

The room was in shadow, the only illumination coming from the windows which were still unshuttered, the grey light of the May twilight, and a little flickering glow from the small fire. She was kneeling at her prie dieu and I had to choke back an exclamation of superstitious fear. I saw Queen Katherine on her knees at her prie dieu, praying with all her heart that she might conceive a son for her husband and that he might turn back to her, away from the Boleyn girls. But then the ghost queen turned her head and it was Anne, my sister, pale and strained, with her flirtatious eyes shadowed with fatigue. At once my heart went out to her and I crossed the room and wrapped my arms around her where she knelt and said, 'Oh Anne.'

She rose to her feet and put her arms around me and her heavy head came down on my shoulder. She did not say that she had missed me, that she was miserably lonely in a court which was turning its attention away from her; but she did not need to. The droop of her shoulders was enough to tell me that queenship was not a great joy to Anne Boleyn in these days.

Gently, I put her in a chair and I took a seat, without permission, opposite her.

'Are you well?' I asked, going to the main point, the only point.

'Yes,' she said. Her lower lip trembled slightly. Her face was very pale with new lines either side of her mouth. For the first time in my life I looked into her face and saw that she resembled our mother, I could see how she would look in old age.

'No pains?'

'None.'

'You look very pale.'

'I'm weary,' she confessed. 'It is draining the strength out of me.'

'How many months?'

'Four,' she said, with the instant recollection of a woman who has been thinking about nothing else.

'You'll feel better soon then,' I said. 'The first three are always the worst.' I nearly said, 'and then the last three', but it was no joke to Anne who had only once carried a child through to the last three months.

'Is the king home?' she asked.

'They told me he was still out hunting, George with him.'

She nodded. 'Is Madge out there with the ladies?'

'Yes,' I said.

'And that Seymour white-faced thing?'

'Yes,' I said, having no difficulty in recognising Jane Seymour from that description.

Anne nodded. 'Well enough then,' she said. 'As long as neither of them are with him then I am content.'

'You should try to be content anyway,' I said gently. 'You don't want a belly full of bile with a baby in there.'

She gave me a swift glance and a hard laugh. 'Oh aye, very content. Did your husband come with you?'

'Not to court,' I said. 'Since you said he could not.'

'Are you still besotted? Or are you weary now of him and his handful of fields?'

'I love him still.' I was not in the mood to rise to Anne's baiting. The thought of William filled me with such peace that I did not want to quarrel with anyone, least of all a woman as pale and weary as this queen.

She gave me a bitter little smile. 'George says that you are the only Boleyn with sense,' she said. 'He says that of the three of us you made the wisest choice. You'll never be wealthy, but you have a husband who loves you, and a healthy baby in the cradle. George's wife looks at him as if she would kill him and eat him, her desire is so mixed with hatred; and Henry flits in and out of my room like a butterfly in the springtime. And those two girls flit after him with nets at the ready.'

I laughed aloud at the thought of the increasingly fat Henry as a butterfly in the springtime. 'Big net,' was all I said.

Anne gleamed for a moment, and then laughed too: her merry familiar laugh. 'Dear God, I'd give anything to be rid of them.'

'I'm here now,' I said. 'I can keep them off you.'

'Yes,' she said. 'And if it goes wrong for me you can help me, can't you?'

'Of course,' I said. 'Whatever else happens, you always have George and you always have me.'

There was a flurry of noise from the outer room: an unmistakable bellow of laughter, the great Tudor roar. Anne heard her husband's joy and she did not smile. 'Now I suppose he'll want his dinner.'

I stopped her as she went to the door. 'Does he know that you're with child?' I asked quickly.

She shook her head. 'No-one knows but you and George,' she said. 'I dare not tell.'

She opened the door and we saw, just as she opened it, Henry tying a locket around the blushing neck of Madge Shelton. At the sight of his wife he flinched but finished his task. 'A little keepsake,' he remarked to Anne. 'A small wager won by this clever girl here. Good evening, my wife.'

'Husband,' Anne said through her teeth. 'Good evening to you.'

He looked past her and saw me. 'Why, Mary!' he exclaimed, beaming with delight. 'The beautiful Lady Carey, back with us again.'

I dropped my curtsey and looked up into his face. 'Lady Stafford, if you please, Your Majesty. I have remarried.'

His quick nod showed that he remembered – and remembered the peal his wife had rung over his head as she banished me from court. As I saw his smile stay constant, and his eyes stay warm on my upturned face, I thought what a poisonous witch my sister was. She had sought and obtained my banishment quite alone, it had not been the will of the king at all. He would have forgiven me at once. If Anne had not needed me to help her hide her pregnancy then she would have left me at the little farmhouse forever.

'And you have a child?' he asked. He could not help a swift glance over my head to Anne, looking from the fertile Boleyn girl to the barren one.

'A girl, Your Majesty,' I said, thanking God that it had not been a son.

'William is a lucky man.'

I smiled up at him intimately. 'I certainly tell him so.'

Henry laughed and reached out a hand to draw me closer. 'Is he not here?' he said, looking around his gentlemen.

'He was not asked . . .' I started.

At once he grasped my meaning. He turned back to his wife. 'Why is Sir William not bidden back to court with his wife?' he asked.

Anne never even wavered. 'Of course he was summoned. I invited them both to come back to us as soon as my dear sister was churched.'

I could do nothing but admire her as she delivered this barefaced lie. Nothing for me to do but accept the lie and then play it for all I was worth. 'He will join me tomorrow if it please Your Majesty. And if I may, I will have my daughter with me too.'

'The court is no place for a baby,' Anne said flatly.

At once Henry rounded on her. 'More the pity. And more the pity I should hear that from my wife. This court is the very place for a baby, as I would have thought you, of all people, would know.'

'I was thinking of the baby's health, my lord,' Anne said coldly. 'I was thinking that she should be brought up in the country.'

'Her mother can be the judge of that,' Henry said grandly.

I smiled, honey sweet, and then I snatched at my chance. 'Indeed, with your permission, I should like to take my baby into the country, to Hever this summer. She can meet my other children.'

'*My* son Henry,' Anne reminded me.

I turned a beguiling gaze upwards to the king.

'Why not?' he said. 'Whatever you wish, Lady Stafford.'

He offered me his arm and I swept him a curtsey and slipped my hand in the crook of his elbow. I gazed up at him as if he were still the most handsome prince in Europe, and not the balding fat man he had become. The clear line of his jaw had thickened. The hair on the top of his head was thin and sparse. The rosebud mouth which had been so kissable in a young face was now a self-indulgent little pout, and his dancing eyes were occluded by the fat of his eyelids and the puff of his cheeks. He looked like a man both indulged and yet unhappy. A man like a sulky child.

I smiled radiantly up at him, I tilted my head towards him, laughed at his remarks, and made him laugh with tales of my buttermaking and my cheesemaking, until we were at the high table and he went to his throne as King of England, and I went to my seat at the table for the ladies in waiting.

❁

We sat long over dinner, this court had become gluttons. There were twenty different meat dishes: game and killed meat, birds and fish. There were fifteen different puddings. I watched Henry taste a little of everything, and continually send for more. Anne sat beside him with a face like ice, picking at her plate, her eyes forever flicking to one side and then the other as if she would see where danger waited.

When the plates were finally taken away there was a masque and then the court set to dancing in earnest. I kept a close watch on the side door to the left of the fireplace, even when I was taking my place in a circle of dancers, even when I was flirting with my old friends of the court. After midnight, my watch was rewarded: the door opened and my husband William slipped in, and looked around for me.

The candles were guttering down and there were so many people dancing and moving around that he was not seen. I excused myself from the dance and went over to him and he drew me at once into an alcove, behind a curtain.

'My love,' he said and took me in his arms. 'It feels like a lifetime.'

'For me too. Is the baby all right? Settled in?'

'I left her and the nurse sound asleep. And I have good lodgings for them and for us too as soon as you can get away from court.'

'I've done better than that,' I said delightedly. 'The king was pleased to see me and he asked for you. You are to come to court tomorrow. We can be here together. He said that we could take Baby Anne to Hever for the summer.'

'Did Anne ask it for you?'

I shook my head. 'It's Anne I have to thank for my exile,' I said. 'She

426

wouldn't even have let me see my children if I had not asked it of the king.'

He gave a low whistle. 'You must have thanked her kindly for that.'

I shook my head. 'No point complaining of her very nature.'

'And how is she?'

'Sour,' I whispered very low. 'Sick. And sad.'

Summer 1535

That night George and I sat in Anne's room as she prepared for bed. The king had said he would lie with her that night and she had bathed and asked me to brush her hair.

'You do make sure he is careful, don't you?' I asked her anxiously. 'It's a sin that he should lie with you at all.'

George gave a short laugh from where he was stretched out on her bed, his boots on her fine covers.

She turned her head under the hairbrush. 'I'm in little danger of rough wooing.'

'What d'you mean?'

'Some nights he cannot do it. Some nights he cannot get hard at all. It's disgusting. I have to lie underneath him while he heaves around and sweats and grunts. And then he gets angry, and he is angry with me! As if I had anything to do with it.'

'Is it drink?' I asked.

She shrugged. 'You know the king. He's always half-drunk by night.'

'If you tell him you're with child . . .' I said.

'I'll have to tell him in June, won't I?' she remarked. 'As soon as it quickens, I'll tell him then. He'll cancel the court's progress and we can all stay at Hampton Court. George will have to ride out and hunt with him and keep that moon-faced Jane off his neck.'

'Archangel Gabriel couldn't keep the women off him,' George said negligently. 'You've set a pattern, Anne, you'll live to regret it. They all of them hold him at arm's length and promise him the earth. It was easier when they were all like pretty Mary here – took a little romp and were paid a couple of manors for it.'

'I think you got the manors,' I said sharply. 'And Father. And William Carey. As I recall, I got a pair of embroidered gloves and a pearl necklace.'

'And a ship named for you, and a horse,' Anne said with her accurate envious memory. 'And gowns without number, and a new bed.'

George laughed. 'You have an inventory as if you were a groom of the household, Anne.' He stretched out a hand for her and pulled her to the bed to lie back on the pillow beside him. I looked at the two of them, as intimate as twins, side by side in the big bed of England.

'I'll leave you,' I said shortly.

'Run off to Sir Nobody,' Anne threw over her shoulder, and twitched the richly embroidered curtains of the bed so they were both shielded from my sight.

❧

William was waiting for me, in the garden, looking out over the river, his face dark.

'What's the matter?'

'He's arrested Fisher,' he said. 'I never thought he'd dare.'

'Bishop Fisher?'

'I thought he had a charmed life. Henry always loved him, and he seemed to be allowed to defend Queen Katherine and emerge unscathed. He's been her man without swerving. She'll grieve for him.'

'But he'll just be in the Tower for a week or so, won't he? And then apologise, or whatever?'

'It depends what they demand of him. He won't take the oath of succession, I'm sure of that. He can't say that Elizabeth is to succeed in the place of Mary, he's written a dozen books and preached a million sermons in defence of the marriage, he can't disinherit her daughter.'

'Then he'll just stay there,' I said.

'I suppose so,' William repeated.

I drew a little closer and put my hand on his arm. 'Why are you so worried?' I asked. 'He'll have his books and his things, his friends will visit him. He'll be released at the end of the summer.'

William turned from the river and took my hands in his. 'I was there when Henry ordered him sent to the Tower,' he said. 'He was at Mass while he was doing his business. Think of that, Mary. He was at Mass when he ordered a bishop to the Tower.'

'He's always done his business while hearing Mass,' I said. I was unwilling to recognise my husband's earnestness. 'It doesn't mean anything.'

'These are Henry's laws,' my husband said, holding my hands and not releasing me. 'The Oath of Succession and then the Supremacy Act, and then the Treason Act. These aren't the laws of the land. These are Henry's laws that set a trap to catch his enemies, and Fisher and More have fallen into it.'

'He's hardly going to behead them . . .' I said reasonably. 'Oh William, really! One is the most revered churchman in the land, and the other was Lord Chancellor. He'd hardly dare behead them.'

'If he dares to try them for treason then none of us is safe.'

I found I had lowered my voice to match him. 'Because?'

'Because he will have found that the Pope does not protect his servants. That English men and women do not rise up against tyranny. That no-one is so well thought of, or so well connected, that they cannot be arrested under a new law of his devising. How long d'you think Queen Katherine will be free once her advisor is imprisoned?'

I pulled my hands away. 'I won't listen to this,' I said. 'It's to fear shadows. My Grandfather Howard was in the Tower for treason and came out smiling. Henry wouldn't execute Thomas More, he loves him. They may be at loggerheads now but More was his greatest friend and joy.'

'What about your Uncle Buckingham?'

'That was different,' I said. 'He was guilty.'

My husband let me go and turned back to the river. 'We'll see,' was all he said. 'Pray God you're right and I am wrong.'

Our prayers were not answered. Henry did the thing that I thought he would never dream of doing. He sent Bishop Fisher and Sir Thomas More to trial for claiming that Queen Katherine had been truly married to him. He let them lay their lives down to declare that he was not the head of the Church, an English Pope. And those two, men without a stain on their conscience, two of the finest men in England, walked out to the scaffold and laid their heads on the blocks as though they had been the lowest of traitors.

They were very quiet days at court, the days in June when Fisher died, when More died. Everyone felt that the world had grown a little more dangerous. If Bishop Fisher could be beheaded, if Thomas More could walk to the scaffold, then who could call themselves safe?

George and I waited with increasing impatience for Anne's baby to quicken in the womb so that she could tell the king that she was with child; but mid-June came and still nothing had happened.

'Could you have mistaken your time?' I asked her.

'Is that likely?' she retorted. 'Do I think of anything else?'

'Could it move so slightly that you cannot feel it?' I asked.

'You tell me,' she said. 'You're the sow that's always in farrow. Could it?'

'I don't know,' I said.

'Yes, you do know,' she said. Her little pursed mouth was shut in a thin bitter line. 'We both know. We both know what's happened. It's died in there. It's five months now and I'm no bigger than when I was three months gone. It's dead inside me.'

I looked at her in horror. 'You must see a physician.'

She snapped her fingers in my face. 'I'd as soon see the devil himself. If Henry knows that there is a dead baby inside me he'll never come near me again.'

'It will make you sick,' I warned her.

She laughed, a shrill bitter laugh. 'It will be the death of me, one way or another. For if I let out one word that this is the second baby I've failed to carry, then I am thrown aside and ruined. What am I to do?'

'I'll go to a midwife myself and ask her if there is something you could take to get rid of it.'

'You'd better make sure she doesn't know it's for me,' Anne said flatly. 'If one whisper of this gets out, then I am lost, Mary.'

'I know,' I said grimly. 'I'll get George to help me.'

❁

That evening, before dinner, the two of us made our way down the river. A private ferryboatman took us, we didn't want the great family barge. George knew a bath house for whores. There was a woman who lived nearby who was reputed to be able to cast spells, or stop a baby, put a curse on a field of cows, or make river trout come to the line. The bath house overlooked the river, with bay windows leaning out over the water. There was a shielded candle in every window, and women seated half-naked by the light, so that they could be seen from the river. George pulled his hat down over his eyes and I drew the hood of my cape forward. We put the boat in at the landing stage, and I ignored the girls leaning out of the windows above our heads and cooing at George.

'Wait here,' George ordered the boatman, as we went up the slippery wet steps. He took my elbow and guided me across the filth of the cobbled street to the house on the corner. He knocked at the door, and as it silently opened, he stood back and let me go in alone. I hesitated on the doorway, peering into the darkness.

'Go on,' George said. An abrupt shove in the small of my back warned

431

me that he was in no mood for delays. 'Go on. We've got to get this for her.'

I nodded and went inside. It was a small room, smoky from the sluggish fire of driftwood burning in the fireplace, furnished with nothing more than a little wooden table and a pair of stools. The woman was seated at the table: an old woman, stoop-backed and grey-haired, a face lined with knowledge, bright blue eyes which saw everything. A little smile revealed a mouthful of blackened teeth.

'A lady of the court,' she remarked, taking in my cloak and the hint of my rich gown at the front opening.

I laid a silver coin on the table. 'That's for your silence,' I said flatly.

She laughed. 'I'll be not much use to you, if I'm silent.'

'I need help.'

'Want someone to love you? Want someone dead?' Her bright gaze scanned me as if she would take me all in. Her grin beamed out again.

'Neither,' I said.

'Baby trouble then.'

I pulled up a stool and sat down, thinking of the world divided so simply into love, death and childbirth. 'It's not for me, it's for my friend.'

She gave a delighted little giggle. 'As ever.'

'She was with child, but she's now in her fifth month and the baby isn't growing and isn't moving.'

At once the old woman was more interested. 'What does she say?'

'She thinks it's dead.'

'Is she still growing stouter?'

'No. She's no bigger than two months ago.'

'Sick in the mornings, her breasts tender?'

'Not now.'

She nodded her head. 'Has she bled?'

'No.'

'Sounds like the baby is dead. You'd better take me to her, so that I can be sure.'

'That's not possible,' I said. 'She's very closely guarded.'

She gave a short laugh. 'You won't believe the houses that I have got in and out.'

'You can't see her.'

'Then we can take a chance. I can give you a drink, it'll make her sick as a dog and the baby will come away.'

I nodded eagerly but she held up a hand. 'But what if she's mistaken? If it's a live baby in there? Just resting awhile? Just gone quiet?'

I looked at her, quite baffled. 'What then?'

432

'You've killed it,' she said simply. 'And that makes you a murderer, and her, and me too. D'you have the stomach for that?'

I shook my head slowly. 'My God, no,' I said, thinking of what would happen to me and mine if anyone knew that I had given the queen a potion to make her miscarry a prince.

I rose to my feet and turned away from the table to look out of the window at the cold grey river. I summoned my memory of Anne as I had seen her at the start of this pregnancy, her higher colour, her swelling breasts; and as she was now, pale, drained, dry-looking.

'Give me the drink. She can be the one to choose whether to take it or no.'

The woman rose from her stool and waddled towards the back of the room. 'That'll be three shillings.'

I said nothing to the absurdly high fee but put the silver coins down on the greasy table in silence. She snatched them up with one quick movement. 'It's not this you need fear,' she said suddenly.

I was halfway to the door but I turned back. 'What d'you mean?'

'It's not the drink but the blade you should fear.'

I felt a cold shiver, as if the grey mist from the river had just crept all over the skin of my back. 'What d'you mean?'

She shook her head, as if she had been asleep for a moment. 'I? Nothing. If it means something to you, then take it to heart. If it means nothing, it means nothing. Let it go.'

I paused for a moment in case she would say anything more, and when she was silent I opened the door and slipped out.

∽

George was waiting, arms folded. When I came out he tucked his hand under my elbow in silence and we hurried down the slippery green steps to the gently rocking boat. In silence we made the longer journey home, the boatman rowing against the current. When he put us off at the palace landing stage I said urgently to George, 'Two things you should know: one is that if the baby is not dead then this drink will kill it, and we'll have that on our consciences.'

'Is there any way we can tell if it's a boy, before she drinks?'

I could have cursed him for the single track of his mind. 'Nobody ever knows that.'

He nodded. 'The other thing?'

'The other thing the old woman said is that we should not fear the drink but fear the blade.'

'What sort of blade?'

'She didn't say.'

'Sword blade? Razor blade? Executioner's axe?'

I shrugged.

'We're Boleyns,' he said simply. 'When you spend your life in the shadow of the throne you're always afraid of blades. Let's get through tonight. Let's get that drink down her and see what happens.'

Anne went down to dinner like a queen, pale-faced, drawn, but with her head high and a smile on her lips. She sat next to Henry, her throne only a little less grand than his, and she chattered to him, and flattered him and enchanted him as she still could do. Whenever the stream of wit paused for even a moment his eyes strayed across the room and rested on the ladies in waiting at their table, perhaps looking towards Madge Shelton, perhaps to Jane Seymour, once even a thoughtful warm smile at me. Anne affected to see nothing, she plied him with questions about his hunting, she praised his health. She picked the nicest morsels from the dishes on the high table and put them on his already loaded plate. She was very much Anne, Anne in every turn of her head and her flickering flirtatious glance from under her eyelashes, but there was something about her determined charm that reminded me of the woman who had sat in that chair before and tried not to see that her husband's attention was drifting elsewhere.

After dinner the king said that he would do some business, so we all knew that he would be carousing with his closest friends. 'I'd better be with him,' George said. 'You'll see she takes it, and stay with her?'

'I'll sleep in her room tonight,' I said. 'The woman said that she'd be sick as a dog.'

He nodded, tightening his lips, and then he turned and went after the king.

Anne told her ladies that she had a headache and that she would sleep early. We left them in the presence chamber, sewing shirts for the poor. They were very diligent as we said goodnight but I knew that once the door was shut behind us there would be the usual endless stream of gossip.

Anne got into her nightdress, and handed me her lice comb. 'You might as well do something useful while we're waiting,' she said ungraciously.

I put the bottle on the table.

'Pour it for me.'

There was something about the dark glass with the glass stopper that repelled me. 'No. This has to be your doing, and your doing alone.'

434

She shrugged like a gambler raising stakes with empty pockets, and poured the drink into a golden cup. She raised it to me as a mock-toast, and threw her head back and drank it. I saw her neck convulse as she forced the three gulps of it down. Then she slammed down the cup and smiled at me, a savage defiant smile. 'Done,' she said. 'Pray God it works easily.'

We waited, I combed her hair, and then a little later she said: 'We might as well go to sleep. Nothing's happening.' And we curled up in bed, as we had slept together in the old days, and we woke just after dawn and she had no pain.

'It hasn't worked,' she said.

I had a small foolish hope that the baby had clung on, that it was a living baby, perhaps a little one, perhaps frail, but clinging on and staying alive, despite the poison.

'I'll go to my bed if you don't want me,' I said.

'Aye,' she said. 'Run off to Sir Nobody and have a sweaty little thump, why don't you?'

I did not reply at once. I knew the tone of envy in my sister's voice and it was the sweetest sound in the world to me. 'But you are queen.'

'Yes. And you are Lady Nobody.'

I smiled. 'That was my choice,' I said, and slipped through the door before she could get the last word.

All day nothing happened. George and I watched Anne as if she were our own child, but although she was pale and complained of the heat of the bright June sun, nothing happened. The king spent the morning at business, seeing petitioners who were in a hurry to catch him, before the court was travelling.

'Anything?' I asked Anne as I watched her dress before dinner.

'No,' she said. 'You'll have to go back to her tomorrow.'

At about midnight, I saw Anne into bed and then went to my own rooms. William was dozing when I got in, but when he saw me he slipped out of bed and untied my laces, as tender and as helpful as a good maid. I laughed at his intent face as he unlaced the waist of my skirt, and then held the skirt wide for me to step out, and then I sighed with pleasure as he rubbed the ridges on my skin where the ribs of the bodice had cut into me.

'Better?' he asked.

'It's always better when I am with you,' I said simply.

He took my hand and led me into bed. I stripped off my petticoat and slid into the warm sheets. At once his warm dry familiar body engulfed

435

me, enveloped me, the scent of him dazzled me, the touch of his naked leg between my thighs aroused me, his warm chest on my arched breasts made me smile with pleasure, and his kisses opened my lips.

We were awakened at two in the morning, while it was still dark, by the quietest of scratches on the door. William was up and out of bed at once, his dagger in one hand. 'Who's there?'

'George. I need Mary.'

William swore softly, threw a cloak around himself, tossed my shift to me and opened the door. 'Is it the queen?'

George shook his head. He could not bear to tell another man our family secrets. He looked past William to me. 'Come, Mary.'

William stepped back from the door, curbing his resentment that my brother should command me out of my own marriage bed. I pulled the shift down over my head and jumped out of bed. I reached for my stomacher and my skirt. 'There's no time,' George said angrily. 'Come now.'

'She'll not leave this room half-naked,' William said flatly.

For a moment George paused to take in William's truculent expression. Then he smiled his charming Boleyn smile. 'She has to go to work,' he said gently. 'This is the family business. Let her go, William. I'll see she comes to no harm. But she has to come now.'

William swung his cloak from his naked shoulders and draped it around me and swiftly kissed me on the forehead as I hurried past. George grabbed my hand and pulled me after him, at the run, to Anne's bedchamber.

She was on the floor before the fire, her arms wrapped around her as if she was hugging herself. On the floor beside her was a bloodstained bundle of cloth. When we opened the door she looked up at us through the trailing locks of her dark hair, and then looked away again, as if she had nothing to say.

'Anne?' I whispered.

I went across the room and sat on the floor beside her. Tentatively I put my arm around her stiff shoulders. She neither leaned back for comfort nor shrugged me off. She was as inflexible as a block of wood. I looked down at the tragic little parcel.

'Was that your baby?'

'Almost without any pain,' she said through her teeth. 'And so fast that it was all done in a moment. I felt my belly turn over as if I wanted to void myself and I got out of bed for the pot and then it was all finished. It was dead. There was hardly any blood. I think it has been dead for months. It has all been a waste of time. All of it. A waste of time.'

I turned to George. 'You have to get rid of that.'

He looked appalled. 'How?'

'Bury it,' I said. 'Get rid of it somehow. This cannot have happened. This whole thing must not have happened.'

Anne slid her white ringed fingers through her hair and pulled. 'Yes,' she said tonelessly. 'It never happened. Like the last time. Like the next time. Nothing ever happens.'

George went to pick the thing up and then checked. He could not bear to touch it. 'I'll get a cape.'

I nodded towards one of the clothes chests that lined the walls. He opened it. A sweet smell of lavender and wormwood filled the room. He pulled out a dark cape. 'Not that one,' Anne said sharply. 'It's trimmed with real ermine.'

He checked at the absurdity of this, but pulled out another, and threw it over the little shape on the floor. It was so tiny that there was nothing of it, even when he wrapped it in the cape and tucked it under his arm.

'I don't know where to dig,' he said quietly to me, keeping a watchful eye on Anne. She was still pulling at her hair as if she wanted pain.

'Go and ask William,' I said, thanking God for my man who would manage this horror for us all. 'He'll help.'

Anne gave a little moan of pain. 'No-one is to know!'

I nodded to George. 'Go!'

He went from the room. The little thing under his arm was so small that it could have been a book wrapped in a cape to keep it dry.

As soon as the door was shut I turned to Anne. Her bed linen was stained and I stripped it off and took her nightgown off her as well. I tore it up and started to burn it on the fire. I pulled a fresh night shift over her head and encouraged her to go back into her bed, to creep under the blankets. She was white as death and her teeth chattered as she lay shrunken, tiny under the thick covers, swamped by the richly embroidered tester and curtains of the great four-posted bed.

'I'll get you some mulled wine.'

There was a jug of wine in the presence chamber and I took it into her room and thrust the hot poker into it. I mixed a little brandy in it as well for good measure and poured it all into her golden cup. I held her shoulders and helped her to drink it. She stopped shivering but she stayed deathly pale.

'Sleep,' I said. 'I'll stay with you, tonight.'

I lifted the covers and crept in beside her. I wrapped her in my arms for the warmth. Her light body with the newly flat belly was as small as a child's. I felt the linen of my night shift grow wet at my shoulder and realised that she was silently weeping, tears pouring out from under her closed eyelids.

437

'Sleep,' I said again, helplessly. 'We can't do anything more tonight. Sleep, Anne.'

She did not open her eyes. 'I shall sleep,' she whispered. 'And I wish to God that I could never wake up.'

Of course she woke in the morning. She woke and she called for her bath and she made them fill it with unbearably hot water, as if she wanted to boil the pain out of her mind and out of her body. She stood in it and scrubbed herself all over and then she subsided into the suds and called for the maids to bring in another ewer of hot water, and another. The king sent word that he was going to matins and Anne replied that she would see him when he broke his fast; she was taking Mass in her bed-chamber. She asked me to fetch the soap and a hard square of linen and scrub her back till it was red. She washed her hair and pinned it on top of her head as she soaked in the boiling water. Her skin flushed crab red as she had them add another ewer of hot water, and then bring her warmed linen sheets to wrap up in.

Anne sat before the fire to dry herself and had them lay out all her finest gowns for her to choose what to wear today and what to take with her when the court set out on its summer progress. I stayed at the back of the room watching her, wondering what this fierce baptism in boiling water meant, what this parade of her wealth told her. They dressed her and she laced tightly so that her breasts were pressed into two tantalising curves of creamy flesh at the neck of her gown. Her glossy black hair was exposed by her pushed-back hood, her long fingers were loaded with rings, she wore her favourite pearl choker with the 'B' for Boleyn at her throat, and she paused before she left the room to look at herself in the mirror, and shot her reflection that knowing, seductive little half-smile.

'Are you feeling all right now?' I asked, coming forward at last.

Her swirling turn made the rich silk of her gown fly outwards and the encrusted diamonds sparkled in the bright light. '*Bien sur*! Why ever not?' she asked. 'Why ever not?'

'No reason at all,' I said. I found I was backing from her room, not from the respect that she liked to see, but from a sense that this was all too much for me. I did not want to be with Anne when she was glittery and hard. When she was like this, I longed for the simplicity and gentleness of William and the world where things were as they appeared.

I found him where I expected him to be, with our baby on his hip, walking by the river. 'I sent the wet nurse for her breakfast,' he said, yielding the baby to me. I put my face to the crown of her head and felt the little pulse gently beating against my cheek. I inhaled the sweet baby smell of her, and closed my eyes with pleasure. William's hand came down into the small of my back and then he held me close.

I rested for a moment, loving his touch, loving the warmth of my baby against my body, loving the sound of the seagulls and the warmth of the sunshine on my face, and then we walked slowly, side by side, on the tow path alongside the river.

'How is the queen this morning?'

'As if none of it had ever been,' I said. 'And there it rests.'

He nodded. 'I was thinking just one thing,' he said tentatively. 'I don't mean to give offence but . . .'

'What?'

'What is it that is wrong with her? That she cannot carry a child?'

'She had Elizabeth.'

'Since then?'

I narrowed my eyes and looked at him. 'What are you thinking?'

'Only what anyone would think, if they knew what I know.'

'And what would anyone think?' I demanded, a little edge to my voice.

'You know what.'

'You tell me.'

He gave a little rueful chuckle. 'Not if you are going to glower at me like that, you look like your uncle. I am shaking in my boots.'

That made me laugh and I shook my head. 'There! I am not glowering. But go on. What would everyone think? What are you thinking, but trying not to say?'

'They would be saying that she must have some sin on her soul, some dealing with the devil or some witchcraft,' he said flatly. 'Don't rail at me, Mary. It is what you would say yourself. I was just thinking perhaps she could confess, or go on a pilgrimage, or wash her conscience clear. I don't know, how can I know? I don't even *want* to know. But she must have done something gravely wrong, mustn't she?'

I turned on my heel and walked slowly away. William caught me up. 'You must wonder . . .'

I shook my head. 'Never,' I said determinedly. 'I don't know half of what she did to become queen. I have no idea what she would do to conceive a son. I don't know, and I don't want to know.'

We walked in silence for a moment. William glanced at my profile. 'If she never gets a son of her own then she'll keep yours,' he said, knowing where my thoughts would be.

'I know that!' I whispered in quiet grief. I tightened my grip on the baby in my arms.

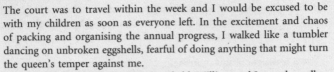

The court was to travel within the week and I would be excused to be with my children as soon as everyone left. In the excitement and chaos of packing and organising the annual progress, I walked like a tumbler dancing on unbroken eggshells, fearful of doing anything that might turn the queen's temper against me.

My good luck held, Anne's temper held. William and I waved goodbye to the royal party as they rode south to the very best that the towns and the great houses of Sussex, Hampshire, Wiltshire, and Dorset could offer. Anne was brilliantly dressed in gold and white, Henry at her side was still a grand king, especially on a big-boned hunter. Anne rode with her mare as close to him as they had always ridden, in those summers only two, three, years ago, when he had been besotted with her and she could see the prize within her grasp.

She could still make him turn to listen to her, she could still make him laugh. She could still lead the court out as if she were a girl riding for pleasure on a summer day. Nobody knew what it cost Anne to ride out and sparkle for the king and wave to the people at the roadside who stared at her with a bitter curiosity but no love. Nobody would ever know.

William and I stood waving until they were out of sight and then we went to find the wet nurse and our baby. As soon as the last of the hundreds of wagons and carts had trundled out of the stable yard and down the West Road we would set off south, to Kent, to Hever, for the summer with my children.

I had planned for this moment and prayed for it on my knees every night for a year. Thank God that the gossip of the court had not reached so far into Kent that my children ever knew what a risk we had run as a family. They had been allowed my letters which had told them that I was married to William and with a baby on the way. They had been told that I had given birth to a girl and that they had a little sister, and the two of them were as excited as I was, longing to see me as I was longing to see them.

They were dawdling on the drawbridge as we rode across the park, I could see Catherine pull Henry to his feet and then they both started to run towards us, Catherine holding her long skirt away from her pounding feet, Henry overtaking her with his stronger stride. I tumbled down from my horse and held out my arms to them both and they flung themselves at me and caught me by the waist and hugged me tight.

They had both grown. I could have wept at how quickly they had grown in my absence. Henry was up to my shoulder, he would have his father's height and weight. Catherine was all but a young woman, as tall as her brother, and graceful. She had the Boleyn hazel-brown eyes and mischievous smile. I pushed her back from me so that I could see her. Her body was forming the curves of a woman, her eyes when they met mine were those of a woman on the brink of adult life: optimistic, trusting. 'Oh Catherine, you are going to be another Boleyn beauty,' I said, and she blushed scarlet and nestled into my embrace.

William got down from his horse and hugged Henry and then turned to Catherine. 'I feel I should kiss your hand,' he said.

She laughed and jumped into his embrace. 'I was so glad when I was told that you were married,' she said. 'Am I to call you Father now?'

'Yes,' he said firmly, as if there had never been any doubt about the matter at all. 'Except when you call me sire.'

She giggled. 'And the baby?'

I went to the wet nurse on her mule and took the baby from her arms. 'Here she is,' I said. 'Your new sister.'

Catherine cooed and took her at once. Henry leaned over her shoulder to pull back the fold of the sheet and look into the tiny face. 'So small,' he said.

'She's grown so much,' I said. 'When she was born she was tiny.'

'Does she cry a lot?' Henry asked.

I smiled. 'Not too much. Not like you. You were a real bawler.'

He grinned at once, a boyish smile. 'Was I really?'

'Dreadful.'

'Still does,' Catherine said with the immediate disrespect of an older sister.

'Do not,' he retorted. 'Anyway, Mother, and, er, Father, would you come inside? There's dinner ready for you soon. We didn't know what time you would be here.'

William turned towards the house and dropped his arm over Henry's shoulders. 'And tell me about your studies,' he invited. 'I'm told you're working with the Cistercian scholars. Are they teaching you Greek as well as Latin?'

Catherine hung back. 'Can I carry her in?'

'You can keep her all the day.' I smiled at her. 'Her nurse will be glad of the rest.'

'And will she wake up soon?' she asked, peering again into the little bundle.

'Yes,' I reassured her. 'And then you shall see her eyes. They are the darkest blue. Very beautiful. And perhaps she'll smile for you.'

Autumn 1535

I received only one letter from Anne, in the autumn:

> *Dear Sister,*
>
> *We are hunting and hawking and the game is good. The king is riding well and has bought a new hunter at a knockdown price. We had the great pleasure of staying with the Seymours at Wulfhall, and Jane was very much in evidence as the daughter of the house. You could break your teeth on her politeness. She walked with the king in the gardens and pointed out the herbs that she uses for cures for the poor, she showed him her needlework and her pet doves. She has fish in the moat which come up to be fed. She likes to supervise the cooking of her father's dinner herself, believing as she does that it is a woman's task to be a handmaiden to men. Altogether charming beyond belief. The king mooned around her like a schoolboy. As you can imagine, I was less enchanted, but I smiled withall, knowing that I am carrying the Ace of Trumps – not up my sleeve but in my belly.*
>
> *Please God that this time all is well. Please God I am writing to you from Winchester and we go on to Windsor where I expect you to meet me. I shall want you by me for all my time. The baby should be born next summer and we will all be safe again. Tell no-one – not even William. It must be a secret until as late as possible in case of any mishap. Only George knows, and now you. I will not tell the king until I am past my third month. I have good reason this time to think that the baby will be strong. Pray for me.*
>
> *Anne*

I put my hand in my pocket and felt for my rosary, and told the beads through my fingers, praying, praying with all the passion I had, that this time Anne's pregnancy would go full term and she would have a boy. I did not think any of us would survive another miscarriage; the secret would creep out, our luck could not survive another disaster, or Anne herself might simply slip over the small step from utterly determined unswerving ambition, into madness.

❁

I was watching my maid pack my dresses into my travelling chest for our return to the court at Windsor when Catherine tapped on my door and came into my room.

I smiled and she came and sat beside me, looking down at the buckles on her shoes, clearly struggling to say something.

'What is it?' I asked her. 'Tell it, Cat, you look ready to choke on it.'

At once her head came up. 'I want to ask you something.'

'Ask it.'

'I know that Henry is to stay with the Cistercians with the other boys until the queen orders him to court.'

'Yes.' I gritted my teeth.

'I wondered if I might come to court with you? I am nearly twelve.'

'You're eleven.'

'That's nearly twelve. How old were you when you left here?'

I made a little grimace. 'I was four. That was something I'd always wanted to spare you. I cried every night until I was five.'

'But I am nearly twelve now.'

I smiled at her insistence. 'You're right. You should come to court. And I'll be there to watch over you. Anne might find a place for you as one of her maids in waiting, and William can watch for you as well.'

I was thinking of the increasing lechery of the court, of how a new Boleyn girl would be the centre of attention, and how my daughter's delicate prettiness seemed to me so much safer in the countryside than at Henry's palaces. 'I suppose it has to happen,' I said. 'But we will need Uncle Howard's permission. If he says yes, then you can come to court with William and me next week.'

Her face lit up. She clapped her hands. 'Shall I have new gowns?'

'I suppose so.'

'And may I have a new horse? I shall have to go hunting, shan't I?'

I ticked the things off on my fingers. 'Four new gowns, a new horse. Anything else?'

'Hoods and a cape. My old one is too small. I've outgrown it.'

'Hoods. Cape.'

'That's all,' she said breathlessly.

'I think we can manage that,' I said. 'But you remember, Miss Catherine. The court is not always a good place for a young maid, especially a pretty young maid. I shall expect you to do as you are told and if there are any flirtations or letters passed then you are to tell me. I won't have you going to court and getting your heart broken.'

'Oh no!' She was dancing round the room like a court jester. 'No. I shall do everything you say, you shall just tell me what to do and I'll do it. Besides, I shouldn't think anyone would even notice me.'

Her skirt swirled around her slim body as her brown hair swung out. I smiled at her. 'Oh they'll notice you,' I said wryly. 'They'll notice you, my daughter.'

Winter 1536

I enjoyed the twelve days of Christmas more than I ever had done before. Anne was with child and glowing with health and confidence, William was at my side, my recognised husband. I had a baby in the cradle and a young beautiful daughter at court. For the Christmas holidays Anne said that I might have her ward Henry at court with us as well. When I sat down to my dinner on twelfth night it was to see my sister on the throne of England and my family around the hall at the best of the tables.

'You look merry,' William said as he took his place opposite me for the dance.

'I am,' I said. 'At last it seems that the Boleyns are where they want to be and we can enjoy it.'

He glanced up to where Anne was starting to lead out the ladies in the complicated configuration of the dance. 'Is she with child?' he asked very quietly.

'Yes,' I whispered back. 'How could you tell?'

'By her eyes,' he said. 'And it's the only time that she can bring herself to be civil to Jane Seymour.'

I giggled at that and looked across the ring of dancers to where Jane, palely virginal in a creamy yellow gown, was waiting, eyes downcast, for her turn to dance. When she stepped forward into the centre of the circle the king watched her as if he would devour her on the spot like a marchpane-iced pudding.

'She is the most angelic woman,' William commented.

'She's a blanched snake,' I said stoutly. 'And you can take that look off your face, because I won't stand for it.'

'Anne stands for it,' William said provocatively.

'He has no permission, believe me.'

'One day she'll overreach herself,' William declared. 'One day he'll be tired of tantrums and a woman like Jane Seymour will seem like a pleasant rest.'

I shook my head. 'She'd bore him to tears in a sennight,' I said. 'He's the king. He likes the hunt and the joust and entertainment. Only a Howard girl can do all of that. Just look at us.'

William looked from Anne, to Madge Shelton, to me and finally to Catherine Carey, my pretty daughter, who sat watching the dancers with the turn of her head the exact mirror image of Anne's own coquettish gesture.

William smiled. 'What a wise man I was to pick the flower of the crop,' he said. 'The best of the Boleyn girls.'

✦

I was with Catherine and Anne in the queen's apartments the next morning. Anne had her ladies sewing the great altar cloth and it reminded me of the work we had all done with Queen Katherine, and the endless stitching of the blue sky which seemed to stretch on and on forever while her fate was being decided. Catherine as the newest and most lowly maid in waiting was allowed only to hem all round the great rectangle of cloth while the other ladies knelt on the floor or pulled up their stools to work on the central body of the pattern. Their gossip was like the cooing of summertime doves, only Jane Parker's voice rang discordantly among them. Anne was holding a needle in her hand but was leaning back to listen to the musicians play. I was disinclined to work altogether. I sat in the windowseat and looked out at the cold garden.

There was a loud knocking on the door and it was flung open. My uncle walked in and looked around for Anne. She rose to her feet.

'What is it?' she asked unceremonially.

'The queen is dead,' he said. It was a measure of his shock that he forgot that she must be called Princess Dowager.

'Dead?'

He nodded.

Anne flushed red and a beaming smile slowly spread over her face. 'Thank God,' she said simply. 'It's all over then.'

'God bless her and take her into His Grace,' Jane Seymour whispered.

Anne's dark eyes flashed with temper. 'And God bless you, Mistress Seymour, if you forget that this Princess Dowager is the woman who defied the king her brother-in-law, trapped him into a false marriage and brought him much distress and pain.'

Jane faced her without flinching. 'I served her as we both did,' she said gently. 'And she was a very kind woman and a good mistress. Of course

I say: "God bless her." With your leave I will go and say a prayer for her.'

Anne looked as if she would very much like to refuse Jane permission to go, but she saw the avid glance of George's wife and remembered that any cat fight would be reported and enlarged on to the court within hours.

'Of course,' she said sweetly. 'Would anyone else like to go to Mass to pray with Jane while I go to celebrate with the king?'

The choice was not a hard one to make. Jane Seymour went alone, and the rest of us went through the great hall and up to the king's apartment.

He greeted Anne with a roar of joy, swept her up and kissed her. You would think he had never been Sir Loyal Heart to his Queen Katherine. You would think it had been his worst enemy who had died and not a woman who had loved him faithfully for twenty-seven years and died with a blessing for him on her lips. He summoned the master of the revels and ordered a feast to be prepared in a hurry, there would be an entertainment and dancing. The court of England was to make merry because one woman who had done nothing wrong had died alone, far from her daughter, and abandoned by her husband. Anne and Henry would wear yellow: the most joyful and sunny of colours. It was the colour of royal mourning in Spain so it was a great jest on the Spanish ambassador who would have to report the ambiguous insult to his master, the Spanish emperor.

I could not force a smile to my face at the sight of Henry and Anne glowing with triumph. I turned away and made for the door. A finger slid against my elbow stopped me. I turned and my uncle was beside me.

'You stay,' he whispered quietly.

'This is a disgrace.'

'Yes. Perhaps. But you stay.'

I would have pulled away but his grip was firm. 'She was your sister's enemy and thus ours. She nearly brought us all down. She nearly won.'

'Because she was right,' I whispered back. 'And we all knew it.'

His smile was genuine. He was truly amused by my indignation. 'Right or not, she's dead now, and your sister is queen without anyone to gainsay her. Spain won't invade, the Pope will lift the excommunication. Hers might have been a just cause; but it dies with her. All we need is for Anne to have a son and we have it all. So you stay and look happy.'

Obediently, I stood beside him as Henry and Anne drew into the bay of a window and talked together. There was something about their heads, so close together, and the rapid ripple of their talk which signalled to everyone that these were the greatest conspirators in the land. I thought that if Jane Seymour had seen them now she would have known that she could never penetrate that unity. When Henry wanted a mind as quick and as unscrupulous as his, it would always be Anne. Jane had gone to pray for the dead queen, Anne would dance on her grave.

The court, left to its own amusements, formed into little knots and couples, to chatter about the death of the queen. William, looking across the room and seeing me standing beside my uncle, my face sulky, came towards me to claim me.

'She's to stay here,' my uncle said. 'No wandering off.'

'She's to follow her own desires,' William said. 'I won't have her ordered.'

My uncle lifted his eyebrows. 'An unusual wife.'

'One who suits me,' William said. He turned to me. 'Did you want to stay or leave?'

'I'll stay now,' I compromised. 'But I won't dance. It's an insult to her memory, and I won't be part of it.'

Jane Parker appeared at William's elbow. 'They're saying she was poisoned,' she said. 'The Dowager Princess. They're saying she died suddenly in great pain, it was something slipped into her food. Who d'you think would have done such a thing?'

Studiously the three of us did not glance towards the royal couple: the two people in all the world who would have benefited most from the death of Katherine.

'It's a scandalous lie. I wouldn't repeat it, if I were you,' my uncle counselled her.

'It's all around the court already,' she defended herself. 'Everyone is asking, if she was poisoned, who did it?'

'Then answer them all that she was not poisoned but died of an excess of spleen,' my uncle replied. 'Just as a woman can die of an excess of slander, I should think. Especially if she slanders a powerful family.'

'This is my family,' Jane reminded him.

'I keep forgetting,' he returned. 'You are so seldom at George's side, you are so seldom working for our benefit that sometimes I forget altogether that you are kin.'

She held his look for a moment only and then her eyes dropped. 'I would be more with George if he was not always with his sister,' she said quietly.

'Mary?' My uncle deliberately misunderstood her.

Her head came up. 'The queen. They are inseparable.'

'Because he knows that the queen must be served and the family must be served. You too should be at her beck and call. You should be at his beck and call.'

'I don't think he wants any woman at his beck and call,' she said mutinously. 'If it is not the queen it is no woman at all for him. He is either with her or with Sir Francis.'

I froze. I did not dare look at William.

'It is your duty to be at his side whether he commands it or not,' my uncle said flatly.

For a moment I thought she would retort, but then she smiled her sly smile and slid away.

Anne summoned me to her privy room in the hour before the dinner. She noticed at once that I was not dressed in yellow for the feast. 'You'd better hurry,' she said.

'I'm not coming.'

For a moment I thought she might challenge me, but she chose to avoid a quarrel. 'Oh very well,' she said. 'But tell everyone that you are sick. I don't want anyone asking questions.'

She glanced at herself in the mirror. 'Can you tell?' she asked. 'I am fatter with this one than the others. It means the baby is growing better, doesn't it? He's strong?'

'Yes,' I said to reassure her. 'And you're looking well.'

She seated herself before her mirror. 'Brush my hair. Nobody does it like you.'

I took off her yellow hood and pulled the thick glossy hair back off her shoulders. She had two brushes made of silver and I used one and then the other, as if I were grooming a horse. Anne tipped back her head and gave herself up to the idle pleasure. 'He should be strong,' she said. 'No-one knows what went into the making of this baby, Mary. No-one will ever know.'

I felt my hands suddenly heavy and unskilled. I was thinking of the witches she might have consulted, of spells she might have undertaken.

'He should be a great prince for England,' she said quietly. 'For I went on a journey to the very gates of hell to get him. You will never know.'

'Don't tell me then,' I said, coward-like.

She laughed shortly. 'Oh yes. Draw your hem back from my mud, little sister. But I have dared things for my country that you could only dream of.'

I forced myself to brush her hair again. 'I'm sure,' I said soothingly.

She was quiet for a moment, then suddenly, she opened her eyes. 'I felt it,' she said in a tone of quiet wonderment. 'Mary, I suddenly felt it.'

'Felt what?'

'Just then, I felt it. I felt the baby. It moved.'

'Where?' I demanded. 'Show me.'

She slapped at her hard boned stomacher in frustration. 'In here! In here! I felt it –' She broke off. I saw her face glow in a way I had never seen before. 'Again,' she whispered. 'A little flutter. It's my child, it's quickened. Praise God I am with child, a live child.'

She rose from her chair, her dark hair still tumbled around her shoulders. 'Run and tell George.'

Even knowing their intimacy I was surprised. 'George?'

'I meant the king.' She corrected herself swiftly. 'Fetch the king to me.'

I ran from the room to the king's apartments. They were dressing him for dinner but there were half a dozen men in the privy chamber with him. I dipped a curtsey at the door and he turned and beamed with pleasure at seeing me. 'Why, it's the other Boleyn girl!' he said. 'The sweet-tempered one.'

More than one man sniggered at the jest. 'The queen begs to see you at once, sire,' I said. 'She has good news for you that cannot keep.'

He raised one of his sandy brows, he was very regal these days. 'So she sends you running like a page, to fetch me like a puppy?'

I curtsied again. 'Sire, it is news I was happy to run for. And you would come for this whistle, if you knew what it was.'

Someone muttered behind me, and the king threw on his golden coat and smoothed the ermine cuff. 'Come then, Lady Mary. You shall lead this eager puppy to the whistle. You could lead me anywhere.'

I rested my hand lightly on top of his outstretched arm, and did not resist as he drew me a little closer. 'Your married life seems to suit you, Mary,' he said intimately as we went down the stairs, half of the gentlemen of the chamber following us. 'You are as pretty as when you were a girl, when you were my little sweetheart.'

I was always wary when Henry grew intimate. 'That's a long time ago,' I said cautiously. 'But Your Grace is twice the prince you were then.'

As soon as the words were out of my mouth I cursed myself for a fool. I had meant to say that he was more powerful, more handsome now. But, idiot that I was, it sounded as if I was telling him that he was twice as fat as he had been then – which was also appallingly true.

He stopped dead on the third stair from the bottom. I was tempted to fall to my knees. I did not dare look up at him. I knew that in all the world there had never been a more incompetent courtier than I with my desire to turn a pretty phrase and my absolute inability to get it right.

There was a great bellow of sound. I peeped up at him and saw, to my intense relief, that he was shouting with laughter. 'Lady Mary, are you run mad?' he demanded.

I was starting to laugh too, out of sheer relief. 'I think so, Your Grace,' I said. 'All I was trying to say was that then you were a young man and I a girl and now you are a king among princes. But it came out . . .'

Again his great shout of laughter drowned me out, and the courtiers on the stairs behind us craned their necks and leaned down, wanting to know what was amusing the king, and why I was torn between blushing for shame, and laughing myself.

Henry grabbed me round the waist and hugged me tight. 'Mary, I adore you,' he said. 'You are the best of the Boleyns, for no-one makes me laugh as you do. Take me to my wife before you say something so dreadful that I shall have to have you beheaded.'

I slipped from his grip and led the way to the queen's rooms, and showed him in, all his gentlemen following. Anne was not in her presence chamber, she was still in her inner room. I tapped on the door, and announced the king. She was still standing with her hair down, her hood in her hand, and that wonderful glow about her.

Henry went in and I shut the door behind him, and stood before it so that no eavesdropper could get close. It was the greatest moment of Anne's career, I wanted her to savour it. She could tell the king that she was pregnant with a baby and for the first time since Elizabeth she had felt a child quicken in her womb.

William came in at the back of the room and saw me, before the door. He touched a shoulder and an elbow and found his way through the crowd. 'Are you on guard?' he asked. 'You've got your arms akimbo like a fishwife guarding her bucket.'

'She's telling him that she's with child. She has the right to do that without some damned Seymour girl popping in.'

George appeared at William's side. 'Telling him?'

'The baby quickened,' I said, smiling up into my brother's face, anticipating his joy as my own. 'She felt it. She sent me for the king at once.'

I was expecting to see his joy but I saw something else; a shadow crossed his face. It was how George looked when he had done something bad. It was George's guilty look. It flashed through his eyes so fast that I was hardly certain that I had seen it, but for a moment I knew with absolute certainty that his conscience was not clear, and I guessed that Anne had taken him as her companion on her journey to the gates of hell to conceive this child for England.

'Oh God, what is it? What have you two done?'

At once he smiled his shallow courtier's smile. 'Nothing! Nothing. How happy they will be! What a couple of days this has been! Katherine dead and the new prince quickened in the womb. *Vivat* Boleyns!'

William smiled at him. 'Your family always impresses me by its ability to see everything in the light of its own interests,' he said politely.

'You mean rejoicing that the queen is dead?'

'Princess Dowager.' William and I spoke together.

George grinned. 'Aye. Her. Of course we celebrate it. Your trouble, William, is that you have no ambition. You don't see that there is in life only ever one goal.'

'And what is that?' William asked.

'More,' George said simply. 'Just more of anything. More of everything.'

❧

All through the cold dark days of January, Anne and I sat together, read together, played cards together and listened to her musicians. George was forever with Anne, as attentive as a devoted husband, forever fetching her drinks and cushions for her back, and she bloomed under his attention. She took a fancy to Catherine and would have her with us too, and I watched Catherine carefully copying the manners of the ladies of the court until she could deal a card pack, or pick up a lute, with the same grace.

'She'll be a true Boleyn girl,' Anne said approvingly of her. 'Thank God she has my nose and not yours.'

'I do thank God for it every night,' I said, though sarcasm was always lost on Anne.

'We could look for a good match for her,' Anne said. 'As my niece she should do very well. The king himself will take an interest.'

'I don't want her married yet, nor against her choice,' I said.

Anne laughed. 'She's a Boleyn girl, she has to marry to suit the family.'

'She's my girl,' I said. 'And I won't have her sold off to the highest bidder. You can get Elizabeth betrothed in the cradle, that's your right. She'll be a princess some day. But my children can be children before they are wed.'

Anne nodded, letting it go. 'Your son is still mine though,' she said, evening the score.

I gritted my teeth. 'I never forget it,' I said quietly.

❀

The weather held very fair. Every morning there was a white ground frost and the scent of the deer was strong for the hounds as they streamed across the park and out into the countryside. The going was hard for the horses. Henry changed his mount two or three times a day, steaming with the heat of his thick winter cape, waiting impatiently for the groom to come running up with the strong big hunter dancing at the end of the reins. He rode like a young man because he felt like a young man again, one who could sire a son on a pretty wife. Katherine was dead and he could forget that she had ever been. Anne was carrying his child and it restored his faith in himself. God was smiling on Henry, as he trusted that God must do. The country was at peace and there was no threat of a Spanish invasion now that the queen was dead. The proof of the decision was in the outcome. Since the country was at peace and Anne with child then God must have agreed with Henry and cast His lot against the Pope and the Spanish emperor. Secure in the knowledge that he and God were of the same mind in this, as in every matter, Henry was a happy man.

Anne was contented. Never before had she felt the world coming to her fingertips. Katherine had been her rival, the shadow queen who had always darkened her own steps to the throne, and now Katherine was dead. Katherine's daughter had threatened the right of Anne's children to rule and now Katherine's daughter had been forced to concede that she would take second place, and Anne's daughter Elizabeth was promised the loyalty of every man, woman and child in the country – and those that refused to promise were either in the Tower or dead on the block. And best of all, Anne had a baby strong and growing inside her.

Henry announced that there was to be a jousting tournament and every man who called himself a man should take his armour and his horse and enter the lists. Henry himself would be riding, his renewed sense of youth and confidence prompted him to take a challenge again. William, complaining mightily of the expense, borrowed his armour from another impoverished knight and rode, taking immense care of his horse, on the first day of the tournament. He kept his seat but the other man was easily declared victor.

'God help me, I have married a coward,' I said when he came to find me in the ladies' tent, Anne seated at the front under the awning and the rest of us, well-wrapped in furs, were standing behind her.

'God bless you, that you have,' he said. 'I brought my hunter out of it without a scratch on him, and I'd rather have that than any reputation for heroism.'

'You are a commoner,' I said, smiling at him.

He slid his arm around my waist and drew me to him for a quick hidden kiss. 'I have the most vulgar of tastes,' he whispered to me. 'For

I love my wife, and I love a bit of peace and quiet, and I love my farm and no dinner is better for me than a slice of bacon and a bite of bread.'

I nestled closer to him. 'D'you want to go home?'

'When you can come too,' he said peaceably. 'When her baby is born and she lets us go.'

Henry rode on the first day of the tournament and won through to the second day. Anne would have been there to watch him but she was sickly in the morning and said that she would come down at noon. She ordered me to sit with her and many of her ladies. The others rode out to the lists, all dressed in their brightest colours, and the gentlemen, some already in armour, riding with them.

'George will take care of the Seymour thing,' Anne said, watching from the window.

'And the king will be thinking of nothing but the joust,' I said reassuringly. 'He loves to win more than anything else.'

We spent the morning at peace in her room. She had her altar cloth spread out for sewing again, and I was tackling one large boring patch of grass while she was doing the cloak of Our Lady at the other end. Between us was a long stretch of revelations: saints going to heaven and devils tumbling down to hell. Then I heard a sudden noise outside the window. A rider, galloping swiftly into court.

'What is it?' Anne lifted her head from her sewing.

I kneeled up on the windowseat to look down. 'Someone riding like a madman into the stable yard. I wonder what . . .'

I bit the next words out of my mouth. Racing out of the stable yard was the royal litter drawn by two stout horses.

'What is it?' Anne asked behind me.

'Nothing,' I said, thinking of her baby. 'Nothing.'

She rose from her chair and looked over my shoulder, but already the royal litter was out of sight.

'Someone riding into the stables,' I said. 'Perhaps the king's horse has cast a shoe. You know how he hates to be unhorsed, even for a moment.'

She nodded but she stayed, leaning on my shoulder, looking out at the road. 'There's Uncle Howard.'

His standard before him, a small party of his men with him, our uncle rode up the track to the palace, and into the stable yard.

Anne resumed her seat. In a little while we heard the palace door bang and heard his feet and those of his men loud on the stairs. Anne raised her head, looked inquiringly as he came into her room. He bowed. There was something in that bow, lower than he usually offered to her, which warned me. Anne rose to her feet, her sewing tumbling off her lap to the floor, her hand to her mouth, her other hand on her loosely laced stomacher.

'Uncle?'

'I regret to inform you that His Majesty has fallen from his horse.'

'He's hurt?'

'Gravely hurt.'

Anne blanched white, and swayed on her feet.

'We need to prepare,' my uncle said firmly.

I thrust Anne into a chair and looked up at him. 'Prepare for what?'

'If he is dead then we need to secure London and the North. Anne must write. She'll have to be Regent until we can establish a council. I shall represent her.'

'Dead?' Anne repeated.

'If he is dead then we have to hold the country together,' my uncle repeated. 'It's a long time until that baby in your belly is a man. We have to make plans. We have to be ready to defend the country. If Henry is dead . . .'

'Dead?' she asked again.

Uncle Howard looked at me. 'Your sister will tell you. There's no time to lose. We have to secure the kingdom.'

Anne's face was blank with shock, as insensate as her husband. She could not imagine a world without him. She was quite incapable of doing my uncle's bidding, or securing the kingdom without the king to rule it.

'I'll do it,' I said quickly. 'I'll draw it up and sign it. You can't ask her, Uncle Howard. She shouldn't be worried, she has the baby to keep safe. Our handwriting is alike, we've passed for each other before. I can write for her, and sign for her too.'

He brightened at that. One Boleyn girl was always much the same as another to him. He pulled a stool over to the writing desk. 'Start,' he said tersely. ' "Be ye well assured . . ." '

Anne lay back in her chair, her hand on her belly, the other at her mouth, staring out of the window. The longer she had to wait, the worse the king must be. A man jolted by a fall is brought quickly home. A man near death is carried more carefully. As Anne waited, looking down to the entrance to the stable yard, I realised that all our safety, all our security was falling apart. If the king died we were all ruined. The country could be pulled apart by every one of the lords fighting on his own account. It would be as it was before Henry's father had pulled it all together: York against Lancaster, and every man for his own. It would be a wild country with every county owning its own master, and no-one able to kneel to the true king.

456

Anne looked back into the room and saw my aghast face, bent over her claim to the regency for the duration of the youth of her child, Elizabeth.

'Dead?' she asked me.

I rose from the table and took her cold hands in my own.

'Please God, no,' I said.

❧

They brought him in, walking so slowly that the litter might have been a bier. George at his head, William and the rest of the gaily dressed jousting party straggling along behind, in frightened silence.

Anne let out a moan and slid to the floor, her gown billowing around her. One of the maids caught her, and we carried her into her bedroom, laid her on the bed and sent a page running for hippocras wine and a physician. I unlaced her and felt her belly, whispering a silent prayer that the baby was still safe inside.

My mother arrived with the wine and took one look as Anne, white-faced, was struggling to sit up.

'Lie quietly,' she said sharply. 'D'you want to spoil everything?'

'Henry?' Anne said.

'He's awake,' my mother lied. 'He took a bad fall but he's all right.'

From the corner of my eye I saw my uncle cross himself and whisper a word of prayer. I had never before seen that stern man call on anyone's help but his own. My daughter Catherine peeped around the door and was waved into the room and given the cup of wine to hold to Anne's lips.

'Come and finish the regency letter,' my uncle said in an undertone. 'That's more important than anything else.'

I took a lingering look at Anne and then went back out to the presence chamber and took up the pen again. We wrote three letters, to the City, to the North, and to parliament, and I signed all three as Anne, Queen of England, while the physician arrived and then a couple of apothecaries. Keeping my head down, in a world falling apart, I was tempting fate to sign myself Queen of England.

The door opened and George came in, looking stunned. 'How is Anne?' he asked.

'Faint,' I said. 'The king?'

'Wandering,' he whispered. 'He doesn't know where he is. He's asking for Katherine.'

'Katherine?' my uncle repeated as quickly as a swordsman draws a blade. 'He's asking for her?'

'He doesn't know where he is. He thinks he's just been unhorsed at a joust years ago.'

'You both go to him,' my uncle said to me. 'And keep him quiet. He's not to mention her name. We can't have him calling for her on his deathbed, he'll dethrone Elizabeth for Princess Mary if this gets out.'

George nodded and led me to the great hall. They had not carried the king upstairs, they were afraid that they would stumble with him. He was a great weight, and he would not lie still. They had laid the litter on two of the tables pushed together, and he was tossing and turning on it, moving restlessly around. George led me through the circle of frightened men and the king saw me. His blue eyes slowly narrowed as he recognised my face.

'I took a fall, Mary.' His voice was pitiful, like a young boy's.

'Poor boy.' I drew close to him and took his hand and held it to my heart. 'Does it hurt?'

'All over,' he said, closing his eyes.

The physician came behind me and whispered. 'Ask him if he can move his feet and his fingers, if he can feel all his parts.'

'Can you move your feet, Henry?'

We all saw his boots twitch. 'Yes.'

'And all your fingers?'

I felt his hand grip mine more strongly.

'Aye.'

'Does it hurt inside you, my love? Does your belly hurt?'

He shook his head. 'It hurts all over.'

I looked at the physician.

'He should be leeched.'

'When you don't even know where he is hurt?'

'He could be bleeding inside.'

'Let me sleep,' Henry said quietly. 'Stay with me, Mary.'

I turned away from the doctor to look down into the king's face. He looked so much younger, lying quietly and drowsily, that I could almost believe that he had been the young prince that I had adored. The fatness of his cheeks fell away as he lay on his back, the beautiful line of his brow was unchanged. This man was the only one who could hold the country together. Without him we would all be ruined: not just the Howard family, not just us Boleyns, but every man and woman and child in every parish in the country. No-one else would stop the lords snapping at the crown. There were four heirs with good claims to the throne: Princess Mary, my niece Elizabeth, my son Henry, and the bastard Henry Fitzroy. The church was in uproar already, the Spanish emperor or the French king would take a mandate from the Pope to come to restore order and then we would never be rid of them.

'Will you get better if you sleep?' I asked him.

He opened his blue eyes and smiled at me. 'Oh yes,' he said in his little voice.

'Will you lie still if we carry you upstairs to your bed?'

He nodded. 'Hold my hand.'

I turned to the physician. 'Should we do that? Get him to bed and let him rest?'

He looked terrified. The future of England was in his hands 'I think so,' he said uncertainly.

'Well, he can't sleep here,' I pointed out.

George stepped forward and picked out half a dozen of the strongest-looking men, and ranged them around the litter. 'You keep hold of his hand, Mary, and keep him still. The rest of you lift when I say the word and go to the stairs. We'll take a rest on the first landing and then go again. One, two, three, now: lift.'

They strained to lift him and to hold the litter level. I went alongside, my hand gripped in the king's. They got into a shuffling stride which kept them all together and we made it up the stairs to the king's apartments. Someone ran on ahead and threw open the double doors into his presence chamber and then beyond, into the privy chamber. They laid the litter on the bed, the king was badly jolted as they put it down, he groaned in bewildered pain. Then we had the task of getting him off the litter and onto his bed. There was nothing for it but for the men to climb on the bed and take him by his shoulders and feet and heave him up, while the others dragged the litter out from underneath him.

I saw the physician's expression at this rough treatment and I realised that if the king was bleeding inside, then we had probably just killed him. He groaned in pain and for a moment I thought it was the death rattle and that we would all be blamed for this. But then he opened his eyes and looked at me.

'Katherine?' he asked.

There was a superstitious hiss from all the men around me. I looked to George. 'Out,' he said shortly. 'Everyone out.'

Sir Francis Weston came towards him and whispered quietly in his ear. George listened attentively and touched Sir Francis's arm in thanks.

'It is the queen's orders that His Majesty be left with the physicians and with his dear sister-in-law, Mary, and with me,' George announced. 'The rest of you can wait outside.'

Reluctantly, they left the room. Outside I heard my uncle stating very loudly that if the king were incapacitated then the queen would be Regent for the Princess Elizabeth, and that no-one should need reminding that they had all, individually, sworn their loyalty to the Princess Elizabeth, his only chosen and legitimate heir.

'Katherine?' Henry asked again, looking up at me.

'No, it's me, Mary,' I said gently. 'Mary Boleyn as was. Mary Stafford now.'

Shakily he took my hand and raised it to his lips. 'My love,' he said softly, and none of us knew which of his many loves he was addressing: the queen who had died still loving him, the queen who was sick with fear in the same palace, or me, the girl he had once loved.

'D'you want to sleep?' I asked anxiously.

His blue gaze was hazy, he looked like a drunkard. 'Sleep. Yes,' he mumbled.

'I'll sit beside you.' George pulled up a chair for me and I sat down without drawing my hand away from the king.

'Pray to God he wakes up,' George said, looking down at Henry's waxy face and his fluttering eyelids.

'Amen,' I said. 'Amen.'

❀

We sat with him till the middle of the afternoon, the physicians at the foot of the bed, George and I at the head, my mother and father forever coming in and out, my uncle away somewhere, plotting.

Henry was sweating and one of the physicians went to ease the covers back from him, but suddenly checked. On his fat calf where he had been injured jousting long ago was a dark ugly stain of blood and pus. His wound, which had never properly healed, had opened up again.

'He should be leeched,' the man said. 'Get the leeches onto that and let them suck out the poison.'

'I can't look,' I confessed shakily to George.

'Go and sit in the window, and don't you dare faint,' he said roughly. 'I'll call you when they've got them on and you can come back to the bedside.'

I stayed in the windowseat, resolutely not looking back, trying not to hear the clink of the jars as they put the black slugs on the king's legs and left them to suck away at the torn flesh. Then George called, 'Come back and sit beside him, you needn't see anything.' And I returned to my place at the head of the bed, only going away when the leeches had sucked themselves into little sated balls of black slime and could be taken off the wound.

In the mid-afternoon, I was holding the king's hand and stroking it, like one might gentle a sick dog, when he suddenly gripped me, his eyes opened and his gaze was clear. 'God's blood,' he said. 'I ache all over.'

'You had a fall from your horse,' I said, trying to judge if he knew where he was.

'I remember,' he said. 'I don't remember coming back to the palace.'

'We carried you in.' George came forward from the windowseat. 'Brought you upstairs. You wanted Mary at your side.'

Henry gave me a mildly surprised smile. 'I did?'

'You weren't yourself,' I said. 'You were wandering. Praise God you're well again.'

'I'll get a message to the queen.' George ordered one of the guards to tell her that the king was awake and well again.

Henry chuckled. 'You must all have been sweating.' He went to move in the bed but he suddenly grimaced with pain. 'God's death! My leg.'

'Your old wound has opened up,' I said. 'They put leeches on it.'

'Leeches. It needs a poultice. Katherine knows how to make it, ask her . . .' He bit his lip. 'Someone should know how to treat it,' he said. 'For God's sake. Someone should know the recipe.' He was silent for a moment. 'Give me wine.'

A page came running with a cup and George held it to the king's lips. Henry drained it. His colour came back and his attention returned to me. 'So who moved first?' he asked curiously. 'Seymour or Howard or Percy? Who was going to keep my throne warm for my daughter and call himself Regent for the whole of her minority?'

George knew Henry too well to be led into a laughing confession. 'The whole court has been on its knees,' he said. 'No-one thought of anything but your health.'

Henry nodded, believing nothing.

'I'll go and tell the court,' George said. 'They will hold a thanksgiving Mass. We were most afraid.'

'Get me some more wine,' Henry said sulkily. 'I ache as if every bone in my body was broken.'

'Shall I leave you?' I asked.

'Stay,' he said carelessly. 'But lift these pillows behind my back. I can feel my back seizing up as I lie here. What idiot laid me so flat?'

I thought of the moment when we shunted him from the litter to the bed. 'We were afraid to move you.'

'Chickens in the farmyard,' he said with mild satisfaction, 'when the cock is taken away.'

'Thank God you were not taken away.'

'Yes,' he said with ungenerous relish. 'It would go hard for the Howards and the Boleyns if I died today. You've made many enemies on your upward climb who would be happy to see you tumble down again.'

'My thoughts were only for Your Highness,' I said carefully.

'And would they have followed my wishes and put Elizabeth on my throne?' he asked with sudden sharpness. 'I suppose you Howards would have got behind one of your own? But what about the others?'

I met his gaze. 'I don't know.'

'If I were not here with no prince to follow after me those oaths might not stick. D'you think they would have been true to the princess?'

I shook my head. 'I don't know. I couldn't say. I wasn't even with the court, I spent all the time in here, watching over you.'

'You would cleave to Elizabeth,' he said. 'Regency to Anne with your uncle behind her, I suppose. A Howard ruling England in all but name. And then a woman to follow a woman, again ruled by a Howard.' He shook his head, his face darkening. 'She must give me a son.' A vein throbbed at his temple and he put his hand to his head as if to press away the pain with his fingertips. 'I'll lie down again,' he said. 'Take these damned pillows away. I can hardly see with the pain behind my eyes. A Howard girl as Regent and a Howard girl to follow her. A promise of nothing but disaster. She must give me a son this time.'

The door opened and Anne came in. She was still very white. She went slowly to Henry's bed and took his hand. His eyes, screwed up with pain, scrutinised her pale face.

'I thought you would die,' she said flatly.

'And what would you have done?'

'I should have done my best as Queen of England,' she returned. She had her hand on her belly as she spoke.

He put his own bigger hand to cover hers. 'You had better have a son in there, madam,' he said coldly. 'I think your best as Queen of England would not be enough. I need a boy to hold this country together, the Princess Elizabeth and your scheming uncle is not what I want to leave behind when I die.'

'I want you to swear you'll never ride in the joust again,' she said passionately.

He turned his head away from her. 'Let me rest,' he said. 'You with your swearing and your promises. God help me, I thought when I put the queen aside that I was getting something better than this.'

It was the bleakest of moments that I had ever seen between them. Anne did not even argue. Her face was as white as his. The two of them looked like ghosts, half-dead of their own fear. What might have been a loving reunion had served only to remind them both how slight was their hold on the country. Anne curtsied to the heavy body on the bed and went out of the room. She walked slowly as if she were carrying a weighty burden and she paused at the door for a moment.

As I watched her, she transformed herself. Her head went back, her lips curved up in a smile. Her shoulders straightened and she rose up, just a little, like a dancer when the music starts. Then she nodded at the guard on the door and he flung it open, and she went out to the buzz of noise of the court, with a face filled with thanksgiving to tell them that the king was well, that he had jested with her about falling from his horse, that he would ride in the joust again as soon as ever he could, and that they were merry.

$$\infty$$

Henry was quiet and thoughtful as he recovered from his fall. The aches in his body gave him a premonition of old age. The wound in his leg wept a mixture of blood and yellow pus, he had to have a thick bandage on it all the time, and when he sat, he propped it up on a footstool. He was humiliated by the sight of it, he who had always been so proud of his strong legs and his dogged stance. Now he limped when he walked and the line of his calf was destroyed by the bulky dressings. Worse than that, he smelled like a dirty hen coop. Henry, who had been the golden Prince of England, acknowledged as the most handsome man in Europe, could see old age coming towards him when he would be lame and in constant pain and stinking like a dirty monk.

Anne was quite incapable of understanding. 'For God's sake, husband, be happy!' she snapped at him. 'You were spared, what else is there?'

'We were both spared,' he said. 'For what would become of you if I were not here?'

'I should do well enough.'

'I think you all do well enough. If I were to die, you and yours would be in my seat while it was still warm.'

She could have held her tongue, but she was in the habit of flaring up at him. 'D'you mean to insult me?' she demanded. 'D'you accuse my family of anything other than complete loyalty?'

The court, waiting for dinner in the great hall, talked a little quieter, straining to hear.

'Howards are loyal firstly to themselves, secondly to their king,' Henry retorted.

I saw Sir John Seymour's head come up and his little secret smile.

'My family have laid down their lives in your service,' Anne snapped.

463

'You and your sister certainly laid down,' Henry's Fool interjected, as quick as a whip, and there was a roar of laughter. I blushed scarlet and I caught William's eye. I saw his hand go to where his sword would be, but it was pointless to rail against a Fool, especially if the king was laughing.

Henry reached over and jovially patted Anne's belly. 'To good purpose,' he said. Irritably, she pushed his hand away. He froze, his good temper dying away in a moment.

'I'm not a horse,' she said sharply. 'I don't like to be patted like one.'

'No,' he said coldly. 'If I had a horse as bad-tempered as you I would feed it to the dogs.'

'You'd do better to ride such a mare and tame her,' she challenged.

We waited for his usual hot response. There was a silence, it stretched into a minute. Anne's smile grew strained.

'Some mares are hardly worth the breaking,' he said quietly.

Only a few people nearest to the high table could have heard him. Anne blenched white and then in an instant turned her head and laughed, a high rippling laugh, as if the king had said something irresistibly funny. Most people kept their heads down and pretended to be talking to their neighbours. Her eyes flicked past me to George and he looked back at her, holding her gaze for a moment, as palpable as a steadying hand.

'More wine, husband?' Anne asked without a quaver in her voice and the gentleman stepped forward and poured for the king and queen, and the dinner began.

Henry was sulky throughout dinner. Not even the dancing and the music lifted his spirits, though he drank and ate even more than usual. He rose to his feet and limped painfully among the court, saying a word here, listening to a gentleman who bowed to him and asked for a favour. He came to our table, where the queen's ladies sat together, and he paused between me and Jane Seymour. We both rose to our feet, neck and neck, and he looked at Jane's downcast smile as she curtsied to him.

'I am weary, Mistress Seymour,' he said. 'I wish we were at Wulfhall and you could make a posset for me, from your herb garden.'

She rose up from her curtsey with the sweetest of smiles. 'I so wish it too,' she said. 'I would do anything to see Your Majesty rested, and eased of his pain.'

The Henry I knew would have said: 'Anything?' for the pleasure of a bawdy jest. But this new Henry pulled out a stool for himself from the table and gestured that we should sit on either side of him. 'You can cure bruises and bumps but not old age,' he said. 'I am forty-five and I never felt my age before.'

'It's just the fall,' Jane said, her voice as sweet and as reassuring as milk dripping into the pail. 'Of course you are hurt and tired, and you must be exhausted by your work for the safety of the kingdom. Night and day I know you think of it.'

'A fine legacy, if I had a son to leave it to,' he said mournfully. They both looked towards the queen. Anne, sparkling with irritation, looked back at them.

'Pray God that the queen has a son this time,' Jane said sweetly.

'Do you truly pray for me, Jane?' he asked very quietly.

She smiled. 'It is my duty to pray for my king.'

'Will you pray for me tonight?' he said, quieter yet. 'When I am sleepless and aching in every bone in my body, and fearful, I should like to think that you are praying for me.'

'I shall,' she said simply. 'It will be as if I were in the room with you, resting my hand on your head, helping you to sleep.'

I bit my lip. At the next table I saw my daughter Catherine, round-eyed, trying to understand this novel form of flirtation done in tones of honeyed piety. The king rose to his feet with a little grunt of pain.

'An arm,' he said over his shoulder. Half a dozen men moved forward for the honour of helping His Majesty back to his throne on the dais. He brushed aside my brother George and chose instead Jane's brother. Anne, George and I watched in silence, as a Seymour helped the king back to his throne.

❀

'I'll kill her,' Anne said grimly.

I was stretched out on her bed, idly leaning on one arm. George sprawled at the fireside, Anne was seated before her mirror, the maid combing her hair.

'I'll do it for you,' I said. 'Setting up to be a saint.'

'She's very good,' George remarked judicially, as one commending an expert dancer. 'Very different from you two. She's sorry for him all the time. I think that's tremendously seductive.'

'Pissy little mistress,' Anne said through her teeth. She took the comb from her maid. 'And you can go.'

George poured us all another glass of wine.

'I should go too,' I said. 'William will be waiting.'

'You stay,' Anne said peremptorily.

'Yes, Your Majesty,' I said obediently.

She gave me a hard, warning look.

'Shall I send the Seymour thing from the court?' she asked George. 'I 'won't have her simpering around the king all day. It makes me furious.'

'Leave her alone,' George recommended. 'When he is well again he'll want something a little more fiery. But stop pulling at him. He was angry with you tonight and you ran towards it.'

'I can't stand him so pitiful,' she said. 'He didn't die, did he? Why should he be in such misery for nothing?'

'He's afraid. And he's not a young man any more.'

'If she simpers at him once again I'll slap her face,' Anne said. 'You can warn her from me, Mary. If I catch her looking at him with that Mother of God smile on her face I'll slap it off her.'

I slithered from the bed. 'I'll say something to her. Perhaps not quite that. Can I go now, Anne? I'm weary.'

'Oh all right,' she said irritably. 'You'll stay with me, won't you, George?'

'Your wife will talk,' I warned him. 'Already she says that you're always here.'

I thought that Anne would shrug it off but she and George exchanged a swift look, and George rose to his feet to go.

'Do I have to be always alone?' Anne demanded. 'Walk alone, pray alone, bed alone?'

George hesitated at the bleak appeal.

'Yes,' I said stoutly. 'You chose to be queen. I warned you it wouldn't bring you joy.'

∾

In the morning Jane Seymour and I found ourselves side by side on the way to Mass. We walked past the king's open door and saw him seated at his table, his injured leg propped before him on a chair, a clerk beside him reading out letters and putting them before him for signature. As Jane went by his door she slowed down and smiled at him, and he paused and watched her, the pen in his hand, the ink drying on the nib.

Jane and I kneeled side by side in the queen's chapel and listened to the Mass celebrated before the altar of the church below us.

'Jane,' I said quietly.

She opened her eyes, she had been far away in prayer.

'Yes, Mary? Forgive me, I was praying.'

'If you go on flirting with the king with those sickly little smiles, one of us Boleyns is going to scratch your eyes out.'

❀

Anne adopted the habit of walking beside the river, up to the bowling green, through the yew tree *allée*, past the tennis courts and back to the

466

palace every day during her pregnancy. I always walked with her and George was always at her side. Most of her ladies came too, and some of the king's gentlemen, since the king was not hunting in the afternoons. George and Sir Francis Weston would walk either side of Anne and make her laugh and take her arm and help her when we went up the steps to the bowling green, and any of our particular circle, Henry Norris, or Sir Thomas Wyatt, or William would walk with me.

One day Anne was weary and cut the walk short. We re-entered the palace with her on George's arm and me a few paces behind her walking with Henry Norris. The guards threw open the doors of her apartments as we came towards them and thus framed a tableau of Jane Seymour leaping from the king's lap and him trying to jump to his feet, brush down his coat, and look nonchalant, but as he was still lame from his fall, he staggered and looked foolish. Anne went in like a whirlwind.

'Get out, slut,' she said sharply to Jane Seymour. Jane dropped a curtsey and scuttled from the room. George tried to sweep Anne through to her inner rooms, but she rounded on the king.

'What were you doing with that thing on your lap? Is she some sort of poultice?'

'We were talking . . .' he said awkwardly.

'Does she whisper so low she has to have her tongue in your ear?'

'I was . . . it was . . .'

'I know what it was!' Anne shouted at him. 'Your whole court knows what it was. We all had the privilege of seeing what it was. A man who says he is too tired to go out for a walk, sprawled at his ease, with some clever little ninny sneaking into his lap.'

'Anne –' he said. Everyone but Anne heard the warning note in his tone.

'I won't tolerate it. She's to leave court!' she snapped.

'The Seymours are loyal friends to the crown and our good servants,' he said pompously. 'They stay.'

'She is no better than a whore in a bath house,' Anne raged at him. 'And she is no friend to me. I won't have her among my ladies.'

'She is a gentle pure young woman and –'

'Pure? What was she doing in your lap? Saying her prayers?'

'That's enough!' he said with a rumble of anger. 'She stays among your ladies. Her family stays at court. You overreach yourself, madam.'

'I do not!' Anne swore. 'I have the say of who attends me. I am queen and these are my rooms. I won't have a woman here I don't like.'

'You will have the attendants I choose for you,' he insisted. 'I am the king.'

'You will not order me,' she said breathlessly, her hand to her heart.

'Anne,' I said. 'Be calm.' She did not even hear me.

'I order everyone,' he said. 'You will do as I bid you for I am your husband and your king.'

'I'll be damned if I do!' she screamed, and turned on her heel and fled to her privy chamber. She opened the door and shouted at him from the threshold. 'You don't master me, Henry!'

But he could not run after her. That was her fatal mistake. If he had been able to run after her then he could have caught her and they could have tumbled into bed together as they had done so many times before. But his leg hurt him and she was young and taunting and instead of being aroused he was baited. He resented her youth and her beauty, he no longer revelled in it.

'It is you who are the whore, not her!' he shouted. 'Don't think I have forgotten what you will do to get into a king's lap. Jane Seymour will never know half the tricks you used on me, madam! French tricks! Whore's tricks! They no longer enchant me; but I don't forget them.'

There was a shocked gasp from the court and George and I exchanged one look of total horror. Anne's door slammed shut and the king turned to his court and George and I met his fulminating glare with the blankness of absolute terror.

He pulled himself to his feet. He said: 'Arm.' Sir John Seymour thrust George aside, and the king leaned on him and went slowly to his own rooms, his gentlemen following him. I watched him go and found that I was swallowing painfully with a dry throat.

George's wife Jane Parker was at my side. 'What tricks did she used to do?'

I had a sudden vivid recollection of coaching her to use her hair, her mouth, her hands on him. George and I had taught her everything that we knew, drawn from George's time in the bath houses of Europe with French whores, Spanish madams, and English sluts, and everything that I knew from wedding and bedding one man and seducing another. We had taken Anne and trained her to do the things that Henry liked, the things all men like, things expressly forbidden by the church. We had taught her to strip naked before him, to raise her shift an inch at a time to show him her privates, we had taught her to lick his cock from the base to the tip with long languorous touches. We had taught her the words he liked and the pictures he wanted in his head. We had given her the skills of a whore and now she was reproached for it. I met George's eyes and I knew he had the same memory.

'Oh Lord save us, Jane,' he said wearily. 'Don't you know that when the king is angry he'll say anything? Nothing, is what she did. Nothing more than a kiss and a caress. The sort of thing that any husband and wife do in their balmy days.' He paused, and corrected himself. 'We didn't, of course; not you and me. But then you're not really a very kissable woman, are you?'

She turned away for a moment as if he had pinched her. 'But of course,' she said, as quiet as a snake going through bracken, '*you* don't really like to kiss women at all unless they are your sisters.'

∾

I left Anne alone for half an hour and then I tapped on her door and slipped into the room. I closed the door on the curious faces of the ladies in waiting and looked around for her. The room was in the darkness of an early winter afternoon, she had not lit the candles and only the firelight flickered on the walls and the ceiling. She was lying face down on her bed and for a moment I thought she was asleep. Then she reared up and I saw her pale face and her dark eyes.

'My God, he was angry.' Her voice was husky from crying.

'You angered him. You ran towards it, Anne.'

'What was I to do? When he insults me before the whole of the court?'

'Be blind,' I counselled her. 'Look the other way. Queen Katherine did.'

'Queen Katherine lost. She looked the other way and I took him. What am I to do to hold him?'

We both said nothing. There was only one answer. There was always only one answer and it was always the same answer.

'I was sick with anger,' she remarked. 'I felt as if I might vomit up my very guts.'

'You must be calm.'

'How can I be calm when Jane Seymour is everywhere I turn?'

I went to the bed and took her hood from her head. 'Let's get you ready for dinner,' I said. 'Go down to dinner looking beautiful and it will all blow over and be forgotten.'

'Not by me,' she said bitterly. 'I won't forget.'

'Then act as if you do,' I advised her. 'Or everyone will remember that he abused you. You had better act as if it was never said and never heard.'

'He called me a whore,' she said resentfully. 'No-one will forget that.'

'We're all whores compared with Jane,' I said cheerfully. 'So what of it? You're his wife now, aren't you? With a legitimate baby in your belly? He can call you what he likes in temper, you can win him back when he is calm. Win him back tonight, Anne.'

I called for her maid and Anne picked out her gown. She chose a gown

469

of silver and white, as if she would assert her purity even when the court had heard her accused of whoreish tricks. Her stomacher was embroidered with pearls and diamonds, the hem of the silvery cloth of the skirt was stitched with silver thread. When she put her hood on her black hair she looked every inch a queen, a snow queen, a queen of speckless beauty.

'Very good,' I said.

Anne gave me a weary smile. 'I have to do it and go on doing it forever,' she said. 'This dance to keep Henry interested. What will happen when I am old and I can dance no more? The girls in my chambers will still be young and beautiful. What happens then?'

I had no comfort to offer her. 'Let's get through this evening. Never mind about years to come. And when you have a son and then more sons you won't mind about getting old.'

She rested her hand on the encrusted stomacher. 'My son,' she said softly.

'Are you ready?'

She nodded and went to the closed door. In the new gesture her shoulders went back and her chin went up, she smiled, her dazzling assured smile, and nodded to the maid to open the door and she went out to face the gossip mill of her own rooms, shining like an angel.

I saw that the family had turned out in support, and knew that my uncle must have heard enough to be fearful. My mother was there, and my father. My uncle was at the rear of the room in amicable conversation with Jane Seymour which gave me pause for a moment. George was on the threshold, I caught his smile and then he went forward to Anne and took her hand. There was a little murmur of interest at her fine gown, at her defiant smile, and then the room eddied as the groups of talkers moved away and re-formed. Sir William Brereton came up and kissed her hand and whispered something about an angel fallen to earth, and Anne laughed and said that she had not fallen but merely arrived on a visit, so the suggestive imagery was neatly turned. Then there was a rustle at the door and Henry stamped into the room with the rest of the court, his lame leg giving him an awkward gait, his round face scored with new lines of pain. He gave Anne a sulky nod.

'Good day, madam,' he said. 'Are you ready to go to dinner?'

'Of course, husband,' she said, as sweet as honey. 'I am glad to see Your Majesty looking so well.'

Her ability to flick from one mood to another was always baffling to him. He checked at her good humour and looked around at the avid faces of the court. 'Have you greeted Sir John Seymour?' he asked her, picking on the one man she would not want to honour.

Anne's smile never wavered. 'Good evening, Sir John,' she said, as mild as his own daughter. 'I hope that you will accept a little gift from me.'

He bowed a little awkwardly. 'I should be honoured, Your Majesty.'

'I want to give you a little carved stool from my privy chambers. A pretty little piece from France. I hope you will like it.'

He bowed again. 'I should be grateful.'

Anne slid a sidelong smile at her husband. 'It is for your daughter,' she said. 'For Jane. To sit on. She seems not to have a seat of her own but she must borrow mine.'

There was a moment's stunned silence and then Henry's great bellow of a laugh. At once the court learned that they could laugh too and the queen's rooms rocked at her jest against Jane. Henry, still laughing, offered his arm to Anne, and she peeped up at him roguishly. He started to lead her from the room and the court took their usual places behind them, and then I heard a gasp, and someone say quietly: 'My God! The queen!'

George cut through the crowd of them like a scythe through grass and grabbed Anne by the hand, pulling her away from Henry. 'Your pardon, Your Majesty, the queen is unwell,' I heard him say swiftly. And then he bent his mouth to Anne's ear and whispered urgently to her. Through the avidly turning faces I saw her profile, I saw the colour drain from her face, and then she pushed her way through them all, George hurrying before her to fling open the door to her privy chamber and pull her in. The people at the back were craning forward, I caught sight of the back of her dress. There was a scarlet stain, blood-red against the silver-white of her gown. She was bleeding. She was losing the baby.

I dived through the press of people to follow her into her room. My mother came behind me and slammed the door on the avid faces staring inwards, on the king who was still looking, bewildered, at the sudden rush of Anne and her family into hiding.

Anne stood alone, facing George, plucking at the back of her gown to see the stain. 'I didn't feel a thing.'

'I'll get a physician,' he said, turning for the door.

'Don't say anything,' my mother cautioned him.

'Say!' I exclaimed. 'They all saw! The king himself saw!'

'It might still be all right. Lie down, Anne.'

Anne went slowly to the bed, her face as white as her hood. 'I don't feel anything,' she repeated.

'Then perhaps nothing is happening,' my mother said. 'Just a little speck.'

She nodded to the maids to take Anne's shoes off, and her stockings. They rolled her on her side and unlaced her stomacher. They peeled off the beautiful white gown with its great stain of scarlet. Her petticoats were drenched in blood. I looked at my mother.

'It might be all right,' she said uncertainly.

I went to Anne and took her hand since it was clear that she would be on her deathbed before our mother would lay a finger on her.

'Don't be afraid,' I whispered.

'This time we can't hide it,' she whispered back. 'They all saw.'

❀

We did everything. We put a warming pan to her feet and the physicians brought a cordial, two cordials, a poultice and a special blanket blessed by a saint. We leeched her and put a hotter pan at her feet. But it was all no good. At midnight she went into labour, in the real struggle and pain of a proper labour, hauling at the sheet knotted from one bedpost to another, groaning at the pain of the baby tearing itself from her body, and then around two in the morning, she gave a sudden scream and the baby came away and there was nothing anyone could do to hold it in.

The midwife receiving it into her hands gave a sudden exclamation.

'What is it?' Anne gasped, her face red from straining, the sweat pouring down her neck.

'It's a monster!' the woman said. 'A monster.'

Anne hissed with fear, and I found myself shrinking from the bed with superstitious terror. In the midwife's bloody hands was a baby horridly malformed, with a spine flayed open and a huge head, twice as large as the spindly little body.

Anne gave a hoarse scream and clambered away from it, scrambling like a frightened cat to the top of the bed, leaving a trail of blood over the sheets and pillows. She shrank back against the bedposts, her hands outstretched as if she would push the very air away.

'Wrap it up!' I exclaimed. 'Take it away!'

The midwife looked at Anne, her face very grave. 'What did you do to get this on you?'

'I did nothing! Nothing!'

'This is not a child from a man, this is a child from a devil.'

'I did nothing!'

I wanted to say 'Nonsense,' but my throat was too tight with my own fear. 'Wrap it up!' I heard the panic in my voice.

My mother turned away from the bed and headed rapidly for the door, with her face as stern as if she was walking away from the executioner's block on Tower Green.

'Mother!' Anne cried out in a little croak.

My mother neither looked back at her nor checked her step. She walked from the room without a word. When the door clicked behind her I thought, this is the end. The end for Anne.

'I have done nothing,' Anne repeated. She turned to me and I thought of the potion from the witch and the night that she lay in the secret room with a gold mask over her face, like a bird's beak. I thought of her journey to the gates of hell and back to get this child for England.

The midwife turned away. 'I shall have to tell the king.'

At once I was between her and the door, barring her way. 'You are not to distress His Majesty,' I said. 'He would not want to know this. These are women's secrets, they should be kept among women. Let us keep this between ourselves and deal with it privately and you shall have the queen's favour, and mine. I shall see that you are well paid for tonight's work and for your discretion. I shall see that you are well paid, Mistress. I promise you.'

She did not even glance up at me. She was holding the bundle wrapped in her arms, the horror of it hidden by the swaddling bands. For one dreadful moment I thought I saw it move, I imagined the little flayed hand putting the cloth aside. She lifted it up towards my face, and I shrank back from it. She took her chance and opened the door.

'You shan't go to the king!' I swore, clinging to her arm.

'Don't you know?' she asked me, her voice almost pitying. 'Don't you know that I am his servant already? That he sent me here to watch and listen for him? I was appointed for this from the moment that the queen first missed her courses.'

'Why?' I gasped.

'Because he doubts her.'

I put my hand to the wall to support me, my head was whirling. 'Doubts her?'

She shrugged. 'He did not know what was wrong with her that she could not carry a child.' She nodded to the limp huddle of cloth. 'Now he will know.'

I licked my dry lips. 'I will pay you anything you ask, to put that down and go to the king and tell him that she has lost a baby but she is able to conceive another,' I said. 'Whatever he is paying you, I will double it. I am a Boleyn, we are not without influence and wealth. You can be one of the Howard servants for the rest of your life.'

'This is my duty,' she said. 'I have been doing it since I was a young girl. I have made a solemn vow to the Virgin Mary never to fail in my task.'

'What task?' I demanded wildly. 'What duty? What are you talking about now?'

'Witch-taking,' she said simply. And then she slipped out of the door with the devil's baby in her arms and was gone.

I shut the door on her and slid the bolt. I wanted no-one to come into the room until the mess was cleaned up, and Anne fit to fight for her life.

'What did she say?' she asked.

Her skin was white and waxy. Her dark eyes were like chips of glass. She was far away from this hot little room and the sense of danger.

'Nothing of importance.'

'What did she say?'

'Nothing. Why don't you sleep now?'

Anne glared at me. 'I will never believe it,' she said flatly, as if she were talking not to me, but to some inquisition. 'You can never make me believe it. I am not some ignorant peasant crying over a relict which is chipwood and pig's blood. I will not be turned from my way by silly fears. I will think and I will do, and I will make the world to my own desire.'

'Anne?'

'I won't be frightened by nothing,' she said staunchly.

'Anne?'

She turned her face away from me, to the wall.

As soon as she was asleep I opened the door and called a Howard – Madge Shelton – into the room to sit with her. The maids swept away the bloodstained sheets and brought clean rushes for the floor. Outside in the presence chamber, the court was waiting for news, the ladies half-dozing, their heads in their hands, some people playing cards to while away the time. George was leaning against a wall in low-voiced conversation with Sir Francis, heads as close as lovers.

William came towards me and took my hand, and I paused for a moment and drew strength from his touch.

'It's bad,' I said shortly. 'I can't tell you now. I have to tell Uncle something. Come with me.'

George was at my side at once. 'How is she?'

'The baby's dead,' I said shortly.

I saw him blanch as white as a maid and he crossed himself. 'Where's Uncle?' I asked, looking round.

'Waiting for news in his rooms like the rest of them.'

'How's the queen?' someone asked me.

'Has she lost the baby?' someone else said.

George stepped forward. 'The queen is sleeping,' he said. 'Resting. She bids you all to go to your beds and in the morning there will be news of her condition.'

'Did she lose the baby?' someone pressed George, looking at me.

'How should I know?' George said blandly, and there was an irritated buzz of disbelief.

'It's dead then,' someone said. 'What is wrong with her that she cannot give him a son?'

'Come on,' William said to George. 'Let's get out of here. The more you say, the worse it will get.'

With my husband and my brother on either side of me we pushed out through the court and down the stair to Uncle Howard's chambers. His dark-liveried servant let us in without a word. My uncle was at the big table, some papers spread out before him, a candle throwing a yellow glow all around the room.

When we entered he nodded to the servant to stir the fire and light another branch of candles.

'Yes?' he asked.

'Anne went into labour and gave birth to a dead baby,' I said flatly.

He nodded, his grave face showing no emotion.

'There were things wrong with it,' I said.

'What sort of things?'

'Its back was flayed open, and its head was big,' I said. I could feel my throat tightening in disgust and I gripped William's hand a little tighter. 'It was a monster.'

Again he nodded as if I were telling him news of a most ordinary and distant nature. But it was George who gave a small strangled exclamation in his throat and felt for the back of a chair to support him. My uncle seemed to pay no attention, but he saw everything.

'I tried to stop the midwife taking it out.'

'Oh?'

'She said that she was already hired by the king.'

'Ah.'

'And when I offered her money to stay or to leave the baby she said that it was her duty to the Virgin Mary to take the baby because she was a . . .'

'A . . . ?'

'A witch-taker,' I whispered.

I felt the odd sensation of the floor floating underneath my feet and all

475

the sounds of the room coming from far away. Then William pressed me into a chair and held a glass of wine to my lips. George did not touch me, he was clinging to the back of the chair and his face was as white as mine.

My uncle was unmoved.

'The king hired a witch-taker to spy on Anne?'

I took another sip of wine and nodded.

'Then she is in very great danger,' he remarked.

There was another long silence.

'Danger?' George whispered, pushing himself upright.

My uncle nodded. 'A suspicious husband is always a danger. A suspicious king even more so.'

'She's done nothing,' George said stoutly. I stole a curious sideways glance at him, hearing him repeat the litany Anne had sworn when she had seen the monster that her body had made.

'Perhaps,' my uncle conceded. 'But the king thinks she has done something, and that is enough to destroy her.'

'And what will you do to protect her?' George asked cautiously.

'You know, George,' my uncle said slowly, 'the last time I had the pleasure of a private conversation with her she said that I might leave the court and be damned to me, she said that she had got where she was by her own efforts and that she owed me nothing, and she threatened me with imprisonment.'

'She's a Howard,' I said, putting the wine aside.

He bowed. 'She was.'

'This is Anne!' I exclaimed. 'We all spent our lives to get her here.'

My uncle nodded. 'And has she repaid us with great thanks? You were exiled from court, as I remember. You'd still be there if she had not needed your service. She has done nothing to recommend me to the king, on the contrary. And George, she favours you, but are you one shilling the richer than when she came to the throne? Did you not do as well when she was his mistress?'

'This is not a matter of favour but a matter of life and death,' George said hotly.

'As soon as she bears a son her position is secure.'

'But he can't make a son!' George shouted. 'He couldn't make a son on Katherine, he cannot make one on her. He is all but impotent! That's why she has been going mad with fear . . .'

There was a deadly silence. 'God forgive you for putting all of us in such danger,' my uncle said coldly. 'It's treason to say such a thing. I did not hear it. You did not say it. Now go.'

William helped me to my feet and the three of us went slowly from the room. On the threshold George spun around, about to complain, but the door silently closed in his face before he could speak.

❁

Anne did not wake until the middle of the morning and then she had a raging temperature. I went to find the king. The court was packing to move to Greenwich Palace and he was away from the noise and the bustle, playing bowls in the garden, surrounded by his favourites, the Seymours very prominent among them. I was glad to see George at his side, looking confident and smiling, and my uncle among the watchers. My father offered the king a wager at good odds and the king took the bet. I waited till the last ball had been rolled and my father, laughing, handed over twenty gold pieces, before I stepped forward and made my curtsey.

The king scowled to see me. I saw at once that neither Boleyn girl was in favour. 'Lady Mary,' he said coolly.

'Your Majesty, I am come from my sister, the queen.'

He nodded.

'She asks that the court delay the move to Greenwich for a week until she has perfectly recovered her health.'

'It's too late,' he said. 'She can join us there when she is well.'

'They have hardly started packing yet.'

'It's too late for her,' he corrected me. There was an instantly suppressed little mutter around the bowling green. 'It is too late for her to ask favours of me. I know what I know.'

I hesitated. A very strong part of me wanted to take him by the collar of his jacket and shake the fat selfishness out of him. I had left my sister sick after a nightmarish childbirth and here was her husband, taking his ease, playing bowls in the sunshine and warning the court that she was far from his favour.

'Then you must know that she, and I, and all we Howards have never swerved for a moment from our love and loyalty to you,' I said. I saw my uncle's scowl at the claim of kinship.

'Let us hope you are not all tested,' the king said unpleasantly. Then he turned from me and beckoned to Jane Seymour. Modestly, eyes downcast, she tiptoed forward from the queen's ladies.

'Walk with me?' he asked in a very different voice.

She curtsied as if it were too much of an honour for her even to speak, and then laid her little hand on his bejewelled sleeve and they walked off together, the court falling into line at a discreet distance behind them.

ॐ

The court was buzzing with rumours which George and I, working alone, could not deny. Once it had been a hanging offence to say one word against Anne. Now there were songs and jokes about her flirtatious court circle, and scandalous insinuations about her inability to carry a child.

'Why doesn't Henry silence them?' I asked of William. 'God knows he has the power of the law to do so.'

He shook his head. 'He is allowing them to say anything,' he said. 'They say she has done everything but sell her soul to the devil.'

'Fools!' I stormed.

Gently he took my hands and unfolded the clenched fingers. 'But Mary. How else would she have made a monstrous child but from a monstrous union? She must have lain in sin.'

'With whom, for God's sake? Do *you* think she has made a contract with the devil?'

'Don't you think she would do so, if it got her a son?' he demanded.

That stopped me. Unhappily, I looked up into his brown eyes. 'Hush,' I said, afraid of the very words. 'I don't want to think it.'

'What if she did perform some witchcraft, and it gave her a monster child?'

'Then?'

'Then he would be right to put her aside.'

For a moment I tried to laugh. 'This is a sorry jest at this sorry time, William.'

'No jest, wife.'

'I can't see it!' I cried in sudden impatience at the way the world had so suddenly turned. 'I can't comprehend what's happened to us!'

Disregarding the fact that we were in the garden and that any of the court could come upon us at any moment, he slipped his arm around my waist and folded me in to him, as intimate as if we were in the stable yard of his farm. 'Love, my love,' he said tenderly. 'She must have done something very bad to give birth to a monster. And you don't even know what it was. Have you never run a secret errand for her? Fetched a midwife? Bought a potion?'

'You yourself . . .' I started.

He nodded. 'And I have buried a dead baby. Please God this matter can be settled quietly and they never ask too many questions.'

❁

The only previous time that the court had abandoned a queen in an empty palace was when the king and Anne had ridden out laughing, and left Queen Katherine alone. Now Henry did it again. Anne watched, unseen, from the window of her bedroom, kneeling up on a chair, still too weak to stand, while he, with Jane Seymour riding at his side, led the progress of the court to Greenwich, his favourite palace.

In the train of merry courtiers behind the laughing king and the new pretty favourite was my family, father, mother, uncle and brother, jockeying for the king's favour, while William and I rode with our children. Catherine was quiet and reserved, and she glanced back at the palace and then looked up at me.

'What is it?' I asked.

'It doesn't seem right to be riding away without the queen,' she said.

'She'll join us later, when she feels well again,' I said comfortingly.

'D'you know where Jane Seymour will have her rooms at Greenwich?' she asked me.

I shook my head. 'Won't she share with another Seymour girl?'

'No,' my young daughter said shortly. 'She says that the king is to give her beautiful apartments of her own, and her own ladies in waiting. So that she can practise her music.'

&

I did not want to believe Catherine but she was quite right. It was given out that Secretary Cromwell himself had given up his rooms at Greenwich so that Mistress Seymour could warble away to her lute without disturbing the other ladies. In fact, Secretary Cromwell's rooms had a private passage connecting the apartment to the king's privy chamber. Jane was ensconced in Greenwich as Anne had been before her, in rival rooms to the queen's apartment, as a rival court.

As soon as the court was settled, a little group of Seymours met and talked and danced and played in Jane's new grand apartments, and the queen's ladies, without the queen to wait on, found their way over to Jane's rooms. The king was there all the time, talking, reading, listening to music or poetry. He dined with Jane informally, in his rooms or hers, with Seymours around the table to laugh at his jests or divert him with gambling, or he took her into dinner in the great hall and sat her near to him, with only the queen's empty throne to remind anyone that there was a Queen of England left behind in an empty palace. Sometimes, as I looked at Jane leaning forward to say something to Henry over my sister's empty seat, I felt as if Anne had never been and there was nothing to stop Jane moving from one chair to the other.

She never wavered in her sweetness to Henry. They must have reared her on a diet of sugar beet in Wiltshire. She was utterly unendingly pleasant to Henry whether he was in a sour mood because of the pain in his leg, or whether he was exultant as a boy crowing in triumph because he had brought down a deer. She was always very calm, she was always very pious – he often found her on her knees before her little prie dieu with her hands clasped on her rosary, and her head uplifted – and she was always unendingly modest.

She set aside the French hood, the stylish half-moon-shaped headdress which Anne had introduced when she first came back to England. Instead, Jane wore a gable hood, like Queen Katherine had done, which only a year ago marked the wearer as someone impossibly dowdy and dull. Henry himself had sworn that he hated Spanish dress, but its very sternness suited Jane's cool beauty as a foil. She wore it like a nun might wear a coif – to demonstrate her disdain for worldly show. But she wore it in palest blue, in softest green, in butter yellow: all clean light colours as if her very palette was mild.

I knew that she was halfway to my sister's place when Madge Shelton, bawdy, flirtatious, loose-living little Madge Shelton, appeared at dinner in a gable hood in pale blue with a high-necked gown to match and her French sleeves remodelled to an English cut. Within days every woman in the court wore a gable hood and walked with her eyes downcast.

Anne joined us in February, riding into court with the greatest show: the royal standard rippling over her head, the Boleyn standard coming along behind her, and a great train of liveried serving men and gentlemen on horseback. George and I were waiting for her on the steps with the great doors open wide behind us, and Henry noticeable by his absence.

'Shall you tell her about Jane's rooms?' George asked me.

'Not I,' I said. 'You can.'

'Francis says to tell her in public. She'll rule her temper in front of the court.'

'You discuss the queen with Francis?'

'You talk with William.'

'He is my husband.'

George nodded, looking towards the first men in Anne's train as they approached the door.

'You trust William?'

'Of course.'

'I feel the same about Francis.'

'It's not the same.'

'How would you know what his love is like to me?'

'I know that it can't be as a man loves a woman.'

'No. I love him as a man loves a man.'

'It's against holy writ.'

He took my hands and smiled his irresistible Boleyn smile. 'Mary, have done. These are dangerous times and the only comfort to me is Francis's love. Let me have that. Because as God is my witness I have few other joys, and I think we are in the greatest of danger.'

Anne's train of escorts rode past and she pulled up her horse beside us with a radiant smile. She was wearing a riding habit in darkest red and a dark red hat set back on her head with a long feather pinned on the brim with a great ruby brooch.

'*Vivat Anna!*' my brother called, responding to her emphatic style.

She looked past us, into the shadows of the great hall, expecting to see the king waiting for her. Her expression did not change when she saw that he was missing.

'Are you well?' I asked, coming forward.

'Of course,' she said brightly. 'Why should I not be?'

I shook my head. 'No reason,' I said cautiously. Clearly, we were to say nothing about this dead baby as we had always said nothing about the others.

'Where is the king?'

'Hunting,' George said.

Anne strode into the palace, servants running before her to throw open the doors.

'He knew I was coming?' she threw over her shoulder.

'Yes,' George replied.

She nodded and waited until we were in her rooms with the doors shut. 'And where are my ladies?'

'Some of them are hunting with the king,' I said. 'Some of them are . . .' I found I did not know how to end the sentence. 'Some of them are not,' I said hopelessly.

She looked past me and raised a dark eyebrow at George. 'Will you tell me what my sister means?' she asked. 'I knew her French and Latin were incomprehensible but now English seems to be beyond her too.'

'Your ladies are flocking to Jane Seymour,' he said flatly. 'The king has given her Thomas Cromwell's apartments, he dines with her every day. She has a little court over there.'

She gasped for a moment and looked from our brother to me. 'Is this true?'

'Yes,' I said.

'He has given her Thomas Cromwell's rooms? He can go straight to her rooms without anyone even knowing?'

481

'Yes.'

'Are they lovers?'

I looked at George.

'No way of knowing,' he said. 'My wager is not.'

'Not?'

'She seems to be refusing to take the addresses of a married man,' he said. 'She is playing on her virtue.'

Anne went to the window, walking slowly, as if she would puzzle out this change in her world. 'What does she hope for?' she asked. 'If she is calling him on and holding him off at the same time?'

Neither of us answered her. Who would know better than us?

Anne turned, her eyes as sharp as a cat's. 'She thinks to put me aside? Is she mad?'

We neither of us answered.

'And Cromwell was ordered out for this shower of Seymours?'

I shook my head. 'Cromwell offered his rooms.'

She nodded slowly. 'So Cromwell is openly against me now.'

She looked to George for comfort, an odd look, as if she were not sure of him. But George had never failed her. Tentatively, he went closer to her and put his hand on her shoulder, brother-like. Instead of turning to him for a hug, she stepped back until he was standing behind her and then she rested her head back against his chest. He gave a sigh and wrapped his arms around her and rocked her gently as they stood, looking out of the window where the Thames sparkled in the wintry sunshine.

'I thought you might be afraid to touch me,' she said softly.

He shook his head. 'Oh, Anne. According to the laws of the land and the church I am anathemetised ten times over before breakfast.'

I shuddered at that; but she giggled like a girl.

'And whatever we have done, it was done for love,' he said gently.

She turned in his arms and looked up at him, scrutinising his face. I realised that I had never in my life seen her look at anyone like that before. She looked at him as if she cared what he felt. He was not just a step on the stair of her ambition. He was her beloved. 'Even when the outcome was monstrous?' she asked.

He shrugged. 'I don't pretend to know the theology. But my mare has dropped a foal with one leg joined to the other and I didn't dip her for a witch. These things happen in nature, they can't always mean something. You were unlucky, nothing more.'

'I won't let it frighten me,' she said staunchly. 'I've seen saint's blood made from the blood of pigs, and holy water scooped up from a stream. Half of this church's teaching is to lead you on, half to frighten you into your place. I won't be bribed onwards, and I won't be frightened. Not by anything. I took a decision to build my own road and I will do it.'

If George had been listening he would have heard the sharp nervous edge in her voice. But he was watching her bright determined face. 'Onwards and upwards, Anna Regina!' he said.

She beamed at him. 'Onwards and upwards. And the next will be a boy.'

She turned in his arms and put her hands on his shoulders and looked up at him, as if he were a trusted lover. 'So what am I to do?'

'You have to get him back,' he said earnestly. 'Don't rail at him, don't let him see your fear. Call him back to you with every trick you know. Enchant him again.'

She hesitated and then she smiled and told him the truth behind the bright face. 'George, I'm ten years older than when I courted him first. I am nearing thirty. He's had only one live child off me, and now he knows that I gave birth to a monster. I will repel him.'

George tightened his grip on her waist. 'You can't repel him,' he said simply. 'Or we all fall. You have to draw him back to you.'

'But it was me who taught him to follow his desires. Worse than that, I filled his stupid head with the new learning. Now he thinks that his desires are God's manifestations. He only has to want something to think that it is God's will. He doesn't have to confirm it with priest, bishop, or Pope. His whims are holy. How can anyone make such a man return to his wife?'

George looked over her head to me for help. I came a little closer. 'He likes comfort,' I said. 'A little soothing. Pet him, tell him he is wonderful, praise him, and be kind to him.'

She looked as blankly at me as if I were speaking Hebrew. 'I am his lover, not his mother,' she said flatly.

'He wants a mother now,' George said. 'He's hurt and he feels old and battered. He fears old age, he fears death. The wound on his leg stinks. He is in terror of dying before he has made a prince for England. What he wants is a woman to be tender to him until he feels better again. Jane Seymour is all sweetness. You have to out-sweeten her.'

She was silent. We all knew that it was not possible to be sweeter than Jane Seymour when she had the crown in her sights. Not even Anne, that most consummate seductress, could out-sweeten Jane Seymour. The brightness had died from her face and for a moment in her thin pallor I saw the hard face of our own mother.

'By God I hope it kills her,' she suddenly swore vindictively. 'If she gets her hand on my crown and her arse on my throne I hope it is the death of her. I hope she dies young. I hope she dies in childbed in the very act of giving him a boy. And I hope the boy dies too.'

George stiffened. He could see from the window the return of the hunting party to court.

'Run downstairs, Mary, and tell the king I am come,' Anne said, not moving from George's embrace.

I ran downstairs as the king was dismounting from his horse. I saw him wince as he stepped to the ground and his weight went onto his injured leg. Jane was riding beside him, a phalanx of Seymours around them. I looked around for my father, for my mother, for my uncle. They were thrust to the back, eclipsed.

'Your Majesty,' I said, sweeping him a curtsey. 'My sister the queen has arrived and bids me to give Your Majesty her compliments.'

Henry looked at me, he was wearing his sulky face, his forehead grooved with pain, his mouth pursed. 'Tell her I am wearied from my riding, I will see her at dinner,' he said shortly.

He went past me with a heavy tread, walking unevenly, favouring his hurt leg. Sir John Seymour helped his daughter from her horse. I noted the new riding gown, the new horse, the diamond winking on her gloved hand. I longed so much to spit some venom at her that I had to bite the tip of my tongue, to make myself smile sweetly at her, and step back as her father and her brother escorted her through the great doors to her apartments – the apartments of the king's favourite.

My father and my mother followed the Seymours, in their train. I waited for them to ask me how Anne was, but they passed me with no more than a nod. 'Anne is well,' I volunteered, as my mother went by.

'Good,' she said coolly.

'Will you not come to wait on her?'

Her face was as blank as a barren woman. It was as if none of us had ever been born to her. 'I will visit her when the king goes to her rooms,' she said.

I knew then that Anne and George and I were on our own.

❧

The ladies returned to Anne's room like a flock of buzzards, uncertain where the best pickings were to be had. I noted, with bitter amusement, the crisis in headgear which Anne's confident return had caused. Some of them went back to French hoods which Anne continued to wear. Some of them stayed in the heavy gable hoods which Jane favoured. All of them were desperate to know whether they should be in the queen's beautiful apartment or over the way with the Seymours. Where might the king come next? Where might he prefer? Madge Shelton wore a gable hood and was trying to wheedle her way into Jane Seymour's circle. Madge for one thought that Anne was in decline.

I entered the room and three women fell silent the moment I approached them. 'What's the news?' I asked.

No-one would tell me. Then Jane Parker, always the most reliable of all scandal mongers, came to my side. 'The king has sent Jane Seymour a gift, a huge purse of gold, and she has refused it.'

I waited.

Jane's eyes were bright with delight. 'She said she could not take such gifts from the king until she was a married woman. It would compromise her.'

I was silent for a moment, trying to decode this arcane statement. 'Compromise her?'

Jane nodded.

'Excuse me,' I said. I made my way through the women to Anne's privy chamber. George was in there with her, Sir Francis Weston with him. 'I would speak with you alone,' I said flatly.

'You can speak in front of Sir Francis,' Anne said.

I took a breath. 'Have you heard about Jane Seymour refusing the king's gift?'

They shook their heads. 'She is supposed to have said that she could not take such gifts from him until she was a married woman, because it might compromise her.'

'Oho,' Sir Francis said.

'I suppose it is nothing more than her flaunting her virtue; but the court's abuzz with it,' I said.

'It reminds the king that she could marry another,' George said. 'He'll hate the sound of that.'

'It parades her virtue,' Anne added.

'And it'll get out,' Sir Francis said. 'This is theatre. She didn't turn down that horse, did she? Or the diamond ring? Or the locket with his picture inside? But the court now thinks, and the world will soon think, that the king is interested in a young woman who has no ambition for wealth. Touché! And all in one tableau.'

Anne gritted her teeth. 'She is insufferable.'

'And there's nothing you can do to pay her back,' George said. 'So don't even think about it. Head up, smile on, and enchant him if you can.'

'There may be mention at dinner of the alliance with Spain,' Sir Francis cautioned her as she rose from her chair. 'Better say nothing against it.'

Anne looked back over her shoulder at him. 'If I have to become Jane Seymour myself, I might as well be set aside,' she said. 'If everything that is me – my wit and my temper and my passion for the reform of the church – has to be denied, then I have set my own self aside. If what the king wants is a biddable wife then I should never have tried for the throne in the first place. If I cannot be me, I might as well not be here at all.'

George went to her, raised her hand and kissed it. 'No, for we all adore you,' he said. 'And this is just a passing whim of the king's. He wants Jane now as he wanted Madge, as he wanted Lady Margaret. He'll come to his senses and come back to you. Look how long the queen held him. He went and came back to her a dozen times. You are his wife, the mother of his princess, just as she was. You can hold him.'

She smiled at that, straightened her shoulders, and nodded to me to open the door. I heard the buzz as she went out, dressed in rich green velvet, emeralds in her ears, diamonds sparkling on her green hood, the golden 'B' on the choker of pearls at her neck.

❀

It grew very cold towards the end of February and the Thames froze outside the palace. The landing stage extended like a path over a floor of white ice, the steps at the landing gate led down to a smooth sheet of glass. The river became like a strange road, which might lead anywhere. In the thinner parts when I looked down I could see the water moving, green and perilous, below the clear sheet of ice.

The gardens, the walkways, the walls and the *allées* around Greenwich all took on a miraculous whiteness as it snowed and then froze and then snowed again. In the pleasure gardens the espaliered walkways were frosted. On the sunny mornings the spiders' webs shone with white crystals like magical lacemaking thrown over the thinnest branches. Every twig, every thinnest blade was lined with white, as if an artist had gone around the whole garden determined to make one see the detail of every branch on every tree.

It was freezing cold at night with an icy wind which blew from the east, a Russian wind. But during the day the sun was very bright and it was delightful to run in the gardens and to play at bowls on the frozen grass while the robins hopped in the dark yew trees of the *allée* and waited for crumbs, and great flocks of cold-loving geese flew overhead with their wings creaking and their long heads extended, searching for open water.

The king declared that we should have a winter fair and that there should be jousting on ice-skates and skate-dancing and a masque for winter with sledges and fire-eaters and Muscovite tumblers. There was a bear baiting, ten times funnier than an ordinary baiting, when the poor animal slid and fell and lunged towards the skidding dogs. One dog raced in for a snap and thought to race out again but found his scrabbling feet had no purchase on the ice and the bear drew him in to his death with one heavy paw on his back. The king roared with laughter at the sight.

They drove down oxen from Smithfield, using the frozen river as a high road, and roasted them on spits over great fires on the riverbank, and the lads ran from kitchen to riverside with hot bread, the kitchen dogs barking and running alongside them all the way, hoping for a mishap.

Jane was a winter princess in white and blue, white fur at her neck and on the hood of her cape. She skated very unsteadily and had to be held up by her brother on one side and her father on the other. They wheeled her towards the king and pushed her, passively beautiful, towards the throne and I thought that to be a Seymour girl must be very like being a Boleyn girl, when your father and your brother thrust you towards the king and you have neither the ability nor the wisdom to race away.

Henry always had a chair for her by his side. The throne for the queen was on his right, as it must be, but on his left there was a seat for Jane if she chose to rest after skating. The king did not skate, his leg was still not healed and there was talk of French physicians or perhaps even a pilgrimage to Canterbury to ease his pain. Only Jane could wipe his frown away, and she managed it by doing nothing. She stood beside him, she let them push her around on skates before him, she flinched at the cockfighting, she gasped at the fire-eater, she behaved as she always had done, as a complete ninny, and it soothed the king in a way that Anne could not do.

Anne came down to dine on the ice with the king for every one of the three days, and seeing her glide about on her sharp whalebone skates with the grace of a Russian dancer, I thought that all we Boleyns were on thin ice this season. The most innocent word from her could make the king scowl, there was no pleasing him. He watched her all the time, with his suspicious piggy eyes screwed up. He rubbed his fingers as he watched her, pulling at the ring on his smallest finger.

Anne tried to dazzle him with her high spirits and her beauty. She kept her temper with him, though he was sour and dull. She danced, she gambled, she laughed, she skated, she was all joy, all light. She threw Jane Seymour into the background, no man ever had eyes for another woman when Anne was in radiant mood. Not even the king could look away from her as she went through the dancing court, her head high, that turn of the neck as someone spoke to her, surrounded by men who wrote poems to her beauty, musicians playing songs for her, the very centre of the excitement of the court at play. The king could not take his eyes off her, but his gaze was no longer entranced. He stared at her as if he would understand something about her, as if he would unravel her charm so that he might see her unwoven, robbed of everything that had made her once so lovely to him. He stared at her like a man might stare at a tapestry that has cost him a fortune and that he suddenly sees one morning as valueless, and wants to unknot. He stared at her as if he could not believe that she had cost him so dear, and repaid him so little. And not even Anne's charm and vivacity could make him think that the bargain was a good one.

While I watched Anne, George and Sir Francis were watching Cromwell. There was a whispered rumour that the king might put Anne aside on grounds that the marriage had been invalid from the start. George and I scoffed at it, but Sir Francis pointed to the fact that parliament was to be dissolved in April, with no good reason given.

'What difference does that make?' George asked him.

'So all the good country knights are back in their shires if the king makes a move against the queen,' Francis answered.

'They'd hardly defend her,' I said. 'They hate her.'

'They might defend the idea of queenship,' he said. 'They were forced to swear against Queen Katherine, they were forced to swear that they denied the Princess Mary, that they recognised Princess Elizabeth. If the king now sets Anne aside they might feel that he has played them for fools, and they won't like that. If he returns to the Pope's view, they might find it a turn-around too quick to swallow.'

'But the queen is dead,' I said, thinking of my old mistress Katherine. 'Even if his marriage to Anne is dissolved, he can't go back to the queen.'

George tutted under his breath at my slowness, but Sir Francis was more patient. 'The Pope's view is still that the marriage with Anne is invalid. And so now Henry is a widower; and free to marry again.'

Instinctively George and Francis and I all looked towards the king. He was rising from his throne on the ice-blue dais. Sir John Seymour and Sir Edward Seymour were either side of him, raising him up. Jane was standing before him, her lips slightly parted on a smile as if she had never seen a more handsome man than this fat invalid.

Anne, skating on the other side of the ice with Henry Norris and Thomas Wyatt, glided over and called casually: 'How now, husband? Are you not staying?'

He looked at her. The colour was whipped into her cheeks by the cold wind, she was wearing her scarlet riding hat with the long feather, and a strand of hair was tickling her cheek. She looked radiant, undeniably beautiful.

'I am in pain,' he said slowly. 'While you have been disporting yourself, I have been suffering. I am going to my rooms to rest.'

'I'll come with you,' she said instantly, gliding forward. 'If I had known I would have stayed at your side, but you told me to go and skate. My poor husband. I shall make you a tisane and sit with you and read to you, if you like.'

He shook his head. 'I would rather sleep,' he said. 'I would rather have silence than your reading.'

Anne flushed. Henry Norris and Thomas Wyatt looked away, wishing themselves elsewhere. The Seymours kept their faces diplomatically bland.

'I will see you at dinner then,' Anne said, curbing her temper. 'And I shall pray that you are rested and free from pain.'

Henry nodded and turned away from her. The Seymours took his arms and helped him over the rich rugs which had been laid on the ice so that he should not slip. Jane, with a meek little smile as if to apologise for being favoured, tripped along in his wake.

'And where d'you think you're going, Mistress Seymour?' Anne's voice was like a whiplash.

The younger woman turned and curtsied to the queen. 'He told me to follow and to read to him,' she said simply, her eyes downcast. 'I can't read Latin very well. But I can read a little French.'

'A little French!' exclaimed my sister, tri-lingual since she was six years old.

'Yes,' Jane said proudly. 'Though I don't understand it all.'

'I wager you understand nothing,' Anne said. 'You can go.'

Spring 1536

The ice melted but the weather hardly seemed to warm. The snowdrops flowered in clumps all around the bowling green, but the green was so waterlogged that we could not play, and the paths themselves were too wet for walking. The king's leg was not healing, it was an open wound and the different potions and poultices they laid on it seemed only to inflame it the more. He began to fear that he would never dance again, and the news that King Francis of France was in high spirits and good health made him all the more sour.

The season of Lent came and so there was no more dancing and no more feasting. No chance either that Anne might seduce him into her bed and get another baby in her belly. No-one, not even the king and the queen, could lie together in Lent and so Anne had to endure the sight of Henry seated on a padded chair, his lame leg resting on a footstool, with Jane reading devotional tracts at his side, in the knowledge that she could not even claim her right as his wife that he should come to her bed.

She was surpassed and overlooked. Every day there were fewer and fewer ladies in her chamber, they were nominated and paid to be ladies in waiting to the queen but they were all in Jane Seymour's rooms. The only ones who stayed faithful were those who were not welcome anyway: our family, Madge Shelton, Aunt Anne, my daughter Catherine, and me. Some days the only gentlemen in her rooms were George and his circle of friends: Sir Francis Weston, Sir Henry Norris, Sir William Brereton. I was mixing with the very men that my husband had warned me against, but Anne had no other friends. We would play cards, or send for the musicians, or if Sir Thomas Wyatt was visiting we would hold a tournament of poetry, each man writing a line of a love sonnet to the most beautiful queen in the world; but there was something hollow at the heart of it, an empty space where the joy should be. It was all falling away from Anne and she did not know how to recapture it.

In the middle days of March she swallowed her pride and sent me to summon our uncle.

'I cannot come now, I have some business to attend to. You may tell the queen I will come to her this afternoon.'

'I did not think that one could tell a queen to wait,' I observed.

In the afternoon when he came, Anne greeted him without any sign of displeasure and drew him into the bay of a window so that they might talk alone. I was close enough to hear them speak, though neither of them ever raised their voices above a polite hiss.

'I need your help against the Seymours,' she said. 'We have to get rid of Jane.'

He shrugged regretfully. 'My niece, you have not always been as helpful to me as I might have wished. There was a moment only a little while ago when you accused me to the king himself. If you were no longer queen I do not think you could become a Howard again.'

'I am a Boleyn girl, a Howard girl,' she whispered, her hand on the golden 'B' at her throat.

'There are many Howard girls,' he said easily. 'My wife the duchess keeps house with half a dozen of them at Lambeth, cousins of yours, all as pretty as you, as Mary, as Madge. All as high-spirited, as hot-blooded. When he is weary of a milksop there will be a Howard girl to warm his bed, there always will be another one.'

'But I am the queen! Not another girl in waiting.'

He nodded. 'I will make you an offer. If George gets the Order of the Garter in April then I will stand by you. See if you can achieve that for the family and we will see what the family can do for you.'

She hesitated. 'I can ask it for him.'

'Do that,' my uncle counselled. 'If you can bring some good to the family then we can make a new contract with you, defend you against your enemies. But this time you must remember, Anne, who your master is.'

She bit the inside of her lip against defiance, she curtsied to him, and she kept her head down.

On 23 April the king gave the Order of the Garter to Sir Nicholas Carew, a friend of the Seymours, nominated by them. My brother George was

overlooked. That night at the feast given to celebrate the new awards, my uncle and Sir John Seymour were seated side by side to share a trencher of good meats, and got on together wonderfully well.

❧

Next day Jane Seymour was sitting with us in the queen's apartments for once, and so the queen's rooms were abuzz with the full complement of the court. The musicians had been called, there was to be dancing. The king was not expected, Anne had challenged him to a game of cards and he had replied coolly that he was much engaged with business.

'What's he doing?' she asked George when he came to her with the king's refusal.

'I don't know. He's seeing the bishops. And he's seeing most of the lords one by one.'

'About me?'

Carefully, neither of them looked towards Jane who was the centre of attention in the queen's own rooms.

'I don't know,' George said miserably. 'I suppose I'd be the last to know. But he did ask what men visit you daily.'

Anne looked quite blank. 'Well, they all do,' she said. 'I am the queen.'

'Certain names have been mentioned,' George said. 'Henry and Francis among them.'

Anne laughed. 'Henry Norris haunts the court for the benefit of Madge.' She turned around and saw him leaning over Madge's shoulder ready to turn the page for her as she sang. 'Sir Henry! Come here, if you please!'

With a word to Madge he came across to the queen and dropped with mock gallantry to one knee. 'I obey!' he said.

'It is time you were married, Sir Henry,' Anne said with pretended severity. 'I cannot have you hanging about my rooms bringing me into disrepute. You must make Madge an offer, I won't have my ladies other than perfectly behaved.'

He laughed outright, as well he might at the thought of Madge being perfectly behaved.

'She is my shield. My heart yearns elsewhere.'

Anne shook her head. 'I don't want pretty speeches,' she said. 'You must make a proposal of marriage to Madge and have done.'

'She is the moon but you are the sun,' Henry replied.

I rolled my eyes at George.

'Don't you sometimes want to kick him?' he whispered loudly.

'The man's an idiot,' I said. 'And this will get us nowhere.'

'I cannot offer Mistress Shelton a whole heart and so I will offer her none,' Henry said, rescuing himself from a whole tangle of politesse. 'My heart belongs to the queen of all the hearts of England.'

'Thank you,' Anne said shortly. 'You can go back to turning pages for the moon.'

Norris laughed, got to his feet and kissed her hand. 'But I cannot afford gossip in my rooms,' Anne warned. 'The king has turned severe since his fall.'

Norris kissed her hand again. 'You shall never have grounds for complaint of me,' he promised her. 'I would lay down my life for you.'

He minced back to Madge who looked up and met my eye. I made a grimace at her and she grinned back. Nothing would ever make that girl behave like a lady.

George leaned over Anne's shoulder. 'You can't scotch rumours one by one. You have to live as though none of them matter at all.'

'I will scotch every single one,' she swore. 'And you find who the king is meeting, and what they are saying about me.'

George could not discover what was happening. He sent me to my father who only looked away and told me to ask my uncle for news. I found my uncle in the stable yard, looking over a new mare he was thinking of buying. The April sunshine was hot in the sheltered yard. I waited in the shade of the gateway until he was done, then I drew close to him.

'Uncle, the king seems much engaged with Master Cromwell, and with the Master Treasurer, and with you. The queen is wondering what business is taking so much time.'

For once he did not turn from me with his bitter smile. He looked me straight in the face and his dark eyes were filled with something I had never seen in him before: pity.

'I should get your son home from his tutors,' he advised quietly. 'He is taught with Henry Norris's boy at the Cistercians, is he not?'

'Yes,' I said, confused at the change of tack.

'I should have nothing to do with Norris, or Brereton, or Weston, or Wyatt, if I were you. And if they sent any letters to you, or love poems or nonsense or tokens, I should burn them.'

'I am a married woman, and I love my husband,' I said, bewildered.

'That is your safeguard,' he agreed. 'Now go. What I know could not help you, and it burdens me alone. Go, Mary. But if I were you I would get both my children into my keeping. And I would leave court.'

I did not go to George and Anne who were anxiously waiting for me, I went straight to the king's rooms to find my husband. He was waiting in the presence chamber, the king was in his private rooms with the inner core of advisors that had kept him busy indoors for all these spring days. As soon as William saw me enter he came across the room and led me into the corridor.

'Bad news?'

'No news at all, it is like a riddle.'

'Whose riddle is it?'

'My uncle's. He tells me to have nothing to do with Henry Norris, William Brereton, Francis Weston or Thomas Wyatt. When I said I did not, he told me to take Henry away from his tutors and keep my children by me and leave court.'

William thought for a moment. 'Where's the riddle?'

'In what he means.'

He shook his head. 'Your uncle would always be a riddle to me,' he said. 'I shan't think what he means, I shall act on his advice. I shall go at once and fetch Henry home to us.'

In two strides he was back in the king's room, he touched a man on his arm and asked him to excuse him if the king called for him, he would be back within four days. Then he was out in the corridor with me, striding towards the stairs so fast that I had to run to keep up with him.

'Why? What d'you think is going to happen?' I asked, thoroughly frightened.

'I don't know. All I know is that if your uncle says that our son should not be with Henry Norris's boy, then I shall get him home. And when I have fetched him here, we are all leaving for Rochford. I don't wait to be warned twice.'

The big door to the yard was open and he ran outside. I snatched up the hem of my gown and ran after him. He shouted in the stable yard and one of the Howard lads came tumbling out and was sent running to tack up William's horse.

'I cannot take him from his tutors without Anne's permission,' I said hastily.

'I'll just get him,' William said. 'We can get permission after – if we need it. Events are going too fast for me. I want us to have your boy safe.' He caught me in his arms and kissed me firmly on the mouth. 'Sweetheart, I hate to leave you here, in the middle of it all.'

'But what could happen?'

He kissed me harder. 'God knows. But your uncle does not issue warnings lightly. I shall fetch our boy and then we will all get clear of this before it drags us down.'

'I'll run and fetch your travelling cape.'

'I'll take one of the grooms'.' He went quickly into the tack room and came out with a common cape of fustian.

'Are you in so much of a hurry you can't wait for your cape?'

'I'd rather go now,' he said simply, and that stolid certainty made me more afraid than I had ever been before for the safety of my son.

'Have you got money?'

'Enough,' he grinned. 'I just won a purse of gold off Sir Edward Seymour. A good cause, isn't it?'

'How long d'you think you will be?'

He thought for a moment. 'Three days, maybe four. No more. I'll ride without stopping. Can you wait four days for me?'

'Yes.'

'If matters get worse then take Catherine and the baby and go. I will bring Henry to you at Rochford, without fail.'

'Yes.'

One more hard kiss and then William put his foot in the stirrup and leaped up into the saddle. The horse was fresh and eager but he held her to a walk as they went under the archway and out onto the road. I shaded my eyes with my hand and watched him go. In the bright sunlight of the stable yard I shivered as if the only man who could save me was leaving.

❀

Jane Seymour did not reappear in the queen's apartments and a strange quietness fell over the sunny rooms. The maids still came in and did their work, the fire was lit, the chairs arranged, the tables laid with fruit and water and wine, everything was prepared for company but none came.

Anne and I, my daughter Catherine, Aunt Anne, and Madge Shelton sat uneasily in the big echoing rooms. My mother never came, she had withdrawn from us as completely as if we had never been born. We never saw my father. My uncle looked through us as if we were panes of Venetian glass.

'I feel like a ghost,' Anne said. We were walking by the river, she was leaning on George's arm. I was walking behind her with Sir Francis Weston, Madge was behind me with Sir William Brereton. I could hardly speak for anxiety. I did not know why my uncle had named these men to me. I did not know what secrets they brought with them. I felt as if there were a conspiracy and at any moment a trap might be sprung and I had walked into it, knowing nothing.

'They are holding some kind of hearing,' George said. 'I got that much from a page who went in to pour the wine for them. Secretary Cromwell, our uncle, the Duke of Suffolk, the rest of them.'

Carefully, my brother and sister did not exchange a glance. 'They can have nothing against me,' Anne said.

'No,' George said. 'But they can trump up charges. Think of what was said against Queen Katherine.'

Anne suddenly rounded on him. 'It's the dead baby,' she said suddenly. 'Isn't it? And the testimony of that foul old midwife with her mad lies.'

George nodded. 'Must be. They have nothing else.'

She whirled on her heel and took off towards the palace. 'I'll show them!' she cried.

George and I ran after her. 'Show them what?'

'Anne!' I cried. 'Don't be too hasty!'

'I have crept around this palace like a little mouse afraid of my own shadow for three months!' she exclaimed. 'You advised me to be sweet. I have been sweet! Now I shall defend myself. They are holding a secret hearing to try me in secret! I shall make them speak out! I shan't be condemned by a pack of old men who have always hated me. I shall show them!'

She ran across the grass to the doorway into the palace. George and I froze for a moment, and then we turned to the others. 'Do go on walking,' I said wildly.

'We will go to the queen,' George said.

Francis put out a quick instinctive hand to keep George with him.

'It's all right,' George reassured him. 'But I'd better go with her.'

George and I ran across the grass and followed Anne into the palace. She was not outside the king's presence chamber and the soldier on the door said she had not been admitted. We drew a blank and waited, wondering where she had gone, when we heard her steps running on the stairs. She had the Princess Elizabeth in her arms, gurgling and laughing at being snatched up from her nursery, watching the flicker of light as Anne ran with her.

She was unbuttoning the child's little gown as she ran. She nodded to the soldier who flung open the door for her and she was into the presence chamber before they realised she was upon them.

'What am I accused of?' she demanded of the king as she was half-over the threshold.

Awkwardly he rose from the head of the table. Anne's angry black gaze raked the noblemen seated around him.

'Who dares say a word against me to my face?'

'Anne,' the king started.

She turned on him. 'You have been filled with lies and poison against me,' she said rapidly. 'I have a right to better treatment. I have been a good wife to you, I have loved you better than any other woman has ever done.'

He leaned on the back of his heavy carved chair. 'Anne . . .'

'I have not brought a son to full term yet but that is not my fault,' she said passionately. 'Katherine did not either. Did you call her a witch for it?'

There was a hiss and a murmur at her naming the most potent word in that casual way. I saw one fist clench with the thumb between second and third finger, making the sign of the cross, to ward off witchcraft.

'But I have given you a princess,' Anne cried out. 'The most beautiful princess that ever was. With your hair and your eyes, undeniably your child. When she was born you said that it was early days and we would have sons. You were not afraid of your shadow then, Henry!'

She had half-stripped the little girl and now she held her out for him to see. Henry flinched back though the child called out 'Papa!' and held out her arms for him.

'Her skin is perfect, she has not a blemish on her body, not a mark anywhere! No-one can tell me that this is not a child blessed by God. No-one can tell me that she is not going to be the greatest princess this country has ever had! I have brought you this blessing, this beautiful child! And I shall bring you more! Can you look at her and not know that she will have a brother as strong and as beautiful as she is?'

Princess Elizabeth looked around at the stern faces. Her lower lip trembled. Anne held her in her arms, her face bright with invitation and challenge. Henry looked at them both, then he turned his head away from his wife, and he ignored his little daughter.

I had thought that Anne would fly into a rage that he did not have the courage to face them, but when he turned his head away the passion suddenly went out of her as if she knew that his mind was made up, and that she would suffer for his stubborn wilful stupidity.

'Oh my God, Henry, what have you done?' she whispered.

He said only one word. He said 'Norfolk!' and my uncle rose from his seat at the table, and looked around for George and for me, hovering in the doorway, not knowing what we should do.

'Take your sister away,' he said to us. 'You should never have allowed her to come here.'

Silently, we stepped into the room. I took little Elizabeth from Anne's arms and she came to me with a cry of pleasure and settled on my hip, her arm around my neck. George put one arm around Anne's waist and drew her from the room.

I looked back as we went out. Henry had not moved. He kept his face turned away from us Boleyns and our little princess until the door shut behind us and we were closed out, and still we did not know what they were discussing, what they had decided, nor what would happen next.

∾

We went back to Anne's rooms, the nursemaid came and took Elizabeth away. I released her with regret, conscious of my desire to hold my own baby. I was thinking of William, wondering how far he was down the road to fetch my son. The sense of foreboding hung over the palace like a storm.

As we opened the door to her private room, a lithe figure sprang forward and Anne screamed and fell back. George had a dagger at the ready, he nearly stabbed before he stopped himself.

'Smeaton!' he said. 'What the devil are you doing here?'

'I came to see the queen,' the lad said.

'For God's sake, I nearly ran you through. You shouldn't be here without invitation. Get out, lad. Go!'

'I have to ask . . . I have to say . . .'

'Out,' George said.

'Will you bear witness for me, Your Majesty?' Smeaton cried over his shoulder as George thrust him towards the door. 'They called me in and asked me so many questions.'

'Wait a minute,' I said urgently. 'Questions about what?'

Anne dropped into the windowseat and looked away. 'What does it matter?' she said. 'They'll be asking everybody everything.'

'They asked if I had been familiar with you, Your Majesty,' the lad said, blushing as scarlet as a girl. 'Or with you, sir,' he said to George. 'They asked if I had been a Ganymede to you. I didn't know what they meant, and then they told me.'

'And you said?' George demanded.

'I said no. I didn't want to tell them . . .'

'Good,' George said. 'Stick to that and don't come near the queen or me or my sister again.'

'But I'm afraid,' the lad said. He was trembling with earnestness, there were tears in his eyes. They had questioned him for hours about vices he had never even heard of. They were hardened old soldiers and princes of the church, they knew more about sin than he would ever learn. And then he had come running to us for help and was finding none.

George took him by the elbow and walked him to the door. 'Get this into your thick and pretty head,' he said flatly. 'You are innocent, and you have told them so, and you just might get away with it. But if they find you here, they will think that you are our lad, suborned by us. So get out and stay out. This is the worst place in the world to come for help.'

He pushed him to the door, but the lad clung to the frame even as the soldier waited outside for a word from George to throw him down the stairs.

'And don't mention Sir Francis,' George said in a rapid undertone. 'Nor anything that you have ever seen or heard. D'you understand? Say nothing.'

The boy still clung on. 'I have said nothing!' he exclaimed. 'I have been true. But what if they ask me again? Who will protect me? Who will stand my friend?'

George nodded to the soldier who made a swift downward chopping blow on the boy's forearm. He released the door with a yelp of pain as George slammed it in his face. 'No-one,' George said grimly. 'Just as no-one will protect us.'

❋

Next day was May Day. Anne should have been woken at dawn with her ladies singing under her window and the maidens processing with peeled willow wands. But no-one had organised it and so, for the first year ever, it did not happen. She woke haggard and pale at the usual time and spent the first hour of the day on her knees at the prie dieu, before going to Mass at the head of her ladies.

Jane followed behind in white and green. The Seymours had brought in the may with flowers and singing, Jane had slept with flowers under her pillow and had, no doubt, dreamed of her husband-to-be. I looked at her bland sweet face and wondered if she knew how high were the stakes in the game she was playing. She smiled back at my hard face and wished me a joyous May morning.

We filed past the king's chapel and he looked away as Anne went by. She kneeled for the prayers and followed them carefully, saying every word, as pious as Jane herself. When the service was over and we were leaving the church the king emerged from his gallery and said briefly to her: 'You will attend the tournament?'

'Yes,' Anne said, surprised. 'Of course.'

'Your brother is in the lists to ride against Henry Norris,' he said, watching her closely.

499

Anne shrugged her shoulders. 'And so?' she asked.

'You will have trouble choosing a champion for that joust.' His every word was heavy with meaning, as if Anne should know what he was talking about.

Anne looked past him to me, as if I might help her. I raised my eyebrows. I did not know either.

'I should favour my brother as every good sister would do,' she said carefully. 'But Henry Norris is a very gentle knight.'

'Perhaps you cannot choose between them,' the king suggested.

There was something pitiful in her puzzled smile. 'No, sire. Which would you want me to choose?'

His face darkened at once. 'Be sure that I shall watch and see who you do choose,' he said with sudden abrupt spite, and he turned away, his limp very pronounced, his sore leg fat with the padding over the wound. Anne wordlessly watched him go.

❧

The afternoon was hot and heavy, low clouds pressed down on the palace and the tiltyard was stultifying in the heat. Every other moment I found I was looking towards the road to London to see if William was returning, though I knew I could not expect him for another two days.

Anne was dressed in silver and white, carrying a white may wand as if she had been maying like a carefree girl in springtime. The knights prepared to joust in the tournament, riding in a circle before the royal gallery, their helmets under their arms, smiling up at the king with the queen seated beside him, and at the ladies behind her.

'Shall you take a wager?' the king asked Anne.

I saw the readiness of her smile at his normal tone of voice.

'Oh yes!' she said.

'Who do you like best for the first joust?'

It was the same question that he had put to her in the chapel.

'I must back my brother,' she said, smiling. 'We Boleyns must stick together.'

'I have lent Norris my own horse,' the king warned her. 'I think you will find he is the better man.'

She laughed. 'Then I shall give my favour to him and put my money on my brother. Would that please Your Majesty?'

He nodded, saying nothing.

Anne took a handkerchief from her gown and leaned towards the edge of the royal gallery and beckoned to Sir Henry Norris. He rode towards her and dipped his lance to her in salute. She reached out with her handkerchief and gracefully, holding the sidling horse still with one hand, he pointed the lance towards her hand and lifted the handkerchief from her in one smooth easy movement. It was beautifully done, the ladies in the gallery applauded and Norris smiled, dropped the lance through his hand, snatched the handkerchief from the top and tucked it into his breastplate.

Everyone was watching Norris but I was watching the king. I saw on his face a look I had never seen before but one I had somehow realised was there, like a shadow. The look he turned on Anne when she gave her kerchief to Norris was that of a man who has used a cup and is going to break it. A man who is weary of a dog and is going to drown it. He had finished with my sister. I saw it in that look. All I did not know was how he would be rid of her.

There was a rumble of thunder, as ominous as the roar of a baited bear, and the king shouted that the tournament should begin. My brother won the first joust, and Norris the second, and then my brother the third. He took his horse back to the lines to let the next challenger take his place and Anne stood up to applaud him.

The king sat still, watching Anne. In the heat of the afternoon his leg began to stink but he took no notice. He was offered drink, some early strawberries. He ate and drank, he took a little wine and some cakes. The jousting went on. Anne turned and smiled at him, engaged him in talk. He sat beside her as if he were her judge, as if it were the day of judgement.

At the end of the joust Anne stood up to deliver the prizes. I did not even see who had won, I was watching the king as Anne gave the prizes and extended her little hand for a kiss. The king heaved himself to his feet and went to the back of the gallery. I saw him point to Henry Norris and beckon him as he left. Norris, stripped of his armour but still on his sweating horse, turned and rode round to meet the king in the rear of the gallery.

'Where's the king going?' Anne said, looking round.

I glanced towards the London road, longing for the sight of William's horse. But there, on the road, was the king's standard, there was the unmistakable bulk of the king on his horse. There was Norris beside him, and a small escort of men. They were riding quickly, west to London.

'Where is he going in such haste?' Anne demanded, uneasily. 'Did he say he was leaving?'

Jane Parker stepped forward. 'Didn't you know?' she asked brightly. 'Secretary Cromwell had that lad Mark Smeaton at his house all last night and has now taken him to the Tower. He sent to tell the king so. Perhaps the king is going to the Tower to see what the lad has confessed to? But why should he take Henry Norris?'

George and I were with Anne in her rooms like prisoners in hiding. We sat in silence. We had a sense of being completely besieged.

'I shall leave at first light,' I said to Anne. 'I am sorry, Anne, I must get Catherine away.'

'Where is William?' George asked.

'He went to fetch Henry home from his tutor.'

Anne's head came up at that. 'Henry is my ward,' she reminded me. 'You cannot take him without my consent.'

For once I did not rise to her. 'For God's sake, Anne, let me keep him safe. This is no time for you and I to quarrel over who can claim what. I shall keep him safe and if I can protect Elizabeth, I shall guard her too.'

She paused for a moment as if even now she would compete with me, but then she nodded. 'Shall we play cards?' she asked lightly. 'I can't sleep. Shall we play all night?'

'All right. Just let me go and make sure that Catherine is sleeping.'

I went to find my daughter. She had been at dinner with the other ladies and told me that the hall was buzzing with gossip. The king's throne was empty. Cromwell was missing too. No-one knew why Smeaton had been arrested. No-one knew why the king had ridden away with Norris. If it had been a mark of special honour then where were they tonight? Where were they dining on this special May Day night?

'Never mind,' I said repressively. 'I want you to pack a few things, a clean shift, and some clean stockings in a bag, and be ready to leave tomorrow.'

'Are we in danger?' She was not surprised, she was a child of the court now, she would never be a girl fresh from the country again.

'I don't know,' I said shortly. 'And I want you strong enough to ride all day, so you must sleep now. D'you promise?'

She nodded. I put her into my bed, and let her rest her head on the pillow where William usually lay. I prayed to God that tomorrow would bring William and Henry back and we all might go together, to where the apple tree leaned low over the road, and the little farm nestled in the sunshine. Then I kissed her goodnight and sent a pageboy running to our lodgings to warn the wet nurse that she must be ready to leave at dawn.

I slipped back to the queen's rooms. Anne was huddled over the fire with George at her side, seated on the hearthrug as if they were both chilled though the windows stood open and the hot airless night did not even stir the hangings.

'Boleyns,' I said, coming quietly through the door.

George turned and put an arm out for me and pulled me down beside him so he could hold us both.

'Bet you we brush through this,' he said stoutly. 'Bet you we rise up and confound them all, and this time next year Anne has a boy in the cradle and I am a Knight of the Garter.'

∽

We spent the night huddled together like vagrants in fear of the beadle, and when the window started to grow light I went quietly down the stairs to the stable yard and threw a stone up at the window where the grooms slept. The first lad who put out his head got the job of pulling my horse out of the stable and tacking her up. But when he had Catherine's hunter in the yard he stopped and shook his head. 'Cast a shoe,' he said.

'What?'

'I'll have to take her to the smith.'

'Can she go now?'

'Smithy won't be open yet.'

'Tell him to open it!'

'Mistress, the forge will be cold. He has to wake and light the fire and get the forge hot and then he can shoe her.'

I swore in my frustration and turned away from him. 'You could take another horse,' the lad suggested, yawning.

I shook my head. It was a long ride and Catherine was not a strong enough rider to manage a new horse. 'No,' I said. 'We'll have to wait for the mare to be shod. Take her to the smith and wake him and get him to shoe her. Then come and find me, wherever I am, and tell me privately that she is ready. And don't tell the rest of the castle.' I glanced anxiously at the dark windows of the palace looking down on me. 'I don't want every fool in the world to know I am riding out.'

He pulled his forelock, his hand cupped empty air. I slid a coin from the pocket of my gown into his grimy palm. 'There's another one for you, if you do this right.'

I went back into the palace. The sentry at the door raised a sleepy eyebrow at me, wondering what I was doing strolling out at dawn and back in again. I knew he would report to someone: Secretary Cromwell, or perhaps my uncle, or perhaps Sir John Seymour, who was now grown so great that he must have men watching for him too.

I hesitated on the stairs. I wanted to go and see Catherine, sleeping sweetly in my big bed; but there was candlelight under the door of the queen's apartments and I felt I belonged to the night-long vigil of the two of them. The sentry stepped to one side and I opened the door and slipped in.

Still they were wakeful, cheek to cheek in the firelight, whispering as soothingly as a pair of doves cooing in the cote. Their heads turned together as I came into the room.

'Not gone?' Anne asked.

'Catherine's horse has cast a shoe. I couldn't go.'

'When will you leave?' George asked.

'As soon as she is shod. I paid a lad to take her to the smith and tell me as soon as she is fit to ride.'

I crossed the room and sat on the hearthrug with them. We all three turned our faces to the fire and watched the flames. 'I wish we could stay here like this, for always,' Anne said dreamily.

'Do you?' I said, surprised. 'I was thinking that this is the worst night of my life. I was wishing that it had never started and that I might wake up in a moment and it could all have been a dream.'

George's smile was dark. 'That's because you don't fear tomorrow,' he said. 'If you feared tomorrow as much as we do, you would wish that the night would go on forever.'

However they wished, it grew steadily lighter, and we heard the servants stirring in the great hall and then a maid clanking up the stairs with a bucket of kindling to light the fire in the queen's bedroom, followed by another with brushes and cloths to wipe the tables for the start of another new day.

Anne rose up from the hearthrug, her face bleak, her cheeks smeared with ash as if she had been mourning in church on Ash Wednesday.

'Have a bath,' George said encouragingly to her. 'It's so early. Send them for your bath and have a hot bath and wash your hair. You'll feel so much better after.'

She smiled at the banality of the suggestion and then she nodded.

George leaned forward and kissed her. 'I'll see you at matins,' he said, and he went from the room.

It was the last time we saw my brother as a free man.

George was not at matins. Anne and I, rosy from our bath and feeling more confident, looked for him but he was not there. Sir Francis did not know where he was, nor Sir William Brereton. Henry Norris had still not returned from London. There was no news of what charge was laid against Mark Smeaton. The weight of fear came down on us again, like the low bellies of the clouds which rested on the palace roofs.

I sent a message to my baby's wet nurse to wait for my coming, we would try to leave within the next hour.

There was a tennis match and Anne had promised to award the prize, a gold coin on a gold chain. She went to the courts and sat under the awning, her head moving, with all the discipline of a dancer, to the left and to the right, her head following the ball but her eyes sightless.

I was standing behind her, waiting for the lad from the stables to come and tell me that the horse was ready, Catherine was at my side, waiting only for my word to run and change into her riding gown, when the gate to the royal enclosure opened behind me and two soldiers of the guard came in with an officer. The moment that I saw them I had the sense of something profound and dreadful happening. I opened my mouth to speak but no words came. Mutely, I touched Anne's shoulder. She turned and looked up at me, and then beyond me to the hard faces of the men.

They did not bow as they should have done. It was that which confirmed our fear. That, and the screaming of a seagull which suddenly flew low over the court and shrieked like an injured girl.

'The Privy Council commands your presence, Your Majesty,' the captain said shortly.

Anne said, 'Oh,' and rose up. She looked at Catherine and she looked at me. She looked around at all her ladies and suddenly their eyes were everywhere but looking at her. They were quite fascinated by the tennis. They had learned Anne's trick, their heads went left, right, while their eyes saw nothing and their ears were on the prick and their hearts were pounding in case she commanded them to go with her.

'I must have my companions,' Anne said flatly. Not one of the little vixens looked around. 'Some lady must come with me.' Her eyes fell on Catherine.

'No,' I said suddenly, seeing what she would do. 'No, Anne. No. I beg you.'

'I can take a companion?' she asked the captain.

'Yes, Your Majesty.'

'I shall take my maid in waiting, Catherine,' she said simply, and then she went quietly out of the gate which the soldier held open for her. Catherine shot one bewildered glance at me and then fell into step behind her queen.

'Catherine!' I said sharply.

She looked back at me, she did not know, poor little girl, what she should do.

'Come along,' Anne said in her dead calm voice, and Catherine gave me a little smile.

'Be of good cheer,' she said suddenly, oddly; as if she were acting a part in a play. Then she turned and followed the queen with all the composure of a princess.

I was too stunned to do anything but watch them go, but the minute they were out of sight I picked up my skirts and fled up the path to the palace to find George, or my father, anyone who might help Anne, and who would get Catherine away from her, safely back to me, and on the road to Rochford.

I ran into the hall and a man caught me as I headed for the stairs, I pushed him away and then I realised it was the one man in the whole world that I wanted. 'William!'

'Love, my love. You know, then?'

'Oh my God, William. They have taken Catherine! They have taken my girl!'

'Arrested Catherine? On what charge?'

'No! She is with Anne. As maid in waiting. And Anne is ordered to the Privy Council.'

'In London?'

'No, meeting here.'

He released me at once, swore briefly, took half a dozen steps in a small circle and then came back to me and caught up my hands. 'We'll just have to wait then, until she comes out.' He scanned my face. 'Don't look like that, Catherine is a little lass. They're questioning the queen, not her. They probably won't even speak to her, and if they do she has nothing to hide.'

I took a shuddering breath and nodded. 'No. She has nothing to hide. She has seen nothing that is not common knowledge. And they would only question her. She is gentry. They wouldn't do anything worse. Where is Henry?'

'Safe. I left him at our lodgings with the wet nurse and the baby. I thought you were running because of your brother.'

'What about him?' I said suddenly, my heart hammering again. 'What about George?'

'They've arrested him.'

'With Anne?' I said. 'To answer to the Privy Council?'

William's face was dark. 'No,' he said. 'They have taken him to the Tower. Henry Norris is there already, the king himself rode with him into the Tower yesterday. And Mark Smeaton – you remember the singer? – he is there too.'

My lips were too numb to frame any words. 'But what is the charge? And why question the queen here?'

He shook his head. 'Nobody knows.'

❁

We waited until noon for any further news. I hovered in the hall outside the chamber where the Privy Council were questioning the queen but I was not allowed into the antechamber for fear that I might listen at the door.

'I don't want to listen, I just want to see my daughter,' I explained to the sentry. He nodded and said nothing, but gestured me back from the threshold.

A little after noon the door opened and a pageboy slipped out and whispered to the sentry. 'You have to go,' the sentry said to me. 'My orders are to clear the way.'

'For what?' I asked.

'You have to go,' he said stubbornly. He gave a shout down the stairs to the great hall and an answering shout came ringing up. They gently pushed me to one side, away from the Privy Council door, away from the stairs, away from the hall, away from the garden door, and then out of the very garden itself. All the other courtiers encountered on the way were thrust to one side too. We all went as we were bid; it was as if we had not recognised how powerful the king was before that moment.

I realised that they had cleared a way from the Privy Council room to the river stairs. I ran to the landing stage where the common people disembarked when they came to the palace. There were no guards on the common landing stage, no-one to stop me standing at the very end of it, straining my eyes to see towards the Greenwich Palace stairs.

I saw them clearly: Anne in her blue gown that she had worn to watch the tennis, Catherine a pace behind her in her yellow gown. I was pleased to see that she had her cloak with her, in case it was cold on the river, then I shook my head at the folly of worrying if she would catch cold when I did not know where they were taking her. I watched them intently, as if by watching I could protect her. They went in the king's barge, not the queen's ship, and the roll of the drum for the rowers sounded to me as ominous and as doleful as the roll of drums when the executioner raises his axe.

'Where are you going?' I shouted as loudly as I could, unable to contain my fear any longer.

Anne did not hear me but I saw the white shape of Catherine's face as she turned towards my voice, and looked all around for me in the palace garden.

'Here! Here!' I shouted more loudly and I waved to her. She looked towards me and she raised her hand in a tiny gesture, and then followed Anne on board the king's barge.

The soldiers pushed off in one smooth motion the moment that they had them on board. The lurch of the boat threw them both into their seats and there was a moment when I lost sight of her. Then I saw her again. She was seated on a little chair, next to Anne, and she was looking out over the water towards me. The oarsmen took the barge into the middle of the river and rowed easily with the inflowing tide.

I did not try to call again, I knew that the rowers' drum would drown out my voice, and I did not want to frighten Catherine, hearing her mother crying out for her. I stood very still and I raised my hand to her so that she could see that I knew where she was, and I knew where she was going, and I would come for her as soon as ever I could.

I sensed but did not look round as William came behind me and raised his hand to our daughter as well. 'Where d'you think they're taking them?' he asked, as if he did not know the answer as well as me.

'You know where,' I said. 'Why ask me? To the worst place we can think of. To the Tower.'

❧

William and I did not delay. We went straight to our room and threw a few clothes into a bag and then hurried to the stables. Henry was waiting with the horses, and he had a quick hug and a bright smile for me before William threw me up into the saddle and mounted his own horse. We took Catherine's horse with us, newly shod. Henry led her alongside his own hunter while William led the wet nurse's broad-backed cob. She was waiting for us and we had her up in the saddle and the baby strapped safely at her breast and then we went quietly out of the palace and up the road to London without telling anyone where we were going nor how long we would be gone.

William took rooms for us behind the Minories, away from the riverside. I could see the Beauchamp Tower where Anne and my daughter were imprisoned. My brother and the other men were somewhere nearby. It was the tower where Anne had spent the night before her coronation. I wondered if she remembered now the great gown that she wore and the silence of the City which warned her then that she would never be a beloved queen.

William ordered the woman of the house to make a dinner for us and went out to gather news. He came back in time to eat and when the woman had served dinner and got herself out of the room he told me what he knew. The inns around the Tower were all buzzing with the news that the queen had been taken up, and the word was that her charge was adultery and witchcraft and no-one knew what else.

I nodded. This sealed Anne's fate. Henry was using the power of gossip, the voice of the mob, to pave the way to an annulment of the marriage, and a new queen. Already in the taverns they were saying that the king was in love again and this time with a beautiful and innocent girl, an English girl from Wiltshire, God bless her, and as devout and sweet as Anne had been over-educated and French-influenced. From somewhere, someone had gathered the certainty that Jane Seymour was a friend to Princess Mary. She had served Queen Katherine well. She prayed in the old ways, she did not read disputatious books nor argue with men who knew better. Her family were not grasping lords but honest honourable men. And it was a fertile family. There could be no doubt but Jane Seymour would have sons where Katherine and Anne had both failed.

'And my brother?'

William shook his head. 'No news.'

I closed my eyes. I could not imagine a world where George was not free to come and go as he pleased. Who could accuse George? Who could blame him for anything, so sweet and so feckless?

'And who is waiting on Anne?' I asked.

'Your aunt, Madge Shelton's mother, and a pair of other ladies.'

I made a face. 'No-one she likes or trusts. But at least she can release Catherine now. She's not alone.'

'I thought you could write. She could have a letter if it was left open. I'll take it to William Kingston, the constable of the Tower and ask him to give it to her.'

I ran down the narrow stairs to the lodging-house keeper and asked her for a piece of paper and a pen. She let me use her writing desk and lit a candle for me as I sat by the window for the last of the light.

> Dear Anne,
> I know that you are served by other ladies now so please release
> Catherine from your service as I need her with me.
> I beg you to let her come away now.
> Mary.

I dripped some candle wax and put my sealing ring into the puddle of wax to show the 'B' for Boleyn. But I left the letter open and gave it to William.

'Good,' he said, reading it quickly. 'I'll take it straightaway. Nobody can think you mean anything other than you say. I'll wait for an answer. Perhaps I'll bring her back with me and we can leave for Rochford tomorrow.'

I nodded. 'I'll wait up.'

Henry and I played cards in front of the little fire on a rickety table sitting on two wooden stools. We were playing for farthings and I was winning all of Henry's pocket money. Then I cheated to let him win a little back, misjudged it, and was bankrupted in earnest. Still William did not come.

At midnight he came in. 'I am sorry to have been so long,' he said to my white face. 'I don't have her.'

I gave a little moan and at once he reached out to me and pulled me close to him. 'I saw her,' he said. 'That was why I was so long. I thought you would want me to see her and know that she was well.'

'Is she distressed?'

'Very calm,' he said with a smile. 'You can go and see her tomorrow yourself at this time, and every day until the queen is released.'

'But she can't come away?'

'The queen wants to keep her and the constable is under instructions to give her whatever she reasonably desires.'

'Surely . . .'

'I tried everything,' William said. 'But it is the queen's right to have attendants, and Catherine is the only one that she actually requested. The others are more or less forced on her. One of them is the constable's own wife, who is there to spy on everything she says.'

'And how is Catherine?'

'You would be proud of her. She sent you her love and said that she would like to stay and serve the queen. She says that Anne is ill and faint and weeping and that she wants to stay with her while she can help.'

I gave a little gasp, half of love and pride, half of impatience. 'She's a little girl, she shouldn't even be there!'

'She is a young woman,' William said. 'She is doing her duty as a young woman should. And she's in no danger. No-one is going to ask her anything. Everyone is clear that she is in the Tower as Anne's companion. No harm will come to her because of it.'

'And is Anne to be charged?'

William glanced towards Henry and then decided that he was old enough to know. 'It looks as if Anne is to be charged with adultery. D'you know what adultery is, Henry?'

The boy blushed a little. 'Yes, sir. It's in the Bible.'

'I believe it is a false charge against your aunt,' William said levelly.
'But it is a charge that the Privy Council has chosen to bring against her.'

At last I was beginning to understand. 'And the others arrested too?
They're charged with her?'

William nodded, tight-lipped. 'Yes. Henry Norris and Mark Smeaton
are to be charged with her, for being her lovers.'

'That's nonsense,' I said flatly.

William nodded.

'And my brother is taken for questioning?'

'Yes,' he said.

Something in his tone of voice alerted me. 'They're not putting him
on the rack?' I asked. 'They're not hurting him?'

'Oh no,' William assured me. 'They won't forget he's gentry. They'll
keep him in the Tower while they question her and the others.'

'But what are they charging him with?'

William hesitated, a glance to my son. 'He's charged with the other
men.'

For a moment I did not understand him. Then I said the word:
'Adultery?'

He nodded.

I was silent. My first thought was to cry out and deny it, but then I
remembered Anne's absolute need for a son, and her certainty that the
king could not give her a healthy baby. I remembered her leaning back
against George and telling him that the church could not be relied upon
to rule on what was and what was not sin. And him telling her that he
could have been excommunicated ten times before breakfast – and she had
laughed. I did not know what Anne might have done in her desperation. I
did not know what George might have dared in his recklessness. I turned
my thoughts away from the two of them, as I had done before. 'What
shall we do?' I asked.

William put his arm around my son and smiled down at him. Henry
was up to his step-father's shoulder now, he looked at him trustingly.

'We'll wait,' William said. 'As soon as this mess is sorted out we'll have
Catherine away and we'll go home to Rochford. And then we'll keep our
heads down for a bit. Because whether Anne is set aside and allowed to
live in a nunnery, or exiled, I think the Boleyns have had their moment.
It's time to go back to making cheese for you, my love.'

❁

The next day there was nothing to do but wait. I let the wet nurse go
away for the day and encouraged William and Henry to stroll about the

town and take their dinner in an ale house while I stayed home and played with the baby. In the afternoon I took her for a little walk down to the river's edge and felt the wind from the sea blowing against our faces. I unswaddled her when I got her home and gave her a cool bath, rumpling her sweet rosy body in a linen sheet and patting her dry, and then let her kick, free of her swaddling bands for a while. I bound her up in fresh bands in time for the others coming in for their dinner and then I left her with the nurse while William and Henry and I went down to the great gate of the Tower and asked if Catherine might come out to see us.

She looked very small as she walked along the inner wall from the Beauchamp Tower to the gateway. But she walked like a Boleyn girl, as if she owned the place, with her head up, looking around her, a pleasant smile to one of the passing guards and then a bright beam to me through the grille as they unlocked the door within the wooden gate and let her slip out.

I wrapped her in my arms. 'My love.'

She hugged me back and then sprang towards Henry. 'Hen!'

'Cat!'

They looked at each other with mutual delight. 'Grown,' she said.

'Fatter,' he replied.

William smiled at me over their heads. 'D'you think they ever use whole sentences?'

'Catherine, I wrote to Anne to ask her to release you,' I said hastily. 'I want you to come away.'

At once she was grave. 'I can't. She is in such distress. You've never seen her like this. I can't just leave her. And the other ladies around her are useless, two of them don't know what they're doing and the other two are my Aunt Boleyn and Aunt Shelton and they sit in a corner all the time and mutter behind their hands. I can't leave her with them.'

'What does she do all day?' Henry asked.

Catherine flushed. 'She cries, and prays. That's why I can't leave her. I just couldn't go. It would be like leaving a baby. She can't care for herself.'

'Are you well fed?' I asked hopelessly. 'Where d'you sleep?'

'I sleep with her,' Catherine said. 'But she hardly sleeps at all. And we could eat as well as we did at court. It's all right, Mother. And it's not for long.'

'How d'you know?'

The captain of the guard leaned forward and said quietly to William, 'Have a care, Sir William.'

William looked at me. 'We gave an undertaking that we would not discuss the matter with Catherine. This is just for us to see her and know that she is well.'

I took a breath. 'Very well. But Catherine, if this goes on for more than a week you will have to come away.'

'I'll do as you say,' she said sweetly.

'Do you need anything? Shall I bring you anything tomorrow?'

'Some clean linen,' she said. 'And the queen needs another gown or two. Can you get them for her from Greenwich?'

'Yes,' I said, resigned. It seemed that all my life I had been running errands for Anne and even now, at this great crisis in our affairs, I was still at her beck and call.

William looked at the captain of the guard. 'Is that well with you, Captain? That my wife brings some linen and gowns for the ladies?'

'Yes, sir,' the man said. He tipped his hat to me. 'Of course.'

I smiled grimly. No-one had imprisoned a queen with no evidence and no charge before. It was difficult to know which was the safe side.

I held Catherine to me once more and felt her smooth hair at the front of her hood just under my chin. I pressed a kiss on her forehead and smelt the scent of her young warm skin. I could hardly bear to let her go but she slipped through the gate and went back down the stone-paved path under the great shadow of the tower and paused and waved, and was gone.

William raised his hand as she went and then turned back to me. 'One thing the Boleyns have never lacked is absolute folly-driven courage,' he said. 'If you were horses I'd have no other breed because you'd jump anything. But as women you are insanely difficult to live with.'

May 1536

I took a boat downriver to Greenwich to fetch the queen's gowns and Catherine's extra linen, leaving William, Henry and the baby behind at the lodgings near the Tower. William was uneasy at my going without him and I was fearful too, it felt like going back into danger, returning to Greenwich Palace; but I preferred to go alone and to know that my son – that precious and rare commodity, a son of the king – was out of sight of the court. I promised to be no longer than a couple of hours and to stop for nothing.

It was an easy matter to get into my rooms but the queen's apartments were sealed on the word of the Privy Council. I thought of finding my uncle and asking him for Anne's gowns and linen and then I concluded that it was not worth drawing attention to another Boleyn girl when the first one was in the Tower for unnamed crimes. I bundled up some gowns of my own for her and was slipping from the room just as Madge Shelton came by. 'Good God, I thought you were arrested,' she said.

'Why?'

'Why is anyone arrested? You were gone. Of course I thought you were in the Tower. Did they let you go after questioning?'

'I've never been arrested at all,' I said patiently. 'I went to London to be with Catherine. She went with Anne as her maid in waiting. She's in the Tower with her still. I just came back for some linen.'

Madge dropped into a windowseat and burst into tears.

I threw a swift glance down the gallery and shifted my bundle from one arm to another. 'Madge, I have to go. What's the matter?'

'Dear God, I thought you were arrested and they would come for me next.'

'Why?'

'It's like being torn apart in the bear pit,' she said. 'They questioned me all morning until I could not tell you what I had seen and heard. They twisted my words around and around and made it sound as if we were a bunch of whores in the whorehouse. I never did anything very wrong. Neither did you. But they have to know everything about everything. They have to know times and places and I felt so ashamed of everything!'

I paused for a moment, picking over the bones of this. 'The Privy Council questioned you?'

'Everyone. All the queen's ladies, the maids, even the servants. Everyone who had ever danced in her rooms. They'd have questioned Purkoy the dog if he hadn't been dead!'

'And what do they ask?'

'Who was bedding who, who was promising what? Who was giving gifts? Who was missing at matins? Everything. Who was in love with the queen, who wrote her poems? Whose songs she sang? Who did she favour? Everything.'

'And what does everyone answer?' I asked.

'Oh we all say nothing at first,' Madge said spiritedly. 'Of course. We all keep our secrets and try to keep those of others. But they know one thing from one person and one from another and in the end they turn you round and catch you out and ask you things you don't know and things you do, and all the time Uncle Howard looks at you as if you are an utter whore, and the Duke of Suffolk is so kind that you explain things to him, and then you find you have said everything you meant to keep secret.'

She finished on a great wail of tears, and mopped her eyes on a scrap of lace. Suddenly she looked up. 'You go! Because if they see you they'll have you in for questioning and the one thing they go on and on about is George and you and the queen and where were you all one night, and what were you doing another night.'

I nodded and walked away from her at once. In a moment I heard her pattering after me. 'If you see Henry Norris will you tell him that I did my very best to say nothing?' she said, as pitiful as a schoolboy hoping not to tell tales. 'They trapped me into saying that the queen and I once gambled for a kiss from him, but I never said more than that. No more than that they would have got from Jane.'

Not even the name of George's poisonous wife made me check, I was in such a hurry to get out of the place. Instead I grabbed Madge Shelton's hand and dragged her along with me as I ran down the stairs and out through the door. 'Jane Parker?'

'She was in there the longest, and she wrote out a statement and she signed it too. It was after she had spoken to them that we all had to go in again and they were asking about George. Nothing but George and the queen and how much they drank together and how often you and he were alone with her, and whether you left them alone.'

'Jane will have traduced him,' I said flatly.

'She was bragging of it,' Madge said. 'And that Seymour thing left court yesterday to stay with the Carews in Surrey, complaining of the heat while the rest of us have our lives picked over and everything torn apart.' Madge ended on a little sob, and I stopped and kissed her on both cheeks.

'Can I come with you?' she asked forlornly.

'No,' I said. 'Go to the duchess at Lambeth, she'll look after you. And don't say that you saw me.'

'I'll try not to,' she said fairly. 'But you don't know what it's like when they turn you round and around and ask you everything, over and over again.'

I nodded and left her, standing at the head of the stone steps: a pretty girl who had come to the most beautiful and elegant court in Europe, and seduced the king himself; and who had now seen the world turn around and the court turn dark and the king turn suspicious and learned that no woman, however flighty or pretty or high-spirited, could think herself safe.

∾

I took the linen to Catherine that night and told her that I could not get the gowns for the queen. I did not tell her why, I did not want to draw any attention to myself nor to our little haven in the lodgings hidden behind the Minories. I did not tell her the other news I had heard from the boatman as he rowed me back to London: that Sir Thomas Wyatt, Anne's old flame who had vied with the king for her attention all those years ago when we had all been doing nothing but playing at love, was arrested and Sir Richard Page, another of our circle, was arrested too.

'They'll come for me soon,' I said to William, sitting over the fire in our little lodging. 'They are picking up everyone who is close to her.'

'You had better stop seeing Catherine every day,' he said. 'I'll go, or we can send a maid. You can follow behind, find a place by the river where you can see her so that you know that she is well.'

The next day we changed our lodgings, and this time we gave a false name. Henry went to the Tower in place of us, dressed like a stable lad delivering Catherine's linen or books for her. He dodged through the crowd to get to the gate, and dodged home after, certain that no-one had followed him. If my uncle had ever understood that a woman can love a girl child, he would have watched Catherine and she would have led him to me. But he never knew that, of course. Few of the Howards ever realised that girls were anything more than counters to play in the marriage game.

And he had other things to do. We realised in the middle of the month that he had been busy indeed when the charges were published. William brought the news home from the bakery where he had been buying our dinner, and waited until I had eaten before he told me.

'My love,' he said gently. 'I don't know how to prepare you for this news.'

I took one look at his grave face and pushed my plate away. 'Just tell me quickly.'

'They have tried and found guilty: Henry Norris, Francis Weston, William Brereton and the lad Mark Smeaton for adultery with the queen your sister.'

For a moment I could not hear him. I could hear the words but it was as if they were coming from a long way away and muffled. Then William pulled back my chair from the table and thrust my head down and the dreamy feeling passed and I could see the floorboards beneath my boots and I struggled against him. 'Let me up, I'm not fainting.'

He released me at once but kneeled at my feet so that he could look into my face. 'I am afraid you must pray for the soul of your brother. They are certain to find against him.'

'He was not tried with the others?'

'No. They were tried in the common court. He and Anne will have to face the peers.'

'Then there will be some excuse. They will have made some arrangement.'

William looked doubtful.

I leaped up from my seat. 'I must go to court,' I said. 'I shouldn't have been skulking here in hiding like a fool. I shall go and tell them that this is wrong. Before it goes any further. If these are found guilty then I must get to court in time to testify that George is innocent, Anne too.'

He moved quicker than I, and was blocking the door before I was even two paces towards it.

'I knew you would say that and you shall not go.'

'William, this is my brother and my sister in the greatest of dangers. I have to save them.'

'No. Because if you raise your head one inch they will have it off as well as theirs. Who d'you think is hearing the evidence against these men? Who will be president of the court against your brother? Your own uncle!

Does he use his influence to save him? Does your father? No. Because they know that Anne has taught the king to be a tyrant and now he is run mad and they cannot prevent his tyranny.'

'I have to defend him,' I said, pushing against his chest. 'This is George, my beloved George. D'you think I want to go to my grave knowing that at the moment of his trial he looked around and saw no-one lift a finger for him? If it is the death of me, I shall go to him.'

Suddenly, William stepped aside. 'Go then,' he said. 'Kiss our baby goodbye before you go, and Henry. I shall tell Catherine that you left your blessing for her. And kiss me farewell. For if you go into that courtroom you will never come out alive. I should think it a certainty that you will be taken up for witchcraft at the very least.'

'For doing what, for God's sake?' I exclaimed. 'What d'you think I have done? What d'you think any of us have done?'

'Anne is to be charged with seducing the king with sorcery. Your brother is said to have helped her. That is why their trials are to be done separately. Forgive me that I didn't tell you it all at once. It's not the sort of news I like to bring to my wife with her dinner. They are accused of being lovers, and of summoning the devil. They're being tried separately not because they will be excused, but because their crimes are too great to be heard in one sitting.'

I gasped and staggered against him. William caught me, and finished what he had to tell me.

'Together they are charged with undoing the king, making him impotent with spells, perhaps with poison. Together they are accused of being lovers and making the baby which was born a monster. Some of this is going to stick, say what you will. You have been party to many late nights in Anne's room. You taught her how to seduce the king, after you had been his lover for years. You found a wise woman for her, you brought a witch into the palace itself. Didn't you? You took out dead babies. I buried one. And there's more than that – more than even I know about. Isn't there? Boleyn secrets that you have not told even me?'

As I turned away, he nodded his head. 'I thought so. Did she take spells and potions to help her conceive?' He looked at me and I nodded again. 'She poisoned Bishop Fisher, poor sainted man, and she has the deaths of three innocent men on her conscience for that. She poisoned Cardinal Wolsey and Queen Katherine . . .'

'You don't know that for sure!' I exclaimed.

He looked hard at me. 'You are her own sister and you cannot offer a better defence than that? That you don't know for sure how many she has killed?'

I hesitated. 'I don't know.'

'She is certainly guilty of dabbling in witchcraft, she is certainly guilty of seducing the king with bawdy behaviour. She is certainly guilty of threatening the queen, the bishop and the cardinal. You cannot defend her, Mary. She is guilty of at least half of the charge.'

'But George . . .' I whispered.

'George went with her in everything she did,' William said. 'And he sinned on his own account. If Sir Francis and the others were to ever confess of what they did with Smeaton and the others they would be hanged for buggery, let alone anything else.'

'He is my brother,' I said. 'I cannot desert him.'

'You can go to your own death,' William said. 'Or you can survive this, bring up your children, and guard Anne's little girl who will be shamed and bastardised and motherless by the end of this week. You can wait out this reign and see what comes next. See what the future holds for the Princess Elizabeth, defend our son Henry against those who will want to set him up as the king's heir or even worse – flaunt him as a pretender. You owe it to your children to protect them. Anne and George have made their own choices. But the Princess Elizabeth and Catherine and Henry have their choices to make in the future. You should be there to help them.'

My hands, which had been in fists against his chest, dropped to my side. 'All right,' I said dully. 'I will let them go to their trial without me. I will not go into court to defend him. But I will go and find my uncle and ask him if something cannot be done to save them.'

I expected him to refuse me this too, but he hesitated. 'Are you sure that he won't have you taken up with them? He has just sat in trial over three men he knew from their boyhood and sent them to be hanged, castrated and quartered. This is not a man in a merciful mood.'

I nodded, thinking hard. 'Very well. I'll go to my father first.'

To my relief, William nodded. 'I'll take you,' he said.

I threw on a cloak over my gown and called to the wet nurse to mind the baby and to keep Henry by her for we were going out for a visit and would only be a little while, and then William and I went from the little lodging house.

'Where is he?' I asked.

'At your uncle's house,' William said. 'Half the court is still at Greenwich but the king keeps to his rooms, he is said to be deeply grieved, but some say that he slips out every night to see Jane Seymour.'

'What happened to Sir Thomas and Sir Richard who were taken up with the others?' I asked.

William shrugged. 'Who knows? No evidence against them, or special pleading, or some kind of favour. Who ever knows when a tyrant runs mad? They are excused; but a little lad like Mark who only ever knew one thing and that was to play the lute is racked until he cries for his mother, and tells them anything they ask him.'

He took my cold hand and tucked it into his elbow. 'Here we are,' he said. 'We'll go in the stable door. I know some of the lads. I'd rather see how the land lies before we go in.'

We went quietly into the stable yard but before William could shout 'Holloa!' up at the window there was a clatter on the cobblestones and my father himself rode into the yard. I darted towards him out of the shadows and his horse shied and he swore at me.

'Forgive me, Father, I must see you.'

'You, is it?' he said abruptly. 'Where have you been hiding this last week?'

'She's been with me,' William said firmly, from behind me. 'Where she should be. And with our children. Catherine is with the queen.'

'Aye, I know,' my father said. 'The only Boleyn girl without a stain on her virtue, and that's only as far as we know.'

'Mary wants to ask you something and then we must go.'

I paused. Now it came to it, I hardly knew what I should ask my father. 'Are George and Anne to be spared?' I asked. 'Is Uncle working for them?'

He gave me a dark bitter glance. 'You would know as much about their doings as anyone,' he said. 'The three of you were as thick as sinners, God knows. You should have been questioned along with the other ladies.'

'Nothing happened,' I said passionately. 'Nothing more than you yourself know about, sir. Nothing more than Uncle himself commanded. He told me to teach Anne, to tell her how to enchant the king. He told her to conceive a baby whatever the price. He told George to stand by her and help her and comfort her. We did nothing more than that was ordered. We only ever did as we were commanded. Is she to die for being an obedient daughter?'

'Don't you bring me into it,' he said quickly. 'I had nothing to do with ordering her. She went her own way, and him and you with her.'

I gasped at his treachery and he dismounted, passed his reins to a groom and would have walked away from me. I ran after him and caught his sleeve. 'But will Uncle find a way to save her?'

He put his mouth to my ear. 'She has to go,' he said. 'The king knows she is barren and he wants another wife. The Seymours have won this round, there'll be no denying them. The marriage will be annulled.'

'Annulled? On what grounds?' I asked.

'Affinity,' he said briefly. 'Since he was your lover, he cannot be her husband.'

I blinked. 'Not me, again.'

'Just so.'

'And what happens to Anne?'

'A nunnery, if she'll go quietly. Otherwise, exile.'

'And George?'

'Exile.'

'And you, sir?'

'If I can survive this, I can survive anything,' he said glumly. 'Now, if you don't want to be called to give evidence against them you'll make yourself scarce and keep out of sight.'

'But could I give evidence for their defence, if I come to court?'

He laughed shortly.

'There *is* no evidence for them,' he reminded me. 'In a treason trial there is no defence. All they can hope for is the clemency of the court and the forgiveness of the king.'

'Should I ask the king for forgiveness for them?'

My father looked at me. 'If your name isn't Seymour then you're not welcome in his sight. If your name is Boleyn then you're due for the axe. Keep out of the way, girl. If you want to serve your sister and your brother, let the business be done as quietly and as quickly as possible.'

William drew me back into the shadow of the stable as we heard a troop of horsemen on the road. 'That's your uncle,' William said. 'Come out this way.'

We went through a stone archway to the double doors where they brought the hay wagons in. A smaller door was cut into the big timbers and William opened it and helped me through. He shut it behind us as the torches flickered into the yard and the soldiers shouted for grooms to help his lordship unsaddle.

William and I went home by dark ways, unseen in the hidden streets of the City. The nurse let us in and showed me the baby asleep in the cradle and Henry in his little pallet bed, the gingery Tudor curls in ringlets around his head.

And then William drew me into the four-poster bed and closed the curtains around us and undressed me, laid me down on the pillows and wrapped himself around me and held me, saying nothing, while I clung to him and could not get warm all night.

Anne was to be tried by the peers in the King's Hall inside the Tower of London. They were afraid to take her through the City to Westminster. The mood of the City which had sulked at her coronation was now turning to defend her. Cromwell's plan had overreached itself. There were few people who could believe that a woman could be so gross as to seduce men when she was pregnant with a baby from her own husband, as the court had claimed she had done. They could not credit that a woman would seek two, three, four lovers under the nose of her husband when her husband was the King of England. Even the women at the dockside who had shouted 'Whore!' at Anne during Queen Katherine's trials now thought that the king had run mad again and was setting aside a legal wife on a pretext, for yet another unknown favourite.

Jane Seymour had moved into the City into the beautiful house of Sir Francis Bryan in the Strand, and it was common knowledge that the king's barge was tied up at the river stairs till well after midnight every night and that there was music and feasting and dancing and masquing while the queen was in the Tower and five good men held as well, four of them under sentence of death.

Henry Percy, Anne's old love, was among the rest of the peers, sitting in judgement on the queen at whose table they had all feasted, whose hand they had all kissed, who had danced with each and every one of them. It must have been an odd experience for them all when she walked into the King's Hall and took a seat before them, the gold 'B' at her throat, her French hood set back to show her dark shining hair, her dark gown setting off her creamy skin. The constant crying and the praying before the little altar in the Tower had left her calm for the day of her trial. She was as confidently lovely as she had been when she came from France, all those years ago, and was set on by my family to take my royal lover from me.

I could have gone along with the common people and taken a place behind the Lord Mayor and the guildsmen and the aldermen, but William was too afraid that I would be seen, and I knew I could not bear to hear the lies they would tell about her. I knew also that I could not bear to hear the truths. The woman from the lodging house went to see the greatest show that London would ever be offered and came home with a garbled account of the list of times and places where the queen had seduced the men of the court by inflaming their desires by kissing with tongues, that she gave them great gifts, that they tried to outdo each other night after night; a story which sometimes touched the truth and sometimes veered off into the wildest of fantasies which anyone who knew the court would have realised could not be true. But it always had that fascination of scandal, it was always erotic, filthy, dark. It was the stuff that people wished that queens might do, that a whore married to a king would be sure to do. It told us much, much more about the dreams of Secretary Cromwell, a low man, than it did about Anne or George or me.

They called no witnesses who had ever seen her touching and blandishing, they called no witnesses to prove that Anne had ill-wished Henry into illness, either. They claimed that the ulcer on his leg and his impotence were her fault too. Anne pleaded not guilty and then tried to explain, to the peers who knew it already, that it was normal for a queen to give little gifts. That it was nothing for her to dance with one man, and then another. That of course poets would dedicate poems to her. That naturally the poems would be love poetry. That the king had never complained, not for one moment, against the tradition of courtly love which ruled every court in Europe.

On the last day of the trial the Earl of Northumberland, Henry Percy, her love from so long ago, went missing. He sent as his excuse that he was too ill to attend. That was when I knew that the verdict would go against her. The lords who had been in Anne's court, who would have sold their own mothers to the galleys to have her favour, gave their verdict, from the lowliest peer to our uncle. One after another, they all said: 'Guilty'. When it came to my uncle he choked on his tears and could barely say the word 'guilty', or speak the sentence: that she should be burned or beheaded on the Green, at the king's pleasure.

The lodging-house woman found a scrap of cloth in her pocket and dabbed at her eyes. She said it did not seem much like justice to her, if a queen had to be burned at the stake for dancing with a couple of young men.

'Very true,' William said judicially, and directed her from the room. When she was gone, he came back to me and took me onto his knee. I curled up like a child, and let him put his arms around me and rock me.

'She will hate to be in a nunnery.'

'She'll have to tolerate whatever the king rules,' he said. 'Exile or a nunnery, she will be glad of it.'

❧

They tried my brother the next day, before they could lose their stomach for the lies. He was accused, as the other men had been, of being her lover and plotting against the king, and like them, he denied it completely. They accused him also of questioning the paternity of the Princess Elizabeth and of laughing at the king's impotence. George, speaking on his sacred oath, fell silent: he could not deny it. The strongest evidence against him was a statement written by Jane Parker, the wife he had always despised.

'They would listen to an aggrieved wife?' I asked William. 'On a hanging matter?'

'He's guilty,' he said simply. 'I'm not one of his intimates but even I've heard him laugh at Henry and say that the man couldn't mount a mare in season, let alone a woman like Anne.'

I shook my head. 'That's bawdy and indiscreet but . . .'

He took my hand. 'It's treason, my love,' he said gently. 'You wouldn't expect it to come to court, but if it does, it is treason just as Thomas More was treasonous to doubt the king's supremacy in the church. This king can say what is a hanging offence and what is not. We gave him that power when we denied the Pope the right to rule the church. We gave Henry the right to rule everything. And now he rules that your sister is a witch and that your brother is her lover, and that they are both enemies of the realm.'

'But he'll let them go,' I insisted.

❁

Every day my boy Henry went to the Tower and met his sister and saw that she was well. Every day William tracked him there and tracked him back, always watching that no-one else was watching. But there were no spies on Henry. It was as if they had done their worst in listening to the queen and entrapping her, in listening to George and his ridiculous indiscretions, and entrapping him.

One day in the middle of May I went with Henry and met my little girl as she walked out of the Tower of London. From where we stood, outside the gate, I could hear the knocking of the nails into the scaffold where they would execute my brother and the four men with him. Catherine was composed. She was a little pale.

'Come home with me,' I urged her. 'And we can go to Rochford, all of us. There's nothing more you can do here.'

She shook her little hooded head. 'Let me stay,' she said. 'I want to stay until Aunt Anne is released to the nunnery and it is over.'

'Is she well?'

'She is. She prays all the time and she prepares herself for a life behind the walls. She knows that she has to give up queenship. She knows that she has to give up the Princess Elizabeth. She knows that she won't be queen now. But it's better since the trial is over. They don't listen to her and watch her the same way. And she is more settled.'

'Have you seen George?' I asked. I tried to keep my voice light but my grief choked me.

Catherine looked up at me, her dark Boleyn eyes filled with pity. 'This is a prison,' she said gently. 'I can't go visiting.'

I shook my head at my own stupidity. 'When I was here before it was one of the many castles of the king. I could walk where I wanted. I should have realised that everything is different now.'

'Will the king marry Jane Seymour?' Catherine asked me. 'She wants to know.'

'You can tell her it is a certainty,' I said. 'He is at her house every night. He is as he was, in the old days, when it was her.'

Catherine nodded. 'I should go,' she said, glancing at the sentry behind her.

'Tell Anne . . .' I broke off. There was too much to send in one message. There were long years of rivalry and then a forced unity and always and ever, underpinning our love for each other, our sense that the other must be bested. How could I send her one word which would acknowledge all of that, and yet tell her that I loved her still, that I was glad I had been her sister, even though I knew she had brought herself to this point and taken George here too? That, though I would never forgive her for what she had done to us all, at the same time, I totally and wholly understood?

'Tell her what?' Catherine hovered, waiting to be released.

'Tell her that I think of her,' I said simply. 'All the time. Every day. The same as always.'

The next day they beheaded my brother alongside his lover Francis Weston, with Henry Norris, William Brereton and Mark Smeaton. They did it on the Green, before Anne's window, and she watched her friends and then her brother die. I walked on the muddy foreshore of the river with my baby on my hip and tried not to know that it was happening. The wind blew gently up the river and a seagull called mournfully over my head. The tideline was a mess of intriguing flotsam: bits of rope, scraps of wood, shells encrusted on weed. I watched my boots and smelled the salt in the air and let my pace rock my baby and tried to understand what had happened to us Boleyns who had been running the country one day and were condemned criminals the next.

I turned for home and found that my face was wet with tears. I had not thought to lose George. I had never thought that Anne and I would have to live our lives without George.

A swordsman was ordered from France to execute Anne. The king was planning a last-minute reprieve and he would extract every drop of drama from it. They built a scaffold for her beheading on the Green outside the Beauchamp Tower.

'The king will release her?' I asked William.

'That's what your father said.'

'He will do it as a great masque,' I said, knowing Henry. 'At the very last moment he will send his pardon and everyone will be so relieved that they will forgive him for the deaths of the others.'

❧

The swordsman was delayed on the road. It would be another day before he was on the platform, waiting for the pardon. Catherine at the gate that night was like a little ghost. 'Archbishop Cranmer came today with the papers to annul the marriage and she signed them. They promised that she would be released if she signed. She can go to a nunnery.'

'Thank God,' I said, knowing only now how deeply I had been afraid. 'When will she be released?'

'Perhaps tomorrow,' Catherine said. 'Then she'll have to live in France.'

'She'll like that,' I said. 'She'll be an abbess in five days, you'll see.'

Catherine gave me a thin smile. The skin below her eyes was almost purple with fatigue.

'Come home now!' I said in sudden anxiety. 'It's all but done.'

'I'll come when it's over,' she said. 'When she goes to France.'

✿

That night, as I lay sleepless, staring up at the tester over the four-poster bed, I said to William, 'The king will keep his word and release her, won't he?'

'Why should he not?' William asked me. 'He has everything he wants. An adultery charge against her so no-one can say that he fathered a monster. The marriage annulled as if it never was. Everyone who impugned his manhood is dead. Why should he kill her? It makes no sense. And he has promised her. She signed the annulment. He is honour-bound to send her to a nunnery.'

❧

The next day a little before nine o'clock they took her out to the scaffold and her ladies, my little Catherine among them, walked behind her.

I was in the crowd, at the back, at Tower Green. From a distance I saw her come out, a little figure in a black gown with a dark cape. She wore a French hood, her hair was held back in a net. She said her final words, I could not hear them and I did not care. It was a nonsense, a piece of the masque, as meaningless as when the king was Robin Hood and we were villagers dressed in green. I waited for the watergate to roll up and the king's barge to rush in with a beat of the drummer and the swirl of oars in the dark water and for the king to stride forward amongst us, and declare Anne forgiven.

I thought he was leaving it so late that he must have ordered the executioner to delay, to wait for the blast of royal trumpets from the river. It was typical of Henry to use this moment for its greatest drama. Now we had to wait for him to make his grand entrance and his speech of forgiveness and then Anne could go to France and I could fetch my daughter and go home.

I watched her turn to the priest for her final prayers, and then take off her French hood, and her necklace. Hidden in my long sleeves I was snapping my fingers with irritation at Anne's vanity and Henry's delay. Why could not the two of them finish this scene quickly and let us all go?

One of her women, not my daughter Catherine, stepped forward and tied a blindfold over my sister's eyes, and then steadied her arm as she knelt in the straw. The woman stepped back, Anne was alone. Like a field of corn bowing down in the wind, the crowd before the scaffold knelt too. Only I stood still, staring over their heads to my sister where she knelt in her black gown with the brave crimson skirt, her eyes blindfolded, her face white.

Behind her the executioner's sword went up and up and up in the morning light. Even then, I looked towards the watergate for Henry to come. And then the sword came down like a flash of lightning, and then her head was off her body and the long rivalry between me and the other Boleyn girl was over.

William pushed me unceremoniously in to one of the alcoves of the wall and thrust his way through the people who were gathering around to see Anne's body wrapped in linen and laid in a box. He scooped Catherine up as if she were no more than a baby and he brought her back through the chattering shocked crowd towards me.

'It's done,' he said tersely to us both. 'Now walk.'

Like a man in a rage he forced us before him, through the gate and out into the City. Blindly, we found our way back to our lodgings, through the crowds which were seething around the Tower and shouting the news to one another that the whore had been beheaded, that the poor lady had been martyred, that the wife had been sacrificed, all the different versions that Anne had carried in one ill-lived life.

Catherine stumbled as her legs gave way and William picked her up and carried her in his arms like a swaddled infant. I saw her head loll against his shoulder and realised that she was half asleep. She had stayed awake for days with my sister as they had waited for the clemency which had been inviolably promised. Even now as I stumbled on the cobbles of the road into the City I realised that it was hard for me to know that the clemency had never come and that the man I had loved as the most golden prince in Christendom had turned into a monster who had broken his word and executed his wife because he could not bear the thought of her living without him and despising him. He had taken George, my beloved George, from me. And he had taken my other self: Anne.

❁

Catherine slept for all that day and all that night, and when she awoke, William had the horses ready and she was on her horse before she could protest. We rode to the river and took a ship downriver to Leigh. She ate while we were on board, Henry beside her. I had my baby on my hip, watching my two older children, thanking God that we were out of the city and that, if we were lucky and kept our wits about us, we might escape notice in the new reign.

Jane Seymour had chosen her wedding clothes on the day that they executed my sister. I did not even blame her for that. Anne or I, would have done the same thing. When Henry changed his mind he always changed it fast, and it was a wise woman who went with him and did not oppose him. Even more so now that he had divorced one faultless wife and beheaded another. Now he knew his power.

Jane would be the new queen and her children, when she had them, would be the next princes or princesses. Or she might wait, as the other queens had waited, every month, desperate to know that she had conceived, knowing each month that it did not happen that Henry's love wore a little thinner, that his patience grew a little shorter. Or Anne's curse of death in childbed, and death to her son, might come true. I did not envy Jane Seymour. I had seen two queens married to King Henry and neither of them had much joy of it.

And as for us Boleyns, my father was right, all we could do now was survive. My uncle had lost a good hand with the death of Anne. He had thrown her onto the gaming table just as he had thrown me or Madge. Whether a girl was fit for seduction or a sop for the king's rage, or even to aim at the highest place in the land, he would always have another Howard girl at the ready. He would play again. But we Boleyns were destroyed. We had lost our most famous girl, Queen Anne, and we had

528

lost George, our heir. And Anne's daughter Elizabeth was a nobody, worth even less than the despised Princess Mary. She would never be called princess again. She would never sit on the throne.

'I'm glad of it,' I said simply to William as the children slept, rocked by the movement of the boat on the ebbing tide. 'I want to live in the country with you. I want to bring up our children to love each other and fear God. I want to find some peace now, I have had enough of playing the great game at court. I have seen the price that has to be paid and it is too high. I just want you. I just want to live at Rochford and love you.'

He put his arm around me and held me close to him against the cold wind that blew steadily off the sea. 'It's agreed,' he said. 'Your part in this is done, please God.' He looked forward to where my two children were in the prow of the boat, looking downriver to the sea, swaying with the rhythmic beat of the oars. 'But those two? They'll be sailing upriver again, back to court and power, sometime in their lives.'

I shook my head in protest.

'They're half Boleyn and half Tudor,' he said. 'My God, what a combination. And their cousin Elizabeth the same. Nobody can say what they will do.'

Author's Note

Mary and William Stafford lived happily together at Rochford. When her parents died (in 1538 and 1539), Mary inherited the whole of the Boleyn family holdings in Essex, and she and William became wealthy land-owners.

She died in 1543 and her son, Henry Carey, rose to become a major advisor and courtier at the court of his cousin, Queen Elizabeth I, the greatest queen England ever had. She made him Viscount Hunsdon. Mary's daughter Catherine married Sir Francis Knollys and founded a great Elizabethan dynasty.

I am indebted to Retha M. Warnicke, whose book *The Rise and Fall of Anne Boleyn* has been a most helpful source for this story. I have followed Warnicke's original and provocative thesis that the homosexual ring around Anne, including her brother George, and her last miscarriage created a climate in which the king could accuse her of witchcraft and perverse sexual practices.

I am very grateful to the following authors, whose books helped me to trace the otherwise untold story of Mary Boleyn, or provided background for the period:

Bindoff, S. T., *Pelican History of England: Tudor England*, Penguin, 1993

Bruce, Marie Louise, *Anne Boleyn*, Collins, 1972

Cressy, David, *Birth, Marriage and Death, ritual religions and the life-cycle in Tudor and Stuart England*, OUP, 1977

Darby, H. C., *A new historical geography of England before 1600*, CUP, 1976

Elton, G. R., *England under the Tudors*, Methuen, 1955

Fletcher, Anthony, *Tudor Rebellions*, Longman, 1968

Guy, John, *Tudor England*, OUP, 1988

Haynes, Alan, *Sex in Elizabethan England*, Sutton, 1997

Loades, David, *The Tudor Court*, Batsford, 1986

Loades, David, *Henry VIII and his Queens*, Sutton, 2000

Mackie, J. D., *Oxford History of England, The Earlier Tudors*, OUP, 1952

Plowden, Alison, *Tudor Women, Queens and Commoners*, Sutton, 1998

Randell, Keith, *Henry VIII and the Reformation in England*, Hodder, 1993

Scarisbrick, J. J., *Yale English Monarchs: Henry VIII*, YUP, 1997

Smith, Baldwin Lacey, *A Tudor Tragedy, the life and times of Catherine Howard*, Cape, 1961

Starkey, David, *The Reign of Henry VIII, Personalities and Politics*, G. Philip, 1985

Starkey, David, *Henry VIII: A European Court in England*, Collins and Brown, 1991

Tillyard, E. M. W., *The Elizabethan World Picture*, Pimlico, 1943

Turner, Robert, *Elizabethan Magic*, Element, 1989

Warnicke, Retha M., *The Rise and Fall of Anne Boleyn*, CUP, 1991

Weir, Alison, *The Six Wives of Henry VIII*, Pimlico, 1997

Young, Joyce, *Penguin Social History of Britain*, Penguin

Philippa Gregory continues the story of the Boleyn family and their inextricable link to the Tudor court in *The Boleyn Inheritance*, now available in paperback. Read on for an extract from this enthralling novel.

Jane Boleyn, Rochester, 31 December 1539

There is to be a bull-baiting after dinner and Lady Anne is shown to the window that overlooks the courtyard so that she can have the best view. As soon as she appears at the window a cheer goes up from the men in the yard below, even though they are bringing out the dogs and it is rare for common men to break off from gambling at such a moment. She smiles and waves to them. She is always easy with the ordinary people, and they like her for it. Everywhere we have been on the road she has a smile for the people who come out to see her, and she will blow a kiss to little children who throw posies of flowers in her litter. Everyone is surprised at this. Not since Katherine of Aragon have we had a queen who is so smiling and pleasant to the common people, and not since Aragon has England relished the novelty of a foreign princess. No doubt this one will learn to be easy with the court too, in time.

I stand beside her on one side and one of her German friends is on the other so that he can tell her what is being said. Lord Lisle is there, of course, and Archbishop Cranmer. He is devoting himself to being pleasing, of course. She may be Cromwell's candidate, and thus an asset for his rival; but his worst fear must have been that the king would bring in a Papist princess, and this reforming archbishop would see his church turned back to the old ways once more.

Some of the court are at the windows to see the baiting, some are gossiping quietly at the back of the room. I cannot hear exactly what is being said, but I think there are more than Lady Browne who think that the Lady Anne is not well-suited to the great position that she has been called on to fill. They judge her harshly for her shyness and her lack of speech. They blame her for her clothes and they laugh at her for not being able to dance or sing or play a lute. This is a cruel court, devoted to frivolity, and she is a girl easy to use as a butt for sarcasm. If this goes on, what will happen? She and the king are all but married. Nothing can stop the wedding. He can hardly send her home in disgrace, can he? For the crime of wearing a heavy hood? Not even the king can do that, surely? Not even this king can do it? It would bring Cromwell's treaty down about his ears, it would bring down Cromwell himself, it would leave England friendless facing France and Spain without any Protestant alliance at our back. The king will never risk it, I am sure. But I cannot imagine what will happen.

Down in the yard below they are getting ready to release the bull, his handler unclips the rope from the ring in his nose, skips out of the way, vaults over the boards and the men who have been sitting on the wooden benches rise to their feet and start to shout bets. The bull is a great animal with heavy shoulders and a thick, ugly head. He turns this way and that, spotting the dogs from one little eye and then the other. The dogs are none too eager to be the first to run in, they are afraid of him in his power and his strength.

I feel a little breathless. I have not seen a bull-baiting since I was last at court, I had forgotten what a savage excitement it is to see the yapping dogs and the great beast that they will pull down. It is rare to see a bull as big as this one, his muzzle scarred from earlier fights, his horns barely blunted. The dogs hang back and bark, sharp, persistent barks with the thrilling sound of fear behind them. He turns from one to another, threatening them with the sweep of his horns, and they fall back into a circle around him.

One rushes in, and at once the bull spins, you would not think such a great animal could move so quickly, his head ploughs low and there is a scream like a human cry from the dog as the horns buffet his body, his bones are broken for sure. He is down and cannot crawl away, he is yelping like a baby, the bull stands over him, his head down, and grinds the side of his great horn into the screaming dog.

I find I am crying out, though whether for the dog or for the bull I couldn't say. There is blood on the cobbles but the bull's attack has left him unguarded to the other dogs, and another darts in and takes a bite at his ear. He turns, but at once another fastens on his throat and hangs there for a moment, his white teeth bared and gleaming in the torchlight, while the bull bellows for the first time and the roar of it makes all the maids scream and me among them, and everyone is now crowding to the windows to see as the bull rakes his head round and the dogs fall back and one of them howls with rage.

I find I am trembling, crying out for the dogs to go on! Go on! I want to see more, I want to see all of it, and Lady Anne beside me is laughing, she is excited too, she points to the bull where his ear is bleeding, and I nod and say, 'He will be so angry! He will kill them for sure!' And then suddenly, a bulky man I don't know, a stranger smelling of sweat and wine and horses, pushes in front of us, into the window bay where we are standing, pushes rudely by me, and says to the Lady Anne, 'I bring you greetings from the King of England,' and he kisses her, full on the mouth.

At once I turn to shout for the guards. This is an old man of nearly fifty, a fat man, old enough to be her father. She thinks at once that he is some drunk fool who has managed to push his way into her chamber. She has greeted a hundred men, a thousand men, with a smile and an extended hand and now this man, wearing a marbled cape and a hood pulled over his head, comes up to her and pushes his face into hers and puts his slobbery mouth on hers.

Then I bite off my shout of alarm, I see his height, and I see the men who have come in with him in matching capes, and I know him at once for the king. At the same moment, like a miracle, at once he does not seem old and fat and distasteful. As soon as I know he is the king I see the prince that I have always seen, the one they called the handsomest prince in Christendom, the one that I was in love with myself. This is Henry, King of England, one of the most powerful men in the entire world, the dancer, the musician, the sportsman, the courtly knight, the lover. This is the idol of the English court, as big as the bull in the yard below us, as dangerous as a bull when wounded, as likely to turn on any challenger and kill.

I don't curtsey because he is in disguise. I learned from Katherine of Aragon herself that one should never see through his disguises, he loves to unmask and wait for everyone to exclaim that they had no idea who the handsome stranger was, that they admired him for himself, without knowing that he was our wonderful young king.

And so, because I cannot warn Lady Anne, the scene in our gallery becomes a baiting to equal what is going on, bloodily, in the courtyard below us. She pushes him away, two firm hands against his fat chest, and her face, sometimes so dull and stolid, is burning with colour. She is a modest woman, an untouched girl, and she is horrified that this man should come and insult her. She rubs the back of her hand over her face to erase the taste of his lips. Then, terribly, she turns her head and spits his saliva from her mouth. She says something in German that needs no translation, clearly it is a curse against this commoner who has presumed to touch her, to breathe his wine-scented breath into her face.

He stumbles back, he, the great king, almost falls back before her contempt. Never in his life has a woman pushed him away, never in his life has he ever seen any expression in any woman's face but desire and welcome. He is stunned. In her flushed face and bright, offended gaze he sees the first honest opinion of himself that he has ever known. In a terrible, blinding flash he sees himself as he really is: an old man, long past his prime, no longer handsome, no longer desirable, a man that a young woman would push roughly away from her because she could not stand his smell, because she could not bear his touch.

He reels back as if he has taken a mortal blow to the face, to his heart. I have never seen him like this before. I can almost see the thoughts running behind his stunned, flabby face. The sudden realisation that he is not handsome, the realisation that he is not desirable, the terrible realisation that he is old and ill and one day he will die. He is no longer the handsomest prince in Christendom, he is a foolish old man who thought that he could put on a cape and a hood and ride out to meet a girl of twenty-four, and she would admire the handsome stranger, and fall in love with the king.

He is shocked to his soul, and now he looks foolish and confused like a muddled grandfather. Lady Anne is magnificent, she is drawn up to her full height and she is angry, she is powerful, she is standing on her dignity and she shoots a look at him which dismisses him from her court as a man that no-one would want to know. 'Leave me,' she says in heavy-accented English, and she turns her shoulder on him as if she would push him away again.

She looks around the room for a guard to arrest this intruder, and she notices for the first time that no-one is springing to save her, we are all appalled, no-one knows what they can say or do to recover this moment: Lady Anne outraged, the king humbled in his own eyes, thrown down before us all. The truth of the king's age and decay is suddenly, painfully, unforgiveably apparent. Lord Southampton steps forwards but is lost for words; Lady Lisle looks at me and I see my shock mirrored in her face. It is a moment of such intense embarrassment that all of us – we skilled flatterers, courtiers, liars – are lost for words. The world we have been building for thirty years, around our prince who is ageless, eternally handsome, irresistibly desirable, has been shattered about our ears – and by a woman we none of us respect.

He turns wordlessly, he almost stumbles as he goes, his stinking leg giving way beneath him, and Katherine Howard, that clever, clever little girl, catches her breath in a gasp of absolute admiration and says to him: 'Ooh! Forgive me, sir! But I am new to court myself, a stranger like you. May I ask – who are you? What is your name?'

Katherine, Rochester,
31 December 1539

I am the only person to see him come in. I don't like bull-baiting, or
bears, or cockfighting, or anything like that, I think it's just downright
nasty – and so I am standing a little back from the windows. And I am
looking round, actually, I am looking at a young man that I had seen
earlier, such a handsome young man with a cheeky smile, when I see the
six of them come in, old men, they must all be thirty at the least, and
the big old king at the front, and they are all wearing the same sort of
cape, like a masquing costume, so I guess at once that it is him, and that
he has come in disguise like a knight errant, silly old fool, and that he
will greet her and she will pretend not to know him, and then there will
be dancing. Really, I am delighted to see him because this makes it a
certainty that there will be dancing and so I am wondering how I can
encourage the handsome young man to be near me in the dance.

When he kisses her it all goes terribly wrong. I can see at once that
she has no idea who he is, someone should have warned her. She thinks
he is just some drunk old man who has staggered in to kiss her for a
wager, and of course she is shocked, and of course quite repelled, because
when he is in a cheap cloak and not surrounded by the greatest court in
the world he does not look at all like a king. In truth, when he is in a
cheap cloak and with his companions, also dressed poorly, he looks like
some common merchant, with a waddling walk and a red nose, who likes
a glass of wine, and hopes to go to court and see his betters. He looks
like the sort of man my uncle would not acknowledge if he called out in
the street. A fat old man, a vulgar old man, like a drunk sheep farmer
on market day. His face is terribly bloated, like a great round dish of
dripping, his hair is thinning and grey, he is monstrously fat, and he has
an old injury in his leg that makes him so lame that he rolls in his walk like

a sailor. Without his crown he is not handsome, he looks like anybody's fat old grandfather.

He falls back, she stands on her dignity, rubbing her mouth to take the smell of his breath away, and then – it is so awful I could almost scream with shock – she turns her head and spits out the taste of him. 'Leave me,' she says and turns her back on him.

There is utter, dreadful silence, nobody says a word, and suddenly I know, as if my own cousin Anne Boleyn is at my side telling me, what I should do. I am not even thinking of the dancing and the young man, for once I am not even thinking of myself, and that almost never happens. I just think, in a flash, that if I pretend not to know him, then he can go on not knowing himself, and the whole sorry masque of this silly old man and his gross vanity will not tumble about our ears. I just feel sorry for him, to tell the truth. I just think that I can spare him this awful embarrassment of bouncing up to a woman and having her slap him down like a smelly old hound. If anyone else had said anything then I would have stayed silent. But nobody says anything and the silence goes on and on, unbearably, and he stumbles back, he almost falls back into me, and his face is all crumpled and confused and I am so sorry for him, poor humbled old fool, that I say, I coo: 'Ooh! Forgive me, sir! But I am new to court myself, a stranger like you. May I ask – who are you?'

Anne, on the road to Dartford, 1 January, 1540

Nothing could be worse, I feel such a fool. I am so glad to be travelling today, seated uncomfortably in the rolling litter, but at least alone. At least I don't have to face any sympathetic, secretly laughing faces, all buzzing with the disaster of my first meeting with the king.

But truly, how should I be blamed? He has a portrait of me, Hans Holbein himself humbled me to the ground with his unsmiling stare, so that the king had my portrait to scrutinise and criticise and study, he has a very good idea of who I am. But I have no picture of him except the picture in my mind that everyone has: of the young prince who came to his throne a golden youth of eighteen, the handsomest prince in the world. I knew well enough that he is all but fifty now. I knew that I was not marrying a handsome boy, not even a handsome prince. I knew I was marrying a king in his prime, even an ageing man. But I did not know what he was like. I had seen no new portrait of him to consider. And I was not expecting . . . that.

Not that he is so bad, perhaps. I can see the man he once was. He has broad shoulders, handsome in a man at any age. He still rides, they tell me, he still hunts except when some wound in his leg is troubling him, he is still active. He runs his country himself, he has not handed over power to more vigorous advisors, he has all his wits about him, as far as one can tell. But he has small, piggy eyes and a small, spoiled mouth, in a great ball of a moon face swelling with fat. His teeth must be very bad, for his breath is very foul. When he grabbed me and kissed me the stink of him was truly awful. When he fell back from me he looked like a spoiled child, ready to cry. But, I must be fair, that was a bad moment for both of us. I daresay, as I thrust him away from me, that I did not appear at my best either.

I wish to God I had not spat.

This is a bad beginning. A bad and undignified beginning. Really, he should not have come on me unprepared and without warning. All very well for them to tell me now that he loves disguising and masquing and pretending to be an ordinary man so that people can discover him with delight. They never told me this before. On the contrary, every day it has been dinned into my head that the English court is formal, that things must be done in a certain way, that I have to learn orders of precedence, that I must never be faulted by calling a junior member of a family to my side before a senior member, that these things matter to the English more than life itself. Every day before I left Cleves, my mother reminded me that the Queen of England must be above reproach, must be a woman of utter royal dignity and coldness, must never be familiar, must never be light, must never be overly-friendly. Every day she told me that the life of a Queen of England depends on her unblemished reputation. She threatened me with the same fate as Anne Boleyn if I was loose and warm and amorous like her.

So why should I ever dream that some fat old drunk would come up and kiss me? How would I ever dream that I am supposed to let an ugly old man kiss me without introduction or warning?

Still, I wish to God that I had not spat out the foul taste of him.

Anyway, perhaps it is not so bad. This morning he has sent me a present, a gift of rich sables, very expensive and very high quality. Little Katherine Howard, who is so sweet that she mistook the king for a stranger and greeted him kindly, has had a brooch of gold from him. Sir Anthony Browne brought the gifts this morning with a pretty speech, and told me that the king has gone ahead to prepare for our official meeting, which will happen at a place called Blackheath, outside the City of London. My ladies say that there will be no surprises between now and then, so I need not be on my guard. They say that this disguising is a favourite game of the king's and once we are married I must be prepared for him to come wearing a false beard or a big hat and ask me to dance, and we will all pretend not to know him. I smile and say how charming, though in truth I am thinking: how odd, and how childlike, and really, how very vain of him, how foolishly vain to hope that people will fall in love with him on sight as a common man, when he looks as he does now. Perhaps when he was young and handsome he could go about in disguise and people would welcome him for his good looks and charm; but surely, for many years now, many years, people must have only pretended to admire him? But I don't speak my thoughts. It is better that I say nothing now, having spoiled the game once already.

The girl who saved the day by greeting him so politely, little Katherine Howard, is one of my new maids in waiting. I call her to me in the bustle of departing this morning, and I thank her, as best I can manage in English, for her help.

She dips a little curtsey, and speaks to me in a rattle of English.

'She says that she is delighted to serve you,' my translator, Lotte, tells me. 'And that she has not been to court before, so she did not recognise the king either.'

'Why then did she speak to a stranger who had come without invitation?' I ask, puzzled. 'Surely, she should have ignored him? Such a rude man, pushing his way in?'

Lotte turns this into English, and I see the girl look at me as if there is more that divides us than language, as if we are on different worlds, as if I come from the snows and fly on white wings.

'*Was?*' I ask in German. I spread out my hands to her and raise my eyebrows. 'What?'

She steps a little closer, she whispers in Lotte's ear without ever taking her eyes from my face. She is such a pretty little thing, like a doll, and so earnest, that I cannot help smiling.

Lotte turns to me, she is near to laughing. 'She says that of course she knew it was the king. Who else would be able to get into the chamber past the guards? Who else is so tall and fat? But the game of the court is to pretend not to know him, and to address him only because he is such a handsome stranger. She says she may be only fourteen, and her grandmother says she is a dolt; but already she knows that every man in England loves to be admired, indeed, the older they are the vainer they get, and surely, men are not so different in Cleves?'

I laugh at her, and at myself. 'No,' I say. 'Tell her that men are not so different in Cleves but that this woman of Cleves is clearly a fool and I shall be guided by her in future even if she is only fourteen, whatever her grandmother calls her.'

But one thing, good m
that he was young, and
for my part I save so much
him as well as he did me
I was to be at liberty;
all the world did set so li
that I thought I could t
him and forsake all other wa
with him; and so I do put n
might once be so happy to
favour and the Queen's
greater man of birth an
you I could never a h
me so well nor a mor

ter Secretary, conſider,
love overcame reaſon. And
oneſty in him, that I loved
nd was in bondage, and glad
that for my part I ſaw that
by me, and he ſo much,
no better way but to take
and to live a poor honeſt life
ubts but we ſhould, if we
ver the Kings gracious
or well I might a had a
higher, but I enſure
e that ſhould a loved
neſt man.